BOOKS BY STUART WOODS

FICTION

Two Dollar Bill†

The Prince of Beverly Hills

Reckless Abandon†

Capital Crimes‡

Dirty Work†

Blood Orchid*

The Short Forever†

Orchid Blues*

Cold Paradise†

L.A. Dead†

The Run‡

Worst Fears Realized†

Orchid Beach*

Swimming to Catalina†

Dead in the Water†

Dirt†

Choke

Imperfect Strangers

Heat

Dead Eyes

L.A. Times

Santa Fe Rules

New York Dead†

Palindrome

Grass Roots‡

White Cargo

Deep Lie‡

Under the Lake

Run Before the Wind‡

Chiefs‡

TRAVEL

*A Romantic's Guide
to the Country Inns of
Britain and Ireland
(1978)*

MEMOIR

Blue Water, Green Skipper

* A Holly Barker Book
† A Stone Barrington Book
‡ A Will Lee Book

STUART WOODS

Dead Paradise

NEW AMERICAN LIBRARY

NEW AMERICAN LIBRARY

Published by New American Library, a division of
Penguin Group (USA) Inc., 375 Hudson Street, New York, New York 10014, USA
Penguin Group (Canada), 90 Eglinton Avenue East, Suite 700, Toronto,
Ontario M4P 2Y3, Canada (a division of Pearson Penguin Canada Inc.)
Penguin Books Ltd., 80 Strand, London WC2R 0RL, England
Penguin Ireland, 25 St. Stephen's Green, Dublin 2, Ireland (a division of Penguin Books Ltd.)
Penguin Group (Australia), 250 Camberwell Road, Camberwell, Victoria 3124,
Australia (a division of Pearson Australia Group Pty. Ltd.)
Penguin Books India Pvt. Ltd., 11 Community Centre, Panchsheel Park,
New Delhi - 110 017, India
Penguin Group (NZ), cnr Airborne and Rosedale Roads, Albany,
Auckland 1310, New Zealand (a division of Pearson New Zealand Ltd.)
Penguin Books (South Africa) (Pty.) Ltd., 24 Sturdee Avenue,
Rosebank, Johannesburg 2196, South Africa

Penguin Books Ltd., Registered Offices:
80 Strand, London WC2R 0RL, England

Published by New American Library, a division of Penguin Group (USA) Inc.
L.A. Dead and *Cold Paradise* were each previously published in G. P. Putnam's Sons and Signet editions.

First New American Library Printing, February 2006
10   9   8   7   6   5   4   3   2

LIBRARY OF CONGRESS CATALOGING-IN-PUBLICATION DATA:
Woods, Stuart.
    [L.A. dead]
    Dead paradise/by Stuart Woods.
        p. cm.
    Contents: L.A. dead—Cold paradise.
ISBN: 0-451-21756-X
        1. Barrington, Stone (Fictitious character)—Fiction. 2. Private investigators—New York
(State)—New York—Fiction. 3. Los Angeles (Calif.)—Fiction. 4. New York (N.Y.)—Fiction.
I. Woods, Stusrt. Cold paradise. II. Title.

PS3537.O642L15 2006
813'.54—dc22   2005054367

Printed in the United States of America

L.A. Dead

*This book is for Barbara Danielson
and Lewis Moore.*

∽ **Chapter 1** ∾

Elaine's, late. Stone Barrington and Dino Bacchetti sat at table number four, looking grim. Elaine joined them.

"So, what's happening here? You two look like you're going to start shooting any minute."

"I'm getting married," Stone said. "Congratulate me."

"Congratulations," Elaine said. "Anybody you know?"

"Hilarious," Stone said.

"It would be, if it weren't so insane," Dino added.

"You and Dolce are really going to do this?" Elaine asked, incredulous.

"Now don't *you* start," Stone growled.

"He won't listen to me," Dino said. "I've been telling him for a year to stay away from her."

"What've you got against your sister-in-law?" Elaine asked him.

"First of all, she's my sister-in-law," Dino replied. "Second, she's evil. Her old man is the devil, and Dolce is his handmaiden."

"Don't start that again, Dino," Stone said. "I don't want to hear it anymore. We're in love, we're getting married, and that's it. What's wrong with that?"

Elaine shrugged. "You're still in love with Arrington," she said. "Everybody knows that."

"What do you mean, 'everybody'?" Stone demanded.

"Me and Dino," Elaine replied.

"Right," Dino chimed in.

"She's married; she has a child," Stone said.

"So?" Elaine queried. "So, she's married to a movie star; nobody ever took a girl away from a movie star? Happens all the time."

"I'm not breaking up anybody's marriage," Stone said, "and Arrington knows it. I've told her so. Anyway, there's the boy."

"Wouldn't be the first kid raised by a stepfather," Elaine said.

"I think it's Stone's kid, anyway," Dino said.

"Dino, I told you, the blood test was done; I saw the lab report. The boy is Vance Calder's, and that's all there is to it. I'm not taking a kid away from his father. Besides, I like Vance."

"What's not to like?" Elaine asked. "He's handsome; he's the biggest star in Hollywood; he's the most charming man I ever met." She sipped her drink. "Present company included," she added.

"Thanks," Stone said. "I needed that."

"So, when's the happy day?" Elaine asked. "You going to be a June bride?"

"Monday," Stone replied. "In Venice."

"This is Thursday," Elaine pointed out. "What the hell are you doing here?"

"We're leaving tonight," Stone said.

"I got news for you. It's after midnight, all the flights have departed."

"We're taking a private jet, belongs to some friend of Eduardo."

"Not bad," Elaine said, looking impressed. "That way, you get to your hotel late enough tomorrow, so you don't have to wait for the people in your room to check out."

"Eduardo has a palazzo," Dino said. "We're being forced to stay there."

"You're going, too?" Elaine asked, incredulous again.

"He's my best man," Stone said glumly.

"If I don't go, my wife will divorce me," Dino said.

"She's Italian," Elaine pointed out. "She won't divorce you."

"The Bianchi family has found a way around that," Dino said. "Remember how Dolce got divorced?"

"I didn't know she was married," Elaine said.

"A youthful indiscretion. She married a capo in the Bonnano family when she was nineteen. It lasted less than three weeks, until she caught him in her bed with her maid of honor."

"So she got a divorce?"

"Not for some years. When it was inconvenient for her to still be married, the guy turned up in New York dead. Took two in the back of the head, a classic hit."

"Let me get this straight," Elaine said, turning toward Stone. "The girl you're marrying on Monday in Venice had her ex popped?"

"Of course not," Stone said hotly. "That's Dino's theory. In the guy's line of work, it was an occupational hazard. Anybody could have had it done."

"Yeah, sure," Dino said. "Funny, it didn't get done until Dolce decided to throw a bag over Stone's head and lead him to the altar."

Stone glanced at his watch. "Dolce and Mary Ann are going to be here any minute. I want you to decide what you're going to do, Dino; are you going to stand up for me, or not? And if you are, I don't want to hear another word about Eduardo and his connections. You married into the family, too, remember?"

"Yeah, with a bun in the oven and a gun to my head. If I hadn't married her, I'd be at the bottom of Sheepshead Bay right now, with a concrete block up my ass."

"You love that girl, Dino," Elaine said, "and the boy, too. You know goddamned well you do."

Dino looked into his drink and said nothing.

"Make up your mind, Dino," Stone said. He looked up to see Dolce and Mary Ann walk into the restaurant. "They're here." He stood up to greet them.

"All right, all right," Dino said. "I guess I can't let you go over there by yourself."

Stone kissed the gorgeous Dolce. She was wearing a cashmere track suit and a huge smile.

"Everybody ready?" she asked. "The car's at the curb, all the bags are in the trunk."

"Everybody's ready," Stone said, shooting a warning glance at Dino.

Elaine stood up and kissed everybody. "Mazeltov," she said. "Send me a postcard."

"Come with us," Stone said. "There's room."

"And who'd mind the store?" she asked.

"You've got plenty of help here."

"They'd steal me blind. Go on, get going; send me a postcard from Venice."

"You bet," Stone said, hugging her.

The foursome left the restaurant. At the curb a spectacular car was waiting.

"What is this?" Stone asked, running a finger along the glossy paintwork.

"It's a Mercedes Maybach," Dolce replied. "The first one in the country. Papa knows somebody in Stuttgart."

"Papa knows somebody *everywhere*," Dino muttered, collecting a sharp elbow in the ribs from Mary Ann.

They piled into the spacious rear seats, facing each other, Pullman style.

"Not bad," Dino admitted, looking around. "I don't suppose there's a phone? I've gotta check in with the cop shop." Dino ran the detective squad at the nineteenth precinct.

"Oh, leave it, Dino," Stone said. "They can get along without you for a week."

Dolce handed Dino a phone, and he began dialing. "Did you pack all my stuff?" Dino asked Mary Ann.

"Everything's in the trunk," she replied. "I ironed your boxer shorts, too." She winked at Dolce. "They love it when you iron their underwear."

"I'll remember that," Dolce laughed.

"Gladys," Dino said into the phone, "I'm off. You've got the number in Venice if anything really important comes up, otherwise I don't want to know, got that? Good. Take care." He hung up. "Okay, I'm cut loose," he said to the others. "What kind of jet we going in, Dolce? I hate those little ones; this better be a G-Four or better."

"Wait and see," Dolce said smugly.

They drove onto the tarmac at Atlantic Aviation at Teterboro Airport, across the Hudson in New Jersey, and up to an airplane that dwarfed everything on the ramp.

"Holy shit!" Dino said as they got out of the limousine. "What the fuck is this?"

"It's a BBJ," Dolce replied, grabbing her jewelry box and cosmetics case from the backseat. The others took their hand luggage from the trunk.

"Sounds like a sandwich."

"A Boeing Business Jet, the biggest thing in the corporate skies."

Hank Esposito, who ran Atlantic Aviation, was at the airplane's stair door to greet them. "You're fueled for maximum range," he said. "You could make it to Tokyo, if you wanted."

"Not a bad idea," Dino said, boarding the airplane.

"*Dino* . . ." Stone warned.

Esposito helped the chauffeur stow the luggage into a forward area of the interior.

The party stepped into a cabin that looked like the living room of a New York City town house.

Stone was flabbergasted. "Where's the fireplace and the grand piano?" he asked.

An Armani-clad stewardess took their hand luggage and showed them through the airplane. Besides the big cabin, there was a conference room and, behind that, two sleeping cabins, each with its own bathroom.

Dino shook his head. "The wages of sin," he said under his breath, avoiding Stone's glance.

As if from a great distance, there was the sound of jet engines revving, and almost imperceptibly, the big airplane began to move.

⟅ **Chapter 2** ⟆

Somewhere over the Atlantic, Stone stirred in his sleep and turned over, bringing his chest against Dolce's naked back. He reached over her and cupped a breast in his hand, resting his cheek on the back of her neck. With thumb and forefinger, he lightly caressed the nipple.

At that moment, a chime sounded and the soft voice of the stewardess spoke. "Ms. Bianchi, we're two hours from our destination. If you and your party would like breakfast, it will be ready in half an hour."

"I think we're going to be late for breakfast," Stone breathed into Dolce's ear.

She turned over, put her feet on the floor, and stood up. "No, we're not," she said.

"You mean you're spurning your intended?"

"I mean I've decided to be a virgin until we're married."

"Isn't it a little late for that?"

"I can start over whenever I like," she said, "and I've just started over."

Shortly, they joined Dino and Mary Ann at the breakfast table. Scrambled eggs and smoked Italian bacon were set before them.

"That was the best night's sleep I've ever had on an airplane," Dino admitted.

"We didn't sleep all *that* much," Mary Ann rejoined, poking him in the ribs.

Stone indicated the large moving map at the front of the cabin. "We're just crossing the Portuguese coast," he said. "Nice tailwind; we're doing over six hundred miles an hour."

The moving map dissolved, and CNN International appeared on the screen.

"Turn that off," Dolce said to the stewardess. "I don't need news for a while."

The stewardess pressed a button, and Vivaldi came softly over hidden speakers. "Better?" she asked.

"Perfect," Dolce said. She turned to Stone and the others. "I have a little announcement," she said.

"Shoot," Stone replied.

"Papa is giving us the Manhattan town house for a wedding present."

Stone stopped eating. His fiancée was referring to a double-width brick-and-granite mansion in the East Sixties that Eduardo Bianchi had built.

He took Dolce's hand. "I'm sorry, my dear, but I can't accept that. It's very generous of Eduardo, but I already have a house, and we'll be living there."

"Don't I have any say in where we live?" Dolce asked.

"You've never asked me very much about my background," Stone said, "so it's time I told you about my family."

"I know all about that," Dolce replied.

"Only what you read in the report Eduardo had done on me. It doesn't tell you everything."

"So, tell me everything," she said.

"My parents were both from wealthy textile manufacturing families in western Massachusetts, the Stones and the Barringtons; they knew each other from childhood. Neither of them liked the plans their families had made for them. When the crash came in 'twenty-nine, both families were hit hard, and both had lost their businesses and most of their fortunes by the early thirties.

"My parents used this upheaval as an opportunity to get out from under their parents' thumbs. My mother left Mount Holyoke, where she was studying art, and my father left Yale, where he was meant to study law, although the only thing he had ever wanted to do was carpentry and wood-working; they married and moved to New York City. My father's family disowned him, because he had joined the Communist party; my mother's family disowned her, because she had married my father.

"They found themselves very broke and living in a Greenwich Village garret. My mother was doing charcoal drawings of tourists in Washington Square for fifty cents a shot, and my father was carrying his toolbox door to door, doing whatever handyman's work he could find, for whatever people would pay him. He was about to go off and join the Civilian Conservation Corps, just to stay alive, when a wonderful thing happened.

"My mother's aunt—her mother's sister—and her new husband bought a house in Turtle Bay, and my aunt hired my father to build her husband a library. That job saved their lives, and when it was done, Aunt Mildred and her husband were so pleased with it that they also commissioned my father to design furniture for the house and my mother to paint pictures for some of the rooms. When their friends saw the house, they immediately began offering him other commissions, and before too many years had passed, both my parents had won reputations for their work. I didn't come along for quite a long time, but by the time that accident had occurred, they could afford me."

Dolce started to speak, but Stone stilled her with a raised hand.

"There's more. Many years later, when Aunt Mildred died, having been preceded by her husband, she left the house to me. I was still a cop then, working with your brother-in-law, and I poured what savings I had into renovating the house, doing a great deal of the work myself, using skills learned in my father's shop. Finally, after leaving the NYPD—by popular request—I was able to earn a good enough living as a lawyer to finish the house. So, you see, the house is not only a part of my family history, it is all I have left of my parents and the work they devoted their lives to. I have no intention of moving out of it, ever. I hope you understand, Dolce."

Nobody moved. Stone and Dolce stared expressionlessly at each other for a very long moment, then Dolce smiled and kissed him. "I understand," she said, "and I won't bring it up again. I'll be proud to live in your house."

"I'll be happy to explain things to Eduardo," Stone said.

"That won't be necessary," Dolce replied. "I'll explain it to him, and, I promise, he'll understand completely."

"Thank you, my dear," Stone said.

"So," Mary Ann said, changing the subject, "what's the plan for Venice?"

"We'll go directly from the airport to Papa's house," Dolce said. "We'll have dinner with him tonight; tomorrow, Saturday, the civil ceremony will be held at the town hall, where we'll be married by the mayor of Venice. Then, on Monday morning, a friend of Papa's from the Vatican, a cardinal, will marry us at St. Mark's, on the square of the same name. After that, Stone and I will go on a honeymoon, the itinerary of which I've kept secret even from him, and the rest of you can go to hell."

"Sounds good," Mary Ann said.

"Who's the cardinal?" Dino asked.

"Bellini," Dolce replied.

"Doesn't he run the Vatican bank?"

"Yes, he does."

"How like Eduardo," Dino said, "to have his daughter married by a priest, a prince of the Church, and an international banker, all wrapped up in one."

"Why two ceremonies?" Stone asked.

Mary Ann spoke up. "To nail you, coming and going," she said, laughing, "so you can never be free of her. The two marriages are codependent; the civil ceremony won't be official until the religious ceremony has taken place, and the priest—pardon me, the cardinal—has signed the marriage certificate."

"It's the Italian equivalent of a royal wedding," Dino said. "It's done these days only for the *very* important, and, as we all know, Eduardo . . ." He trailed off when he caught Stone's look.

"Eat your eggs, Dino," Mary Ann sighed.

⤳ Chapter 3 ⤶

The gleaming mahogany motor launch, the Venetian equivalent of a lim-ousine, glided up the Grand Canal in the bright, spring sunshine. Stone looked about him, trying to keep his mouth from dropping open. It was his first visit to the city. The four of them sat in a leather banquette at the stern of the boat, keeping quiet. Nothing they could say could bur-nish the glories of Venice.

The boat slowed and turned into a smaller canal, and shortly, came to a stop before a flight of stone steps, worn from centuries of footsteps. Two men dressed as gondoliers held the craft still with long boat hooks and helped the women ashore. As they reached the stone jetty, a pair of double doors ahead of them swung open, as if by magic, and Eduardo Bianchi came toward them, his arms outstretched, a smile on his handsome face. He embraced his daughters, shook hands fairly warmly with his son-in-law, then turned to Stone and placed both hands on his shoulders. "And my new son," he said, embracing him.

"Very nearly," Stone said. "It's good to see you, Eduardo, and it's very kind of you to arrange all this for us. Dolce and I are very grateful."

"Come into the house," Eduardo said, walking them toward the open doors. "You must be exhausted after your flight."

"Not really; it's hard to know how we could have been made more comfortable in the air," Stone said. "Once again, our gratitude."

Eduardo shrugged. "A friend insisted," he said. "Your luggage will be taken to your rooms. Would you like to freshen up, girls?"

The girls, dismissed, followed a maid down a hallway.

"Come into the garden," Eduardo said. "We will have lunch in a little while, but in the meantime, would you like some refreshment?"

"Perhaps some iced tea," Stone said. Dino remained silent. Eduardo ushered them through French doors into a large, enclosed courtyard, which had been beautifully planted, and showed them to comfortable chairs. Unbidden, a servant appeared with pitchers of iced drinks, and they were served.

"First of all, I must clear the air," Eduardo said. "I quite understand that you may be very attached to your own house; I would not impose mine on you."

Stone was once again astonished at Eduardo's apparently extrasensory intuition. "Thank you, Eduardo. It was a magnificent offer, but you are quite right—I am very attached to my own house. It is much caught up with my family's history in New York. Fortunately, Dolce has consented to live there."

"She is a smart girl," Eduardo said, smiling slightly. "I would have been disappointed in her, if she had begun her marriage by attempting to move her husband from a home he loves."

"I expect she will find my taste in interior decoration inadequate, and I have steeled myself for the upheaval."

"You are smart, too," Eduardo said. He turned to his son-in-law. "Dino, how goes it among New York's finest?"

"Still the finest," Dino replied.

"Are you arresting many innocent Italian-American businessmen these days?" Eduardo asked impishly.

"There aren't many left," Dino said. "We've already rehoused most of them upstate."

Eduardo turned back to Stone. "Dino disapproves of my family's former colleagues," he said. "But he is an honest policeman, and there are not many of those. Many of his other colleagues have also been 'rehoused upstate,' as he so gracefully puts it. Dino has my respect, even if he will not accept my affection."

"Eduardo," Dino said, spreading his hands, "when I have retired, I will be yours to corrupt."

Eduardo laughed aloud, something Stone had never heard him do. "Dino will always be incorruptible," Eduardo said. "But I still have hopes of his friendship." Eduardo glanced toward the French doors and stood up.

Stone and Dino stood with him. A tall, thin man with wavy salt-and-pepper hair was approaching. He wore a black blazer with gold buttons, gray silk trousers, and a striped shirt, open at the neck, where an ascot had been tied.

"Carmen," Eduardo said, "may I present my son-in-law, Dino Bacchetti."

To Stone's astonishment, Dino bowed his head and kissed the heavy ring on the man's right hand.

"And this is my son-in-law-to-be, Stone Barrington."

The man extended his hand, and Stone shook it. "Your Eminence," he said, "how do you do?"

"Quite well, thank you, Stone." Bellini held onto Stone's hand and stared into his face. "He has good eyes, Eduardo," he said to Bianchi.

Stone was surprised that the cardinal spoke with an American accent.

"My son," Bellini said to Stone, "it is my understanding that you are not a Roman Catholic."

"I am a believer, Your Eminence," Stone said, "but not a registered one."

Bellini laughed and waved them to their seats. He accepted a fruit juice from the servant, then reached into an inside pocket and took out a thick, white envelope sealed with red wax, and handed it to Eduardo. "Here is the necessary dispensation," he said. "The Holy Father sends his greetings and his blessing."

"Thank you, Carmen," Eduardo said, accepting the envelope.

If Stone understood this transaction correctly, he now had papal approval to marry Dolce. He was embarrassed that the necessity had never occurred to him. "Your Eminence, I am surprised that your accent is American. Did you attend university there?"

"Yes, and preparatory school and elementary school before that. I was born and raised in Brooklyn. Eduardo and I used to steal fruit together, before the Jesuits got hold of me." He said something to Eduardo in what seemed to Stone flawless Italian, raising a chuckle. He turned back to Stone. "I understand that you are engaged in the practice of law."

"That's correct."

"If I may torture the scriptures a little, it is probably easier for a camel to pass through the eye of a needle than for a lawyer to enter the Kingdom of Heaven."

"I tread as narrow a path as my feet will follow," Stone replied.

Bellini smiled. "I should hate to oppose this young man in court," he said to Eduardo.

"Are you a lawyer, as well?" Stone asked.

"I was trained as such at Harvard," Bellini replied, "and my work requires me still to employ those skills from time to time—after which I immediately visit my confessor. I should hate to die with the practice of law on my soul."

"I understand you also dabble in banking."

"Yes, but there is nothing so pure as money, used properly. I am required to ask you, Stone, if you have ever been married."

"No, Your Eminence; I've come close, but I've never been in serious trouble."

"And do you willingly consent to your wife's devout practice of her religion?"

"Willingly, Your Eminence. To deny Dolce anything could be dangerous to my health."

Bellini seemed to try not to laugh, but Dino couldn't help himself.

The women arrived, and they all moved to a table set in the center of the garden, where they feasted on antipasti, a pasta with lobster sauce, and a glittering white wine, served from frosted pitchers. During most of lunch, Eduardo and the cardinal conversed seriously in Italian.

When they got up from the table, Stone sidled over to Dino. "What were Eduardo and Bellini talking about at lunch?" he asked.

"Not you, pal," Dino said. "They were doing business." He glanced at his father-in-law to be sure he would not be overheard. "Eduardo still doesn't know how much Italian I understand."

Stone and Dolce took a walk together through the narrow streets of Venice, becoming hopelessly lost. They did a little window shopping and talked happily. Stone tried to find out where they were honeymooning, but Dolce would reveal nothing.

They returned to the palazzo in the late afternoon, ready for a nap. Stone was shown to a suite—sitting room and bedroom—that overlooked the Grand Canal. He dozed off to the sounds of motorboats and of water lapping against stone.

He dreamed something that disturbed him, but when he awoke, he couldn't remember what it was. He joined the others for cocktails with a strange sense of foreboding.

At cocktails, Eduardo's sister, Rosaria, was present; she was a large woman who perpetually wore the black dresses of a widow. Stone had met her at Eduardo's home in New York, where she had kept house for her brother since his wife's death. Her younger niece was named for her, but the family had always called her Dolce.

The cardinal was now dressed in a beautifully cut black suit.

Half an hour later they were all shown aboard Eduardo's motor launch and transported to dinner at the world-famous Harry's Bar. Stone suspected that Eduardo's presence alone would be cause for considerable deference from the restaurant's staff, but the presence of a cardinal sent them into paroxysms of service. Stone had never seen so many waiters move so fast and from so crouched a position.

They dined on a variety of antipasti and thinly sliced calf's liver with a sherry sauce, with a saffron risotto on the side. The wines were superlative, and by the time they had been returned to the Bianchi palazzo, Stone was a little drunk, more than a little jet-lagged, and ready for bed. Dolce left him at his door with a kiss and vanished down the hallway.

Stone died for ten hours.

Chapter 4

At nine o'clock the following morning, Stone was resurrected by a servant bearing a tray of bloodred orange juice, toast, prosciutto, sliced figs, small pastries, and coffee. A corner of the huge tray held that day's *International Herald Tribune* and the previous day's *New York Times*. By the time he had breakfasted and done the crossword puzzle, it was after ten.

The servant knocked and entered. "Mister Bianchi requests that you be downstairs at eleven o'clock," he said. "The civil ceremony is to be at noon." He disappeared.

Stone shaved and showered then went to the huge cupboard where his clothes hung, all freshly pressed. He dressed in a white linen suit he had bought for the occasion, a pale yellow, Sea Island cotton shirt, a tie with muted stripes, and tan alligator oxfords. Finally, he tucked a yellow silk square into his breast pocket, stuffed his trouser pockets with the usual contents, including some lire, and consulted the mirror. It occurred to him that he might never look so good again.

The group gathered in the central hall of the palazzo. Dolce wore a dazzling white silk dress that showed a becoming amount of very fine leg and wore only a single strand of pearls for jewelry, along with the five-carat, emerald-cut diamond engagement ring supplied by a man of Stone's acquaintance in the diamond district of New York.

"You are very beautiful," Stone said to Dolce, kissing her.

"Funny, that's what I was going to say about you," Dolce replied. "I love the suit."

"It's my wedding dress," Stone explained.

Dino and Mary Ann were well turned out, and to Stone's astonishment, Aunt Rosaria wore a dress of white lace. She was, apparently, out of mourning, at least for the day.

"Is the cardinal coming?" Stone asked Dino.

"No," Dino replied. "Cardinals don't attend civil marriage ceremonies."

"I suppose not," Stone said.

They were escorted to the palazzo's jetty where a small fleet of gondolas, garlanded with flowers, awaited, and they were rowed down a bewildering series of canals to the town hall, where the mayor awaited on the jetty.

Moments later, the party was arranged before an impossibly ornate desk in the mayor's office. Much Italian was spoken. At one point, the mayor turned to Stone, his eyebrows lifted high.

"Say '*sì*,' " Dino whispered.

"*Sì*," Stone said.

Dolce also said, "*Sì*," then an ornate document was produced and signed by Stone and Dolce, then by the mayor and the witnesses. The mayor said something else, delivered sternly.

Dino translated. "He says, 'Remember, you are not yet entitled to the pleasures of the marriage chamber.' "

Back on the jetty outside the town hall, Stone discovered that the gondolas had been replaced by Eduardo's motor launch, and shortly, they were moving fast over open water, toward an island.

Dolce, who held fast to Stone's arm, explained. "Papa has taken the Cipriani Hotel for lunch."

"You mean the dining room?"

"I mean the entire hotel; Papa has many guests. There will be many people at lunch, but don't worry about remembering their names; they don't matter."

Stone nodded.

The hotel occupied the entire island, and lunch was held in its garden.

"Not much chance of party crashers," Dino commented as they walked into the garden. "Unless they swim well." He looked around at the huge crowd of guests who were applauding their entrance—middle-aged and elderly Italians, dressed for Sunday, who were demonstratively affectionate with Dolce and who behaved toward Eduardo pretty much as if he were the Pope. Stone was introduced to each of them, but the flood of Italian names passed him by.

"Who are these people?" he asked Dolce.

"Distant relatives and business acquaintances," she replied tersely.

Stone could not see any family resemblance. "Who are these people?" he asked Dino, when he had a chance.

"I can't prove it," Dino said, "but my guess is you'd have a real problem placing a bet, buying a whore, or getting a fix anywhere in Italy right now."

"Come on, Dino."

"You'll notice that, although there's a band and lots of food, there's no photographer?"

Stone looked around and couldn't see a camera in anybody's hands.

"My guess is, the wedding pictures will be taken Monday, at the church, and that none of these people will be there, which is okay with me. I certainly don't want to be photographed with any of them."

It was late afternoon before they returned to the palazzo. Stone was told to be downstairs at eight for cocktails, then he was allowed to stagger to his room, strip, and fall facedown on the bed, until he was shaken awake by a servant and told to dress. He'd had the bad dream again, but he still couldn't remember it.

Aunt Rosaria had prepared what Stone assumed was their wedding dinner. They ate sumptuously, then adjourned early, everyone being tired from the day's festivities.

"Sleep as late as you like," Eduardo said to the group. "Mass is at eleven tomorrow morning."

Each retired to his own room. Stone, having had a three-hour nap, was not yet sleepy; he changed into a sweater and decided to go for a walk.

He was almost immediately lost. There was a dearth of signs pointing to anywhere, except St. Mark's Square, and he didn't want to go there. Instead, he just wandered.

An hour later, he found himself approaching what he recognized from photographs as the Rialto Bridge. As he climbed its arc, a woman's head appeared from the opposite direction, rising as she walked backward toward him, apparently talking to someone following her. Immediately, Stone knew her.

The shining hair, the slim figure, the elegant clothes, the shape of her calves. It was Arrington. His heart did strange things in his chest, and he was suddenly overcome with the unexpected thrill of seeing her. Then he remembered that she was now Mrs. Vance Calder, of Los Angeles, Malibu, and Palm Springs, that she had borne Vance's child, and that he had sworn her off for life.

Stone was struck heavily by the fact that his reaction to seeing her was not appropriate for a man who would be married on the morrow, and he was suddenly flooded with what had been pent-up doubts about marrying Dolce. In a second, every reservation he had ever had about marriage, in general, and Dolce, in particular, swept over him, filling him with a sickening panic.

On Arrington came, still walking backward, talking and laughing with someone who was still climbing the other side of the bridge, probably Vance Calder. Stone recovered quickly enough to place himself in her path, so that she would bump into him. She would be surprised, they would laugh, Vance would greet him warmly, and they would congratulate him, on hearing of his plans.

She ran into him harder than he had anticipated, jarring them both. Then she turned, and she wasn't Arrington. She was American, younger, not as beautiful; the man following her up the bridge was young, too, and beefy.

"I'm awfully sorry," Stone said to her.

Her young man arrived. "You did that on purpose."

"I apologize," Stone said. "I thought the lady was someone I knew."

"Yeah, sure," the young man said, advancing toward Stone.

"Don't," the girl said, grabbing at his arm. "He apologized; let it go."

The man hesitated, then turned and followed the woman down the bridge.

Stone was embarrassed, but more important, he found himself depressed that the woman had not been Arrington. He stood at the top of the bridge, leaning against the stone railing, looking down the canal, wondering if the universe had just sent him a message.

⤚ **Chapter 5** ⤙

Stone was having the unpleasant dream again, and in it, someone was knocking loudly on a door. Then someone was shaking him, and he woke up this time, remembering that Arrington had been in the dream.

A servant was bending over him. "Signore Bianchi asks that you come to the library at once," the man said. "It is not necessary to dress."

"All right," Stone replied sleepily. He looked at his bedside clock and saw that it was shortly before eight A.M. He found a large terry robe in the wardrobe, put it on over his bedclothes, found his slippers, and, smoothing down his hair, hurried to the central hall, where the servant directed him to the library, a room he had not yet seen.

It was a large room, the walls of which were lined from top to bottom with leather-bound volumes, leaving room for only a few pictures. Stone thought he recognized a Turner oil of the Grand Canal. Eduardo, the cardinal, and Dino, all in dressing gowns or robes, stood before the fireplace.

"Good morning," Stone said. "Is something wrong?"

None of the men seemed to want to speak first. Finally, Eduardo spoke. "We have had some bad news from the States." He turned to his son-in-law. "Dino?"

Dino flinched as if he had been struck, then he began. "My office called a few minutes ago: Rick Grant from the LAPD called and left a message."

Stone knew Rick Grant; he was a detective assigned to the office of the chief of police of Los Angeles, who had been helpful to him on an earlier visit to California. "What is it?"

Dino took a deep breath. "Vance Calder is dead."

"I am very upset about this," Eduardo said. "Vance was my friend, too."

Stone knew that Eduardo was a stockholder, with Vance, in Centurion Studios and had been an investor in some of Vance's films. "How?" he asked Dino.

"He was shot. Last night, in his home."

"Murdered?"

"Yes; shot once in the head."

"Is Arrington all right?" He steeled himself for the answer.

"Yes; she's in a local hospital."

"Was she hurt?"

"No."

"Who shot Vance?"

"That's undetermined," Dino said. "But when I got back to Rick, he told me he thinks Arrington might be a suspect."

Stone found a sofa and sat down. "Jesus Christ," he said, then remembered in whose company he was. "Forgive me, Your Eminence."

The cardinal nodded soberly.

"I wouldn't put too much stock in that theory," Dino said. "You and I both know that, in cases like this, the spouse is always a suspect until cleared."

Stone nodded. He was trying to think what to do next but not getting anywhere.

The cardinal came and sat down beside him. "Stone," he said, putting a fatherly hand on his shoulder, "I am aware of your previous relationship with Arrington. Eduardo and I have discussed this at some length, and we agree that it would be extremely unwise to go forward with the wedding until this . . . situation has been, in some way, resolved."

Stone looked at the man but said nothing.

Eduardo came and stood next to Stone. "This is very complicated," he said. "Both Dolce and I are friends of Vance's, and you, of course, were very close to Arrington. There will be many emotions at work for a while, so many and so confused that to proceed with the marriage at this time would be folly."

"Does Dolce know about this?"

Eduardo shook his head. "I am going to go and wake her now and tell her; this is my duty, not yours."

"I will come, too," the cardinal said. "She may need me."

Stone nodded. "All right. Tell her we'll talk the minute she's ready."

Eduardo and the cardinal left the room.

"What haven't you told me?" Stone asked Dino.

"Rick says Arrington hasn't made any kind of statement yet. She apparently can't remember what happened. They've put her under sedation in a private clinic, but . . ."

"But what?"

"Before she went under, she was asking for you; she said she wouldn't talk to anybody but you."

"I'll have to call her," Stone said.

"I told you, she's under sedation, and Rick didn't know the name of the place where they'd taken her."

"How about Peter? Where is he?"

"The servants are taking care of him; he has a nanny. Rick said his people had spoken to Arrington's mother, and she's on her way out there from Virginia."

"That's good."

"Did Rick say anything else at all?"

"No. He was going to make some calls, and he said he'd get back to me the minute he found out anything more."

Stone walked to the windows and looked out into the lovely garden. "Dino," he said, "did Arrington know that Dolce and I were being married this weekend?"

"I have no idea. Did you tell her?"

Stone shook his head. "I haven't talked with her since last summer; Dolce and I had dinner with them in Connecticut, at their place in Roxbury. It's only a few miles from my new place in Washington."

"And how did that go?"

"Not well. Dolce was very catty, obviously jealous. The next morning, Arrington showed up at my cottage and, well, sort of threw herself at me."

"And how did you handle that?" Dino asked.

"I managed to keep her pretty much at arm's length—though, God knows, that wasn't what I wanted. I told her I wouldn't do anything to harm her marriage, and that was pretty much that. A couple of minutes after she left, Vance showed up—I think he must have been following her. He asked if he had anything to worry about from me, and I told him he didn't. He thanked me and left. That was the last time I saw either of them."

"Sounds as though you handled the situation about as well as it could be handled."

"God, I hope so; I hope none of this has anything to do with Arrington and me."

"I hope so, too," Dino said, "but I'm not going to count on it."

"Come on, Dino, you don't really think she . . ."

"I don't know what to think," Dino said.

Eduardo and the cardinal returned, and Dolce was with them, her face streaked with tears. She came and put her arms around Stone.

Stone had never seen her cry, and it hurt him. "I'm sorry about all this, Dolce," he said to her.

"It's not your fault," she said. "You didn't have any control over her."

"Now, let's not jump to conclusions," he said. "We don't know what happened yet."

"All right, I'll give her the benefit of the doubt."

"You'd better get ready to go, Stone," Eduardo said.

"Go?"

"You're going to Los Angeles, of course," Eduardo said. "She asked for you, and she may not have anyone else."

"Her mother is on the way."

"Her mother can take care of the child, of course, but this is going to be a very difficult situation, given Vance's fame and position in the film community."

"Go, Stone," Dolce said. "We can't have this hanging over us; go and do what you can, then come back to me."

"Come with me," Stone said, wanting her protection from Arrington as much as her company.

"No, that wouldn't do. You're going to have to deal with Arrington on your own."

"My friend's jet is not available today," Eduardo said, "but there's a train at nine-thirty for Milano, and a one o'clock flight from there to Los Angeles. If you miss that, the trip will become much more complicated."

Stone held Dolce away from him and looked into her face. "You're sure about this?"

"I'm sure," Dolce said. "I hate it, but it's the only thing to be done; I know that."

He hugged her again, then left and went to his room, where he found that a servant had already packed most of his things. Half an hour later, he stood on the palazzo's jetty with Dino, Eduardo, the cardinal, and Dolce. He shook hands with Eduardo and Bellini. The cardinal gave him a card. "If I can ever be of service to you, please call me. Of course, I'll make myself available for a service when this situation has been sorted out."

"Thank you, Your Eminence," Stone said. He turned to Dolce and kissed her silently, then motioned Dino into the launch. "Ride with me," he said.

"Have you heard any more from Rick?" Stone asked as the launch pulled away from the jetty.

"No, but it's the middle of the night in L.A. Where will you be staying?"

"At the Bel-Air Hotel. Oh, will you call and book me a room?"

"I'll let Eduardo handle it; you'll get a better room."

A few minutes later they docked at the steps to the Venice train station. Eduardo's butler met them there with Stone's train and airplane tickets and took his bags. Dino walked him to the train.

"I wish you could come with me and help make some sense of this."

Dino shook his head. "I'm due back in the office first thing Wednesday. Call me when you've got your feet on the ground, and I'll help, if I can."

The train was beginning to move, and Stone jumped on. He and Dino managed a handshake before the train pulled out of the station.

Stone found his compartment and sat down. Stress often made him drowsy, and he dozed off almost immediately.

⌁ Chapter 6 ⌁

Even a first-class transatlantic airline seat seemed oddly spartan after the pleasures of the Boeing Business Jet, but Stone managed to make himself comfortable. A flight attendant came around with papers; none of the English-language papers had the story yet, but he caught Vance's name in the headlines of an Italian journal.

He managed to sleep some more and had a decent dinner, which, for him, was lunch, then the lights dimmed, and Vance Calder's face appeared on the cabin's movie screen. It was a report from CNN International and mentioned no more than the bare bones of the story, which Stone already knew. He'd have to wait until LAX for more news.

He thought about another flight, how if Arrington hadn't missed it, things would have been very different. They had planned a winter sailing holiday on the island of St. Mark's, in the Caribbean, and he had planned, once at sea, to ask her to marry him. She had called him at the airport as the flight was boarding and said she had just gotten out of an editorial meeting at *The New Yorker*, for which she sometimes wrote pieces. There was no way for her to make the plane, but she would be on the same flight the following day. The airplane had taken off in the first flurries of what would become a major blizzard in New York, and there was no flight the next day, or the day after that. Then he had a fax from her, saying *The New Yorker* wanted a profile of Vance Calder, who hadn't given a magazine interview in twenty years. It was a huge opportunity for her, and she had begged to be allowed to miss their holiday. He had grudgingly agreed and had put the newly purchased engagement ring back into his suitcase, to await a return to New York.

Then he had been caught up in an extraordinary situation in St. Mark's, had become involved in a murder trial, and by the time he was ready to return to the city, there was a fax from Arrington saying that, after a whirlwind romance, she had married Vance Calder.

After that had come news of her pregnancy and her uncertainty about the identity of the father. The paternity test had come back in Vance's favor, and that was that. Now Vance was dead, and Arrington had turned Stone's life upside down once again.

Stone looked up at the cabin screen again. A film was starting, and it was Vance Calder's latest and last. Stone watched it through, once again amazed at how the actor's presence on screen held an audience, even himself, even now.

The time change was in Stone's favor, and they reached LAX in the early evening. Stone stepped off the airplane and found Rick Grant waiting for him. The LAPD detective was in his fifties, graying, but trim-looking. They greeted each other warmly.

"Give me your baggage claim checks," Rick said, and Stone complied. He handed them to another man. "The Bel-Air?" he asked Stone.

"Yes."

Rick guided Stone through a doorway, down a flight of stairs, and out onto the tarmac, where an unmarked police car was waiting. Rick drove. "You all right?" he asked.

"Well, it's three o'clock in the morning where I just came from, but after some sleep I'll be okay. How about you? How's the job?"

"I made captain; that's about it."

"How's Barbara?" Stone had introduced Rick to Barbara Tierney, who was now his wife.

"Extremely well; in fact, she's pregnant."

"At your age? You dog."

"How about that? I thought I was all through with child rearing."

"Bring me up to date on what happened, Rick, and don't leave anything out."

"The Brentwood station caught the case on Saturday evening, about seven P.M. Calder's Filipino butler called it in. There was a patrol car there in three minutes, and the detectives were there two minutes after that. Calder's body was lying in the central hallway of the house, facedown. He'd taken one bullet here," he tapped his own head at the right rear, "from about three feet. He was still breathing when the patrol car got there, but dead when the detectives arrived."

"The gun?"

"Nine-millimeter automatic; Calder owned one, and it hasn't turned up, in spite of a *very* thorough search."

"Where was Arrington when it happened?"

"In the bathtub, apparently. They were going out to dinner later.

The butler heard the shot and sent the maid to find her. She was still in a robe when the detectives arrived. They noted the strong smell of perfume; there was a large bottle of Chanel No. 5 on her dressing table."

"And that made them suspicious, I guess."

"Yeah."

"But how would Arrington know that perfume can remove the residue from the hands of someone who's fired a gun?"

Rick shrugged. "It's the sort of thing that pops up on the news or in a television movie. Anybody could know it."

"Did Arrington say anything to the detectives?"

"She was distraught, of course, but she seemed willing to talk; then she fainted. By this time, an ambulance had arrived, and the EMTs revived her. When she came to, she seemed disoriented—gave her name as Arrington Carter and didn't recognize the maid or her surroundings. The maid called her doctor, and he arrived pretty quickly. He had the EMTs load her up and take her to a toney private hospital, the Judson Clinic, in Beverly Hills. After the crime scene team arrived, they went to the clinic to question Arrington but were told she'd been sedated and would be out for at least twenty-four hours."

"Anything missing from the house?"

"Calder's jewelry box, which, the butler said, had half a dozen watches and some diamond jewelry in it, and the gun. None of Arrington's stuff had been taken, according to the maid."

"So, Calder could have interrupted a burglary and gotten shot with his own gun for his trouble."

"That's one scenario," Rick said.

"And I guess another is that Arrington shot Vance during a quarrel, hid the gun and the jewelry box, scrubbed her shooting hand and arm with Chanel No. 5 and jumped into a tub, just in time to be found by the maid."

"That's about it."

"Any other scenarios?"

"Nope, just the two."

"How's the voting going?"

Rick shrugged. "I'd say the burglar is losing, at the moment."

"Are you serious?"

"I think the detectives would have felt better about her, if she'd kept her head and told them a convincing story. They weren't too keen on the hysterics and fainting."

"They think she was acting?"

"They think it's a good possibility. I'd find her a shrink, if I were you, and a lawyer, too. A good one."

The two men rode along in silence for a few minutes. Shortly, Rick turned off the freeway and onto Sunset Boulevard. A couple of minutes later he turned left onto Stone Canyon, toward the Bel-Air Hotel.

"Is there anything else you want to ask me, Stone?" Rick said. "Next time we meet, we might not be able to talk to each other so freely."

"I can't think of anything else right now. Any advice?"

"Yeah, get Centurion Studios involved; they're equipped to handle something like this, and I understand that Calder was a major stockholder, as well as their biggest star."

"I'll call Lou Regenstein tomorrow morning," Stone replied.

Rick turned into the hotel parking lot and stopped at the front entrance. "Good luck with this, Stone," he said. "Don't hesitate to call, but don't be surprised if I clam up or can't help. I'll do what I can."

"Thanks for all you've done, Rick, and thanks for meeting my flight, too."

"Your luggage will be here soon."

Stone shook his hand and got out of the car. He walked over the bridge to the front entrance of the hotel and into the lobby. "My name is Barrington," he said to the young woman at the desk. "I believe I have a reservation."

"Oh, yes, Mr. Barrington," she replied. "We've been expecting you." She picked up a phone and dialed a number. "Mr. Barrington is here."

A moment later a young man arrived at the desk. "Good evening, Mr. Barrington, and welcome back. My name is Robert Goodwood; I'm the duty manager. Did you have any luggage?"

"It's being delivered from the airport," Stone said.

"Then I'll show you to your suite."

The young man led the way outdoors and briskly up a walkway, asking about Stone's flight and making chitchat. He turned down another walkway and arrived at a doorway hidden behind dense plantings, unlocked it and showed Stone in.

Stone was impressed with the size and beauty of the suite, but concerned about the cost.

As if anticipating him, Goodwood said, "Mr. Bianchi has insisted that your stay here is for his account."

"Thank you," Stone said.

"I'll send your luggage along as soon as it arrives. Can I do anything else for you?"

"Please send me the New York and L.A. papers."

"Of course." Goodwood gave Stone the key and left.

Stone left the suite's door open for the bellman, shucked off his coat, loosened his tie, sat down on a sofa, and picked up the phone.

"Yes, Mr. Barrington?" the operator said.

"Would you find the number of the Judson Clinic, which is in Beverly Hills, and ring it?" he asked.

"Of course; I'll ring it now."

Apparently the hotel knew of the hospital.

"The Judson Clinic," a woman's voice breathed into the phone.

"My name is Stone Barrington," he said. "I'm a friend of Mrs. Arrington Calder. Can you connect me with her room, please?"

"I'm afraid we have no guest by that name or anything like it," the woman said.

"In that case, please take my name—Stone Barrington—and tell Mrs. Calder that I'm at the Bel-Air Hotel, when she feels like calling."

"Good night," the woman said, and hung up.

The bellman arrived with the luggage and the papers. "Shall I unpack anything, Mr. Barrington?" he asked.

"You can hang up the suits in the large case," Stone said. The man did as he was asked, Stone tipped him, and he left.

Stone picked up the papers. Vance had made the lower-right-hand corner of *The New York Times* front page and the upper-right-hand corner of the *Los Angeles Times*. The obituary in the L.A. paper took up a whole page. There was nothing in the news report he didn't already know.

Stone ordered an omelet from room service and ate it slowly, trying to stay awake, hoping Arrington would call. At eleven o'clock, he gave up and went to bed.

Tomorrow was going to be a busy day.

Chapter 7

The telephone woke Stone. He checked the bedside clock: just after nine A.M. He swung his legs over the side of the bed and picked up the phone. "Hello?"

"Is this Stone Barrington?"

"Yes."

"This is Dr. James Judson, of the Judson Clinic."

"Good morning. How is Arrington?"

"She's been asking for you. I'm sorry the woman who answered the telephone last night didn't know that."

"When can I see her?"

"She's still sleeping at the moment, but why don't you come over here around noon? If she isn't awake by then, I'll wake her, and the two of you can talk."

"What is her condition?"

"Surprisingly good, but there are complications; we can talk about that when you arrive." He gave Stone the address.

"I'll see you at noon," Stone said. He hung up, then pressed the button for the concierge and ordered a rental car for eleven-thirty, then he called room service and ordered a large breakfast. While he was waiting for it to arrive, he called Centurion Studios and asked for Lou Regenstein, its chairman.

"Good morning, executive offices," a woman's voice said.

"Lou Regenstein, please; this is Stone Barrington."

"May I ask what this is about?"

"He'll know." Stone had met Regenstein the year before, when he was in Los Angeles on another matter involving Vance and Arrington.

A moment later, Regenstein was on the line. "Stone, I'm so glad to hear from you; you've heard what's happened, I'm sure."

"That's why I'm here; I got in last evening."

"I've been going nuts; the police won't tell me where Arrington is, and the coroner won't release Vance's body to a funeral home without her permission."

"Arrington is in a hospital; I'm going to see her at noon today."

"Is she all right? Was she hurt in the shooting?"

"She's fine, from all accounts. I'll be talking to her doctor, too."

"What can I do to help?"

"Lou, who is the best criminal lawyer in L.A.?"

"Marc Blumberg, hands down; does Arrington need him?"

"Yes, if only to contain the situation."

"He's a personal friend of mine; I'll call him right now. Where can he see Arrington?"

"I want to see her before she talks to another lawyer," Stone said. "Tell Blumberg to expect a call from me at some point, and to deny that he's representing Arrington, if the press should call in the meantime."

"All right." Regenstein gave him Blumberg's number. "Remember, Stone, Centurion is at Arrington's disposal—anything she needs; you, too. Look, I've had an idea: You're going to need some place to get things done while you're here. I'll make Vance's bungalow available to you for as long as you need it."

"Thank you, Lou; it would be good to have some office facilities."

"You remember Vance's secretary, Betty Southard?"

Indeed he did; Stone and Betty had spent considerable time together during his last visit to town, much of it in bed. "Of course."

"She's there, holding down the fort; I'll let her know you're coming, and I'll leave a pass for you at the main gate."

"Thank you, Lou, I'll be in touch later." Stone hung up and called his own office, in New York.

"Stone Barrington's office," Joan Robertson said.

"Hi, it's Stone."

"Oh, Stone, I'm so glad you called. Have you heard about Vance Calder?"

"Yes, I'm in L.A. now, at the Bel-Air Hotel."

"What's going on?"

"I haven't had time to find out, but I want you to go into our computer boilerplate, print out some documents and fax them to me soonest."

"What do you want?"

Stone dictated a list of the documents, then hung up. Breakfast arrived and he turned on the TV news while he ate. The local channels were going nuts; the biggest star in Hollywood had been murdered, and they couldn't find out *anything*. They were treading water as fast as they could, recycling what little information they had. They couldn't find Arrington, the police wouldn't issue anything but the most basic statement, Centurion had no comment, except to express deep loss and regret, and no friend of either Vance's or Arrington's would talk to the press, even off the record, not that any of them knew anything. That was good, he thought.

The phone rang. "Hello?"

"Mr. Barrington?"

"Yes."

"This is Hillary Carter, Arrington's mother."

"How are you, Mrs. Carter?"

"Terrible, of course, but I'm glad you're here. Arrington badly needs someone to take charge of things."

"Have you seen her?"

"Only for a few minutes, yesterday, and she was semiconscious. She was asking for you, though."

"I'm seeing her at noon today."

"Oh, good. The doctor doesn't want her to see Peter, yet; I don't know why."

"I'll see if I can find out."

"I'm at Vance's house, now, and the situation here is nearly out of hand. I've had to call the police to keep people from climbing over the fence."

"I'll see if I can arrange some private security."

"That would be a very good idea, I think."

"Is Peter all right?"

"Yes, but he wants his mother and father, and I'm having to stall him. What I'd like to do is to get him out of this zoo and take him home to Virginia with me. Arrington is quite happy for him to come with me."

"That might be a good idea. Can I call you after I've seen Arrington?"

"Yes, please; I'll give you Vance's most secret number. The press hasn't learned about it, yet."

Stone wrote down the number.

"I'm so sorry we've never met face to face," Mrs. Carter said. "Arrington has always spoken so well of you."

"Mrs. Carter, do you have any objection to my taking over all of Arrington's legal decisions and contacts with . . . everyone outside the family?"

"I'd be very grateful if you would, but of course, I'd like to be consulted about any medical treatment beyond what she's getting now."

"Of course. I'll talk to you later today." He said good-bye and hung up. There was a knock on the door, and an envelope was slid under it. Stone checked the contents and found the documents Joan had faxed to him.

He telephoned Lou Regenstein.

"Yes, Stone?"

"I've just spoken with Arrington's mother, who is at Vance's house with her grandson. She says the press there is out of hand, and she's had to call the police. Can you arrange for some private security to take over that?"

"Of course; how many men do you want?"

"She says they're coming over the fence, and my recollection is that they've got a large piece of property there."

"Something like eight acres," Regenstein said.

"I should think half a dozen men inside the fence, two in the house and a car patrolling the perimeter of the place, twenty-four hours a day, for the time being."

"Consider it done; anything else?"

"Mrs. Carter wants to take Peter back to Virginia with her. Do you think you could arrange transportation?"

"The Centurion jet is at her disposal," Regenstein said. "I'll have a crew standing by in an hour."

"I shouldn't think she'd need it until later today. Is it at Burbank?"

"Yes, but the press would know that. I'll have it moved to Santa Monica and hangared at the Supermarine terminal, until she's ready to leave."

"Thank you, Lou. I'll call you later."

There was nothing else to do, Stone reflected. Dino would be in the air, now, on his way back to New York. He checked his notebook, dialed the palazzo number in Venice, and asked for Eduardo.

"Stone?"

"Yes, Eduardo?"

"This is Carmen Bellini. Eduardo and Dolce are on their way back to New York. I'm spending a couple of more days here to rest, at his suggestion. Are you in Los Angeles?"

"Yes." Stone told him most of what he knew so far. "If Eduardo contacts you before I reach him, please pass on that information."

"Certainly. Is there anything I can do for you?"

"Pray for Arrington," Stone said.

He hung up, and it suddenly occurred to him that, since he had left Venice, he had not thought of Dolce once.

⌁ Chapter 8 ⌁

Stone collected his rental car, a Mercedes E430, and drove to the Judson Clinic, arriving at noon. The place was housed in what had been a residence, a very large one, on a quiet Beverly Hills street, set well back from the road. The reception desk was in the marble foyer, and Stone asked for Dr. Judson.

A moment later, a man appeared on the upstairs landing, waving him up. Stone climbed the floating staircase and was greeted by a distinguished-looking man in his sixties, wearing a well-cut suit. Stone thought he would make an impressive witness, if it came to that.

"Mr. Barrington? I'm Jim Judson."

"Please, call me Stone."

"Thanks. Come into my office, and let's talk for a moment, before we see Arrington."

Stone followed him into a large, sunny office and took a seat on a sofa, while Judson sat across from him in a comfortable chair.

"I want to tell you what I know, thus far, so that you'll be prepared when you see Arrington," he said.

"Please do."

"Arrington was brought here by an ambulance on Saturday evening, at the request of her personal physician, Dr. Lansing Drake, a well-known Beverly Hills doctor. She was alternately hysterical, disoriented, and lethargic. Dr. Drake explained briefly what had occurred at her residence, and he and I agreed that she should be sedated. I injected her with twenty milligrams of Valium, and she slept peacefully through the night.

"When she awoke on Sunday morning she seemed quite calm and normal, and she immediately asked that you be contacted. She said that you were on an island in the Caribbean called St. Mark's, and that she was supposed to meet you there. My staff made repeated attempts to contact you there, without success. I reassured her that we would find you, and she seemed to accept that. She slept much of the morning, had a good lunch. When she questioned why she was here, I said that she had collapsed at home, and that I thought it a good idea for her to remain here for observation for a day or two. She accepted that.

"Late in the afternoon, her mother arrived, having flown in from Virginia. I was in the room when they met, and it became immediately apparent that Arrington was very disoriented. She seemed not to understand that she was married to Vance Calder, saying that she was supposed to interview him, but that she had changed her mind and had decided to meet you in St. Mark's instead. When her mother mentioned Peter, her son, she became disturbed again, but after a few moments seemed to understand that she had a son and that Calder was the father. Her mother, quite wisely, turned the conversation to trivial things, and after a few minutes she left. Arrington immediately went to sleep again."

"And what do you make of all this?" Stone asked.

"It seems clear that Arrington is undergoing periods of anterograde amnesia, brought on by the shock of her husband's murder. Anterograde amnesia is a condition during which the great mass of old memories, prior to a certain point, remain intact, while the subject does not have access to more recent memories, or those memories are intermittent or scrambled—this, as opposed to retrograde amnesia, during which the subject may lose memory of all prior events, even her identity."

"Forgive me, Jim, are you a psychologist?"

"A psychiatrist. This is, primarily, a psychiatric clinic, although we do some work with patients who have substance abuse problems."

"Is Arrington likely to recover all her memory?"

"Yes, if the basis for her amnesia is emotional, not physical, and that seems the case. Her mother had spoken with her on the previous Sunday and said that at that time she seemed perfectly normal. If she should show signs of not recovering her memory, then I think a brain scan would be in order, to rule out a physical basis for her problem."

"Does she know that Vance is dead?"

"That's hard to say; I haven't asked her that, directly, and when the police came here, I refused to allow her to be questioned."

"You did the right thing," Stone said.

"Arrington seems to have an idea that something may be wrong, but she tends to divert the conversation if it heads in a direction she doesn't want it to go. She may very well be, unconsciously, protecting herself emotionally from a situation that she is not yet ready to confront."

"I see. Perhaps it's time to explain to her what has happened?"

"Perhaps it is. She'll have to be told sooner or later, and since she seems to have an emotional attachment to you, it might be best that she hear it from you."

"All right. Jim, I should tell you that, for the moment, I am acting as Arrington's attorney, as well as her friend, and that, given the circumstances, you may be asked questions by the police. Should that occur, I advise you to rest on doctor-patient confidentiality and decline to answer. At a later date, with Arrington's concurrence, I may ask you to give a statement to the police or the district attorney."

"I understand completely."

"Shall we go and see Arrington, then?"

"Please follow me." Judson led the way from his office, down a hallway to the last door on the right-hand side. He knocked softly.

"Come in," a woman's voice replied.

Judson opened the door. "Arrington, I've brought someone to see you," he said. He stepped aside and ushered Stone into the room.

The room appeared much like a guest room in a sumptuous home, except for the elevated hospital bed. On the far side of the room, a cabinet had, apparently, once held a television set, which had been removed. Sunlight streamed through the windows, which were open above a garden at the rear of the house. Arrington sat up in bed and held out her arms. "Stone!" she cried.

Stone went to her and took her in his arms, kissing her on the cheek. To his surprise, she turned his head and gave him a wet kiss on the mouth. Stone glanced at the doctor, who evinced surprise.

"How are you feeling?" he asked.

"Much better. For a while, all I was doing was sleeping. What took you so long to get here?"

"I had to come a great distance," he replied. "Do you feel well enough to talk for a while?"

"Yes, I do; I feel very well, actually. I'm not quite sure why Dr. Judson is keeping me here."

"Your mother came to see you yesterday, remember?"

"Of course. We had a very nice visit. I'm sorry to have alarmed her; it was a long way for her to come, to find me perfectly well."

"She wanted to be sure Peter was all right without you."

Arrington's face clouded slightly. "Yes, she told me. I'm a little confused about that."

"How so?"

"Well, apparently—this is very embarrassing—I had forgotten that I'm his mother."

"That's all right," the doctor interjected. "Don't worry about that."

"Did you remember who Peter's father is?"

"Yes, after I was prompted, I'm ashamed to say. Stone, I'm so sorry; I wanted a chance to explain to you about Vance and me. I wrote to you in St. Mark's, but I suppose you must have already left there by the time the letter arrived. Can I explain?"

"Yes, go ahead," Stone said, sitting on the side of the bed.

She took his hand in both of hers. "Stone, I think I knew that you were going to ask me to marry you when I arrived in St. Mark's. Am I right, or am I being presumptuous?"

"You're right; I was going to ask you. I had a ring, even."

"I think I felt . . . a little panic about that, as if I weren't really ready to be your wife. I think that may be why I missed the first flight. The snow-storm was something of a relief, I'm afraid."

"You were a free woman," Stone said. "You didn't have to marry me."

"Then Vance arrived in town, and although we'd known each other before, something was different this time."

Stone recalled that Arrington had been with Vance, at a dinner party, when they had first been introduced.

"We spent all our time together, working on the interview, which turned into a *very* long conversation about everything in the world, and before I knew it, we were in love. I can't explain it; it just happened."

"It's like that, sometimes," Stone said.

"Do you hate me for it?"

"I could never hate you."

"Oh, I'm so relieved," she said, squeezing his hand. "I don't think I could be happy without you in my life—as a friend, I mean." She blushed a little.

"I feel the same way," Stone said. "And it's because I'm your friend that I have to tell you some things, now." Stone took a deep breath, looked directly into her large eyes, and told her.

⟿ Chapter 9 ⟿

Arrington stared at Stone as he spoke, her eyes wide and unblinking. Gradually, tears rimmed her eyes, then spilled down her cheeks. She seemed unable to speak.

Stone stopped talking for a moment. "Do you remember any of this?" he asked.

She shook her head, spilling more tears.

"What's the last thing you remember before Saturday?" Dr. Judson asked.

She closed her eyes tightly. "Someone cutting the grass," she said.

"And what day was that?"

"I'm not sure. I had a brief conversation with . . . Geraldo, his name is. I asked him not to cut the grass quite so closely. We agreed on two inches; I remember that."

"Do you remember what plans you and Vance had for Saturday night?" Judson asked.

She shook her head. "I'd have to look at the book."

"What book is that?"

"The book that Vance and I keep our schedules together in. I have my own book, too, for things I don't do with him, and he has his own book that Betty keeps."

"And who is Betty?"

"Betty Southard, his personal assistant; she works in his office at the studio."

"What were you doing immediately before you spoke to Geraldo?" the doctor asked.

"I was cutting flowers in the garden," she said.

"And what did you do after you finished cutting the flowers and speaking to Geraldo?"

Her shoulders sagged. "I don't remember. I suppose I must have gone back into the house, but I can't remember doing it."

"What jewelry had you planned to wear Saturday night?" Stone asked.

"Diamonds," she replied. "It was black tie."

"Who was the host?"

"What?"

"The host of the dinner party?"

"What dinner party?"

"The one on Saturday night."

She looked lost. "I don't remember."

"Did you take your jewelry out of the safe?"

"I don't know."

"What is the last thing you remember Vance saying to you?" Judson asked.

"He said I should wear the diamonds. He was taking his jewelry box out of the safe; I remember that."

"What else was in the safe?"

"I remember who was having the dinner party," she said. "It was Lou Regenstein."

"Did you enjoy the party?" Judson asked.

"I don't remember the party," she said.

"Arrington," Stone said, "does Vance own a gun?"

"I think so," she replied. "At least, he said he did. I've never seen a gun in the house."

"Do you know how to fire a gun?" Stone asked.

"My father taught me to fire a rifle, a twenty-two, when I was sixteen."

"Did he teach you how to fire a pistol, too?"

She shook her head. "I don't think I've ever even held a pistol."

"Well," Dr. Judson said, "I think we've covered about enough for now."

"Is Peter all right?" Arrington asked.

"Your mother wants to take him back to Virginia with her for a visit."

"I think that's a good idea," Arrington said, nodding. "I want to say good-bye to him."

"Suppose you telephone him," the doctor said.

"Yes, I could do that." She turned to Stone. "Tell me the truth. I'm not crazy, and I want to know. Is Vance dead?"

"Yes," Stone replied. "I'm afraid he is."

She was silent, seeming to think hard. "Who's taking care of everything?" she asked finally.

"You mean the house? The servants are there."

"No, I mean, there has to be a funeral; things have to be done; decisions made. I don't know if I can do this."

"I'll help in any way I can," Stone said. He had intended to bring this up, himself.

"Oh, would you handle things, Stone? There are legal matters, too, I'm sure."

"Who is your lawyer?" Stone asked.

"You are, I guess; I don't have another one. Vance has one, but I can't think of his name."

"Would you like me to represent you both legally and personally?" Stone asked.

"Oh, yes, please, Stone. I'd feel so much better, if I knew you were handling everything."

"What about medical decisions?"

"I'll make those myself," she said. "Unless I'm not able to, then I'd like you to make those decisions, too."

Stone opened a hotel envelope and took out a sheaf of papers. "Dr. Judson, do you believe that Arrington is capable of making decisions about her affairs?"

"I don't see any reason why she shouldn't," the doctor replied.

"Do you have a notary public here?"

"My secretary," he said, picking up a phone.

The woman arrived shortly with her stamp.

Stone explained each of the documents to Arrington—a general power of attorney, a medical authorization, an agreement appointing him as her attorney, and a letter addressed "To whom it may concern," stating that Stone had authority to act on her behalf in all matters, business and personal. When everything had been signed, notarized, and witnessed by the doctor, Stone kissed Arrington good-bye.

"I'll be back to see you tomorrow and bring you up to date on events," he said. "Why don't you call your mother now, and say good-bye to Peter?"

"All right. Stone, I'd like it very much if you would stay in our . . . my home; it would be comforting to know you are there. Manolo and the staff will make you comfortable in the guest house, and use the phones, the cars, anything you need."

"Thank you, I may do that," Stone said. "I'm going to go over there now and drive your mother and Peter to the airport. Will you tell her I'm on my way?"

"Yes, of course."

"Is there another way to the house besides through the front gate?"

"Yes, there's a service entrance about a hundred yards down the road, and there's a utility service road into the back of the property; you enter it from the street behind. I'll tell Manolo to open it for you."

"Thanks, that would be good." He kissed her again and left with the doctor. "What did you think, Jim?" Stone asked as they walked down the corridor.

"My diagnosis hasn't changed. She seems to remember something about that night, the thing about the jewelry; I'd like to know exactly when the conversation with the lawn man took place."

"So would I," Stone said. He thanked the doctor, then drove to Vance's house, entering through the utility road, where a servant stood waiting to close the gate behind him. He parked in a graveled area near the back door and went inside, where he was greeted by Manolo, the Filipino butler.

"It's good to see you again, Mr. Barrington."

"Thank you, Manolo," Stone replied. "I wish the circumstances were different. Mrs. Calder has suggested I move into the guest house."

"Yes, Mrs. Calder's mother passed on that message," Manolo said. "The guest house is all ready for you."

"I'm going to take Arrington's mother and Peter to the airport now, and after that I'll go back to the Bel-Air, return my rental car, and take a cab back here. Mrs. Calder suggested I use one of her cars."

"Of course, and I'll give you a remote that will open the back gate, too," Manolo said. "I'm afraid the media have the front gate staked out—permanently, it seems."

A man approached Stone. "Are you Mr. Barrington?"

"Yes."

"My name is Wilson; I'm commanding the security detail here."

"Good; what kind of vehicles do you have available?"

"I've got a Chrysler van with blacked-out windows, and two unmarked patrol cars."

"I'd like you to drive Mrs. Carter and the boy to Supermarine, at Santa Monica Airport. The Centurion Studios jet is waiting there to fly them to Virginia."

Mrs. Carter appeared in the hallway, a handsome little boy of two holding her hand. "Hello, Stone," she said. "Have you met Peter?"

Stone knelt and took the boy's small hand. "Not since he was a baby," he said. "Peter, you're getting to be a big boy."

"Yes, I am," the boy said gravely.

There was something familiar in the child's face, Stone thought—some characteristic of Vance or Arrington, he wasn't sure just what. "You're going to get to ride on a jet airplane this afternoon," he said.

"I know," Peter replied. "My bags are all packed."

Two maids appeared, carrying the luggage, and everyone was bundled into the van.

"I'll lead the way out the back," Stone said, "and I'd like a patrol car to follow us. If necessary, I'd like that car to block the road."

"I understand," Wilson replied. He spoke softly into a handheld radio. "My people are assembling out back, now. Shall we go?"

"Manolo," Stone said, "I'd like to talk with you when I get back."

"Of course, Mr. Barrington," Manolo replied. "I thought you might wish to." He handed Stone a small remote control for the rear gate.

"By the way," Stone said, "on what days is the lawn mowed?"

"The man is here today," the butler replied. "Ordinarily, it's on Fridays, but he was ill last Friday."

"When was the last time he was here?"

"A week ago Friday."

"Do you recall Mrs. Calder having a conversation with him on that day?"

"Yes, she asked him not to cut the lawn so closely. She asked me to see that it was done."

"A week ago Friday?"

"Yes, sir."

"Thank you, Manolo. And do you recall if Mr. and Mrs. Calder went out that evening?"

Manolo looked thoughtful. "Yes, they went to Mr. Regenstein's home for dinner. I drove them; the chauffeur was on vacation."

"Was it a black-tie dinner?"

"Yes, sir; Mr. Calder was dressed in a dinner suit."

"And do you remember what jewelry Mrs. Calder wore?"

"She wore diamonds," he said. "She usually does, when it's a black-tie event."

"Thank you, Manolo; I should be back in a couple of hours."

"Will you be dining here, then?"

"Yes, I think I will," Stone said.

"I'll tell the cook."

"Something simple, please; a steak will be fine."

"Of course."

Stone helped Mrs. Carter and Peter into the van, then got into his own car. They made it out the back way undetected.

⌒ Chapter 10 ⌒

Stone saw Mrs. Carter and Peter off on the Centurion jet, then returned to the Bel-Air, checked out, left his rent-a-car with the parking attendant, and took a cab back to the Calder residence. He had thought of returning through the rear entrance, but he didn't want a cab driver to know about that, so he called Manolo and asked him to be ready to open the front gate. There was only a single television van at the gate when he arrived, and the occupants took an immediate interest in him, but before they could reach the cab with a camera, he was safely inside. Before he got out of the cab, he handed the driver a hundred-dollar bill. "That's for not talking to the TV people about who you delivered here," he said.

"Thank you, sir," the man said, "but I don't know who you are, anyway."

"Just don't stop when you go out the gate."

Manolo and a maid took Stone's bags through the central hallway of the house, out the back, and around the pool to the guest house. Stone thought the little house was even nicer than the suite at the Bel-Air. While the maid unpacked for him and pressed his clothes, Stone walked back into the house with Manolo.

"You said you wished to speak with me, Mr. Barrington?"

"Yes, Manolo; it's important that I know everything that happened here on Saturday night. Please tell me what you saw and heard."

"I was in my quarters, a little cottage out behind the kitchen entrance, when I heard a noise."

"How would you characterize the noise?"

"A bang. I didn't react at first, but I was curious, so I left my quarters, entered the house through the kitchen door and walked into the central hall." He led the way into the house.

"Which door did you come through?" Stone asked.

"That one," Manolo replied, pointing to a door down the hall.

"And what did you see and hear?"

"I saw Mr. Calder lying right there," he said. "He was lying . . . he . . ."

"Can you show me?"

"Yessir." Manolo walked to the spot and lay down on his side, then rolled partly onto his belly. "Like this," he said. "Can I get up, now?"

"Yes, of course."

Manolo stood up. "He had a hole in his head here," he said, pointing to the right rear of his own head. "It was bleeding."

"Did you think he was alive?"

"Yessir, he was. I felt his pulse in his neck."

"What did you do then?"

"I went to the phone there," he pointed to a table, "and called nine-one-one and asked for the police and an ambulance quick."

"What next?"

"The maid, Isabel, came into the hall from the kitchen; I told her to go and see if Mrs. Calder was all right, and she went toward the master suite, there, through the living room, and through that door."

"How much time elapsed between the time you heard the shot and the time you found Mr. Calder?"

"I didn't go right away; I kept listening and wondering if I had heard what I heard. I expect it may have been two or three minutes."

"Which—two or three?"

"Closer to three, I guess. I wasn't running."

"Were those doors open?" Stone asked, pointing to the French doors that led to the pool, guest house, and gardens.

"One of them was," Manolo said. "It was wide open, in a way it wouldn't ordinarily be. Normally, it would either be closed, or both doors would be latched open."

"What happened next?"

"Mrs. Calder came running into the hall with the maid; she was wearing a robe and dripping water."

"What did she do or say?"

"She yelled out, 'Vance!' and then she got closer and saw the wound, and she backed away from him. She was making this noise, sort of like a scream, but not as loud, and she said, 'No, no!' a couple of times. I told Isabel to take her into the bedroom, that I would see to Mr. Calder and that an ambulance was on the way."

"Manolo, when Mrs. Calder came in, did you smell anything?"

"Well, yessir, I guess she smelled real sweet, having just got out of the tub."

Stone looked at the Saltillo tiles that formed the floor and saw a dark stain on the grout between the tiles.

"I couldn't get that out," Manolo said. "I tried, but I couldn't."

"What happened next, Manolo?"

"Two uniformed police officers arrived—they rang the bell, and I let them in the gate. They looked at Mr. Calder and felt his pulse, but they didn't move him. One of them talked to somebody on a walkie-talkie. Not long after that, another police car arrived, this time, plainclothesmen. They went and talked to Mrs. Calder, and I followed them, but she wasn't making any sense; she was hysterical and didn't seem to know where she was or what had happened."

"Show me where the master suite is, please."

Manolo led him through the living room and through a set of double doors, then through a small foyer and into a large bedroom, which contained a king-size bed, a fireplace, and a sofa and chairs in front of a hearth. "Mrs. Calder's dressing room and bath are through here," he said, leading the way through a door to one side of the bed. There was another foyer, and to the left, a very large room, filled with hanging clothes, cubicles for sweaters and blouses, shoe racks, and a three-way mirror. To the right was a large bathroom with a big tub and a dressing table. On top of the dressing table was a large perfume bottle, emblazoned with the name "Chanel," and next to that a bottle of bath oil with the same brand name. Stone smelled them both.

"Now, can I see Mr. Calder's dressing room?" Stone asked.

"Right this way, sir."

They walked back into the bedroom, around the bed, and through another door. The arrangement was the same but both the dressing room and bath were smaller and decorated in a more masculine style.

"Where is Mr. Calder's safe?" Stone asked.

Manolo went to a mirror over a chest of drawers, pressed it, and it swung open to reveal a steel safe door, approximately fifteen by twenty inches, a size that would fit between the structural studs. An electronic keypad, not a combination lock, was imbedded in the door.

"Do you know the combination?" Stone asked.

"Yessir, it's one-five-three-eight. You press the star key first, then the numbers, then the pound key, then turn that knob."

Stone opened the safe, which was empty. "What did Mr. Calder keep in here?" he asked.

"He kept his jewelry box and a gun," Manolo said.

"Do you know what kind of gun it was?"

"I don't know the brand of it, but it was an automatic pistol. There was a box of ammunition, too, that said nine millimeter, but the police took that."

"What was in the jewelry box?"

"Watches and other jewelry. Mr. Calder liked watches, and he had six or seven. There were some cuff links and studs, too; a nice selection."

"What did the box look like?"

"It was about a foot long by, I guess, eight inches wide, and maybe three or four inches deep. Deep enough to have the watches on mounts that displayed them when you opened the box. It was made out of brown alligator skin."

"The safe is pretty shallow," Stone said.

"The box would just fit into it, lying flat on the shelf, there. The pistol was at the bottom, along with the box of bullets."

Stone took one more look around. "Thank you, Manolo, that's all I need. Where is Mr. Calder's study? I'd like to make some phone calls."

"The main door is off the living room," Manolo said, "but you can get there this way, too." He walked to a double rack of suits, took hold of the wooden frame, and pulled. The rack swung outward. Then he pressed on the wall, and a door swung open, offering entry to the study.

Stone followed the butler into the study, then watched as he swung the door shut. Closed, it was a bookcase like the others in the room.

"Mr. Calder liked little secret things like that," Manolo said, smiling. "What time would you like dinner, Mr. Barrington?"

"Seven o'clock would be fine."

"And how do you like your beef cooked?"

"Medium, please."

"Would you like it served in the dining room or in the guest house?"

"In the guest house, I think."

"We'll see you at seven, then," Manolo said, and left the room.

Stone turned to examine Vance Calder's study.

∽ Chapter 11 ∼

Three Academy Awards gazed at Stone from the mantel of the small fireplace in the room. Stone knew that Vance had been nominated seven times and had won three. The room was paneled in antique pine that radiated a soft glow where the light struck it; there were some good pictures and many books. The room was extremely neat, as if it were about to be photographed for *Architectural Digest*.

Stone sat down at Calder's desk, and as he did, the phone rang. He checked the line buttons and saw that it was the third line, the most secret number. He picked it up. "Hello?"

There was a brief silence. "Who is this?" a woman's voice asked.

"Who's calling?"

"Stone?"

"Dolce?"

"I've been trying to reach you; the Bel-Air said you had checked out."

"I did, an hour ago. I'm staying in the Calders' guest house."

"With Arrington?"

"In the guest house. Arrington is in a hospital."

"What's wrong with her?"

"I don't think I should go into that on the phone; the press, as you can imagine, is taking an intense interest in all this. I wouldn't put it past some of the yellower journals to tap the phones."

"So you can't give me any information?"

"Not about Vance and Arrington, but *I'm* fine; I'm sure you wanted to know that."

"I don't like any of this, Stone."

"Neither do I; I'd much rather be in Venice with you."

"Sicily."

"What?"

"I was going to take you to Sicily, to show you where my family came from. I'm there now, on our honeymoon."

"I'm sorry to miss it; can I have a raincheck?"

"We'll see," she said, and there was petulance in her voice.

"Dolce, in Venice, you encouraged me to come here and help; that's what I'm doing."

"I had Papa and the cardinal to deal with. And exactly how are you helping?"

"I can't go into that, for the reasons I've just explained. Perhaps I can call you tomorrow from another number."

"Yes, do that." She gave him her number and the dialing codes for Sicily.

"How are you feeling?" he asked.

"Randy, actually. There's a rather interesting looking goatherd on the property; I was thinking of inviting him in for a drink."

"I can sympathize with your feelings," he replied. "I'd rather not be sleeping alone, myself."

"Then don't," she said. "I don't plan to."

"I meant that I'd rather be sleeping with you."

"You'd be my first choice, too," she said, "but you're not here, are you?"

Stone hardly knew what to say to that. Dolce had been mildly difficult, at times, but she had never behaved like this. He was shocked.

"No answer?"

"What can I say?"

"Say good night," she said, then hung up.

"Well," Stone said aloud, "that was very peculiar." He turned his attention back to the desk and began opening drawers. The contents were pretty much the same as in his own desk, but they were much more neatly arranged. He had never seen anything quite like it, in fact; it was as if a servant had come in and arranged the contents of the desk every day. He looked around for filing cabinets, but there were none. Apparently, all business was done from Vance's studio office.

Stone opened the center drawer, and, to his surprise, it pulled right out of the desk, into his lap. The drawer was lacking at least eight inches in what he had expected to be its depth. But why? He examined the bottom and sides of the drawer, which seemed perfectly normal, then he looked at the back. At the bottom of the rear of the drawer were two small brass hooks. Then he noticed that the drawer was slightly shallower than it might have been expected to be. He set the drawer on the desktop and looked at it for a minute. There was no apparent reason for the drawer to have hooks at its back. Unless . . . He took hold of the two drawer pulls and twisted, first to the left, then to the right. They moved clockwise for, perhaps, thirty degrees. He looked at the hooks on the back of the drawer; instead of lying flat, they were now positioned vertically.

He turned the knobs counterclockwise, and the hooks returned to their horizontal position. He reinserted the drawer all the way into the desk, turned the drawer pulls clockwise again, then opened the drawer all the way. The hooks had engaged another, smaller drawer that accounted for the missing depth, and in that drawer were some sealed envelopes, which he began opening.

The envelopes contained a copy of Vance's will, a note to Arrington with instructions in the event of his death, and two insurance policies, with a value of five million dollars each, payable to Vance's estate.

He placed the will on the desk and read it. There was a long list of bequests, most of them for a hundred thousand dollars or more. Two, to universities, were for a million dollars, for the establishment of chairs in the theatrical arts, and one was personal, in the same amount, to his secretary, Betty Southard. Arrington and Lou Regenstein had been appointed executors. The will was dated less than a month before. If everything else in Vance's estate was as well organized as his will, Stone reflected, then his affairs were as neatly arranged as his desk drawers. Stone made a note of the law firm that had drawn the will, then he replaced the documents in the secret compartment, closed the drawer, turned the pulls counterclockwise, and opened it again, just to check. Everything was as before.

Stone then went to the bedroom and searched it thoroughly; he assumed that the police had done the same thing and that the maid had tidied the place after them. Maybe that was why Vance's desk drawers were so neat. He found nothing but the ordinary detritus of wealthy married couples' lives—keys, address books, family photographs, bedside books, remote controls. Stone realized that the room did not appear to have a television set. He pressed the power button, and the lid of an old trunk at the foot of the bed opened, and a very large TV set rose from its depths and switched on.

The local news was on, and it was about Vance. A handsome young woman gazed into the teleprompter and read: "Vance Calder's widow has still not been questioned by the police. Greg Harrow has this report."

The scene shifted to the Calders' front gate, where a young man in an Italian suit spoke gravely. "Amanda, police department sources tell us that, as yet, there are no suspects in the murder of Vance Calder, and that his widow is still hospitalized, with no sign of emerging to speak. The investigating detectives want very much to talk to her, but her doctor refuses to allow her to be interviewed. Some of my colleagues in the media have been to every private hospital in the L.A./Beverly Hills area, without finding out where she is a patient. It had been suggested that she may have been taken to the Calder Palm Springs home, or to their Malibu beach house, but both those residences are dark, and during the past twenty-four hours, only one vehicle, a taxicab, has arrived here at the Calder Bel-Air home, and the driver refused to talk to the media. There was one man in the taxi, and he, apparently, remained at the house. Centurion Studios has issued a press release expressing the sorrow of everyone there at the news of Calder's death and asking that the media leave Arrington Calder alone and allow her to rebuild her shattered life. The Calders' only child, Peter, may still be at the Bel-Air house, cared for by the servants, but he has not been spotted here. All we have seen here is security, and plenty of it. A private service has the house and grounds completely sealed off, and no one, except the taxi, has arrived or departed today. We'll keep you posted as details come in."

Stone switched off the TV set, pleased with the news. He could hardly have written it better himself, but he knew the lid could not be kept on for much longer. He picked up the phone and called Rick Grant's home number.

"Hi, Stone, how's it going?"

"As well as can be expected," Stone said. "Let me give you a number where you, and only you, can reach me." He dictated the number. "You can also reach me at Vance Calder's offices at Centurion, as of tomorrow. I'm going to work out of there."

"Anything new?"

"Not much. Arrington is still under a doctor's care."

"How much longer?"

"You can tell your people that I'll make her available at the earliest possible moment."

"Tell them yourself," he said. "That would be better. The lead detectives on the investigation are Sam Durkee and Ted Bryant, out of Brentwood." He gave Stone the number.

"I'll call them tomorrow morning."

"These are decent guys, Stone, and Durkee, in particular, is a very good detective, but unless they start getting cooperation from Arrington, they're going to begin leaking stuff to the media, and that would not be good for her."

"We're not hiding anything; Arrington really hasn't been up to questioning, but she's getting better."

"I'm glad to hear it. Anything else I can do for you?"

"Not a thing, Rick; I'll call Durkee tomorrow."

"Good night, then; Barbara sends her best."

"My best to her, too." Stone hung up and felt a hunger pang. He walked back out to the guest house, where he found Manolo setting a small table and the maid hanging his clothes in the closet, having pressed them.

He sat down to his steak and half a bottle of good Cabernet and tried to forget both Arrington and Dolce as he watched a movie on television. He was unable to forget either of them.

⟫ **Chapter 12** ⟪

It was a perfect southern California morning, cool and sunny. Stone swam a few laps in the pool, then put on a guest's terrycloth robe and breakfasted by the pool, looking over the *Los Angeles Times* and *The New York Times*, which had arrived with his breakfast. The Vance Calder story had been relegated to the inside pages of the New York newspaper, and was struggling to cling to the front page of the L.A. journal, but it wasn't going to go away, he knew. The moment a fragment of new information surfaced, there would be headlines again.

He showered, shaved, dressed, and walked into the house, carrying his briefcase. He retrieved the documents from the secret compartment of Vance's desk and put them into his briefcase, then he rang for Manolo. "I'd like to use one of the Calders' cars," he told the butler.

"Of course, Mr. Barrington, right this way." He led Stone to a door that opened into the garage, which had enough room for six cars, but held only four: a Bentley Arnage; two Mercedes SL600s, one black and one white; and a Mercedes station wagon. "The nanny and I use the station wagon for household errands, unless you'd like it," Manolo said.

The Bentley was too much, Stone thought. "No, I'll take one of the other Mercedes—the black one, I suppose. That was Mr. Calder's wasn't it?"

"Yes, sir. The white one is Mrs. Calder's. You'll find the keys in the car."

Stone had used the black convertible once before, when in L.A., and he recalled that it did not have vanity plates, so it would not be immediately recognized by the media. In fact, he reckoned, a black Mercedes convertible would, in Beverly Hills and Bel-Air, be a practically anonymous car. He backed out of the garage, drove around the house and, using his remote, let himself out of the utility gate and onto the street beyond. He checked to be sure that he was not followed, then drove to Centurion Studios.

The guard was momentarily confused to see Vance Calder's car arrive with a different driver, but when Stone gave his name, he was immediately issued a studio pass.

"The one on the windshield will get this car in," the guard said. "Use the other pass, if you drive a different car."

"Can you direct me to Mr. Calder's bungalow, please?" The guard gave him directions, and five minutes later, he had parked in Vance's reserved parking spot. The bungalow was just that; it looked like one of the older, smaller Beverly Hills houses below Wilshire. Stone walked through the front door into a living room.

A panel in the wall slid open, and Betty Southard stuck her head through the opening. "I knew you'd turn up," she said. She left her office, walked into the living room and gave him a big hug and a kiss. "I'm glad to see you again," she said.

"I'm glad to see you, too; I'm going to need a lot of your help."

"Lou Regenstein called and said you'd be using Vance's office." She waved him into a panelled study, much the same as the one at the house, but larger, with a conference table at one end. "Make yourself at home," she said. "The phones are straightforward; you can make your own calls, or I'll place them for you, depending on whether you want to impress somebody."

"Thank you, Betty," Stone said, placing his briefcase on the desk. "I have some personal news for you; have you seen Vance's will?"

"Not the new one; he made that recently, and he hadn't brought a copy to the office."

"You're a beneficiary," Stone said. "He left you a million dollars."

Betty's jaw dropped, and a hand went to her mouth. "I think I'd better sit down," she said, and she did, taking a chair by the desk. Stone sat down behind it. "You didn't know?"

"I hadn't a clue," she said. "I mean, I suppose I would have expected something after fifteen years with him—I joined him at twelve, you know," she said archly.

Stone laughed. "Now you're a rich woman; what are you going to do?"

Betty sighed. "I haven't the foggiest idea," she said. "Lou has told me I could have my pick of jobs at the studio, but I don't know, I might just retire. I've saved some money, and I've done well in the bull market, and there's a studio pension, too; Vance got me fully vested in that last year, as a Christmas present."

"Then you can be a woman of leisure."

"A lady who lunches? I'm not sure I could handle that. Certainly, I'll stay on long enough to help you settle Vance's affairs—and Arrington's, too," she said darkly. "I'm sure she'll have a lot to settle."

"And what does that mean?" Stone asked.

"Oh, I don't know. I guess you know that Arrington and I have never gotten along too well—yes, you can call it jealousy, if you like, but there were other reasons."

"Tell me about them."

"Stone, tell me straight: Did Arrington shoot Vance?"

"I haven't the slightest reason to think so," Stone replied. "And I don't know why it even occurred to you to ask the question."

"As I understand it, the police have not cleared her."

"They haven't even talked to her, but I expect them to clear her when they do. She's at the Judson Clinic."

"Is she ill?"

"Not exactly, but she's been better. When she saw Vance on the floor of their home with a bullet in his head she pretty much went to pieces."

"Yes, she would, wouldn't she?" Betty said with a hint of sarcasm.

Stone ignored that. "I hope she can get the police interview out of the way soon, maybe even today. It will depend on what her doctor says."

"Look, I certainly don't have any evidence, but—call it woman's intuition, if you like—I think Arrington is perfectly capable of having killed Vance, then pretending to break down, just to keep from having to talk to the police."

"Tell me why you think that."

"Just for starters, I think Vance was miserable in the marriage. Oh, he never said so, in so many words, but I knew him as well as anybody, and I think that, in spite of his constant good humor, he was unhappy."

"Give me some example of his unhappiness."

"I can't. It was just the odd comment, the raised eyebrow when Arrington was mentioned. He did love Peter, though; I've never seen a man love a child so much."

"Anything more specific?"

"No, certainly nothing I could testify to under oath."

Stone relaxed a little inside; he hadn't realized he had become so tense. "Well, I hope you'll keep your feelings to yourself. If you think of anything specific you can tell me, I want to hear about it, though."

"Of course."

Stone glanced at his watch. "Let's get started. Will you get me Dr. James Judson at the Judson Clinic?"

Betty placed the call from the conference table phone, then left the room and closed the door.

"Good morning, Jim, it's Stone Barrington."

"Good morning, Stone."

"How's your patient this morning?"

"She's very well, I think. I believe she's about ready to go home."

"Not just yet," Stone said. "She's going to have to talk to the police, and I'd like her to do it from a hospital bed."

"I understand. When do you want them to see her?"

"Today, if you think it's all right."

"I think it should be. She's mentioned that she expects them to come, so we may as well get it over with. I'd like to be with her when they question her, though."

"Of course, and I will be, too. How about early afternoon?"

"All right; I'll prepare her."

"I'll do some preparation, too, before they arrive. I'll let you know the exact time, after I've talked to them."

"I'll wait to hear from you, before I tell Arrington."

"I'm working from Mr. Calder's office at the studio, should you need to reach me." Stone gave him the number, then hung up. He found the intercom and buzzed Betty.

"Yes, Stone?"

"Now get me Detective Sam Durkee at the Brentwood LAPD station."

After a short wait, Betty buzzed him, and he picked up the phone. "Detective Durkee?"

"That's right."

"My name is Stone Barrington; I'm handling the affairs of Mrs. Vance Calder."

"I know your name from Rick Grant," Durkee said. "Rick says you're an ex–homicide detective."

"That's right; NYPD."

"Then you'll understand what we have to do."

"Of course. I've just spoken to Mrs. Calder's doctor, and he says you can interview her this afternoon. How about two o'clock at the Judson Clinic?"

"That's good for me; I'll bring my partner, Ted Bryant."

"You have to understand her condition," Stone said. "She's been very badly shaken up, and there are some big gaps in her memory."

"Oh? How big?"

"When I spoke with her yesterday, the last thing she could remember was a conversation with her gardener eight days before the homicide. I've confirmed the date with her butler."

"So, basically, when we question her, she's going to say she remembers nothing?"

"Her doctor says she may recover some of her memories, but I can't promise you anything. For a while, she didn't remember being married to Calder, but she's gotten past that, so she may remember even more. I can tell you that she has no hesitation about talking to you; she wants her husband's murderer caught and prosecuted."

"Well, we'll certainly try to make that wish come true," Durkee said.

"There have to be some ground rules: Both her doctor and I will be present at the interview, and if either of us, for any reason, feels she shouldn't continue, we'll stop it."

"Understood," Durkee said dryly. "See you at two o'clock."

Stone hung up and began to think about this interview. It was crucial, he knew, for Arrington to convince them she was innocent. If she couldn't do that, her life was going to change even more dramatically than it already had.

⤳ **Chapter 13** ⤳

Stone could have spotted the two men as detectives in any city in the United States. They were both middle-aged, dressed in middling suits that revealed bulges under the left arm to anyone looking for them. Sam Durkee was at least six-four and beefy in build; Stone made him as an ex-athlete. Ted Bryant was shorter, bald, and pudgy. He didn't expect either of them to be stupid, and his plan was to be as cooperative as humanly possible, without handing them his client on a platter.

He shook their hands, then led them upstairs to Arrington's room. She was sitting up in bed wearing cotton pajamas; Dr. Judson was at her bedside. Stone made the introductions, and everybody pulled up a chair.

Durkee took the lead. "Mrs. Calder," he said, "first, I want to offer the department's condolences on your loss."

"Thank you," Arrington said, managing a wan smile.

"I hope you understand that there are questions we must ask, if we're to apprehend your husband's killer; I know this won't be pleasant, but we'll keep it as short as we can, and we'd like the fullest answers you can give us."

"I'll do my best," Arrington replied.

"What do you recall about the evening your husband was shot?"

"Absolutely nothing, I'm afraid. I remember going to the hairdresser's the day before, the Friday, but I don't remember driving home, or anything after that, until I woke up here."

A Friday memory was progress, Stone thought.

"Are you beginning to pick up pieces of your memory?" Bryant asked.

"It seems so," she said. "Every day, I remember a little more."

"Are you aware that your husband owned a gun?"

"He told me so, but I never saw it."

"Was he the sort of man who would have used a gun to defend his home?"

"He certainly was; I'm sure that's why he owned it."

"Do you know where he kept the gun?"

"No."

Stone spoke up. "The butler told me that Mr. Calder kept a nine-millimeter pistol in the same safe where he kept his jewelry."

"Thank you," Durkee replied. "Mrs. Calder, how would you characterize your marriage?"

"As a very happy one," Arrington replied.

"Did you and your husband ever quarrel?"

"Of course." She smiled a little. "But our quarrels were almost always good-humored. You might call them mock quarrels. We argued about lots of things, but always with respect and affection."

"You say your quarrels were 'almost' always good-humored. Did they ever become violent?"

"You mean, did Vance ever hit me? Certainly not."

"Did you ever hit him?"

She looked down. "I can remember slapping him, once and only once. He'd said something that offended me."

"What did he do when you slapped him?"

"He apologized, and it never happened again. My husband was a gentleman in every possible sense of the word."

"When you argued, what did you argue about?"

"He would give me a hard time, sometimes, about how much shopping I did. Vance had a tailor, a shirtmaker, and a bootmaker; he ordered his clothes from swatches, so shopping was very simple for him. I think it both amused and horrified him to learn how women shop. He could never understand why I would buy things, then take them back the next day."

"Any other subjects you argued about?"

"Sometimes we'd disagree on child rearing. Vance believed strongly in corporal punishment, and I didn't. He'd been brought up that way by his parents, and in English schools, and he thought if it was good enough for him, it was good enough for his son."

"Did he use corporal punishment often with your child?"

"Rarely, and then only a palm applied to the bottom."

"And you disagreed with that?"

"Yes. I was never struck as a child, and I didn't want Peter to be."

"What else did you disagree about?"

She shrugged. "I can't think of anything else specifically."

"What about women?"

"There were one or two of my friends he didn't like much, but he tolerated them for my sake."

"That's not what I mean," Durkee said. "Are you aware that your husband had a reputation for sleeping with his leading ladies?"

Arrington smiled. "That was before we were married. My husband walked the straight and narrow."

"And if you had learned that he didn't, might that have provoked a quarrel?"

"It might have provoked a divorce," Arrington replied. "When we married, I let him know in no uncertain terms what I expected of him in that regard."

"And what did you expect?"

"Fidelity."

"Were you always faithful to him?"

"Always," she replied.

"Was there any man in your past for whom you still felt . . . affection?"

Stone was a little uncomfortable with this, but he kept a straight face and waited for her answer.

"I feel affection for a number of friends," Arrington replied, "but I was as faithful to my husband as he was to me."

Stone didn't like this answer, and he saw the two detectives exchange a glance.

Arrington saw it, too. "What I mean is, I was faithful to him, and he was faithful to me."

"Mrs. Calder, are you acquainted with a woman named Charlene Joiner?"

"Of course; she costarred with my husband in a film."

"Were you and Ms. Joiner friends?"

"No; we met a few times, and our relationship was cordial, but I wouldn't call us friends. The last time I saw her was when she and Vance cohosted a political fund-raiser at our house."

"Would it surprise you to learn that your husband, while he was filming with Ms. Joiner, was spending considerable periods of time in her trailer?"

"No; I suppose they had lines to read together."

Bryant spoke up. "Mrs. Calder, when did you become aware that your husband was having sex with Ms. Joiner?"

"I was not and am not aware of that," she replied icily.

"Come on, Mrs. Calder," Bryant said impatiently, "while they were filming together, your husband stopped having sex with you, didn't he?"

They were good cop/bad copping her, and Stone hoped Arrington had the sense to realize it. He made no move to stop them.

"My husband and I had a very satisfactory sex life, and I can't remember any period of our marriage when that wasn't the case," Arrington replied firmly.

"Do you not recall ever telling another woman that your husband had stopped making love to you?"

Arrington frowned. "Ah," she said, "I think I know what you're getting at. A friend of mine once complained to me that *her* husband had stopped sleeping with her, and I believe I tried to commiserate by telling her that all couples went through periods like that. I think you must have spoken with Beverly Walters."

"Do you deny telling Mrs. Walters that your husband had stopped fucking you?" Bryant demanded.

Stone began to speak, but Arrington held up a hand and stopped him.

"I think Mrs. Walters may have inferred a bit more than I meant to imply," she said, and her color was rising.

"Mrs. Calder," Durkee said, breaking in, "if you had learned that your husband was having sex once, sometimes twice a day with Ms. Joiner in her trailer, would that have made you angry?"

"Hypothetically? Yes, I suppose it would have hurt me badly."

"When you are hurt by a man, do you respond angrily?"

"I have a temper, Detective Durkee, but on the occasions when it comes out, I have never harmed another human being."

"When was the last time you fired a handgun?" Bryant asked suddenly.

"I have never fired a pistol," she replied.

"But you know how, don't you?"

"I have never, to the best of my recollection, even held a handgun."

"Mrs. Calder," Durkee asked, "where is your husband's jewelry box?"

"I'd like very much to know, Detective; I had hoped that, by now, you might be able to tell me."

"Where did you hide the jewelry box and the pistol?"

"I didn't hide either of them anywhere," she replied.

"But you say you don't remember anything about the shooting. How could you remember not hiding them?"

"To the very best of my recollection, I have not handled either my husband's jewelry box or his gun."

"Mrs. Calder, do you recall hearing or reading somewhere that perfume applied to the hands and arms removes any trace of having fired a weapon?"

"No, I don't."

"What kind of perfume do you use?"

"I use several, but my favorite is Chanel No. 5."

"Did you use that the night your husband was shot?"

"I don't remember the night my husband was shot."

"Would you use perfume before taking a bath?"

Arrington looked at him as if he were mad. "No."

"Then why would you reek of perfume on getting out of a bath?"

"I use bath oil, Detective, of the same scent as my perfume, but generally speaking, I never reek."

Stone suppressed a smile. He sensed that the two detectives were running out of questions, but he didn't rush them.

"Mrs. Calder," Durkee said, "I have to tell you that, after investigating your husband's murder very thoroughly, we have concluded that the two of you were alone in the house when he was shot."

"That hardly seems possible," Arrington replied. "Otherwise, where are the jewelry box and the gun?"

"We believe you hid them after shooting your husband."

"Where? Have you searched our house?"

"We haven't found them—yet," Bryant said.

"Let me know when you do," Arrington said. "Otherwise, I'll have to file an insurance claim."

Durkee stood up. "I believe that's all for now," he said, turning to Stone. "I want to be notified when she leaves the hospital, and I want to know where she goes."

"I'll give you a call," Stone said, walking both men toward the door.

When they were outside, Bryant turned to Stone. "She killed him," he said.

"Nonsense," Stone said. "It's obvious that someone got into the house. Haven't you found any evidence of anyone else?"

The two detectives exchanged a glance.

"I want disclosure," Stone said.

"Are you licensed to practice law in the state of California?" Bryant asked.

"No."

"My advice is to get her a lawyer who is. I'm sure the D.A. will disclose to him."

Stone watched as the two detectives walked to their car. He didn't like the way this was going.

⟫ **Chapter 14** ⟪

Stone arrived back at Vance's studio bungalow to find a message from Lou Regenstein, whom he'd been meaning to call anyway. He got the studio head on the phone.

"How is Arrington?" Lou asked.

"Much better. Her doctor says she can go home tomorrow."

"Have you given any thought to funeral arrangements?"

"I was going to ask you the same thing. I'm sure the studio can do a much better job of this than I can."

"I have a suggestion," Lou said.

"Go ahead."

"We have a cathedral set on our biggest sound stage right now. I'd like to hold a memorial service for Vance there and, in addition to his friends, invite many of the studio employees who have worked with Vance over the years."

"That sounds good to me," Stone said.

"I'd like to invite a small media pool and allow them to tape the service. I think that will go a long way toward keeping them off Arrington's back right now."

"Why don't you give Arrington a call at the Judson Clinic and discuss it with her? I think she's up to it now; she saw the police this afternoon."

"Is Arrington facing any legal difficulties?" Lou asked.

"It's too soon to tell, Lou; the police, not having a suspect, quite naturally look at the spouse. I think we'll just have to wait for them to get past that."

"Have you called Marc Blumberg, my lawyer friend, yet?"

"Not yet; I hope we won't need him. Also, there's a downside to calling him; if somebody in his firm leaked the call to the press, it would make it look as though we expected Arrington to be charged."

"I understand," Lou said. "I'll call Arrington now."

Stone hung up and glanced at his watch. It would be midnight in Sicily, now, and he hadn't called Dolce yet. He knew she liked to stay up late, so he dialed the number.

It rang once, before being picked up by a machine. "I'm entertaining a guest right now," Dolce's voice said, "so go away."

Stone hung up, angry, and tried to think of something else. He thought of Marc Blumberg and dialed his number.

"Mr. Blumberg's office," a woman said.

"My name is Stone Barrington; I'm calling Mr. Blumberg at the suggestion of Lou Regenstein."

"And how can Mr. Blumberg help you, Mr. Barrington?"

He obviously wasn't going to get past this woman without telling her the purpose of his call, and he had no intention of doing that. "Please ask Mr. Blumberg to call me at Centurion Studios." He gave her the number and hung up.

Betty Southard came into the office. "I was passing and heard you mention a Blumberg. Marc Blumberg?"

Stone nodded.

"Is Arrington in *that* much trouble?"

"It's just a precaution," Stone replied. "I think it's best to be ready for anything."

"I suppose so," she said. "How about some dinner tonight?"

"I'd like that," Stone said. He hadn't been looking forward to being sequestered at the Calder house, and Dolce's behavior had removed any guilt he might have felt about seeing another woman. "Book us at your favorite restaurant."

"Pick me up at seven-thirty?"

"Sure."

"You remember the address?"

"How could I forget?"

The phone rang, and Betty picked up the one on the desk. "Mr. Calder's bungalow." She handed the phone to Stone. "Marc Blumberg."

"Thank you for returning my call, Mr. Blumberg," Stone said. "Lou Regenstein has suggested we meet to discuss something very important."

"Of course," Blumberg said. "Tomorrow morning okay?"

Stone could hear diary pages turning. "I'd rather not come to your office, for reasons I'll explain later. Would it be possible for you to meet me at Centurion Studios after office hours?"

"I'll be finished here by five-thirty," Blumberg replied. "I could be there by six, but I'll only have about forty-five minutes; I have to get home and change for dinner."

"Six will be fine," Stone said. "I'll leave instructions for you at the gate." He hung up. "Betty," he said, "will you have a pass and directions to the bungalow at the main gate? Blumberg is coming here at six."

"Consider it done," she replied.

"Do you mind if I don't change for dinner?" he asked. "I won't have time to go back to Vance's."

"No problem. When is Arrington getting out of the hospital?"

"Tomorrow, I hope."

"Do you think you should be living at the house then?"

"You have a dirty mind."

"You bet I do; I have two suggestions."

"What?"

"The first is, move in with me. I managed to make you comfortable the last time you were here."

"I think it's best that I just move back to the Bel-Air," Stone said. "What's your second suggestion?"

"Vance has . . . had a place at Malibu; I think that might be enough distance between you and Arrington, and I've got the keys."

"That's a thought," Stone said. "I'll let you know."

Marc Blumberg bustled into the bungalow promptly at six, a small, fit-looking, deeply tanned man of fifty in a perfectly cut suit and gleaming shoes.

Stone shook his hand. "Can I get you a drink?"

"I'm okay," Blumberg said, taking a seat on a leather sofa. "I believe I've heard of you, Stone. May I call you Stone?"

Stone sat down beside him. "Of course."

"And I'm Marc. I remember that business in St. Mark's a few years back, when you defended the woman on a murder charge. Saw it on *60 Minutes,* I think."

"Yes, that was a difficult one."

"Pity she was hanged."

"Yes."

"I remember from Lou that you're a friend of Mrs. . . . the Calders. I take it I'm here to talk about another murder trial."

"Let's call this a precautionary meeting."

"It's always wise to take precautions. Has Arrington talked to the police yet?"

"Earlier this afternoon."

"I should have been there for that," Blumberg said.

"I didn't want to appear to be running scared," Stone said. "You'd have been happy with the way it went." He gave Blumberg a detailed rundown of Arrington's questioning.

"That sounds okay," Blumberg said. "You handled it well."

"Thank you."

"Sounds as though they don't have another suspect."

"That's how I read it. They went through the drill the night of the murder, and they didn't come up with anything, and that disturbs them. Cops like early indications, and when they don't find them, they look at the household."

"Anybody in the house besides Arrington?"

"No. The butler and maid were in their quarters; the butler found Vance and called the police."

"What was the scene like?"

"Vance was dressed in tuxedo trousers and a pleated shirt, no tie. They were going to a black-tie dinner at Lou's house a little later. He was found lying facedown in the central hallway of the house, one bullet here." Stone pointed at the spot.

"You used to be a cop didn't you?"

"Yes."

"Have you got a scenario for this that doesn't involve Arrington shooting Vance?"

"Here's how I read it," Stone said. "Arrington was in the bathtub; Vance was getting dressed. His safe was open, containing his jewelry box, a nine-millimeter automatic, and a box of cartridges. He either walked in on a burglary, or a burglar walked in on him, probably the former. The burglar took the jewelry box and the gun, walked Vance into the central hallway and shot him."

"Any struggle?"

"Looks like an execution to me. My guess is, Vance saw it coming and turned away. That's why the wound in the back of the head." Stone stood up, held out his hands in the "no, no" position, then half turned away from his imaginary assailant.

"Makes sense," Blumberg said.

"For Arrington to have done it, she would have to have gone to the safe, taken out the gun, cocked it, flipped off the safety, then either marched her husband out into the hall, or gone looking for him and found him there. That doesn't fit a domestic quarrel."

"It fits a cold-blooded, premeditated murder," Blumberg said. "How do you figure the chances of that?"

"Unlikely in the extreme."

"I'm glad to hear it. So what we've got is an innocent woman who loved her husband, who is a suspect only because the police haven't done their job and found the real killer."

"In a nutshell," Stone said. "A couple of other things you should know: I got the impression from the detectives that they might have other evidence we don't know about. They refused to disclose it to me, said they'd talk to a California lawyer."

"We'll get it, don't worry. What's the other thing?"

"The police talked to a woman named Beverly Walters, who told them Vance was screwing an actress named Charlene Joiner; they took that as Arrington's motive for the shooting."

"I know her; she's a complete bitch, and she could give us trouble at a trial. Charlene Joiner, huh? If it's true, Vance was a lucky guy."

"Yeah, I've seen some of her pictures."

"Tell me, Stone, what's your role in all this?" Blumberg asked. "Family friend?"

"That, and for the moment, Arrington's personal representative. I have her confidence and a power of attorney."

Blumberg looked Stone in the eye. "You and Arrington ever have a thing, Stone?"

"We were living together in New York when she suddenly married Vance."

"You want me to represent her?"

"If it becomes necessary."

"I think you're right about my presence being a red flag; the media would play that big. Here's what we do. I don't so much as even speak to Arrington, unless we find out she's going to be arrested."

"I might be able to get advance notice of that, if it happens."

"Good. If you do, I surrender her to the D.A. I can arrange that. From then on, I'm her lawyer, not you; I'm running the case."

Stone shook his head. "If it comes to that I'll want to be involved every step of the way."

"That's not how I work."

"Then I can only thank you for your time," Stone said.

Blumberg thought for a moment. "What do you want?"

"Second chair; partner in decision-making; no move without my agreement."

"All right," Blumberg said. "Are you licensed in California?"

"No."

"I'll deal with that. I'll want a hundred-thousand-dollar retainer up front, against a half-million-dollar fee, the remainder payable before the trial starts."

"To include all your expenses," Stone said.

"Agreed. If I can stop it before it goes to trial, I'll bill her at a thousand dollars an hour."

"To include your associates and staff."

"Done." Blumberg held out his hand, and Stone shook it.

"I'll draft a letter appointing you and get a check drawn, immediately after any arrest."

"When is Arrington returning home?"

"Tomorrow, I think."

"Where are you living while you're here?"

"In the Calders' guest house."

"I don't want the two of you to spend so much as a single night under the same roof. Move out before she gets home."

"All right."

Blumberg looked at his watch and stood up. "I've got to run," he said.

"One thing, Marc," Stone said. "I don't want you to mention this to *any-body*—staff, wife—*anybody*."

"That goes without saying," Blumberg replied.

Stone walked him to his car. "Thanks for coming," he said.

"Don't worry about a thing," Blumberg said breezily. "I'll get her off."

Stone waved good-bye, then went to his own car. You probably will, he thought, but I hope to God it doesn't come to that.

He went back to his desk, called Dolce again and got the same message. It only made him angrier. He was glad to be having some company tonight.

⤷ **Chapter 15** ⤶

Stone and Betty sat at a good table at Spago Beverly Hills. "I remember when this was another restaurant," he said. "I had lunch here a couple of times, in the garden."

"I'll give you a little Beverly Hills gossip," Betty said. "You know why the old place failed, after many years as a success?"

"Tell me."

"The story is, a group of prominent wives were having lunch here, when they overheard the owner make an anti-Semitic remark. They told their friends, their friends told their friends, and within two weeks, the place was empty. It went out of business not long afterward."

"I'll bet you're full of Beverly Hills gossip," Stone said.

"You bet I am."

"Then tell me, was Vance sleeping with Charlene Joiner?"

Betty smiled. "What do you know about Charlene Joiner?"

"Just what I read in the papers during the presidential campaign. She had once had an affair with Will Lee, back when he was first running for the Senate, and the Republicans tried to make something of it."

"Well, let me tell you; Charlene is some piece of work. She has cut a swath through the rich and powerful in this town, and she has done it very cleverly, choosing her partners carefully, as much for their discretion as for what they can do for her career."

"Sounds like a smart girl."

"Smart, and from what I can glean, spectacular in the sack, in a town where outstanding is ordinary."

"But was Vance sleeping with her?"

Betty toyed with her drink.

"I don't think it would be disloyal of you to tell me."

"Yes, I know; Vance is dead, but sometimes I feel as though he's just on location, or something, and that he might walk into the bungalow at any moment."

"If you feel you'd be betraying a confidence, I understand."

"This has something to do with Arrington, doesn't it?" she asked.

"It might, before this is all over. It's important that I know whether this is just a rumor, or if it's true."

Stone looked up to see a lush-looking brunette in her mid-thirties walk up to their table. She was fashionably dressed, coiffed, and made up, and Stone thought her breasts seemed too large for the rest of her.

"Hello, Betty," the woman said, her voice dripping with sympathy. "How are you doing, sweetie?"

Stone stood up.

"Hi, Beverly," Betty replied. "Oh, Stone, this is Beverly Walters; Beverly, this is Stone Barrington."

"Arrington's friend?" she held out a hand. "She's told me so much about you."

"How do you do?" Stone said.

"How long are you in town for?"

"Not very long," Stone replied.

She fished a card from her handbag and handed it to him. "Call me; maybe I can help."

Stone pocketed the card. "Thank you."

"Betty, I'm so sorry about Vance; I know how close you were."

"Thanks, Beverly," Betty replied, without much enthusiasm.

"Call me, if you want to bend an ear," the woman said. She gave Stone a little wave and walked back to her table.

"Steer clear of *her*," Betty said through clenched teeth.

"She's the source of the rumor I'm trying to confirm," Stone said. "She told the police that Vance was sleeping with Charlene Joiner."

"She doesn't know anything; she's just inventing gossip."

Their dinner arrived.

"Betty, one more time: Was Vance sleeping with her?"

"All right, I'll tell you about Vance. It was his practice to sleep with *all* his leading ladies, and a lot of those in supporting roles, too."

"Even after he was married?"

"He never wavered. He'd either have them back to the bungalow for lunch or to his trailer. You haven't seen the trailer, have you? It is *very* comfortable."

"*All* his leading ladies?"

"You go back and watch *any* film that Vance starred in, and you may wonder why the love scenes are so convincing. Well, they were convincing, because they had been *very* well rehearsed."

"And how many pictures did Vance make after he was married?"

Betty counted on her fingers. "Four," she said.

"You think Arrington knew about this?"

"I don't think Vance was shortchanging her, if that's what you mean."

"This Walters woman told police that Arrington had complained to her that Vance had stopped sleeping with her, and that the reason was an affair with Charlene Joiner."

Betty shook her head. "That just doesn't ring true. Vance was a sexual athlete his whole life. He was in superb physical condition, and he *loved* sex. He could have made a very nice living doing porno movies, because he had both the equipment and the endurance for the work. It's much more likely that Arrington would have complained of *too much* sex, rather than not enough."

"How do you know about all this?"

"Because I know *everything* about Vance Calder. I worked for him for fifteen years, and I got the job while in bed with him. I was a script girl on one of his pictures, and we were fucking each other for most of the shoot. Toward the end of the picture, he offered me the job. He told me, quite frankly, that our little affair was going to end with the wrap, and I knew he was telling the truth. I took the job, because it was better than the one I had, and we didn't make love again. But he never kept secrets from me. Maybe that's why he left me the million dollars—because he knew I could make that much writing a tell-all book. I could, too."

"I'll bet you could."

"So, now you know what you want to know?"

"I do."

"Now you tell me something," she said.

"Anything."

"The last time you were in L.A., you and I had a rather delicious time together."

"We certainly did."

"Why do I get the feeling that isn't going to happen this time?"

"Things have changed," Stone said. He told her about Dolce and why he had been in Venice.

Betty nodded. "I understand," she said. "I don't like it much, but I understand."

"Thank you for not liking it," Stone replied.

⤳ Chapter 16 ⤳

Stone slipped into the estate through the utility entrance, parked his car in back and walked to the guest house. He got out of yesterday's clothes, slipped into a robe, called Manolo, and ordered breakfast. As soon as he set down the phone, it rang.

"Hello?"

"Stone?" It was Arrington, and she sounded agitated. "I've been trying to reach you since last night—where have you been?"

"Right here," he lied. "I was tired, so I unhooked the phone. I just plugged it in again so I could order breakfast. How are you feeling?"

"I'm feeling very well, thank you. The doctor says I can leave this morning. He wants to check me over once more, but I should be ready to go by ten. Will you come and get me, please?"

"Of course. I'll be there at ten sharp."

"Oh, good. Will you bring me some clothes? Ask Isabel, the maid, to put together an outfit—slacks and a blouse, shoes, stockings, and underwear. They brought me here practically naked, and I don't have anything to wear."

"Sure. I'll call Isabel, and I'll see you there at ten." He started to tell her he was moving out of the house, but he thought it might be best to wait until he saw her.

"See you then, darling," she said and hung up.

Stone called the maid and asked her to put the clothing into his car; then, as he promised he would, he called Sam Durkee at the Brentwood station.

"Durkee."

"Morning, Sam. It's Stone Barrington."

"Oh, yeah."

"You asked me to let you know when Mrs. Calder was leaving the clinic; it's this morning." He paused for a moment, native caution coming into play. "At ten-thirty."

"Hey, Ted," Durkee called out, "Vance Calder's widow is getting out at ten-thirty." His voice returned to the receiver. "Thanks for letting us know," he said.

"Do you need to speak with her again?" Stone asked.

"Not at the moment."

"If you do, call me at Centurion Studios, and I'll arrange it. The operator there will find me."

"Sure thing."

"Good-bye." Stone hung up, wishing he hadn't called Durkee; he had a funny feeling about this.

At nine-fifteen, as Stone was finishing breakfast, the phone rang.

"Hello?"

"Stone? It's Jim Judson, at the clinic."

"Morning, Jim; is Arrington still going to be ready to leave at ten?"

"I'm not sure if you'll want her to," Judson replied. "As we speak, the press is gathering outside. There are three television vans with satellite dishes, and at least a dozen reporters."

"Ah," Stone said, once again regretting his call to Durkee. "I think this calls for a change in plans."

"I thought you might think so."

"Is there another way out of the building besides the front door?"

"We have a small parking lot for staff at the west end of the building. You enter it from near the front door, but the exit is around the corner. From my office, I can see media people staking that out, too, but only a handful of them."

Stone had a look at his street map of Beverly Hills. "All right, here's what we do," Stone said. "Can you find a nurse's uniform that will fit Arrington?"

"Yes, I suppose so."

"Get her dressed in the uniform, cap and all, and borrow a car—the older and more modest, the better—from one of your staff. Have Arrington walk out to the parking lot, get into the car, and leave by the side-street exit. Have her turn left, then take her first right. I'll be waiting there. She'll leave the borrowed car there for you to pick up."

"All right. When do you want her to leave the building?"

Stone looked at his watch. "Half an hour?"

"Fine."

"How is she this morning?"

"She's all right, but you might still find her a little fragile. She still hasn't remembered anything between her hair appointment the day before the murder and waking up here the day after."

"Thanks, Jim; I'll speak to you later, if I have any questions." Stone hung up, then checked his map again. He'd have to pass a corner near the clinic to position himself where he wanted to be; he hoped his car would be anonymous enough. He called Manolo. "I'd like to take the station wagon today," he said.

"Of course, Mr. Barrington; I'll have Isabel put the clothes in that car. The keys are in it."

Stone drove out the utility exit and made his way toward the Judson Clinic. He had to stop at a traffic light on the corner half a block from the clinic, and as he waited, Sam Durkee and Ted Bryant drove past him on the cross street, toward the clinic. "You sons of bitches," Stone muttered. The light changed and he drove straight ahead, past the exit from the employees' parking lot, which a small group of reporters had staked out. He turned right at the next corner and pulled over, leaving the engine running.

Ten minutes passed, and, right on time, Arrington appeared, driving an elderly Honda. She parked the car, ran over to the Mercedes station wagon, and got in. "Thank you for getting me out of there, Stone," she said, planting a kiss on his cheek.

Stone pulled out of his parking space. "Your clothes are in the backseat. Did anybody recognize you?"

"Nope; they hardly gave me a glance. I wasn't what they were expecting, I guess." She began undressing.

Stone tried to keep his eyes straight ahead and failed. "I don't think we should go to the Bel-Air house," he said.

"Shall we just check into a motel, then?" she suggested.

"How about the Malibu house?"

"I don't have a key with me."

"Betty gave me one; I was going to move out there today."

"All right, let's go to Malibu; I have clothes and everything I need out there, except maybe some groceries."

Stone made his way to the freeway, then got off at Santa Monica Boulevard and drove toward the ocean. Soon, they were on the Pacific Coast Highway.

"God!" Arrington exclaimed. "It feels so good to be out of that place."

"Seemed like a very nice place," Stone said.

"Oh, it is, and they were wonderful to me, but I still felt like a prisoner. Now I feel free again!" She turned to him. "Why were you going to move to the Malibu house? Weren't you comfortable in Bel-Air?"

"Oh, yes, and Manolo was taking very good care of me. But, at the moment, it's important that you and I not be living under the same roof."

"Why not?"

"You're going to be under a lot of scrutiny for a while, and having an old boyfriend living at your house would give the press just a little too much to write about."

"I suppose you're right," she said. "God, but I hate living under a microscope. How long is this going to go on?"

"Weeks, maybe months. If the police find Vance's killer, that will help it go away. How is Peter?"

"He's wonderful. We talked this morning, and he's having a great time in Virginia. Mother keeps horses, and she has a pony for him. I want him to stay there until this is over."

"That's a good idea, I think."

"Drive straight through the town," she said. "The house is in the Malibu Colony, just past the little business district."

Stone followed her instructions, and turned through a gate, where they were stopped by a security guard.

"It's me, Steve," she said to the man.

"Welcome back, Mrs. Calder," he replied.

"If anybody asks, I'm not here," she said. "This is Mr. Barrington; he'll be coming and going."

"I'll put his name on the list."

Stone followed Arrington's directions to the house, a large stone and cedar contemporary on the beach. He gave her the key, and she opened the door and punched in the security code. He made a note of the code.

Stone went to the phone and called Betty.

"Where are you?" she asked.

"I've taken Arrington to the Malibu house; there was a mob of press at the clinic."

"The police have called here twice."

"Guy named Durkee?"

"That's right."

"If he calls again, tell him you haven't heard from me today."

"All right; are you coming in at all?"

"Maybe later." He gave her his cell phone number. "You can reach me there in an emergency. If you call here, let it ring once, hang up, and call again."

"You were wonderful last night," she said. "This morning, too."

"Same here," he replied.

"Oh, she's there, huh?"

"I'll talk to you later." He hung up.

"I want to take a bath," Arrington said. "Join me?"

"Thanks, I've just showered," he replied.

"Oh, it's going to be like that, is it?"

"You're a grieving widow, and I'm an old family friend."

"We'll see." She went upstairs.

Stone found Vance's study and picked up the phone. It was time to call Marc Blumberg.

ꙍ Chapter 17 ꙍ

Marc Blumberg came on the line. "Congratulations on getting her out of the Judson place," he said. "I passed the clinic on the way to work this morning; there were a lot of disappointed TV people out on the street."

"The cops leaked it to the media," Stone said. "I made the mistake of giving them advance notice."

"I saw a cop car there this morning, with Durkee in it."

"I saw them, too; do you think they were just there to watch the fun?"

"I think they were there to arrest Arrington," Blumberg said.

"Why do you think that?"

"I heard from a source at the LAPD that they have a witness who says Arrington expressed an interest in killing Vance."

"I don't believe it," Stone said.

"I don't believe she'd say that, either," Blumberg replied, "but I do believe that someone might say she did."

"Any idea who?"

"Not yet. I think it's time for me to call the D.A. and express our desire to cooperate, offer to let them question Arrington."

"They're not going to like what she has to say. She still has a memory gap from the day before the killing until she woke up in the clinic. They're probably going to want a polygraph, too."

"I'll have the usual reasons for not cooperating on that, plus there's the memory loss; she can't lie about what she can't remember."

"They'd want to ask her if she *can* remember," Stone said. "If she says she can't, and the needle jumps, they'll be all over her."

"I think we should consider doing a polygraph of our own," Blumberg said.

"And leak it to the press?"

"Right."

"Couldn't hurt."

"Where is she now?"

"At the Malibu house; I'm with her." Stone gave him the phone number.

"Have any funeral arrangements been made yet?"

"Lou Regenstein is handling that; he plans to do it on a sound stage at the studio."

"Good idea; that'll keep the public at arm's length. Stone, I think they're going to arrest Arrington, but I think I can hold them off, until after the funeral."

"What do you think the charge will be?"

"If they have faith in their witness, it could be murder one."

"Shit," Stone said. "And that will mean no bail. I don't want to see her in jail for weeks or months, waiting for a trial."

"Neither do I," Blumberg said. "There's an outside chance that I could get house arrest, under police guard, with high bail. Can she raise it?"

"How high are we talking about?"

"At least a million; maybe as high as ten million."

"I'll have to talk to Vance's lawyer and financial people about that," Stone said. "I've been putting it off, hoping the situation would be resolved. There are two big insurance policies, but they're not going to pay, if Arrington is arrested."

"Is she the beneficiary?"

"No, the estate is, but she's the principal heir."

"If the estate is the beneficiary, the insurance company has to pay; no way around it for them. But, of course, there's a law against a murderer profiting from his crime, so probate would be another story. However, we could offer to sign over Arrington's interest in the estate to secure a high bail; a judge might go for it, because until she's convicted, she's innocent."

"Any precedent for that?"

"I'll get somebody researching; we'll do a brief."

"Good; I'll get on to the Calders' financial people and see how liquid she is."

"Okay. If the police show up there and want to arrest Arrington or take her in for questioning, tell them her doctor has ordered her to bed and to call their captain or the D.A. before proceeding."

"Right." Stone said good-bye and hung up. Immediately, the phone rang. "Hello?"

"Stone, it's Betty; Manolo just called and said the police are at the Bel-Air house with a search warrant, tearing the place apart."

"Call him back and tell him not to impede them in any way," Stone replied. "I'll call him later."

"All right. Anything else?"

"Did Vance have a principal financial adviser?"

"He pretty much managed his own affairs," she replied, "but the person who would have the greatest grasp of his affairs is Marvin Kitman, his accountant. His lawyer is Bradford Crane."

Stone jotted down both numbers. "Call both of them, and tell them I'm handling Arrington's affairs. There's a power of attorney in Vance's office desk, giving me full authority; fax that to both of them."

"All right. Are you still out of touch, if the police call again?"

"I am. I'll talk to you later." Stone hung up to see Arrington coming down the stairs. She was wearing a thin, silk dressing gown, and judging from the way she was lit from behind by a large window on the stair landing, nothing else.

"Ah, that's better," she said, heading for the bar. "Can I fix you a drink?"

"It's a little early for me, and for you, too. Come and sit down, Arrington; we have to talk."

"I'm having a Virgin Mary," she said, pouring tomato cocktail over ice, "or, as Vance used to call it when he was dieting, a 'bloody awful.'" She came and sat down beside him on the sofa, drawing a leg under her, exposing an expanse of inner thigh. "I'm here," she said, placing her hand on his.

Stone took her hand. "I've got to explain your situation to you," he said, "and you're going to have to take what I tell you seriously."

She withdrew her hand. "All right, go ahead."

"I've retained a criminal trial lawyer to represent you, a man named Marc Blumberg."

"I know him a little," Arrington said. "His wife is in my yoga class. But why do I need a criminal lawyer?"

"Because there's a good possibility that you may be charged with Vance's murder."

"But that's ridiculous!" she said. "Utter nonsense!"

"I know it is, but you have to understand how the police work. They suspect you, because you were the only one in the house when Vance was shot."

"Except the murderer," she said.

"They think you hid the gun somewhere in the house, and they're over there right now with a search warrant."

"Suppose they find it? What then?"

"Then they'll check it for your fingerprints."

"Complete nonsense."

"What I'm trying to tell you is that you have to be prepared to be arrested and charged."

"You mean go to jail?"

"It's possible that, in such a case, bail could be denied by a judge, and you'd have to remain in custody until the trial was over."

"Oh, God," she said, bringing both hands to her face, "I don't think I could take that."

"Blumberg is exploring every possible option as to bail, and you might have to raise a very large sum of money. Are you acquainted enough with Vance's financial affairs to know whether that would be readily available?"

"I only know that Vance was very well off. I mean, we lived splendidly, as you know, but I never took an interest in his finances, and he never sat me down and explained things to me."

"I'm going to be calling his lawyer and accountant to discuss things with them. I'll know more after that, and I can explain your situation to you then." Stone thought for a moment. "Do you know if Vance had any life insurance?" He felt very sneaky asking this, but he wanted to know her answer.

"I've no idea," she replied. "My assumption is that he was rich enough not to need life insurance."

Stone breathed a little easier. "Did you have a joint bank account?"

"Yes, but I had my own account. Vance put money into it as necessary.

There was a household account that Betty paid all our bills from—she signed the checks on that one—and we had the joint account, which Vance used pretty much as his own; I almost never signed checks on that one. I don't know what other accounts he had, because all that sort of mail went to his office, not to the house."

"Do you have any idea how much cash you have immediately available?"

"Vance put twenty-five thousand dollars in my account a few days before he was killed, and I probably had five or six thousand dollars in there already. So, thirty thousand, maybe? I've no idea what the joint account balance is."

"I'll check into that," Stone said. He took a deep breath. "There's something I have to ask you, Arrington, and I want the straightest answer you can give me."

"Shoot."

"Did you ever tell anyone that you were considering killing Vance?"

"Of course not!"

"Something else, and this is even more important. I have to know this: Do you think that it is within the realm of possibility that, during the time you can't remember, you and Vance had such a serious fight that you might have killed him?"

"Absolutely not!" she cried. "How can you even ask? Don't you know me any better than that?"

"As a lawyer I sometimes have to ask unpleasant questions, even of people I know very well."

She moved across the sofa, her dressing gown falling open, and put her arms around his neck, pressing herself to him. "Oh, Stone, I'm so afraid," she said. "And I'm so glad you're here."

Stone could feel the familiar contours of her body against him. He should have pushed her away, but he couldn't bring himself to do so. "I'm here for as long as you need me," he said, stroking her hair.

They remained like that for what seemed a long time; she took his face in her hands and kissed him.

Then the doorbell began to ring repeatedly, and someone was knocking loudly.

⤷ Chapter 18 ⤶

Stone opened the door. A steely-looking man in his sixties, carrying a large case, stood on the doorstep.

"I'm Harold Beame," the man said. "Marc Blumberg sent me; you Stone Barrington?"

"Yes, come in."

"Marc didn't want to come himself; he figured there'd be press at the gate, and he was right."

"Might they have recognized you? Marc says you're well-known to the press."

"My car windows are heavily tinted, and they wouldn't recognize the car. Where's my subject?"

"She's upstairs; I'll get her in a minute." He led the man into the study. "Can I see your list of questions?"

"Sure." Beame handed over a sheaf of papers. "Marc faxed them to me."

Stone read through the list. They were tough questions, designed not for a milk run polygraph, but for learning the truth. Apparently, Blumberg wanted very much to know if his client was really innocent. "Fine," Stone said. "I'll get Mrs. Calder." He went upstairs and found Arrington at her dressing table. She was wearing a cotton shift over her bikini and was brushing her hair.

"Mr. Beame is downstairs in the study; he's ready for you."

"I'll be right with him." She seemed entirely serene.

"This is nothing to worry about; just give a truthful answer to each question."

"I'm not worried," she said. "I have nothing to hide."

Stone walked her downstairs to the study. "Do you mind if I sit in?" he asked Beame.

"I mind," Beame said. "It has to be just me and my subject; I don't want her to have any distractions."

Stone left the two of them alone in the study and walked out to the rear deck of the house. Beyond a carefully tended beach, the blue Pacific stretched out before him. He took off his jacket and stretched out in a lounge chair. He'd had hardly any time to himself, and he was grateful for the break.

He thought of Dolce, and his thoughts were still angry. He felt some

guilt about her, but he told himself he was now a free man. Dolce's behavior had made him want out of the relationship; he couldn't imagine a
lifetime with a woman who behaved that way. He should have taken Dino's
advice, he thought, and he'd certainly take it now. He would have to call
Dolce and tell her flatly that it was over.

He thought of Arrington, and his thoughts were not pure. They had
lived together for nearly a year, and during all that time, he had been happier than he had ever been with a woman. He had been crushed when she
had married Vance Calder, a fact he had tried to hide from himself, without success. Now she was a free woman again—except, she might not be
free for long. He had to get her out of this mess, and if he could, then they
could see if they might still have some sort of life together. He thought
about the money, and it annoyed him. Eduardo Bianchi's money, and his
casual gift of the Manhattan house, had bothered him; he was accustomed
to making his own way in the world, and the thought of a wife who was half
a billionaire was, somehow, disturbing. He thought of Arrington's son,
Peter. He liked the child, and he thought he could get used to being a
stepfather. He might even be good at it, if he used his own father as a
model. He took a deep breath and dozed off.

Arrington was shaking him, and he opened his eyes. The sun was lower
in the sky, and the air was cooler.

"We're all done," she said.

"How'd it go?"

"You'll have to ask Mr. Beame."

Stone walked into the study and found Beame packing his equipment.
"Want to give me a first reaction?" Stone asked.

"Marc said I could," Beame replied. "I'll send him a written report, but
I can tell you now that she aced it." He frowned. "Funny, I don't think I've
ever had a subject who was more relaxed, less nervous. I don't think she
was tanked up on valium, or anything like that; I can still get good read-
ings when they try that."

"I don't think she was," Stone said.

"Anyway, if she can pass with me, she can pass with anybody."

Stone realized that his pulse had increased, and now he could relax.
"Thank you; I'm glad to hear it."

Beame smiled. "It's a lot easier to represent an innocent client than a
guilty one, isn't it?"

"Yes, it is. When you leave, make sure that crowd at the gate doesn't see
your face. I assume your windshield isn't blacked out."

"I'll wear a hat and dark glasses, and don't worry, the car is registered
to a corporate name. If they run the plates, they'll come up dry."

Stone showed Beame to the door and thanked him, then he went back out to the terrace. Arrington was out of the shift, now, stretched out on a lounge in her bikini, and there was a cocktail pitcher on the table next to her.

"It's not too early for a drink now, is it?" she asked. "I made one of your favorites."

Stone poured the drinks into two martini glasses, handed her one and stretched out on the lounge next to her. He sipped the drink. "A vodka gimlet," he said. "It's been a long time."

"Poor deprived Stone," she said.

"I think I associated the drink with you."

She smiled. "I'm glad you waited until now to have one."

"You passed the polygraph with flying colors," he said.

"I know."

"You know? Arrington, you haven't been taking tranquilizers, have you?"

"Of course not. You told me just to tell the truth, didn't you?" She smiled again. "Are you relieved?"

Stone laughed. "Yes, I'm relieved."

"There was always the possibility that I'd killed Vance, wasn't there?"

"I never believed that," he said truthfully.

She reached over and took his hand. "I know you didn't; I could tell."

They sat in silence for a minute or two and sipped their drinks.

Finally, Arrington spoke. "I told you last year I'd leave Vance for you, remember?"

"I remember."

"You were terribly proper, and I was angry with you for not taking me up on it, but I must admit, I admired you for the way you behaved."

Stone said nothing.

"I'm free now, Stone; I hope that makes a difference to you."

"It does, but there's something that troubles me, and I'm not quite sure how to deal with it."

"I'm listening."

"I've spoken with Vance's accountant and lawyer, and as soon as we're past this thing with the police and the will is probated, you're going to be a very rich woman."

"Well, I suppose I assumed that," Arrington said. "How rich?"

"Half a billion dollars."

Her jaw dropped. "Half a *billion*? Is that what you said?"

"That's what I said. In fact, right now, you're a multimillionaire. You and Vance have a joint stock account that's currently worth more than fifteen million dollars."

"I guess I thought that's what the whole estate would be worth. I guess I don't think about money, much. I don't even pay much attention to the trust Daddy left me."

"You don't have to think about this right now, but you will have to later on."

"I suppose so." She looked at him narrowly. "Are you troubled by my newfound wealth, Stone?"

"Well, yes. I guess I'll just have to get used to it."

"I was wealthy before, you know. Daddy's trust fund is a fat one, worth about twelve million, last time I checked. It never bothered you before."

"I didn't know the details," he replied. "I didn't know you were all that rich."

"Poor baby," she said, patting his cheek.

Stone took a deep breath. "Now, there's something about me you have to know."

"What's that?"

"You remember Dolce."

"Eduardo Bianchi's daughter? How could I forget that dinner party in Connecticut last summer?"

"Dolce and I were to have been married last weekend, in Venice."

Arrington sat up and looked at him, surprised. "Oh?"

He started to tell her about the preliminary, but thought better of it. What did it matter? "But before it could take place, I was on a plane to L.A."

Arrington placed a hand on her breast. "Close call," she said. "Whew!" Then she sat back. "Are you in love with her?"

"I'm . . . a little confused about that," Stone said.

She took his hand again. "Let me help clear your mind."

"I'll admit, I had misgivings, even before going to Venice, but she was pretty overwhelming."

"I can imagine," Arrington said tartly.

"Now, I think I must have been crazy. Dino has been telling me that since the moment I met her."

"Dino is a very smart man," Arrington said. "Listen to him. I know how overwhelming a moment can be; that's how I came to marry Vance. You're well out of that relationship."

"I'm not exactly out of it, yet," Stone replied. "I still have to speak to her; she's been . . . unavailable when I've called her. She's in Sicily."

"That's just about far enough away," Arrington said. "That should make it easier for you."

"I'm going to have to tell Eduardo, too."

"I can understand how facing him might be more daunting than telling Dolce."

"He's been very kind to me; he made it plain that he was very happy about my becoming his son-in-law."

"He's a nice man, but try not to make him angry. He would make a bad enemy, from what Vance has told me about him."

"Yes, I know; or, at least, that's what Dino keeps telling me. God knows, I don't want him for an enemy."

"Well, I wouldn't let too much time pass before squaring this with both Eduardo and Dolce," Arrington said. "It won't get any easier."

"I know," Stone replied.

The phone on the table between them rang, and Arrington picked it up. "Yes? Oh, hello, Manolo; yes, I'm very well, thank you. I'll be spending a couple of days out here." She listened for a moment. "Did the police make much of a mess? Well, I'm sure you and Isabel can handle it. Yes, he's right here." She handed the phone to Stone. "Manolo wants to speak to you."

Stone took the phone. "Hello, Manolo."

"Good evening, Mr. Barrington. A lady has been telephoning you here; she's called several times. A Miss Bianchi?"

"Yes, I know her; I'll call her tomorrow."

"She left a number."

Stone realized he had left Dolce's number in Sicily at the Bel-Air house. He took out a pen and notebook. "Please give it to me."

Manolo repeated the number; Stone thanked him and hung up.

"Dolce called?" Arrington asked.

"Yes." He looked at his notebook. "She seems to be at the Bel-Air Hotel."

"Why don't you call her from the study," Arrington said. "I don't want to hear this conversation."

"Good idea." Stone went into the study and dialed the hotel number.

"Bel-Air Hotel," the operator said.

"Miss Dolce Bianchi, please."

"One moment. I'm sorry, sir, but we don't have anyone by that name registered."

Stone was baffled for a moment, then he had a terrible thought. "Do you have a Mrs. Stone Barrington?"

"Yes, sir; I'll connect you."

As the phone rang, Stone gritted his teeth.

⤳ **Chapter 19** ⤳

The phone rang and rang, and for a moment, Stone thought she'd be out. He was sighing with relief when Dolce, a little breathless, picked it up.

"Hello?"

Stone couldn't quite bring himself to speak.

"Stone, don't you hang up on me," she said.

"I'm here."

"I'm sorry I took so long to answer; I was in the shower."

"We need to talk," he said.

"Come on over; I'll order dinner for us."

"I won't be able to stay for dinner; I have another commitment." This was almost true.

"I'll be waiting."

"It'll take me at least half an hour, depending on traffic. See you then," he said hurriedly, before she asked where he'd be coming from. He hung up and went back out to the deck. "I'm going to go and see her now," he said.

Arrington stood up, put her arms around him and gave him a soulful kiss. For the first time—for the first time since she'd run off with Vance—he responded the way he wanted to. Arrington stepped back and patted him on the cheek. "Poor Stone," she said. "Don't worry, you can handle it." She turned him around, pointed him toward the door, and gave him a spank on the backside, like a coach sending in a quarterback with a new play. "I'll order in some food and fix us some dinner," she called, as he reached the door.

"Don't start cooking until I call," he said. "I don't know how long this is going to take."

The mob at the Colony gate had boiled down to one TV van and a photographer, and although they stared at him as he drove through, they didn't seem to connect him with Vance Calder's widow. A few miles down the Pacific Coast Highway, there was an accident that held up traffic for half an hour, giving Stone more time than he wanted to think.

Women, he reflected, usually broke it off with him, for lack of commitment. He had never been in the position of breaking off an engagement, and he dreaded the thought. By the time he got past the accident and made it to the hotel, he was an hour late.

Dolce opened the door and threw herself into his arms. "Oh, God, I've missed you," she whispered into his ear. It did not make Stone feel any better that she was naked. It seemed that women had been flaunting nakedness all day, and he had never been very good at resisting it. He pushed her into the suite and closed the door. "Please put something on; we have to talk."

Dolce grabbed a robe and led him into the living room. Stone chose an armchair so he wouldn't have to share the sofa with her. "I'm sorry you came here," he said. "It was the wrong thing to do under the circumstances."

"What circumstances?" she asked.

"Arrington is in trouble, and until I can get her out of it, I can't think about anything else."

"She killed Vance, didn't she? I *knew* it."

"She did not," Stone said.

"I could smell it as soon as I arrived in this town. The newspapers and TV know she's guilty, don't they?"

"They don't know anything, except the hints the cops are dropping."

"The cops know she's guilty, don't they?"

"Dolce, she passed a lie detector test this afternoon, a tough one, by a real expert."

"You need to think she's innocent, don't you, Stone? I know you; you have to believe that."

"I *do* believe that," Stone said, although Dolce was still shaking her head. "The police are trying to railroad her, because they can't find the real perpetrator, and I can't let that happen."

"Are you still in love with her, Stone?"

"Maybe; I haven't had time to think about that." In truth, he'd hardly thought of anything else. "Dolce, we very nearly made a terrible mistake. Let's both be grateful that we were spared a marriage that would never have worked."

"Why would it never have worked?"

"Because we're so different, temperamentally. We could never live with each other."

"Funny, I thought we had been living with each other for the past few months."

"Not permanently; we were playing at living together."

"*I* wasn't playing," she said.

"You know what I mean. We were . . . acting our parts, that's all. It would never have worked. I wish you hadn't come."

"Stone, I'm here because you're my husband, and you need me."

"Dolce, I am *not* your husband, and I'd appreciate it if you'd tell the hotel that."

"Have you forgotten that we were married last Saturday, in Venice, by the mayor of the city?"

"You know as well as I do, that ceremony is not valid without a religious ceremony to follow."

"We took vows."

"I said '*sì*' when prompted; I have no idea what the mayor said to me."

Dolce recited something in Italian. " 'Til death us do part," she translated.

"Well, that's what happened with your previous husband, isn't it?" he shot back, then immediately regretted having said it.

"And it could happen again!" Dolce spat.

"Is that what we've come to? You're threatening me?"

Dolce stood up and came toward him. "Stone, let's not do this to each other; come to bed."

Stone stood up and backed away from her. The robe had come undone, and he fought the urge to touch her. "No, no. I have to leave, Dolce, and you should leave, too, and go back to New York or Sicily or wherever."

"Papa is going to be *very* disappointed," she said in a low voice.

That really did sound like a threat, Stone thought. "I'll call him tomorrow and explain things."

"Explain what? That you're abandoning me? Leaving me at the altar? He'll just *love* hearing that. You don't know Papa as well as you think you do. He has a terrible temper, especially when someone he loves has been wronged."

Stone was backing toward the door. "I haven't *wronged* you, Dolce; I've just explained how I feel. I'm doing you a favor by withdrawing from this situation now, instead of later, when it would hurt us both a lot more." He was reaching for the doorknob behind him.

"You're my husband, Stone," Dolce was saying, "and you always will be, for as long as you live," she added threateningly.

"Good-bye, Dolce," Stone said. He got the door open and hurried out, closing it carefully behind him.

He had gone only a few steps when he heard a large object crash against the door and shatter. On the way through the lobby, he stopped at the front desk. "I'm Stone Barrington," he said to the young woman.

"Yes, Mr. Barrington," she said. "Are you checking in again?"

"No, and please be advised that the woman in suite 336 is Miss Dolce Bianchi, not Mrs. Stone Barrington. Will you let the telephone operator know that, please?"

"Of course," the young woman said, looking nonplussed. "Whatever you say, Mr. Barrington."

Stone got the station wagon from the attendant and headed back toward Malibu. Before he had even reached Sunset, the car phone rang.

"Hello?"

"Stone," Arrington said, "I'm on my way back to Bel-Air."

"Why and how?" Stone asked.

"I caught sight of a photographer on the beach with a great big lens, and I guess it just creeped me out. Manolo came and got me; he had to smuggle me past the gate in the trunk."

"All right, I'll meet you at the house. Tell Manolo to use the utility entrance." He said good-bye and hung up. How long, he wondered, had that photographer been on the beach?

Chapter 20

Stone got to the house first. He parked the car, went into the house and out to the guest house, where he started packing his clothes. He had his bags in Vance's Mercedes by the time Arrington arrived.

She came in through the front door, took a few steps, and froze, staring down the central hallway. "That's where he was, isn't it?" she asked Stone, nodding toward the spot.

"You remember?" Stone asked.

She nodded again.

He turned to the butler. "Manolo, will you fix us some dinner, please? Anything will do."

"Of course, Mr. Barrington," the butler said, and disappeared into the kitchen.

Stone took Arrington's hand and walked her to the bedroom. He sat her on the bed and sat down beside her. "What else do you remember?" he asked. "This is important."

Arrington wrinkled her brow. "Just Vance lying there, bleeding."

"Do you remember anything immediately before that?"

"I don't think so."

"Do you remember hearing the shot?"

She shook her head. "No. Just Vance lying there."

"Do you remember the police and the paramedics arriving?"

"No. Nothing until I woke up in the clinic." She laid her head on his shoulder. "When is this going to be over, Stone?"

"Not for a while," Stone replied. "We've still got the funeral on Friday, and on Saturday, we have to take you to the district attorney's office."

"Will they put me in jail?"

"I hope not; Marc Blumberg's working on that."

"I'm so glad you're here," she said. She put her hand on his cheek and drew him closer, kissing him.

Stone pulled back. "Listen to me carefully," he said. "You and I cannot be seen by *anybody* being . . . affectionate with each other."

"Only Manolo and Maria are here."

"And they'd both be shocked, if they walked in here and found us kissing. If they were called to testify in court, they'd have to tell the truth. Your husband has been dead for less than a week; you have to be seen to be the grieving widow for some time to come; I cannot tell you how important that is to your future."

She nodded. "I understand." She took his hand. "But it's important for you to know that I still love you. I never stopped."

Stone squeezed her hand but could not bring himself to respond. "Go freshen up for dinner," he said.

They dined in the smaller of the two dining rooms, on pasta and a bottle of California Chardonnay. They chatted about old times in New York, but as dinner wore on, Arrington seemed increasingly tired.

"I think you're going to have to put me to bed," she said finally.

Stone rang for Manolo. "We'll get Isabel; she'll put you to bed."

Arrington nodded sleepily. "I wish you were coming to bed with me."

"Shhh," Stone said. He turned her over to Isabel, got the keys and the alarm code for the Colony house from Manolo, then drove back to Malibu. He chose the guest room nearest the kitchen, unpacked, soaked in a tub for a while, and fell asleep.

He was awakened by the telephone. Nine-thirty, he saw by the bedside clock. He had slept like a stone.

"Hello?"

"Stone?"

"Yes."

"It's Marc Blumberg."

"Good morning, Marc."

"No, it's not."

"What's the problem?"

"The problem is, there is a very nice color photograph of you and Arrington in each other's arms, on the cover of the *National Inquisitor*. She's wearing a very tiny bikini."

"Oh, God," Stone groaned.

"Did the two of you spend the night together?"

"No, we didn't. I had to go into L.A., and while I was gone, Arrington spotted the photographer on the beach. Her butler came and drove her to the Bel-Air house. I met them there, we had dinner, then I moved out of the guest house and out here."

"Did the media outside the gates figure out that Arrington left?"

"No, I don't think so; she left in the trunk of the car."

"Did any media see you return to the house last night?"

"There was a TV truck there, but they paid little attention to me."

"So they think she's still there, and that you spent the night together."

"I suppose they could draw that conclusion."

"All right, I'm going to have to hold a press conference and try to contain this."

"I suppose that's the right thing to do."

"The upside is, you were fully clothed and were seen to leave after kissing her, while she remained on the deck. The photograph is a little ambiguous, too; I can claim that you were simply consoling her. The *Inquisitor* hasn't figured out who you are, yet; I'll describe you as a family friend who drove her home from the clinic."

"All right."

"They're going to put all this together sooner or later, probably sooner, so be prepared for some attention. Tell me, does Vance's bungalow at Centurion have a bedroom?"

"Yes, it does."

"I want you to move out of the Malibu house and into the bungalow this morning."

"All right. I'm very sorry about this, Marc. It was all very innocent."

"Don't worry about it; damage control is part of what I do. I'd just like there to be as little damage as possible to have to control."

"I understand."

"Now, listen: I don't want you to leave by the Colony gate."

"I'm afraid that's the only way out, Marc."

"Here's what you do. Pack your bags into the car and leave it in front of the house, with the key in the ignition. Then walk south along the beach about a mile, and you'll come to a restaurant. Walk through the building and be in the parking lot at, say, eleven o'clock. One of my people will pick up the car at the house and drive it to the restaurant."

"All right."

"Now, for God's sake, don't wear a business suit for your walk down the beach. Blend in."

"Will do."

"What kind of car is it?"

"A black Mercedes SL600 convertible."

"Be there at eleven. I'll call you around noon at the studio." Blumberg hung up.

Stone made himself some breakfast, then packed his bags, put them into the car, then showered and dressed in a guest bathing suit. He grabbed a towel and left the house by the front door. He walked down a couple of houses and cut through a yard and onto the beach.

It was a beautiful California morning, and Stone enjoyed the walk. He was passed by other people in bathing suits, joggers, and people walking their dogs. He got to the restaurant a little early, had a cup of coffee, then walked out into the parking lot. An attractive young woman was standing beside the Mercedes, waiting.

"Good morning, I'm Stone Barrington," he said, offering his hand.

"Hi, I'm Liz Raymond, one of Marc's associates," she replied.

"Can I drop you anywhere?"

"I'll be picked up here," the woman said. "Nice swimsuit."

"Thanks, it's borrowed."

"See you later," she said, as a car pulled up. She got into it and was driven away.

Stone drove to Centurion, gave the guard at the gate a wave, and drove to the bungalow. He walked inside with his bags to be greeted by an astonished Betty Southard.

"Well, now," she said, "you've just topped Vance. He never walked in here in a bathing suit."

"It's a long story," Stone said.

"I'll bet, and I've got all day," she replied.

⤳ Chapter 21 ⤳

Stone explained his appearance, then he pointed at three large canvas bags on the floor near Betty's office door. "What are those?" he asked.

"Arrington's mail," she said.

"I'm sorry, I don't understand."

"After Vance's death, his fans kept writing. I've got two girls in the back room sorting it now. Those are the bags we haven't gotten to yet."

"I don't believe it."

"Well, believe this: Right now, opinion is running about sixty-forty in favor of Arrington being a murderess."

" 'Murderess.' That has a quaint Victorian ring to it."

"I guess I'm just a quaint, Victorian girl," she replied.

Stone picked up his bags. "Where's the bedroom?" he asked. "Marc Blumberg wants me to move in here."

"Somewhere the *Inquisitor* can't find you?"

"I was just hugging her," he lied.

"Come on, I'll show you." She led the way down a hall and into a comfortably furnished bedroom with an adjacent bath and dressing room. "Want me to unpack for you?" she asked.

"Thanks, I can manage," he replied, laughing. "Go back to your mail; I want to get dressed." Betty left the room, and Stone got out of the swimsuit and into some clothes.

Betty appeared in the doorway. "Marc Blumberg's holding a press conference on TV." She switched on a set at the foot of the bed, and the two of them sat down to watch it as, on television, a secretary opened a set of double doors and the press poured into Blumberg's office, where he awaited them, seated behind an impressive desk.

"Thank you, ladies and gentlemen," Blumberg said, remaining seated. "I have a brief statement for you regarding the investigation into the death of Vance Calder. Can we hold the flash cameras until I've finished, please?"

When everything had quieted down, Blumberg began. "I have been retained by Vance Calder's widow, Arrington, to represent her during the investigation of her husband's death, not because she has anything to fear from the investigation, but because she wants to be sure that the Los Angeles Police Department is leaving no stone unturned in the pursuit of her husband's murderer."

"What about the photograph in today's *Inquisitor*?" somebody asked.

"I'll get to that in a minute," Blumberg replied. "Now, if I may continue?" He stared the room into silence. "Good. This is what we know so far: Last Saturday night, Mr. and Mrs. Calder were getting ready to go to a dinner party at the home of Lou Regenstein, chairman of Centurion Pictures. Mr. Calder was dressing, and Mrs. Calder was in the bathtub. A servant heard a loud noise, and when he investigated, found Mr. Calder lying in the central hallway of the house, near death, having received a gunshot wound to the head. The servant summoned the police and an ambulance, then sent a maid to let Mrs. Calder know what had happened.

"When Mrs. Calder saw her husband, she collapsed and had to be treated for shock by the paramedics when they arrived. Her personal physician was summoned; he sedated her and arranged for her to be moved immediately to a private clinic, where she remained until yesterday.

She asked for a family friend, a New York attorney, Mr. Stone Barrington, to come to Los Angeles to handle her affairs, and Mr. Barrington was summoned from Italy, where he was on vacation.

"When Mr. Barrington arrived, he spoke with Mrs. Calder's physician about her condition and learned that she was unable to remember anything that had happened between midafternoon last Friday and the time when she awoke in the clinic on Sunday morning. The moment Mrs. Calder was up to it, Mr. Barrington invited the police to interview her at the clinic, and yesterday, he picked her up there and took her to her Malibu home, where he hoped she might have some privacy to continue her recovery.

"Sadly, a tabloid photographer violated her privacy and photographed her with Mr. Barrington as she took the sun on a rear deck of the house. Mr. Barrington then left the house, giving her a hug before leaving, and that, ladies and gentlemen, was the photograph that was so outrageously misrepresented in the tabloid's pages.

"I am sorry to tell you that, as of this moment, the LAPD is treating Mrs. Calder as a suspect, and that later in the week, she will be interviewed by the district attorney's office. In anticipation of that meeting I arranged yesterday for her to receive a thorough polygraph examination from Mr. Harold Beame, formerly with the FBI, who is a renowned examiner. I am pleased to tell you that Mr. Beame has reported that, in his expert opinion, Mrs. Calder answered truthfully every question put to her. I can tell you that they were very tough questions; I know, because I wrote them myself."

This got a laugh from the group.

"However, when we meet with the district attorney, I intend to volunteer Mrs. Calder for another polygraph, administered by a qualified examiner of his choosing. Further, at that meeting, Mrs. Calder will answer every question put to her by members of the district attorney's office.

"Finally, Mrs. Calder has authorized me to offer a reward of $100,000 for any information leading to the arrest and conviction of her husband's killer." He held up a placard with a telephone number on it. "We ask that anyone with such information call both the police *and* this number. We wouldn't want anything to get lost in the shuffle at the LAPD."

Another laugh.

"That's all I have to tell you, at the moment, and I won't be answering any questions today. However, you may rest assured that I will be in contact with the media when there is anything of significance to report."

With that, Blumberg got up and marched out of his office, ignoring the questions shouted by the crowd.

Betty switched off the set. "Well, I guess that puts the ball in the D.A.'s court, doesn't it?"

"I believe it does," Stone agreed. "That was a very impressive perform-
ance."

"Did you approve the reward?"

"No, but I would have, if asked. I think it's a good idea. It might turn
up something and, at the very least, it will keep the police busy with leads
from people who want the money."

A phone on the bedside table rang, and Betty answered it. "It's Marc
Blumberg," she said, handing Stone the phone.

"Hi, Marc; I saw your press conference. Very good, and you have my approval on the reward money."

"I thought I would have," Blumberg answered. "I want to meet with Arrington this afternoon; where shall we do it?"

"How about three o'clock at her house? You know where it is?"

"Yes, and that's fine."

"There's a utility entrance at the rear of the property. . . ."

"No," Blumberg interrupted, "I'll go in the front way; let the press see
me."

"Whatever you think best."

"Just keep that phrase in mind, and we'll get along great, Stone. See
you at three." He hung up.

The phone rang again immediately, and Betty answered it. "It's Arrington," she said, handing Stone the phone again.

"Hi."

"I just saw Marc Blumberg on TV; was that your idea?"

"No, it was his, but I wholeheartedly approve."

"I haven't seen this rag, but I take it the photographer I saw was responsible."

"Yes; that should give you some idea of how careful you have to be.
Marc Blumberg is coming to the house at three this afternoon; be ready
to meet him, and don't wear a bikini."

She laughed. "Touché. Will you be here?"

"Yes."

"See you then."

Stone hung up and turned to Betty. "Will you make some notes on the
tenor of the mail you're receiving? I expect Blumberg will want to know
about it."

"Sure; I'll go add it all up now." Betty left the room.

Stone finished dressing. For the first time, he was beginning to feel
some optimism about the way things were going. Marc Blumberg was a
considerable force, when aroused, and Stone was glad to have him on Arrington's side.

◌৹ **Chapter 22** ৎ◌

He had been dreading this call, but he couldn't put it off any longer. Stone dialed Eduardo Bianchi's private telephone number in New York. As usual, he got only the beep from an answering machine, no message.

"Eduardo, it's Stone Barrington. I would be grateful if you could call me sometime today; there's something important I have to talk to you about." He left the numbers of both the bungalow and the Calder house.

Then he called Dino. He could not remember when so much time had passed without a conversation with his friend, and he knew he had been putting off this one, because he knew what Dino would say.

"She's guilty," Dino said, after Stone had brought him up to date.

"No, she's not."

"You just don't want to believe it, because you think she killed him so she could have you."

Stone winced at the truth. "She passed a polygraph yesterday, aced it," he said lamely.

"Yeah, I saw Blumberg's press conference on CNN. I don't believe it; she must have been on drugs, or something."

"The examiner told me drugs couldn't fool him." It had occurred to him that Arrington had seemed eerily calm since she had left the clinic.

"Look, Stone, I've been getting updates from Rick Grant, and while they may not have her cold, his people really believe she whacked her husband."

"I'm aware of their opinion," Stone said. "But don't judge her so soon. I'm here, on the spot, up to my ears in this, and my instincts tell me she's innocent."

"Stone, nobody's *innocent*, you know that. Everybody's guilty of *something*."

"Not murder; not Arrington. She doesn't have it in her."

"Whatever you say, pal."

"There's something else."

"What?"

"I ended it with Dolce last night."

"Good news, at last! What made you see the light?"

"We had a transatlantic conversation that I didn't like the tone of, for one thing."

"And Arrington's free, for another thing?"

"There is that," Stone admitted sheepishly. "It was something I hadn't expected."

"Have you told Eduardo?"

"I have a call in to him now."

"That should be an interesting conversation."

"Any advice as to how I should handle it?"

"Oh, I don't know; how do you feel about South America?"

"Come on, Dino; how should I break it to him?"

"Right between the eyes, dead straight; he might respect that."

"I hope so."

"Then again, he might not. He dotes on that girl; if he thinks you've done her wrong, well . . ."

"Well, what?"

"You might not be well for very long."

"Dino, this isn't Sicily."

"To Eduardo, *everywhere* is Sicily."

"I see your point," Stone said.

"I think everything is going to depend on what Dolce says to Eduardo," Dino said. "How pissed off was she when you broke it to her?"

"Pretty pissed off."

"Oh."

"Yeah."

"Maybe she'll cool off before she talks to the old man."

"Maybe."

"For your sake, I hope so."

"Thanks."

"You want me to take some time off, come out there?"

"I don't know what you could do, Dino, except keep me company. That, I wouldn't mind."

"You let me know if something comes up and you need me, okay?"

"Okay."

"I got a meeting; talk to you later."

Stone hung up. Why did everybody think Arrington was guilty, except him? Was he completely nuts? Blinded by how he felt about her? He made himself a sandwich in the bungalow's kitchen, then went into Betty's office. "How's the mail coming?"

Betty consulted a steno pad. "Nearly done," she said, "and opinion is running about two to one against Arrington."

"Swell," Stone said. He looked at his watch. "I've got to run; I'm meeting Marc Blumberg at the house."

Stone took the rear entrance, then watched through a front window as Marc Blumberg drove very slowly through the mob of press, through the gates, and up to the house. The lawyer certainly knew how to make an entrance.

Arrington appeared from the bedroom just as Blumberg entered the house. She gave Stone a peck on the cheek, then shook hands with Blumberg.

"How are you, Marc? It's been a long time."

"I'm terrific, Arrington, and I hope you are, too."

"I'm all right, I guess. How is Arlene?"

"Very well."

"Tell her I miss my yoga class with her."

"I know she misses you, too."

Manolo stepped up. "May I get you anything, Mr. Blumberg?"

"No, thanks," Blumberg replied. "Let's get down to work. Arrington, I want to talk with you alone at some length; where can we do that?"

"Vance's study would be a good place," she replied. "Can Stone be there?"

"Sorry, this is just you and me." He took a folder from his briefcase and handed it to Stone. "You might take a look at this while we're talking. We'll be a while."

Stone accepted the folder and watched as Arrington led Marc Blumberg into Vance's study and closed the door. He asked Manolo for some iced tea, then went out onto the rear terrace, took a seat, and opened the folder. Inside was the medical examiner's report on Vance Calder's autopsy.

Manolo brought the tea and left him alone. He began to read. Death as the result of a single gunshot to the right occipital region of the head. No news there. Subject: a well-developed male of fifty-two years, seven months, six feet two, a hundred and ninety pounds. Stone's own height and weight. Drugs present in bloodstream: Zyrtec, an antihistamine; alcohol content: .03, a drink or two.

He was surprised at the number of scars found on Vance's body: two-inch scar over left collarbone—sutured; one-and-one-half-inch scar, inside of left wrist, unsutured, secondary tissue present; two-and-one-half-inch surgical scar, right shoulder; one-inch abdominal surgical scar; three-inch surgical scar, left knee; two-inch scar, sutured, right thigh; several small scars on both hands. X rays revealed some old broken bones—right femur, left tibia, and a broken nose. That, he reflected, had given Vance's face additional character, kept him from looking pretty. All in all, though, it sounded as though Vance had led a rougher life than that of a pampered movie star. He noted the absence of any cosmetic surgical scars. Vance Calder had been the real thing.

More than an hour passed before Arrington and Marc Blumberg emerged from the study. Arrington looked decidedly pale and shaken, while Blumberg was his usual, cool, well-pressed self.

"I'm going to go lie down for a few minutes," Arrington said, and went into the bedroom.

"Well," Stone said, "do you think she's innocent?"

"She's my client," Blumberg replied, "so she's innocent."

"Come on, Marc, I want an opinion. So far, everybody I know except me thinks she did it."

"It doesn't matter," Blumberg said.

"It doesn't matter?"

"Not to me, Stone; but then I'm not in love with her."

Stone was surprised at this, but he said nothing.

"She's innocent until proven guilty, and I'm going to keep her that way."

"How are you going to handle the D.A. on Saturday?"

"I'm not going to handle him," Blumberg replied. "I'm going to stay out of his way, and let him at her."

"You really think that's a good idea?"

"Listen, the D.A.'s questioning is going to be nothing, compared with what I just put her through. I dragged her back and forth across the stones of her story for an hour, and she never budged from it. The woman is a rock, and the D.A. is not going to make a dent in her. She's a good actress, too."

"Actress?"

"She'll have a jury on her side from the moment she opens her mouth, and I don't have the slightest qualm about having her testify. O.J.'s team was smart to keep him off the stand—the prosecution would have gutted him, just as happened in the civil trial, but they won't lay a glove on Arrington, trust me."

"You think it'll go to trial?"

"Not unless they've got a lot more than I think they've got. We'll find out about that on Saturday morning. What did you think of the autopsy report?"

"Pretty straightforward. He sure had a lot of scars."

"I asked Arrington about that; he did most of his own stunt work. Over the years, it took its toll."

"That would explain it," Stone said. "God, I hope this doesn't go to trial."

"I wouldn't mind, if it did," Blumberg said with a small smile. "A trial would be a lot of fun."

Chapter 23

Stone got out of the Bentley and went around to the other side, where Manolo was holding the rear door open for Arrington and her son, Peter, and his grandmother, who had brought him back for the service, at the insistence of Marc Blumberg.

Stone took her left hand, tucked it under his arm while she held Peter's hand with her right, and led the little group through the open rear door of the sound stage, past a large truck with satellite dishes on top. The soft strains of a pipe organ wafted through the huge space. Schubert, he thought.

As he led them to a front pew, he took in the atmosphere, which was fragmented, and a little unreal. The cathedral set was not complete, being composed of only those parts necessary for the shooting of a scene. Everything at the rear—the choir loft, the organ and its pipes, the pulpit (or whatever it was called in a Catholic or Anglican church)—looked like the real thing, while other parts of the ceiling and stained glass windows were incomplete. A coffin of highly polished walnut rested in front of the pulpit. Stone wondered if Vance Calder's body was really inside, or if it was just a prop.

He deposited Arrington and Peter next to her mother on the front pew, then walked to the side of the seating area and stood. From there, he had an excellent view of the crowd. Perhaps twenty pews had been placed on the concrete floor, and they were packed with Hollywood aristocracy. Stone recognized several movie stars, and he was sure that the others were the crème de la crème of producers, writers, and directors. Two pews behind Arrington he was surprised to spot Charlene Joiner, the costar of Vance's last film, with whom he had, apparently, been sleeping. At the other end of the pew sat Dolce, accompanied by her father. Dolce pointedly ignored him, but Eduardo gave him a grave glance, and they exchanged somber nods. Eduardo had not returned his phone call.

Behind the twenty pews was a sea of folding chairs, occupied by the working folk of Centurion Studios—directors, carpenters, grips, bit players, script ladies, and all the other people who made movies happen. Stone counted four large television cameras—the studio kind, not the handheld news models, and he realized that they must be feeding to the big truck outside. A boy's choir began to sing, and Stone turned to find that the youngsters had filed into the choir loft while he had been looking at the crowd. It took him a moment to realize that their moving lips were not in synch with the music: That was recorded, and the boys were, apparently, child actors. The organist, too, was faking it; only the choir director seemed to truly understand the music. The whole scene was gorgeously lit.

As the strains of the choir died, and the boys stopped moving their lips, a richly costumed priest (or actor?) walked onto the set and began speaking in Latin. If he was an actor, Stone reflected, he certainly had his lines down pat. Stone was glad the coffin was not open, if indeed Vance's body was inside, because this was the first funeral service he had ever attended where he was wearing the corpse's suit.

The clothes he had brought with him had been chosen for Venice, and Dolce had insisted on light colors. When he had confessed to Arrington that he had nothing suitable for a funeral, she had suggested he wear some of Vance's clothes, which had turned out to fit him very well—so well, in fact, that Arrington was insisting that he have all of Vance's clothes, the thought of which made him uncomfortable.

"Look," she had said, "if you don't take all these perfectly beautiful suits, jackets, and shirts, they'll end up being sold at some ghastly celebrity auction. Please, Stone, you'd be doing me a great favor."

So now he stood staring at the coffin, wearing the deceased's dark blue Douglas Hayward chalk-stripe suit, his handmade, sweetly comfortable Lobb shoes, and his Turnbull & Asser silk shirt and necktie. The underwear and socks were, mercifully, his own.

The eulogies began, led by Lou Regenstein. They were kept short, and the speakers had, apparently, been chosen by occupation: There was an actor, a director, a producer, and an entertainment lawyer. Each, of course, spoke of Vance's endearing personal qualities and gift for friendship, but his Oscars, New York Film Critics' Awards, and his business acumen were all covered at some length, as well.

When the service ended, the coffin was opened, and Vance's body was, indeed, inside. Those in the pews were directed past the coffin to Arrington, who stood alone, well to one side of the coffin, while those in the folding chairs to the rear were directed out the hangarlike doors at the front of the sound stage.

After speaking words of condolence, the mourners divided into two groups—some were directed toward the main doors, while the truly close friends and business associates were sent out the rear door, where their cars waited to take them to the cemetery.

Stone stood near the rear door and, shortly, Eduardo Bianchi drifted over, while Dolce remained in the line of mourners. Eduardo, dressed in a severely cut black silk suit, held out his hand and shook Stone's warmly. "Stone, I'm sorry not to have returned your call yesterday, but I was en route to Los Angeles and did not receive your message until this morning."

"That's quite all right, Eduardo," Stone replied. "It's good to see you."

"I expect that you called to tell me of yours and Dolce's . . . ah, difficulties. She had, of course, already told me."

"I'm sorry that I couldn't tell you myself," Stone said. "This is not easy, of course, but I believe it is the best thing for Dolce. I'm not sure what it is for me."

"I understand that these things sometimes do not work out," Eduardo said. "People's lives are complicated, are they not?"

"They certainly are," Stone agreed.

"I understand that Dolce can be a difficult woman, and I know that Vance's death has, perhaps, meant a sudden change in your life. I want you to know that I remain fond of you, Stone, in spite of all that has happened. I had hoped to have you for a son, but I will be content, if I must, to have you for a friend."

"Thank you, Eduardo, for understanding. I will always be very pleased to be your friend and to have you as mine." To Stone's surprise, Eduardo embraced him, then turned and walked back to join Dolce in the receiving line.

The drive to Forest Lawn was quiet, except for Arrington's patiently answering Peter's questions about the service and who all the people were. Stone was glad he didn't have to answer the questions himself.

At the brief graveside service, Stone stood to one side again, and when it was over, he was surprised to be approached by Charlene Joiner, who held out her hand and introduced herself.

"I'd like to speak to you privately, if I may," she said.

Her accent was Southern, and Stone remembered that she was from the same small Georgia town, Delano, as Betty Southard.

"This is probably not the best time," Stone replied. "I'm staying at Vance's bungalow at the studio. You can reach me there."

"I'll call over the weekend," she said, then turned and went to her car.

After the service, Stone drove Arrington, Peter, and her mother home to Bel-Air. All the way, he wondered what Charlene Joiner could possibly have to say to him.

Later, he met Vance's accountant at the Calders' bank, where he signed a very large note on Arrington's behalf and drew a number of cashier's checks. Now he was ready for the district attorney.

⤜ **Chapter 24** ⤏

On Saturday morning, Stone arrived at the Bel-Air house, entering through the utility entrance, as usual. Marc Blumberg arrived moments later, and since Arrington was not quite ready, they had a moment to talk.

"Where do we stand on bail?" Blumberg asked.

Stone took an envelope from his pocket. "First of all," he said, handing Blumberg a check, "here is your half-million-dollar retainer."

"Thank you very much," Blumberg said, pocketing the check.

Stone displayed the remaining contents of the envelope. "I also have a cashier's check for five million dollars, made out to the court, and five others for a million each, so we can handle any amount of bail up to ten million dollars immediately. If more is required, I can write checks on Arrington's account for another five million."

"I like a lawyer who comes prepared," Blumberg said. "Now, at this meeting, I don't want you to say anything at all."

Stone shrugged. "All right."

"It may get rough, and you may feel the need to come to Arrington's rescue, but allow me to make the decision as to when that becomes necessary. If we can get through this questioning without either of us having to speak, then we'll have won our point."

"I understand. If they arrest her, though, she's going to have to spend the weekend in jail. We're not going to get a judge for a bail hearing on a Saturday."

"Let me worry about that," Blumberg said. "And if, for any reason, we can't get bail, I'll arrange for her to be segregated at the county jail."

Arrington walked into the room, wearing a simple black suit and carrying a small suitcase. "Good morning, all," she said, and held up the bag. "I've brought a few things, in case I have to stay."

Stone was relieved that he had not had to suggest that to her.

"Let's go, then," Blumberg said. "I've hired a limo to take us all in comfort. We'll go out the back way, and we'll enter the courthouse through the basement parking lot."

The three of them joined Blumberg's associate, Liz Raymond, in the long black car and departed the property by way of the utility gate, unobserved. The ride to the courthouse was very quiet.

On reaching the courthouse, they drove into the underground garage and stopped at the elevators, where detectives Durkee and Bryant were waiting.

"Hello, Sam, Ted," Blumberg said, shaking their hands. Stone ignored them.

The group rode upstairs in the elevator, walked down a hallway, and entered a large conference room, where the district attorney and two of his assistants, a man and a woman, awaited, along with a stenographer. Blumberg introduced the D.A., Dan Reeves, and the two A.D.A.s, Bill Marshall, who was black, and Helen Chu, who was Asian. No hands were shaken.

"Please be seated," Reeves said, and they all sat down around the table.

"As I understand it," Reeves said, "you are here to surrender Mrs. Calder."

Blumberg held up a hand. "Before any charge is made, I request that you question my client. It's my belief that, when you are done, you will see that an arrest is unnecessary."

"All right; do you have any objection to a stenographic record being made?"

"None whatsoever. I'd also like to volunteer my client for a polygraph; you choose the examiner."

"Yes, I saw your press conference," Reeves said dryly. "Shall we begin?"

"By all means."

Reeves dictated the names of those present and started to ask his first question, but Blumberg interrupted.

"I'd like the record to show that my client is here voluntarily and is willing to answer all questions."

"So noted," the D.A. said. "Mrs. Calder, you understand you are here because you are a suspect in the murder of your husband, Vance Calder?"

"I understand it, but I don't understand it," Arrington replied in a calm voice.

"Beg pardon?"

"I mean, I accept your characterization of my visit here, but I don't understand why I'm a suspect."

"That will become apparent as we proceed," Reeves said. "Mrs. Calder, please recount the events as you recall them on the evening of your husband's death."

"I have only one memory of that evening," Arrington said. "I remember being shown my husband's body as it lay on the floor of the central hallway of our house. Apart from that single image, I have no recollection of anything between midafternoon the previous day and the following morning, when I woke up at the Judson Clinic."

Blumberg spoke up. "For the record, Dr. James Judson, an eminent psychiatrist, is available to testify that Mrs. Calder is suffering from a kind of amnesia, brought on by the shock of her husband's violent death."

"So you have no recollection of shooting your husband?" Reeves asked.

"I would never have shot my husband," Arrington replied, "but I have no recollection of the events of that evening."

"So you don't know if you shot him?"

"I know that I would *never* do such a thing."

"But you don't *know*."

"Asked and answered," Blumberg said. "Perfectly clear."

"Mrs. Calder, is it possible that, while delusional, you might have shot your husband?"

"I have never been delusional," Arrington replied. "My doctor has explained to me that my amnesia has nothing to do with delusion."

"Have you ever threatened to kill your husband?"

"Certainly not."

Reeves took a small tape recorder from a credenza behind him and placed it on the table. "This is an excerpt from an interview with a friend of yours, Mrs. Beverly Walters."

"An acquaintance, not a friend," Arrington replied.

Reeves pressed a button.

"I told Arrington," Beverly Walters's voice said, "that I had it on good authority that Vance, during the filming of his last picture, was sleeping with his costar, Charlene Joiner, on a regular basis. She pooh-poohed this. I asked her if she would divorce Vance, if she found out that it was true. She replied, and these are her exact words, 'I wouldn't divorce him, I'd shoot him.' And this was two days before Vance was killed."

Reeves stopped the machine. "Do you recall this conversation with Mrs. Walters?"

"Yes, I do," Arrington replied.

"So you admit having said that you would not divorce your husband on learning of his adultery, but shoot him, instead?"

"I spoke those words in jest, and Mrs. Walters took them as such. We both had a good laugh about it."

"But you don't deny having said that you would shoot your husband?"

"Mr. Reeves, how many times have you said, in jest, that you would kill somebody, maybe even your wife? This is common parlance, and we all do it. I had no evidence of adultery on my husband's part. I regarded him at that time, and still do, as a faithful husband."

"But Mrs. Walters had just told you that she, quote, had it on good authority, unquote, that your husband was actually committing adultery with his costar, Ms. Joiner."

"Mr. Reeves, I would never accept Beverly Walters's word about such a thing. She is an inveterate and vicious gossip, who enjoys stirring up trouble, and that is why she is an acquaintance, and not a friend of mine. If her husband were not an occasional business associate of my husband, I would not see her at all."

"But she said she had it on good authority."

"'Good authority,' to Beverly Walters, is something she heard at the hairdresser's or read in a scandal sheet. Did you ask her to substantiate this rumor she was spreading?"

Reeves didn't reply.

"I assure you that if I were a murderous person, I would have been much more likely to shoot Beverly Walters than my husband."

Stone had to suppress a smile.

"Mrs. Calder, did you and your husband ever fight?"

"Occasionally—perhaps rarely would be a better choice of words."

"Physically fight?"

"No, never."

"I will reserve the right to present evidence to the contrary at a later date," Reeves said. "That concludes the questioning," he said to the stenographer. "Thank you; you may leave us now."

The stenographer took her machine and left the room.

Stone was surprised that Arrington's questioning had been so brief, and that no further evidence against her had been offered.

"Mrs. Calder," the district attorney said, "you are under arrest on a charge of second-degree murder. Please stand up."

Arrington stood, and the two police detectives began to handcuff her.

⌁ Chapter 25 ⌁

On Sunday morning, Stone got up and went out for the papers. He'd have to arrange daily delivery, he thought. The studio, ordinarily a hive of activity, was dead on a Sunday. He drove through the empty streets, inquired of the guard at the gate where to get a paper, and for his trouble was rewarded with a *New York Times* and a *Los Angeles Times*.

"We get a few delivered for folks who are working over the weekend," the guard said.

Stone returned to the bungalow, and as he entered, the phone was ringing. He picked it up.

"Stone Barrington?"

"Yes."

"This is Charlene Joiner."

"Good morning."

"As I mentioned at the funeral, I'd like to get together with you; I have some information you might find interesting."

"All right," Stone said.

"Why don't you come to lunch? There'll be some other people here, but we can find a moment to talk."

"Thank you, I will," Stone replied.

"Do you know the Malibu Colony?"

"Yes, I've been to the Calder house there."

"I'm six doors down," she said. She gave him the house number. "One o'clock, and California casual."

"See you then." He hung up, wondering what information she might have for him and what "California casual" meant.

Betty had left Danish pastries in the fridge for him; he made himself some coffee and spent the morning reading the papers. The L.A. paper had a front-page story about Arrington's arrest, while the New York paper had a blurb on the front page and an inside story—this seemed to be the standard coverage. Marc Blumberg had issued a press release, detailing Arrington's willingness to answer all questions. "I don't expect this to go to trial," he said, "if the LAPD does its job, but should it do so, Mrs. Calder will testify without fear of any question."

Stone thought that was immoderate; things might change before the trial, and they might not want her to testify. Still, it sounded good now, and helped create the impression that Arrington had nothing to fear from a trial. He was troubled by the D.A.'s reluctance to disclose the evidence against her. Normally, they would use the press to reinforce the idea that they had a strong case.

He passed through the Malibu Colony gate a little after one, then drove to Charlene Joiner's house. A uniformed maid opened the door for him and took him out to a rear terrace. Charlene and another woman were sitting beside the pool, talking, both wearing swimsuits. Charlene stood up, wrapped a colorful sarong skirt around her lower body, and came to greet him, hand out.

"Hello, Stone," she said, taking his hand and leading him toward the other woman. "This is Ilsa Berends," she said.

Stone recognized the actress from her films. She was in her early forties, he thought, but in wonderful shape. "How do you do, Miss Berends," he said. "I've enjoyed your work in films." He turned to Charlene. "Yours, too. In fact I saw one on the airplane from Milan."

"You were in Milan recently?" Berends asked.

"Venice, really; I flew out of Milan."

"Vacation?" Charlene asked.

"Sort of," Stone replied. He turned to see another woman arriving, and she was another recognizable actress, though he could not remember her name. Five minutes later, two more arrived.

Charlene introduced everyone. "I'm afraid you're going to be in the middle of a hen party," she said. "You're our only man."

"The pleasure is mine," Stone replied. A houseman brought everyone mimosas, and half an hour later, they sat down to lunch.

The conversation was about L.A. matters—films, gossip, and shopping.

"I understand you're a friend of Arrington Calder," Ilsa Berends said to Stone.

It was the first question addressed to him by anyone. "That's right," Stone said.

"I also hear you used to live together," the actress said. This got everyone's attention.

"I think I'll stand on attorney-client privilege," Stone replied.

Everyone laughed.

"Were you there when Arrington was arrested?" another woman asked.

"I was at the meeting at the D.A.'s office, where Arrington had voluntarily appeared and answered questions."

"I think she did it," the youngest woman, who could only have been in her early twenties, said.

"Certainly not," Stone replied.

"The loyal attorney," Berends said.

"So far, the district attorney seems to have no evidence against her."

"Except Beverly Walters's statement," Charlene said.

Stone was astonished. "How did you know about that?" he asked.

Everybody laughed.

"Because Beverly has told everyone she knows about it," Charlene replied. "She would never be involved in anything like this without telling all of Beverly Hills."

"Well, I can tell you that her version of the conversation is different from Arrington's. It was an entirely innocent remark."

"Innocent, that she said she was going to kill her husband?" Berends asked.

"Haven't you ever said you were going to kill somebody?"

"No, not seriously."

"Neither has Arrington—seriously."

"You're sweet, standing up for her like that. You really think she's innocent?"

"I really do," Stone said. "Or I wouldn't say so."

"So, what's your strategy going to be at trial?" somebody asked.

"That will be for Marc Blumberg to decide; he's the lead attorney in the case. I'm just helping out when I can and handling Arrington's personal affairs."

"Oh, so Arrington had affairs, too?" someone asked.

"Her business affairs," Stone said, wagging a finger at her. "There's an estate to settle and a lot of other things to be taken care of."

"Didn't Vance have a lawyer?"

"Yes, but Arrington is entitled to her own representation."

"So, what have you handled for her?"

"Ladies, you'll have to forgive me; I've said about all I can."

"Oh, shoot," Berends said. "And there was *so* much I wanted to know."

"I'm sorry to disappoint you," Stone said.

The absence of further information seemed to cast a pall over the luncheon, and soon the women began leaving. Finally, Stone was left alone with Charlene Joiner.

"Thank you, Ramon," she said to the houseman, who was clearing the dishes. "Just put those things in the dishwasher, and you and Reba can go. Thank you for coming in today." She watched the man go into the kitchen, then turned to Stone. "Alone at last," she said, standing up and slipping out of the sarong. "I hope you don't mind if I get some sun."

"Not at all," Stone said. To his surprise, she didn't stop with the sarong; she unhooked her bra, freeing her breasts, and shucked off the bikini bottom. He noted that there were no sun lines on her body.

She stretched like a cat. She was tall and slender, and she obviously took very good care of herself. Her legs were long, her hips were narrow, and her breasts were impressive.

"They're original equipment," she said, catching Stone's glance.

Stone laughed. "I'm glad to hear it. You said you had some information for me." He tried to keep his tone light and his breathing regular.

She settled on the chaise beside his, turned her face to the sun and closed her eyes. "Yes, I do. It may not be important, but I thought you ought to know about it."

"I'm all ears."

"Vance and I use the same gardening service, which takes care of the grounds of both his Malibu and Bel-Air houses. The man, whose name is Felipe, was due here on Monday morning to cut the grass and do some gardening work, and he didn't show up. I called the service, and they sent somebody else that afternoon."

Stone waited for this to become relevant. "Go on."

"The man who came in the afternoon didn't do a very good job, so I called his boss and asked when Felipe would be back. He said he had called Felipe's house—he apparently lived with a sister—and was told that he had returned to Mexico over the weekend, and he didn't know when he'd be back."

"Did Felipe also work at the Calders' house?"

"Yes; he worked there last Friday and on Saturday, the day Vance was killed."

"And he suddenly went back to Mexico on the Sunday?"

"On the Saturday night, according to his boss."

"So he couldn't have been questioned by the police," Stone said. "That *is* interesting."

"I thought you might think so. The man did good work, but once I caught him in my house. He said he was looking for a drink of water, but he wasn't in the kitchen; he was in the living room."

"Did he know where the kitchen was?"

"Yes, he had been in there before. I think he fancied Reba, my maid."

"You think he might have stolen something?"

"I think he would have, left to his own devices. I told him not to come into the house again. If he wanted water, he was to ask Reba to bring it to him. There's a staff toilet off the kitchen he could use. His full name is Felipe Cordova; his boss says he's from Tijuana."

"Thank you for telling me this," Stone said. "There's something I'd like to ask you; it's a rude question, but I'd appreciate a straight answer."

"Was I fucking Vance Calder?" she asked.

"That's the question."

She laughed. "Sweetie, all of the women here today have fucked Vance, at one time or another."

"*All* of them?"

"Every one of them is a member of the I Fucked Vance Calder Club. The club is bigger than that, of course; we're only the tip of the nipple."

"Let's get back to my original question."

"You bet I was fucking him, and loving it." She smiled. "So was he."

"Where did these meetings take place?"

"You mean where did we fuck? I hate euphemisms. In his bungalow at the studio; in his trailer, when we were on location; in his Colony house just down the street; and here. Right up until the day before his death."

"How often did this happen?"

"Every day we could manage it; sometimes twice a day. Vance was always ready," she said, "and so was I." She turned toward him and placed a hand on his arm. "In fact," she said, "I'm ready right now."

Stone patted her hand. "That's a kind thought," he said, "but it's very likely that you're going to be called as a witness for the prosecution at Arrington's trial, and . . ."

"I'll bet you could get me to say whatever you wanted me to," Charlene said, getting up and sitting on the edge of his chaise.

"That would be suborning perjury," Stone said, trying to keep his voice calm. "My advice to you is to tell the truth."

"I'll tell you the truth," she said, and her hand went smoothly to his crotch. "I want you right now, and," she squeezed gently, "I can tell you want me."

"I'm afraid . . ."

She squeezed harder. "Stone," she said, "you don't want to turn down the best piece of ass on the North American continent, do you?"

Stone got to his feet, and his condition was something of an embarrassment. She got up, too. "Charlene," he said, "I don't doubt you for a moment, but, believe me, it could mean big trouble for both of us."

"It might be worth it," she said, rubbing her body against his.

Stone was backing away, but he could not bring himself to disagree. "I have to leave," he said, turning for the door.

"All right," she sighed, "but when this trial is over, you call me, you hear?"

Stone waved and walked quickly through the house and to his car. When he was finally behind the wheel, he noticed that he was breathing harder than the effort had required.

Chapter 26

Stone drove slowly back to the studio, top down, trying to enjoy the California weather, instead of thinking about Charlene Joiner. He had read the newspaper accounts of her long-ago affair with the senator and presidential candidate Will Lee, and he had every sympathy for the senator. She was extraordinarily beautiful, all over, and, if Betty Southard's account of her prowess in bed was true, the senator was lucky to get out with his scalp.

He could not make the randiness go away. Just when he thought he had it under control, he passed the public beach area near Sunset, and a girl walking along the sand in a bikini got him going again. Stone sighed and tried to think pure thoughts.

As he walked into the studio bungalow, the phone was ringing, and Betty answered it.

"It's for you," she said.

Stone went into the study and picked up the phone. "Hello?"

"Stone, it's Rick Grant."

"Hi, Rick, what's up?"

"I just wanted to see how you're doing. I heard about the scene at the D.A.'s office. Blumberg pulled that one out of the fire."

"At least, temporarily."

"It was a shitty thing for the D.A. to do—try to make her spend the weekend in jail."

"Do I detect a sympathetic note?"

"Sort of."

"Rick, what have they got on her that they're not telling us?"

"I can't get into that," Rick replied, "but there is something I can tell you."

"Please do."

"They found a good footprint outside the French doors leading to the pool. A Nike, size twelve."

"That's interesting."

"The guy had walked through some sprinkler-dampened dirt, or something; there was only one good one, but they got a photograph of it."

"I learned something else," Stone said.

"Tell me."

"There was a Mexican gardener there, on both the Friday and Saturday, but he left the country Saturday night, went back to Tijuana, so he couldn't have been questioned by Durkee and Bryant."

"That's very interesting," Rick admitted.

"What's more, another customer of the same gardening service caught the guy in her living room, once. She thought he would have stolen something, left to his own devices."

"Pretty good; now you've got another suspect. That should take some of the heat off Arrington."

"It will, if Durkee and Bryant investigate—find the guy and bring him back."

"I wouldn't count on that," Rick said. "Getting somebody back from the Mexicans almost never happens. Unless he comes back across the border voluntarily, well, you're not going to see him. Do you know his name?"

"Felipe Cordova, and he's from Tijuana. Had you heard about this guy from your people?"

"No, and that's puzzling; I'll check into it. I'll pass this on to Durkee, and we'll see what happens."

"I'll tell you what I think, Rick: I think Durkee and Bryant, and now the D.A., have the hots for Arrington as a suspect, and they don't want to know anything that points to anybody else."

"Could be," Rick admitted. "Wouldn't be the first time that's happened."

"Happens all the time," Stone said. "In New York, and everywhere else. The path of least resistance, never mind who really did it; nail *somebody*."

"We've all seen that."

"And the high profile of this case has got them salivating for a high-profile perp."

"Could be."

"I think it's the O.J. thing," Stone said. "They lost that one, and now they want a big conviction to salvage their reputations."

"Possibly."

"Will you let me know what you hear about the Mexican gardener?"

"I'll do that."

"Talk to you later," Stone said into the phone, and hung up. He walked into Betty's office, but she was not at her desk. He felt the need for a shower and went into the bedroom. He undressed and stretched out on the bed, thinking to relax for a few minutes. Then Betty came out of the bathroom, and she was naked.

"Oh!" she said. "Sorry, I thought you'd be on the phone for a while."

"It's okay, Betty," he said, getting up. "It's not the first time we've seen each other in the buff."

She walked over and put her arms around him. "I just want to see if this feels as good as I remember. It does."

"It certainly does," Stone agreed. Then, before he could get into trouble, he held her off a few inches. "If I'm not careful, you'll seduce me," he said.

Betty laughed.

Then there was a blinding flash of light, followed by another. Stone and Betty both turned toward the door, astonished. The flash came again, then there was the sound of running feet leaving the cottage.

Stone blinked, trying to regain his vision.

"What the hell was that?" Betty cried.

"I don't know; what's the number for the main gate?"

Betty dialed the number and handed the phone to Stone.

"Main gate," the guard said.

"This is Stone Barrington; we've had an intruder in Mr. Calder's bungalow. Who's come in this morning?"

"In the last half-hour, only Mrs. Barrington," the man replied.

"There *is no Mrs. Barrington!*" Stone yelled. "Don't let her in here again!" He hung up and turned to Betty. "I'm sorry, it was Dolce; I didn't even know she was still in town."

"Well," Betty said, "ask her if I can have a set of prints."

"That would be funny, if I weren't so pissed off."

"Where were we?" Betty asked.

But Stone was already dressing.

"Where are you going?"

"I'm going to put a stop to this thing with Dolce."

"And how are you going to do that?"

"I'll talk to her."

"Lotsa luck," Betty said. "Looks to me as though you're past talking."

Chapter 27

Stone parked Vance Calder's Mercedes in the upper parking lot of the Bel-Air Hotel and walked quickly to Dolce's suite. He was going to have to have this out with her, once and for all. He rapped sharply on the door and waited.

A moment later the door was opened by a white-haired woman in her sixties, dressed in a hotel robe. "Yes?" she said, looking at him suspiciously.

"May I see Miss Bianchi, please?"

"I'm sorry, you have the wrong room," the woman replied, starting to close the door.

"May I ask, when did you check in?"

"About noon," she replied and firmly shut the door.

Stone walked down to the lobby and the front desk. "Yes, Mr. Barrington?" the young woman at the desk said. "Are you checking in again?"

"No, I'm looking for Miss Dolce Bianchi. Has she changed rooms?"

"Let me check," the woman said, tapping some computer keys. "I'm afraid I don't see a Miss Bianchi."

"Try Mrs. Stone Barrington," Stone said, through clenched teeth.

"Ah, yes. Mrs. Barrington checked out last night."

"And her forwarding address?"

She checked the computer screen and read off the address of Eduardo's house in Manhattan.

"Thank you," Stone said.

"Of course," she replied. "We're always happy to see you, Mr. Barrington."

"Thank you, and by the way, would you inform the management that there is *no* Mrs. Stone Barrington? The woman's name is Dolce Bianchi, and should she check in again, I would be grateful if you would not allow her to use my name in the hotel."

"I'll speak to the manager about it," the woman replied, looking baffled.

"Thank you very much," Stone said, managing a smile for the woman. He walked back to the parking lot, switched on the ignition, and called the Bianchi house in Manhattan. He got an answering machine for his trouble. Frustrated, he called Dino's number at home.

"Hello?" Mary Ann, Dino's wife, answered.

"Hi, Mary Ann, it's Stone."

"Hi, Stone," she said cheerfully, then her voice took on a sympathetic tone. "I'm sorry things didn't work out in Venice."

"Thank you, but I think it was for the best."

"Well, since you're not too broken up about it, I don't mind telling you, I think you're lucky to be out of that relationship. I mean, Dolce's my sister, and I love her, but you're far too nice a guy to have to put up with her."

"She registered at the Bel-Air as Mrs. Stone Barrington," he said.

"Oh, Jesus," Mary Ann breathed. "That's just like her."

"She checked out yesterday and said she was returning to New York, but there's no answer at the Manhattan house. Have you heard from her? I want to talk to her."

"Not a word; I knew she went to Vance Calder's funeral, and I thought she was still in L.A. Hang on, Dino wants to speak to you."

"So how's the bridegroom?" Dino asked.

"Don't start. She checked into the Bel-Air as Mrs. Stone Barrington. Are you sure that civil ceremony has no force in law?"

"That's my understanding, but I'm not an Italian lawyer," Dino replied. "Is Dolce giving you a hard time?"

"I'm staying at Vance Calder's cottage at Centurion Studios, and she barged in there this afternoon with a camera and caught me in bed with Betty Southard, Vance's secretary."

Dino began laughing.

Stone held the phone away from his ear for a moment. "It's not funny, Dino. I can't have her going around pretending to be Mrs. Barrington and behaving like a wronged wife."

"Listen, pal, you're talking to the guy who warned you off her, remember?"

"Don't rub it in. What am I going to do about her?"

"I guess you could talk to Eduardo; you two are such good buddies. Maybe he'll spank her, or something."

"Yeah, sure."

"I can't think of anybody else who could handle her."

"Neither can I."

"You got the Brooklyn number?"

"Yes."

"That's what I'd do, in your shoes—that, and talk to an Italian lawyer."

"Thanks, I'll talk to you later." Stone punched off, and it occurred to him that he knew an Italian lawyer. He dug out his wallet and found the cardinal's card. He looked at his watch; it would be early evening in Italy. He called the operator, got the dialing code for Rome, and punched in the number.

"Pronto," a deep voice said.

"Good evening," Stone said. "My name is Stone Barrington; may I speak with Cardinal Bellini, please?"

"Stone, how good to hear from you," Bellini said, switching to English.

"Thank you; I'm sorry to bother you, but I need some advice regarding Italian law, and I didn't know anyone else to call."

"Of course; how can I help you?"

"You'll recall that, before my sudden departure from Venice, Dolce and I went through some sort of civil ceremony at the mayor's office."

"I do."

"But I had to leave Venice before the ceremony at St. Mark's."

"Yes, yes."

"My question is, does the civil ceremony, without the church ceremony, have any legal force?"

"Not in the eyes of the church," Bellini replied.

"How about in the eyes of the Italian government?"

"Well, it is possible to be legally married in Italy in a civil ceremony." Stone's heart sank.

"Can you tell me what this is about, Stone? Is something wrong?"

"I don't want to burden you with this, Your Eminence," Stone said.

"Not at all," the cardinal replied. "I have plenty of time."

Stone poured it all out—Arrington; Arrington and Vance Calder; Dolce; everything.

"Well," the cardinal said when he had finished, "it seems you've reconsidered your intentions toward Dolce."

"I'm afraid I've been forced to."

"Then it's fortunate that this occurred before you took vows in the church."

"Yes, it is. However, I'm concerned about my marital status under Italian law. Is it possible that I am legally married?"

"Yes, it is possible."

Stone groaned.

"I can see how, given the circumstances, this might concern you, Stone. Before I can give you any sort of definitive answer, I'd like to do a bit of research. I'm leaving Rome tomorrow morning for a meeting in Paris, and it may be a few days, perhaps longer, before I can look into this. Let's leave it that I'll phone you as soon as I have more information."

"Thank you, Your Eminence." Stone gave him the Centurion number, thanked him again, and hung up.

He started the car and drove slowly back to the studio. When he reached the cottage it was dark, except for a lamp in the window. Betty had gone.

Stone rarely drank alone, but he went to the bar and poured himself a stiff bourbon. What had he gotten himself into? Was he married? If so, the Italians didn't have divorce, did they? He had not wanted to question a cardinal of the Church about a divorce. He collapsed in a chair and pulled at the bourbon. For a while, he allowed himself a wallow in self-pity.

⮶ Chapter 28 ⮷

Stone was signing documents faxed to him from New York by his secretary when Betty buzzed him.

"Rick Grant on line one."

Stone picked up the phone. "Hi, Rick."

"Good morning, Stone. I had a chat with Durkee about this missing Mexican gardener, and I have to tell you that he and his partner don't seem to have the slightest interest in him."

"I suppose they're not interested in the footprint they found outside the house, either."

"Not much. It's a Nike athletic shoe, size twelve, right foot, with a cut across the heel. I got that much out of Durkee."

"Can you get me a copy of the photograph of the footprint?"

"I think you're better off asking for that in discovery."

Rick obviously didn't want to get more involved than he already was. "Maybe you're right."

"I thought of something, though."

"What's that?"

"I told you how tough it was to get suspects out of Mexico, but there might be something you can do."

"Tell me."

"I know a guy named Brandy Garcia. Brandy is a Latino hustler, does a little of everything to make a buck. He's been a coyote, running illegals across the border, he's run an employment agency for recently arrived Latinos, he may even have smuggled some drugs in his time, I don't know. But he's well connected below the border, especially in Tijuana, where he's from, and he might be able to find this guy, Felipe Cordova, for you."

"Sounds good."

"Trouble is, Cordova is not a suspect, so even if you found him and the Mexicans were willing to extradite him, nobody would arrest him."

"That's discouraging," Stone replied.

"I know. But you might try to talk to him, if Brandy can find him."

"How do I get hold of Brandy Garcia?"

"I left a message on an answering machine, giving him your number. He may or may not call; I don't know if he's even in the country."

"Okay, I'll wait to hear from him."

"Good luck."

"Thanks, Rick." Stone hung up.

Twenty minutes later Betty buzzed him. "There's somebody on the phone, who says his name is Brandy Garcia; says Rick Grant told him to call."

"Put him through," Stone said. There was a click. "Hello?"

"Mr. Barrington?"

"Yes."

"My name is Brandy Garcia; Rick Grant said I might be of some service to you." The accent was slight.

"Yes, I spoke to Rick. Can we meet someplace?"

"You free for lunch?"

"How about a drink?"

"Okay: the Polo Lounge at the Beverly Hills Hotel at twelve-thirty?"

"All right."

"See you then." Garcia hung up.

Stone opened his briefcase, found a bank envelope, and counted out some money.

Stone drove up to the portico of the Beverly Hills Hotel and turned his car over to the valet. Walking inside, he thought that the place looked very fresh and new. It was the first time he'd visited the hotel since its multi-million-dollar renovation by its owner, the Sultan of Brunei.

He walked into the Polo Lounge and looked around, seeing nobody who fit the name of Brandy Garcia. The headwaiter approached.

"May I help you, sir?"

"I'm to meet a Mr. Garcia here," Stone said.

"Mr. Barrington?"

"Yes."

"Come this way, please." He led Stone through the restaurant, out into the garden, and to a table in a shady spot near the rear hedge. A man stood up to greet him.

"Brandy Garcia," he said, extending a hand.

"Stone Barrington," Stone replied, shaking it. Garcia was slightly flashily dressed, in the California style, and perfectly barbered, with a well-trimmed moustache. He bore a striking resemblance to the old-time Mexican movie actor Gilbert Roland.

Garcia indicated a seat. "Please," he said.

"I don't think I'll have time for lunch," Stone said.

Garcia shrugged. "Have a drink, then; I'll have lunch."

They both sat down. There was a large snifter of cognac already before Garcia. "So you're a friend of Rick's?" Garcia asked.

"Yes."

"I've known Rick a long time; good guy. Rick was the first person to tell me I look like Gilbert Roland." He appeared to be cultivating the resemblance.

"Oh," Stone said.

"You think I look like him?"

"Yes, I think you do."

This seemed to please Garcia. The waiter brought them a menu. "Please. Order something. It would please me."

Stone suppressed a sigh. "All right. I'll have the lobster salad and a glass of the house chardonnay."

"Same here," Garcia said, ogling two good-looking women as they were seated at the next table, "but I'll stick with brandy. So," he said, finally, "Rick says you're looking for somebody."

"Yes, I am."

"What is his name?"

"Felipe Cordova."

Garcia shook his head slowly. "I don't know him," he said, as if this were surprising.

"I'm told he's from Tijuana," Stone said.

"My hometown!" Garcia said, looking pleased.

"He was working as a gardener in Los Angeles until recently." Stone tore a page from his notebook. "He was living with his sister; this is her name and address. He suddenly left L.A. on a Saturday night, the same night a murder was committed."

Garcia's eyebrows went up. "The Vance Calder murder?"

"Yes," Stone admitted. He had not wanted to share this information.

"I read the papers, I watch TV," Garcia said. "Your name was familiar to me."

"I want to find Cordova, talk to him."

"Not arrest him?"

Stone shook his head. "The police don't consider him a suspect. I just want to find out what he knows about that night."

Garcia nodded sagely. "There are some difficulties here," he said.

The waiter arrived with their lunch.

"What difficulties?" Stone asked.

"Tijuana is a difficult place, even for someone with my connections. And maybe Señor Cordova doesn't want to talk to you. That would make him harder to find."

Stone read this as a nudge for more money. "Can you find him?"

"Probably, but it will take time and effort."

"I'm quite willing to pay for your time," Stone said.

Garcia pushed a huge forkful of lobster into his mouth and chewed reflectively. Finally, he swallowed. "And if I find him, then what?"

"Arrange a meeting," Stone said.

Garcia chuckled. "You mean a nice lunch, like this?" He waved a hand.

"I just want an hour with the man."

"How, ah, *hard* do you wish to talk to him?"

"I don't want to beat answers out of him, if that's what you mean."

"Are you willing to pay him to sit still for this, ah, conversation, then?"

"Yes, within reason."

"I am not reasonable," Garcia said. "I will require five thousand dollars for my services, half now and half when you see Cordova."

"I don't have twenty-five hundred dollars on me," Stone said. "I can give you a thousand now and the rest in cash when we meet Cordova."

Garcia nodded gravely. "For a friend of Rick's that is agreeable."

Stone took a stack of ten one-hundred-dollar bills from his pocket, folded them and slipped them under Garcia's napkin. "When?"

"Within a week or so, I think," Garcia replied, pocketing the money.

"You have my number."

Garcia suddenly looked at his wristwatch. "Oh, I have to run," he said, standing up. "I will be in touch." He turned and walked back into the hotel without another word.

Stone finished his lunch and paid the check.

⌒ **Chapter 29** ⌒

As Stone walked back into the Calder bungalow at Centurion, he could see Betty in her office, leaning back in her chair and waving the phone. "It's Joan Robertson, in New York," she called out.

Stone went to Vance's office, picked up the phone, and spoke to his secretary. "What's up?" he asked.

"Oh, Stone, I'm so glad I got you," Joan said breathlessly. "Water is coming down the stairs."

"What do you mean?"

"I mean that the main stairs of the house look like a tributary of the Hudson River. It's been raining hard here for three days."

"Oh, shit," Stone said. When he had inherited the house, the roof had seemed the one thing that didn't need renovating. It was old, but it was of slate, which could last a hundred years or more. Now it occurred to Stone that the house was over a hundred years old, and so was the roof. "Here's what you do," he said. "Call a guy named Billy Foote; he's in my phone book. Billy was my helper when I was renovating the house, and he can do almost anything. Tell him to buy a whole lot of plastic sheeting and to get up on the roof and tack it down everywhere. That'll stop the worst of it."

"Okay, then what?" Joan asked sensibly.

Stone realized he didn't know a roofer, let alone one qualified to tackle a slate roof. "Let me think for a minute," he said.

"Listen, Stone, I think you ought to get back here. There are clients you need to see, instead of just talking on the phone, and there's going to be damage to the house as a result of all the water coming in. Please come back."

Stone knew she was right. "I'll be home as soon as humanly possible," he said. "Call Billy, and tell him to hire whatever help he can and to start asking around about roofers who can deal with slate."

"All right," she said, then hung up.

Stone buzzed Betty.

"Yes?"

"Get me on the red-eye," he said. "I've got to go back to New York for a few days."

"Right; you want a car to meet you at the airport?"

"Good idea. I'm going over to Arrington's; you can reach me there, if you need me."

"Okay."

Stone packed his bags and loaded them into Vance's car.

Betty came out of the bungalow. "When are you coming back?" Betty asked.

"As soon as I can," Stone replied, giving her a kiss on the cheek.

"Stone, I think I'm going to be getting out of here pretty soon. Do you think you'll need me much longer?"

"I'd appreciate it if you'd hang around at least until I get back from New York.

"Don't worry, I'll clean up Vance's affairs for you, and I'll find somebody to do the job for Arrington when I'm gone. Now you get back to New York, and I'll see you when I see you." She gave him a sharp slap on the rump to send him on his way, and went back to her office.

All the way to Arrington's he thought about his house, how he loved it, and what must be happening to it. He called Joan on the car phone.

"Yes, Stone?"

"You'd better call Chubb Insurance and have them get somebody over there in a hurry. Tell them I need a recommendation for a roofer."

"Will do."

He entered the Calder property through the utility entrance, as had become his habit. Arrington heard the car pull up and met him at the back door.

She slipped her arms around his neck and kissed him. "I missed you," she said.

"How are you?"

"Bored rigid, as a matter of fact." She kissed him again. "And randy."

"Now, now, now, now . . ." Stone said, holding her away from him. "We can't allow ourselves to think that way, you know that."

"Come on in, and let me fix you a drink."

"I could use one," he replied. They settled in the little sitting room off the master suite. "I have to go back to New York for a little while," he said.

"Oh, no," she replied. "You're all I've got right now, Stone."

Stone explained about the roof and his impatient clients. "If there's as much water as Joan says there is, then it's going to take me some time to get things sorted out."

"But what will I do without you here?"

"Marc Blumberg is in charge of your case, anyway; I'm just an adviser."

"Marc is good, but he's no smarter than you are," she said.

"Thank you, but we're on his turf, and he knows it a lot better than I do. Who else could have gotten you bail on a Saturday?"

"I suppose you're right."

"I'll call every day," he said.

"You getting the red-eye?"

"Yes."

"Let's have some dinner before you go, then." She picked up a phone, buzzed Manolo, and ordered food. "And after dinner, will you please drive Mr. Barrington to the airport?" She thanked him and hung up. "I don't know what I would have done without Manolo," she said. "He's the most intensely loyal person I've ever met, besides you. Do you know that as soon as Vance was buried, he started getting offers from people, some of them my friends? And he turned down every one of them. He and Maria have just been wonderful."

"You're lucky to have them," Stone agreed. "On the subject of loyal help, Betty Southard told me this afternoon that she's going to leave as soon as Vance's affairs are settled, probably move to Hawaii."

"I don't blame her," Arrington said. "She's never liked me, particularly, so maybe it's best."

"She said she'd find somebody to work for you."

"Good."

"I'd like to wash up before dinner; will you excuse me?"

"Use Vance's bathroom; it's the closest," she said, pointing to the hallway.

Stone left her and found the bathroom. As he came back up the hallway, past Vance's dressing room, he thought something was odd, but he wasn't sure what. He walked back to the bathroom and looked at the wall backing up onto the dressing room, then he walked down the hallway and looked at the dressing room. There was something wrong with the proportions, but the bourbon he had just had on an empty stomach was keeping him from figuring it out. He went back and joined Arrington.

"How old is this house?" he asked.

"It was built during the twenties," she said, "but when Vance bought it in the seventies, he gutted it and started over."

"Did he make a lot of changes?"

"He changed everything; he might as well have torn it down and started over, but Vance was too keen on costs to waste the shell of a perfectly good house. After we were married, I redecorated the master suite, with his approval on fabrics and so forth."

"Did you tear down any walls then?"

"No, the space was already divided as you see it. Even though Vance was a bachelor when he rebuilt the house, he provided for what he called 'the putative woman.' "

Stone laughed.

They had dinner in the small dining room and talked about old times, which weren't really that old, Stone reflected. A lot had happened in the few years they had known each other.

"I think I'd go back to Virginia, if I were allowed to leave town," Arrington said, "and just spend a few weeks or months. Do a lot of riding. I miss that."

"You've got room for horses here," Stone said.

"You're right; there's actually an old stable on the property, and there are still riding trails in the neighborhood. Did you know that the Bel-Air Hotel is built on property where Robert Young used to own a riding stable?"

"No, I didn't know that."

"Maybe when this is all over, I'll buy a couple of horses. Do you ride?"

"You're talking to a city kid, you know. I mean, I rode a little at summer camp as a boy, but that was about it."

"I'm going to redecorate this house, too," she said. "I don't want to sell it; it's unique, and I love it so. I didn't do a lot about the place, except for the master suite, when I moved in, and I'm tired of even that. You did such a good job on your house; will you consult?"

"I'll consult, when I get back," Stone said. He thought it was good that she was looking past the trial, instead of obsessing about it. He wanted her optimistic; otherwise, she'd come apart.

They talked on into the evening, easily, the way people do who know each other well. Then Manolo brought the Bentley around, with Stone's luggage already in the trunk.

"Don't stay any longer than you have to," Arrington said, kissing him lightly. "And by the way, it's time you sent me a bill. I can't have you devoting all your working time to me, and after all, I'm a rich woman."

"I'll probably overcharge you," Stone said.

"That would not be possible," she said, kissing him again, this time more longingly.

Stone allowed himself to enjoy it, and the drive to the airport passed in a haze of good wine and rekindled desire.

He checked his luggage, got to the gate, and boarded with only a couple of minutes to spare. The flight attendant was closing the door to the airplane, when she suddenly reopened it and stepped back.

Dolce got onto the airplane, and the flight attendant closed the door behind her.

Chapter 30

S tone was sitting in the first-row window seat of the first-class section, and he watched like a trapped rabbit, as Dolce, cobralike, glided past, ignoring him, and took a seat somewhere behind him.

"Would you like a drink, Mr. Barrington?" the attendant asked.

"A Wild Turkey on the rocks," he replied without hesitation, "and make it a double." When the drink arrived, he drank it more quickly than he usually would have, and by the time the flight reached its cruising altitude, he had fallen asleep.

Sometime in the night he awoke, needing the bathroom. On the way back to his seat, he looked toward the rear of the compartment and saw Dolce, sitting on the aisle three rows behind his seat, gazing unblinkingly at him. It was unnerving, he thought. He slept only fitfully for the rest of the flight.

When the door opened at the gate, Stone was the first off the airplane, nearly running up the ramp into the terminal. His bags were among the first to be seen in baggage claim, and a driver stood by with his name written on a shirt cardboard. He pointed at the bags and followed the driver to the waiting car.

He felt hungover from having the bourbon so close to bedtime, and the weather did not improve his mood. It was still raining heavily, the result of a close brush from a tropical storm off the coast, and even though the driver handled his bags, he got very wet between the car and his front door.

He tipped the driver generously, opened the door, and stepped inside his house, shoving his bags ahead of him. He tapped the security code into the keypad and looked around. The stairs had been stripped of their runner, which was piled on the living room floor, on top of a fine old Oriental carpet that had come with the house, both of them sodden. A smell of dampness permeated the place.

He put his bags on the elevator and pressed the button, then he walked up the stairs slowly, surveying the damage, which, if not catastrophic, was still awful. Thank God for insurance, he thought. He walked into his upstairs sitting room, where there was more wet carpet, and watermarks on the wall next to the stairs, where the water from the breached roof had run down. At least it had stopped, he thought, though it was still raining hard outside. Billy Foote must have gotten the plastic cover over the roof. His beautiful house, nearly ruined. He thought about how hard he had worked to restore it. Now a few days' rain . . .

The security system beeped, signaling that Joan was arriving for work. He picked up a phone and buzzed her.

"Hi. Was your flight okay?"

"As okay as could be expected. Thanks for getting Billy over here."

"He did a good job. The insurance adjustor got here in a hurry, and he's sending a roofer to bid for the job as soon as it stops raining, if it ever does, and the carpet cleaners are coming this morning to take away all the wet rugs."

Stone looked around his bedroom. "Tell them to throw away the carpet up here," he said. "It's time to replace it, I think, and the stairway runner, too. I do want to save the Oriental in the living room, though."

"Okay."

"Any calls?"

"None that can't wait until this afternoon," she said. "You probably need some sleep."

"That's true. I'll check with you later." He hung up, got undressed, went into a guest room, where the carpets were still dry, and got into bed.

He woke up around noon, showered, shaved, dressed, and went downstairs, where his housekeeper, Helene, had left a sandwich for him. He had just finished it when the front doorbell rang. That would be the carpet people, he thought, and instead of using the intercom, he went to the front door and opened it. Eduardo Bianchi stood on his doorstep, glumly holding an umbrella. The Mercedes Maybach idled at the curb.

"Eduardo!" Stone said, surprised. He had almost never seen the man anywhere except on his own turf. "Come in."

"Thank you, Stone. I'm sorry to barge in, but I heard you were back from California, and I wonder if you could spare me a few minutes?"

"Of course," Stone said, taking the umbrella, and helping the older man off with his coat. "Come on back to my study. Would you like some coffee?"

"Thank you, yes," Eduardo replied, rubbing his hands together briskly. "It's terrible out there."

Stone settled him in a chair in his study, then made some espresso and brought in a pot and two cups on a tray.

"So, you're back in New York for a while, I hope?" Eduardo asked.

"I'm afraid not," Stone said. He explained the problem with the roof. "I have some clients to see, too, then I have to get back to L.A. I'm afraid Arrington still needs me there."

"Ah, Arrington," Eduardo said slowly. "A most unfortunate situation for her. Do you think she will be acquitted?"

"I think she's innocent, and I'll do everything I can to see that she is. Marc Blumberg, an L.A. lawyer, is her lead counsel; I'm just advising."

Eduardo nodded. "I know Marc; he's a good man, right for this."

Stone was not surprised, since Eduardo seemed to know everybody on both coasts. He waited for his near-father-in-law to come to the point of his visit.

"Dolce is back, too," he said.

"I know," Stone replied. "I caught a glimpse of her on the airplane, but we didn't talk."

Eduardo shook his head. "This is all very sad," he said. "I do not like seeing her so upset."

"I'm very sorry for upsetting her," Stone said, "but I could not do otherwise under the circumstances."

"What are your intentions toward Arrington?" Eduardo asked, as if he had the right to.

"Quite frankly, I don't know," Stone said. "She has some serious difficulties to overcome, and, if Blumberg and I are successful in defending her, I don't know what her plans are after that. I'm not sure she knows, either."

"And your plans?"

"I haven't made any. Every time I do, it all seems to come back to Arrington, one way or another."

"You are in love with her, then?"

Stone sighed. He had been avoiding the question. "I think I have to finally face the fact that I have been for a long time."

"Why did you not marry her when you had the opportunity?" Eduardo asked.

"I intended to," Stone replied. "We were going on a sailing holiday together in the islands. I had planned to pop the question down there. She was delayed in joining me, because she had been asked to write a magazine piece about Vance. The next thing I knew, they were married."

Eduardo nodded. "Vance could do that," he said. "He was a very powerful personality, difficult for a young woman to resist." Eduardo set down his coffee cup and crossed his legs. "Now we come to Dolce," he said. "My daughter is very unhappy. What are your intentions toward her?"

Stone took a deep breath. "Dolce and I have talked about this," he said. "I've told her that I think it would be a terrible mistake for both of us, should we marry."

"Why?" Eduardo asked, and his eyes had narrowed.

"This business with Arrington has taught me that I'm not free of her," Stone replied, "as I thought I was. Vance's sudden death was a great shock, and not just because I liked him."

"Arrington is once again available, then?"

"Well, she's no longer married."

"Has she expressed an interest in rekindling your relationship with her?"

"Yes," Stone said, surprising himself with his willingness to discuss this with Eduardo.

"And there is the child," Eduardo said.

"Yes; there was a time when we both thought he might be mine, but the blood tests . . ."

"And who conducted these tests?" Eduardo asked.

"Why do you want to know?"

"Indulge me, please."

Stone went to his desk and rummaged in a bottom drawer. The report was still there. He handed it to Eduardo.

Eduardo read the document carefully. "This would seem conclusive," he said.

"Yes."

"Who employed these 'Hemolab' people?" he asked, reading the name of the laboratory from the letterhead.

"Arrington, I suppose."

Eduardo nodded and handed back the document and stood up. "I am sorry to have taken your time, Stone," he said, "but I had to explore this with you in order to know what to do."

Stone wasn't sure what he meant by that. "You are always welcome here, Eduardo."

"Thank you," he replied.

Stone followed him to the door, helped him on with his coat, and handed him his umbrella.

"Dolce is ill, you know," Eduardo said suddenly.

"What? What's wrong with her?"

"Her heart is ill; it has always been so, I think. I had hoped you could make her well, but I see, now, that it will not happen."

"What can I do to help, Eduardo?"

"Nothing, I think, short of marrying her, and after what you have told me today, I think that would destroy both of you."

"Is there anything I can do?"

Eduardo turned and looked at Stone, and his eyes were ineffably sad. "You can only keep away from her," he said. "I think she may be . . . dangerous." Then, without another word, he turned and walked down the steps and back to his car.

Stone watched as the limousine moved off down the street, and the shiver that ran through him was not caused by the dampness.

～ **Chapter 31** ～

Stone met with his anxious clients and soothed their nerves. He spoke to the insurance agent and got approval to begin repairs, then, because he could not bear to look at his damaged house, he went downtown to ABC Carpets and picked out new ones, arranging for their people to measure and install them. As he got in and out of taxicabs, he caught himself looking around to see if he had unwanted company, but he did not see Dolce.

At half past eight he was at Elaine's, giving her a kiss on arrival and being shown to his usual table.

Elaine sat down for a minute. "So," she said, "you're up to your ass in this Vance Calder thing."

"I'm afraid so."

"I always liked Arrington," she said. "I wouldn't have thought she could kill anybody."

"I don't think she did."

"Can you prove it?"

"I guess the only way I can prove that is by proving somebody else did it. Otherwise, even if she's tried and acquitted, too many people will believe she's guilty, and a smart lawyer got her off."

"I hear she's got a smart lawyer—besides you, I mean."

"That's right; he's doing a good job, so far."

"Stone." She looked at him sadly.

"Yes?"

"Sometimes people do things you wouldn't think they could do. People get stressed, you know, and the cork pops."

Stone nodded.

"If you want to get through this okay, you'd better get used to the idea that you may be wrong about her."

"I don't think I am."

"Protect yourself; don't tear out your guts hoping."

It was the first advice he'd ever gotten from her. "I'll try," he said. He looked up to see Dino and Mary Ann coming through the door. He especially wanted to see Mary Ann.

Everybody hugged, kissed, sat down, and ordered drinks.

"You got a little sun," Dino said, inspecting him.

"Out there, you get it just walking around."

Elaine got up to greet some customers, giving his shoulder a squeeze as she left.

"What was that?" Dino asked.

"Encouragement," Stone replied. "I think she thinks Arrington did it."

"Doesn't everybody?" Dino asked.

"Do you?"

"Let's put it this way: I think I'm probably more objective about it than you are."

"Oh."

"Let me ask you something, Stone: If you all of a sudden found out for sure that she did it, would you try to get her off, anyway?"

"That's my job."

"You're not her lawyer; Blumberg is."

Stone looked into his drink. "It's still my job."

"Oh," Dino said, "it's like that."

"Well!" Mary Ann interjected. "Isn't it nice to all be together again, and right here at home!"

"Don't try to cheer him up," Dino said to his wife. "It won't work."

Michael, the headwaiter, brought menus, and they studied them silently for a minute, then ordered. Stone ordered another drink, too.

"Two before dinner," Dino said.

"He's entitled," Mary Ann pointed out.

They chatted in a desultory manner until dinner arrived, then ate, mostly in silence.

"Mary Ann," Stone said, when the dishes had been taken away, "your father came to see me this afternoon."

"He did?" she asked, surprised. "Where?"

"At my house."

"That's interesting," she said. "He doesn't do much calling on people. What did he want?"

"To know my intentions toward Arrington and Dolce."

"Is that all? What did you tell him?"

"That I don't know what my intentions are toward Arrington, but that Dolce and I are not getting married."

"That wasn't what he wanted to hear, I'm sure."

"I know, but I had to be honest with him."

"That's always the best policy with Papa."

"When he left, he said something that scared me a little."

Dino spoke up. "That's what he does best."

"What did he say?" Mary Ann asked.

"He said Dolce is ill, and that she might be dangerous."

"Oh," Mary Ann said quietly.

"What did he mean by that?"

Mary Ann didn't seem to be able to look at him.

"I think Stone needs to know, honey," Dino said. "Answer his question."

Mary Ann sighed. "When Dolce doesn't get what she wants, she . . . reacts badly."

"Now, *there's* news," Dino snorted.

"Exactly *how* does she react badly?" Stone asked.

"She, ah, breaks things," Mary Ann said slowly. "People, too."

"Go on."

"When she was, I guess, six, Papa gave her a puppy. She tried to train it, but it wouldn't do what she told it to. It was like she expected it to understand complete sentences, you know? Well, she . . . I don't want to say what she did."

"She broke the puppy?" Dino asked.

"Sort of," Mary Ann replied. Her face made it clear she wasn't going to say any more.

"I think she's been stalking me," Stone said.

"What?" Mary Ann said.

"She's shown up in a couple of places where I was. Unexpectedly, you might say. She registered at the Bel-Air as Mrs. Stone Barrington. She was on my flight home last night."

"Oh, shit," Dino breathed.

"I thought about trying to talk to her again, but I don't even want to be in the same room with her."

"That's a good policy," Dino said.

"I don't know what to do," Stone admitted.

"I'd watch my back, if I were you," Dino said. "Remember what happened to the husband . . ."

"Oh, shut up, Dino," Mary Ann spat. "She's my sister; don't talk that way about her."

"I'm sorry, hon, but Stone's in a jam, here, and we've got to help him figure this out."

"Well, you're not helping by . . . what you're saying."

"Are you carrying?" Dino asked.

"Dino!" his wife nearly shouted.

"It wouldn't surprise me if Dolce is," Dino continued, ignoring her.

"No, I'm not," Stone said. "I don't think it's come to that."

"Listen, Stone," Dino said. "At the point when it comes to that, it's going to be too late to go home and get a piece."

Their waiter stepped up with a dessert tray.

"Nothing for me," Stone said.

"I'll have the cheesecake," Dino said.

"Nothing for him," Mary Ann said, pointing a thumb at her husband. "Especially not the cheesecake."

Dino sighed.

"Nothing for anybody," Mary Ann said to the waiter.

They got a check, and declined the offer of an after-dinner drink from Elaine. Dino grabbed the check and signed it, before Stone could react.

"That's completely out of character, Dino," Stone said, chuckling.

"Who knows how many more opportunities I'll have," Dino replied, getting an elbow in the ribs from Mary Ann for his trouble.

They made their farewells to Elaine and started out of the restaurant. As they shuffled toward the door, Stone felt Dino slip something fairly heavy into his coat pocket.

"Don't leave home without it," Dino whispered.

⌐ Chapter 32 ⌐

Stone reached into his coat pocket, took out the pistol, and placed it on the bedside table. It was a little .32 automatic, not a service weapon, but the kind of small gun a cop might keep in an ankle holster, as a backup.

He undressed, got into bed, and tried to watch the late news, but finally turned it off. He was still groggy from the sleep upset of taking the red-eye, and the conversation at dinner had depressed him.

He drifted off immediately and fell into a deep sleep. He dreamed, and something was out of place in his dream—a high-pitched squeal, as if from a great distance. Then the squeal stopped.

Stone sat straight up in bed, wide awake. The squeal was the sound the security system made to warn that it was about to go off; it stopped only when the proper four-digit code was entered, and it had stopped. Then he remembered that Dolce knew the code.

He got out of bed as silently as he could and rearranged the pillows under the duvet, to give the impression he was still in bed, then he picked up Dino's pistol, tiptoed to his dressing room, and stood just inside the door. There was enough light coming through the windows to let him see the bed.

He heard the light footsteps on the stairs, which were now bare of the carpet runner. They approached slowly, quietly, until they reached the bedroom, where they stopped. She was letting her eyes become accustomed to the nearly dark room. Then she began to move forward again, and she came into Stone's view.

She was wearing a black raincoat with the hood up, so her face was still in darkness, and Stone thought she looked like the angel of death; she carried a short, thick club in her right hand. She reached the bed and stopped, then, holding the club at her side, she reached out with her left hand and began to pull back the covers.

"Freeze!" Stone said. "There's a gun pointed at your head."

She turned slowly to face him, but the shadow of the hood still obscured her face.

"Drop what's in your hand," he said.

She released the club, and it fell to the bare wood floor with a soft thud.

"Now, reach behind you and turn on the lamp, and keep your hands where I can see them."

She turned away and switched on the lamp, then turned back toward him, brushing off the hood. Instead of the black, Sicilian coif Stone had expected, honey-colored hair fell around her shoulders.

"Why are you pointing a gun at me, Stone?" she asked.

Stone's mouth fell open. "Arrington! What the hell are you doing here?"

"Could you point the gun somewhere else before we continue this conversation?"

Stone put the pistol on the dressing room chest of drawers and turned back to her.

She looked down, amused. "You're still pointing something at me," she said, unbuckling her belt and shucking off the raincoat. She was wearing black slacks and a soft, gray cashmere sweater. At her feet, on the floor, was the folding umbrella she had dropped.

Stone grabbed a cotton robe from the dressing room and slipped into it.

"Aw," she said, disappointed, "I liked you as you were. Don't I get a kiss?"

Stone crossed the room and gave her a small kiss, then held her at arm's length. "I'll ask you again: What the hell are you doing here?"

"Aren't you glad to see me?"

"Of course not! You've jumped bail, for God's sake, don't you understand that? The judge confined you to your house!"

"Don't worry, he'll never miss me."

"Arrington, let me explain this to you. As of this moment, you've forfeited two million dollars in bail."

"It's worth it to see you," she said. "I missed you."

"You could be arrested at any moment, and if you are, you won't get bail again; you'll have to stay in jail until the trial."

"Nobody's going to arrest me," she said. "Nobody knows I'm out of the house, except Manolo and Isabel, and certainly nobody knows I'm in New York. Manolo has instructions to tell anyone who calls that I'm not feeling well, and to take a message. I can return any calls from here."

Stone sat down on the edge of the bed and put his face in his hands. "I'm an officer of the court," he moaned. "I'm supposed to call the police or arrest you myself."

"Oooooo, arrest me," she purred.

Stone heard the sound of a zipper and looked up. She was stepping out of her slacks, and she had already shucked off the sweater, leaving only her panties.

She looked around, hands on her hips. "Now where are those pesky handcuffs? You must have some around here somewhere, being an ex-cop, and all."

Stone put his face back in his hands, and a moment later he felt her slip into the bed. Her fingernails moved down his back, and he started to get up, but she grabbed the belt of his robe and pulled him back onto the bed.

"I know Marc Blumberg said we couldn't be alone together in my house, but now we're alone together in *your* house, aren't we? So we're playing by the rules." She reached around him and tugged the belt loose, then pulled the robe off his shoulders. She dug her fingers into his hair, pulled him back onto the bed, and ran a fingernail along his penis, which responded with a jerk. "I *knew* you'd be glad to see me!" she said, then she pulled his face to hers and kissed him softly.

"This wasn't supposed to happen," Stone said, when he could free his lips for a moment.

She pulled his body toward hers. "Well, if I'm going to be arrested and carted off to jail, it seems only fair that I should have a last meal." She bent over him and kissed the tip of his penis. "I believe I'm entitled to have anything I want to eat, isn't that the tradition?" Then she began to concentrate on her repast.

Stone stood it for as long as he could, which was a little while, then he pulled her up beside him. She curled a leg over his body, opening herself to him. He slid inside her and, lying face-to-face, they began to make love, slowly.

"It's been way, way too long," Arrington said, moving with him and kissing his face.

"You're right," Stone breathed, admitting it as much to himself as to her.

"Tell me you've missed me."

"I've missed you."

"Tell me you've missed *this*."

"I can't tell you how much I've missed this," he moaned. "There are no words."

"Then *show* me," she said.

And he did.

⤚ Chapter 33 ⤙

Stone lay, naked, on his back, drained and weirdly happy, for a lawyer whose client seemed to be trying to go to jail. It was a little after ten A.M., and they had made love twice since sunup. He heard the shower go on in his bathroom and the sound of the glass door closing. He wanted to enjoy the moment, but he couldn't; he was faced with the problem of how to get Arrington back into the Los Angeles jurisdiction without getting her arrested and himself into very deep trouble.

A moment later, she came back, wearing his robe and rubbing her wet hair with a towel. "Good morning!" she said, as happy as if she were a free woman.

"Good morning." He managed a smile.

She sat down on the bed, took his wilted penis in her hand, and kissed it. "Aw," she said. "Did it die?"

"For the moment," he admitted. "Tell me, how did you get here? Exactly, I mean; I want a blow-by-blow account."

"Well, let's see: First I called the airline and made a reservation, then I put a few things into that little bag over there," she said, pointing to the top of the stairs, where she had left it, "then I left a note for Manolo, got into my car, left the house by the utility gate, which you have come to know and love, and I drove to the airport. I parked the car, walked into the terminal, gave the young lady at the ticket counter my credit card—the one that's still in my maiden name—and she gave me a ticket. Then I got on the plane, and when I arrived in New York, I took a cab here. Did I leave out anything?"

"Yes; your picture has been all over the L.A. and New York papers and *People* magazine, for Christ's sake; why didn't anyone recognize you?"

"I wore a disguise," she said. She went to her bag, unzipped it, and took out a silk Hermes scarf and a pair of dark glasses; she wrapped the scarf tightly around her head and put on the shades. "With this and no makeup, my own mother wouldn't recognize me."

"Why so few clothes?" he asked.

"I have a wardrobe in our apartment at the Carlyle," she said. "I was going to send you up there to get me a few things. I thought it would be foolish to dally in baggage claim, so I traveled light."

Stone sat up and put his feet on the floor. "Well, you were certainly right not to do anything foolish."

"Was that sarcasm I heard?"

"Irony."

"Oh. Shall I fix you some breakfast?"

"Oh, no; Helene will be downstairs by now; she can fix it. I don't want *anyone* to see you."

"Then I shall be served in bed," she said, sitting cross-legged among the pillows.

The phone rang, and Stone picked it up. "Hello?"

"Hi, it's Betty."

"Good morning; you're up early."

"Yep. When I got into the office, there was a message from someone named Brandy Garcia; ring a bell?"

"Yes; what was the message?"

"He said he'd found what you wanted, and he'd call again."

"If he does, tell him to call me at this number."

"Will do. How's New York?"

"It is as ever."

"Good; when are you coming back?"

"As soon as . . ." he stopped. The Centurion airplane, he thought. "Can you switch me to Lou Regenstein's office?"

"I could, but he wouldn't be in this early, and anyway, he's in New York."

"He is? Where?"

"I don't know, but I could ask his secretary when she gets in."

"Hang on." He covered the phone and turned to Arrington. "Do you have any idea where Lou Regenstein stays when he's in the city?"

"At the Carlyle," she said. "He has an apartment there, too."

"Never mind," he said to Betty. "I'll talk to you later." He hung up.

"You want to call Lou?"

"Yes; what's the number of the Carlyle?"

She found her handbag and her address book. "Here's the private line to his apartment." She read it to him as he dialed.

"Hello," Lou Regenstein's voice said.

"Lou, it's Stone."

"Hi, Stone, what's up?"

"How long are you in New York for?"

"About thirty seconds; I was on the way out the door to Teterboro Airport when you called."

"You going back to L.A.?"

"Yep. Where are you?"

"I'm in New York. Can you give, ah, a friend and me a lift?"

"Sure; how fast can you get to Teterboro?"

"Is an hour fast enough?"

"That's fine; see you there."

"Lou, will there be anyone else on the airplane?"

"Nope, just you and me—and your friend. Anybody I know?"

"I'll surprise you," Stone said. "See you in an hour." He hung up and turned to Arrington. "Get dressed," he said, "and put on your disguise."

"I'll have to dry my hair," she said.

"Then do it fast." He picked up the phone and buzzed Joan Robertson. "Morning."

"Good morning."

"I've got to leave for L.A. in half an hour; I want to drive, so will you come along and drive the car back?"

"Sure; I'll put the answering machine on."

"See you downstairs in a few minutes."

While Arrington dried her hair, Stone packed, put his bags in the elevator, and pressed the down button. Then he grabbed a quick shower and shave and threw on some casual clothes. "Ready?" he asked Arrington.

"Ready," she said, getting into her raincoat, wrapping the scarf around her head and slipping on her dark glasses.

They took the stairs to the ground floor. Stone led her through the door to the garage, put their bags into the trunk of the car, and opened a rear door for her. "You wait here while I get Joan, and don't talk on the way to the airport; I don't want her to know who you are."

Arrington shrugged. "Whatever you say." She got into the car and closed the door.

Stone went to his office, signed a couple of letters, and brought Joan back to the car. "There's someone in the backseat," he said. "Please don't look, and please don't ask any questions."

"Okay," Joan replied.

He opened the passenger door. "You sit up here; I'll drive."

Stone pressed the remote button on the sun visor and started the car, all in one motion. He had visions of Dolce waiting for him in the street, and he wasn't going to give her time to react. He reversed out of the garage, across the sidewalk, and into the street, causing a cabby to slam on his brakes and blow his horn. He pressed the remote button again, put the car into gear and was off, checking his mirrors. He thought for a moment that he saw a dark-haired woman across the street from his house, but he wasn't sure it was Dolce. He made the light and crossed Third Avenue. He would take the tunnel.

The car was something special—a Mercedes E55, which was an E-Class sedan with a souped-up big V-8, a special suspension, and the acceleration of an aircraft carrier catapult launcher. Something else for which he was grateful, at the moment: The car had been manufactured with a level of armor that would repel small-arms fire. He had been car shopping when it was delivered to the showroom and had bought it in five minutes, on a whim, at another time in his life when he feared that somebody might be shooting at him.

Rush hour was over, and he made it to the Atlantic Aviation terminal in twenty-five minutes, without getting arrested, all the while dictating a stream of instructions to Joan about what had to be done in the way of re-pairing the house.

At the chain-link gate to the ramp, he buzzed the intercom and gave the tail number of the Centurion jet. The gate slid open and he drove onto the ramp and to the big Gulfstream Four. He parked at the bottom of the airstair door, gave the bags to the second officer, who was waiting for them, and gave Joan a peck on the cheek. "Thanks for not asking any questions," he said. "One of these days, I'll explain."

Joan leaned forward and whispered, "She's just as beautiful as her pic-tures." Then she took the keys, got into the car, and headed for the gate.

Stone led Arrington up the stairs and into the airplane. Lou Regenstein was sitting on a couch, reading *The New York Times.* He looked up as Ar-rington took off her glasses and scarf. "Holy shit," he said. "What are you . . ."

Stone held up a hand. "Don't ask. You have not seen what you're seeing."

"Well," Lou said, standing up and hugging Arrington. "You're the nicest-looking invisible lady I've ever seen."

The airplane began to move, and Stone began to breathe again.

Chapter 34

With the time change in their favor, it was late afternoon when the G-IV touched down at Santa Monica airport. There was a short taxi to Supermarine, where Lou Regenstein's stretch Mercedes limousine was waiting at the bottom of the airstair when the engines stopped. It took a minute to load their luggage, then they were headed toward the freeway.

"May I use your phone, Lou?" Arrington asked. "I want to call home."

"Of course."

She dialed the number. "Hello, Manolo, I'm . . ." She stopped and held her hand over the phone. "Something's wrong," she said. "Manolo just called me, 'sir.' "

Stone took the phone. "Manolo, it's Mr. Barrington; is there someone there?"

"Yes, sir," Manolo said smoothly. "I'm afraid she's resting at the moment. Can I have her call you back? There are some gentlemen waiting to see her now."

"Gentlemen? The police?"

"Yes, sir," Manolo said, sounding relieved that Stone had caught on.

"Just arrived?"

"Yes, sir."

"Do this: Go and knock on Mrs. Calder's bedroom door and pretend to speak to her, then put the policemen in Mr. Calder's study, and tell them she's getting dressed, and she'll be a few minutes. Give them some coffee to keep them occupied."

"Yes, Mr. Regenstein, I'll tell her you called," Manolo said, then hung up.

Stone put the phone back in its cradle.

"Trouble?" Lou asked.

Stone nodded. "Tell your driver to get moving; the cops are at the house."

Lou picked up the phone and pressed the intercom button. "Get us to the Calder place pronto," he said.

Stone took the phone and told the driver how to find the utility gate.

Arrington looked out the window. She seemed finally to have grasped what a difficult position she had put herself in.

Ten hair-raising minutes later, the limousine pulled into the rear drive and stopped at the gate.

"We'll walk from here, Lou," Stone said. "Please ask your driver to leave our bags at Vance's bungalow." He shook hands with Lou, grabbed Arrington's hand and practically dragged her from the car.

"I don't have the remote control for the gate with me," he said. "Is there some other way to open it?"

"Not that I know of," Arrington said, jogging to keep up with him.

"We'll have to go over the fence, then." He hustled her into the woods beside the gate and made a stirrup with his hands, then practically threw her over the fence. She landed in a pile of leaves, and a moment later, he joined her. She was laughing.

"I'm sorry, this is so ridiculous," she said.

"We'll laugh about it later," Stone said, taking her hand and starting to run. They made it to the rear of the house, and Stone looked into the living room. "All clear," he said. "Now here's what you do: Go into your room, brush your hair, then go into Vance's study, looking ill. You don't feel well at all. Let me do the talking."

She nodded, then ran into the house and through the living room, toward the master suite.

Stone took a couple of deep breaths, made sure there were no leaves stuck to his clothes, then went into the study. Durkee and Bryant were drinking coffee and looking at Vance's Oscars, while Manolo stood, watching them.

"Afternoon, gentlemen, what can I do for you?"

"We're here to see Mrs. Calder," Durkee said.

Manolo spoke up. "I let Mrs. Calder know the gentlemen are here, Mr. Barrington. She'll be out shortly."

"Thank you, Manolo, that's all." He took a chair. "So, to what do we owe the honor of your visit?"

"We just want to see Mrs. Calder," Durkee said.

"She won't be answering any questions," Stone replied. "Surely, you knew that."

"We had a tip that she was in New York," Durkee said. "Show her to me; I'm getting tired of waiting."

Arrington chose that moment to enter the room. "Stone," she said drowsily, "what's this about? I was asleep."

"Sorry to wake you, Mrs. Calder," Durkee said.

"Are you satisfied?" Stone asked.

"I guess so."

Stone turned Arrington around and led her to the bedroom door. "You can go back to bed," he said. "Are you going to want dinner later, or do you want to just sleep?"

"I want to sleep," she said.

"Do you want Dr. Drake?"

"No, I think I'll be all right in the morning." She left the room, and Stone closed the door behind her.

He turned back to the two cops. "A tip? What kind of tip?"

"An anonymous call," Durkee said. "A woman. Said the lady had jumped bail."

Stone shook his head. "As long as you're here, tell me something."

"What's that?"

"Why haven't you interviewed the gardener, Cordova?"

"We have no reason to," Durkee said. "He's not a suspect."

"Do you think he might be connected to the footprint you found outside the back door to the house?"

Durkee and Bryant exchanged a glance. "Nah," Durkee said. "Anybody could have made it."

"A size-twelve Nike, and *anybody* could have made it?"

"Our investigation has not found the footprint or the gardener to be relevant," Durkee said. "Anyway, Cordova's in Mexico, and we'd never find him there."

"Have you made any effort?" Stone demanded.

"I told you, he's not relevant to our investigation. The murderer is in that bedroom."

Bryant spoke up. "Let's get out of here."

"By the way, Mr. Barrington, what are you doing here?" Durkee asked, with a smirk.

"I was working in the guest house," Stone replied. "I'm one of her lawyers."

"Nice work, if you can get it," Bryant said.

Stone opened the door to the study. "Manolo," he called, "show these officers the door, please." He turned to the two detectives. "And don't come back here again, without a warrant. You won't be let in."

The detectives left, and when Stone was sure they were off the property, he went into the bedroom and found Arrington at her dressing table, applying makeup. "Why are you putting on makeup?" he asked. "I hope you don't think you're going anywhere."

"Why don't we go to Spago for dinner?" she asked archly.

"Do you have any idea how lucky you just were?"

"Don't, Stone; I'm converted. I'm sorry I gave you a bad time." She smiled. "Not *very* sorry, though. I enjoyed my trip to New York."

"Give me your car keys," he said.

"Why?"

"Because I've got to get it back from the airport. Manolo can drive me."

She dug into her purse. "I took Vance's car," she said. "It's in short-term parking; the ticket is over the sun visor."

"I'll talk to you tomorrow," he said, kissing the top of her head.

"Won't you come back for dinner?" she asked, disappointed.

"I'm beat; I hardly got any sleep last night, remember?"

She smiled. "I remember." She stood up and kissed him. "I don't think I'll ever forget."

"Neither will I," he said, kissing her. Then he went to find Manolo, and they headed for LAX.

It was getting dark by the time he got back to the bungalow at Centurion. He checked the answering machine on Betty's desk, saw the red light blinking, and pressed the button.

"Mr. Barrington," Brandy Garcia's voice said, sounding exasperated. "I call here, and the lady says call New York; then I call New York, and the lady says to call here. I've got the item you want, and I'm going to call just one more time."

Then, as Stone stood there, the phone rang. "Hello?"

"Mr. Barrington?"

"Yes. Brandy?"

"Hey, Stone; I found your man."

"Where is he?"

"In Tijuana, of course."

"All right, you found him; now how do *I* find him?"

"You come to Tijuana."

"When?"

"Tomorrow afternoon; it's not a bad drive, three to four hours, depending on traffic. What kind of car will you be in?"

"A Mercedes convertible, black."

"No, no, you don't want to be driving around Tijuana in that. You park your car at the border, and walk across; I'll have somebody meet you."

"All right, what time?"

"Say three o'clock?"

"I'll be there."

"Wear a red baseball cap, so my man will know you."

"All right."

"Cordova wants a thousand dollars to meet with you."

"For as long as I want?"

"How long do you want?"

"Maybe an hour, maybe more."

"He'll do that, and Stone?"

"Yes?"

"Don't forget the rest of *my* money, too."

"See you at three o'clock."

⚒ Chapter 35 ⚒

Stone took the freeway to San Diego and made it in three and a half hours. He had some lunch at a taco joint near the border, then put the money and his little dictating recorder into his pockets, put on the red baseball cap he'd bought at the Centurion Studios shop, parked the car, and walked to the border crossing. He was questioned by a uniformed officer.

"What's the purpose of your visit to Mexico?" the man asked.

"A business meeting."

"What kind of business?"

"I'm a lawyer," Stone replied. "I'm interviewing a witness."

"Let's see some ID."

Stone showed his U.S. passport.

"Are you carrying more than five thousand dollars in cash or negotiable instruments?"

Stone was not about to lie about this. "Yes."

"How much?"

"About seven thousand."

The man handed him a declaration. "What's the money for?"

"I have to pay the man who located the witness for me."

"Fill out the form."

Stone did as he was told, handed it over, and was waved across the border.

"You better be careful, carrying that much money," the officer said.

"Thanks, I will." Stone walked slowly down the busy street, waiting for somebody to recognize him. He saw no one, and no one seemed to take note of him. He had never been to Mexico before, and he was nervous. Everything he had read about the place in the newspapers had led him to believe that the country was a vast criminal enterprise, with drug dealers and kidnappers on every corner and a corrupt police force. So far, he didn't like it.

A block from the border, he sat down at one of two tables outside a little restaurant. A waiter appeared. "*Cerveza,*" Stone said, exhausting his Spanish. A moment later, he was drinking an icy Carta Blanca, the only thing he intended to allow past his lips on this trip. He had finished the beer and was wondering if he had come on a fool's errand when a small boy dressed in ragged jeans and sneakers ran up to him.

"Señor Stone?" the boy asked.

Stone nodded.

The boy beckoned him to come.

Stone left five dollars on the table and followed the boy. They turned a corner and came to a Lincoln Continental of a fifties vintage, a giant, four-door land yacht of an automobile. Brandy Garcia sat at the wheel and beckoned him to the passenger side.

"Give the boy something," Garcia said.

Stone gave the boy five dollars and stuck the red baseball cap on his head.

The boy turned the cap backward, grinned, and disappeared into the street crowd.

Stone got into the car and waited for Garcia to drive off, but he simply sat there. "Well?"

"I want the rest of my money, first," Garcia said.

Stone took a precounted thousand dollars from a pocket and handed it over. "The rest when I'm sitting down with Cordova."

"Fair enough," Brandy said, and put the car into gear. "Pretty nice buggy, eh?"

"Nicely restored," Stone admitted. "I haven't seen one of these in years."

Garcia turned a corner and sped down the street, oblivious of the pedestrians diving out of his way. "I got three more beauties at my house," he said. "I got a Stingray Corvette, a '57 Chevy Bel-Air coupe with the big V-8, and a '52 Caddy convertible, yellow. All mint."

"Well," Stone said, "I guess the Lincoln is the closest thing we're going to get to inconspicuous."

Garcia laughed and turned another corner. "Everybody knows me in Tijuana," he said. "Why be inconspicuous?"

Soon they were leaving the busy part of town and driving down a dirt street. The houses were getting farther apart, and after a while there were very few houses. Garcia slowed and turned down a dirt road; a mile later, he turned into a driveway and drove a hundred yards to a little stucco house in a grove of trees, with an oversized garage to one side.

"Here we are," Garcia said, parking next to a beat-up Volkswagen and getting out of the car. "Cordova is already here; that's his car," he said, jerking a thumb in the direction of the VW. Stone quickly memorized the license plate number before he followed Garcia into the house.

"How's Cordova's English?" Stone asked, as they walked through a tiled living room and out onto a patio.

"Ask him yourself," Garcia said, nodding toward a large man seated at a patio table next to a small swimming pool, hunched over a beer. "That's Felipe Cordova, and you owe me another three grand."

Stone handed him the money, then walked to the table and took a seat opposite the man, getting a look at his shoes on the way. He saw the swoosh logo. "Felipe Cordova?"

The man nodded.

Stone offered his hand. "My name is Barrington."

Cordova shook it limply, saying nothing.

"You have any problem with English, or you want Brandy to translate?"

Cordova looked at Garcia, who was stepping back into the house, and Stone took the opportunity to switch on the little recorder in his shirt pocket.

"English is okay," he said, "but I got another problem—a thousand. bucks."

Stone counted out five hundred and placed it on the table. "The rest when we're finished, and if you tell me the truth, there might be a bonus."

"What you want to know?" Cordova asked.

"You work for a gardening service in L.A.?"

"Yeah."

"You work sometimes for Charlene Joiner, in Malibu?"

Cordova smiled a little. "Oh, yeah."

"You work for Mr. and Mrs. Calder, in Bel-Air?"

"Yeah."

"You were at their house the day Mr. Calder was shot." It wasn't a question.

"I don't know nothing about that," Cordova said.

"Thanks for your time," Stone said. "You can leave."

Cordova didn't move. "What about my other five hundred?"

"If you want that, you'll have to start earning it," Stone said.

Cordova glared at him for a moment. "I didn't cut the grass that day."

"No, you were there to burgle the place."

Cordova chuckled. "Shit, man," he said.

"I'm not here to arrest you; I think you know the cops aren't going to find you here. They're not even looking for you."

"What makes you think I'm a burglar?" Cordova asked.

"Those Nikes you're wearing cost a hundred and eighty bucks," Stone said. "You didn't buy them cutting grass."

"Shit, man . . ."

Stone slammed his hand on the table. "Shit is right," he said. "That's all I'm getting from you."

"Okay, okay, so what do you want to know?"

"Did Calder catch you in the house?"

"I never got into the house," Cordova replied.

"You were right outside the door; you were seen," Stone lied.

"By who?"

"By Manolo's wife; you didn't see her."

"Then you know I didn't get in the house. I only got as far as the back door. I went in through a little gate where we take the equipment in."

"And what did you see at the back door?"

"First, I heard something."

"Like what?"

"Like a gun going off."

"How many times?"

"Once. I was almost to the back door when I heard it. I took a few more steps, and I looked through the door. It was a glass door, you know? With panes?"

"I know. What did you see?"

"I saw Mr. Calder lying on the floor in the hall, and blood was coming out of his head."

"What else did you see?"

"I saw the gun on the floor beside Mr. Calder."

"What kind of gun?"

"An automatic; I don't know what kind."

"What color?"

"Silver."

"What else did you see?"

"I saw a woman running down the hall."

Stone's stomach suddenly felt hollow, and he couldn't speak.

Cordova went on. "She was wearing one of them robes made out of that towel stuff." He rubbed his fingers together.

"Terrycloth?"

"Yeah. It had this . . ." He moved his hands around his head.

"Hood?"

"Yeah, a hood. She was barefoot; I don't think she had nothing on, except the robe."

"Could you see her body?"

"No, just her feet."

"Did you see her face?" Stone held his breath.

"No."

Stone let out the breath.

"But it was Mrs. Calder."

Stone's stomach flip-flopped. "If you didn't see her face, how do you know it was Mrs. Calder?"

"C'mon, man, who else would it be, naked and in a robe in the Calders' house?"

"But you didn't see her face."

"No, but it was her. Same size and everything; same ass, you know?"

"Which way was she running?"

"Away from me—that's all I know, man; I got the hell out of there, you know? I was over that fence and out of there in a big hurry."

Stone took him through it again, made him repeat every statement, but nothing changed. Finally, there was nothing else to ask. He shelled out another five hundred, and Cordova put it in his pocket.

"You want to make another three hundred?" Stone asked.

"Sure."

Stone put the money on the table. "Sell me your shoes."

"Huh?"

"I'll give you three hundred dollars for your shoes."

Cordova grinned. "Sure, man." He shucked off the Nikes and put them on the table. They were dirty, beat up, and huge. He put the money in his pocket, gave a little wave, and lumbered toward the house, padding along in his stocking feet.

Garcia came out of the house. "How'd it go?" he asked.

"Great," Stone said. "Just great. Get me back to the border."

"I see you got yourself some shoes." He held his nose.

"Just get me back, Brandy," Stone said, feeling sick.

⤳ Chapter 36 ⤳

Stone drove back toward Los Angeles in a fog, torn between what he had believed had happened to Vance Calder and what Felipe Cordova had told him. He had thought Cordova had murdered Vance, but every instinct he had developed as a cop, interrogating witnesses, told him that Cordova had told him the truth in their interview.

"I've been fooled before," he said aloud to himself. Cordova still could have done it; maybe he was a better liar than Stone had thought. The only good thing about Cordova was that the LAPD had not questioned him, didn't want to. He would not like to see the Mexican on the stand, testifying against Arrington.

The car phone rang. Stone punched the send button, so he could talk hands free. "Hello?"

"Hi, it's Betty. Joan called from New York, said to tell you that everything was in hand with the house. The roofer is going to start in a couple of days, and it will take him a week to finish."

"Good news," Stone said.

"She also said that Dolce was waiting at the house when she got back from Teterboro, and that she told her that you'd returned to L.A. Does that mean we can expect more candid snaps?"

"I certainly hope not. I've already told the guard at the gate not to let her into the studio again, but maybe you'd better call and reinforce that."

"Will do."

"Any other calls?"

"Marc Blumberg called, said he just wanted to catch up with you. He's at his Palm Springs house; you want the number?"

Stone fished a pen and his notebook out of his pocket. "Shoot."

Betty dictated the number, and he jotted it down, careful to keep the car on track.

"Your bags are piled up in the entrance hall; want me to unpack for you?"

"Thanks, I'd appreciate that. I was too tired to bother last night."

"I'll send your laundry out, too."

"Thanks again."

"Stone you sound funny—depressed."

"I'm just tired," he replied. "The round-trip cross-country flight messed with my internal clock."

"Want to have dinner tonight?"

He knew what that meant. "Give me a rain check, if you will; I just want to get some rest."

"Okay, call if you need anything."

Stone punched the end button, then dialed Marc Blumberg's Palm Springs number and punched the send button again.

"Hello?"

"Marc, it's Stone."

"Hi, there, you in the car?"

"Yeah, I'm just north of San Diego."

"What are you doing down there?"

"I've been to Tijuana to meet with Felipe Cordova, of Nike footprint fame."

"What did he have to say for himself?"

"It's a long story; why don't we get together when you're back in L.A.?"

"Why don't you come here, instead? I'll give you some dinner and put you up for the night. You could be here in a couple of hours."

"Okay, why not?"

"You got a map?"

"Yes."

"Take I-15 to just short of Temecula, then cut east over the mountains."

"Okay, what's the address?"

Blumberg gave him the street and number and directions to the house.

"See you in a while." He hung up, then saw a sign for I-15 just in time to make the turn.

He found the turnoff for Palm Springs and followed the curving mountain road, enjoying the drive. His head began to clear, and almost without effort, things started to line up in his mind. First of all, he still believed Arrington was innocent; second, he felt that Cordova was the best suspect; third, he was going to do whatever it took to get Arrington out of this. He forced himself to consider the possibility that Arrington had shot Vance. If so, he rationalized, it must somehow have been self-defense. He could not let her be convicted, especially after what had happened in New York. He was in her thrall again, if he had ever been out of it, and all he wanted at the moment was a future with Arrington in it. By the time he had found Marc Blumberg's house, his ducks were all in a row.

The house was a large contemporary, sculpted of native stone and big timbers, on several acres of desert. Marc greeted him warmly and led him out to the pool. The sun was low in the sky, and the desert air was growing cool. A tall, very beautiful woman was stretched out on a chaise next to the outside bar.

"This is Vanessa Pike," Marc said. "Vanessa, meet Stone Barrington."

The two shook hands. It was difficult for Stone not to appreciate her beauty, especially since she was wearing only the bottom of her bikini.

"What'll you drink?" Marc asked them both.

"I'll have a gin and tonic," Vanessa replied.

"So will I," Stone echoed.

Marc motioned him to a chair opposite Vanessa, who showed no inclination to cover herself, soaking up the waning rays of afternoon sun.

"Aren't you getting chilly?" Stone asked.

"I'm rarely chilly," she replied, with a level gaze.

"I believe you," Stone said.

Marc came back with the drinks and joined them. "So, how'd you ever find Cordova?"

"A friend at the LAPD put me in touch with a guy named Brandy Garcia, who knows the territory down there."

"I've heard about him," Blumberg said. "A real hustler."

"Took him less than a week to find Cordova."

"Where'd you meet?"

"At Garcia's house. He seems to be doing very well for himself."

"I don't get it; why would Cordova talk to you?"

"Because I paid him a thousand dollars, plus another three hundred for his shoes."

"You got the Nikes?"

"I did."

"Was there a cut on the sole?"

"There was; they're in my car; they'll match the photograph the cops took."

"Now that is great! What did Cordova say?"

Stone took a deep breath and told the lie. "Denied everything; wasn't at the house that day, went to Mexico, because somebody in the family was sick."

"You couldn't shake his story?"

Stone shook his head. "No way to disprove it, without telling him about the footprint, and I didn't want to tip him off about that."

"You think there's any way of getting him back, so the cops can question him?"

"No, short of arranging another meeting and kidnapping him, and I don't think a judge would look kindly on that, not even a judge you play golf with."

"You're right about that."

"He's not coming back to L.A. anytime soon; he's gone to ground, and I doubt if we'll ever see him again."

"Well, we've got the shoes," Blumberg said.

"You think that's enough to win a motion to dismiss?"

"Maybe; I'd like to think about that. I'd really like to have more."

"Like a confession from Cordova?"

Marc grinned. "That would do it, I think."

Stone got serious. "We can't let this go to trial, Marc."

"Oh, I think I could win it," Marc replied cockily.

"Probably, but I don't want to take the chance, and I don't want Arrington to have to live with half the world thinking she murdered her husband."

"We'll go for the motion to dismiss, when I'm ready," Marc said, "and we'll play it big in the press, sow some doubt amongst the jury pool. Even if we lose, we can do ourselves some good."

"Let's don't lose," Stone said.

A Latino in a white jacket came out of the house. "Dinner is served, whenever you're ready, Mr. Blumberg."

"Thank you, Pedro," Marc said. "We'll be right in."

"May I use a phone?" Stone asked.

"Sure; go into my study, first door on your left." Marc pointed the way.

Stone went into the study, closed the door behind him, and picked up the phone on the desk. He checked his notebook and dialed the number for Brandy Garcia.

"Buenos dias," Garcia's voice said. "Leave me a message, okay?" There was a beep.

"Give your friend in Tijuana a message," Stone said. "Tell him there's a warrant out for him. Tell him to go where even *you* can't find him." He hung up the phone and went in to dinner.

Vanessa was sitting at a small table alone. She patted a chair next to her.

Stone was relieved that she had put on a sweater. He sat down. "Where's Marc?"

"He's down in the wine cellar, getting us something to drink."

Marc returned with a bottle of claret, opened it, tasted it, poured them each a glass, and sat down. He raised his glass. "To motions to dismiss," he said, "and to Vanessa."

"I'll drink to both," Stone said, raising his glass.

⌦ Chapter 37 ⌫

When Stone came down to breakfast, Marc was just finishing his coffee. Stone took a seat, and Pedro came and took his order for bacon and eggs.

"Sleep well?" Marc asked.

"Probably better than you did," Stone replied, trying not to smirk. "Where's Vanessa?"

"Still asleep. Tired." Marc smirked.

"I see."

"You should give Vanessa a call sometime," Marc said. "There's nothing serious between the two of us, and she's really a very nice girl."

"It's a thought," Stone said noncommitally.

"I wouldn't like to see you all alone in L.A. Might affect your work on the case, that sort of frustration. And since Arrington is off limits . . ."

"You're too kind, Marc."

"I certainly am."

"Listen, Marc, I was thinking last night: Instead of making an announcement to the press about Cordova, why don't you just leak it a little at a time. Do you know a reporter you can trust not to reveal his sources?"

"You have a point: If the press gets wind of a suspect that the police have ignored, then the cops will look bad, and we won't appear to have had anything to do with it. I like it, and I know just the reporter at the *L.A. Times*."

"Our judge, whoever he turns out to be, will probably hear about it, too, and when we demonstrate in court that the rumors of another suspect are true . . ."

"That is delightfully Machiavellian, Stone," Marc said. "You surprise me."

Stone didn't know how to reply to that. His breakfast arrived, and he enjoyed it, while Blumberg talked about golf in Palm Springs.

"You play? I'll give you a game this morning."

"I've hit a few balls; that's about it."

"You should take some lessons; that's how to get started."

"Golf in Manhattan is tough," Stone said. "I think you pretty much have to drive to Westchester, and that's if you can get into a club."

"Why do I have the feeling you aren't telling me the truth about Felipe Cordova?" Marc asked, suddenly changing the subject.

"I don't know, Marc," Stone replied, surprised. "Why do you feel that way?"

"You think Cordova didn't kill Vance, don't you?"

"He told a very convincing story."

"But you want the LAPD and the D.A. and a judge to think he did it."

"Just that he's a viable suspect, and the cops have ignored him. Shows a lack of good faith on their part."

"Let me ask you this: What happens if I get the charges against Arrington dismissed, then the cops find Cordova?"

"I don't think we'll ever see Cordova again; he's too scared."

"You said he denied everything, and you didn't contradict him by telling him about the shoeprint at Vance's house."

"That's right."

"So what happens to his story when the cops tell him about the shoeprint?"

"First, they have to find him; he's in Mexico, probably not in Tijuana anymore. You know the problems with finding somebody down there, not to mention the difficulties of getting a suspect extradited."

"I'm talking worst case, here, Stone; I have to protect myself. If, by some miracle, the cops find Cordova in Mexico, or, more likely, he comes back to this country and gets arrested for speeding, or something. I have to know what he's going to say."

"My guess is, he'll try to implicate Arrington. He knows about the murder, knows she's been charged. He'll do everything he can to see that she takes the fall. That's my guess."

"I suppose that makes sense," Marc said. "You know, I've tried a lot of cases in my time, and a lot of them murders, too, but I don't think I've ever tried one where my second chair was in love with the defendant."

Stone kept eating his eggs.

"You're a bright guy, Stone, and I suspect a very good lawyer, so I'm going to rely on you not to do anything that will get *me* hung."

"I would never do anything like that," Stone replied truthfully.

"I can see how you might not want to tell me everything you know, to save Arrington's very beautiful ass, how you might even lie to me. That's okay, as long as it doesn't interfere with how I handle my case, and as long as it doesn't get me disbarred or damage my credibility with the D.A. and the judges in this town. That credibility is the most valuable asset I have in defending a client, and I don't want to lose it. I hope I make myself perfectly clear."

"Perfectly clear, Marc," Stone said, finishing his coffee. He looked at his watch. "Well, I think I'd better be getting back to L.A. Thanks for your hospitality."

Marc stood up and shook his hand. "And don't forget, if you get horny, call Vanessa; don't go sneaking into Arrington's bedroom. If that got out, it could screw us all." He handed Stone his card, with Vanessa's number scrawled on the back.

Stone nodded and put the card into his pocket. "I take your point." He left the house, got into the car, which smelled of Felipe Cordova's Nikes, and headed back toward L.A.

He was back at Centurion Studios by eleven-thirty, and Betty met him at the door of the bungalow, looking rattled.

"What's wrong?" he asked, tucking a finger under her chin and lifting her head.

"I've just had a very peculiar conversation with Dolce, if you can call it a conversation," she said. "Actually, it was more of a tirade."

"Oh, God; what did she say?"

"She went into some detail about what she would do to me if I ever, as she put it, 'touch him again.' She means you, I believe."

"I'm sorry about that, Betty; this has nothing to do with you, really."

"That's not the impression I got," Betty said. "Frankly, she sounded nuts to me. I'm scared."

"Tell you what," Stone said. "Why don't you take a trip to Hawaii, do some scouting for just the right place when you bail out of L.A."

Betty brightened. "You think you could get along without me for a while? Careful how you answer that."

Stone laughed. "It'll be tough, but I'll manage."

"Maybe that's not such a bad idea," Betty said. "I'll get you some help from the studio secretarial pool, then call the travel agent." She headed for her office.

"Any other calls?" he asked.

"Brandy Garcia called; said his friend has already got your message."

"I've no idea what *that* means," he replied, covering his ass.

"Oh, and I almost forgot: Dolce says you're to meet her at the Bel-Air for lunch at one o'clock."

"*She's in L.A.?*"

"Yep. And she said, 'tell him to be there without fail, or I'll get mad.' "
Stone gave a low moan.

Betty picked up her phone and dialed a number. "Try to keep her busy
long enough for me to get out of town, okay?" she called to him.

"I wish I could reverse our roles," Stone replied.

Chapter 38

Stone arrived at the Bel-Air on time and with trepidations. What will I do
if she starts shooting? he asked himself. What if she only makes a scene?
What then? He liked to think he had had less than his share of arguments
with women, and that he managed that by being easy to get along with. He
had a dread of public disagreements, especially in the middle of places
like the Bel-Air Hotel.

He wasn't sure where to meet her, so he wandered slowly through the
lobby and outside again, toward the restaurant. Then he saw her, seated at
a table in the middle of the garden café, wearing a silk print dress, her hair
pinned to the top of her head, revealing her long, beautiful neck. Her
chin rested on her interlocked fingers, and her mien was serene.

"Oh hello, Mr. Barrington," the headwaiter said as he approached.
"Mrs. Barrington is waiting, and may I congratulate you?"

Stone leaned over and spoke quietly, but with conviction. "There is *no*
Mrs. Barrington," he said. "The lady's name is Miss Bianchi."

"Yes, sir," the man said, a little flustered. "Whatever you say." He led
Stone to the table and pulled out a chair for him.

Stone sat down and allowed her to lean over and brush his cheek with
her lips.

"Hello, my darling," she purred.

"Good afternoon, Dolce."

"I hope you're enjoying your stay in Los Angeles."

"I can't say that I am," he replied, looking at the menu.

"Poor baby," she said, patting his cheek. "Maybe it's time to go back
home to New York—yet again."

"Not for a while."

"But what's to keep us here?" she asked, all innocence.

"Business is keeping *me* here," he replied.

The waiter appeared. Dolce ordered a lobster salad and a glass of chardonnay, and Stone, the taco soup and iced tea.

"Why are you in L.A.?" he asked, hoping for a rational answer. She began rummaging in a large handbag for something, and Stone leaned away from her, fearing she might come up with a weapon.

She came up with a lipstick and began applying it. "I want to be with my husband," she said, consulting a compact mirror.

"Your husband is dead," Stone said through clenched teeth.

"You look perfectly well to me," she replied, gazing levelly at him.

"Dolce . . ."

"And how is the murderess, Mrs. Calder?"

"Dolce . . ."

"I think I will be quite happy when they put her away."

"Dolce . . ."

"Vance was such a lovely man, and we were such good friends. I think it would be terribly unfair, if she got away with it."

"Dolce, stop it!"

"My goodness, Stone, keep your voice down. We don't want a public scene, do we?"

Stone decided to treat this as a negotiation. "Just tell me what you want," he said.

Her eyebrows shot up. "What *I* want? Why, I want whatever my darling husband wants. What do *you* want, dear?"

"I want to end this little charade of yours; I want us to go our separate ways in an amicable manner." He paused and decided to fire the last arrow in his quiver. "I want to be with Arrington."

Her eyebrows dropped, and her eyes narrowed. "Believe me when I tell you, my darling, that I will never, ever allow that to happen, and you had better get used to the idea now."

Stone felt his gorge rising, but the waiter appeared with their lunch, allowing him to cool down for a moment before continuing. "I don't understand," he said.

"You asked me to marry you, did you not?"

"Yes, but . . ."

"And I married you, in Venice, did I not?"

"That wasn't a legal marriage."

"Oh, Stone, now you're beginning to sound like a lawyer."

"I *am* a lawyer, and I know when I'm married and when I'm not."

"I'm afraid not, sweetie," she said, attacking her lobster salad. "You seem unable to face reality; you're in complete denial."

Stone nearly choked on his soup.

"*I* am in denial?"

"A serious case of denial, I fear."

"Let's talk about denial, Dolce. I've explained to you, in the clearest possible terms, that I no longer wish to continue my relationship with you. I've explained why."

"I seem to remember your saying something about that, but I hardly took you seriously," she said.

This was maddening. "Dolce, I do not love you; I thought I did for a while, but now I realize I don't."

She laughed. "And I suppose you think you love Arrington?"

"Yes, I do." Funny, he hadn't said that to Arrington.

"But Stone, how can you love a woman who has murdered her husband? How do you know you won't be next?"

"That's a very strange thing for *you* to say," Stone said under his breath, trying to control his temper. "I seem to remember that you once had a husband who is now dead of extremely unnatural causes."

"That was the business he chose, if I may paraphrase Don Corleone, and he had to live with it." She speared a chunk of lobster. "Or die with it. You might remember that."

"I chose a different business, and I am choosing a different woman." My God, he thought, what do I have to say to get through to her?

Dolce shook her head. "No, Stone; you haven't yet come to the point where you have to make a real choice." She chewed her lobster. "But you will."

"Is that some sort of threat, Dolce?"

"Call it a prediction, but take it any way you like."

"Why would you want a man who doesn't want you?" he demanded. "Why do you demean yourself?"

She put down her fork, and her eyes narrowed again. "You do not know me as well as you will after a while," she said, "but when you do come to know me, you will look back on that remark as dangerous folly."

"That's it," Stone said, putting down his spoon. "One last time, for the record: I do not love you; I will not marry you; I *have not* married you. I love another woman, and I believe I always will. I want nothing more to do with you, ever. I cannot make it any clearer than that." He stood up. "Good-bye, Dolce."

"No, my darling," she replied smoothly, "merely *au revoir*."

"Dolce," he said, "California has a very strong law against stalking; don't make me publicly humiliate you." He turned and walked out of the café.

All the way back to the studio he ran the conversation through his head, over and over. It had been like talking to a marble sculpture, except that a sculpture does not make threats. Or had she made threats? Was there anything in her words that could be used against her? He admitted there was not. What was he going to do? How could he get this woman off his back? More important, how could he get her off his back without grievously offending her father, whom he did not want for an enemy?

He parked in front of the bungalow and, finding it locked, used his key. On Betty's desk there was a note, stuck to a package.

"I've taken your advice, lover; I'm on a late afternoon plane. I'll call you in a couple of days to see how you're making out. A girl from the pool will be in tomorrow morning to do for you, although she probably won't do for you as I do. Take care of yourself."

He turned to the package, which was an overnight air envelope with a Rome return address. He opened it, and two sheets of paper fell out. The top one was a heavy sheet of cream-colored writing paper. Stone read the handwritten letter:

> The Vatican
> Rome
>
> Dear Stone,
>   I have made the investigations I told you I would, speaking personally to the mayor of Venice. I have concluded that you and Dolce are legally married in Italy, and that the proper documents, which you both signed, have been duly registered. The marriage would be considered valid anywhere in the world.
>   I know this was not the news you wanted. I would offer advice on an annulment, but you are not a Catholic, and, you surely understand, I cannot offer advice on divorce.
>   You remain in my thoughts and prayers. If there is any other help I can give you, please let me know.
>
> Warmly,
> Bellini

Stone looked at the other piece of paper. It was printed in Italian, bore his and Dolce's names, and appeared to be a certificate of marriage.

"Oh, shit," he said.

⤳ Chapter 39 ⤶

Stone called Dino. "Do you remember telling me, on the way to Italy, that there would be two marriage ceremonies, a civil one and a religious one?"

"Sure. Why do you ask?"

"You remember telling me that the civil ceremony wasn't legal until the religious ceremony had been performed?"

"Sure. Why do you ask?"

"Where did you get that information?"

"Which information?"

"The information that one ceremony didn't count without the other?"

"I said one wouldn't be legal, without the other. I didn't say it wouldn't *count.*"

"Where did you get that information?"

"From Mary Ann."

"Is Mary Ann an authority on Italian marital law?"

"All women are authorities on marital law, in any country."

"Do you know where Mary Ann got that information?"

"No, why?"

"Because I want to strangle the person who gave it to her."

"My guess is, that would be Dolce. Good luck on strangling her without getting offed yourself. What the fuck is this about, Stone?"

"I called Bellini to ask him about this. I just got a letter from him, along with a copy of my marriage certificate."

"You mean the ceremony is valid, legally?"

"Yes."

Dino began giggling. "Oh, Jesus!" he managed to get out.

"This isn't funny, Dino. I just had lunch with Dolce, where I made it as clear as possible that I was not married to her and didn't intend to be."

"Let me guess: She didn't buy that."

"You could put it that way. She as much as said she'd kill me or, maybe, Arrington if I continue to deny the marriage."

"Well, if I were you, I'd take the threat seriously."

"I *am* taking it seriously."

"What's your next move? I'm dying to hear."

"I haven't the faintest idea."

"Want a suggestion?"

"If it's a serious one."

"First, I'd see a divorce lawyer; then I'd watch my ass. Arrington's, too, which isn't too much of a chore, if I correctly recall her ass."

"Do you have any idea what it takes to get a divorce in Italy?"

"Nope; that's why I suggested a divorce lawyer. Listen, pal, be thankful you didn't get married in the Italian church. Then you'd *really* be in deep shit."

"Dino, I don't think I ever thanked you properly."

"Thanked me for what?"

"For advising me to stay away from Dolce."

"You didn't take my advice; why are you thanking me?"

"It was good advice, even if I didn't take it."

"Well, I'm glad you remember; saves me from saying I told you so."

"I'm happy to save you the trouble."

"Listen, Stone, this isn't all bad, you know?"

"It isn't? What's not all bad about it?"

"You've got the perfect means of staying single now. Every time some broad presses you to marry her, all you've got to say is, that you're already married, and your wife won't give you a divorce." Dino suppressed a laugh, but not well. "And you'll be telling the truth. Millions of guys would envy you!"

"You don't happen to know an Italian divorce lawyer, do you?"

"Nope, and can you imagine what will happen if you get one, and then he finds out who you're trying to divorce?"

"What?"

"Come on, Stone, Eduardo is probably better known to Italian lawyers than to American ones."

"You really know how to make a guy's day, Dino."

"Always happy to spread a little cheer."

"See you around."

"Bye."

Stone hung up, looked at his watch, then called Marc Blumberg's office.

"Yeah, Stone?"

"Marc, I'm glad you're back from Palm Springs. Can I come and see you? I need some legal advice, on a subject not connected to our present case."

"Sure, come on over; I'll make time."

Stone was surprised to find Vanessa Pike in Marc's office, and relieved to see her fully dressed. "Hi, Vanessa," he said.

"I was going to run Vanessa home, as soon as I made a couple of calls," Marc said. "What can I do for you?" He looked at Stone, then at Vanessa. "Honey, can you go powder your nose?"

Vanessa got up, opened a door in the corner of Blumberg's large office, and closed it behind her.

"What's up?" Marc asked.

"You do divorce work, don't you?"

"Who are we talking about getting divorced?"

"Me."

"Sure, I do divorce work, but first the client has to be married."

Stone placed the letter from Bellini and the marriage certificate on Marc's desk.

Marc read the letter. "Wow," he said. "You're pals with Cardinal Bellini?"

"He was supposed to officiate at my wedding, in Venice. We had a civil ceremony on a Saturday, and it was my understanding that it wasn't valid until we had the religious ceremony. The call came about Vance's death before that could take place, and the next thing I knew, I was on a plane for L.A."

"This Bellini is a real heavyweight, you know," Marc said, and there was awe in his voice.

"Marc, focus, please! This is a marriage in name only; it wasn't even consummated—at least, *after* the ceremony."

"And who is . . ." He looked at the marriage certificate. ". . . Rosaria Bianchi?" His face fell. "She's not . . . she couldn't be . . ."

Stone nodded dumbly.

"Eduardo Bianchi's daughter?" His eyebrows went up. "Stone, I'm looking at you in a whole new light, here."

"I want out of this so-called marriage, Marc. How do I go about that?"

"Before we go into that, Stone, let me ask you something, something serious."

"What?"

"Are you looking to piss off Eduardo Bianchi? I assume you know exactly who he is."

"I know who he is, and I like him. He likes me, I think, or he did when he thought I was going to be his son-in-law."

"Have you told him about this?"

"He was at the ceremony, Marc."

"I mean, have you told him you want a divorce from his daughter?"

"I don't think he even knows the marriage is valid, but he knows that Dolce and I are no longer together. He was pretty understanding about it."

"Well, for your sake, I hope to hell he's going to be understanding about it. I wouldn't want to be in your shoes, if he decides *not* to be understanding."

"Marc, what am I going to do? How do I get out of this?"

"Well, assuming that you can find a way to stay alive, the situation shouldn't be all that bad. I once worked with an attorney in Milan on a divorce case." He looked at his watch. "It's too late there to call him now, but I'll call him in the morning, and we can see where we stand. I'm assuming Ms. Bianchi wants out, too."

"Don't assume that," Stone said.

"What should I assume?"

"Assume the worst."

Vanessa came out of the powder room. "May I reappear now?"

"Sure, honey," Marc said, "we're done, for the moment."

Stone got up to leave.

"Oh, Stone," Marc said, "would you mind giving Vanessa a lift home? I've still got some work here."

"Sure."

"If it's not out of your way," Vanessa said.

Stone shrugged. "I don't know where I'm going, anyway."

⤚ Chapter 40 ⤙

Stone followed Vanessa's instructions to a quiet street up in the Hollywood Hills, above Sunset Boulevard, where they turned into the driveway of a pretty, New England–style, shingled cottage. They had been quiet all the way.

"You all right?" she asked, when they had stopped.

"Yes, sure," Stone said.

"Tell you what: Why don't you come in, and I'll fix you some dinner?"

"I don't want to put you to any trouble, Vanessa."

"I gotta eat, you gotta eat," she replied.

"Okay." He got out of the car, followed her to the front door and waited while she unlocked it and entered the security system code. The house was larger than it had seemed from the outside, and prettily decorated and furnished.

"There's a wet bar over there," she said, pointing to a cabinet. "Fix us a drink; I'll have a Johnny Walker Black on the rocks."

Stone opened the cabinet, found the scotch, and found a bottle of Wild Turkey, too. He poured the drinks and followed her into the kitchen. There was a counter separating the cooking area from a sitting room, and he took a stool there. He wondered if she would now strip to the waist and walk around as she had in Palm Springs.

Vanessa turned out to be something of a mind reader. "Don't worry," she said, "I'm not going to take any clothes off. That was Marc's idea, in Palm Springs."

"Marc's idea? Why would he ask you to do that?"

"Oh, I was already fairly naked; he just asked me not to get dressed. Marc is concerned about you."

"Concerned how?"

"He thinks you need . . . companionship." She began rummaging in the refrigerator.

"Oh."

"Marc is a very kind man; I owe him a lot."

"Why?"

"I was in the middle of an awful divorce, and my lawyer was intimidated by my ex's lawyer. I ran into Marc at a cocktail party and complained about it, and he said he'd fix it. He did. He renegotiated my settlement, got me the Bel-Air house and a lot of money. I sold that house, bought this place, and invested the difference. If not for Marc, I'd probably be working as a secretary somewhere. As it is, I'm well fixed."

"Good for him," Stone said.

"He thinks that if you're fucking Arrington, it could hurt his case."

"He has made that point," Stone said.

"You two were an item before she married Vance, weren't you?"

"Yes, we were."

"Will you be again, assuming she doesn't go to prison?"

"Hard to say," Stone replied.

"Is that what you want?"

"Sometimes I do; other times, I don't know," he admitted.

Vanessa smiled. "I think it's what you want." She switched on the gas grill of the restaurant-style stove and put the steaks on, then started to make a salad.

Stone watched her move expertly around the kitchen. She was beautiful, smart, and, he did not doubt, affectionate. But Arrington was on his mind, and he could not get that out of the way.

They had finished dinner and were sipping a brandy before the living room fireplace.

"I'm having a tough time making a decision," Vanessa said.

"Anything I can do to help?"

"I'm in something of an ethical quandary. I've promised a friend to keep something in confidence, but to do that might harm someone else."

"That's a tough one," Stone said.

"The person who might be harmed is not a particular friend, though I have nothing against this person."

"Then why are you having so much trouble keeping your promise to your friend?"

"Because it might help Marc—and you—if I told you about it."

"Is there some way you can give me a hint without breaking your word to your friend?"

"I'm not sure. Perhaps if I tell you a little about it without revealing the friend's identity?"

"Sounds good to me."

"Marc says that he's worried that the police might have more on Arrington than he knows about."

"I've been worried about that, too."

"Well, you're both right to be worried."

Stone sucked in a breath. "Can you tell me any more?"

"I'm sorry," she said. "I don't think I can." She sipped her brandy. "It's just that there may very well have been a witness to what happened that night."

"You mean the Mexican gardener?"

"No, someone else. That's all I can say."

"Have you told Marc about this?"

"No, he'd just browbeat it out of me, and I'd feel terrible. I don't think you would try to do that."

Funny, Stone thought, he had been thinking about doing just that. "Well," Stone said, "if you can ever see your way clear to tell me more, I'd like to hear it."

"I think that's unlikely," she replied.

Stone looked at his watch. "I'd better go; it's getting late."

She walked him to the door, and he gave her a peck on the cheek. "Thanks for dinner," he said, "and for the good company. I needed it."

"I'm sorry I can't be of more help," she said.

"You've at least confirmed our suspicions," Stone said, "and that's a help." He waved and started toward his car. She waited until he had backed out of the drive before closing the door.

The street was dark, and there were a few cars parked along the curb. As Stone put the car into gear and drove away, he noticed headlights appear in his rearview mirror. Funny, he thought, he hadn't seen a car coming when he'd backed out. He watched the lights in the mirror until he reached Sunset, then lost them in the traffic.

ᕤ Chapter 41 ᕥ

Stone was wakened by the sound of someone entering the bungalow. Since Betty was now in Hawaii, he wasn't expecting anybody, so he got into a robe and padded into the front room in his bare feet.

A young woman was seated at Betty's desk; she looked up, startled. "Oh," she said. "I didn't know you were here."

"I'm here," Stone said. "But why are you?"

"I'm Louise Bremen, from the secretarial pool; Betty wanted a temp while she's on vacation."

"Oh, of course; I'd forgotten. I'm Stone Barrington." He walked over and shook her hand.

"Anything special you want done?" she asked.

"Just sort the Calder mail and separate the bills. Betty uses a computer program to pay them."

"Quicken? I know that."

"Good; you can write the checks, and I'll sign them. I'm a signatory on the Calder accounts."

"Sure; can I make you some coffee?"

"I'll do it, as soon as I've had a shower," Stone said. He went back to his bedroom, showered, shaved, and returned to the kitchenette. He was having breakfast when the phone rang, and Louise called out, "Marc Blumberg for you."

Stone picked up the phone. "Marc?"

"Yes, I . . ."

"I'm glad you called. I had dinner with Vanessa last night, and she pretty much confirmed our suspicion that the police have something on Arrington they haven't disclosed. Seems there was another witness to what happened when Vance was shot."

"And who was that?"

"She wouldn't say; she said she had been told in confidence."

"And why didn't she tell *me* that? She certainly had plenty of opportunity."

"She said she was afraid you'd browbeat the name out of her. She seemed very serious about keeping the confidence. I think you ought to take her to lunch and press the point."

There was a long silence on the other end.

"Marc?"

"You haven't been watching television this morning, have you?"

"No; I guess I slept a little late. I'm having breakfast now."

"Vanessa is dead."

"What?"

"Her house burned to the ground last night. TV says the cops haven't ruled out arson."

"But I was with her; we had dinner."

"Must have been later than that. It's the husband, I know it is."

"She told me about the divorce; was he that angry?"

"As angry as I've seen a husband in thirty years of practice. I got her a terrific settlement, and I wouldn't have been surprised if he'd taken a shot at *me.*"

Stone found a kitchen stool and sat down. "I can't believe it," he said.

"Was she all right when you left her?"

"She was fine; she cooked dinner, and . . ."

"How late were you there?"

"I guess I left a little before eleven."

"You'd better talk to the cops, I guess."

"I suppose so, though I can't really tell them much."

"Did Vanessa give any hint at all about who her friend, the witness, might be?"

"No; in fact, she went to the trouble of avoiding mention of even the gender."

"It's bound to be a woman; Vanessa doesn't . . . didn't have men friends, except for me."

"Do you know who her female friends were?"

"She ran around with a group that hung around with Charlene Joiner. I don't know who the others were. You think you could look into that?"

"Sure, I'll be glad to."

"I've got to go; what with Vanessa's affairs to handle, I've got a lot on my desk this morning."

"Thanks, Marc; I'll get back to you if I find out anything." Stone hung up and wolfed down the rest of his muffin, while dialing Rick Grant.

"Captain Grant."

"Rick, it's Stone Barrington."

"Morning, Stone; what's up?"

"I've just heard from Marc Blumberg that a woman I was with last evening died in a fire last night."

"That thing in the Hollywood Hills?"

"Yes; Vanessa Pike was her name."

"Looks like a murder, from what I hear."

"I thought I should talk to the investigating officers."

"Yes, you should. Hang on a minute."

Stone waited on hold while he finished his coffee.

Rick came back on the line. "You know where the house is?"

"Yes."

"Meet me there in, say, forty-five minutes."

"All right."

They hung up, and Stone went to his desk and signed the checks Louise had printed out, then he got into his car and drove to Vanessa's house.

He smelled it before he saw it, the odor of burning wood, not at all unpleasant. He saw Rick Grant getting out of a car ahead of him and parked behind him.

The two men shook hands, and Rick lead Stone through the police tape. The house was nothing more than a smoking ruin. Rick went to two men in suits who were standing on the front lawn, talking to a fire department captain in uniform.

"Morning, Al, Bruce," Rick said. "Stone, these are detectives Alvino Rivera and Bruce Goldman. This is a former NYPD detective, Stone Barrington."

Stone shook hands and he and Rick were introduced to the fireman, whose name was Hinson.

"Stone, tell Al and Rick about last night."

Stone gave a brief account of his evening with Vanessa.

"Did she say anything about her husband?" Goldman asked, when Stone had finished.

"She told me about the divorce and her settlement. I gathered it wasn't an amiable thing. Her lawyer, Marc Blumberg, who introduced me to her, said the man was very angry about what he had to give her."

"She show any signs of stress or nervousness when talking about her husband?" Rivera asked.

"No, it seemed to be in the past, at least, to her."

"Does the husband look good for this?" Rick asked.

"Maybe. We questioned him this morning at his house. We still have to check out his alibi, but it sounds tight. If he's responsible, then he probably hired a pro."

The fireman spoke up. "The fire was started with gasoline near the master bedroom windows," he said. "We found a can, apparently from the victim's own garage. The perp had wheeled over a gas grill next to the house, and when the fire got going, the propane tank exploded. It must have been full, or nearly so, because it did a lot of damage. The explosion probably killed the woman."

"We haven't heard from the M.E. yet," Goldman said, "but that sounds right."

"You're a lawyer, right?" Rivera said to Stone.

"Right."

"You're in town about the Calder thing?"

"Right."

"When you left last night, did you notice anybody hanging around the street?"

"When I backed out of the driveway, there were no moving cars visible on the street, just parked ones, but as I drove down the block toward Sunset, I saw some headlights in my rearview mirror. My guess is, somebody was waiting in the street, then started up and followed me to Sunset. I lost the car after I turned."

"Any idea of what kind of car?"

"No, all I saw was headlights."

"So the guy was hanging around, waiting for you to leave and for her to go to sleep."

"Could be. I didn't notice anybody following when we drove *to* the house, but I wasn't watching my mirror especially."

"What was your relationship to Mrs. Pike?" Goldman asked.

"I met her the day before yesterday in Palm Springs, at Marc Blumberg's house. Late yesterday afternoon, I had a meeting with Blumberg in his office, right after he returned from the Springs, and she was there. He asked me to give her a lift home, and she invited me to stay for dinner. That was it."

"Did you have sex with her?" Rivera asked.

"No."

"Ever met the husband?"

"No; I don't even know his name."

"Daniel Pike; big-time producer/director."

"I've heard of him."

"You know any of her friends?"

"Blumberg says she's friendly with a group that hangs around with Charlene Joiner."

"Joiner, the movie star?"

"One and the same."

"We'll talk to her."

Rick spoke up. "Anything else you fellows require of Stone?"

"Not at the moment."

"You can reach me through the switchboard at Centurion Studios," Stone said. "I've got a temporary office there, and here's my New York number." He handed them his card.

"You here for long?"

"Until the Calder thing is done."

"Good luck on that one," Goldman said. "I hear the wife is toast."

"Don't believe everything you hear," Stone said.

He and Rick turned and walked back to their cars.

"Thanks for coming over here, Rick," Stone said. "They might not have been as nice, if you hadn't been here."

"Glad to do it. Stone, do you know something you didn't tell those guys?"

"No, that's everything."

"Good," Rick said, shaking hands. He got into his car and drove away.

Stone got back into his car. Well, almost everything, he thought. He had one other thought, but it was completely crazy, and he dismissed it.

⤳ **Chapter 42** ⤳

Back at the studio bungalow, Stone called the Centurion switchboard. "Good morning, this is Stone Barrington, at the Vance Calder bungalow."

"Good morning, Mr. Barrington," a woman replied, "how can I help you?"

"Can you tell me if Charlene Joiner is working on the lot today?"

"Yes, she is; shall I connect you to her dressing room?"

"Thank you, yes."

The phone rang, and an answering machine picked up. Charlene's honeyed Southern voice said, "Hey. I'm shooting, or something, at the moment, but I'll get back to you, if you're worth getting back to." A beep followed.

"Charlene, this is Stone Barrington. I'd like to see you sometime today, if you have a moment. You can reach me at Vance's bungalow. By the way, you should expect a call from the police, too, about Vanessa Pike's death." He hung up.

Louise Bremen came and knocked on the door. "Mrs. Barrington called," she said.

"Louise, there is no Mrs. Barrington," Stone replied, keeping his tone light. "Just a woman who claims to be that. Her name is Dolce Bianchi; what's her number?"

"She didn't leave a number," Louise said. "She just said you'd be hearing from her, and she kind of chuckled."

"Call the Bel-Air Hotel, and see if there's anybody registered under either name. If so, buzz me, and I'll talk to her."

"All right. Oh, and Mrs. Calder called, too."

"I'll return the call after I've spoken to Miss Bianchi."

A couple of minutes passed, and the phone buzzed. Stone picked it up. "Dolce?"

"No, Mr. Barrington," Louise said. "The Bel-Air says she's not registered there."

"Thanks, Louise. Try the Beverly Hills and the dozen best hotels after that, too. Ask about both names." He hung up the phone and thought for a minute. Actually, he admitted to himself, Dolce *did* have a right to call herself Mrs. Barrington, given the latest news from Italy, but it grated on him to hear her do it. Now he allowed himself to think about whether Dolce might have had anything to do with the torching of Vanessa's house and her death in the fire. Crazy, it certainly was, and he could not bring himself to believe that Dolce would have had anything to do with it, based simply on the fact of his visit there. He thought of mentioning it to the police, but dismissed the idea. He had no evidence whatsoever, and it might seem to the police like an attempt on his part to use them to rid himself of a troublesome woman. Still, he had to consider: If Dolce had been involved in Vanessa's death, might she try to harm Arrington? All the extra security he had arranged to guard the Calder estate was gone, since the press had lost some interest in her. Then he had a thought. He dialed Arrington's number.

"Hello?"

"Hi, it's Stone."

"Where are you? I've missed you."

"Same here, but I've been busy. I'm at the bungalow at the moment. Tell me, you're awfully alone there; how would you like some houseguests? The judge didn't bar that."

"I'd like *you* for a houseguest," she replied.

"I was thinking of Dino and Mary Ann, if I can get them out here."

"Oh, I'd love to see them! I've got cabin fever in a big way, and since you're being so standoffish, their company would be very welcome."

"I don't *feel* standoffish," Stone said. "Circumstances are keeping us apart."

"Would you visit me, if Dino and Mary Ann were here?"

"I think that would be perfectly kosher."

"Then, by all means, invite them!"

"I'll call you back." He hung up and dialed Dino's office.

"Lieutenant Bacchetti."

"Dino, it's Stone."

"How's sunny California?"

"You said you had some time off coming; why don't you come out here and see for yourself? And bring Mary Ann?"

"You in some kind of trouble, pal?"

"Maybe, I'm not sure."

"Dolce?"

"Possibly. A woman I had dinner with, somebody I'd met twice, died in a fire last night, not long after I left her house. It was arson, and they suspect her ex-husband, but . . ."

"And how can Mary Ann and I help?"

"You can come and stay at Arrington's."

"As extra security?"

"As houseguests. She says she'd love to see you both. She's been stuck alone in the house for too long, and cabin fever is setting in. There's a wonderful guest house, and some acreage; Mary Ann would love it."

"Hang on," Dino said, and put Stone on hold.

Stone tapped his fingers, waiting. He was beginning to feel a little cabin feverish, himself, even if he wasn't confined to quarters, and he missed his dinners with Dino at Elaine's.

"I'm back," Dino said. "Mary Ann's on board; we'll be out there tomorrow afternoon."

"That's great," Stone said. "I'll arrange for Arrington's butler to meet you at the airport, and we'll all have dinner together. The butler's name is Manolo; call Arrington's and leave your flight time with either him or her."

"Will do."

"Tell Mary Ann not to bring a lot of clothes; she can buy everything she needs on Rodeo Drive."

"Yeah, sure. If you mention that, I'll shoot you."

"Speaking of shooting, bring something, and will you stop by my house and bring me the Walther from my safe? Joan will open it for you; give her a call. And that little piece you loaned me is on my bedside table."

"Okay, see you tomorrow." Dino hung up.

Stone called Arrington and told her the news.

"I'll have Isabel plan something special for dinner," she said.

"Sounds great. Dino will let you know their flight time."

"Why don't you and I have dinner tonight?"

"Behave yourself."

"Oh, all right; just be here at seven tomorrow evening."

"I wouldn't miss it." Stone said good-bye and hung up. Almost immediately, the phone buzzed.

"Yes?"

"Charlene Joiner on line one."

He punched the button. "Hello, Charlene, how are you?"

"Terrible," she replied. "I'm very upset about Vanessa."

"It was a very bad thing."

"Did you know her, Stone?"

"I met her at Marc Blumberg's Palm Springs place a couple of days ago."

"You were right about the police; they're on their way over here now. Maybe you and I should talk before I meet them."

"No, you don't need a lawyer; just answer their questions truthfully. If we met first, it might make them think I'm involving myself in their case even more than I'm already involved."

"How are you already involved?"

"I had dinner at Vanessa's house last night; apparently, I was the last person to see her alive."

"Lucky Vanessa! At least she went with a smile on her face."

"It wasn't like that, Charlene," Stone said. "When can we get together?"

"Why don't you come over here for lunch? I'll be done with the police by then, say one o'clock, and I don't have to be back on the set until three."

"All right, where are you?"

"In the biggest fucking RV you ever saw," she said, "parked at the rear of sound stage six. It's got 'Georgia Peach' painted on the side."

"I'll find it. See you at one."

"I'll look forward."

⤚ Chapter 43 ⤙

Stone found the RV at the back of the sound stage, and Charlene had not overstated its size. It looked as long as a Greyhound bus, and it, indeed, had "Georgia Peach" painted on the side. Stone was about to get out of his car when he saw the two policemen, Rivera and Goldman, leaving the big vehicle. He waited until they had driven away before getting out of his car.

He knocked on the RV door and, a moment later, it was opened by a plump middle-aged woman wearing horn-rimmed glasses, with a pencil stuck in her hair.

"You Barrington?" she asked.

"That's me."

"I'm Sheila, come on in." She sat down at a desk behind the driver's seat and pointed at a door a few feet away. "Charlene's expecting you."

Stone rapped on the door.

"Come on in, Stone," came the voice through the door.

Stone opened the door and stepped into a surprisingly well-furnished room. It contained a sofa, coffee table and a couple of comfortable chairs, a desk, a dressing table, and a king-size bed. Charlene's voice came from what Stone presumed to be the bathroom, the door of which was ajar. "Have a seat," she called. "I'm just getting undressed."

"What?"

"Sit down. You want a drink?"

"I'm okay at the moment."

Charlene stuck her head out the door. "You don't mind if I'm naked, do you?" It was a rhetorical question. Before Stone could reply, she stepped into the room, and, unlike the last time he had seen her, she was not even wearing her bikini bottom. "I hope you're not too, too shy," she said, "but I'm shooting a nude scene this afternoon, and I can't have any marks on my body from clothes or underwear."

Stone sat down on the sofa. "I won't complain," he said, but he felt like complaining. Why were women always walking around naked in front of him just when he was trying to be good? He was struck anew at how beautiful she was—tall, slender, with breasts that were original equipment, not options, and she was a lovely, tawny color. "Did you greet the cops this way?"

"For them, I put on a robe, but it left this little mark where I tied it around the waist, see?" She pointed at a slightly red spot.

"Can't have that, can we?" Stone said lamely.

"The director would go nuts," she said. "Once I turned up with pantie marks and he shut down production until the next day, and I got a call from Lou Regenstein about it. You sure you don't want something to drink? Some iced tea, maybe?"

"All right, that would be nice."

She went to a small fridge, opened the door, and bent over, presenting a backside for the ages.

Stone took a deep breath and let it out slowly. There was not a hint of fat or cellulite anywhere. How did Hollywood do it?

She came back with a pitcher of iced tea and two glasses, then poured them both one and sat down on the sofa.

She pulled a leg under her, and Stone could not help but notice that she had recently experienced a clever bikini wax.

"The fuzz were very nice," she said.

"I'll bet."

She giggled. "I don't think they'd ever seen a movie star up close before. I mean, not this close, but close. You're by way of being an old acquaintance, so I don't mind."

"Neither do I," Stone said truthfully.

"Vanessa's death really shook me up," she said, but she didn't look shaken. "People my age are not supposed to die."

"You think the ex-husband did it?"

"I can't think of anybody else with a motive," she replied, shaking her head. "Vanessa was a sweet girl. You said you were with her last night?"

"Yes, I gave her a lift home from Marc Blumberg's office, and she asked me to stay for dinner."

"Oh, speaking of food, it should be here in a minute." As if on cue, there was a rap on the door, and Charlene got up and went into the bathroom. "You let them in, sugar; I don't want to give the waiter a coronary."

"You don't seem to mind giving me one," Stone said, walking to the door. He heard a giggle from the bathroom.

Two waiters came in and, in a flash, had arranged two lobster salads and a bottle of chardonnay on the coffee table. They were gone just as quickly, and Charlene returned, just as naked.

"I'm starved!" she said, sitting down and attacking the lobster.

Stone poured them both a glass of wine. "Charlene, who were Vanessa's best friends?"

"You met most of them at my house," Charlene replied. "The ladies who lunch? The whole group was there, except for Vanessa and Beverly."

"Beverly Walters?"

"Yep. You know her?"

"I met her briefly in a restaurant once."

"Beverly's all right, I guess, but she wouldn't be in the group, if it hadn't been for Vanessa."

"What's Beverly's story?"

Charlene shrugged. "She's a Beverly Hills housewife, I guess. She came out here to be an actress and ended up giving blow jobs for walk-ons. Her husband saved her from that; now all she does is have lunch and shop."

Stone tried the lobster; it was perfect, tender, and sweet. "Where'd the food come from?" he asked.

"From the studio commissary; have you been there, yet?"

"No."

"You'll have to come with me, sometime, sugar; that would do wonders for your reputation around here."

"You're not exactly shy, are you, Charlene?"

"You ever noticed *anything* shy about me, sugar?"

"No, I haven't. Tell me, was this group of ladies with you on the day Vance was shot?"

"Was it a Saturday? Yes, it was. I remember now. Sure, they were all there that day; we have a regular Saturday thing at my house."

"How late?"

"Later than usual, as I recall. Everybody's mostly gone by five or six, but a couple of people stayed right through dinner. I think it's *cleansing* to have dinner without a man occasionally."

"What time did Vanessa leave?"

"She didn't stay for dinner. I remember, they left, because Beverly had a dinner party to go to that night, and she had to get home and change. I don't know what Vanessa was doing."

"They left together?"

"Yes, they came and left in Vanessa's car."

"That's promising," Stone said, half to himself.

"Promising? How do you mean?"

"Sorry, I was thinking aloud."

Charlene, having eaten a third of her lunch, grabbed her wineglass and half reclined on the sofa, resting her feet in Stone's lap.

The view was transfixing, Stone thought, trying to concentrate on his lobster instead. "Are you and Beverly close at all?" he asked.

"Not very. Like I said, she's not my favorite person."

"I understand that Beverly is . . . talkative."

"Well, that's an understatement! We had to listen to every detail of every affair she had."

"Did she ever sleep with Vance?"

"Sugar, if Vance had ever had a social disease, half of Beverly Hills would have come down with it."

"I mean, did she ever talk about having an affair with him?"

"She tried, but she was late to the party; the rest of us had already had Vance."

"Vanessa, too?"

"Sure, and before she was divorced. Vance didn't discriminate against married women."

"Who is Beverly married to?"

"A producer on the lot, here: Gordon Walters. That's her entree around town; if she were ever divorced, she'd never get asked to dinner. Gordy's a sweetheart, but Beverly isn't all that popular. Everybody knows you can't tell her anything. It would be like putting it on a loudspeaker at Spago."

"Charlene, I wonder if you'd do a favor for me."

"Sugar," she said, poking him in the crotch with a toe. "I've been *trying*."

"Another kind of favor."

"Sure, if I can."

"Have lunch with Beverly Walters; see if you can find out what happened after she and Vanessa left your house that Saturday."

"Why do you want to know?"

"You can't share this with the ladies," Stone said.

She made a little cross with a long fingernail on her left breast.

"Beverly is a witness against Arrington, in this shooting thing. She's testified that Arrington told her she wanted to kill Vance. Arrington was joking, of course."

"Of course," Charlene said dryly.

"It's possible that Beverly might have been at Vance's house that evening, and that she might have seen something. I can't let Arrington go into court without knowing what Beverly saw. Do you think you could worm that out of her?"

"Shoot, Stone, I could worm Beverly's genetic code out of her, if she knew it."

"Vanessa said something about this to me, and I wouldn't like for Beverly to know that. Vanessa felt she was breaking a confidence, just by mentioning the possibility."

"That sounds like Vanessa," Charlene said, looking misty for a moment. "She'd be true blue, even to Beverly."

"When do you think you could see her?"

"She'll be over at the house on Saturday, with the others, I'm sure; we'll have some commiserating to do over Vanessa."

"I'd appreciate any help you could give me."

Charlene smiled a small smile. "How *much* would you appreciate it?"

"A lot," Stone said.

"I don't believe you," Charlene replied. "It's Arrington, isn't it? She's why I can't get you in the sack."

"We're old and good friends," Stone said.

Charlene laughed. "Well, at least you didn't say you were *just* good friends. I don't blame you, Stone; she's perfectly gorgeous. I'd hop into bed with her in a minute."

Stone laughed, put down his fork, and stood up. "I'll tell her you said so, if the occasion should ever arise. I've got to get going. Thanks for the lunch, and, especially, for your help."

Charlene put down her wineglass, arose, and came toward Stone. She snaked one arm around his neck, hooked one leg around his and kissed him, long and deep.

Stone enjoyed the moment.

"Just you remember," she said, "you owe me one."

Stone released himself and made his way out of the RV. On the short drive back to the bungalow, Stone made a concerted effort to forget how Charlene Joiner had looked naked, and failed.

⤳ Chapter 44 ⤳

Stone spent the evening alone in Vance's bungalow, heating a frozen dinner and watching one of Vance's movies from a selection of video-tapes in the study. It turned out to be one in which Charlene Joiner had costarred, and that didn't help him think pure thoughts. Her ability as an actress actually lived up to her beauty, which surprised him, though it was not the first of her movies he had seen.

He slept fitfully, then devoted the following day to a combination of Calder Estate business and correspondence FedExed by Joan from New York, which kept his mind off naked women, living and dead. The noon news said that Daniel Pike was not a suspect in his ex-wife's death, but he didn't believe it. The police had probably leaked that information to make Pike think he was safe. He'd done the same thing, himself, in his time.

Arrington called early in the afternoon. "Dino and Mary Ann are arriving at three," she said, "and Manolo is meeting them. I can't wait to see them!"

"Same here," Stone said, and he meant it. Cut off from Arrington most of the time, he craved affectionate company.

"You be here at seven," she said.

"Can I bring anything?"

"Yes, but I don't think you'll share, in your present mood."

"When this is over, I'll share until you cry for mercy."

"Promises, promises! Bye." She hung up.

Stone left the studio at six-thirty, which would make him fashionably late to Arrington's. Then, after no more than a mile, the car's steering felt funny, and he pulled over. The rear tire was flat. He thought of changing it himself, but there was a gas station a block away, and he didn't want to get his fresh clothes dirty, so he hiked down there and brought back a mechanic to do the work. As a result, he was half an hour late to dinner.

He entered through the front gate, for a change, and noted that there were no TV vans or reporters about. Manolo let him in and es-corted him into the living room where Arrington, Dino, and Mary Ann sat on sofas before the fireplace. Another woman was there, too, but her back was to him.

He hugged Dino and Mary Ann, but when he went to embrace Arrington, she kept an elbow between them. "And look who else is here!" she cried, waving a hand toward the sofa. The other woman turned around.

"Dolce," Stone said weakly. "I've been trying to reach you."

"Well, you can reach me now," Dolce replied, patting the sofa next to her.

Stone started to take another seat, but Arrington took his arm tightly and guided him next to Dolce. "Dolce has told me your wonderful news!" Arrington said brightly, showing lots of teeth. "Let me congratulate you!"

Stone looked at Dino and Mary Ann, both of whom looked extremely uncomfortable. He sat down next to Dolce and submitted to a kiss on the cheek.

"My darling," she said, "how handsome you look tonight."

"I'm sorry I'm late," Stone said to Arrington, ignoring Dolce. "I had a flat tire on the way."

"Of course you did, Stone," she replied, as if he were lying.

Manolo brought him a Wild Turkey on the rocks, and Stone sipped it. This whole thing was insane; what was Dolce doing here? He discovered that he was sweating. "How was your flight?" he asked Dino and Mary Ann.

"Pretty much the same as being moved around the Chicago Stockyards with an electric cattle prod," Dino replied gamely, trying to hold up his end.

"Heh, heh," Stone said, taking a big swig of the bourbon. He stole a glance at Dolce, who was smiling broadly. He hoped she wasn't armed.

Across the coffee table, on the sofa opposite, Arrington was smiling just as broadly. She emptied a martini glass and motioned to Manolo for another. "Well, isn't this fun!" she said. "Old friends together again. How long has it been?"

"A long time," Mary Ann replied, as if it had not been long enough.

"Oh, Stone," Dino said, standing up. "I brought you something; come out to the guest house for a minute."

"Excuse me," Stone said to Arrington.

"Hurry back, now!" she replied.

Stone followed Dino out the back door and toward the guest house. "What the fuck is going on?" he demanded.

"How should I know?" Dino replied. "I didn't know Dolce was coming until she got here, ten minutes before you did. Mary Ann must have invited her, but she didn't say a goddamned thing to me about it." He opened the door to the guest house and led the way in.

"And she told Arrington we were married in Venice?"

"You bet she did, pal, and she laid it on thick. Arrington was smiling a lot, but she would have killed her, if there had been anything sharp lying around." Dino went to his suitcase and handed Stone his little Walther automatic, in its chamois shoulder holster.

"What am I going to do with this now?" Stone asked.

"I'd wear it if I were you," Dino replied. "You might need it before the evening is over."

Stone shucked off his jacket and slipped into the shoulder holster.

"My thirty-two automatic wasn't on your bedside table, where you said it would be, and it wasn't in your safe, either."

"That's weird," Stone said. "Helene wouldn't have touched it when she was cleaning; she hates guns, and Joan wouldn't have had any reason to be upstairs."

"I asked Joan about it, and she said she hadn't seen it."

Stone checked the Walther; it was loaded. He put the safety on and returned it to the holster.

"You're going to need a local permit for that, aren't you?" Dino asked.

"Rick Grant got me one last year when I was out here; it's in my pocket. Can you think of some way to get Dolce out of here? I've got to explain to Arrington what's going on."

"I thought you would have explained it to her a long time ago," Dino said. "That girl is *really* pissed off."

"I realize I should have," Stone said, "but I just didn't want to bring up Dolce while Arrington is in all this trouble."

"Well, *you're* the one who's in trouble, now, and we'd better get back in there, so you can face the music."

They went back into the house, and found Mary Ann struggling to keep some sort of conversation going.

Manolo came into the room. "Dinner is served, Mrs. Calder," he said.

Everyone rose and marched into the dining room.

"Now let's see," Arrington said, surveying the beautifully laid table. "We'll have Mr. and Mrs. Bacchetti to my left, and Mr. and Mrs. Barrington, here, to my right."

Stone winced as if lashed. Everybody sat down, and a cold soup was served.

"This is a beautiful house," Dino said.

"Thank you, Dino; Vance let me redo the place after we were married, so I can take full credit. Stone, where are you and Dolce going to make your home?"

Stone dropped his spoon into his soup bowl, splashing gazpacho over his jacket.

Dolce took up the slack. "Papa offered to give us his Manhattan place, but Stone has insisted that we live in his house," she said. "I'm *so* looking forward to redecorating the place. It's a little . . . *seedy* right now."

Stone could not suppress a groan. Dolce knew that Arrington had had a big hand in decorating his house. The soup was taken away, before Arrington could throw it at Dolce.

"And how is your father?" Arrington asked solicitously. "And all those *business* associates of his? The ones with the broken noses?"

Stone stood up. "Excuse me." He left the table.

Arrington caught up with him at the front door. "Running away, are you? You complete shit! You *married* that bitch?"

"I have a lot to explain to you," Stone said. "Can we have lunch tomorrow?"

"Lunch? I don't ever want to see you again! Not as long as I live!"

"Arrington, you're going to have to listen to me about this."

"The hell I do!" she hissed, then pushed him out the front door and slammed it behind him.

Stone was already in his car when he saw Dolce in his rearview mirror, coming out of the house. The gates opened for him, and he floored the accelerator.

He made a couple of quick turns, headed nowhere, just trying to be sure that Dolce wasn't following him. He made the freeway, then got off at Santa Monica Boulevard, so he could keep an eye on several blocks behind him. Sweat was pouring off him, and he was breathing rapidly. When he had to stop for a traffic light he took the opportunity to put the car's top down, and the breeze began to cool him. His breathing slowed, and he began to feel nearly normal, except that he was numb between the ears. He did his best to drive both Dolce and Arrington out of his head, tried to think of nothing. For a while he was in a nearly semiconscious state, driving by instinct, uncaring of his direction.

When his head cleared he found himself at a traffic light in Malibu. He dug his notebook out of his pocket, looked up the number and dialed the hands-free phone.

"Hello?" she said, her voice low and inviting.

"It's Stone; I'm in Malibu. Are you alone?"

"I sure am," she replied.

"Not for long." He headed for the Colony.

⤳ **Chapter 45** ⤳

Charlene met him at the door, wearing nothing but a short silk robe. Neither of them said a word. He kissed her, then, without stopping, lifted her off her feet.

She climbed him like a tree and locked her legs around him. "Straight ahead," she said, removing her lips from his just long enough to speak. "Hang a right at the end of the hall."

He followed her directions and came into a large bedroom only steps from the sand. The sliding doors to the beach were open, and a breeze billowed the sheer curtains. She unlocked her legs and dropped to the floor, tearing at his clothes. Together they got him undressed and her robe disappeared. They dived at the bed.

Stone had been erect since she'd answered the phone, and Charlene wasn't interested in foreplay. He was inside her before they were fully on the bed, and she was already wet. They made love hungrily, rolling about on the king-size bed, he on top, then she. There were no words, only sounds—yells, bleats, cries, moans. The breeze from the Pacific blew over their bodies, drying their sweat, keeping them going. She came slowly to a climax, and Stone followed her more swiftly, penetrating her fully. More sounds, followed by gasps for breath, then they were both lying on their backs, sucking in wind.

"Good God!" she managed to say finally. "I've done a lot of fucking in my time, but I don't think I ever had a running start before."

"I was in a hurry," he panted.

"Oh, I'm not complaining, sugar."

He turned and reached for her. "Again," he said.

She pushed him onto his back. "Now you take it easy," she said. "My call for tomorrow isn't until eleven, and you've got to last until then. I don't want you to leave in an ambulance."

Stone burst out laughing. "Oh, I feel wonderful," he laughed. "First time in I don't know how long."

"You've been wound a little tight, haven't you?"

"You wouldn't believe how tight."

"Well, I think I've just had a demonstration, and if it took you that long to start unwinding . . ."

"I think I may live now, if Dolce doesn't shoot me."

"Dolce? Is there somebody I don't know about?"

"My *wife*, God help me."

"Sugar, I believe we've skipped a part of your bio," she said, rising onto one elbow and tossing her hair over her shoulder.

"Paper marriage," he said. "Piece of paper, nothing more. Trouble is, it's an *Italian* piece of paper."

"Baby, you're not making any sense. Did you get drunk in Vegas, or something?"

"Happened in Venice," he panted. "The real one, not the Vegas one. Glorious place to get married."

"Did she Shanghai you?"

"I went voluntarily, I'm afraid. I don't know *what* I was thinking."

"So, what's the next level of that relationship?"

"The next level is divorce, and I have a feeling it's not going to be easy, since it has to happen in Italy."

"I don't understand how . . . wait a minute; you came out here just to help Arrington, didn't you?"

"Yes."

"Were you in Venice when you heard about Vance?"

"Yes. We'd had the civil ceremony; we were due for the big one, in St. Mark's, the next day. When I heard about Vance, I dropped everything."

"Including Dolce?"

"Turned out that way."

"How did she take it?"

"Badly."

"And now you think she wants to shoot you?"

"Oh, no; she'd rather have me drawn and quartered and the pieces barbecued."

"What does she *want*?"

"Me, dead or alive."

"You mean she still wants to be married to you?"

"Apparently so. She's been introducing herself to the world as Mrs. Stone Barrington."

"Oops."

"Yeah, oops."

"Who is this girl?"

"Her last name is Bianchi."

"Wait a minute: at Vance's funeral I saw you talking to . . ."

"Her father."

"I've heard a little about him," she said. "Sounds like this could be tricky."

"Well put. Tricky."

She pushed his hair off his forehead with her fingers and kissed him. "I could hide you here for a few months," she said.

"I don't think I could survive that."

She giggled. "Probably not, but you'd last a while. What made you show up here tonight? Where were you earlier this evening?"

"I went to Arrington's house for dinner. Dolce was there."

"Well, that must have been a teensy bit awkward."

"You could say that. You could say I'm lucky I got out of there before the two of them tore me to pieces."

"And how did this little soiree come about?"

"I don't have the faintest idea. I arrived, and they were both there. I don't think I've ever been at such a complete loss."

"Poor baby," she said. "I suppose you need consoling."

"Oh, yes. Console me."

She swapped ends and began kissing him lightly, getting an instantaneous response.

He placed a hand on her buttocks and pulled her to his face, searching with his tongue.

She took him into her mouth.

He found her.

They remained in that position for a long time.

⤳ Chapter 46 ⤳

Stone stood, his hands against the tile wall of the shower, his head under the heavy stream of water. His knees were trembling. He had no idea what time it was, except that the sun was up.

The bronzed-glass door opened, and Charlene stepped in. She grabbed a bottle of something, sprayed it on his back, and began soaping his body. "How you doing, sugar?"

"I'm shattered," he said. "I can hardly stand up."

"I can't imagine how that happened," she giggled. "All we did was make love."

"How many times?"

"Several," she replied. "Who's counting?"

He leaned back against the tile and let her soap him. "I have the strange but almost certain feeling that sometime early this morning I passed some sort of physical peak in my life, and that everything from here on is downhill."

"Sugar," she said, "that's the sort of peak that most men hit at eighteen. You should be pleased with yourself."

"I'm never going to be the same again; I can hardly stand up. You may have to carry me out of here."

She pulled him back under the shower and rinsed him, then turned off the shower. "Maybe if you hold my hand you can make it." She led him out of the stall, dried him and herself with fat towels, and found robes for them both. "Come on, hon; breakfast is on the table."

He followed her through the sliding doors and onto a terrace over-looking the beach. When they sat down a low wall cleverly blocked the view from the sand, but still allowed them a panorama of the sea. It was nicely private.

She removed the covers from two plates. His was eggs, home fries, sausages, and muffins; hers was a slice of melon.

"Why do I have so much and you so little?" he asked, digging in.

"Because you need your strength, and I need to keep my ass looking the way it does without surgery."

"It looks wonderful, especially up close."

"You should know; you were in and out of there a few times."

Stone sneezed.

"God bless you."

"I hope I'm not getting a cold."

"I don't think you can get a cold from anal sex."

"Good point; maybe I'm just allergic to something."

"For a while there, I thought you might be allergic to me."

Stone shook his head. "Not in the least."

"Then what took you so long to knock on my door?"

"Call it misplaced loyalties."

"That's it," she agreed. "Neither one of them deserves you." She smiled. "Only me. Tell me, do you always wear a gun to assignations?"

"What?"

"I seem to recall removing a shoulder holster from your body, along with everything else. Did you feel you needed a lot of protection from me?"

"A friend brought it out from New York for me. No offense."

"None taken."

Stone finished his eggs and poured them some coffee. "When are you going to see Beverly Walters?"

"Yesterday."

"You've already talked to her?"

"Well, you didn't give me a chance to tell you last night."

"What did she say?"

"She was coy, which is unlike Beverly. Normally, she spills everything, usually without being asked."

"But not yesterday?"

Charlene shook her head. "She had a secret, and she wasn't going to tell me. I couldn't worm it out of her."

"She was there, I think. She must have seen what happened."

"If I were you, I'd be worried."

"I am."

"What's your next move?"

"I don't know. We could depose her, get her under oath."

"Why?"

"The idea is to find out what the prosecution witness knows."

Charlene sighed. "The problem with that, Stone, is you don't *want* to know."

She had a point, he thought.

Stone got back to the studio bungalow a little before eleven. Louise Bremen, from the studio secretarial pool, was at Betty's desk. "Good morning," she said, handing him a phone message. It was from Dino, and the return number was at the Calder guest house.

"Good morning," he replied, pocketing the message.

"Oh, you've spilled something on your jacket," Louise said.

Stone had forgotten about the gazpacho from the night before.

"Take it off, and I'll send it over to wardrobe for you; they'll get the stain out."

"Thanks," Stone said. He went into the bedroom, took off the jacket, and put the Walther and its holster into a drawer, then he took the jacket back to Louise. "Have we heard anything from Dolce Bianchi?"

"Not a peep," she replied.

"Good." He went into the study and called Dino.

"Hello."

"Hi."

Dino spoke softly, as if he didn't want to be overheard. "Let's meet for lunch," he whispered.

"Okay, come over here, and we'll go to the studio commissary. Borrow a car from Manolo; he'll give you directions."

"In an hour?"

"Good." They both hung up. Stone buzzed Louise and asked her to arrange a studio pass for Dino.

Dino was introduced to Louise, then Stone showed him around the bungalow.

"These movie stars live pretty well, don't they?" he said.

"Better than cops and lawyers."

"Better than anybody. That guest house we're staying in is nicer than any home I've ever had."

"The pleasures of money."

"I'm hungry; let's eat. We can talk over lunch."

Stone drove him slowly through the studio streets, pointing out the exterior street set and the sound stages.

"It's like a city, isn't it?" Dino said.

"It has just about everything a city has, except crime."

"Yeah, that happens in Bel-Air and Beverly Hills."

Stone parked outside the commissary, which was a brick building with a walled garden. Stone showed the hostess his VIP studio pass, and they were given a table outside, surrounded by recognizable faces.

Dino took it all in, pointing out a movie star or two, then they ordered lunch.

"All right, what happened after I left last night?" Stone asked.

"Not much. What could compare to the scene just before you left?"

"What was Dolce doing there?"

"Mary Ann invited her, with Arrington's permission. It was an innocent thing on both their parts, I guess."

"How innocent could it be? Mary Ann was in Venice; she knew everything."

"She thought Arrington knew everything, too. You didn't tell her?"

"I hadn't found the right moment," Stone said.

"She was pretty upset after you left, even though she tried not to show it. I tried to smooth things over, but she wouldn't talk about you."

"I've never been double-teamed like that," Stone said.

"I felt sorry for you, but there was nothing I could do. You're going to have to find some way to square things with Arrington."

"As far as I'm concerned, the ball's in her court. I was ambushed, and I didn't like it."

"That wasn't her intention, Stone."

"Maybe not, but the result was the same."

"Fortunately, Dolce left when you did. Did you go together?"

"No, I outran her."

"You can't run forever."

"What else can I do? You can't talk to her like a normal human being. I've got Marc Blumberg working on an Italian divorce."

"I have a feeling this is not going to be as easy as divorce."

"Funny, I have the same feeling," Stone replied.

When they got back to the bungalow, Louise came into the study. "Lou Regenstein's secretary called. Lou would like you to come to an impromptu dinner party he's giving for some friends at his house tonight.

He says to bring somebody, if you'd like. It's at seven-thirty." She laid the address on his desk.

"Let me make a call," Stone said. He found the number for Charlene's RV and dialed it.

"Hey, sugar," she said. "How you feeling?"

"I think I've recovered my health. Would you like to go to a dinner party tonight?"

"Sure, but I won't be done here until six-thirty or seven."

"Have you got something that you could wear? We could leave from here."

"I've got just the thing," she said. "I wore it in a scene this morning."

"Pick you up at the RV about seven-fifteen?"

"Seven-fifteenish."

"See you then." He hung up. "Call Lou's secretary and tell her I'd love to come, and I'm bringing a date."

Louise went back to her desk to make the call.

"Who's the date?" Dino asked.

"Charlene Joiner."

Dino's eyebrows went up. "You kidding me?"

"Nope," Stone replied smugly. "She's a new friend."

"One of these days, you're going to screw yourself right into the ground," Dino said.

⤳ Chapter 47 ⤳

Charlene kept Stone waiting for only fifteen minutes. When she emerged from her dressing room she was wearing flowing cream-colored silk pants and a filmy patterned blouse. Stone noticed in a nanosecond that the blouse was so sheer that nipples were readily in view.

"So *that's* what L.A. women wear to dinner parties." He laughed, kissing her.

"They do if they have the right equipment," Charlene replied, wrapping a light cashmere stole around her shoulders.

"You're going to be very popular tonight," Stone said.

"With the men, anyway. Whose house are we going to?"

"It's a surprise."

"I love a surprise," she said, settling into the car. "This is Vance's car, isn't it?"

"It is. I borrowed it."

"Such an incestuous town," she said.

With Charlene's help he found the house, or rather, estate, in Holmby Hills. Stone was beginning to believe that everybody in L.A. lived on four or five acres. He stopped in the circular driveway, and a valet took the car. As they approached the house, the front door was opened by a butler, and they stepped into a large foyer. From across the living room beyond, Lou Regenstein headed toward them.

"Oh, my God," Charlene said under her breath.

"What's wrong?"

"I'll tell you later," she whispered.

"Stone!" Lou cried, his hand out. "And Charlene!" He looked a little panicky. "What a surprise!"

"For me too, Lou," she replied, accepting a peck on the cheek. She whipped off the stole, handed it to the butler, and swept into the room at Stone's side, her back arched, breasts held high.

Lou led them toward a tall, handsome woman of about fifty, who was talking to another couple. "Livia," he said. "You haven't met Stone."

"How do you do?" the woman said, taking Stone's hand. Then she turned toward Charlene, and her eyes narrowed.

"And of course, you know Charlene Joiner," Lou said.

"Of course," she replied icily, then turned and walked away.

There was something going on here, Stone thought, and he wasn't sure he wanted to know what it was.

Lou quickly turned to the couple Livia had been talking to. "And this is Lansing Drake and his wife, Christina."

Stone took the man's hand. "It's Dr. Drake, isn't it?"

"Yes, and your name?"

"I'm sorry," Lou said, "this is Stone Barrington, a friend of Vance's and Arrington's."

For a split second, the doctor looked as though he had been struck across the face, then he recovered. "Nice to meet you," he mumbled, then turned to Charlene. "And of course, I know you," he said, chuckling, his eyes pointing below her shoulders.

"Of course you do," Charlene said.

Lou's attention was drawn to the front door, where other guests were arriving. "The bar is over there," he said to Stone, pointing across the room. "Please excuse me."

Dr. Drake and his wife had suddenly engaged someone else in conversation, so Stone lead Charlene toward the bar.

"Pill pusher to the stars," Charlene said.

"Yes, I've heard of him; he's Arrington's doctor. What were you talking about at the front door?"

"If you hadn't been surprising me, I'd have warned you," she said.

"Warned me about what?"

"Livia; she hates me with a vengeance. Poor Lou is going to get it between the shoulder blades tonight."

"Who is she?"

"Lou's wife."

"I didn't know he even *had* a wife. Nobody's ever mentioned her to me."

"Nobody ever does, least of all Lou. They've had an arm's-length marriage for twenty years. Word has it they occupy different wings of this house. They're only seen together when he entertains here, or at industry events, like the Oscars."

"And why does she hate you?"

"You don't want to know."

"You're probably right." They reached the bar; Charlene had a San Pellegrino, and Stone had his usual bourbon.

"Did you see the look on the doctor's face when he met you?" Charlene asked.

"Yes; I thought he was going to break and run for a minute."

"This is going to be a very weird evening," Charlene said.

Stone looked toward the front door and nearly choked on his drink. "You don't know how weird," he said.

Charlene followed his gaze. "That, I suppose, is the fabled Dolce."

"It is," Stone replied, "and the man with her is her father, Eduardo."

Charlene linked her arm in Stone's. "Well, come on, then," she said. "I want to be introduced."

There was nothing else for it, Stone thought; may as well brazen it out. He walked toward the two, wishing to God he were on another continent. "Good evening, Eduardo," he said. "Hello, Dolce."

Eduardo took his hand, but not before a shocked glance at Charlene's highly visible breasts. "Stone," he managed to say.

Dolce said nothing, but shot a look at Charlene that would have set a lesser woman on fire.

"Eduardo, this is Charlene Joiner. Charlene, this is Eduardo Bianchi and his daughter, Dolce."

"I'm so pleased to meet you both," Charlene said, offering them a broad smile, in addition to everything else.

"Enchanted," Eduardo said stiffly.

"Oh, yes," Dolce said dryly, looking Charlene up and down. "Enchanted."

"Charlene is one of Lou's biggest stars," Stone said, because he could not think of anything else to say.

"I never go to the pictures," Eduardo said, "but I can certainly believe you are a star."

"Oh, Eduardo, you're sweet," Charlene giggled. She turned and snaked an arm through his. "Come on, and I'll get you a drink." She led him away, leaving Stone suddenly with Dolce, the very last place he wanted to be.

"Alone at last," Dolce said archly.

"Dolce, I . . ."

"Are you fucking her?"

"Now, listen. I . . ."

"Of course you are. That's what you do best, isn't it?"

"Will you listen . . ."

"I'm sure she's *very* good in the sack."

"Dolce . . ."

"Is she, Stone? Does she give good head?"

"For Christ's sake, keep your voice . . ."

"I'll bet she's spent more time on her knees than Esther Williams spent in the pool."

"Dolce, if you don't . . ."

"Oh, good, a martini," Dolce said, as a waiter approached with a tray. She took one, tossed it into Stone's face, returned the glass to the tray, and walked away.

The room was suddenly silent. Then Charlene's laugh cut through the quiet. "I don't *believe* you," she was saying to Eduardo, who, uncharacteristically, seemed to be laughing, too.

"Dinner is served!" the butler called out, and the guests began filtering toward the dining room.

Charlene came, took Stone by the arm, and turned him toward dinner.

"Let's get out of here," Stone said, dabbing at his face with a handkerchief.

"Are you kidding?" Charlene laughed, dragging him toward the dining room. "I wouldn't miss this dinner for anything!"

⤜ Chapter 48 ⤛

There were sixteen at dinner. Stone found himself near the center of the long, narrow table, on his hostess's left. Directly across from him was Dr. Lansing Drake, who had landed with Dolce on his right and Charlene on his left. Most men, Stone reflected, would have been delighted to find themselves bracketed by two such beautiful women, but Dr. Drake looked decidedly uncomfortable, and when Stone nodded to him, he looked at his plate, then up and down the table, as if seeking an escape route.

The woman to Stone's left seemed to be in her eighties and deaf, while the handsome and chilly Livia, to Stone's right, seemed disinclined to acknowledge his presence. Dolce, across the table, shot him long, hostile looks whenever his eyes wandered her way. Only Charlene seemed happy. She had drawn Eduardo, to her left, and between her large eyes and her beautiful breasts, she seemed to have him mesmerized.

"How long have you known that woman?" a deep, whiskey-scarred voice asked.

Stone jerked to attention. Livia had spoken to him. "Oh, we met only recently. This is the first time we've been out." That was, strictly speaking, the truth. They had done all sorts of things at home, but they had not been out.

"I would be careful, if I were you," Livia said. "She probably has a social disease."

"I beg your pardon?" Stone said, astonished that a hostess would say such a thing to her guest about his companion.

"More than likely, a *fatal* social disease," Livia said, ignoring his reaction.

"Mrs. Regenstein . . ."

"I detest that name; call me Livia."

"You detest your husband's name?"

"And my husband, as well."

"Then why are you married to him?"

"I find it convenient; I have for more than twenty years. But enough about me; let's talk about you. What did you do to little Miss Bianchi that would invite a drink in the face?"

"My private life," Stone said, "unlike yours, is private."

"You're going to be a bore, aren't you?" she asked.

"You will probably think so."

"Who are you, anyway?"

"My name is Stone Barrington."

"Ah, yes, Louis has mentioned you. You're that disreputable lawyer from New York who was screwing Arrington Calder just before she married Vance, aren't you?"

Stone looked across the table, caught Charlene's eye and jerked his head toward the door. Then he turned to Livia Regenstein. "Good-bye, you miserable bitch," he said quietly, then he got up and walked out of the dining room. He waited a moment for Charlene to catch up, then led her toward the front door.

While Charlene was waiting for her wrap, and the valet was bringing Stone's car, Lou Regenstein caught up with them. "What's wrong, Stone? Why are you leaving?"

"Lou, I must apologize; I'm afraid I don't have a scorecard for the games that are played in this town. I'm sorry if I made your wife and your guests uncomfortable."

"It's I who should apologize," Lou said. "Livia can be hard to take."

"I'll see you soon," Stone said. They shook hands, and he and Charlene left the house.

Stone put the top down. "I need some air," he said, turning down the street. "I hope it won't disturb your hair."

"Don't worry about it," Charlene replied. "Well, that was quite an evening. What were you and Livia talking about, dare I ask?"

"You, mostly," Stone said.

"Oh. I may as well tell you. For a short time Livia and I shared a lover."

"Not Lou, I hope."

"No, someone much younger. Soon after I came into the picture, the man stopped seeing Livia. Livia has been livid ever since."

"This is my fault; I should have told you where we were having dinner."

"Listen, sugar, don't worry about it; I didn't have half as bad a time as you."

"What were you and Eduardo talking about?"

"The movie business, mostly."

"He seemed fascinated."

"I'm sure he was. He spoke well of you, too."

"Did he?"

"He said you were a gentleman."

"And that was just before I caused a scene by walking out of an elegant dinner party."

"I'm sure his opinion of you hasn't changed."

"You know, until this week, I had never in my life walked out of any dinner party, and now, in the space of three days, I've walked out of two."

"Are you upset?"

"Not really; I must be getting used to it."

"I guess folks out here aren't working with quite the same social graces as their counterparts in New York."

Stone reached Sunset and turned toward the studio. "How'd you happen to come out here?"

"You want the fan magazine version, or the truth?"

"The truth will do nicely."

"Hang a left here," she said. "There's a nice little restaurant down the street, and we haven't had dinner."

Stone followed directions. "No, we haven't."

The restaurant was not all that small, but it was very elegant, and the headwaiter, spotting Charlene, had them at a special table in seconds. They ordered drinks and dinner.

"Okay, now tell me your story," he said.

"It's a strange one," she said. "I'm from Meriwether County, Georgia, near a little town called Delano."

"That's where Betty Southard, Vance's secretary, is from."

"True, but she was older than I, so we didn't really know each other. Anyway, I was pretty much a country girl, and I had this boyfriend who murdered a girl, in Greenville, the county seat. The court appointed a lawyer named Will Lee to defend my boyfriend."

"Wait a minute, is this the senator from Georgia? The presidential candidate?"

"Yes, but not at that time. Old Senator Carr, who Will worked for, had a stroke, and Will ran for his seat, but the judge wouldn't let him out of defending Larry, my boyfriend, even though it was during the campaign. As you might imagine, the trial attracted a lot of press coverage."

"I think I remember this vaguely," Stone said, "but not the outcome."

"Larry was convicted and sentenced to death. A tabloid paid me for my story, and all of a sudden, Hollywood was sniffing around. Next thing I knew I was out here, with a part in a movie. Then there was another part and another, and the rest is pulp fiction."

"Amazing. Was the boyfriend executed?"

She shook her head. "I went to see the governor of Georgia and personally, ah, interceded on his behalf. His sentence was commuted to life without parole. We still correspond."

"Was he guilty?"

"Oh, yes."

"That's the damndest story I ever heard."

"There's more."

"Tell me."

"Will Lee and I had a little one-time encounter that became a side issue in the presidential race."

"That was you?"

"I'm afraid so. When I'm old and washed up, somebody's going to make a really bad TV movie about all this, and then I'm going to write my memoirs."

"I'm sure it will be a hot seller."

"You better believe it, sugar."

After dinner, he drove her back to her car at Centurion, and they said good night.

"One thing," he said to her.

"What's that, baby?" she asked, putting her arms around his neck.

"Dolce has taken this whole business hard. After tonight's events, I think you should be careful."

"You mean, watch my back?"

"Yes, that's what I mean."

She kissed him. "Sugar," she said, "Dolce doesn't want to mess with me."

"I hope you're right."

She kissed him again. "Should I go armed?"

"Do you own a gun?"

She nodded. "All legal-like, too."

"Try not to shoot at anybody; you might hit me."

"I shoot what I aim at, sugar." She kissed him again, then got into her car. "By the way," she said, as she put the top down. "There's going to be a kind of memorial for Vanessa tomorrow at my house. Will you come?"

Stone nodded. "Sure."

"Just a few people. Six o'clock."

"I'll be there."

She gave a little wave and drove away.

⤳ **Chapter 49** ⤳

The memorial for Vanessa Pike at Charlene's house seemed more of a memorial cocktail party, Stone reflected as he walked into the well-populated living room. Everyone had a drink, even if, in the California style, it was designer fizzy water, and there was a buffet at one end of the room laden with raw vegetables, melon, and other low-fat delicacies.

Charlene came and gave him a virtuous peck on the cheek. "I think you'll know a few people," she said. "Mingle while I greet."

Stone nodded, went to the bar, and waited while the barman ransacked the house for a bottle of bourbon. He would not bear his grief in sobriety, no matter what the West Coast convention. While he waited, he surveyed the room, picking out most of the women he had met on his first visit to the house, along with Dr. Lansing Drake and his wife and, somewhat to his relief, Marc Blumberg. At least he'd have somebody to talk to. He collected his drink and joined Marc.

"What've you been up to?" Marc asked.

"Not much," Stone said.

"I think it's about time to go for a motion to dismiss," Marc said.

"I'm not so sure about that," Stone replied.

"Why not?"

"Because I think it's quite possible that Beverly Walters was there when Vance was shot, and she's the prosecution's prime witness."

"Are you sure she was there?"

"As sure as I can be without putting her under oath and asking her."

Marc mulled that over for a moment. "I wonder if she hates Arrington that much, that she'd testify?"

"She hates her enough to testify to a conversation in which Arrington, apparently in jest, says she'd kill Vance if she caught him with another woman."

"You have a point," Marc admitted.

"Have you heard anything new from the investigation into Vanessa's death?" Stone asked.

"They've cleared the husband," Marc replied, nodding toward two men across the room.

Stone followed his gaze and found the two cops he'd met after the fire at Vanessa's. "What are they doing here?"

"They must think the murderer is present," Marc said. "Such a person might call attention to himself by his absence."

"Have you caught them staring at anybody?" Stone asked, glancing out the big windows toward the beach.

"They're staring at you right now," Marc said.

Stone looked back toward the two detectives and found that Marc was not lying. Both men gazed gravely back at him. Stone raised his glass a little and nodded; both men nodded back. "You think I'm all they've got?"

"I guess so."

"What do you suppose they think my motive is?"

"Who knows?"

"I mean, I met her only twice, both times in your company. Did you notice any murderous intentions on my part?"

Marc shrugged. "Nothing obvious."

"I suppose they've questioned you about those meetings."

"In some depth."

"Do I need a lawyer?"

"*Everybody* needs a lawyer."

Stone laughed.

"But probably not you, not yet."

"That's a relief; I'm not sure I could afford you."

"Probably not."

"Excuse me; I need the powder room." Stone set down his glass. He left the lawyer and walked down a hallway to the first-floor half-bath. The door was ajar and he stepped inside and switched on the light. He reached behind him to close the door, but felt a pressure on it. Then he was pushed forward into the little room and someone stepped in behind him and closed the door. Stone turned to find Beverly Walters sharing the john with him.

"What the hell are you doing here?" he demanded.

She reached behind her and turned the lock. "Same as you; grieving for Vanessa."

"I mean in this toilet."

"I wanted to talk to you."

"We can't talk; you're a witness against my client. Surely you must understand that."

"Of course; that's why we're talking in here."

"We're not talking at all," Stone said. "There are two police officers here, and they work for the same department that's investigating Vance's murder. They would certainly report it if they saw us talking." He started around her, but she took hold of his lapels and stopped him.

"Listen to me," she said.

"I *can't* listen to you," he replied, trying to free himself.

She clung to him. "I'm going to testify against Arrington," she said.

"I believe I'm aware of that," Stone replied, taking hold of her wrists and trying to disengage.

"But you don't know what I'm going to say."

"I've already heard you testify once."

"But you didn't hear everything. I saw Vance murdered."

"Ms. Walters, please let me out of here."

"I can put Arrington in prison, don't you understand?"

"You can try," Stone said, "but I expect to have something to say about that, and so does Marc Blumberg. You're not going to get a free ride on the stand."

"I want you to tell Arrington that I'm sorry. That I'm fond of her. That I don't want to do it."

"Don't want to do it?" Stone asked, growing angry. "Then why did you talk to the police?"

"I felt I had to."

"We'll, you're an admirable citizen, Ms. Walters, but now I want you to get out of my way."

"Never mind," she said. "I'll leave." She turned, unlocked the door, opened it, and closed it behind her.

Stone locked the door. What the hell was wrong with the woman? He used the john, taking his time, then washed his hands and opened the door slowly. He peeked down the hall, saw no one, then left and went back to where Marc Blumberg was still standing.

"That took a long time," Marc said. "You all right?"

"I'm extremely pissed off," Stone said. He told Marc what had happened.

"Maybe she's crazy," Marc said. "Maybe that's our approach to questioning her. I'll put somebody on her and see if we can come up with some other erratic behavior."

"She said she saw Vance murdered, and she's going to testify to that."

"Well, at least we know what she's going to say on the stand."

There was a clinking of a knife on glass, and they turned toward the sound. Charlene was standing on the steps to the foyer; they made a little stage. She asked for everyone's attention, then a series of people came up and said a few words about Vanessa. They kept it light, but the crowd looked somber.

Finally, Charlene looked at Beverly Walters. "Beverly, I'm sure you'd like to say something; you and Vanessa were so close."

Walters looked down and shook her head, dabbing at her eyes with a tissue.

"Of course," Charlene said. "We all know how you feel. Everybody, please stay as long as you like. There'll be a light supper in a few minutes."

She stepped down and made her way across the room toward Stone and Marc Blumberg.

"You handled that gracefully," Stone said.

"It's about all I can do for Vanessa," Charlene replied.

Marc spoke up. "Is Beverly Walters usually so reticent?"

Charlene snorted. "Beverly would normally not miss a chance to be the center of attention."

Marc nodded at the two police officers across the room. "I think she's getting quite a lot of attention," he said.

Stone looked at the two men, who had eyes for no one except Beverly Walters.

⤜ Chapter 50 ⤛

Stone and Charlene sat on the patio overlooking the sea. The guests had all gone, and they were having a cold supper.

"Tell me everything you know about Beverly Walters," he said.

"Haven't I already?"

"I've heard bits and pieces, but I'd like to hear what you know about her."

Charlene took a deep breath, swelling her lovely breasts. "Well, she came out here as an actress. She'd had a nice part on Broadway, and somebody at Centurion saw her and brought her out to test her. She had a few small parts, but she didn't seem to be going anywhere, then she met Gordon, her husband, on a picture, and pretty soon they were married."

"Did she screw around after she was married?"

"Sugar, you have to remember where you are. It would have been a lot more noteworthy if she *hadn't* screwed around, and nobody took note of that."

"Did she ever sleep with Vance?"

"If she did she never talked about it, but I wouldn't be surprised. Quite apart from Vance's talents as a lover, lots of women would have slept with him just to be able to say they did. Beverly would have been one of those."

"But she never said she did?"

"Not to me, and I suppose, not to any woman I know, because I would have heard about it within minutes."

"Lots of people knew Vance slept around?"

"They did before he got married, but after that, he became a lot more discreet."

"He didn't stop sleeping around, he just became more discreet about it?"

"That's about right. As part of being more discreet, he might have slept with fewer women. I never discussed it with him."

"I don't mean to pry, but when you and Vance were sleeping together, it was after he was married?"

"Sure, you mean to pry, but I don't mind. Yes, it was afterward."

"Where did you meet?"

"My RV or his."

"Ever at his bungalow?"

"Once or twice, late, after Betty had gone for the day."

"He wouldn't have wanted Betty to know?"

"I guess not. Word was, they once had a thing going. Maybe he thought she might be jealous."

Stone picked at his salmon and sipped his wine.

"What are you thinking, Stone?"

"Sorry, I was just letting my mind wander. Sometimes that helps me sort things out."

"Have you sorted something out?"

"No."

Charlene laughed.

"Beverly did something strange tonight."

"What did she do?"

Stone told her about the incident in the powder room.

"She was probably hoping you'd ravish her on the spot."

"No, it wasn't like that."

Charlene shrugged. "Did you talk to Dr. Lansing Drake at all?"

"No," Stone replied.

"He seemed to get a little skittish when I mentioned you."

"He behaved oddly at dinner last night, too. Why might he feel uncomfortable around me?"

"Damned if I know."

"Tell me about Dr. Drake."

"He's the doctor of choice in Beverly Hills and Bel-Air," Charlene said. "Why?"

"He's pretty easygoing; if somebody wants a Valium prescription, he's not going to give them a hard time about it. He knows how to keep his mouth shut, too. I'll bet he's cured more cases of the clap and gotten more people secretly into rehab than any doctor in town."

"Is he a decent doctor?"

"There are jokes about that, but I've never heard anybody say he really screwed up on something. I mean, he hasn't killed anybody that I know of. I think his principal talent is that he knows when to refer somebody to a specialist. That's his motto: When in doubt, refer. He can't get into too much trouble that way."

"I gather he's pretty social."

"Oh, he doesn't miss too many parties. He's not on everybody's A list, but he probably makes most B-plus lists. I think that's where he gets most of his business. People sidle up to him at a party and ask him about a rash, or something, and the next thing you know they're his patients. He's very charming."

"Did Vance go to him?"

"Oh, Vance thought he was Albert fucking Schweitzer. I've heard him talk about Lansing in the most glowing terms."

"So Vance trusted him."

"Implicitly."

"Is he your doctor?"

"For anything up to and including a skinned knee. I've got a gynecologist who gets most of my business. I'm a healthy girl; I've never really been sick with anything worse than the flu."

"I'm glad to hear it."

"As a matter of fact, I'm feeling particularly healthy tonight. You don't have to be anywhere, do you?"

"I'm happy where I am," he replied.

She stood up, took him by the hand, and led him into the house and toward her bedroom. Once there, she unzipped her dress and let it fall to the floor.

"Promise you won't ruin *my* health," he said.

"Sugar," she replied, working on his buttons, "I'm not making any such promise."

"Be gentle," he said.

"Maybe," she replied, leading him toward the bed, and not by the hand.

Chapter 51

Stone made it back to the Centurion bungalow, tired but happy, around ten A.M. Louise was at her desk, and she handed him a message from Brandy Garcia.

"He works from an answering machine," Stone said to the secretary. "Call and leave a message that he can reach me now."

"Dino Bacchetti called, too. He said you have the number."

"Right, I'll call him." Stone shaved and changed into fresh clothes, then went into the study. He was about to call Dino when Louise buzzed him.

"Brandy Garcia on line one."

Stone picked up the phone. "Hello?"

Garcia wasted no time on pleasantries. "I thought you should know that our mutual acquaintance from Tijuana is back in town."

"What?"

"Apparently, his sister—the one he lived with when he was here—is sick, and he's taking care of her kids."

"I thought you told him to lose himself."

"I did, my friend, but I can't follow him all over Mexico to make sure he stays down there."

"Do you have a number for his sister's house?"

"Got a pencil?"

"Shoot." Stone jotted down the number. "Call him and tell him to keep his head down."

"Will do, Chief." Garcia hung up.

Stone sighed. It was bad enough that Beverly Walters was going to testify, but if Cordova appeared in court, he might lend credence to her story. He called Marc Blumberg.

"Morning, Stone. Where'd you sleep last night?"

"None of your business," Stone replied.

Blumberg laughed. "You seemed to be hanging back when everybody else was leaving."

"We had dinner, and that's all you need to know."

"Okay, okay, what's up?"

"Our friend Cordova has turned up in L.A. again."

"That's bad," Blumberg replied. "I filed a motion to dismiss this morning. I hope we can get a hearing scheduled before the police find him."

"The one thing we've got going for us is that the police aren't looking for Cordova, although he doesn't know that."

"Do you know where to find him?"

"Yes. I can get a message to him if the police suddenly get interested."

"You want to prep Arrington, or shall I?"

"You'd better do it; she's not speaking to me at the moment."

"Oh? What went wrong?"

"It's too complicated to go into. Let's just say that she got angry about something she didn't have a good reason to be angry about."

"Stone, you are the only man I know whose relations with women are more complicated than mine."

"That's not how I planned it, believe me. Will you call Arrington?"

"Okay, whatever you say."

"How are you planning to handle Beverly Walters?"

"I'm planning to shred her on the stand."

"She may have been sleeping with Vance; I'm still working on finding out."

"Even if she wasn't, I think I'll ask her anyway. Several times, maybe. Anything we can do to damage her credibility puts us one step closer to getting Arrington out of this."

"I think you're right. Let me make another call to see if I can find out more."

"Let me know when you do."

"See you later." Stone hung up and buzzed Louise. "What time is it in Hawaii?" he asked.

"Three or four hours earlier than here, I think."

"You've got Betty Southard's hotel number, haven't you?"

"She's moved to a rented cottage, and I have the number."

"Go ahead and get her on the phone, and let's hope she's an early riser."

"I'll buzz you."

Stone sat thinking about Beverly Walters and Felipe Cordova and what they could mean to the charges against Arrington. The phone buzzed, and Stone picked it up. "Betty?"

"Aloha, stranger," she said.

"Hope I didn't get you up."

"You know I'm an early riser," she said. "Wish you were here to get my heart started in the morning."

"A pleasant thought, but I'm still needed here. You enjoying yourself?"

"So much that I'm thinking of making a permanent move here. Will you come see me?"

"When you least expect it."

"Why'd you call? Surely not just to wake me up."

"I wanted to ask you something."

"Go ahead."

"Beverly Walters. Did she and Vance ever have a thing?"

"Why do you ask?"

"Because she's the key prosecution witness against Arrington, and I need to know as much as possible about her."

"Vance didn't keep much from me, but he never mentioned Beverly in those terms. Anyway, he was pretty tight with her husband, Gordon."

"If he was sleeping with her, where do you think it might have happened?"

"In his RV, more than likely, but just about any place that was convenient."

"Did he ever bring her to the bungalow?"

"Not when I was around, but he didn't do that with his women, except maybe after hours. A few mornings there were signs in the bungalow that someone had been there."

"When was the last time you can remember?"

"No more than a day or two before he was shot."

"Did you ever find anything in the bungalow belonging to a woman?"

"Once or twice—a lipstick or a scarf. When I did, I just left it on Vance's desk and said nothing about it."

"Anything that you could identify as belonging to Walters?"

"Come to think of it, the lipstick I found was one I've seen her wear, but I suppose that's a pretty tenuous connection, isn't it?"

"Yes, it is. Nothing else?"

"Nothing I can think of. I'll call you if I think of anything else."

"Thanks, I'd appreciate that. It could be important."

"How's Arrington bearing up?"

"I don't know, to tell you the truth. She's not communicating with me at the moment."

"Uh oh; I don't want to know about that."

"Good, because I'm not going to tell you about it. What do you have planned for the day?"

"The beach, of course. Can't you hear the surf over the phone?"

"You know, I think I can."

"That's all you need to know about my day."

"You take care, then."

"Bye-bye."

Stone hung up. That had been a disappointment. He called Dino.

"Yes?"

"It's me. How's it going?"

"I'm having a lovely time sitting around the pool, while Mary Ann and Arrington talk and giggle."

"Any thaw there?"

"A little, maybe; I'll have to pump Mary Ann. My guess is, though, if you want her to talk to you, you're going to have to make the first move."

"What did I do?"

"Nothing, nothing, just got married. That seems to have disappointed her."

"But . . ."

"Listen, Stone, you don't have to convince me. She's behaved badly and won't admit it. I'm just saying that you're going to have to make the first move, whether it's logical or not. It's how women work."

"Tell me about it."

"I shouldn't have to. What's up with you? Anything happening?"

"Marc Blumberg has filed for a motion to dismiss the charges against Arrington, so he'll probably turn up over there pretty soon to prep her for her testimony."

"What are the chances of shutting this thing down early?"

"In my view? Two: slim and very slim."

"I guess you've got to make the effort."

"You bet. I don't want to hang around L.A. for another six months waiting for this to come to trial. I'm getting homesick for a little New York grit in my teeth, you know?"

"Yeah? Funny, I'm getting to like it here. Think the LAPD could use another detective?"

"You wouldn't last a month out here, Dino. It's all too easy; you're a New Yorker; you like things tough."

"Call Arrington and make nice, then maybe we can all have dinner together."

"Without Dolce?"

"Without Mrs. Barrington."

"Don't say that."

"Call her."

"Okay; see you later." Stone hung up and stared at the phone. He might as well get it over with.

⁓ Chapter 52 ⸙

Manolo answered the phone. "Good morning, Manolo," Stone said. "It's Stone Barrington. May I speak with Mrs. Calder?"

"Good morning, Mr. Barrington; it's good to hear from you. I'll see if she's in."

She'd damned well better be in, Stone thought. Next time she decamps I'll let her wait out the trial in jail. "Thank you."

She kept him waiting for a long time. This wasn't going to be easy. "Yes?" she said finally, coldly.

"Good morning."

"What can I do for you?"

"You can be civil, for a start."

"I'm listening; what do you want?"

"I invited Dino and Mary Ann out here as much for me as for you. I'd like to see them. Shall we try dinner again?"

"Oh, I do hope Mrs. Barrington can make it."

"I hope not. And she's Mrs. Barrington only in her own mind, nowhere else."

"How did that happen, Stone? Did you get drunk and wake up married?"

"I could ask you the same question, but I think we should do our best to put our respective marriages behind us and get on with our lives."

Long silence. "You have a point," she admitted finally.

"If it makes any difference, I was on the rebound," he said.

There was another silence while she thought about that. "Come for dinner at seven," she said, then hung up.

Stone chose his clothes carefully—a tan tropical wool suit, brown alligator loafers, and a pale yellow silk shirt, open at the collar, as a concession to L.A. Arrington had always responded to well-dressed men, and he wanted very much for her to respond. He entered through the front gate, the TV crew having departed for more sordid pastures, and parked in front of the house.

Manolo greeted him, beaming. "Good evening, Mr. Barrington," he said. "It's good to see you back here." There was relief in his voice, as if he'd feared that Stone might never be allowed in the house again.

"Good evening, Manolo," Stone said.

"They're having drinks out by the pool; shall I pour you a Wild Turkey?"

"I feel like something breezier," Stone said. "How about a vodka gimlet, straight up?"

"Of course."

Stone followed Manolo down the broad central hallway, past the spot where Vance Calder had bled out his life on the tiles, and emerged into the garden, past the spot where Felipe Cordova had left his big shoeprint. Where had Beverly Walters stood? he wondered.

Dino waved from a seat near the pool bar, where he, Mary Ann, and Arrington sat in thickly cushioned bamboo chairs around a coffee table. He gave Dino a wave and pecked the two women on the cheek as if there had never been a scene at their last meeting. Manolo went behind the bar and expertly mixed Stone's drink, then brought it to him in a frosty glass on a silver tray.

"Thank you, Manolo," he said.

"That looks good," Arrington said. She pulled his hand toward her and sipped from his drink. "Oh, a vodka gimlet. Let's all have one, Manolo." Manolo went back to work while, at the other end of the pool, Isabel set a table for dinner.

"I thought we'd dine outside," Arrington said. "Such a perfect California evening."

"It certainly is," Stone agreed. This was going well, and he was relieved.

"You know, before I married Vance I had always hated L.A., but evenings like this changed my mind. I mean, there's smog and traffic, and everybody talks about nothing but the business, but on evenings like this, you could almost forgive them."

"I think Dino has caught the L.A. bug, too," Stone said, smiling. "He was inquiring only today whether the LAPD would have him."

"What?" Mary Ann said. "Dino live out here? He wouldn't last a month."

"My very words to him."

"Maybe I wouldn't have to cop for a living," Dino said. "Maybe I'd become an actor. I could do all those parts Joe Pesci does, and better, too."

"You know, Dino, I believe you could," Arrington laughed. "Want me to call Lou Regenstein at Centurion and get you a screen test?"

"Nah, I don't test, and I don't audition," Dino said, waving a hand. "My agent would never let me do that . . . if I had an agent."

"That's it, Dino," Arrington said. "Play hard to get. Movie people want most the things they can't have. Your price would double."

Then, it seemed to Stone, the clock began to run backward, and they all became the people they had been before all this had happened. They were old friends, easy together, enjoying the evening and each other. The gimlets seemed to help, too. Soon they were laughing loudly at small jokes. Then Manolo called them to dinner.

No soup this time, Stone reflected; nothing to be dumped in his lap, and no Dolce to screw up their evening. They began with seared foie gras, crisp on the outside, melting inside, with a cold Château Coutet, a sweet, white Bordeaux. That was followed by a thick, perfect veal chop and a bottle of Beringer Reserve Cabernet Sauvignon. Dessert was an orange crème brûlée and more of the Coutet.

Coffee was served in Vance's study, before a fire, as the desert night had become chilly. The women excused themselves, and Stone and Dino declined Manolo's offer of Vance's cigars.

"Looks like the bloom is back on the rose," Dino said.

"The atmosphere is certainly warmer," Stone agreed.

"Arrington and Mary Ann spent the afternoon talking about you, I think. Mary Ann probably told her how lost you were without her, and how when Dolce came along, you were ripe for the picking."

"That's embarrassingly close to the truth," Stone said. "Have you heard anything from Dolce?"

"She and Mary Ann had breakfast together at the Bel-Air this morning."

"Is that where she's staying?"

"She's been cagey about where she's staying. I don't like it, frankly; I don't think this is over."

"Neither do I."

"Are you carrying?"

"No, and I don't know why I asked you to bring a weapon out here. A moment of paranoia, I guess."

"If Dolce is mad at you, it's not paranoid to go armed. If I were you, I wouldn't leave home without it."

"I'd feel a fool, wearing a gun these days," Stone said. "It took some getting used to when I was on the force, but now . . . well, it just seems, I don't know, belligerent."

"You've never liked guns, have you?"

"No, I guess not. I mean, I admire a well-made tool, and I guess that's what a gun is. Some of them are beautiful things, like the Walther, but I never liked the Glocks; they're ugly."

The women came back, and Manolo poured their coffee.

"Did Marc Blumberg see you today?" Stone asked Arrington.

"He came in time for lunch, and by the time he left, I was 'prepped,' as he put it. Sounds as though someone had shaved my pubic hair and painted my belly orange."

Dino made a face. "Such imagery! Only a woman could put it that way."

"Men are such babies," Mary Ann said. "So easily shocked. Dino, you couldn't make it as a woman for a single day."

"And I wouldn't want to try," Dino said.

They chatted for another hour, then Stone rose and announced his departure. Dino was stifling yawns by this time, too, and he and Mary Ann departed for the guest house.

Arrington walked Stone to the door. "I'm sorry about my behavior last time," she said. "I realize now that it wasn't your fault, that you were the victim."

"Hardly that," Stone said. "I knew what I was getting into."

"No, you didn't," she said at the door, resting her head on his shoulder. "You never do."

Stone put a finger under her chin, raised her head, and kissed her lightly. "I'm glad you and I are all right again."

"So am I."

"If it's any help, I'm already working on an Italian divorce."

"Any kind will do."

"I'd better go."

"Good night, sweet prince."

"And angels sing me to my rest? Not just yet, I hope."

He walked toward the car, then he stopped and turned. She was still standing in the doorway. "Arrington?"

"Yes?"

"I seem to recall that you never wore terrycloth robes."

"What a good memory you have. I always liked plain cotton or silk. What an odd thing to remember."

"Oh, I remember a lot more," he said, as he waved good night and got into the car.

All the way back to Centurion he thought about what she used to wear.

≈ **Chapter 53** ≈

The following morning Marc Blumberg called and asked Stone to come to his office to discuss the motion to dismiss. Stone left Centurion and on his way passed the spot where he'd had the flat tire, reminding him that he had left the damaged tire at a service station for repair. He stopped to pick it up, and as he opened the trunk he saw Felipe Cordova's Nikes. He'd completely forgotten about them.

He arrived at Blumberg's office and was shown in and given coffee, while Marc finished a meeting in his conference room. Shortly, the lawyer came into his office and sat down at his desk.

"So," said Stone, "what's your plan? Who are we going to call?"

"Nobody," Marc replied. "That's my plan."

"Come again?"

"My plan is to cross-examine the prosecution's witnesses to within an inch of their lives. After all, it's they who have to make a case, not we."

"You don't think we ought to try?" Stone asked doubtfully.

"Let me ask you something, Stone: Can we prove Arrington didn't shoot Vance?"

"Maybe not."

"If we could prove she didn't do it, we'd be home free, but we can't. So we're going to have to cast so much doubt on the prosecution's case that the judge will throw it out."

"And how are we going to do that?" Stone asked.

"I know Beverly Walters better than you," Marc replied.

"How well, Marc?"

"Well enough, trust me."

"All right, I'll trust you."

"Have you got any other ideas about how we might proceed?"

Stone took a deep breath. "I think we ought to call Felipe Cordova."

"I thought he was lost in darkest Mexico."

"He was, but he's back in L.A. Brandy Garcia gave me a heads up."

"Doesn't it bother you that the prosecution would call Cordova, if they knew what we knew about his actions that night?"

"No."

"Stone, we're going to have Beverly Walters on the stand saying she saw Arrington shoot Vance, while Arrington doesn't remember *what* she did or didn't do. Cordova is just going to back up Beverly's story, isn't he?"

"I don't think so," Stone said.

"And why not?"

"A couple of reasons. First, Vanessa Pike told me she drove Beverly to the Calder house, and that Beverly saw what happened from the rear of the house, at the doors to the pool."

"Wait a minute. What Vanessa told you was that she drove *somebody* to Vance's; she didn't say who."

"But we know it was Beverly."

"How do we know that?"

"Because Charlene Joiner says that the two of them left her house together, after a day lying around the pool."

"At what time?"

"At just about the time it would have taken for them to drive to the Calder house and arrive at the time Vance was being shot."

"Will Charlene testify to that?"

"Yes, to that and more."

"What else?"

"She'll testify that Beverly was wearing a terrycloth robe over a bathing suit when she left her house."

"So?"

"Cordova says he saw a woman next to Vance's body, and she was wearing a terrycloth robe."

"Did he see her face?"

"No."

"Then it could have been Arrington."

"Arrington doesn't wear terrycloth robes. She likes plain cotton or silk."

"Can we prove that?"

"We can call her maid, who would know her wardrobe intimately, and who got her out of the tub and into a robe."

"I like it," Blumberg said. "But how are we going to put Beverly in the house?"

"I think she'll admit being outside, and it's a short step from the back door into the hallway where Vance died. And there's this, Marc: I'd be willing to bet that Cordova is not mentioned in Beverly's story, because she didn't see him."

"Yeah, but can Cordova prove he was there?"

"The police can; they've got a photograph of his shoeprint."

"But you have the shoe."

"Yes, it's in the trunk of my car. I bought the shoes from Cordova in Mexico."

"Nikes, weren't they?"

"Right."

"There are millions of pairs of Nikes out there."

"There aren't millions of size twelves, and remember, Cordova's have a cut across the heel of the sole that shows up in the photograph."

"You know, Stone, I think we're awfully close to being able to prove that Arrington didn't kill Vance."

"Close but not quite there. Cordova didn't see Beverly shoot him."

"And we don't have a motive."

"Or the weapon."

"Shit!" Blumberg said. "What could her motive be?"

"I think they were sleeping together. It could be that he told her to get lost, and she reacted badly."

"Could be, but how do we prove that?"

"I wish Vanessa were still alive; she could probably tell us."

"I'd give a million bucks for that gun with her prints on it."

"So would I," Stone agreed, "but it doesn't look as though we're ever going to find it."

"I'd give a lot for a witness who could put Beverly in the sack with Vance, too."

"Oddly enough, Beverly is known among her friends as a blabbermouth, but apparently, she never blabbed about a relationship with Vance."

"Except maybe to Vanessa."

"Maybe, but we'll never know."

Marc suddenly stood up. "Jesus," he said, "I just thought of something. Vanessa kept a diary."

"How do you know that?"

"She kept it in her handbag, and she'd write in it at odd moments. I tried to read it once, but it was one of those things like high school girls have, with a tiny lock on it."

"I know the kind you mean," Stone said.

Marc sat down again. "But it must have been in the house with her; it would have burned."

"I think I can find out about that," Stone said.

"How? From the investigating officer?"

"I have a friend in the department."

"Use my phone," Marc said, pointing across the room to a phone on a coffee table.

Stone went to the phone and dialed Rick Grant's direct line.

"Captain Grant."

"Rick, it's Stone Barrington. Can we meet somewhere?"

"I don't think that's a good idea, Stone."

"Why not?"

"You're defending Arrington Calder, and, I have to tell you, the investigators on the Vanessa Pike case are looking at you funny."

"All right, then will you do this for me? Call those officers and ask them if they found Vanessa's diary in their search of the premises after the fire."

"Why?"

"Because, if it still exists, it may have some information about Vance Calder's murder."

"If that's true, then it would have to go to Durkee and his partner, too."

"All I want is a copy. We could subpoena it, if we have to."

"All right, I'll check on it and get back to you."

"Thanks, Rick." He hung up and turned back to Marc. "If we hit paydirt in the diary, then we can demand that the cops get a search warrant for Beverly's house. Maybe the gun is there."

"Wouldn't that be nice?" Blumberg said.

Stone stood up suddenly.

"Where are you going?"

"To Vanessa's house. I don't think I feel comfortable with the cops seeing that diary before we do."

"Let me know what you find."

Stone headed for the door.

Chapter 54

Stone drove slowly up Vanessa's street and down again, making sure that nobody from the police or fire departments was at the site. Satisfied, he parked across the street and got out of the car.

The house was a sad shell, with most of the roof gone and with large gaps in the walls. He ducked under the yellow police tape and stepped through one of the gaps into what had been the living room. The acrid smell of burned dwelling filled his nostrils, and with a shudder, he thought he detected a faint whiff of seared meat. A few charred sticks of what had been furniture remained in the room and the remains of the sofa were recognizable. He recalled that he and Vanessa had sat there, sipping their drinks and talking, no more than an hour before she had died.

He walked on a runner of plastic sheeting that had been placed there like a sidewalk by the fire department investigators, to avoid disturbing evidence. As he moved through the rooms he noticed that the ash around him had a smooth surface, and telltale marks showed that the debris had been raked, in search of evidence. If anything were left of Vanessa's diary, which he doubted, then the investigators would surely have found it. His trip here had been for naught. Her purse and the diary had probably been in the kitchen, and there was no longer a kitchen.

Then he turned and saw something he hadn't seen before: the garage. He hadn't seen it, because on his last visit, the house had been in the way, but now he could look through a giant, charred hole and see the little building. It seemed older than the house, or maybe it had just not been updated over the years, the way the house had been. It looked like something out of the twenties, a meager, clapboard structure with two doors, the old-fashioned kind that featured a brass handle in the middle of the door. One turned the handle, lifted, and the door rose. Surely electric openers would have been added by this time.

He tried the doors. The first didn't move, but the second operated as it had been designed to. It took some effort, but he got the door halfway open and stepped under it. He tried a light switch on the wall, but nothing happened. The power had either been interrupted by the fire or turned off by the fire department.

A single car, a Mazda Miata, was in the garage. It was red, small, and cute, and he reflected that Vanessa would have looked good in it, her hair blowing in the wind. The top was up, and he tried the passenger door: locked. He walked around the car and tried the driver's door, with success. He found the trunk release and popped the lid. There was a spare, flat, and the jack, and an old pair of sneakers—nothing else.

He went back to the driver's door and tried to sit in the seat, but found himself jammed, until he could locate the release and move the seat backward. The courtesy lights illuminated the interior, and he looked around.

Women made a terrible mess of cars, he thought. The most fastidious woman seemed unable to avoid the buildup of used Kleenex, fast-food wrappers, and old paper cups in her automobile. He checked the tiny glove compartment, which held only a couple of parking tickets and a lipstick tube. There were some road maps in a door pocket, and nothing behind the sun visors. He got out of the car, and as he did, moved the driver's seat forward and checked behind it. Nothing there. He reached across and felt behind the passenger seat, and he came in contact with something made of canvas.

He reached over, unlocked the passenger door from the inside, then walked around the car and opened the door. He moved the seat forward and extracted a beat-up canvas carryall bearing the logo of a bookstore chain. He set it on top of the car and checked its contents. Inside was a thick book on interior design, a wrinkled bikini, a bottle of suntan lotion, and a leather-covered book with a binding flap that ended in a brass tip secured by a tiny lock. Stamped on the front of the book, in gilded letters, was "My Diary." If the cops had thought to search the car, they had done a lousy job, Stone thought. He tried opening it, but the lock held.

He put the carryall back where he had found it, closed the car doors, returned the garage door to its original position, and walked back to his car. He was tempted to try to open the diary here, but he decided it might be best to do it elsewhere. He drove back to Marc Blumberg's building.

He walked into Marc's office, smiling, holding up the leather diary.

Marc took it and turned it over in his hands. "It's not burned at all," he said.

"It wasn't in the house," Stone replied. "I found it in her car, in the garage."

"Can you pick a lock, or shall I pry it open?" Marc asked.

"Hang on a minute; what's our legal position? I took this from her car with nobody's permission. Given that, do we want to break into it?"

"We can open it with the permission of her executor," Marc said.

"Do you know who he is?"

Marc grinned. "You're looking at him. Here's a paper clip."

Stone straightened the wire and began probing the lock. It was simple; one turn and it was open. He set the diary on Marc's desk and began flipping pages, while the two of them bent over it.

"Funny, I don't recognize any names," Marc said. "We knew a lot of the same people."

"Maybe she's giving people code names; if somebody got into the diary, it might save embarrassment."

"Let's start at the end and work backward," Marc said. They began reading; Vanessa had written in a small, but very legible, hand.

"Look, in the last entry she says she's going to Palm Springs to 'Herbert's' house. I wonder why she called me Herbert?"

"I guess you just look like a Herbert, Marc."

"Yeah." He flipped back further in the book. "There's mention here of a Hilda, quite often. Think that could be Beverly?"

"We need a context to figure this out," Stone said, turning pages. "Here, the pages are dated; this is the day Vance was shot. There's mention of Hilda, Magda, and Jake."

"Jake was Vance's character in one of his recent movies," Marc said. "*Fear Everything*, I think."

"She mentions lunch around the pool at Magda's. That must be Charlene Joiner. Here we go!" He began reading aloud. "'When we left Magda's, Hilda insisted on going to Jake's house, which I thought was nuts. She knew about this service entrance at the rear of the property. I wouldn't get out of the car, but Hilda, bold as brass, walked to the house. Hilda has admitted screwing Jake, but, Jesus, I never thought she'd have the guts to go to his house. She must have been gone ten minutes, then there was a noise, and a minute later, she came running back, breathless, and told me to get the hell out of there. She wouldn't say what happened but I'd be willing to bet that she ran into Mrs. Jake.

God, that must have been embarrassing! She was still breathing hard when I dropped her off at her house. I've never seen her so discombobulated. I know I'll eventually hear about this from somebody else, even though she won't discuss it. Hilda can never keep her mouth shut for long—she'll either brag about this, or try for sympathy. Jesus, I'm so glad I didn't go with her!'"

"Well, *that's* pretty clear," Marc said, "but I'd feel a lot better if she had just said that she'd watched Beverly shoot Vance."

"All we've really got here is what Vanessa told me."

"Yeah, we've got to get Beverly to admit that she's Hilda, or get corroboration from Charlene on the stand that they were at her house that day."

Stone was flipping forward through the pages, looking at the dates after Vance's murder. "Look at this," he said. "'Hilda keeps trying to tell me something, but she can't get it out. She seems very guilty about something. Having seen the papers, it's not hard to figure out that Jake was killed while we were at his house, but Hilda won't tell me what she saw there. I keep thinking maybe I should go to the police. I've got to ask Herbert about this, but how am I going to do that without betraying Hilda's confidence?'"

"I wish to God she had asked me," Marc said. "Maybe I could have done something to prevent her death."

"Wait a minute," Stone said, "are you thinking that Beverly set the fire at Vanessa's, because she knew too much?"

"It wouldn't be the first murder that was committed to cover up another murder," Marc said.

Stone sat down heavily, feeling enormously relieved.

"You look kind of funny, Stone," Marc commented. "Was it something I said?"

"Yes, it was," Stone replied. "I had never connected Beverly with Vanessa's death, but what you're saying makes perfectly good sense. I'm afraid that I thought someone else . . ." He stopped himself.

"That someone else murdered Vanessa?"

Stone nodded.

"Who?"

"I'd rather not say. If you're right, then it doesn't make any difference."

"I guess not." Marc picked up the phone.

"Who are you calling?"

"The D.A. I want him to see this diary. If we're lucky, maybe we won't need the motion hearing."

"Marc," Stone said, "we don't have anything we didn't before. Beverly has obviously already told the D.A. that she was at Vance's that night; otherwise, how else could she be a witness?"

"You're right, but I have to turn this over to either the D.A. or the police, anyway, and it at least independently establishes that Beverly was there. She won't know what's in the diary, so maybe I can use it to rattle her at the hearing."

"Call the D.A.," Stone said.

⤳ Chapter 55 ⤳

The cab crawled up the street. From the rear seat Stone checked the house numbers, but most of them were missing, like a lot of other things in this neighborhood. Stone had taken a taxi, because he did not want to park a Mercedes SL600 on this block.

As it turned out, the house number was unnecessary, because Felipe Cordova was sitting on his sister's front porch, drinking from a large beer bottle, while two small children played on the patchy front lawn.

"Wait for me," Stone said to the driver.

"How long you going to be?" the driver asked. "I don't like it around here."

"A couple of minutes; I'll make it worth your while."

"Okay, mister, but hurry, okay?"

Stone got out of the cab, let himself through the chain-link front gate, and approached the house.

Cordova watched him come, curious at first, until he recognized Stone. "Hey, Mr. Lawyer," he said, raising the quart in salute. "You back to see me again?"

Stone pulled up a rickety porch chair and sat down. "Yes, Felipe, and I've brought good news."

"I always like good news," Felipe replied happily.

"The police are no longer looking for you," Stone said.

"Hey, that *is* good news."

"But you and I have a little official business."

Cordova's eyes narrowed. "Official?"

"Nothing to worry about," Stone said, taking the subpoena from his pocket and handing it to the man. "I just need you to testify in court."

Cordova examined the document. "The day after tomorrow?"

"That's right. Ten A.M.; the address is there." He pointed.

"What's this about?"

"I just want you to answer the same questions I asked you in Mexico. And I want the same answers."

"How much do I get paid?"

"That's the bad news, Felipe; I can't pay a witness. That could get us both put in jail."

Cordova frowned. "I'm going to have expenses, man."

"You can send a bill for your expenses, your *reasonable* expenses, like cab fare and lunch, to this lawyer." He handed Cordova Marc Blumberg's card. "See that it doesn't come to more than a hundred bucks."

"Suppose I don't want to testify?"

"Then the police *will* be looking for you, and if you leave the country, you won't be able to come back. The border patrol will have you in their computer, and you don't want that, do you?"

Cordova shook his head.

"Relax, Felipe; there's nothing to this. When you get to the courthouse, you sit on a bench outside the courtroom until you're called, and then you take the stand, swear the oath on the Bible, and you answer questions."

"Just like on *Perry Mason*?"

"Just like that, except on *Perry Mason*, the witness is always the murderer. We know you're not the murderer; we just want you to tell about the woman you saw in the house, the one in the terrycloth bathrobe."

"Oh, yeah."

Stone stood up. "Be sure you remember that word, Felipe: *terrycloth*. I'll see you there at ten A.M. the day after tomorrow, and remember, that document means you *have* to testify or be arrested. You understand?"

Cordova nodded.

Stone patted him on the back and went back to his cab. "Okay," he said, "back to Centurion Studios." He took out his cell phone and called Marc Blumberg. "He's been served."

"You think he'll show, or should I send somebody out there?"

"He'll show."

When Stone arrived at the studio bungalow, Dino and Mary Ann were waiting for him.

"So this was Vance's cottage?" Mary Ann asked while being shown around.

"This was his office and dressing room," Stone replied. "Of course, he had an RV that served as a dressing room, too. All the stars seem to have them."

A young man pulled a golf cart to the front door and got out.

"Here's your tour guide," Stone said.

"Dino, don't you want to go?"

"I've already seen enough; I'll hang out with Stone," Dino replied.

"Then we'll get some dinner," Stone said. The phone rang, and Louise answered it.

"Stone, it's for you; the lady sounds upset."

Stone went into the study and picked up the phone. "Hello?"

"Stone, it's Charlene," she whispered.

"Why are you whispering?"

"Somebody just took a shot at me."

"Where are you?"

"At home. Somebody fired right through the sliding doors to the pool."

"Are you hurt?"

"No."

"Call nine-one-one. I'll be there as fast as I can."

"Hurry."

Stone hung up the phone. "Come on," he said to Dino. "I'll explain on the way. Louise, when Mrs. Bacchetti gets back, tell her we'll be back soon, all right?"

"Sure."

Stone grabbed the Walther automatic and its shoulder holster from a desk drawer, then ran for the car with Dino right behind him.

"What's this about?" Dino asked as they cleared the front gate and turned into the boulevard.

"You're about to meet a movie star," Stone said.

When they pulled up in front of the Malibu Colony house, there were no police cars in sight. Stone wondered about that, but he was relieved that there was no ambulance, either.

The front door was ajar, and Stone walked in cautiously, stopping to listen. He heard nothing. It was getting dark outside, and there were no lights on in the house. "Charlene?" he called out.

"Stone?" her voice came from somewhere at the back of the house.

Stone walked quickly down the hallway, followed by Dino. "In here," Charlene's voice said from somewhere to the right.

They turned into the sitting room of the master suite. Charlene was crouched behind the little bar, and she had a nine-millimeter automatic pistol in her hand. She rushed to Stone and threw an arm around him. She was naked. "I'm so glad you're here," she said, the gun at her side.

"This is my friend Dino Bacchetti," Stone said.

"Nice to meet you," Dino said, looking her up and down. He reached out and took the pistol from her, removed the clip, and ejected a cartridge from the chamber.

"Why don't you get into some clothes," Stone said.

She ran into the bedroom.

Stone looked around. The big glass door to the pool side patio had shattered, and glass was everywhere.

Charlene returned, tying the sash on a dressing gown and wearing shoes.

"Where are the police?" Stone asked. "Surely they've had time to get here."

"I didn't call the police," she said.

"Why not?"

"I called you, instead."

"Start at the beginning, and tell me what happened."

"I was lying on the sofa there, reading a script, when I heard two shots. The glass door shattered, and I rolled off the sofa onto the floor and crawled over to the bar as fast as I could. My gun was in a drawer there."

"Dino, will you take a look around out back?"

"Sure."

"Wait a minute," Charlene said. She went to a wall switch and turned on the lights around the pool. "That'll help."

Dino slapped the clip back into Charlene's gun, worked the action, then went outside, the pistol hanging at his side.

"Do you think this was a serious attempt on your life?" Stone asked.

"Come here," Charlene replied, leading him around the sofa and pointing.

Stone looked at the two neat holes halfway down the back cushion.

"My head was right under the holes," Charlene said.

"You should have called the police immediately; they should be trying to find out who did this."

"I know who did it," Charlene said. "I saw her."

Stone's innards froze. "Her?"

"I believe these days she calls herself Mrs. Stone Barrington."

"Oh, Jesus," Stone said.

ꘖ Chapter 56 ꘖ

Stone found a paring knife behind the bar and cut into the sofa, just as Dino returned from the pool area.

"It's clear out there," he said. "The guy must have come up from the beach, since no traffic passed us on the way in here." He looked at what Stone was doing. "Whatcha got there?"

"Two slugs," Stone said, holding them up. "And it wasn't a guy."

Dino took the two lumps and looked closely at them. "Holy shit," he said.

"What?"

"These are mine." He held one up and pointed. "See? I made a mark there on each one, so if I ever got involved in a shootout, I'd know which slugs came from my weapon. These came from the thirty-two automatic I loaned you, Stone. How'd that happen?"

"It seems that Dolce took the gun from my house."

Dino groaned. "Are the cops coming?"

"I didn't call them," Charlene said.

"Why not?" Stone asked. "I told you to call nine-one-one."

"Two reasons: First, the tabloids would make my life hell if they found out that somebody shot up my house; second, I know who her father is."

Stone nodded. "All right."

"Also, once I had the Beretta in my hand, I figured I could handle her."

"Yeah, I thought I could handle her, too," Stone said. He turned to Dino. "Is Eduardo still in L.A.?"

Dino nodded. "At the Bel-Air."

Stone turned back to Charlene. "You want to come with us? Maybe you shouldn't stay here tonight."

"I'll come with you," she said. "I'll sleep at the studio in my RV; let me get some things." She disappeared into the bedroom again.

Stone picked up the phone, dialed the Bel-Air, and asked for Eduardo. "Yes?"

"Eduardo, it's Stone Barrington."

"Good evening, Stone."

"It's important that I come and see you right away."

"Of course; I'll be here."

"I'll be there in an hour."

"Have you had dinner?"

"No."

"I'll order something."

"Thank you." He hung up as Charlene emerged from her bedroom, wearing jeans and a sweater and carrying a small duffel.

They drove into town, not talking much, Charlene wedged into the space behind the two front seats. Stone dropped Dino at the bungalow. "Tell Mary Ann I'm sorry I can't have dinner, but don't tell her what's happened."

"I'll send her back to Arrington's with the car," Dino said. "I'm coming with you."

"You don't have to, Dino."

"I'm coming."

"I'll be right back." He drove Charlene to her RV and got her settled there. "Will you be all right here?"

"Sure, I will. The fridge is full; I'll eat something and watch TV. Will you come back later?"

"Probably not," Stone said. "I have to take care of this."

"I understand."

"And thanks for not calling the police."

She gave him a little kiss. "Go safely." She held up the Beretta. "You want this?"

"Thanks, I have my own." He left her and drove back to the bungalow for Dino. Mary Ann was about to leave in Arrington's station wagon, and Stone traded cars with her.

"Don't hurt her, Stone," Mary Ann said.

"I don't intend to," Stone replied.

Stone drove to the upper end of the Bel-Air Hotel complex and parked the station wagon. Followed by Dino, he found the upstairs suite and rang the bell. Eduardo, wearing a cashmere dressing gown, opened the door and ushered them in.

"Good evening, Stone, Dino," he said.

"I'm sorry to disturb you, Eduardo," Stone replied.

"Not at all. Come and have an aperitif; dinner will be here soon." He pointed at the bar in the living room. "Please help yourselves; I'll have a Strega." He picked up the phone and told room service there would be three for dinner, then he joined Stone and Dino.

Stone poured three Stregas and handed two of them to Eduardo and Dino. They raised their glasses and sipped.

"Come, sit," Eduardo said, motioning them to a sofa. "Why have you come to see me?" he asked when they were settled.

"Eduardo," Stone said, "I'm sorry to have to tell you this, but about two hours ago, Dolce attempted to kill Charlene Joiner, the actress you met the other evening at the Regensteins'.".

Eduardo winced, and his hand went to his forehead. His face showed no incredulity, simply painful resignation. "How did this occur?"

"Dolce apparently drove out to Malibu, parked her car, and approached Charlene's house from the beach. She fired two bullets through a sliding-glass door at Charlene, who was lying on a sofa, reading."

"Was Miss Joiner harmed?"

"No, only frightened."

"Do you think Dolce seriously tried to kill her?"

"I'm afraid I do, and she came very close."

"Where would Dolce have gotten a gun out here?" Eduardo asked. He seemed to be thinking quickly.

"Apparently, she took it from my house in New York without my knowledge. The gun belonged to Dino; he had loaned it to me."

"Does she still have the gun?"

Dino spoke up. "I saw no sign of it outside Miss Joiner's house, so I assume she does."

"Are the police involved?"

"No," Stone replied. "Charlene called me, instead of the police, and she has no intention of involving them."

"Thank God for that," Eduardo said. "This would have been so much more difficult."

"It's difficult enough," Stone said. "I feel responsible."

Eduardo shook his head. "No, no, Stone; something like this has been coming for a long time. If it hadn't been you, it would have been someone else."

"Why do you say that, Eduardo?" Dino asked. "Has she ever done anything like this before?"

Eduardo shrugged. "Since she was a little girl she always reacted violently if denied something she wanted."

The doorbell rang, and Dino jumped up. "I'll get it," he said.

"Dolce is all right most of the time," Eduardo said to Stone. "But she occasionally has these . . ." He didn't finish the sentence. "I had hoped that if she were happily married, she might be all right." He stopped talking while the waiter set the dining table, then he motioned for his guests to take seats.

He poured them some wine and waited until they had begun to eat their pasta before continuing. "She's seen a psychiatrist from time to time, but she always discontinued treatment after a few sessions. Her doctor advised me at one point to have her hospitalized for a while, but instead I took her to Sicily, and after some time there, she seemed better."

"What can I do to help?" Stone asked.

"I'll have to ask her doctor to recommend some place out here where she can be treated," Eduardo replied.

"I believe I know a good place," Stone said. He told Eduardo about the Judson Clinic and Arrington's stay there. "Would you like me to call Dr. Judson?"

"I would be very grateful if you would do so," Eduardo replied.

Stone left the table, called the clinic, and asked them to get in touch with Judson and have him telephone him at the Bel-Air. "I'm sure they'll be able to find him," he said when he had returned. "I was very impressed with Judson," he told Eduardo.

"Good," Eduardo said. "I'll get in touch with her own doctor and ask him to come out here and consult."

"I expect that, after treatment, she'll be all right," Stone said.

"I hope so," Eduardo replied, but he did not sound hopeful.

The phone rang and Stone answered it. "Hello?"

"May I speak with Stone Barrington, please?"

"Speaking."

"Stone, this is Jim Judson, returning your call."

Stone briefly explained the circumstances. "Do you think you could admit her to your clinic? Her father will be in touch with her doctor in New York and ask him to come out here."

"Of course," Judson replied. "When can you bring her to the clinic?"

"I'm not sure," Stone said. "We have to find her."

"Is she likely to be violent?"

"That's a possibility, but I don't really know."

"I'll have my people prepare, then. When you're ready to bring her here, just call the main number. I'll alert the front desk. If you need an ambulance or restraints, just let them know."

"Thank you, Jim; I'll be in touch." Stone hung up and returned to the table. "Dr. Judson will admit her," he said.

"But now we have to find her," Dino said. "Where do we look?"

Eduardo sighed. "I know where she is," he said sadly. "She's at the home of some friends of mine who are out of the country. We'll go there together."

Stone shook his head. "Dino and I can do this, Eduardo. Dolce is already angry with me; let's not make her angry with you, too."

Eduardo nodded. He found a pad, wrote down the address, and handed it to Stone. "I know I don't have to ask you to be gentle with her."

"Of course, I will be."

"But be careful," Eduardo said. "Don't allow her to endanger you or Dino."

Stone nodded and shook Eduardo's hand. "When this is done," Eduardo said, "there's something else I must talk with you about. Please call me."

"I'll call you as soon as we get Dolce to the clinic." He and Dino left before dessert arrived.

⌦ Chapter 57 ⌦

With Dino navigating, Stone found the house. It was on Mulholland Drive, high above the city, a contemporary structure anchored to the mountainside by a cradle of steel beams. The front door was at street level, but the rear deck, Stone noticed, was high above the rocky hillside. The house was dark, but there was a sedan with a Hertz sticker on the bumper parked in the carport.

Stone parked on the roadside and headed for the front door, but Dino stopped him.

"Give me a couple of minutes to get around back," he said.

"Dino, the back of the house is at least fifty feet off the ground."

"Just give me a couple of minutes."

Stone stood at the roadside and looked out at what was nearly an aerial view of Los Angeles—a carpet of lights arranged in a neat grid, disappearing into a distant bank of smog, with a new moon hanging overhead. The air seemed clearer up here, he thought, taking a deep breath of mountain air. How had it come to this? he wondered. What had started as a passionate affair and had ripened into something even better was now broken into many pieces, ruined by Dolce's obsession with him and his own bond with Arrington. He didn't know where this would all end, but nothing looked promising. He glanced at his watch, then started up the driveway to the house.

The house's entry was dark, but as he approached, his feet crunching on gravel, he saw that the front door was ajar. He stopped and listened for a moment. Music was coming from somewhere in the interior of the house—a Mozart symphony, he thought, though he couldn't place it. Some instinct told him not to ring the doorbell. He pushed the door open a little and stepped inside into a foyer. He could hear the music better now. It seemed to be coming from the living room, beyond. He moved forward. A little moon and starlight came through the sliding-glass doors to the deck, on the other side of the living room. He walked down a couple of steps. He could see the dim outlines of furniture. Then the silence was broken.

"I knew you'd come, Stone," Dolce said.

Stone jumped and looked around, but he couldn't find her. "Do you mind if we turn on a light?"

"I prefer the dark," she said. "It's better for what I have to do."

"You don't have to do anything, Dolce," he said. "Just relax; let's sit down and talk for a little while."

"Talking's over," she said. "We're way beyond talk, now."

"No, we can always talk."

The sound of two light pistol shots cracked the silence, and Stone dove for the floor, but not before the muzzle flash illuminated her, standing with her back to the fireplace, holding the pistol in both hands, combat-style.

"Stop it, Dolce!" he shouted. "Don't make things worse." He crawled behind a sofa, while wondering why his own gun was not in his hand.

She fired again, and he felt the thud against the sofa. "Things can always get worse," she said. Then he heard a sharp thud, and something large made of glass shattered against the stone floor.

"Stone?" It was Dino's voice. "Are you hit?"

"No," Stone replied. "Can I stand up?"

"Yes. She's out."

Stone stood up, found a lamp at the end of the sofa and switched it on. Dino stood before the fireplace, a short-barreled .38 in his hand, looking down. Stone came around the sofa and saw Dolce crumpled on the floor among the shards of the glass coffee table. Dino was standing on the hand that held the .32 automatic. Stone went to her and gently turned her over. "What did you hit her with?" he asked.

"The edge of my hand, across the back of the neck. I'm sure I didn't hurt her." He picked up the .32, removed the clip, worked the action, and slipped it into his jacket pocket. Stone picked up the ejected cartridge and handed it to Dino. "We'd better find the spent shells," he said. "Otherwise, when the owners return home they'll be calling the police."

Dino rummaged around the broken glass and recovered the shell casings. "I've got three," he said. "There was only one more, in the breech."

Stone found a phone and called the clinic. "This is Stone Barrington," he said to the woman who answered.

"Yes, Mr. Barrington, we've been expecting your call."

"We're on our way there."

"Will you require any sort of restraints?"

"I don't know," he replied. "Best be ready, though."

"We'll expect you shortly. Do you know how to get into the garage?"

"Yes."

"You'll be met there and brought up in the elevator."

"Good." Stone hung up, got his arms under Dolce, and picked her up. "Let's get her to the car," he said.

Dino closed the front door behind them, then got into the rear seat of the station wagon, helping Stone move Dolce's unconscious form into the car, then Stone went around to the driver's side.

"I hope to God we can get out of here before the cops show up," Dino said. "Some neighbor must have heard the shots."

Stone started the car and headed down Mulholland. "They'll find an empty house," he said.

"And a mess. Eduardo had better send somebody up there to clean up."

"I'll mention it to him."

They got as far as Sunset Boulevard before Dolce began to come to.

"Easy, Dolce," Stone said. "You just lie here and rest."

"Stone?" she said.

"I'm here, Dolce," he said from the front seat. "Just lie quietly. We'll have you home soon." He turned up Sunset and began making his way toward the Judson Clinic.

"Where's home?" she asked dreamily.

It was a good question, Stone thought, and he didn't have an answer.

There were two beefy men in orderlies' uniforms waiting in the garage with a gurney. Stone stopped the car, got out, and helped Dino remove Dolce.

"Where are we?" she asked. Her hand went to the back of her neck. "I've got a headache."

"We'll get you something for that," one of the orderlies said. "Why don't you hop up here and we'll get you upstairs and to bed."

"I don't want to go to bed," she said, looking around the garage. "It's early, and I'm a late person."

"We won't need the gurney," Stone said. "Come on, Dolce, let's go upstairs and get you something for your headache." He reached for her arm, but she stiffened and tried to pull away.

Dino stepped up and helped hold her as they got her onto the elevator.

An orderly pressed a button. "We've got a room ready," he said.

"What hotel is this?" Dolce asked.

"The Judson," an orderly replied.

"Never heard of it. I want to go to the Bel-Air."

"The Bel-Air is full," Stone said.

"Never mind, Papa keeps a suite there; I want to go to the Bel-Air."

"Eduardo said to take you here," Stone said. "He'll come and see you in the morning."

The elevator stopped, and the party moved down the hallway, with Stone and Dino holding tightly onto Dolce. They got her into a room, where a nurse was waiting.

"Oh, no," Dolce said, struggling. "I know this place. I've been to a place like this."

The nurse came forward, a syringe in her hand.

Stone turned Dolce's face toward him. "It's going to be all right," he said.

She whirled when she felt the needle in her arm, but Stone and Dino held her tightly.

"Oh, no," Dolce said again. "I don't want to . . ."

"Put her on the bed," the nurse said to the two orderlies, and in a moment they had her stretched out. She turned to Stone and Dino. "She'll be out in a minute, and she'll sleep for twelve hours."

Stone stood at the bedside and held her hand until her eyes had closed and she was breathing deeply.

A few minutes later Stone and Dino took the elevator back to the garage and got into the car.

"I don't ever want to have to do that again," Stone said.

"Then you'd better get a divorce," Dino replied.

⸙ Chapter 58 ⸙

Stone looked in the bathroom mirror; he did not much like himself this morning. Watching Dolce being sedated had shaken him badly, and later, explaining to Eduardo what had happened had not improved his state of mind. He had not slept much, and he was due at Marc Blumberg's office to prepare for tomorrow's hearing. He got into a hot shower and let the water run. The phone was buzzing when he got out.

It was Eduardo. "I saw her early this morning," he said.

"How was she?"

"Still sleeping; I just sat and looked at her. Her own doctor will be here today."

"Is there anything I can do, Eduardo?"

"Everything is being done that can be done. Later, if her doctor thinks you could be helpful, perhaps you could see her."

"Of course."

"I would like to take her to New York as soon as she is able to travel. Dr. Judson said he would consult with her doctor about that. If possible, I will take her home to Brooklyn and have her treated there."

"Perhaps she would be happier there," Stone said, not knowing what else to say.

"Stone, there is something else I must tell you about."

"What is it, Eduardo?"

"When I was at your house in New York we talked about the blood tests you took when Arrington's child was born."

"Yes, I remember."

"The tests were conducted by a laboratory here, in Los Angeles, called Hemolab."

"Yes."

"I think you should know that tests conducted by this company have, in the past, been known to be . . . manipulated. I cannot go into any detail about this, and I cannot discuss my reasons. Suffice it to say that this information is not just my opinion, but more substantial."

Again, Stone didn't know what to say.

"I don't know if, in your case, the results were accurate or not, and I have no way of investigating. You might wish to have the tests repeated by another laboratory."

"Thank you, Eduardo; I'll give that some thought." He would certainly do that.

"I must go now."

"I'll call you tonight to hear about Dolce."

"Thank you; I'll be in my suite all evening. Good-bye."

Stone hung up and sat on the bed, rattled by what Eduardo had said. He looked at the bedside clock: nearly eight; he was due at Marc Blumberg's office at nine to prepare for the hearing the following day. He shaved and dressed, then he called Dino.

"How you doing, pal?" Dino asked.

"I've been better."

"What do you need?" Dino could always read him.

"I'd appreciate it if you'd do something for me."

"Name it."

"Wait until midafternoon, then call the office of a Dr. Lansing Drake, in Beverly Hills. Tell him Arrington recommended him, that you're having abdominal pains, and that you'd like to see him late this afternoon. Then call me at Marc Blumberg's office and tell me what time he'll see you."

"You want me to go and fake it with this doctor?"

"No, no; I just want you to make the appointment, so that if he calls back to confirm who you are, he won't get me on the phone instead."

"Okay, I can do that. Dinner tonight?"

"Sure, if I don't have too much homework to do."

"Talk to you this afternoon, then."

"Bye." Stone was about to leave when the phone buzzed again. "Yes, Louise?"

"Brandy Garcia is on one."

Stone picked up the phone. "Yes, Brandy?"

"Stone, what's going on with Felipe Cordova? He called me last night, and he was upset."

"I subpoenaed him to testify at a hearing, that's all. He's at no risk by doing that."

"Yeah, but yesterday afternoon, he got *another* subpoena for the same time and place, this one from the D.A. And they searched his house, too. He didn't know what they were looking for."

Stone thought about that for a moment. "Somebody's got his wires crossed, that's all. There's nothing for him to worry about."

"He doesn't like this, Stone. I think he might bolt."

"Brandy, there's a thousand bucks in it for you if you can see that he shows up for that hearing."

"What am I going to tell him?"

"Tell him nobody's going to put him in jail; tell him anything you like, just have him there. Lead him by the hand."

"Okay, I'll do it for the grand. What are you going to give him?"

"I've already told him that I can't pay him to testify."

"I could give him a couple hundred, though?"

"Sorry, I didn't hear that; must be trouble on the line. Have him there, Brandy."

"You got it."

Stone sat in Marc Blumberg's office.

"I don't like this much," Marc was saying.

"What's the difference who he's testifying for? We know what he's going to say."

"Do we?"

"I think so. It might be more effective to let the D.A. get his story into the record, then bring out our points on cross."

"Okay, I buy that. Now, let's get started."

They worked through lunch, and at midafternoon, Dino called.

"Hi."

"Hi. I've got an appointment."

"When?"

"As soon as I can get there."

"Thanks, Dino."

"Dinner?"

"Meet me at the studio at seven."

"See you then."

Stone hung up and turned to Marc. "Are we about done? There's somewhere I have to be."

"Go ahead; I'll see you at the courthouse tomorrow morning."

Stone looked up Drake's address in the phone book.

"My name is Bacchetti," Stone said to the receptionist.

"Oh, yes, Mr. Bacchetti," she replied. "Will you wait in examination room B, down the hall? And undress down to your shorts."

Stone found the room, which contained an examination table, a sink, and a cabinet for supplies. He did not undress; he sat down in the only chair and waited. A couple of minutes later, Dr. Lansing Drake entered the room, preoccupied with a clipboard in his hand.

"Mr. Bacchetti," he said, not looking up. "Just a moment, please." He went to the sink, washed his hands, then turned around. "Now, what seems to be . . ." His jaw dropped.

"I'm Stone Barrington, Dr. Drake; we met recently at Lou Regenstein's."

"I don't understand," Drake said nervously, looking toward the exit.

Stone got up and leaned on the door. "I won't keep you long, Doctor. My name will be familiar to you, because a while back, you submitted a sample of my blood, along with one from Vance Calder, to a company called Hemolab, for a paternity test."

"I don't recall," the doctor replied.

"Oh, I think you do," Stone said.

"Vance Calder was my patient," Drake said. "I have to respect his confidence."

"Vance is dead, Doctor, and now you have to deal with me. You can do it here, quietly, or you can do it in court. What's it going to be?"

Drake sagged against the examination table. "If Arrington should learn of this conversation . . ."

"I don't think that will be necessary. What I want to know, quite simply, is if the tests were run again by another laboratory, would the results be the same?"

Drake gazed out the window. "I honestly don't know."

"Do you deny altering the test results?"

Drake looked back at him. "I most certainly do." He looked away again. "That is, I don't know if the results were tampered with."

"And why don't you know?"

Drake sighed. "Vance came to me and said it was essential that the test prove that he was the father of the child. I conveyed that to someone at Hemolab."

"So I'm the child's father?"

"I said I don't know. I simply made Vance's wishes known. For all I know, he *was* the father. I suppose it could have gone either way, or there would have been no need for the test."

"Yes," Stone said, "it could have gone either way. I want to see the original test results."

"I'm afraid that will be impossible. At Vance's request, once the report was issued, the blood samples and the records were destroyed. The lab never knew who he was; the two subjects were simply labeled A and B."

"Then you knew when you saw the results."

"No, I didn't. I didn't care, really. I wrote a letter saying that Vance was the father, that's all. I don't know if he was or not."

"So, the test was just to have something to show Arrington?"

"I suppose. But if you ever tell her that, I'll deny even speaking to you."

"Thank you, Doctor," Stone said. He left the office and went back to his car.

Dino looked across the dinner table at Stone. "Are you sure you want to know?"

"Of course, I want to know; wouldn't you?"

"I'm not sure," Dino replied. "Under the circumstances."

"What circumstances?"

Dino shrugged. "The present circumstances."

Stone thought about that. Arrington might still go to prison. In that case, he'd want to raise the boy—if he was the father. But if she were freed, then what? He and Arrington and their son would live happily ever after? That is, if the boy was, indeed, his son and not Vance's.

"If you've got to know, then here's what you have to do," Dino said. "You and Arrington and the boy have to go together to have blood drawn, two samples of both yours and the boy's. She sends one set to a lab, and you send them to another. Then you compare results, and you'll know."

"Yes, I suppose we would."

"But if the news of the test should get out, well, you'd have a tabloid shitstorm on your hands."

"Yes, we would."

"I think you need to do some more thinking."

"I think you're right.

⤳ Chapter 59 ⤳

Manolo drove Stone, Arrington, and Isabel to the courthouse, while Dino and Mary Ann followed in the station wagon. This time, they could not avoid the press, since the hearing had been placed on the court calendar, which was public. Even the underground garage was covered by the TV cameras, and it took both Stone and Manolo to keep them from following the group into the elevator.

There was another gauntlet to run, between the elevator and the courtroom, but Stone was relieved to see Felipe Cordova sitting outside the courtroom, with Brandy Garcia at his side. Brandy winked at him as they passed. Stone told Isabel to wait to be called, then he took Arrington into the courtroom, where Marc Blumberg met them at the defense table. Dino and Mary Ann found seats. Stone set down his briefcase and a shopping bag he had been carrying.

"Okay, we've been over this," Marc said to Arrington. "You'll testify as before, unless . . ."

"Unless what?" Arrington asked.

"Unless you've regained your memory."

She shook her head. "I don't remember anything after that Friday night, until I woke up in the clinic."

"Just checking," Marc said.

The judge entered, and the bailiff called the court to order.

"I'm hearing a motion to dismiss this morning, I believe," the judge said.

Marc Blumberg rose. "Yes, Your Honor. I would ask that the District Attorney's office present its witnesses, followed by defense witnesses."

The judge turned to the prosecution table. "Ms. Chu?"

The young woman rose. "The District Attorney calls Detective Sam Durkee."

Durkee took the stand, and under questioning, established that the murder had taken place.

When it was Marc Blumberg's turn, he rose. "Detective, you've testified that Mr. Calder was shot with a nine-millimeter semiautomatic pistol."

"Yes."

"Did you find the weapon?"

"No."

"Did you search the Calder house and grounds thoroughly?"

"Yes."

"How many times?"

"Three, over two days."

"And no weapon?"

"No."

"Did you search any other house for the weapon?"

"Yes, we searched the home of Felipe Cordova, the Calders' gardener."

"Oh? When?"

"Yesterday."

"I'm glad you got around to it. Did you find the weapon?"

"No."

"Did you search the house or grounds of Beverly Walters?"

"No."

"Why not?"

"Because she's not a suspect."

"I see. You say you searched the Calder house thoroughly. In your search, did you find a white terrycloth robe?"

"No, but I wasn't looking for one."

"When you arrived at the Calder house and first saw Mrs. Calder, what was she wearing?"

"A bathrobe, or a dressing gown, I guess you could call it."

"What was it made of?"

"I'm not sure; some sort of smooth fabric."

"Could it have been either cotton or silk?"

"Yes, I suppose it could have been."

"Could it have been terrycloth?"

"No, I'm sure it wasn't."

"What color was it?"

"It was some sort of floral pattern, brightly colored."

"No further questions."

The D.A. called the medical examiner and elicited testimony on the autopsy results, then, "Your Honor, the District Attorney calls Beverly Walters."

Beverly Walters appeared through a side door and was sworn. Chu began by taking her through her previous story of having heard Arrington threaten to kill her husband, then she continued. "Ms. Walters, where were you on the afternoon of the evening Vance Calder was murdered?"

"I was at the home of a friend, at a swimming party."

"And after you left the party, where did you go?"

"I went to Vance Calder's home."

"And how did you enter the grounds?"

"Through a rear entrance."

"Did you ring the doorbell?"

"No, I entered through the door to the pool and sneaked into Mr. Calder's dressing room."

"Was Mr. Calder present?"

"Yes."

"Where was Mrs. Calder?"

"She was taking a bath, I believe. That was what Mr. Calder told me when I spoke with him earlier."

"Having reached the dressing room, what did you do?"

"Mr. Calder and I made love."

"In his dressing room?"

"On a sofa in his dressing room."

"Was this the first time you and Mr. Calder had made love?"

"No, we had done so on a number of occasions."

"And where did these trysts take place?"

"In his trailer at Centurion Studios, in his bungalow there, and at his home, always in his dressing room."

"On the earlier occasions, when you made love in the dressing room, was Mrs. Calder present in the house?"

"Yes. We timed the meetings for when Arrington was in the tub. When they went out in the evenings, she was as regular as clockwork; she'd spend half an hour in the bath."

"Why did you take these risks?"

"Vance found it exciting, knowing that Arrington was in the house. He loved taking chances."

"After you had made love that evening, what did you do?"

"When we had finished, Vance began getting dressed and said I should leave, that Arrington—Mrs. Calder—would be getting out of her bath soon."

"And did you leave?"

"Yes, I left through the same door I had entered by."

"And after leaving, did you have occasion to return to the house?"

"Yes."

"Why?"

"I heard a gunshot."

"How did you know it was a gunshot?"

"I didn't, at first, but when I peeked back through the glass doors, I saw Mr. Calder lying on the floor of the hallway. Mrs. Calder was standing next to him, holding a gun in her hand."

"She was just standing there? Was she doing anything else?"

"She was screaming at him."

"What was she saying?"

"I don't know exactly; it was pretty garbled. I did hear her say 'son of a bitch.'"

"Was Mrs. Calder directing this abuse at Mr. Calder?"

"Yes. There was no one else there."

"What did you do then?"

"I ran back to the car. I didn't want Arrington to shoot me, too."

Stone glanced at Arrington. Her face had reddened.

⊰ Chapter 60 ⊱

Chu turned to the defense table. "Your witness, Mr. Blumberg."

Marc stood. "Mrs. Walters—it is *Mrs.* Walters, isn't it?"

"Yes," she replied, her mouth turning down.

"What were you wearing on this occasion?"

"I wasn't wearing anything," Walters replied. There was a titter among the reporters present.

"I mean when you arrived at the Calder residence. What were you wearing then?"

"I was wearing a robe. I had removed my swimsuit in the car."

"What sort of a robe?"

"A terrycloth robe."

"What color?"

"White."

"Did the robe have a hood?"

"Yes."

"When you left Mr. Calder's dressing room, you were wearing the white terrycloth robe with the hood?"

"Yes."

"Was the hood up?"

"Yes, my hair was still wet."

"You and Vance Calder argued on that occasion, didn't you?"

She looked startled. "I don't know what you mean."

"He was all finished with you, wasn't he? And he told you so?"

"No, *I* told *him* we were finished."

"And he didn't like that?"

"No, he didn't."

"So you did argue."

Walters flushed. "If you could call it that."

"No further questions," Marc said. "I ask that the witness be instructed to remain available; I may wish to recall her."

"The witness will remain available," the judge said.

Chu stood again. "The District Attorney calls Felipe Cordova."

The bailiff brought Cordova into the courtroom; he was sworn and took the stand.

"Mr. Cordova," Chu said, "you were gardener to the Calders?"

"I cut the grass every week."

"Were you present at the Calder residence on the evening Mr. Calder was murdered?"

"Yes."

"For what reason?"

"I was looking to steal something, if I could." He didn't appear to be embarrassed by this answer.

"Did you have occasion to approach the rear door of the house and look inside?"

"Yes."

"Why?"

"I heard a noise, like a gun."

"When you looked inside, what did you see?"

"I saw Mr. Calder, lying on the floor bleeding, and Mrs. Calder standing there, and a gun was on the floor."

"And what did you do?"

"I ran. I didn't want to be caught there."

"Your witness," Chu said to Blumberg.

Marc stood. "Mr. Cordova, you say you saw Mrs. Calder standing next to Mr. Calder's body?"

"Yes."

"How was she dressed?"

"In a bathrobe."

"What kind of bathrobe?"

"You know, the terry kind."

"Terrycloth?"

"Yes."

"What color?"

"White."

"Did the robe have a hood?"

"Yes, she was wearing the hood."

"Did you see her face?"

"Not exactly."

"Was she facing you?"

"Not exactly."

"Well, if you didn't see her face, how do you know it was Mrs. Calder?"

"I seen her before, you know, and I recognized her shape." He made a female shape with his hands, and the courtroom tittered again.

"Since you never saw her face, is it possible that the woman you saw was not Mrs. Calder, but another woman?"

Cordova shrugged. "Maybe."

Marc turned to the judge. "Your Honor, could we have Mrs. Walters back for a moment to try something?"

The judge waved both lawyers forward. "Just what do you want to try, Mr. Blumberg?"

"I'd like for Mrs. Walters to try on a robe for Mr. Cordova."

"I've no objection, Your Honor," Ms. Chu said.

"Go ahead. Bailiff, bring Mrs. Walters back to the courtroom."

Beverly Walters returned, looking wary.

"Mrs. Walters," the judge said, "I'd like you to put on a bathrobe for the court."

Walters nodded, and Stone handed Marc a white terrycloth robe. He held it for the woman, and she put it on.

"Please put up the hood, step out of your shoes, and face the rear of the courtroom, Mrs. Walters," Marc said. She followed his instructions, and he turned to Cordova. "What about it, Mr. Cordova? Could this be the woman you saw?" He made the woman shape with his hands.

"Yeah, she could be," Cordova said.

"No further questions," Marc said.

Ms. Chu was on her feet. "Your Honor, now I'd like for Mrs. Calder to try on the robe for Mr. Cordova."

"Any objection, Mr. Blumberg?" the judge asked.

"None whatsoever, Your Honor."

The courtroom watched as Arrington slipped into the white robe and turned her back on Cordova.

"Mr. Cordova," Chu said, "could this be the woman you saw?"

Cordova nodded. "Yeah. I guess it could be either one of them; they look pretty much the same."

"No further questions, Your Honor. That concludes the District Attorney's presentation."

"Mr. Blumberg," the judge said, "do you have any witnesses?"

"Your Honor, we call Isabel Sanchez."

Isabel came into the courtroom, was sworn, and took the stand.

"Your Honor, my colleague, Mr. Stone Barrington of the New York Bar, will question this witness."

The judge nodded assent.

"Mrs. Sanchez," Stone began, "are you and your husband employed by Mrs. Arrington Calder?"

"Yes, we are," Isabel replied.

"How long have you worked for her?"

"Since she married Mr. Calder. We worked for fifteen years for him before they married."

"Do you, personally, perform the duties of a maid in the household?"

"Yes."

"Do your duties require you to deal with Mrs. Calder's wardrobe?"

"Yes, I do her laundry—her underthings and washables—and I gather things to be sent to the dry cleaners and an outside laundry."

"Would you say that you are familiar with Mrs. Calder's wardrobe?"

"Oh, yes, very familiar. I know her clothes as well as I know my own."

"Tell me, does Mrs. Calder own a terrycloth robe?"

"Yes, she does. She has terrycloth robes for the guest house, four of them, for the two bedrooms."

"What color are the guest house robes?"

"They are bright yellow."

Stone held up the white robe. "Is this Mrs. Calder's robe?"

"No."

"Of course not, since it was bought yesterday at the gift shop of the Beverly Hills Hotel. Does she own one like it?"

"No, she doesn't."

Stone went to the shopping bag and pulled out a bright yellow robe. "Is this the color of the guest house robes?"

"Yes."

He handed her the robe. "Take a look at it. Is this one of the guest house robes?"

Isabel examined the robe and its label. "Yes, it is."

He held up the two robes together. "These robes are very different colors, aren't they?"

"Yes, they are."

"Could you mistake one of these robes for the other?"

"No, they're different colors."

Stone held up the white robe. "Does Mrs. Calder own a robe this color?"

"No, she does not. And Mrs. Calder never wears terrycloth, even around the pool."

"Do you know why?"

"She doesn't like it; she likes Sea Island cotton or silk. I've never once seen her wear a terrycloth robe."

"No further questions, Your Honor," Stone said. "And that concludes our presentation of witnesses."

"Ms. Chu, closing?"

Chu stood, looking chastened. "We have nothing further, Judge."

"Mr. Blumberg?"

"I believe the evidence speaks for itself, Your Honor. The District Attorney's own witnesses have exonerated my client."

"Mr. Blumberg, I believe you are correct. Your motion for dismissal of charges is granted, with prejudice." He turned to the D.A.'s table. "Ms. Chu, I believe you and the police may wish to speak further with Mrs. Walters." He rapped his gavel. "Mrs. Calder, you are free to go, with the court's apologies. Court is adjourned."

Arrington stood and turned to Marc and Stone. "What does 'with prejudice' mean?"

"It means the D.A. can't bring these charges against you again. You're a free woman."

"If it's all right," she said, "I'd like to leave by the front door."

"I'll tell Manolo to bring the car around front," Stone said.

She grabbed Stone's hand, and they made their way through the crowd of press. He passed Dino. "Follow Manolo in your car," he said. Dino nodded and, with Mary Ann, made his way from the courtroom.

"Mrs. Calder will have a statement on the front steps of the courthouse," Marc shouted over the din, and the press dutifully followed them outside. Microphones were set up on the steps, and Marc shouted for silence.

He faced the reporters, apparently relishing the moment. "Justice has been done," he said. "Arrington Calder is a free woman, and I only wish the police and the District Attorney's office had done their work earlier, instead of waiting for us to do it for them. Now Mrs. Calder would like to say a few words."

Arrington stepped up to the microphones. "I want to thank my attorneys, Marc Blumberg and Stone Barrington," she said. "But I have no thanks whatsoever for the media, who have made my life a living hell these past weeks. These are the last words I will ever speak to a camera or a reporter. *Good-bye!*" She stepped back.

Suddenly, a reporter in the front of the group held up a tabloid newspaper. "Mr. Barrington!" he shouted.

Stone, who had been about to lead Arrington away, turned and looked at the paper. What he saw was himself and Betty Southard quite naked, covering half the page. Both were looking at the camera, and black bars covered strategic areas of their bodies.

"Oh, shit," Stone said involuntarily.

Chapter 61

Arrington took one look at the paper and stalked off. Stone followed her as quickly as he could, with reporters shouting questions at him from both sides. He got Arrington into the rear seat of the Bentley, but before he could climb in, she slammed the door and hammered down the lock button. Stone was left on the sidewalk, surrounded by cameras and screaming reporters.

Marc Blumberg grabbed his arm and pulled him toward the curb as Dino and Mary Ann drove up in the Mercedes station wagon, and they both got into the rear seat. Dino drove away, while reporters scattered from his path.

"You can drop me at the garage entrance around the corner," Marc said.

Dino glanced back at him. "Congratulations; you sure nailed Beverly Walters. How did you know she and Vance had an argument?"

"I figured he dumped her. *Everybody* dumps Beverly, sooner or later, and I figured she didn't like it. At least she admitted to an argument." Marc turned to Stone. "By the way, I had a call early this morning from my attorney friend in Milan, about the possibility of divorce."

"And?" Stone asked.

"The news isn't good. In order to get a civil divorce in Italy, the two of you have to appear before a magistrate and mutually request the action."

"Can't I sue?"

"Yes, but in a contested divorce, you'd have to subpoena her, and you can't do that in the United States. You'd have to serve her in Italy."

Stone winced. "Good God."

The car stopped at the entrance to the garage, and at that moment, there was a ringing noise.

Marc took a small cell phone from an inside pocket. "Yes?"

He smiled broadly. "Sure, I'll see her. I'll go right now." He closed the phone and stuck it back into his pocket. "That was my office," he said. "Beverly Walters has been arrested for Vance's murder, and she wants me to represent her."

"Are you going to?" Stone asked.

"Sure, why not? Since the charges against Arrington were dismissed with prejudice, there's no conflict. Anyway, it's an easy acquittal."

Mary Ann turned around. "Acquittal? After what was said in court today?"

"Sure. My guess is that, since she wasn't a suspect, she was never Mirandized, so everything she told the police and everything she said in court is inadmissible. The only testimony against her is Cordova's, and he's already admitted that he couldn't distinguish between Beverly and Arrington in the robe."

"What about Vanessa Pike's murder?" Stone asked.

"There's no evidence against her," Marc replied, "or they would already have arrested her. Anyway, she may not have murdered Vanessa."

That was true, Stone thought, and the other possible suspect was in a mental hospital.

Marc opened the car door and offered Stone his hand. "Thanks for the fun," he said. "Now I've gotta go see my new client."

"And thank you, Marc. I'll get you a check tomorrow."

Dino drove away and pointed the car toward Bel-Air. "Hey, what was all that crowd of reporters after you about?"

Stone sighed and told them what had happened.

"Did Arrington see the paper?"

He nodded. "I'm afraid so."

They arrived back at the Calder house to find Manolo loading suitcases into the Bentley.

"Manolo," Stone asked, "is Mrs. Calder going somewhere?"

"Yes, sir," Manolo replied. "But you better ask her about that."

"She certainly packed fast," Stone said.

"Oh, she packed before we went to court," Manolo said. "And on the way home, she called Mr. Regenstein from the car. The Centurion airplane is waiting for her at Santa Monica."

Stone went into the house, followed by Dino and Mary Ann. Arrington was coming out of the bedroom. He stopped her. "Can we talk?" he asked.

"I don't think we have anything to talk about," she said. "I'm going to Virginia to be with Peter and my mother, and I don't know when I'm coming back. Why don't you join Betty Southard in Hawaii? The two of you were made for each other. Or, perhaps, you could move in with Charlene Joiner."

He took her arm, but she snatched it away.

"Good-bye, Dino, Mary Ann," she said, kissing them both. "I'm sorry your stay wasn't as pleasant as it might have been."

"Don't worry about it," Dino replied.

"Something I want to know," Stone said. "The amnesia: Was it real?"

"It was at first. After I came home from the clinic, everything gradually came back to me."

"So what happened that evening?"

"I don't think I'm going to tell you," she said. "You still think I might have killed Vance, don't you?"

"No, I don't."

"Sure you do, Stone. Anyway, you'll never know for sure, will you?" And with that she turned and walked out of the house. A moment later, the Bentley could be heard driving away.

Isabel came into the room. "Lunch is served out by the pool," she said.

Dino took Stone's arm. "Come on, pal. You could use some lunch, and probably a drink, too."

Stone followed him outside, and the three of them sat down. Isabel brought a large Caesar salad with chunks of chicken and served them.

"You did very well this morning, Isabel," Stone said. "Thank you very much."

"All I did was tell the truth," Isabel replied. She opened a bottle of chardonnay and left them to their lunch.

They chatted in a desultory way about the events of the past weeks, and Stone felt depressed. He finished his salad and tossed off the remainder of his wine. "Excuse me a minute," he said, getting up. "I have to make a phone call."

"There's a phone," Dino said, pointing at the pool bar.

"This one is private," Stone replied. "I'll go inside." He went into the living room and looked around for a phone, but didn't see one, so he went into Vance's study and sat at the desk. Someone had left the bookcase/door to the dressing room open. He got out his notebook and dialed.

"Hello?"

"Betty, it's Stone."

"Well, hello there. I heard about the court thing this morning on the news. Congratulations."

"Thanks, but Marc Blumberg carried most of the water. Listen, I called about something else, something you have to know about."

"Dolce's dirty pictures? I probably saw them before you did; it's earlier here, remember?"

"I'm so sorry about that, Betty."

"Don't worry about it; it's made me a lot more interesting to people here. I've already had three dinner invitations this morning."

Stone laughed. "You're amazing."

"I don't imagine the pictures went down quite as well for you. They must have caused problems."

"Well, what can I do about it?"

"Treasure the photographs, sweetie; I will. Bye, now."

Stone hung up laughing. Then he noticed that something seemed to have changed in the dressing room. He got up and walked through the doorway. The dressing room was empty of all Vance's clothes; only bare racks were left. The chesterfield sofa, where Vance's trysts with Beverly Walters had occurred, was all that was left in the room.

He was about to turn and go back outside to join Dino and Mary Ann when he remembered something. He walked to Vance's bathroom, looked inside, then down the little hallway that separated it from the dressing room. He had noticed something odd here before and had forgotten about it.

He went into the bathroom and, with his outstretched arms, measured the distance to the door from the wall of the bathroom that backed onto the dressing room. Holding out his arms, he walked into the hallway and held his arms up to the wall of the little corridor. Then he measured the distance from the wall containing the dressing room safe to the door, and marked that off on the corridor wall. Most people wouldn't have noticed, he thought, but with his experience of remodeling his own house, he had. The wall containing the safe appeared to be about eighteen inches deep, instead of the usual four or six inches.

He went back into the dressing room, trying to remember the combination to the safe. "One-five-three-eight," he said aloud, then tapped the number into the keypad and opened the door. The safe was about four and a half inches deep; it was the kind meant to be installed in a standard-depth wall between the studs. Or it appeared to be. He rapped on the sides of the safe, which made a shallow metallic noise, then he rapped on the rear wall of the safe, which made a deeper, hollower sound. Something was very odd here.

He rapped harder, and the rear wall of the safe seemed to move a little. Then, with his fingertips, he pressed hard on the rear wall. It gave an eighth of an inch. Then there was a click, and the seemingly fixed steel plate swung outward an inch. Stone hooked a finger around the plate and pulled it toward him, revealing a twelve-inch-deep second compartment in the safe. Inside, Stone saw two things: Vance Calder's jewelry box and a nine-millimeter semiautomatic pistol.

"My God!" he said aloud. "Arrington killed him." Then from behind him, a male voice spoke.

"I thought so, too."

Stone turned to find Manolo standing there. "What?"

"When I found Mr. Calder dead, I thought Mrs. Calder had shot him. They had had a big argument about something earlier; there was lots of shouting and screaming. It wasn't their first."

"What have you done, Manolo?"

"When I heard the shot and found Mr. Calder, the gun was on the floor beside him, where whoever shot him had dropped it. I thought Mrs. Calder had done it, and my immediate thought—I'm not sure why—was to protect her. So I took the gun and put it in the hidden compartment of the safe, and, so the police would think it was a robbery, I put his jewelry box in there, too, and closed it. They never figured it out."

Stone took a pen from his pocket, stuck it through the trigger guard of the pistol and lifted it from the safe. "Then it will have the fingerprints of the killer on it. Now we'll know for sure who killed Vance."

Manolo shook his head. "I'm afraid not, Mr. Barrington; I wiped the gun clean before I hid it. I was so sure that Mrs. Calder had done it. Of course, after this morning in court, I don't think so anymore."

"Does Arrington know you hid the pistol?"

"No. I never told her."

Stone put the pistol on top of the chest of drawers, then, weak at the knees, sat down on the sofa. "So we'll never know for sure."

"I know," Manolo said. "I'm a little surprised that you don't, Mr. Barrington." He picked up the pistol by the trigger guard, put it back in the safe's rear compartment, and closed it.

"I'll leave it there for a while, then I'll get rid of it and send the jewelry box to Mrs. Calder."

Stone was beyond arguing with him.

Chapter 62

Stone stayed in L.A. for a couple of more days, paying the last of the bills to come to the bungalow and seeing that Vance Calder's estate was released to Arrington.

After he had packed his bags and was ready to leave the bungalow, Lou Regenstein came into Vance's study.

"Good morning, Lou."

"You on your way home, Stone?"

"Yes, I'm done here. Louise can pack up Vance's things and send them to the house. Manolo and Isabel are still there."

"Have you talked to Arrington?"

"No, she isn't speaking to me."

"I should think she'd be grateful to you for everything you've done for her."

"Maybe, but there are other things she's not grateful to me for."

"The business in the tabloid?"

Stone nodded. "Among other things."

"Well, I want you to know that I am certainly grateful to you. Arrington is now the second-largest stockholder in Centurion, after me, and together, the two of us control the company. If she'd gone to prison, God knows what would have happened here."

"I'm glad it worked out all right."

"Is there anything I can do for you, Stone?"

"You can have someone drive Vance's car back to the house," he said, holding out the keys.

Lou accepted the keys. "I'll have my driver take you to the airport." Lou picked up the phone and gave the order. "He'll be here in a minute."

Stone looked around. "What will happen to Vance's bungalow?"

"Charlene Joiner is moving in, as soon as we've redecorated it to her specifications. She's Centurion's biggest star now."

"She deserves it."

They chatted for a few minutes, then Lou's chauffeur knocked at the door. "Shall I take your bags, Mr. Barrington?"

"Yes, thank you." He shook hands with Lou. "Thanks for all your help."

"Stone, you'll always have friends at Centurion. If there's ever anything, anything at all, we can do for you, just let me know."

"When you speak to Arrington, tell her I'm thinking of her."

"Of course."

Stone left the bungalow and was about to get into Lou's limousine, when Charlene drove up in a convertible.

"Leaving without saying good-bye?" she called out.

Stone walked over to the car. "It's been a weird couple of days; I was going to call you from New York."

"I get to New York once in a while. Shall I call you?"

He gave her his card. "I'd be hurt, if you didn't." He leaned over and kissed her, then she drove away. Before she turned the corner, she waved, without looking back.

Stone got into the limo and settled into the deep-cushioned seat. He'd be home by bedtime.

Back in Turtle Bay, he let himself into the house. Joan had left for the day, but there was a note on the table in the foyer.

"A shipment arrived for you yesterday," she wrote. "It's in the living room. And there was an envelope delivered by messenger this morning."

Stone saw the envelope on the table and tucked it under his arm. He picked up his suitcases and started for the elevator, then he looked into the living room and set down the cases. Standing in the center of the living room was a clothes rack, and on it hung at least twenty suits. He walked into the room and looked around. On the floor were half a dozen large boxes filled with Vance Calder's Turnbull & Asser shirts and ties. Then he noticed a note pinned to one of the suits.

> You would do me a great favor by accepting these. Or you can just send them to the Goodwill.
>
> I love you,
> Arrington

His heart gave a little leap, but then he saw that the note was dated a week before their parting scene, and it sank again.

He'd think about this later. Right now, he was tired from the trip. He picked up the suitcases, got into the elevator, and rode up to the master suite. Once there, he unpacked, then undressed and got into a nightshirt. Then he remembered the envelope.

He sat down on the bed and opened it. There were some papers and a cover letter, in a neat hand, on Eduardo Bianchi's personal letterhead.

I thought you might like to have these. This ends the matter. I hope to see you soon.

Eduardo

Stone set the letter aside and looked at the papers. There were only two: One was the original of the marriage certificate he and Dolce had signed in Venice; the other was the page from the ledger they and their witnesses had signed in the mayor's office. These made up the whole record of his brief, disastrous marriage.

He took them to the fireplace, struck a match, and watched until they had been consumed. Then he got into bed, and with a profound sense of relief, tinged with sorrow, Stone fell asleep.

Cold Paradise

This book is for
Marvin and Rita Ginsky.

⌁ Chapter 1 ⌁

Elaine's, late.

Stone Barrington finished his osso buco as Elaine wandered over from another table and sat down.

"So?" she asked.

" 'So?' What kind of question is that?"

"It means, 'tell me everything.'"

Stone looked up to see Dino struggling to shut the front door behind him. Dino was his former partner, now a lieutenant, head of the detective squad at the 19th Precinct.

Dino came over, sloughing off a heavy topcoat. "Jesus," he said, hanging up his coat, muffler and hat. "There's already six inches of snow out there, and there's at least thirty knots of wind."

"How are we going to get home?" Stone wondered aloud.

"Don't worry, my driver's out there now, putting the chains on the car." Dino now rated a car and driver from the NYPD.

Stone shook his head. "Poor bastard. It's tough enough being a cop without drawing you for a boss."

"What do you mean?" Dino demanded, offended. "The kid's getting an education working for me. They don't teach this stuff at the academy."

"What, how to put chains on a lieutenant's car?"

"All he has to do is watch me, and he learns."

Stone rolled his eyes, but let this pass. They drank their champagne in silence for a moment.

"So?" Dino asked, finally.

"That's what I just asked him," Elaine said.

"So, I'm back." Stone had returned from an extended stay in LA a few days before.

"I knew that," Dino said. "So?"

"Can't either of you speak in complete sentences?"

"So," Dino said, "how's Mrs. Barrington?"

"Dino," Stone said, "if you're going to start calling her that, I'm going to start carrying a gun."

"I heard," Elaine said.

"I'm not surprised," Stone replied. "Dino has a big mouth."

"So, how is she?" Dino demanded.

"I talked to Eduardo today," Stone said. "Her shrink doesn't want me to see her. Not for a while."

"That's convenient," Dino said.

"You bet it is," Stone agreed.

"You feeling guilty, Stone?" Elaine asked.

"Sure he is," Dino said. "If he had just taken my advice . . ."

"Mine, too," Elaine echoed.

"All right, all right," Stone said. "If I had only taken your advice."

"Arrington is for you," Elaine said.

"Arrington isn't exactly speaking to me," Stone said.

"What does that mean?"

"It means that if I call her, she's civil, but if I try to reason with her, she excuses herself and hangs up."

"How's the boy?" Dino asked.

"Peter's fine."

"Does he know who his father is yet?"

"Look, Dino, *I* don't know who his father is. It could just as well have been Vance as me. Not even Arrington knows. Nobody will, until we do the DNA testing."

"And when does that happen?"

"Arrington won't discuss it."

"Keep after her."

"I don't know if it's worth it," Stone said wearily. "I'm not sure it would make any difference."

"Give her time," Dino said. "She'll come around."

"You're a font of wisdom, Dino. Know any other relationship clichés?"

"Every eligible man in the country is going to be after her," Elaine said.

"What?" Stone asked.

"She's Vance Calder's widow, dummy, and as such, she's very, very rich. Not to mention gorgeous. You'd better get your ass down to Virginia and win her back."

"She knows where to find me," Stone said.

Elaine rolled her eyes.

Another blast of frigid air blew into the room as the front door opened again.

"It's your pal Eggers," Dino said, nodding toward the door.

Bill Eggers came over to the table. He didn't unbutton his coat. "Hi, Elaine, hi, Dino," he said, then he turned to Stone. "I've been calling you all evening. I should have known I'd find you here." Bill Eggers was the managing partner of Woodman & Weld, the extremely prestigious law firm with which Stone was associated, in a very quiet way.

"My home away from home," Stone said. "What's up?"

"I've got a client in the car that you have to see tomorrow morning."

"Bring him in. I'll buy him a drink."

"He won't come in."

"Who is he?"

"No names, for the moment."

"You have secrets from us, Bill?" Elaine asked.

"You bet I do," Eggers replied. "Ten o'clock sharp, Stone?"

"Ten o'clock is fine; sharp depends on the snow. Your office?"

"Penthouse One, at the Four Seasons. He doesn't want to be seen with you."

"Tell him to go fuck himself," Stone said.

"Stone," Eggers said, "get this thing done and get it done right, and you could end up a rich man."

"Ten o'clock, *sharp,*" Stone said.

⤳ **Chapter 2** ⤳

Stone left his house in Turtle Bay early. Eighteen inches of snow had fallen the night before, and the city was a mess. Cabs were few, and he would have to hoof it to 57th Street and the Four Seasons Hotel.

He was clad in a sheepskin coat, cashmere-lined gloves, a soft, felt hat and rubber boots over his shoes. The sidewalks on his block had not been cleared, but the street had been plowed, and he walked up the middle of it all the way to Park Avenue, unmolested by any traffic. The city was peculiarly quiet, the silence punctuated only by the occasional blast of a taxi's horn and, twice, the sound of car striking car. He made it to the Four Seasons ten minutes early.

It was said to be the most expensive hotel in the city, a soaring, very modern skyscraper set on the broad, crosstown street between Madison and Park. A gust of wind propelled him into the lobby, and he was immediately too warm. He found a checkroom and unburdened himself of his outer clothing, and shortly, the elevator deposited him on a high floor. He rang the bell beside the double doors and, immediately, a uniformed butler opened the door.

"Yes, sir?"

"My name is Barrington. I'm expected."

"Of course, sir, please come in."

Stone was ushered through a foyer into a huge living room with a spectacular view of the city looking south, or what would have been a spectacular view if not for the clouds enveloping the tops of the taller buildings.

Bill Eggers came off a sofa by the windows and shook his hand. "Sit down," he said, "and let me brief you."

Stone sat down, and immediately he heard another man's voice coming from an adjoining room through an open door. "Bill?" the voice said. "Come on in."

Eggers stood up. "I'm sorry," he said to Stone, "but there's no time. Just listen a lot and follow my lead. Say yes to anything he says."

"Not if he propositions me," Stone said, but Eggers was already leading the way into the next room. Stone followed, and a very tall, very slender man in his mid-thirties came around a desk and shook Eggers's hand. "How are you, Bill?"

"Very well, Thad," Eggers replied. "Let me introduce a colleague of mine. This is Stone Barrington. Stone, this is Thad Shames."

"How do you do?" Stone said, shaking the man's hand. He knew just enough about him to know who he was, but no more than that. Software came into the equation, and multimillions. Stone didn't follow finance or business very closely.

"Good to meet you, Stone," Shames said. "Bill says you can solve my problem?"

Stone glanced at Eggers. "Yes," he said, more confidently than he felt. Shames was dressed in a nicely cut dark suit, but his shirt seemed to have been laundered but not pressed. His tie was loose, and the button-down collar's tips were not buttoned. Shames waved them both to a pair of facing sofas and, as he sat down and crossed his legs, revealed that he was also wearing a battered pair of suede Mephisto's, a French athletic shoe. His blond, nearly pink hair was curly and tousled and had not been cut for months. He was clean-shaven, but Stone doubted that he could raise a beard.

"I've got a press conference at the Waldorf in an hour," Shames said, "so I'll make this as quick as I can."

Stone and Eggers nodded automatically, like mechanical birds.

"I've met this spectacular woman," Shames said, then waited for a reaction.

"Good," Eggers replied.

"Yes," Stone said.

"I think I'm in love."

The two lawyers nodded gravely.

"Congratulations," Eggers said.

"Yes," Stone echoed.

"This is a lot more important than I'm making it sound," Shames said, grinning. "I've never been married, and, well . . ."

Not getting laid, Stone thought. *Horny. Vulnerable rich guy.*

"Anyway, she's just spectacular. I feel so lucky."

He doesn't realize yet she's taken him, Stone thought.

"What's her name?" Eggers asked.

"That's just the thing," Shames said, blushing. "I'm not sure I know."

"When did you meet her?" Eggers asked.

"Last weekend."

"Where?"

"In the Hamptons."

"At this time of the year?"

"Oh, it's getting awfully chic out there in winter, now," Shames replied. "All the most interesting people go out there on winter weekends. You don't have to put up with the summer tourists and all their traffic."

"Sounds great," Eggers said. "Who introduced you to, ah, her?"

"Nobody, actually. We met at this big party at some movie guy's house—I get those guys mixed up—and after talking for a few minutes, we got the hell out of there and went to Jerry Della Femina's for dinner. We had a great time."

"Good," Eggers replied.

"Yes," Stone said.

"She said her name was Liz," Shames said.

"Maybe that's her name," Stone chanced, but shut up at a glare from Eggers.

"I'm not sure," Shames said.

"Do you have some reason to think her name might not be Liz?" Eggers asked.

"Not really, just a feeling. She wouldn't give me a last name or even tell me where she lives."

"How can Stone and I help, Thad?"

"I want you to find her for me."

This time, Stone glared at Eggers, but Eggers avoided the look.

The butler appeared at the door. "Excuse me, Mr. Shames, but your office is on line one."

Shames stood up. "I'd better take this in the other room," he said. "Please excuse me for a moment." He left, closing the door behind him.

"I know you have some questions," Eggers said.

"Just one," Stone replied. "Are you out of your fucking mind?"

"Now, Stone . . ."

"What am I, some seedy shamus, tracking down women for rich men?"

"Stone . . ."

Stone stood up. "Call me when you've got something of substance, Bill."

Eggers didn't move. "The press conference he's holding is to announce an initial public offering of stock in a new company he's started. Shames has taken two other companies public in the past eight years, and they're both multibillion-dollar, worldwide corporations now. How would you like to have ten thousand shares of the new company at the opening price?"

Stone looked at him warily. "Tell me about it."

"I don't know all that much, except that it's supposed to be an astonishing new technology for the Internet, and that Thaddeus Shames is doing it."

Stone knew enough to know how spectacular a lot of Internet stocks had been in the market. "What's it going to open at?"

"The price hasn't been set yet; probably around twenty dollars a share. Last week an Internet IPO happened, and the stock went up eight hundred percent the first day."

Stone sat down.

Shames returned to the room, and Eggers stood up.

"Thad, Stone is going to take this on. I've got a meeting back at the office, so I'll leave the two of you to continue." He shook hands with Shames and Stone and left.

"Bill told you about my new IPO?" Shames asked.

"Yes," Stone said. *You bet he did.* Stone had already calculated how much of his portfolio he'd have to liquidate to buy the new stock.

"This girl is really wonderful," Shames said.

"I'll help you in any way I can," Stone said.

"Walk me to the car, and I'll tell you everything I know on the way."

I'll bet we'll have time left over, Stone thought. "Sure. And, Thad?"

"Yes?"

"Why don't you let me walk you across the street and get you a new shirt for this press conference."

"Across the street?"

"Turnbull and Asser is right across from the hotel. Won't take a minute."

Shames looked down at his shirt. "Guess it couldn't hurt," he said.

"They have shoes, too."

⤸ Chapter 3 ⤷

As they passed through the living room of the huge suite, a woman's voice rang out.

"Thad?"

Shames and Stone stopped and turned. An attractive young woman wearing a chef's smock was waving from the adjacent dining room.

"Yes, Callie?" Shames replied.

"Do you have any idea how many for lunch, yet? I'm turning it over to the caterers, and they'd sure like to know."

"Oh, I don't know. Tell them to plan for a hundred. If there are leftovers we can donate them to a good cause."

"Right," she said. "See you in PB."

Shames rang for the elevator. "Now, about Liz," he said to Stone. "What do you want to know?"

"Describe her appearance."

Shames held a hand across his chest. "She comes up to about here."

"Five-five, five-six?"

"I guess."

"Was she wearing heels?"

"I'm not sure."

"Hair color?"

"A dark brunette."

"Long? Short?"

"To her shoulders; maybe a bit longer."

"How old was she?"

"Thirtyish, I guess."

"Weight?"

"Mediumish, I suppose."

"Body?"

"Attractive."

"Anything else distinctive about her appearance? Nose?"

"Turned up."

"Eyes?"

"Blue, I think."

Jesus, Stone thought, *I'm glad the girl didn't commit a crime; she'd get away with it.*

The elevator arrived, and they got on.

"Let's talk about her name again, Thad. What made you think that Liz might not be her real name?"

"Just a feeling."

"Try to remember if she said anything specific about her name."

"I asked her, 'What's your name?' And she said, 'Liz will do.' And I said, 'What's your last name?' And she said, 'Just Liz.'"

"Well, she's pretty cagey. Do you think she knew who you were?"

"If she did, she didn't give any sign of it. She asked me what I did, and I told her."

"What did you tell her?"

"I said I was a software entrepreneur. She said, 'Like Bill Gates?' And I said, 'Well, not quite on that scale.' That was the only time we talked about work."

"You didn't ask her what she did?"

"Oh, yeah, I did. She said, 'I'm retired.' And I said, 'From what?' And she said, 'From marriage.'"

"So she divorced well?"

"I guess."

"How was she dressed?"

The elevator reached the ground floor, and they went to the checkroom.

"She was wearing this sort of dress."

"Did it look expensive?"

"I guess. I mean, she looked beautiful in it, and it was a pretty expensive crowd at the party."

"How about jewelry?"

"I think she was wearing earrings. Yes, diamond earrings. Those little stud things, you know? Except they weren't all that little."

"Wedding or engagement ring?"

"A big diamond, but not on her left hand."

"So she didn't return her engagement ring after the divorce."

"I guess not."

"Necklace? Bracelet?"

"A gold necklace and a gold bracelet, I think with diamonds. Nothing flashy, though."

"How about her speech; any sort of accent? Southern? Midwestern?"

"American. No accent that caught my attention."

Stone got into his coat, and they left the hotel. "Right across the street, there," he said, pointing to the shop. He led the way, avoiding ice patches and slush in the gutters. "Don't you have a coat?" he asked.

"It's in the car," Shames said, nodding at a stretched black Mercedes that was making a U-turn, following them.

Stone held the shop door open for Shames, then pointed the way upstairs. They emerged onto the second floor and went into the shirt and tie room.

"Gosh!" Shames said. "I've never seen so many colors. You pick out something for me."

"What size?"

"Sixteen. The sleeves usually aren't long enough for me."

"These will be pretty long," Stone said. A salesman showed them the sixteens. Stone riffled through them and picked out a blue-and-white narrow-striped shirt. "How about this?"

"Fine."

Stone picked out a tie and a complementary silk pocket square and handed them to a saleslady. "Send these down to the shoe shop, please." He led the way back downstairs to the shoe shop.

"This is a really nice place," Shames said, looking around.

"You'd never heard of it?"

"No, and it's right across the street from the hotel, too."

A salesman approached, and Stone helped the man choose some dignified oxfords and some socks.

Shames handed the man a credit card.

"There's a dressing room," Stone said, pointing. "Why don't you put those things on?" He waited, and when Shames returned, he had made a mess of tying the tie. Stone retied it for him and stuffed the silk handkerchief into his breast pocket. "You could pass for a captain of industry," Stone said. "That's a really nice suit."

"I had it made in London. This is the only time I've worn it." Shames signed the credit card chit and checked himself out in a mirror. "Something doesn't look quite right," he said. "What is it?"

"There's a barbershop at the Waldorf," Stone replied, glancing at his watch. "Make the crowd wait for you."

"Okay, I guess I could use a trim."

They stepped back into the street, where the Mercedes was waiting. "Ride down to the Waldorf with me," Shames said. "You can drop me, and the car will take you to your place to pack and then to the airport."

"Sorry?" Stone said, getting into the car. He wasn't sure he had understood.

"To Teterboro. My airplane is out there."

"I don't understand."

"Well, you'll have to go to Palm Beach."

"Why?"

"Because that's where she is. Didn't I mention that?"

"I don't believe you did," Stone said. "Why do you think she's in Palm Beach?"

"I ran into a guy I know at dinner last night who was at the party in the Hamptons. He recognized her at LaGuardia yesterday. She was boarding a flight for Palm Beach."

"You think she lives in Palm Beach?"

"I've no idea."

They drove down Park Avenue, then the driver made a U-turn and stopped in front of the Waldorf.

"Oh," Shames said, reaching into an inside pocket and extracting an envelope. "Here's some expense money."

Stone took the envelope. "Thanks."

"You can stay at my place down there," Shames said, handing him a card. "Not in the house; the house is being renovated, and it's a complete mess."

"Guest house?" Stone asked.

"No, my boat is moored out back. You can stay aboard. There's some crew aboard, I think. They'll get you settled. Anything else I can tell you?"

"I can't think of anything," Stone said. "If you think of something, please call me."

"Okay. You can reach me through my office. The number's on the other side of the card. I'll be down to Palm Beach in a few days. See you then." He offered Stone his hand, grabbed a ratty-looking overcoat from the front seat, got out of the car and walked into the Waldorf.

"Where to, sir?" the driver asked.

Stone gave him the address. "I have to pack some clothes, then I guess we're going to Teterboro. Jesus, I didn't ask him *where* in Teterboro."

"Atlantic Aviation," the driver replied.

"Thanks," Stone said. He wished he'd had time to find Shames an overcoat. His had been awful.

He sat back in the seat and thought about his first move when he got to Palm Beach. All he could think of at the moment was to stop every thirty-ish brunette he saw and ask if her name was Liz and if she had had dinner in the Hamptons last weekend with an extremely tall geek. Stone sighed.

Chapter 4

When he got home, Stone ran upstairs and started packing. He'd never been to Palm Beach before, but he assumed it would be warm, so he took tropical-weight suits and jackets. He thought about a dinner jacket and threw it in, just in case. He changed into a lightweight suit, took his bags back downstairs, opened the door and waved the driver to come and get them, then he went downstairs to his office. His secretary, Joan Robertson, was working at her desk.

"Oh, good, you made it in," he said.

"My husband drove me. Otherwise, I wouldn't have. Why are you wearing that suit? You'll freeze."

"I'm off to Palm Beach."

Joan rolled her eyes. "Just back from LA a couple of days ago, and now off to Florida. Why don't *I* ever get to go where it's warm?"

"Someday," he said. He looked into the envelope Thad Shames had given him; a thick stack of hundreds, at least ten thousand dollars. He counted off two thousand, stuck them in a pocket and tossed Joan the rest. "Put this in the safe for hard times." He jotted down the address and phone number from Shames's card and handed it to her. "This is where I'll be."

"How long?"

"Who knows? No more than a few days, I hope."

"Have fun. Oh, I almost forgot." She handed him a slip of paper. "A Mrs. Winston Harding the Third called this morning, wants to talk to you?"

Stone looked at the paper. "Who is she?"

"I've no idea. She sounds terribly upper class, though. She said she needed to talk to you about an important legal matter, and that you came highly recommended."

"Did she say by whom?"

"Nope, but she sounds like money to me. I wouldn't waste any time getting back to her."

Stone stuffed the paper into a pocket. "I'll call her from Palm Beach." He ran for the car.

At Teterboro, the car drove him up to the airstair door of a Gulfstream V, and the driver carried his bags on and stowed them.

"Mr. Barrington?" a uniformed crewman asked.

"That's me."

"We're ready to taxi. Please find a seat and buckle up."

Stone chose from a dozen comfortable chairs and fastened his seat belt. As the airplane started to move, the young woman he'd seen in Shames's Four Seasons suite came out of a compartment and sat down near him.

"Hi," she said. "I'm Callie Hodges."

"I'm Stone Barrington." They shook hands.

"I heard you were coming to Palm Beach with us," she said.

Stone looked around the airplane. "Who's 'us'?"

"The pilots and me. We're all that's aboard today."

"What do you do for Thad?" Stone asked.

"I'm his chef and party planner. I pretty much go where he goes. I'll fix you some lunch after the seat belt sign goes off."

"Thanks, I haven't eaten."

The big corporate jet taxied to runway 24, paused for a minute, then rolled onto the runway and started moving faster. Shortly, they were climbing into a thick overcast, and in less than five minutes they broke out into sunshine and clear skies.

Callie unbuckled her seat belt. "Would you like something to drink before lunch?"

"A glass of wine with lunch will be fine."

"Be right back." She disappeared into the galley.

Stone picked up a *New York Times* and leafed through it. On the front page of the business section there was an article about Shames's coming press conference, with speculation about the announcement.

Callie returned with a tray bearing a large lobster salad and a glass of white wine, then she went and got a tray for herself. "I'll join you, if you don't mind."

. "Please do. How long have you worked for Thad?"

"A little over a year," she said. "You?"

Stone looked at his watch. "Less than three hours. I'm doing a legal investigation for him."

"Thad's a character," she said. "You'll like working for him."

"I hope so. I don't know much about him, except that he's in computer software, in a pretty big way, I gather."

She smiled. "A pretty big way, yes. The last *Forbes 400* put his net worth at five point eight billion dollars."

Stone blinked. He had spent a lot of time around the rich, but not *that* rich. "So this new venture of his is a pretty big deal, then?"

"I hope so," she said, "because I've got a nice little bundle of stock options."

"So what's it like, working for the superrich?"

"Insane," she said, "but I've gotten used to Thad's quirks."

"He has a lot of them?"

"Thad is *all* quirk," she laughed. "The superrich are one thing, but the *newly* superrich are something else entirely. Thad's a big child, really, and he's grown accustomed to instant gratification. Whatever you're doing for him, my advice is to do it in a hurry."

"I'll try," Stone said. "The salad is delicious; wonderful dressing."

"Thank you, kind sir."

"Have you spent a lot of time in Palm Beach?"

"Oh, yes. Thad's had his place there for a couple of years, and he's mostly back and forth from there to New York. Of course, the house has been under construction for all that time, so we live on the boat."

"That's what he told me."

"You're staying aboard, then?"

"I am."

"Good. I'll cook you dinner tonight."

"Why don't I take you out?" Stone asked. "I should get to know the lay of the land."

"I'd love that."

"Book us at some place you like."

"Will do." She turned her attention to her lunch.

She was very attractive, Stone thought. Late twenties or early thirties, tall, slender, a blond ponytail, nice tan. He finished his lunch and she took their trays away.

"Is there a phone on the airplane?" he asked her.

"In the arm of your chair," she said. "It's a satellite phone, but it works like a cell phone." She headed for the galley.

Stone dug the slip of paper from his pocket and looked at it. Mrs. Winston Harding III, in the 561 area code. Where was that? He dialed the number.

"Hello," a low female voice said immediately.

"May I speak with Mrs. Winston Harding, please? My name is Stone Barrington."

"Oh, Mr. Barrington, this is Mrs. Harding. How good of you to ring me back so promptly. You sound a little funny. Are you in a car?"

"In an airplane," Stone said. "Tell me, where is the five-six-one area code?"

"Palm Beach, Florida," she said.

"Oh. Oddly enough, that's where I'm flying to."

"How convenient," she said. "I wonder if we might meet while you're here? I'm in need of some very good legal counsel."

"Of course. Who recommended me, may I ask?"

"No one, really. It was something I read about you once. Let's have lunch tomorrow. Do you know a restaurant called Renato's?"

"No, this will be my first visit to Palm Beach."

"It's in the heart of town, in a little cul-de-sac off Worth Avenue, right across the street from the Everglades Club. Anyone can tell you."

"I expect I can find it."

"Twelve-thirty, then, in the garden?"

"Fine. How will I recognize you?"

"I'll recognize you," she said. "See you tomorrow." She hung up.

Stone replaced the phone in the arm of the chair. Winston Harding.

Sounded faintly familiar, but he couldn't place the man. Hard to tell much about Mrs. Harding from her voice, even her age. He pictured her as in her fifties, but she could be younger, he supposed. Or older.

He settled back into his chair and returned his attention to the *Times.* Soon, he dozed off.

Chapter 5

Stone was wakened by a slight jar and the screech of rubber on pavement. He opened his eyes to see airport buildings rushing past the airplane's windows as the pilot deployed the thrust reversers.

"You slept very well," Callie said. She was back in her seat.

"It's one of the things I do best," he replied.

"I guess I'll have to figure out the other things for myself," she said, with a little smile.

The airplane taxied to a stop in front of a terminal, and the copilot came out of the cockpit and lowered the airstair door. A lineman entered the airplane, and the copilot showed him where the luggage was stored.

Stone followed Callie down the stairs to a waiting car, a Jaguar XK8 convertible, top down. The lineman was stowing their luggage in the trunk and behind the seat.

"Hop in," Callie said.

Stone got into the passenger seat, and a minute later they were out of the airport, rolling east. The temperature was in the mid-seventies, and the sun was shining brightly.

"Quite a difference from New York, huh?" Callie said.

"Where are we now?" Stone asked.

"We're in West Palm, and in a couple of minutes we'll cross onto the island of Palm Beach, if traffic isn't too screwed up on the bridge. They're replacing it, and it's taking forever."

Traffic was screwed up on the bridge, and it took forever before they were waved across and Callie was able to drive quickly again. They passed between a double row of very tall royal palms.

"This your first trip here?" she asked.

"Yes, it is. In fact, the only place I've ever been in Florida is Miami—twice, both times to pick up people in handcuffs."

She looked at him. "What kind of lawyer are you?"

"One who used to be a cop."

She made a few quick turns and suddenly, they were on the beach, driving past huge, ugly stucco mansions. "Thought I'd give you a little tour on the way to the house," she said. "That's Mar a Lago over there—the home of Marjorie Meriwether Post, now owned by the awful Donald Trump. He's turned it into a club. Some of these palaces have tunnels to the beach." She turned down Worth Avenue. "This is the shopping heart of Palm Beach," she said. "All the famous stores are here." They drove past Saks Fifth Avenue, Ralph Lauren and dozens of smaller shops.

"Where is the Everglades Club?" he asked.

"Down at the end. Why do you ask?"

"I have a lunch date for tomorrow at a place called Renato's, which is supposed to be across the street."

"Here comes the Everglades Club on the left," she said, "and on the right is a little alley full of shops, and Renato's is at the end."

"What's the Everglades Club?"

"Palm Beach's most desirable club, or the snottiest, depending on your point of view."

"And what is your point of view?"

"It's the snottiest. Not only are Jews not allowed as members, they can't even visit as guests, and I'm half-Jewish."

"I didn't know that sort of thing still existed in this country."

"You've led a sheltered life," she said. She turned left and began driving through a series of quiet streets lined with large houses and sheltered by tropical vegetation.

"This is beautiful," he said.

"Certainly is. The most desirable houses are either on the beach or on the Inland Waterway, which in Palm Beach is called Lake Worth. Thad's place is on Lake Worth. It's more sheltered for the boat." Shortly, she turned the Jaguar through a large gate into a circular drive and stopped before a palazzo that seemed to have been airlifted from Venice. "Here we are. Leave the luggage. Somebody will get it."

Stone followed her to the huge double front doors. She pushed and a door swung back to reveal a central hallway that ran straight through the house. The hall was a gallery, hung with large oils. Stone recognized a Turner.

"Oh, good," she said. "They've finished redoing the hall." She led Stone out the back door and into gorgeously planted gardens.

Stone looked back. "You'd never know the house was under construction," he said.

"The outside is all finished, now, so all the equipment and tools are inside." They passed through the gardens and onto a broad lawn, beyond which Lake Worth gleamed in the sunlight.

Blocking most of the view, however, was a very large, very beautiful old yacht.

"That's *Toscana,*" Callie said.

"She's glorious."

"She was built in Italy in the thirties. Thad spent two years both restoring her to her original condition and almost invisibly modernizing every system on board."

"How big is she?"

"Two hundred and twenty-two feet, but with only seven cabins, so everyone aboard can be comfortable. Thad gives me the smallest one, but that's bigger than the big cabins on lesser yachts."

A small Hispanic young man wearing a smart uniform of white shirt and shorts came down the gangplank to meet them.

"Stone, this is Juanito, *Toscana*'s chief steward. Juanito, this is Mr. Barrington."

"Welcome aboard," Juanito said. "Mr. Barrington is in cabin number two. Mr. Thad phoned to say he was coming."

"I'll show him aboard," Callie said. "Our luggage is in the Jag."

Juanito found a handcart and ran off toward the house.

Stone followed Callie into the main saloon, and it was as if they had stepped into a much earlier decade. "My God," he said, "it might have been launched yesterday."

"Yes, Thad did a really good job on the restoration. Come on, I'll show you to your cabin. Thad has given you the best one, after the master stateroom." She led the way down a central passage off the saloon and opened a heavy mahogany door on the starboard side. "Here you are."

Stone stepped into a cabin paneled in mahogany with white painted trim. There was a carved marble fireplace on one side of the room, with a sofa and a pair of chairs facing it, and behind them, a large bed with a canopy, trimmed in nautical-looking fabric. Out the large porthole was a view of the water. "Marvelous," he said.

"Your bath is in here," Callie said, switching on a light.

More marble, with a large tub and a separate shower stall. "I've never seen anything like this vessel," Stone said, "although I once sank a yacht nearly as large."

"Run her on the rocks?"

"No, I was just angry with her owner."

Callie looked at him, unsure whether he was serious. "I wouldn't mention that to Thad," she said. "You might make him nervous."

Juanito appeared with Stone's luggage. "May I unpack for you, Mr. Barrington?"

"Thank you, Juanito, yes."

"And would you like your suits pressed?"

"Thank you again."

"My cabin is down the hall," Callie said, grabbing the single small duffel that had accompanied her. "Why don't you poke around, take a look at *Toscana?* Dinner at eight all right? I booked from the airplane."

"Fine. How are we dressing?"

"It's an elegant place, and the crowd will be elegantly dressed, at least, as they define elegant."

"See you a little before eight," Stone said. He left Juanito to do his work and began to explore the big yacht. There were two other cabins on the starboard side, and another three on the port side. Stone took a narrow staircase up a deck and emerged under a broad awning covering an expanse of teak decking. The superstructure was forward, and a set of doors led to what he suspected was the master stateroom. He took another staircase and came to the bridge, where a man in his mid-thirties, wearing the same white uniform as Juanito, except with more stripes on his shoulder boards, was sitting at the chart table.

"G'day," the young man said with an Australian twang. "You must be Mr. Barrington."

"That's right," Stone said, offering his hand.

"I'm Gary Stringfellow, the captain," he said.

"Good to meet you."

"Juanito show you to your cabin?"

"Yes, I'm just having a look around. This is quite some bridge." It was all mahogany and brass.

"Yes. In the rebuilding, we tried to keep it much as it was when the yacht was built, except, of course, we have every piece of modern gear known to man."

"I can see that."

"Wander at will," Gary said. "I have some work to do. Just let Juanito know if you need anything."

"Thanks, I will." Stone continued his tour, working his way forward to the stern, then aft to a broad sundeck, where he shucked off his coat, loosened his tie and collapsed into a chair.

Juanito appeared, as if by magic, bearing a silver tray and a frosty glass. "I thought you might like a gin and tonic," he said.

"Thank you, Juanito. You're psychic." Stone took the drink, and Juanito disappeared, only to return a moment later with a cordless phone.

"A call for you, Mr. Barrington," he said.

Stone accepted the instrument. "Hello?"

"It's Bill. How was your flight?"

"You're full of surprises, Bill, I'll give you that."

"I had meant to brief you before you met Thad, but there was no time. I take it you understand his problem?"

"Yes, it's sort of like being back in high school—the geek wants to date the beauty queen."

"Thad is impulsive, but he takes these things seriously. Do the best job for him you can, and it will react to your benefit."

"It already has," Stone said. "After all, I'm sitting on a yacht in Palm Beach with a gin and tonic frozen to my fist, while you're in New York, freezing your ass off."

"That was unkind."

"It's no fun being in Florida in winter if you can't gloat a little."

"Yeah, yeah. Listen, Stone, take this assignment seriously, all right? Thad is very important to the firm. We're doing all the legal work on his IPO, and I'm his personal attorney. Clients don't get any bigger than Thad Shames."

"I get the picture," Stone replied.

"Keep me posted," Eggers said, "and don't let anything go wrong." He hung up.

Stone put his feet up, sipped his drink and watched the yachts sail by. This was wonderful. Tomorrow he'd find the girl and she and Shames would live happily ever after. What could possibly go wrong?

⤙ Chapter 6 ⤚

Stone reappeared on the afterdeck just before eight, showered, shaved and wearing a gray linen suit, a cream-colored silk shirt, a yellow tie and black alligator shoes. He took a long look at the lights of West Palm, and then he was joined by Callie.

"Good evening," she said.

He turned to look at her and was stunned by the transformation. Her hair was loose around her shoulders, and she was wearing a tight-fitting, short dress of a dark brown espresso color. It was cut fairly low, showing off handsome breasts and a good tan. When she smiled, her teeth practically glowed in the dark. "Good evening," he said, when he got his breath back.

"Shall we go?" She led him back through the gardens, their way lighted by low lamps along the path, through the house and to the car. "Would you like to drive?" She held out the keys.

Stone took them. "Sure. I haven't driven one of these." He opened the door for her, then went around to the driver's side. The engine purred, rather than roared, to life, and he pulled into the lamplit street and accelerated. "Nice. What kind of power?"

"A two-hundred-and-ninety-horsepower V-eight."

"Very smooth, too. Is it yours?"

"Yes."

"Cooking must pay better than I thought."

"Well, I don't have rent, utilities or any other household expenses to worry about, and it helps when your boss gives you an interest-free loan."

"Sounds as though you've made yourself important to Thad."

"I try." She directed him through a number of turns and shortly they pulled up before a restaurant called Cafe L'Europe. A valet took the car.

"I would have thought the 'el, apostrophe' was a little much," Stone said as they entered.

"A great deal about Palm Beach is a little much," she said.

They were shown to a table near the center of the room. "What would you like to drink?" Stone asked.

"A Tanqueray martini, please."

"And a vodka gimlet," Stone told the waiter. "This is a very good table," he said to her.

"I booked it in Thad's name," she replied.

"Smart move." Menus and a wine list were brought.

Callie closed her menu. "I'm sick of thinking about food," she said. "Order for me."

"Anything you don't eat?"

"I can't think of anything."

The waiter returned. "Are you ready to order, sir?"

"Yes," Stone said. "We'll start with the beluga caviar and iced Absolut Citron," he said. "For the main course, the rack of lamb, medium rare." He opened the wine list. "And a bottle of the Phelps Insignia 'ninety-one."

"Very good, sir." He went away.

They sat back and sipped their drinks until the caviar came, then they ate it slowly, sipping the lemon vodka and making it all last. A couple came into the restaurant, the young woman wearing a sleeveless sweater with the name "Chanel" emblazoned across her chest, in two-inch-high letters.

"A billboard," Stone said.

"Typical of Palm Beach," Callie replied.

"Eurotrash?"

"Just trash. There's a lot of it about. Oh, there are still some old-line families around, living quietly, if grandly, but mostly it's what you see here—people who somehow got ahold of a lot of money and want everybody to know it. They've bid up the real estate out of sight. A nice little house on a couple of acres is now three million bucks, and last week I saw an ad for what was advertised as the last vacant beachfront lot in Palm Beach—all one and a half acres of it—and they're asking eight and a half million."

Stone nearly choked on his vodka.

The waiter had just taken away the dishes when three people, two women and a man, entered the restaurant and were shown to a table by the street windows. Stone followed their progress closely. One of the women, a redhead, had something very familiar about her.

Callie kicked him under the table. "I thought that in this dress, I might get your undivided attention."

"I'm sorry," Stone said, "but I think I know one of the women. Except she's a redhead, and the woman I knew was a blonde, like you. Well, not as beautiful as you."

"She must have been important," Callie said. "Tell me about her."

"It's not a short story," Stone said. "More of a novella."

"I've got all night."

"All right."

Dinner arrived, and Stone tasted the wine. "Decant it, please," he said to the waiter.

When that was done, Callie said, "Continue."

"Oh, yes. A few years back I scheduled a sailing charter out of St. Marks. You know it?"

"Yes, we've been in there on *Toscana.*"

"My girlfriend was supposed to follow, but she got snowed into New York, then she got a magazine assignment to interview Vance Calder."

"Lucky girl," she said. "My favorite movie star."

"Everybody's favorite. That's why she couldn't turn it down. Anyway, I was stuck there alone, and one morning I was having breakfast in the cockpit of the boat, and something odd happened. A yacht of about fifty feet sailed into the harbor, the mainsail ripped, and nobody aboard but a beautiful blonde. After customs had cleared the boat, the police came and took her away.

"The following day I was passing the town hall and there was some sort of hearing under way, and I went in. Turned out to be an inquest. The girl, whose name was Allison Manning, had been sailing across the Atlantic with her husband, who was the writer Paul Manning . . ."

"I've read his stuff," she said. "He's good."

"Yes. Anyway, her testimony is that they're halfway across, and he winches her up the mast to fix something, then cleats the line. She finishes the job and looks down to find him lying in the cockpit, turning blue. She's stuck at the top of the mast, but eventually she manages to shinny down. He's dead, probably of a heart attack. He's the sailor, and she's the cook and bottle-washer, and now she's in the middle of the Atlantic Ocean, alone, her husband starting to rot in the heat. She buries him at sea and, in a considerable act of seamanship for somebody who isn't a sailor, manages to get the yacht across the Atlantic to St. Marks."

"This is beginning to sound familiar. Wasn't there something about it on *Sixty Minutes* a while back?"

"Then you know the story?"

"No, go on. Tell me everything."

"St. Marks's Minister of Justice doesn't buy her story, and he charges her with murdering her husband. Stone to the rescue. I offer to help. She's tried. With the help of a local barrister, I represent her. Long story short, she's convicted and sentenced to hang."

"Jesus."

"Yes. I call New York and pull out all the stops on publicity. *Sixty Minutes* shows up, and many telegrams are sent to the prime minister, demanding she be released. On the day of the execution, fully expecting a pardon, I and the barrister and a priest visit her in her cell. Suddenly she's taken out, and the three of us are locked in. A minute later, we hear the trap sprung on the gallows."

"That's horrible," she said. "I don't think I knew the end of the story. I must have been traveling at the time."

"There's more. Turns out her husband wasn't dead; it was all an insurance scam. He'd lost a ton of weight and shaved off a beard and was unrecognizable, and he was there, in St. Marks, posing as a magazine writer covering the story."

"And he didn't stop the hanging?"

"No. What's more, in order to cover up his new identity, he engineered a light airplane crash in which his ex-wife and two others died."

"And he got away with it?"

"Fortunately, no. He turned up in New York a few weeks later, demanding his yacht."

"What?"

"Didn't I mention that Allison, by way of my fee, gave me the yacht?"

"No."

"Well, she did."

"And now Paul Manning wanted it back?"

"He did."

"What did you do?"

"I'd been expecting him to show up, so I made a phone call, and the police came and took him away. He was extradited to St. Marks, where he was tried, then hanged for the three murders."

"God, what a story. And what made you think of it tonight?"

"I thought of it because Allison Manning is sitting right over there by the windows."

Callie's head spun around.

Stone tapped her on the arm. "Don't stare. I don't want her to see me."

"You're sure?"

"She's dyed her hair red, but that is Allison in the flesh, and very nice flesh it is."

"How could she possibly be here if she was hanged in St. Marks?"

"I didn't finish my story. Unbeknownst to me, Allison had, through the local barrister, arranged to deliver a cashier's check for one million dollars into the prime minister's hands. Accordingly, the execution was faked, and Allison departed the island in a fast yacht she had chartered for the purpose."

"That didn't make it into the *Sixty Minutes* report, did it?"

"It did not. And I may have violated attorney-client confidentiality by telling you."

"Where did Allison get a million dollars?"

"Paul Manning had been insured for twelve million dollars, and the insurance company had already paid."

"So she skipped St. Marks with all that money?"

"Much to the annoyance of her husband."

"But he got his comeuppance."

"He did."

"And you got the yacht."

"I did."

"Do you still have it?"

"No. I sold it in Fort Lauderdale."

"You said you'd never been anywhere in Florida except Miami."

"I forgot about Lauderdale."

"How much did you get for the yacht?"

"A million, six."

"And what did you do with it?"

"I gave the IRS a large chunk, and the rest is in a sock, under my mattress."

She threw back her head and laughed. When she had recovered herself, she asked, "Why do you suppose Allison Manning is in Palm Beach?"

"I have no idea."

They got back to *Toscana* around eleven and stood on the afterdeck, watching the moon come up.

"If you will forgive me," she said, "I'm going to turn in. It was a long day, and I've had a lot to drink."

"I'm hurt," he replied, "but I'll get over it."

She leaned into him and kissed him, just long enough to be interesting; creamy lips, warm tongue. "Sleep well."

"Now I won't sleep at all," Stone said.

"Oh, good," she replied, then walked off toward her cabin.

☙ **Chapter 7** ☙

Late the following morning, Stone borrowed Callie's Jaguar, drove downtown and found a parking space on Worth Avenue. He arrived at Renato's five minutes early and presented himself to the headwaiter. "I'm meeting a Mrs. Harding," he said.

"Oh, yes," the man replied. "We have you in the garden." He led Stone to a table under overhanging bougainvillea and left a pair of menus. Stone sipped some mineral water and waited for Mrs. Winston Harding to appear. When she arrived, Stone choked on his mineral water. This, he had not been expecting.

She was only fashionably late, wearing blue slacks and a matching cashmere sweater, pearls at the neck, the very picture of the fashionable young matron. He tended to remember her in short shorts, with a shirt tied below her breasts, revealing an enticing midsection, and he tried to make the adjustment.

Stone stood to greet her. "Hello, Allison," he said.

"Shhh," she whispered, hugging him, her breasts pressing against him for an extra moment. "We don't use that name here."

He held her chair and ordered a cosmopolitan for her. "Brad," she said to the headwaiter, "this is Stone Barrington. I'm sure you'll be seeing more of him."

The headwaiter shook Stone's hand, then went to get her drink.

"So what is this Mrs. Winston Harding business?"

"That, my love, is my name these days. It's good to see you." She smiled, leaning forward to allow her breasts to be seen down the V-necked sweater.

"And you," he said. "You disappeared over the horizon in that rented yacht, and I thought I'd never see you again. I've often wondered where you got to."

"Oh, all over," she said, smiling. "I've seen the world since last I saw you. I started with a cruise in the Pacific and the Far East, and I just kept going. A year later, I met Winston Harding in London, and a few weeks later we were married in Houston, his home. Winston was a property developer."

"Was?"

"I'm a widow now."

"My condolences. Was there insurance involved?"

She blushed a little. "That was an evil thing to say. He died of a heart attack. He was fifty-five."

"My apologies."

"But there was insurance involved, and a great deal else. Let's order."

She chose the poached salmon, and Stone the rigatoni with a sauce of wild boar sausage and cream. He ordered a bottle of Frascati.

"Well, Palm Beach must be the perfect spot for a wealthy widow," Stone said.

"We bought the house the year after we were married," she replied. "I hardly chose it for widowhood; it just worked out that way. Funny, it's worth three times what Winston paid for it."

"I've heard the market is hot."

"And so am I," she said. She stopped talking while their lunch was served. "In a manner of speaking," she said, when the waiter had left.

"I should think you would have cooled off considerably," Stone said. "After all, you're dead."

"Being dead has its advantages," she said, "but if you run into someone you used to know, it can come as a shock to them."

"Has that happened to you?"

"From time to time, but I've always managed to duck out before we came face-to-face."

"I think I prefer you as a blonde, though."

She laughed. "I'm probably the only redhead in Palm Beach with blond roots."

"So you're finding it a strain, being dead?"

"I'd rather be alive."

"Well, there is the insurance company," Stone said.

"That's why I called you. I want you to represent me in squaring things with those people."

Stone blinked. "You mean you want to give them back their twelve million dollars?"

"Of course not," she said. "Well, not all of it. I thought you might negotiate a settlement. What do you think the chances are of that?"

"I think the insurance company would be very surprised to get *any* of their money back."

"How little do you think I could give them?"

"Who knows? After they get over their initial shock, they'll probably begin to wonder who wants to give it to them. After all, both the culprits are dead."

"I read about your part in sending Paul back to St. Marks," she said.

"I hope you derived some satisfaction from that," Stone replied. "After all, he could have stopped your 'execution' at any time, and he didn't."

She shrugged. "Well, that's all in the past, isn't it?"

"Apparently not, if you're still suffering the aftereffects."

"Stone, I've always been an honest person. You mustn't think I'm some sort of career criminal."

"I don't. I've always thought it was Paul's idea to screw the insurance company."

"It was. Of course, I went along with it, after he'd spent a few months persuading me. Who knew it would end the way it did?"

"Did you love him?"

"Oh, God, did I love him, and for years! It had begun to wear off, though, by the time we hatched the plot. My plan was to take half the money and kiss Paul good-bye." She smiled. "That's when I fell into your bed."

"As I recall, it was *your* bed, but it hardly matters. I had just had the shock of my girl running off with somebody else, so I was easy."

"Yes, you were," she said, her voice low. "Maybe, now that I'm going to be legal again, we could see something of each other."

Stone shook his head. "For the moment, all I can do is represent you in trying to put things right with the insurance company. If I spend any more time with you than that, then I'm a part of a criminal conspiracy."

"But once I'm legal again . . ."

"That's different."

"I mean, I don't want to start using my old name again, or anything like that. I just want to know that I can cross a border without popping up in some computer."

"Not much chance of that, since you're supposed to be dead."

"I still have my old passport. I used it, until I married Winston, then I used my old birth certificate to get a new one."

"Did he know about your past?"

She shook her head. "Not the bad part. I reinvented my life without Paul Manning, and he believed me. He was a dear soul. He never doubted me."

"Well, I think you're right to want to settle this thing with the insurance company. How high will you go?"

She looked thoughtful. "Five million?"

"I should think they'd be *delighted* to get that much back. They wrote off the money a long time ago. Can you afford it?"

"Oh, yes. I still had ten million when I met Winston, and he had a considerable estate. Also, the market has been *very* kind to me."

"You'd need to square things with the IRS."

"How?"

"I don't know, maybe file an amended return. Get a good accountant and let him handle it. It's worth the money to be righteous again."

"Yes, I suppose it is."

"Well, Allison . . . I'm sorry, what do you call yourself these days?"

"Elizabeth."

"That's nice. I . . ." Stone stopped. No, it couldn't be.

"I've had to be so wary all the time. Only last weekend, I met the most interesting man, but he's apparently pretty well known, and I just didn't want to get into anything like that until I had my life in order, so I got all nervous and just walked away from him."

Yes, it could be. "And where were you last weekend?"

"In Easthampton."

"Did you dine at Jerry Della Femina's?"

Her jaw dropped. "How could you know that?"

"You're Liz," he said.

"You know Thad, what's his name?"

"Shames."

"Well, I'll be damned."

"Not if I can square things with the insurance company." Stone got out his cell phone and notebook and dialed a number. "This is Stone Barrington. Is he available?"

"Who are you calling?" she asked.

"Yes, tell him it's important."

Shames came onto the line. "Stone? Anything to report?"

"There's someone here who'd like to speak with you," Stone said. He handed the phone to Liz.

She took it, baffled. "Hello? Yes, this is Liz. Oh, it's you! We were just talking about you. Well, yes, I'd like to see you again. Saturday? I believe I'm free. All right, I'll look forward to seeing you then." She handed the phone back to Stone.

"Stone, bring her to the party on Saturday night, aboard *Toscana*. Seven o'clock."

"All right."

"See you then. Gotta run."

Stone returned the cell phone to his pocket.

"So, you're a matchmaker, as well?"

"Glad to be of service."

"He is well known, isn't he?"

"Yes, in the worlds of computer software and Wall Street, he's something of a celebrity."

"I don't know about these things. I never read the *Wall Street Journal.*"

"Neither do I."

She frowned.

"Anything wrong?"

"There is something else."

"What's that?"

"Paul Manning."

"He's dead."

She shook her head. "No, he's not."

"But he went back to St. Marks and was . . ." Stone stopped. "You bought him out, didn't you?"

She nodded sheepishly. "I called Sir Leslie, the barrister, remember?"

"Oh, yes. How much did it cost you?"

"Half a million."

"You got a volume discount?"

"Stone, I couldn't just let him be hanged."

"Why not? He's a triple murderer. And, when he thought you were going to be executed, he didn't lift a hand to save you from the gallows."

"That's true, of course, but still . . ."

A terrible thought struck Stone. "Please tell me Paul doesn't know you're alive."

She slumped. "I'm afraid he does. Sir Leslie let it slip."

"Good God. Where is Paul?"

"I don't know, but he was in Easthampton last weekend."

"You saw him?"

"I was in a shop on Sunday afternoon, and he passed by in the street."

"You're sure it was Paul?"

"Absolutely sure. He's kept all that weight off, and he's had a nose job, but I recognized him just by the way he walked."

"Did he see you?"

"No. I mean, I don't think so. Still, I got the hell out of the Hamptons, and as soon as I got to Palm Beach, I changed my hair color. What can I do about this, Stone?"

"It's the money he wants, isn't it? You could try buying him off."

"Will you deal with that for me?"

"Well, there are two problems with that. First, I don't know where to find him. Second, the last time he saw me, he wanted to kill me, and since I got him arrested, imprisoned and nearly hanged in St. Marks, I doubt if he feels any more kindly toward me. In fact, it makes me nervous just knowing he's out there somewhere."

"Apparently, he wants to kill me, too," she said. "At least, that's what he told Sir Leslie."

"Grateful, isn't he?"

"Stone, what am I going to do?"

"Well, Allison—excuse me, *Liz*—since we don't know how to find him, I suppose we're going to have to wait for him to find you."

She nodded. "Or you."

⮿ Chapter 8 ⮾

After lunch, when Allison, now Liz, had left him, Stone took a drive
around Palm Beach before returning to the yacht. He thought about
Paul Manning and how he would not like to renew his acquaintance with
the man. During his career as a police officer, Stone had known a number
of people who would have preferred to see him dead, rather than alive,
but all of them were either dead themselves, or safely locked away in
prison. Except Paul Manning. He flipped open his cell phone and dialed
his office number.

"Stone Barrington's office," Joan said.

"Hi, it's me."

"Hi. How's Palm Beach?"

"Sunny and warm."

"Oh, shit."

Stone laughed. "Joan, have you told anyone I'm in Palm Beach?"

"No," she said.

"Has anybody inquired about my whereabouts?"

"I don't think anybody cares," she said archly.

"Thanks. Will you check my old files for one on the Boston Mutual Insurance Company? There's an investigator there I'd like to speak to, and
I can't remember his name."

"You want to hold? I've got most of that stuff scanned into the computer."

"Go ahead and look." Stone made a couple of turns. He was now in a
handsome residential neighborhood off North County Road, which pretty
much served as Palm Beach's main street.

"I've got it," she said. "He's the chief investigative officer for Boston
Mutual."

"That's the guy. Name and phone number?" He pulled to the curb and
got out his notebook.

"Frank Stendahl." She gave him the number.

Stone wrote it down. "Any other calls?"

She read him a short list, and he gave her instructions on handling
them, then he hung up and dialed Frank Stendahl's number. He had met
Stendahl in St. Marks, when the man had come to investigate the claim on
Paul Manning's insurance policy and had ended up testifying at Allison's
trial. Stone had involved him in the capture of Paul Manning later, but the

murder charges against Manning had taken precedence over Boston Mutual's insurance fraud charges, and, since Allison had made their twelve million dollars disappear before she was "hanged," Manning had had no money left for them to go after.

"Stendahl," a gruff voice said.

"Frank, it's Stone Barrington."

Stendahl's voice warmed. "Stone, how are you?"

"Very well, thanks. How's the weather in Boston?"

"Don't ask."

"I won't. Tell me, Frank, how do you think your company would feel about getting back some of the money you paid out on the Paul Manning policy?"

"You planning to reimburse us, Stone?" Suspicion had crept into the investigator's voice.

"Certainly not," Stone replied. "But it might be possible to recover a part of the sum."

"How?"

"Let's just say that I have a client who is interested in clearing up the matter. Not the whole twelve million, of course, but a decent fraction."

"How decent a fraction?"

"How about a million dollars?"

"How about six million?"

"It's not going to happen, Frank."

"And what do we have to do to get this money?"

"Nothing, really. Just agree to a settlement and sign a release."

"Releasing who from what?"

"Releasing anybody from any liability connected with the fraud."

Stendahl was silent.

"Frank?"

"I'm just trying to figure this out," he said. "Who's your client?"

"I'm afraid that's confidential and will have to remain so."

"I just don't get it, Stone," Stendahl said. "Both the people responsible for the fraud are dead, and the money vanished into thin air, or at least into some offshore account we could never find. Who would want to give us a million bucks out of the goodness of his heart?"

"I'm afraid I can't help you there, Frank. I was contacted and instructed to contact your company and make the offer. That's all I can tell you."

"I just don't get it," Stendahl said again.

"You want me to tell my client you said no?"

"Of course not," Stendahl nearly shouted. "I'll have to take this upstairs, see what they have to say."

"I can have the money in your account twenty-four hours after I receive the release."

"I'll tell them that."

"And, Frank, it's going to be an iron-clad release—broad and deep, covering anything anybody could ever have done to Boston Mutual in the matter of this policy."

"Stone, do you have any idea how hard it would be for an insurance executive ever to sign such a document? It would turn his liver to rock candy."

"Maybe a million dollars would melt it."

"Where can I reach you?"

Stone gave him the cell phone number. "I'm in Florida," he said.

Stendahl groaned and hung up.

Stone called his office again and dictated a release. "Type that up, leaving the amount blank, and have it ready to fax to Stendahl," he said.

"Will do," Joan replied.

Stone pulled back into traffic. On the way back to the yacht, he passed West Indies Drive, where Elizabeth Harding's house was. He was going to have to get used to that name.

"Liz," he said aloud. "Liz, Liz, Liz." He thought about the nights he had spent with her aboard the yacht in St. Marks, and the memory stirred more in him than he was comfortable with. After all, he was pimping—well, that was too strong a word—*representing* Thad Shames in the matter of Liz Harding, and sleeping with the woman his client was chasing would probably violate *some* canon of legal ethics.

He was back on board *Toscana*, sipping a rum and tonic on the afterdeck, when his cell phone rang.

"Stone Barrington."

"It's Stendahl. I'm with our CEO and CFO, and I'm going to put you on the speakerphone."

"Okay."

Stendahl's voice became hollow. "Now, Stone, our people are not willing to enter into this transaction without knowing more about your client and his reasons for making this offer."

"Frank, gentlemen, client-attorney confidentiality prevents me from telling you any more than I already have about my client's identity or motives. This is a very simple proposition: I will wire-transfer one million dollars into Boston Mutual's account in return for a release of criminal and civil liability in the matter of the Paul Manning policy for anyone who ever had anything to do with it."

Another voice spoke. "This is Morrison, CFO of the company," it said. "Five million, and that's our best offer."

"Mr. Morrison," Stone said, *"I'm* doing the offering, and while I'm at it, I'll give you our last, best offer to settle this matter. One million, five hundred thousand dollars, and that's it. You have only to accept or reject, but I must tell you, that if you reject this offer, when this phone call is over, you will never hear of this matter again. You simply have to decide whether you'd rather be out twelve million dollars or ten million, five." Stone stopped talking and waited.

"Hang on," Stendahl said, and the call went on hold.

Stone waited, tapping his fingers against his glass. If they stood firm, he could always come back with five million later. After all, that's what Liz Harding had said she would pay.

"We're back," Stendahl said.

"This is Shanklin, the CEO of the company," a new voice said. "We accept, pending a legal review of the form of the release."

"Give me a fax number," Stone said, then wrote it down. "Gentlemen, you'll have the release in five minutes. Sign and fax it to my office, along with your bank account number, and FedEx the original. Upon receipt of the original, I will wire-transfer the funds to your account."

"We're waiting," Stendahl said.

Stone punched off and speed-dialed his office. When Joan answered, he said, "Insert the amount of one million five hundred thousand dollars in the document, print it out and fax it to Stendahl pronto; he's waiting for it." He gave her the number, then hung up.

Stone sat and sipped his drink, watching the afternoon grow later. Half an hour later, his cell phone rang. "Hello?"

"It's Joan. They signed the document and faxed it back to us."

"Great," Stone said. He found Juanito, got the yacht's fax number, gave it to Joan and asked her to fax the document to him, then he called Liz Harding.

"It's Stone," he said when she had answered. "I have news."

"Tell me," she said.

"Boston Mutual has accepted an offer of one point five million to settle the matter and release you from any civil or criminal liability."

"Oh, Stone," she gushed. "I can't tell you how wonderful it is to hear that."

"Now listen," he said. "It's three-thirty. I want you to call or fax your bank right this minute and instruct them to wire-transfer the funds to my firm's trust account in New York. It's too late for them to do it today, but instruct them to wire the funds immediately upon opening on Monday morning. That way, I can have the funds wired to Boston the same day, and this transaction will be complete."

"Then I'm a free woman?"

"I've no doubt that you're a very expensive woman, but you'll be free when that money hits their bank account. I have a copy of the release being faxed to me, and I'll give it to you tomorrow night, when I pick you up. And I want you to fax a copy of the instructions to your bank to me aboard the yacht." He gave her the fax number. "Now get moving."

"Okay!"

Half an hour later, he had both faxes in hand. He took a long swig of his drink and reflected on a good day's work. There was some small doubt tickling the back of his brain, but before he could summon it up, the rum flushed it away.

Chapter 9

Stone was taking a nap in his cabin when there was a knock on his door. "Come in," he called out.

The door opened and Callie Hodges stuck her head in. "Sorry, I didn't mean to wake you."

Stone sat up on his elbows. "It's all right. How are you?"

"I'm good. You free for dinner?"

"Sure."

"I'll cook for you, then."

"Sounds wonderful."

"Find the galley when you're awake," she said. "I'll be the one in the apron."

"Be there shortly," he said. "I'd like to grab a shower."

"Half an hour is fine," she said, then closed the door.

Stone went into the bathroom, a little groggy, and inspected his face. The shave was okay. He stripped and got into the shower, and by the time he emerged, he was awake again. He dried his hair, slipped into a polo shirt and chinos and made his way forward. He found the galley a deck below the bridge, off the dining room. Callie was, indeed, wearing an apron, and, it appeared, nothing else.

"Hi," she said. "Make us a drink?" She pointed to the butler's pantry, and when she turned back to the stove he was a little disappointed to see that she was wearing a strapless top and shorts under her apron.

"What would you like?" Stone asked.

"You were drinking vodka gimlets last night, weren't you?"

"That's right. Would you like to try one?"

"Love to."

Stone measured the vodka and Rose's sweetened lime juice into a shaker, shook the liquid cold and strained it into two martini glasses. He took them back into the galley and handed one to Callie. "Try that."

She sipped the icy drink. "Mmmm . . . perfect!"

"What are you cooking?"

"Risotto," she said, stirring a pot with her free hand. "It has to be constantly stirred until it's done."

"I love risotto," he said.

"Any kind of food you don't love?"

"I never eat raw animals," he said, "or anything that might still be alive, like an oyster."

"You don't like oysters? You don't know what you're missing."

"Last time I saw somebody eat oysters, he squeezed some lemon juice onto them, and they flinched. I never eat anything that can still flinch."

"Anything else?"

Stone thought. "Celery and green peppers. I think that's it."

"There's a bottle of chardonnay in the little wine fridge, there," she said, nodding. "Will you open it? This is almost ready."

Stone found a bottle of Ferarri-Carano Reserve and opened it. "Where are we dining?"

She was spooning risotto onto two large plates. "Follow me," she said, picking them up. She led the way through a swinging door into a small dining room, where a table was set for two. "The big dining room is through that door," she said. "We can seat up to sixteen in there."

"This is lovely," Stone said, sliding her chair under her and taking his own. He tasted the wine and poured two glasses.

"Dig in," she said. "Don't let it get cold."

Stone tasted the risotto, which contained fresh shrimp and asparagus. "Superb. Where'd you learn to cook?"

"At my father's knee," she said. "My mother preferred his cooking to hers, so she never entered the kitchen if she could help it. Later, I did a course at Cordon Bleu, in London, and I worked for a while for Prudence Leith, who has a London restaurant and catering service there. I learned a lot from Prue."

"How'd you come to work for Thad Shames?"

"Last summer I was cooking for a movie producer and his wife in the Hamptons, and Thad came to dinner. The producer was a real shit. He enjoyed ordering me around and complaining about my attitude."

"Did you have an attitude?"

"Probably. Anyway, he was particularly bad that night, complaining about the food, when everyone else was complimenting it. Finally, I'd had enough. I put dessert on the table and told him I was quitting, and he could do the dishes, then I walked out. I went to my room and packed my suitcase and started walking toward the village, up the dark road. Then Thad pulled up in a car and offered me a lift. He asked where I was going, and I said I didn't know. He offered me a job cooking for him, drove me back to his place, installed me in the guest house, and I've worked for him ever since. The job has grown to include lots of other duties, and I've enjoyed it."

"What would you be doing if you weren't working for Thad?" Stone asked.

"Probably working in a restaurant and hating it. I don't like a big kitchen, and you have no social life at all. This job is perfect for me. You aren't married, are you?"

"No."

"Ever married?"

"No. Well, once for about fifteen minutes. It was sort of annulled."

"And where is the ex-wife today?"

"Under full-time psychiatric care. I have that effect on women."

She laughed. "I won't pry. I just wanted to know if you were free before . . ."

"Before what?"

"Before I seduced you."

"If I weren't free, would it matter?"

"It certainly would," she said. "I've learned not to get involved with married men."

"I won't ask how. Where are you from?"

"I was born in a small town in Georgia, called Delano, but I grew up mostly in Kent, Connecticut."

"I have a little house in Washington, Connecticut."

"Nice town."

"Your folks still there?"

"Both dead. Daddy was a small-town lawyer and banker; my mother wrote short stories and poetry, sometimes for *The New Yorker.*"

"One of them was Jewish, you said?"

"Mother. She was a New York girl through and through. They met in the city at a party, and she married him and moved to Connecticut with him. She always missed living in New York. How about you?"

"Born and bred in the city. My father was a cabinet and furniture maker, my mother, a painter."

"Were they good at it?"

"They were. Dad has work in some of the city's better houses and apartments; Mother has two pictures in the permanent collection of the Metropolitan Museum. Mother and Dad are both gone, now."

"So we're both orphans?"

"We are, I guess."

They finished the risotto, and Callie served them a salad, then dessert—old-fashioned chocolate cake.

They took their coffee onto the afterdeck and settled into the banquette that ran around the stern railing.

"So, did you have a productive day?"

"I did."

"How did your lunch with the dead lady go?"

"Very well. I believe I solved her problem."

Callie set down her coffee cup. "Now," she said, "how do I go about seducing you? Do I just stick my tongue in your ear, or what?"

"It's easier than that." Stone took her face in his hands and kissed her for quite a long time. Their temperatures rose quickly.

"There may be crew about," she breathed between kisses. "We'd better go to your cabin."

"Oh, yes," Stone said.

She took his hand and led him forward. In less than a minute they were standing at the end of his bed, undressing each other. In Callie's case, it was quick; she was wearing only the two pieces. She sat on the bed and watched him peel off his clothes.

He knelt before her and began kissing the inside of her thighs, as she ran her fingers through his hair. He pushed her back on the bed and explored her delta, kissing the soft, blond fur at the edges. She gave a little shudder as he took her into his mouth. It took only a minute for her to come, and when she was finished, she pulled him onto her by his ears and felt for him, guiding him in.

"I love the first time," she said, as they made love. "It's always so . . ."

"So new," Stone panted.

"And exciting."

"Sometimes it gets better as it goes along," he said, thrusting.

She thrust back. "We'll see," she said, and they both came together.

Chapter 10

When Stone awoke his cabin was filled with sunshine, and it was past eleven o'clock. He never slept that late, and he was surprised. Callie was gone, and her side of the bed had been made. He shaved and showered, got into some slacks and a polo shirt and, since the palms outside were moving with the breeze, tied a light cashmere sweater around his shoulders.

He found Callie on the afterdeck in a bikini, reading a novel.

"Good morning," he said, kissing her.

She kissed him back. "You slept late," she said.

"Something I rarely do. I must have been tired."

She chuckled. "I should hope so."

"You look awfully fresh," he said.

"I've only been up for half an hour."

"Good book?"

"Starts really well. A writer I haven't read before, but I saw a good review in the *Times Book Review* last week. Fellow named . . ." She looked at
the cover. "Frederick James."

"I don't know him, either."

"A first novel, the review said. You had breakfast?"

"No, I was considering waiting for lunch."

"How about brunch? I'll take you to the Breakers."

"Isn't that a hotel?"

"Yes, and it has a nice beach club."

"Am I dressed properly?"

"Very." She stood up. "I'll get into some real clothes." She put down the
book and walked off toward her cabin.

Stone sat down and picked up the book. He read a couple of pages, and
by the time she returned, he had read thirty. "You're right," he said, "it
starts well." He looked up at her. "You look wonderful."

"Thank you, sir." She was wearing a yellow shift that set off her tan.

They walked through the main house, and as they were about to get
into her car, a small procession of Mercedes convertibles pulled into the
driveway behind them, and a man got out of one and came toward them,
carrying a clipboard.

"Where could I find Mr. Shames?" he asked.

"He's on his way to Palm Beach, but he won't be arriving until this afternoon."

"Are you Ms. Hodges?"

"I am."

"Oh, good. You can sign for the cars."

She looked at the three convertibles. "Sign for them?"

"I'm delivering them from the dealer," the man said. "Mr. Shames ordered them some time ago."

"Sure, I'll sign," Callie said, and did so. "Just leave the keys in them."

"They're all registered. You want me to show you how everything
works?"

"We'll figure it out," she said, getting into her car. She pulled out of the
drive and headed toward the beach.

"Thad has bought *three* Mercedes convertibles?"

"He does things like that. Come to think of it, he mentioned this a few weeks ago, and I had forgotten. He bought them for himself and the guests on the yacht to use."

"I'm unaccustomed to people who buy expensive cars three at a time."

"Well, if you're going to work for Thad, you'd better get used to that sort of thing."

"Actually, my work here is nearly done," Stone said. "I thought I'd fly home tomorrow."

She glanced at him. "Whatever your work was, it seems to have been conducted in restaurants. You haven't been anywhere else here, have you?"

"I guess I haven't," Stone replied, "and you're right."

"Can you tell me about it now?"

"Afraid not."

"This is all very mysterious."

"It isn't, really, or at least, it wasn't until I got here."

"This has to have something to do with the lady in the restaurant the other night."

"Could be."

"What's her name again?"

"Elizabeth Harding."

"That wasn't what you told me the other night. It was Alice, or something like that."

"Allison. Allison Manning."

"Oh, yeah, Paul Manning's wife."

"Widow." Then it occurred to Stone that she wasn't Manning's widow, since he was still alive. He made a mental note to think about that later.

A guard let them through a gate and they drove down a narrow road beside a golf course.

"The Breakers has golf, tennis, the beach, the works," Callie said. She parked the car. "Come on, I'll show you the inside of the place before we eat." She led the way into a huge, twin-towered building and into a lobby that looked like some part of an Italianate cathedral.

"Jesus," Stone said.

"Yeah. It was built by Henry Flagler, the railroad magnate, who seems to have built just about everything on the east coast of Florida. Come on, let's get some lunch." She led him out of the hotel and through another security gate, where she flashed a photo ID. A minute later, they were seated on a broad terrace, overlooking a huge swimming pool and the sea.

The sun shone brightly, but the breeze made it cool, and Stone put on his sweater.

"You dress well," she said.

"Thanks. So do you."

"Are your suits, by any chance, made by Doug Hayward?"

"Yes. How did you know?"

"I've met a number of men who go to him, and I dragged Thad in there once and made him have a suit made. Doug's a nice man, isn't he?"

"I've never met him."

"Oh? How can he make your clothes without meeting you?"

"I inherited a lot of stuff from a friend who died last year. It was all from Hayward."

They ordered lunch.

"Nice friend," she said.

"Well, I've known his wife for a while. She insisted I take the clothes. In fact, she just shipped them to me and said I could send them to the Goodwill, if I didn't want them. She was afraid they'd end up in some celebrity auction."

"Celebrity? Who was he?"

"Your favorite movie star, Vance Calder."

"Holy mackerel. I've been dining with Vance Calder's clothes?"

"You have, indeed."

"Who killed Vance Calder, anyway?"

"Good question. There were suspects, but no conviction."

Their lunch came, and Stone dove into a chicken Caesar salad. "How much time do you spend here?" Stone asked.

"Quite a lot, it seems. Thad does more entertaining here than in New York, so I've just camped out on the yacht."

"Does he have a New York apartment?"

"He keeps that suite you saw at the Four Seasons."

Stone shook his head.

"Yes, I know, it's a lot of money. Thad would really prefer to live in hotels full-time, but he thought he ought to have a home somewhere, so he bought the Palm Beach house. I think he bought it as much for dockage for the yacht as for the house, but he's got a big-time designer doing the place up. There's a warehouse in West Palm already bursting with stuff that's ready to move in, as soon as the builders are gone."

"Which is when?"

"Shouldn't be long, now. What will happen is, the painters will finish, and the next day a parade of moving vans will arrive, and by nightfall, the place will be furnished."

Stone laughed. "When I think of how long it took me to get settled in my house."

"And where is your house?"

"I inherited one in Turtle Bay from a great-aunt, and I spent a couple of years renovating it. Did a lot of the work myself."

"You seem to inherit everything—clothes, houses."

"Just those things, nothing else."

"What sort of work did you do on your house?"

"Carpentry, mostly, but a little of everything."

"And where did you learn to be a carpenter?"

"Same place you learned to cook: at my father's knee."

"Oh, right, I forgot; he was a cabinetmaker."

"He was more than that, really; he was a kind of artist in wood."

Somewhere, a cell phone rang. Callie picked up her straw handbag and rummaged in it, finally coming up with a phone. "Hello? Oh, hi. Where are you? Okay, I'll be back at the house by the time you get there. Oh, and the cars came. The Mercedes convertibles? Remember? See you shortly." She hung up. "That was Thad. He's just landed." She laughed. "He'd forgotten all about ordering the cars. Come on, eat up and let's get back."

Stone ate up, wondering about the kind of man who could order three Mercedeses, then forget about it. The longer he hung around Thad Shames, the more bizarre things got.

⋙ Chapter 11 ⋘

Stone and Callie arrived back at the house simultaneously with Thad Shames, who climbed out of the back of a limo and tossed two briefcases to Juanito.

"Hey, Callie, hey, Stone!" Shames called out.

"Hey, boss," Callie said. She pointed at the convertibles. "There are your cars."

Shames looked them over. "Nice," he said. He bent over, removed the keys and tossed them to Stone. "Use it while you're here," he said.

Stone walked along with him toward the house. "Actually, I was hoping to get a lift back to New York with you on Sunday," Stone said. "Not much more I can do here."

"Sorry, I'm headed to the Coast on Sunday," Shames replied. "Why don't you stick around for a few days and relax a bit? Callie could use the company, and I can tell she likes you. You got anything urgent waiting for you in New York?"

"Nothing that couldn't wait a few days, I guess," Stone admitted.

"It's settled, then."

They walked through the house, and Shames inspected the work done on the central hallway. "Oh," he said to Callie, "I think we'll have cocktails and dinner in the house. Big buffet, okay?"

"But Thad, the house isn't finished being painted," Callie replied.

"It will be by morning," he said.

"But there's no furniture."

"It's on its way; I called from the airplane. The painters will work straight through the night, the furniture comes at eight A.M., and tomorrow evening we'll turn our party into a housewarming."

"Whatever you say, boss."

"It's black tie, right?"

"That's what I put on the invitations."

"How many acceptances?"

"Fifty couples, give or take."

"Nice-sized group. Feed them well."

"I thought Maine lobster, a bourride—that's a garlicky French fish stew—and tenderloin of beef for the carnivores. Lots of other stuff, too."

"Whatever you say, Callie." They had reached the yacht, and Shames led the way aboard, followed by Juanito with the two briefcases. He had apparently brought no other luggage. "Let's talk a minute, Stone," Shames said, beckoning to him to follow.

Stone followed him to the owner's cabin, the first time he had seen it. They walked into a large, gorgeously furnished sitting room. Juanito deposited the two briefcases on a big desk and left.

"What do you think of *Toscana*?" Shames asked.

"She's a dream," Stone replied. "I've never seen anything like her."

"Neither has anybody else," Shames laughed. "She's my favorite thing. If I had to give up everything but one, I'd keep her."

"I can understand that."

"I wish we had time for a cruise out to the Bahamas this weekend, but I really do have to be on the Coast by Sunday night. We're having another announcement shindig out there on Monday morning."

"Just what is this new technology your company is going to make?" Stone asked.

"It consists of a circuitboard that replaces the modem in a computer, plus some extraordinary software we're developing for both e-companies and users that gives every customer what very nearly amounts to a T-1 Internet connection over ordinary telephone lines, twenty-four hours a day, for a monthly fee of less than fifty dollars."

Stone knew that a T-1 was the fastest Internet connection, and that it required a special phone line to be installed. "That's very impressive," he said.

"Don't worry, I've already allocated your shares. Bill Eggers will buy them for you the day before the initial public offering."

"Thank you, Thad. That's very generous."

"You'll be tempted to sell them the first week, but don't; hang on to them."

"I'll take your advice."

Juanito appeared with two frosty gin and tonics. They touched glasses and drank.

"Now," Shames said, "tell me about Liz."

"I had lunch with her yesterday," Stone replied. "She was apologetic about rushing away from Easthampton, but she had to come back here."

"She lives here?"

"Here and in Houston. She's a widow, not a divorcée."

"How long?"

"Last year sometime. She seems excited about seeing you again."

Shames grinned like a schoolboy. "That sounds good."

"Thad, I have a lot else to tell you about Liz Harding," Stone said, adopting a serious mien.

"That sounds bad."

"It's not, necessarily, but there are things that, since you're my client, I have to tell you about her."

"I'll just shut up and listen," Shames said.

Stone started at the beginning and told Shames the story of Allison/Liz—all of it, leaving out nothing except his own affair with Allison. When he had finished, he polished off the rest of his drink, sat back and waited for questions. There weren't any.

"That's extraordinary," Shames said. He got to his feet. "I think I'll have a nap before dinner. Will you excuse me?"

Stone got up. "Of course. Thad, I want to be sure you understand about the husband, Paul Manning."

"Ex-husband, isn't he?"

"Ex–Paul Manning. She doesn't know what he's calling himself these days."

"Well, if he's legally dead, she's twice-widowed, isn't she?"

"In a manner of speaking. I'm not sure what the legal ramifications are. I've never run into anything quite like this before."

"She considers herself single?"

"Yes, she does."

"Then as far as I'm concerned, she's single, and that's an end to it."

"It is," Stone said, "unless Paul Manning turns up. I think you have to consider him a dangerous man."

"Well, he doesn't sound stupid, so I don't think he's dangerous. He's gotten away with a triple murder and major insurance fraud, so I think he has to count himself lucky, don't you?"

"I suppose."

"Don't worry about Manning, Stone. He's not going to risk screwing up his life by exposing his own past."

"I hope you're right," Stone said.

"You will pick up Liz tomorrow night? I have a lot on my plate, what with all these guests coming."

"Of course."

"Thanks." Shames disappeared into the bedroom and closed the door behind him.

Stone went back to his own cabin. Thad was right, of course. Paul Manning wasn't stupid, and, if Stone could just find him and talk to him, he'd be a rich man from the settlement Allison/Liz wanted to make with him. And then, he thought, sighing, he'd be free of this whole business, Thad Shames would have the girl of his dreams, and everybody could get on with the business of living happily ever after.

Sometime after midnight, Stone was wakened from a deep sleep by someone crawling into bed with him. He had been dreaming, and what was happening seemed an extension of his dream.

"Arrington?" he said sleepily.

"Whoa!" Callie said, sitting up and crossing her legs.

Stone shook himself fully awake. "Callie? What's happening?"

"You were about to get made love to," she said, "but you spoke to the wrong girl."

"I'm sorry. I was dreaming. I thought you were . . . somebody else at first."

"Stone, I know very well that Arrington is Vance Calder's wife—rather, widow. The whole world knows. Why would you be dreaming of her crawling into bed with you?"

"I don't remember exactly what I was dreaming," Stone said, sitting up in bed and dragging a couple of pillows behind him.

"That doesn't answer my question," she said. "But if it's none of my business, tell me so, and I'll get out of here."

"No, no," he said, stroking her hair. "Arrington and I were . . . close, before she married Vance. We don't have a relationship now, at least not a very good one."

"You're sure about this? I don't want to intrude where I'm not wanted."

He pulled her head down onto his shoulder, and she stretched out beside him. "You're wanted," he said.

She ran a hand down his belly until it stopped at his penis. She held it in her hand. "Oh!" she exclaimed, "it's alive!"

"Alive and well," he replied.

She rolled on top of him, sat up and guided him inside her. She bent down and put her lips close to his ear. "You'd better be telling the truth about Arrington Calder," she whispered, "or this will never happen again."

~ Chapter 12 ~

Stone was awakened by conflicting smells—one chemical, one culinary. He sat up in bed in time to see Callie enter his cabin, bearing a covered tray, kicking the door shut behind her.

"Smells good," he said. "But what's the other odor?"

"Paint," she replied. "The painters finished their work last night, and all the windows in the house are open. The decorators and moving people are in there now, working like beavers." She set the tray on the bed between them and whipped off the cover. "Voilà!" she said. "Brie omelettes!"

Stone picked up a plate and dug in. "Fantastic!" He sipped some orange juice.

"We've got the yacht to ourselves this morning," she said. "Thad has already made a lot of phone calls and had a business breakfast aboard and has taken a party into town for some shopping."

"I can't believe he's putting that house together in a day," Stone said.

"Oh, he's had the designers shopping for a year. They've planned out every room, right down to the pictures on the walls."

"It took me a year to get my house to that state."

"You must not have been newly superrich," she said.

"Good guess."

"What are your plans for today?"

"Plans? Me? I never have plans. I just sit back and let you and Thad do it for me. I don't think I've made a decision of any kind since I met the two of you. What do you have planned for me today?"

"Absolutely nothing. I plan to get some sun, do some reading and rest up for tonight."

"Oh, that's right. You're going to be pretty busy, aren't you?"

"Not if the caterers don't want to get fired. They're turning up at five, and I'll show them the kitchens and where to set up. After that, they'd better not bother me because I'll be partying."

"Well, I think your plan for the day sounds good. I'll join you, if that's all right."

"It's all right," she said. "By the way, do you need to rent a dinner jacket? I know a place."

"Nope. I brought one, just in case."

"Always prepared, aren't you?" She finished off her omelette, took his plate, poured him a large mug of coffee and stood up. "I'll get this stuff back to the galley, and I'll see you on the afterdeck later."

"Okay." Stone watched her go, then he got up, showered, put on a swimsuit, grabbed a terry robe from the closet and walked back to the fantail. Callie was already stretched out on a chaise, wearing only her bikini bottom, reading.

"Hi, want something good to read?"

"Sure."

She tossed him a book. "I just finished it. It's great."

Stone looked at the book: *Tumult* by Frederick James. "Oh, yes, I read some pages yesterday. Starts well."

"Ends well, too. Enjoy."

Stone read through the morning, broke for sandwiches and closed the book at five.

"Good?"

"Good."

"Thad liked it, too. He had me send the author an invitation to the party tonight, but we never heard from him. I guess his publisher didn't forward it." She looked at her watch. "I've got to get over to the house and brief the caterers," she said. "I'll see you at the party."

"Think I'll have a nap," Stone said. He went back to his cabin and slept for half an hour, then he shaved, showered and dressed in Vance Calder's ecru raw silk dinner jacket, a silk evening shirt and a black tie. He walked back to the house and through the central hallway, dodging frantic caterers and decorators, got into his borrowed Mercedes E430 convertible and drove into town. Shortly, he pulled up in front of Liz Harding's house. He walked across the driveway, his evening shoes crunching on the pea gravel. The doorbell was set in an intercom box. He pressed it and it made a noise like a telephone ringing.

"Hello?"

"It's Stone."

"Oh, Stone. The door's unlocked; let yourself in, and I'll be down in a few minutes."

"Okay." She clicked off, and Stone opened the door and walked into the house. It was quite beautiful, Queen Anne in style, not terribly large, but made of good materials—marble floors, walnut paneling, beautiful moldings. He found the living room and continued to explore, ending up in a handsome little library with many leather-bound volumes. A small bar had been set up on a butler's tray, and he poured himself some chilled mineral water, then he wandered around the room. A collection of silver-framed photographs rested on the mantel, and Stone inspected them. They were all of Liz Harding with a hand-some, silver-haired man, clearly Winston Harding, taken in various cities and on various beaches.

"He was handsome, wasn't he?" she said.

Stone turned and found her standing in the doorway, wearing a white silk dress and a gorgeous diamond necklace, with matching earrings. Her hair was blond again.

"Yes, he was, and you are very beautiful," Stone said.

She came and gave him a little hug, careful not to muss her makeup. "And so are you," she said. "That's the most beautiful dinner jacket I've ever seen."

"Thank you," Stone replied. He decided to stop telling people that the clothes were Vance Calder's, and to start taking credit himself.

"Would you like a drink before we go?" she asked.

"I think we're already fashionably late," he replied. "Why don't we just go to the party?"

She took his arm, and he led her out to the car.

"Drive slowly," she said. "The hair."

"I like it blond."

"So do I. It's my natural color."

"I remember."

"Stone!" she said, laughing and blushing.

"That wasn't what I meant, but I remember that, too."

"You're awful."

"I know."

"Still, we had some good times, didn't we? You were getting over a girl, as I recall."

"And you were helping."

"I did what I could," she said.

Stone drove slowly through the town and finally turned into the drive-way of Thad Shames's house. Or tried to; there were half a dozen cars ahead of him. Music wafted through the open windows. Finally, he gave the keys to a valet and extracted Liz from the car. He was beginning to think of her as Liz by now. They walked through the open doors of the house and into the living room. A big band was playing Rodgers & Hart at the other end, and people were dancing.

"How spectacular!" Liz said. "I mean, in spectacular good taste!"

"It certainly is," Stone agreed. "Would you believe that twenty-four hours ago, this was an empty, unpainted house?"

"No, I would not," she replied. She sniffed the air. "Still, there is that faint odor."

Stone spotted Thad Shames across the room, towering over his guests. "I think there's someone over there who'd like to see you," he said, taking her arm and leading her across the room.

Shames spotted them coming and went to meet them, or rather, Liz.

"Well, hello," he said, taking both her hands and kissing her on both cheeks.

"Will you excuse me?" Stone asked. They didn't seem to notice, so he left them and made his way across the large room to where the bar had been set up on a long table. "A gin and tonic," Stone said to the bartender.

"Coming up," the bartender replied.

Stone saw Callie across the room and waved to her. She waved back, but seemed to have no interest in joining him.

"Here you are," the bartender said.

"Thank you," Stone replied, accepting the drink.

"You know," a voice behind him said, "I think you may look better in that dinner jacket than the original owner did."

Stone turned around and found Arrington Carter Calder standing there, looking gorgeous. Before she put her arms around his neck and kissed him, he could see, over her shoulder, Callie Hodges making her way toward them.

⤳ Chapter 13 ⤶

Her lips melted into Stone's, and her body was against his, and only the thought of Callie approaching made him take hold of Arrington's shoulders and hold her back. He smiled broadly for effect. "It's good to see you, Arrington."

Then Callie was upon them. "Well, Stone," she said, "who's this?"

"Callie, I'd like you to meet Arrington Calder," Stone said, trying not to dab at his lips.

"Well, clearly, you two have met before tonight," Callie said. "How do you do, Arrington?"

"Very well, Callie. I believe we talked on the phone this morning."

"Yes. Thad very much wanted to have you here. Have you seen him yet?"

"Yes, when I arrived."

"I hope your room is comfortable."

"It is, indeed, though it smells a little of paint."

"We apologize," Callie said. "I understand you and Stone know each other."

"We're old friends," Arrington said.

"Yes," Stone echoed, wanting somehow to guide this conversation, if he could. "And how did you manage to get Arrington here so quickly, Callie?"

"We sent the airplane for her this morning," Callie said sweetly.

"Twenty-four hours ago," Arrington said, "who knew I'd be in Palm Beach tonight?"

"Yes," Stone replied, casting a sharp glance at Callie. "Who knew?"

Callie suddenly seemed flustered. "Please excuse me, I have to welcome somebody," she said. She had not even glanced at the door, but she made off in that direction.

"And how do you know Thad Shames?" Stone asked.

"Vance and I met him in Los Angeles early last year. Vance was an early investor in some of his companies. And how do you happen to be here, Stone?"

"I've been doing some work for Thad, which involved coming to Palm Beach."

"What sort of work?"

"I'm afraid it's confidential."

"Show me around the house, will you?" she said.

"We'll explore together," Stone said. "This is the first time I've been inside, except for the central hallway. I'm staying on the yacht, out back."

"Then follow me," Arrington said, taking his hand and starting out. She led him among handsome couples of various ages, beautifully dressed and coiffed. They walked across the central hall and into a large, two-story library, stocked with matched sets of books, some of them, apparently, quite old.

They found the dining room, which had been set up for a buffet, then climbed the central stairs to the second floor.

"Where are we going?" Stone asked.

"Just exploring," Arrington replied, towing him along. "That must be the master suite," she said, pointing at a large set of doors. They walked on farther. "Let's see what a bedroom looks like," she said, suddenly opening a door, tugging him inside and closing it behind her.

They were in a large, sumptuously furnished room with a huge, canopied bed, elaborate draperies and antique furniture. Stone saw a stack of luggage in a corner, and as they walked toward the windows, he saw the initials *ACC* stamped on the cases. "This is your room?" he asked.

"Oh, look, there's the yacht," she said, standing at the window. The moon was coming up and a streak of its light fell on the vessel. In the foreground, the gardens were lit with Japanese lanterns. She turned, took Stone's face in her hands and kissed him again.

Stone felt her against him, the familiar curves of her body, the cool tips of her fingers against his skin, and he responded appropriately.

"Oh, I can feel you," she whispered, moving her hips forward. She tugged at his bow tie, and it came undone.

Suddenly, Stone was uncomfortable, and he held her away. "I can't do this," he said, "not with the way things have been between us."

"I'd like for things to be as they were," she said.

"A lot has happened since then."

"Most of it to me," she said.

"I'm aware of that. But every time something happens to you, it seems to happen to me, too."

"Poor baby," she cooed.

"Which brings up the matter of Peter," Stone said.

She stepped back from him. "Do we have to talk about that now?"

"Now is as good a time as any, and better than most."

"Why do you have to be certain who Peter's father is?" she asked. "I'm not sure *I* want to know."

"I don't understand that, but I'm sure you can understand why I want to know," Stone said. "If you put your mind to it."

She turned away from him. "Men!"

"Do you find it so odd that a man would want to know if he had a son?"

"I don't want to talk about it anymore," she said. "Let's go back downstairs." She headed for the door.

Stone followed close behind her. Two couples were coming down the hall toward them, apparently touring the house. They smiled knowingly at Stone as they passed. What the hell was that about? he wondered, then he realized that his tie was untied and hurriedly retied it. He ran down the stairs after Arrington, caught up with her on the landing overlooking the living room and stopped her.

"Listen to me," he said. "You and I cannot have a normal relationship until we settle the question of Peter."

"Why can't you just leave it alone?" she said. "I really don't want to know."

"Then you don't want to know me," Stone replied.

She ran down the stairs, and he followed more slowly. People were looking up at them, among the crowd, Callie. Stone let Arrington make her way across the room, and he turned toward the bar and ordered another drink.

A moment later, Callie appeared at his side. "Oh, your tie is all mussed," she said. "Let me fix it for you." She tugged at the bow until she was satisfied. "Well, it didn't take the two of you long, did it?"

"What?" Stone asked, distracted, then he caught her meaning. "Oh, don't be ridiculous."

"Am I being ridiculous?" she asked. "A woman scorned, I suppose."

"Scorned? You invited her here, didn't you? Not Thad."

"I suggested it to Thad," she said. "I wanted to know where I stood."

"If you wanted to know where you stood, you could have simply asked me," Stone said, trying to keep the anger from his voice. "There was no need to send a jet to Virginia and haul her down here; no need to pull the scabs off old wounds."

"I'm sorry," Callie said sheepishly.

"You should be. You shouldn't interfere in other people's lives, especially when you don't have a clue what's going on."

"Listen, Stone," Callie said, now sounding angry herself. "I don't know about you, but I don't sleep casually with people, especially when there's something else going on in their lives. If you and Arrington are in love with each other, I'd rather know it now, not later."

"I didn't bring her down here," Stone said, *"you* did. I'd be grateful if you'd stop meddling in my life." He set down his drink, turned and walked out of the room. He made his way past couples in the gardens, then to the yacht, where he made himself a large drink at the bar in the saloon and sat on the afterdeck, drinking it, watching the moonlight on the water, trying to banish the thought of both Arrington and Callie from his mind.

Later, the music stopped and the sound of slamming car doors and diminishing voices told him the party was ending. He knew he couldn't sleep for a while, so he made himself another drink.

Then Juanito was at his elbow with a cordless phone. "Mr. Barrington, Mr. Thad is calling for you," he said.

Stone took the phone. "Hello?"

"Stone, please come over to Liz's house right away," Shames said. "I've already called the police."

Stone started to ask why, but Shames had already hung up.

⤜ Chapter 14 ⤝

Stone drove quickly, but not too quickly, through the streets of Palm Beach. It was well after midnight, now, and traffic was light, but he did not wish to attract the attention of a traffic cop at this moment. He swung into West Indies Drive and, shortly, into the driveway of Liz's house. One of Thad Shames's Mercedes convertibles was parked outside and, beside it, what was obviously an unmarked police car. The front door of the house stood wide open.

Stone walked quickly inside and looked around. No one was in sight. "Hello!" he called out.

"In here," came a man's voice through the living room and to his left. Stone followed the sound and arrived in the study. Shames and Liz, who appeared to be unharmed, and a man in a police officer's uniform with stars on the shoulders stood in the center of the room, which was a mess. All the pictures on the mantel had been swept onto the floor, a large mirror on one wall had been shattered and much of the furniture had been overturned, reducing some small porcelain figurines to shards.

"What's happened?" Stone asked.

"We're not sure," Shames replied. "Stone, this is Chief Dan Griggs of the Palm Beach Police Department. Chief, this is my and Mrs. Harding's attorney, Stone Barrington."

The chief offered his hand. "I thought I knew all the attorneys in town," he said. "Good to meet you, Mr. Barrington."

Stone shook the man's hand. "And you, Chief. I'm based in New York; that's why we haven't met. What's happened here tonight?"

Shames spoke up. "Liz and I arrived to find the front door open and the place a mess."

"The whole place? The living room looked all right."

"I've had a look around," the chief said. "This is the only room that was disturbed."

"Anything missing?" Stone asked.

Liz spoke up. "I can't find anything gone, just broken."

"What about the door? Was it forced?"

Griggs shook his head. "Either it wasn't locked, or somebody had a key."

"I'm afraid it may not have been locked," Liz said sheepishly. "I tend to forget. Anyway, Chief Griggs and his men take such good care of us all that it hardly seems necessary."

"I thank you, Mrs. Harding," the chief said, obviously pleased, "but we'd really prefer you to lock your doors."

"I'll make a point of it from now on."

"So this is vandalism?" Stone asked.

"Looks that way to me," Griggs replied. "Nothing taken, only this room messed up; nothing else to call it."

"Chief, have you had other incidents like this in town?"

Griggs shook his head. "We might get some spray paint on a building or a bridge sometimes—teenagers, you know—but I can't recall an incident of vandalism in a private home, unless it was connected to a burglary."

"No known perpetrators of this sort of thing around town?"

"None in our files."

"Chief, why don't you and I take a walk through the house. Liz, Thad, will you excuse us for a couple of minutes?"

"Of course," they said together.

Stone and the chief left the room, and Stone led him toward the stairs. "Let's take a look up here."

Griggs followed him, but at the top, stopped. "I've already walked through here with Mrs. Harding," he said.

"I know," Stone replied, "but I wanted to make you aware of a situation."

"Go right ahead," Griggs said.

"Mrs. Harding was formerly married to a man named Paul Manning, a well-known writer. Her name was Allison Manning, at the time."

"Why'd she change it to Elizabeth?"

"To get away from Manning."

"And you think he did this?"

"Very possibly. The photographs on the mantel were of Mrs. Harding and her late husband. Looks like a jealous rage to me."

Griggs nodded and wrote something in his notebook. "Mr. Barrington, your name is familiar. Were you ever on the police force in New York?"

Stone nodded. "For fourteen years."

"I've got it," the chief said. "The Sasha Nijinsky case."

"That's right. I retired about that time; disability."

"You look pretty healthy to me."

"Bullet in the knee."

"Hope you got the son of a bitch."

"My partner did."

"Allison Manning," the chief mused. "Something about an island?"

"That's right. She was accused of murdering her husband, but, of course, he wasn't dead."

"Saw something about it on *Sixty Minutes*."

"Yes. It got a lot of press at the time."

"You're a pretty high-profile lawyer up there, aren't you?"

"Not when I can help it."

"You got a card?"

Stone handed him one, and he pocketed it. "About this Paul Manning. You think we're going to hear from him again?"

"I wouldn't be surprised."

"You think he might harm Mrs. Harding?"

"That's a possibility."

"I'll look into it."

"Chief, I hope you'll keep all this background information in confidence. I'm sure Mrs. Harding wouldn't want people to connect her with a past incident that was very traumatic for her."

"We have a lot of well-known people in Palm Beach, and I run a very discreet department," Griggs said.

"I'm sure you do, and I appreciate your discretion."

"Can we go back downstairs, now?"

"Yes, I just wanted to discuss all this with you privately."

They started down the stairs.

"Tell you what," Griggs said. "I'll put a man on the house for a while. Nobody'll notice him, not even Mrs. Harding."

"I'd be grateful for that," Stone said.

"Of course, I can't keep people on this forever, if nothing happens."

"I understand completely. I'm going to suggest to Mr. Shames that he invite Mrs. Harding to stay at his house. He's going out of town for a while, but I'm sure his staff could make her comfortable there."

"Good idea," Griggs said.

"Maybe your man could stay in the house?"

"With Mrs. Harding's permission, sure."

"I'll have a word with her."

They reached the study.

"Liz is going to come back to the house with me," Shames said. "She'll stay with us, at least until I get back from the Coast."

"Good idea," Stone said. "Liz, the chief would like to have one of his men stay in the house. Is that all right?"

"Oh, yes," Liz said. "That would be wonderful." She went to a desk drawer, found a spare key and gave it to the chief, along with the alarm code.

"Well, if you folks don't need me anymore, I'll be going," the chief said. "I'll have a man here in half an hour."

Hands were shaken all around, and the chief departed.

"I'd better pack some things," Liz said, and left the room.

Shames turned to Stone. "It's this Manning guy, isn't it?"

"Very likely," Stone said. "This has none of the markings of a random crime—nothing taken, only one room disturbed."

"So, he's tracked her down."

"It looks that way."

"I'm glad you're staying on for a while, Stone. I feel better knowing you're here to take care of her."

"I'll let Woodman and Weld know."

"I'll call Bill Eggers and arrange everything."

"Thank you."

Shames was quiet for a moment. "Stone," he said finally, "you think he's going to try to kill her?"

"I think if that's what he had in mind, he'd already have tried. This was obviously to frighten her."

"It worked," Thad said. "She was a mess for a few minutes after we got here. There are some guns on the boat. I'll have Juanito make them available to you."

"I hope I won't need a gun," Stone said. "But you never know."

Stone followed Thad and Liz back to the house, and when they were safely inside, he walked back to the yacht and his cabin. His adrenaline was still a little high, and he got out of his dinner jacket and the rest of his clothes and into a hot shower. He was drying himself when he heard a soft knock at the cabin door. He got into a robe and went to answer it.

He opened the door to find Callie Hodges standing there, in a silk dressing gown, holding a 9mm semiautomatic pistol.

⋙ Chapter 15 ⋘

Stone stared at the armed young woman. "My money or my life?"

"Don't be ridiculous," she said, handing him the gun. "Thad wanted you to have this. I can't imagine why. What's happened?"

"Nothing serious," he replied. He checked that the safety was on, then tossed the gun onto the bed.

"May I come in for a minute?" she asked.

"Sure." He stood back and allowed her to enter.

She went and sat on the sofa before the fireplace. "Would you like a fire?" she asked. "It's cool tonight."

"All right." He went and sat on the sofa beside her, keeping some distance between them.

She found a box of long matches, checked to be sure the flue was open and lit the fire. The kindling caught, and the fire blazed cheerily. She switched off the ceiling light and sat down on the sofa again. "I want to apologize to you for my behavior today."

Stone didn't say anything. He was still annoyed with her.

"I was interfering in your life without any idea of the consequences. I hope having Arrington here didn't make things worse between you."

"They were already pretty bad," he replied. "I suppose I had a chance to make it up with her, but I didn't like the terms."

"You accept my apology?"

"I do," he said, his voice softening, "and I appreciate it."

"You don't have to explain anything to me. I don't have the right to ask."

"I'll explain anyway," Stone said. "I told you about my trip to the islands, where I met Allison Manning, now Liz Harding, but I didn't tell you that, at the time, Arrington and I were living together in New York. We were supposed to fly down together, but she was delayed and missed the flight, and then there was a snowstorm, and she was stuck there for another day. She was a magazine writer, and *The New Yorker* asked her to do a profile of Vance Calder, whom she already knew. She accepted, and the next thing I knew, she had gone back to California with him, and they were married, almost overnight."

"That must have come as a shock."

"It did. A bigger shock came later, when she told me she was pregnant."

"With your child or Vance's?"

"She didn't know. It could have been either of us. In due course, she had the child, I supplied a blood sample, and so did Vance. She called to say that the boy was Vance's, and that was that."

"I'm sorry."

"There's more. When Vance died, I went out to help Arrington handle the situation, and in so doing, I learned that Vance may have been in control of the test results."

"So, you're the father?"

"It may be that the results showed that Vance really was, but if not, he could have had the report changed."

"So you may be the father and you may not?"

"Right."

"So why don't you do the test again?"

"Arrington doesn't want it done."

"Why not?"

"I don't know."

"You'd think she'd want to know for sure who the father of the child is."

"You'd think."

"Who does he look like?"

"He looks like both Vance and my father."

She laughed. "I'm sorry, but it's a little . . ."

"Yes, I know, funny." He smiled himself.

"So that's how you left it with Arrington?"

"That's it."

"Let me ask you something," she said. "If the test were done, and the child turned out to be yours, what would you want to do about it?"

"I'm not sure, except I'd want him to know, eventually, and I'd like to have some part in his life."

"What about Arrington? Wouldn't you want her back?"

"Arrington and I seem to be . . . I think the expression is 'star-crossed.' She's a volatile person, and every time we have seemed to be getting close to each other again, something happens to blow it up."

"And that's what happened tonight?"

"I told her that if she didn't want to know who the boy's father is, then she didn't want to know me."

"Then how, may I ask, did your tie get mussed up?"

Stone laughed. "Arrington had just pulled it loose when I made my little speech, and she stalked out."

"Out of where?"

"Out of her room."

"And how did you get to her room?"

"On foot."

Callie laughed again.

"I thought we were touring the house. I didn't know where her room was."

"So you were led down the garden path?"

"In a manner of speaking."

Callie stroked his cheek with the backs of her fingers. "Poor Stone," she said. "Between Arrington and me, you've had a rough time tonight, haven't you?"

"Beset from all sides," Stone said, kissing her fingertips.

"Can I make it up to you?" she asked, sliding across the sofa toward him.

"You can try," Stone said.

She put her hand on his leg under the robe and slid it up his thigh. "How's this?" she asked.

"It's a start," he replied.

She untied his robe and took it away, then untied her own robe, letting it drop to the floor. She pressed him back on the sofa, knelt beside him and kissed his penis.

Stone made a little noise.

She took him into her mouth and played gently with him, rubbing a nipple, getting the response she wanted at both ends. She held his testicles in one hand, doing inventive things with her tongue, then she stopped for a moment. "This is just for you," she said. "You don't have to wait for me."

"I want you now," Stone said, panting a little.

"Maybe later," she said, taking him into her mouth again. She pushed his legs apart and pulled his knees up, then began exploring the cleft of his buttocks with her fingers.

"I'm going to explode soon," Stone said.

"Not yet," she replied, then began again. She moved her head slowly up and down, beginning with the tip, then pressing until nearly the whole length of him had disappeared.

Stone couldn't find words, only noises.

Then Stone exploded, and she stayed with him for another minute, prolonging the orgasm, keeping him going until he could only cry out and collapse back onto the sofa.

Finally, cradling his testicles in a hand, she laid her head on his belly and kissed it softly. "How are you?" she asked.

"I can't make a fist," he replied.

"You hardly need to," she laughed.

They remained that way for a moment, then she climbed onto the sofa with him and lay on top of him, nestling her head into his shoulder.

"There's something else I should tell you," he said, "just so you won't think I'm keeping anything from you."

"I'm listening."

"When I heard about Arrington and Vance—I was on the island of St. Marks, at the time—Allison Manning and I had . . ."

She raised her head. "Each other?"

"Yes. I was angry with Arrington, and Allison . . ."

"Was there?"

"Yes."

She laid her head back down. "Well, Allison is somewhere down the road, and I'm here, so just stay away from her."

"That may be difficult," he said.

"What do you mean?"

"Somebody broke into her house this evening and trashed a room. Thad has brought her back here. He's asked me to look after her while he's on the Coast."

She raised her head again. "Where's that gun?"

He pulled her head back down. "Not to worry."

"How do I know that?"

"Let me show you," he said. He rolled her onto her back and knelt beside the sofa, the way she had. With his tongue, he explored her soft fur. "How's that for reassurance?" he asked.

She pulled his head back into her lap. "It's a start," she said.

⤳ Chapter 16 ⤷

Stone was still sleeping soundly when he was awakened by the sound of his cabin door opening. He lifted his head and saw Callie approaching with a breakfast tray. She was fully dressed.

He sat up on his elbows. "What time is it?"

"A little after nine," she said, setting the tray down on the bed. "I've been up since six, seeing that everybody got breakfast before Thad and Arrington left for the Coast."

"They're gone?"

"Half an hour ago. After our conversation of last night I didn't think you'd want to get up early to say good-bye."

Stone laughed. "After our, ah, 'conversation' of last night, I don't know that I *could* have gotten up. I may spend the day in bed."

"I'd spend it with you, but there are some odds and ends with the painters and builders that I have to deal with. And, by the way, your friend Allison—sorry, Liz—is moving onto the yacht, into Thad's cabin."

"Why?"

"She complained that the odor of drying paint gave her a headache. I'd like to give her a permanent one."

"What have you got against Liz Harding?"

"Her past with you, of course, and now she'll be right down the corridor. See that your door is securely locked before retiring, please."

"Then how will you get in?"

"I have a key," she said smugly, "and I know how to use it."

"Fear not, you've rendered me incapable with another woman. I'm not sure I can walk."

"Don't walk, eat," she said, stuffing a croissant into his mouth. She walked to the door, then turned back. "You're going to need your strength," she said. "See you tonight."

Stone bit off a bite of the croissant and lay back on the bed, chewing.

At mid-morning, showered, shaved and dressed, Stone ventured out of his cabin and found Liz Harding sitting on an afterdeck sofa, reading a book about Palm Beach.

"Good morning," he said. "Feeling better today?"

"Feeling safer," she said, "since I'm here with you." Her voice was kittenish.

"You're not here with me," he said. "You're here with Thad."

"But you'll protect me while he's gone."

"Yes, but I'm not expecting anything untoward to happen. Are you?"

She closed her book and tossed it onto the coffee table. "I don't know anymore," she said. "It took me a year after I left St. Marks before I began to relax, and the marriage to Winston before I felt really safe. But after last night . . ."

"It may just have been some teenaged vandal," Stone said. "I wouldn't worry about it."

"I hope you're right," she replied. "Now, I want to do some shopping, and I don't think I'd feel safe unless you were with me."

"All right, I'll tag along. Since I'm staying longer than I'd planned, I could probably use a few things myself."

"I'll get my purse," she said.

They found a parking spot on Worth Avenue and strolled slowly down the street. Stone glanced around occasionally, looking for anyone resembling Paul Manning. Liz had said he'd had a nose job, so Stone concentrated on tall men. Manning was at least six-three, he remembered. Everyone he saw was comfortingly short.

He sat in the husband's chair in a shop as Liz tried on dresses. He flipped idly through one of several Palm Beach magazines, which featured grinning people in lavish clothes, photographed at parties, and many shots of overdecorated interiors of huge houses. There were ads for Rolls-Royces and Ferraris and many for jewelry.

They went into the Polo Ralph Lauren shop, where Stone bought some extra underwear and socks, along with a spare cashmere sweater for the cool evenings he had not anticipated.

He followed Liz into a jewelry shop and looked at a Cartier Tank Francaise wristwatch, while she tried on a diamond bracelet.

"You like?" she asked, holding out her wrist.

"I like."

"I like your watch, too."

Stone gave it back to the saleslady. "It's beautiful, but . . ." The "but" was twenty grand, he thought.

Liz bought the bracelet, which came to nearly thirty thousand dollars, Stone noted. "I'll wear it for Thad, when he comes back," she said.

"When is he coming back? He didn't tell me."

"Tomorrow or the next day, depending on how his business goes."

"Don't forget to call your insurance company to put the bracelet on your policy."

"Thank you. I would have forgotten. I did call my bank about the settlement with the life insurance company. The funds will be wired to your bank today."

"Good. I'd like to get that settled as soon as possible."

"Me, too," she said.

"I'll call my office when we get back to the yacht." As he spoke, he felt his cell phone vibrate in his pocket. "Excuse me," he said, answering it. "Hello?"

"Hi, it's Joan."

"How are things in the big city?"

"Running smoothly. The bank called. Mrs. Harding's money is in your trust account. You want me to complete the transaction with the insurance company?"

"Please."

"I'll get the wire off now, and we should have a confirmation today, I expect."

"Great. What else is happening?"

"One or two calls; I put them off. When are you coming back?"

"Thad Shames has asked me to stay on a few days. I'll let you know later in the week."

"Okay. Remember, sunshine causes skin cancer."

"Thanks for reminding me." He punched off and turned to Liz. "The money's on its way to the insurance company."

"Wonderful. Can I buy you lunch to celebrate? We can go back to Renato's."

"Sure. I liked it there."

They ate pasta and chatted. "Now that you're going to be a truly free woman, what are your plans?" he asked.

"Well, I think that depends on how it goes with Thad," she said. "So far, so good. He's very sweet . . . and virile." She smiled.

Stone laughed. "He'd have to be to keep up with you, as I recall."

"We were quite something for a short time, weren't we?"

"I guess we were, at that."

"You were the first man I'd slept with besides Paul for a very long time, and I found the experience, well, liberating."

"I'm glad."

"I have the distinct impression that you're liberating Callie Hodges, at the moment."

"I didn't say that," he blustered.

"You didn't have to. I took one look at her this morning—or rather she took one look at me—and I knew. She knows we slept together, doesn't she?"

Stone nodded and sipped his wine. "I thought it best to tell her."

"You getting serious about this girl?"

"Too soon to say," Stone said, uncomfortable.

She placed her hand on his. "I'm sorry to embarrass you, Stone. It's just that I think I envy her a little. Maybe more than a little."

Stone didn't know what to say.

"But," Liz said, "we must learn to be content with our lot, mustn't we? Lord knows, I have no complaints. I was just feeling a little greedy."

"I'm flattered," Stone said.

They walked back to the car, and as Stone opened the door for Liz, he noticed that the rear tire on the curb side had gone flat. He squatted and examined it. There was a large hole in the tread, too big a hole for a slow leak. It was as if somebody had plunged a knife into it.

Stone shrugged off his jacket and tossed it into the rear seat. "I'm afraid we've got a flat," he said. "It'll just take a couple of minutes to change."

"Why don't you call the Mercedes service people?" she asked. "They'll come and change it."

"It'll only take a minute." He opened the trunk and went to work. He thought about it as he cranked the jack. Was somebody really crazy enough to slash a tire in broad daylight in the middle of Worth Avenue?

⌐ Chapter 17 ⌐

Stone spent the afternoon reading, and late in the day Joan Robertson called from New York.

"We've closed with the insurance company," she said, "and I've wired the funds. Want me to fax you a fully executed copy of the document?"

"Please," Stone replied. "I expect Mrs. Harding would like to have it."

"Right away." She paused. "Stone?"

"Yes?"

"There's something I think I ought to mention. It seemed like nothing, really, but I just have a feeling . . ."

"What is it?"

"You've had some phone calls the last few days, from a man who wouldn't give his name."

"What did he say?"

"He wanted to speak to you; then, when I told him you were away, he wanted to know where you were."

"Did you tell him?"

"No, I felt uneasy about it. I just told him that I'd have you call him, but he wouldn't leave a number."

"How did he sound?"

"Nice, at first, then insistent. He was very annoyed that I wouldn't tell him where you were."

"And he wouldn't leave a number?"

"No, but I nailed him on caller ID. The first two times he called from the Brooke Hotel, on Park Avenue."

"Did the readout give a room number?"

"No, just the phone number. I called it and got the hotel operator. Then, after that when he called, the caller ID didn't report a number, said it was outside the area or something."

"When were the first phone calls?"

"Thursday and Friday."

"Okay, if he calls back again, give him my cell phone number."

"You sure? I have this creepy feeling."

"I'm sure. He won't know where I am."

"Okay."

"Anything else?"

"Everything else seems normal," she said.

"Talk to you later, then." He hung up and thought about the calls for a few minutes, then he dialed the number of Bob Berman, an ex-cop who sometimes undertook investigative work for him, particularly work that Stone could pretend not to know about.

"Hello," Bob said.

"Hi, it's Stone."

"How you doing?"

"Pretty good. I'm in Florida at the moment."

"You're just trying to hurt me, aren't you?"

"Yes. You up for some work?"

"Sure. What you got?"

"I've had a couple of phone calls that are worrying Joan. The first two came from the Brooke Hotel, on Park—she got that from caller ID. You know anybody at the Brooke? Maybe somebody in security, an ex-cop?"

"Nah, not a soul. You got a room number?"

"No."

"Could the calls have come from a pay phone?"

"No, the number reported was the hotel's."

"Would the guest list for that time help?"

"Maybe," Stone said. "How hard would it be to get it?"

"I might be able to hack into their computer," Bob replied. "Depends on how tough their security firewall is. My guess is, if a travel agent can get in to check availability, I can get in. I know a guy at the phone company. He can give me a list of all their lines. Probably cost five hundred, though."

"Spend the money," Stone said. "At least I can see if there's a familiar name on the list."

"What day did the guy call?"

"Thursday and Friday. I suppose the guest list for either day would do. See if you can get the home addresses of the guests, too."

"I'm on it," Bob said.

"Call me on my cell phone when you get something."

"Will do." Bob hung up.

Juanito appeared with an envelope. "A fax for you, Mr. Barrington," he said.

"Thank you, Juanito," Stone said, accepting the envelope. He opened it to find the fully executed agreement with the insurance company.

"And you have a telephone call," Juanito said, handing him a cordless phone.

"Hello?"

"Mr. Barrington?"

"Yes?"

"This is Dan Griggs, from the Palm Beach Police Department."

"How are you, Chief?"

"Okay, I guess. I ran a check on this Paul Manning fellow. He's dead. He was hanged for murder on a Caribbean island called St. Marks a few years ago."

"I'm sorry, Chief, I should have given you a heads up on that."

"You knew he was dead?" The chief sounded annoyed.

"He's not dead. St. Marks is a small, independent nation with a strange justice system and a greedy prime minister. He was bought out."

"Bought out of a hanging?"

"For half a million dollars."

"I never heard of anything like that," Griggs said.

"There are some places where it happens."

"So you think we might have a murderer loose around here?"

"It's possible. I still don't have any concrete evidence of that, but if I come across any, I'll let you know."

"How many people did he kill?"

"Three."

"Well, I think I'd like to see him in my jail."

"I'm afraid there's nothing to arrest him for, yet," Stone said.

"Three murders isn't enough? Isn't there any evidence against him?"

"It happened in another country, and my guess is the evidence no longer exists. According to the record, he was tried, convicted and executed, so, in a legal sense, he's not only protected by the law on double jeopardy, he no longer exists."

"Except he does."

"He does."

"You got a description of this man? I'd like to distribute it to my people."

"Tall, six-three or -four, on the slender side when I knew him, although he used to be a lot heavier, I'm told. Hair could be any color. He had a prominent nose when I knew him, though he's apparently had a nose job, so I'm not sure I'd recognize him on sight."

"So, tall is all we've got?"

"That's about it. He might have gotten heavier, but I doubt if he's gotten any shorter."

The chief laughed. "I guess not. Okay, he's tall and dead. I'll let my people know."

"I'll call you if I learn anything else," Stone said. The two men said good-bye and hung up.

Liz appeared on the afterdeck in a bikini, looking fetching.

"I've got something for you," Stone said, handing her the envelope.

She took out the agreement and read it swiftly. "My get-out-of-jail-free pass," she said, smiling.

"Well, not exactly free," Stone reminded her.

"It's worth every penny." She put her arms around him and gave him a big kiss, reminding him, for a moment, how much he had enjoyed her embrace in the past.

Stone looked over her shoulder and saw Callie coming up the gangplank. "All in a day's work," he said, gently removing her arms from his neck.

She tucked the document into her purse. "I'm going up on the top deck and catch some sun," she said.

"See you later." He watched her climb the stairs, then turned to greet Callie.

"I can't leave you alone for a minute, can I?" she said, poking him in the ribs.

"Just her sincere thanks for a job well done," he replied.

"What kind of job?" she demanded, her eyes narrowing.

"A professional job," he said, giving her a kiss.

"If she does it again, *I'm* going to do a professional job on *her,*" Callie said.

"Say, have you, by any chance, seen a tall man hanging around the house or the neighborhood?"

"No, but . . ."

"But what?"

"There was a tall man at the party I didn't know and didn't invite."

"How tall?"

"Real tall; taller than you."

"Hair color?"

"Dark, going gray."

"Nose?"

"Straight. Rather nice-looking man. I started to work my way over to him to find out if he was a crasher, but at that moment you arrived with Liz, which distracted me, and when I looked for him again, he was gone."

"Would you recognize him if you saw him again?"

"Yes."

"If you see him again—anywhere—I want to know about it."

"Okay," she said. "But why?"

"Let's just say that I'd like to speak with him."

☙ Chapter 18 ❧

Callie cooked dinner for the three of them, taking her time about it, and it was nearly ten when they sat down.

"You're a superb cook, Callie," Liz said, tasting her sweetbreads.

"Thank you, Liz," Callie replied. She turned to Stone. "Compliments, please."

"Wonderful," Stone said. "Everything is wonderful."

"A little quicker about it next time, if you want to continue to dine so well."

"I could not be more grateful," Stone said, tugging an imaginary forelock.

"Praise accepted," Callie replied.

They ate in silence for a while, not even bothering with desultory conversation. Callie finished, got up and went for dessert.

"Callie is very attractive," Liz said.

"Yes, she is."

"I think I'm a little jealous. I had an awfully good time in your bed—or rather, in mine—and I haven't forgotten a moment of it."

"Neither have I," Stone said, "but if quoted, I'll deny I said that."

"She's very attractive," Liz said, looking across the room at Callie.

"You said that before."

"Why don't we try . . ." She stopped.

"Try what?"

"Oh, what the hell—why don't we try a threesome?"

Stone nearly choked on his wine.

"What, do you find the idea so repulsive?"

"Hardly," Stone said, recovering himself. "It might just be too much of a good thing."

"Are you afraid she won't?"

"I've no idea how she would react, and I'm not going to find out."

"I'll feel her out," Liz said. "So to speak. Don't worry, I'll be subtle."

"Now listen," Stone said, but then he looked up to see Callie returning with dessert. He shot Liz a glance and turned to receive a warm crème brûlée. "Looks wonderful," Stone said.

Callie sat down. "So what have you two been talking about?" she asked, looking at Liz, then at Stone.

"Sex," Liz said.

Stone gulped.

"What about sex?"

"Are you for it, or agin' it?"

Callie laughed. "I'm all for it," she said.

Stone felt panic rising in his chest. This conversation was out of control—out of his control, anyway. At that moment, Juanito appeared with the cordless phone. Stone could have kissed him.

"For you, Mr. Barrington," the steward said.

Stone took the phone. "Hello?"

"Stone, it's Dan Griggs. I'm sorry to call you so late."

"That's all right, Dan. What's up?"

"One of my men—a plainclothesman—has spotted somebody matching the description of this Paul Manning."

"Where?"

"Downtown, at a bar and restaurant called Taboo." He gave Stone the address.

"He's still there?"

"At the bar, talking to a woman. You want me to have him picked up?"

"No, Dan, I'll go down there myself."

"Okay. My man will be around if you need backup. His name is Detective Riley—short, good-looking, wears sharp suits."

"I'll call you later," Stone said. He hung up and turned to the two women. "Something's come up. I have to go downtown," he said.

"I'll come with you," Callie said.

Stone had to think only for a nanosecond. He didn't trust the two of them alone together. "All right," he said. "Liz, do you mind?"

"No, go ahead. I'm going to have a brandy and turn in."

"Let's go," he said to Callie. He led the way off the yacht and to the car.

"Where are we going?" Callie asked.

"You know a bar called Taboo?"

"Sure."

"Get me there."

"Okay, but why are we going there?"

"A man answering the description of the man you saw at the party is there. I want to know if it's the same man."

"Who is he?"

"I can't really answer that until I've talked to Liz."

"He's part of the legal matter?"

"Yes."

"Take a left, then a right," she said.

Stone followed her directions.

"Is that why you wanted me to come along, so I could identify him?"

"Yep."

"I got the feeling you didn't want Liz and me talking about sex."

"I can't imagine how you got that idea," Stone said.

"Well, you were obviously uncomfortable with the turn the conversation was taking. What was Liz talking about?"

"Nothing, really."

"Well, I suppose I'll have to ask her, if I want to know."

"Oh, all right," Stone said. "She suggested that she and you and I have a threesome. I want to point out that it was *she* who raised the subject, and I said absolutely nothing to encourage her."

"Turn right again," Callie said.

Stone turned.

"So what did you tell her?"

"I didn't tell her anything. I was too surprised."

"What were you *going* to tell her, after you'd recovered from your surprise?"

"I wasn't going to tell her anything."

"Why? Did the idea not appeal to you?"

Stone turned and looked at her.

"Keep your eyes on the road," she said. "And take the next left."

Stone turned left.

"Have you ever been in a threesome?" she asked.

"No," he said.

"I have, once."

"Really?" he asked, surprised.

"In college, with two guys. We were all good friends. It was just a one-time romp."

"You astonish me."

"For such a sophisticated man, you can be so . . . naive. Didn't you think I would enjoy having two men?"

"Did you?"

"Very much, although we were all so embarrassed the next morning, we never repeated the experience."

"Why were you embarrassed?"

"We were very young," she said. There was a long pause. "I'm older, now, but I've never been in bed with a woman—in a threesome, I mean."

"And not in a threesome?"

"Oh, sure. Most girls have tried that. It's not such a big deal as it is with men."

"I've heard other women say that."

"So, what do you think?"

"About what?"

"About a threesome, with Liz and me?"

Stone looked up ahead and saw an awning, with the restaurant's name emblazoned on it. "There's Taboo," he said, grateful for an excuse to avoid answering.

A valet took the car, and Stone and Callie went inside. The bar was straight ahead, and Stone saw Paul Manning immediately.

⌁ Chapter 19 ⌁

The bar was up front, the restaurant at the rear. The place was subtly lit, and a pianist was playing quiet jazz underneath the conversation at the busy bar. Stone spotted Detective Riley leaning against the piano, holding a glass apparently filled with mineral water. Riley motioned toward the bar, but Stone was already staring at Manning's back.

He nodded at Riley and turned to Callie. "See the tall man at the middle of the bar, talking to the brunette?"

"Yes."

"Is that the man you saw at the party?"

"Looks like him from behind, but I can't see his face."

"Come on." Stone took her arm and guided her toward the couple. The brunette, looking past her companion, flicked an eye toward them, then turned back to her conversation.

Stone stopped a pace from the couple. "Paul!" he said, loudly enough to be sure he could be heard.

The man's head jerked around in an instantaneous reaction.

"That's the man," Callie whispered.

"I'm Stone Barrington. I'm sure you remember."

The man turned fully around and regarded Stone, his brow wrinkled. His hair was longish and dark, flecked with gray. "I don't believe we've met," he said, "but weren't you at the Shames party the other night?"

Stone looked at him carefully. The face was thin, the nose straight. He was the right age, and there was a resemblance to the Paul Manning he had known, but the nose seemed to change everything. "Yes, I was, but we met some time ago, in St. Marks."

"I'm sorry," the man said. "I put into St. Marks a few years ago on a sailing charter, but I don't recall meeting you there."

"I'm sure you remember your wife," Stone said.

The brunette looked up sharply at the man.

"My wife died last year," he said.

"Oh, longer ago than that," Stone said.

"I think I would remember when my wife died," the man said quietly.

The brunette spoke up. "You didn't tell me, Paul. I'm sorry."

"I hadn't had time, yet, but thank you," he said to her. He offered his hand to Stone. "I'm Paul Bartlett, and this lovely lady is Charmaine Tallman," he said. "Perhaps you've mistaken me for someone else."

Stone nodded at the woman and shook the man's hand. "Stone Barrington."

"Do you live in Palm Beach, Stone?"

"No. How about you?"

"I arrived a couple of weeks ago."

"How long do you plan to stay?" Stone asked.

"Actually, I'm house-hunting. I sold my business late last year, and I suppose I'm taking early retirement."

"What sort of business?"

"Graphic design."

"Where?"

"Minneapolis. I thought I'd try somewhere with a warmer winter. Florida seemed attractive. Where are you from, Stone?"

"New York," Stone replied. The man displayed not a hint of nerves. Could he be mistaken?

"Did you think I was another Paul?"

"Does the name Paul Manning ring a bell?"

"Writer? I read some of his stuff a few years ago, but not recently."

"How did you come to be at the Shames party?" Callie asked.

"I came with the Wilkeses," he said. "We just stopped by for a drink on the way to another dinner."

"How do you know the Wilkeses?"

"From Minneapolis. I used to do a lot of his company's design work—product packaging, mostly."

Callie nodded.

"Does the name Allison ring a bell?" Stone asked.

"I had a secretary named Allison, once."

Out of the corner of his eye, Stone saw Detective Riley moving slowly past them. He stopped a few feet behind Paul Bartlett.

"I can't get past the feeling that you think I'm someone else."

"I can't get past that, myself," Stone replied. "What was the name of your firm?"

"Bartlett and Bishop," he replied. "We were bought out by a New York–based firm. May I offer you a drink?"

"Thanks, but we have to be going," Stone said. "Perhaps I'll see you again. Where are you staying?"

"At the Chesterfield," Bartlett replied. "Call me anytime."

"Thanks. Ready, Callie?"

"Sure."

Stone gave the couple a small wave and guided Callie out of the bar.

On the sidewalk, as they waited for their car to be brought around, the policeman approached them. "Mr. Barrington? I'm Dave Riley."

Stone shook his hand. "Of course. Chief Griggs said you'd be here."

"Was that your man?"

"I'm not sure," Stone said. "He's the right size and age, but I haven't seen him for a few years, and I'm told he's had his nose altered. Did you hear any of our conversation?"

"I got his name and his story about the business."

"Can you check that out? Maybe get a photograph of Paul Bartlett?"

"I'll see what I can do," Riley said.

The car arrived. Stone thanked the detective and he and Callie got in and drove away.

"What he said about the Wilkeses rings true," she said. "He was standing near them when I saw him, and Mr. Wilkes does have a lot of business interests in the Midwest."

"At first I was sure it was Manning," Stone said. "But now . . . well, let's see what the police turn up."

"Why are the police involved?"

Stone took a deep breath. "I've already told you about Allison; Manning was her husband." He told her the story.

"And you think Manning is in Palm Beach? What evidence do you have of that?"

"Nothing concrete," Stone said. "Just a hunch, brought on by the trashing of Liz's study at her house."

"Bizarre," Callie said.

"Indeed."

They pulled into the driveway of the Shames house, got out and walked toward the yacht.

"So," Callie said, "what about this threesome?"

"Well, there are problems about that," Stone said, trying to think of some.

"What sort of problems? I'm certainly not one of them. I think she's very attractive."

"She's my client, and she's the girlfriend of another client, for a start."

"And where in the canon of legal ethics does it say you can't sleep with a client?"

"I, ah, can't quote you chapter and verse, but believe me, it's inadvisable."

"Come on, Stone, what's the real reason? You're a red-blooded American boy. You must harbor the fantasy of two women in bed with you—and with each other."

"I can't deny that," Stone said, reaching the gangplank and helping her aboard. "I suppose the main reason is that I wouldn't want to share you with anybody, not even another beautiful woman."

"Now, that was the politic thing to say," she said, smiling at him. "But is there some other reason?"

"Apart from what I've already said, it just doesn't feel right," he replied.

"Now, *that's* the best reason you've given me," she said. "Maybe another time."

"You never know," Stone replied.

"I can tell you're interested," Callie said.

"How?"

She rubbed the back of her hand across the front of his trousers. "Let's just say, it shows."

Stone laughed and pulled her to him. "Think you could be satisfied with just me?"

"I expect so," she replied, leading him toward his cabin.

ᥰ Chapter 20 ᥱ

Stone had a late breakfast the following morning and was finishing his coffee, when Juanito came aboard from the house with a Federal Express package for Stone. He ripped it open.

Joan wrote in a note: "Bob Berman brought this by for you. He said you'd know what it is."

Stone lifted a four-inch-thick stack of computer paper out of the box and looked at the first page. It was a computerized registration form for the Brooke Hotel in Manhattan. The fanfold paper opened to reveal what appeared to be the entire guest list for the Brooke on the previous Friday.

Liz came on deck looking fresh and new in a short linen dress. "Good morning," she said. "What's that?"

"I had some phone calls from a Manhattan hotel last week; fellow asked for me and wouldn't leave a number."

"You think it might have been Paul?"

"Maybe. It would be a big help if you would go through these registration forms and see if any of the names seem familiar to you—not just people you know, but names that Paul might have chosen for a new identity."

"Sure, I'll be glad to."

"When you've done that, I'd like you to take a ride with me."

"Where?"

"I met a man last night who could possibly be Paul, but I couldn't be sure. The nose was different, as you said, and that seemed to change everything. Anyway, I haven't seen him for some years, and I'm not sure how good I'd be at identifying him. I'd like to see if we can spot him around his hotel and let you get a look at him."

"Okay, and I can tell you that when I saw him in Easthampton he looked very different from his old self. I spotted him as much by his walk and his body language as by his appearance."

"What sort of hair did he have?"

"His natural dark, going gray; that hadn't changed."

"How long?"

"Not too long; longer than yours, though."

"Does the name Paul Bartlett ring any bells?"

"Just the Paul. But if Paul were hiding out, I don't think he'd use his real first name. He's a lot smarter than that."

"Sit down, and let's go through this hotel list together."

"Okay. Can I have some coffee first?"

Stone rang for Juanito and ordered the coffee, then they started going through the stack of fanfold paper. They had gone through only a dozen or so names when Liz stopped. "Garland," she said. "Donald Garland."

"Familiar?"

"Garland was Paul's mother's maiden name. Donald was his father's first name."

"Do you know how to contact them? Maybe he's been in touch."

"Both dead," Liz said.

"Mr. Garland is from San Francisco," Stone read from the document. "Says here he's with Golden Gate Publishing, and he lives in Pacific Heights. When it's opening time out there, I'll check him out."

They continued to read through the list for a while, then Juanito appeared with the telephone. "For you, Mr. Barrington."

"Yes?"

"It's Dan Griggs."

"Morning, Dan. I expect Dave Riley briefed you on last night's events."

"Yes, and we've checked out Mr. Bartlett. He's from Minneapolis, as he said, and he did sell his design firm last year."

"Oh," Stone said. "I guess that lets him out."

"Not necessarily," Griggs said. "He had owned the firm for only two years when he sold it, and I haven't been able to find out anything about him before that, which is unusual."

"I thought I'd take Mrs. Harding over to his hotel this morning and see if we can spot him. She thinks she can identify Paul Manning."

"It's a nice thought, but he checked out this morning; said he was going back to Minneapolis on business."

"He doesn't have a business," Stone pointed out.

"I'm checking with the airlines to see if he was on any outbound flight this morning," Griggs said. "I'll let you know if I come up with anything."

"Thanks, Dan," Stone said, and hung up.

Liz was still going through the guest list. "I haven't come across anything else yet," she said.

"Paul Bartlett has checked out of his hotel," Stone said. "Said he was returning to Minneapolis on business. Did Paul Manning have any connection with Minneapolis?"

"No, but he wouldn't have settled in a place where anybody knew him."

"How recognizable would he have been to his readers? Did he do a lot of book signings? Have his photograph on the book jackets?"

"The only photograph of Paul that ever appeared on a book jacket or in a press release from his publishers would have been one taken when he was very heavy and had a full beard. He would be completely unrecognizable to any reader now."

"Bartlett recently sold a graphic design business. Did Paul have any design inclinations?"

"He was a fine arts major at Syracuse," Liz said. "He drew and painted quite well."

"Did he take any design courses? Anything that would give him the skills he would need for graphic design?"

"I don't really know," she said. "He didn't talk about college all that much."

Callie appeared on deck. "What are you two doing?" she asked.

Stone explained the stack of paper.

"And how did you get the guest list of a New York hotel?"

"You don't want to know."

Juanito came back with the phone for Stone.

"Hello."

"It's Dan Griggs. Paul Bartlett didn't take any flight out this morning, and he didn't charter any aircraft on the field, but he did turn in his rental car at Hertz, at the airport."

"That doesn't make any sense," Stone said. "Why would he drive to the airport and turn in his car, then not fly out? How would he leave the airport without transportation?"

"I'll check the local cab companies and see if a driver picked up anyone answering his description," Griggs said.

"You might check if he rented a car from another company, too, and if so, what kind and what license number. Might be nice to get his driver's license info from Hertz, too."

"I got that. It lists a Minneapolis address."

"Issued when?"

"Two years, three months ago."

"Can you check with the Minnesota motor vehicle department and find out if it was a renewal or a new license, and if he turned in a license from another state?"

"Sure, that's pretty easy."

"Oh, and what's his date of birth on the license?"

Griggs told him, and he repeated it to Liz.

"Eighteen months younger than Paul," she said.

"Keep me posted," Stone said to Griggs, and hung up.

Liz was still going through the hotel list.

"Anything at all?" Stone asked.

"Just Garland so far," she said. "Pity the hotel doesn't photograph its guests."

"I'll bet it won't be long before they start that," Stone said. "That'll make it easier to track fugitives."

"And errant husbands," Liz said. "I wonder if there's a Mrs. Bartlett."

"He said she died last year."

"Might be interesting to check with the Minneapolis police department and find out if that's true and, if so, how she died," Liz said.

"You know something, Mrs. Harding," Stone said. "You'd make a good cop." He picked up the phone and called Dan Griggs.

"It's Stone. Bartlett said his wife died last year. Can you check with the Minneapolis PD and see if there was foul play suspected?"

"Sure can do that," Griggs said. "Bartlett's driver's license was issued after a driving test, not swapped for another state's."

"Now that's *really* interesting," Stone said. "How many middle-aged men take driving tests?"

"Only those who learned to drive late in life, and that's not likely—and those who haven't driven for a long time or who've been out of the country long enough for their licenses to expire."

"And people who need new identities."

"Right. Something else: I talked with the Hertz clerk at the airport, and she said Bartlett was picked up by somebody in a BMW. She could see the curb from her desk."

"So he could still be in town."

"Or on a road trip."

"Yeah. Dan, could you check with an outfit called Golden Gate Publishing in San Francisco and find out if their employee Donald Garland matches Bartlett's description?"

"Okay. They open in an hour out there. How'd you get onto this Garland?"

"You'd rather not know, but there's an outside chance he could be Manning."

"I'll get somebody on it."

"Thanks." Stone hung up and gazed across Lake Worth.

"What?" Liz asked.

"Somebody picked up Bartlett at the airport. I wonder why."

Callie was leafing through the hotel guest list.

"Callie? Where do the Wilkeses live?"

"On North County Road."

"Let's go see them."

⤳ **Chapter 21** ⤝

"Tell me about the Wilkeses," Stone said. "What are their first names?" They were driving up North County Road. To their right, usually behind high hedges, were houses that fronted the beach.

"Frank and Margaret," she said. "He founded a chain of fast-food restaurants in the Midwest, and later, he bought some other companies. He's very rich." She pointed. "The house is the next one."

Stone pulled up to a wrought-iron gate, which was tightly shut. A section of hedge prevented the house from being seen from the street.

"I think I'm uncomfortable just ringing the bell," Callie said.

Stone handed her his cell phone. "Tell them we're in the neighborhood, and we're calling at the suggestion of Thad Shames."

Callie made the call, chatted brightly with Mrs. Wilkes for a couple of minutes, then hung up. "Okay," she said, "they'll see us."

Stone pulled up to the gates, reached out the window, rang the bell and the gates opened. The driveway was longer than Stone had expected, and they emerged in a cobblestoned circle with a fountain in its center. The house was an old one, in the Florida Spanish style, and appeared to have been carefully restored. Stone and Callie got out of the car and rang the front doorbell.

The door was answered by Margaret Wilkes, dressed for golf in a plaid skirt and polo shirt. "Callie, come in," she said. "How nice to see you."

"Mrs. Wilkes, this is Stone Barrington, a friend of Thad's."

"How do you do?" Stone said, and shook her extended hand.

"Please come back to the terrace," she said. A houseman appeared from the rear of the house. "Bobby, please bring us a pitcher of lemonade."

Frank Wilkes rose from a wicker sofa on the rear terrace to greet them, and introductions were made. The terrace overlooked a large pool and a garden, with the Atlantic beyond. Both the Wilkeses were charming and unpretentious.

After the lemonade had been served, Stone got to the point. "Mr. and Mrs. Wilkes . . ."

"Please, Frank and Margaret," Wilkes said.

"Thank you. I'm here, on Thad Shames's behalf, to inquire about a Mr. Paul Bartlett, of Minneapolis. You know him, I believe."

"Yes, of course," Wilkes replied. "For several years."

"May I ask just how many years?"

"Well, let's see: He had a design business in Minneapolis, and he and his partner made a presentation to us, oh, a little over two years ago. That's when we first met. We hired them to redesign all our paper products—plates, sandwich cartons, the hats for the counter people, that sort of thing. Why do you want to know about Paul? Is he in some sort of difficulties?"

"Oh, no, nothing like that. It's just that he bears a resemblance to someone I used to know and that Thad is interested in. We only want to know that he's who he says he is."

"I see," Wilkes said. Clearly, he did not. "Who did you think he might be?"

"Did you meet Mrs. Winston Harding at Thad Shames's party?"

"No."

"Mrs. Harding is a close friend of Thad's. The man we're interested in was someone she knew in the past, who dropped out of sight a few years ago. No one knows what happened to him, but there are indications that he might be in Palm Beach. Someone noticed that Mr. Bartlett resembled this man, whose name is Paul Manning."

"Well, why don't you ask Paul about this?"

"I did, last night, but he pretty much denied being Manning."

"But you're not convinced?"

"Thad has asked me to investigate the possibility that Bartlett and Manning are the same man."

"Then why don't you arrange for Paul and Mrs. Harding to meet? Surely that would answer the question."

"I had hoped to do that, but Mrs. Harding doesn't wish to see him. Also, Mr. Bartlett checked out of his hotel this morning."

"That's news to me," Wilkes said.

"I just wondered if you had any knowledge of Bartlett's background before you first met him."

"I saw a résumé at the time," Wilkes said. "He had a broad background in advertising and graphics design, worked for several places in New York, as I recall."

"Did you check with any of his former employers for a reference?"

"No. We would ordinarily do that with a prospective employee, but we dealt with Paul as an outside contractor, and frankly, we were more interested in the presentation he prepared for us than in what he had done in the past. We were very enthusiastic about the work, and that was all that mattered."

"Do you know anyone who has known Paul Bartlett much longer than you have?"

Wilkes thought about that for a moment. "No, I don't believe I do."

"Did you know Mr. Bartlett's wife?"

Margaret Wilkes spoke up. "Oh, yes. In fact, we introduced them. Such a shame about Frances."

"I understand she's deceased?"

"Yes, in an accident last year. Terrible thing."

"How did it happen?"

"She and Paul were out driving on a Sunday afternoon, and they swerved to miss hitting a deer. Frances was thrown through the windshield and killed instantly."

"Who was driving?"

"Paul was, but he was wearing a seat belt."

"There was no passenger-side air bag," Wilkes said, "and apparently the buckle on Frances's seat belt failed or was defective. I urged Paul to sue the car company, but he didn't have the heart. He just wanted to put it behind him. That's why he sold his company."

"Do you know if he made a lot of money on the sale?"

"I shouldn't think so; they were a fairly new company. I think the people who bought them wanted the talent they employed and me for a client more than anything else. Of course, Paul would be quite well fixed, though."

"How is that?" Stone asked.

"Well, Frances was very wealthy. She'd lost her husband a few months before she and Paul met, and he'd left a considerable fortune."

"I see," Stone said.

"Mr. Barrington," Margaret Wilkes said, "you're beginning to frighten me. Are you thinking that Paul might somehow have caused Frances's death?"

"At this moment, I have no real reason to think so, Mrs. Wilkes. I'm simply concerned with learning whether he is, or once was, Paul Manning."

"This Manning," Wilkes said, "what was his relationship to Mrs. Harding?"

"He was her first husband."

"And what sort of man is he?"

"Not a very nice one, I'm afraid."

"Was this just some domestic dispute?"

"More than that," Stone said. "Manning murdered three people."

"Good God!" Wilkes said. "He's dangerous, then?"

"Manning certainly is, but please remember, I have no evidence yet that Manning and Bartlett are the same man."

"Well, I hope to God you'll find out!" Wilkes said.

"I know this is upsetting to you and Mrs. Wilkes," Stone said, "and I apologize for that."

"No, no, if Paul is this Manning, then we certainly want to know. I assume you'll have him arrested."

"We'll take whatever measures are appropriate," Stone said.

"I'll hardly know what to say to Paul when we see him," Mrs. Wilkes said.

"Do you expect to see him anytime soon?"

"Why, yes. He's coming to dinner tonight."

"Here, in this house?"

"Yes," she said.

Wilkes spoke up. "Perhaps you'd better come, too," he said.

⟿ Chapter 22 ⟿

The three of them stood on the afterdeck, Stone in black tie, Callie in a silk dress and Liz in a terry robe.

"I wish you'd come with us," Stone said to Liz.

Liz shook her head. "I don't want to see him," she said.

Callie patted her small purse. "I've got a camera in here," she said. "I'll get his picture."

"All right, let's go," Stone said. "I've no idea what time we'll be back, but I've asked Juanito to keep an eye on you."

"Thank you, Stone," Liz said.

Stone and Callie walked to the car and drove north.

"What do you think is going to happen?" Callie said.

"I don't think anything will happen. I'll contrive to stand next to Bartlett, and you'll take our photograph, come hell or high water."

"Have you alerted the police?"

"No. If he is Manning, he's not charged with anything. I just want an opportunity to get him alone and to put an offer to him."

"What sort of offer?"

"Liz is willing to pay him to go away."

"Oh. And you think that will work?"

"I can only hope so."

"What if he still denies being Manning?"

"I've got a friend in New York working on Bartlett's background. Maybe we'll be able to present him with some evidence that he's not who he says he is."

"Tonight?"

"Probably not that soon, although my friend has my cell phone number."

"This is kind of exciting," Callie said, giggling.

"All in a day's work," Stone said dryly.

The gates of the Wilkes house were open, and a valet took their car. Stone and Callie walked into the house and were greeted by Frank and Margaret Wilkes in the foyer.

"Stone, Callie, welcome," Mrs. Wilkes said.

"Thank you for asking us, Margaret," Stone replied. "Is he here yet?"

"No. In fact, he called and said he couldn't make it in time for drinks, but he'd be here for dinner."

"Did he say why?"

"No. Why don't you two go on out to the terrace and have a drink. Frank and I will be along as soon as all our guests have arrived."

"Thank you, we will." Stone led Callie through the house and out to the same terrace where they had sat earlier that day. A dozen couples had already arrived and were drinking and talking to the tune of a light jazz trio, which was set up beside the pool.

Callie saw some people she knew and introduced Stone. A waiter brought them drinks, and they chatted with the other guests. Soon the crowd had swelled to around fifty, and the Wilkeses joined their guests on the terrace.

Margaret Wilkes tugged at Stone's sleeve and whispered, "I've arranged the place cards so that you and Paul are at the same table."

"Thank you," Stone said.

Conversation continued for another half hour, then they were called to dinner. The very large dining hall had been set up with tables of eight, and Stone and Callie found their place cards and Paul Bartlett's. Callie was seated next to Bartlett, and Stone was two places away. They had barely introduced themselves to their dinner partners and sat down, when Paul Bartlett entered the dining room, stopped to kiss his hostess on the cheek, then made his way to his place.

He looked surprised to find Stone and Callie there. They shook hands. "I hadn't expected to see you again so soon, Stone," he said. "How did you come to be here?"

"Callie is a friend of the Wilkeses," Stone said. "They were kind enough to ask us."

"Oh," he replied, but he didn't seem satisfied with the answer.

The first course was served, and Stone and Callie exchanged a glance and a shrug. No opportunity to get a photograph at dinner. It would have to be later.

The woman on Stone's right was deep in conversation with Bartlett, to the exclusion of Stone, who had to occupy himself with the dinner companion on his left, a handsome woman in her seventies.

"And who are you?" she asked him, with a touch of imperiousness.

"My name is Stone Barrington."

"And how do you know the Wilkeses?" There was suspicion in the question.

"My companion for the evening is a friend of theirs," Stone said, nodding in Callie's direction.

"Goodness," the woman said, taking in Callie. "One wouldn't think *she* would need a walker."

"A walker?" Stone asked.

"Isn't that what you are?"

"I'm afraid I don't understand."

"Of course you do, darling. My name is Lila Baldwin. Perhaps you could give me your card, for the future?" She nodded toward her own date, a sleekly handsome man in his thirties, who sat next to Callie. "I'm afraid I've had about all of Carlton that I can bear for one season."

Stone gave the woman his card, then the penny dropped. The woman thought he was for hire as an escort, maybe more. "If you should ever need an attorney, please call me," he said.

"Attorney?" She looked at the card, holding it at arm's length. She apparently didn't want to be seen in her glasses.

"Woodman and Weld, in New York," Stone said.

She looked at him more closely, squinting. "Your firm did my estate planning," she said. "A lovely man named William Eggers."

"I know him well," Stone said.

"You don't look like an estate planner," she said, accusingly.

"No, that's a little out of my line," he replied. "I'm more of a generalist."

"And what sort of problem would I hire you for?" she asked.

"Oh, nothing specific. If you should have a problem of any sort, call Bill Eggers, and he'll know if I'm your man."

"Oh, I think you could be my man, no matter what my problem was," she said.

Stone was trying to come up with an answer to that when his tiny cell phone, clipped to his waistband, began to vibrate silently. "Would you excuse me for just a moment?" he said. "I'll be right back." He stood up and walked toward the dining room door, fishing out the phone and opening it, but keeping it concealed in his hand until he was out in the hall.

"Hello?"

"It's me," Bob Berman said.

"Have you got something?"

"This guy's an amateur," Bob said. "His identity is paper thin. There's nothing in his credit report going back more than two and a half years. His driver's license is green as grass, and he's only got one credit card, one of those that's guaranteed by a savings account. No mortgage or bank loans on the record, only a car loan, from a high-interest loan company."

"His design company must have done business with a bank."

"Probably, but I'll bet his partner did all the financial stuff. Bartlett would never survive even the most minimal credit check for any substantial business. There's not even a history of other bank accounts, nothing in the New York credit bureaus, either."

"Anything on who he really is?"

"If you can get a fingerprint on a bar glass or something, I could run that. Otherwise, I'll need a lot more time to nail him down."

"I'll have a shot at it," Stone said. "Call me if you come up with anything else."

"Will do,"

Stone returned to his table, stopping to whisper in Callie's ear. "It's looking good. When dinner's over, try to slip a glass or something with his fingerprints on it into your purse."

"Love to," she said.

Stone returned to his seat and the attentions of Lila Baldwin, glancing at Paul Bartlett, who seemed to be having a good time. Stone wanted to end his good time.

Chapter 23

The woman sitting between Stone and Paul Bartlett got up between courses and went to the powder room, and Stone took the opportunity.

"Paul, I was out at the airport this morning. Did I see you leave in a BMW?"

Bartlett looked at him as if Stone had seriously invaded his privacy. "Were you following me?" he demanded.

"Of course not," Stone said. "I was at the airport, and I saw you, that's all. I didn't mean to upset you."

Bartlett waved a hand. "Sorry, I guess I'm being paranoid."

Stone wondered what he had to be paranoid about.

"I took my rental car back to Hertz. I bought a car this morning, and the salesman picked me up and drove me to the dealership."

"Oh, what did you buy?"

"A Bentley."

"Very nice."

"Were you considering one?"

"No, the Bentley is out of my league. If you're making that sort of investment, you must have decided to stay on in Palm Beach."

"Well, I am looking for a house."

Callie was on her feet, digging into her purse. "Let me get a shot of you two," she said. "Stone, move over a seat."

Bartlett waved her away. "No, please. I don't enjoy being photographed." When Callie seemed to persist, he nearly barked at her. "Sit down," he said. "Please. I take a Muslim view of photography: It steals one's soul."

"If one has a soul," Stone said.

Bartlett shot a glance at Stone, picked up a liqueur glass, downed the contents and stood up. "Excuse me," he said.

"You're not leaving," Callie said.

"Terrible headache," Bartlett replied.

"Still at the Chesterfield?" Stone asked.

"Sure, call me anytime. Good night." He strode toward his hostess's table, spoke to her for a moment, kissed her on the cheek and left the room.

Callie reached over, picked up the small liqueur glass, wrapped it in a tissue from her purse and dropped it into her bag. "Better than a photograph," she said.

Stone looked up to see Frank Wilkes coming toward them. He sat down in Bartlett's chair. "Paul has abandoned us, I see."

"Yes, he seemed uncomfortable."

"Stone, after speaking with him, do you think he may be the man you're looking for?"

"I think he may be," Stone said, "but even if he's not, he's not the man he says he is."

"Then who is he?"

"I hope to know more about that soon, Frank. I'll let you know when I find out."

"I'd appreciate that. Margaret and I introduced him to Frances, his wife, and the thought that he might have had something to do with her death is, naturally, very disturbing to us."

"I can understand that. Can you tell me everything you remember about the accident?"

"It was on a Sunday afternoon, I remember. Paul and I had a golf date, and Frances picked him up at the clubhouse when we had finished—must have been around six. They were on the way home when . . ." He stopped.

"No, they weren't on the way home. We played at the Manitou Ridge Golf Club, in the Minneapolis suburbs, and their house—Frances's house—is west of there. The accident happened along the shore of White Bear Lake, which is east—no, northeast of the club. After the funeral, I remember asking Paul what they were doing out in that direction. He said Frances had wanted to go for a drive along the lake. I didn't say anything at the time, but that seemed odd to me. I can't explain why, exactly, but it seemed out of character for Frances to want to do something as idle as go for a drive. She was the sort of person who would never take the long way home, if there was a shorter route."

"And what do you remember about the accident itself?"

"The papers said that they were coming around a curve when a deer jumped out of the brush, and in trying to avoid it, Paul went off the road and smashed into a tree. Frances went through the windshield and hit the tree, killing her instantly."

"You said earlier today there was something wrong with the seat belt?"

"Yes, I remember reading that. I told Paul he should sue, but he wanted no part of that."

"Do you remember anything else about the accident or its aftermath that struck you as odd?"

Wilkes thought about it. "A few weeks later I was playing golf with a friend of mine, Arthur Welch, who was Frances's lawyer. He mentioned that Paul had sold Frances's house, and that surprised me."

"Why?"

"Well, I knew that when Frances and Paul married, she insisted on a prenuptial agreement that severely limited any inheritance for him in the event of her death. The bulk of her estate was to go to a local art museum. When Arthur told me Paul had sold the house, I mentioned the prenup, and he told me that Frances had rescinded the prenup and had made a new will."

"When?"

"Less than a month before her death."

"I see."

Wilkes rubbed his forehead. "I think I see, too. I didn't want to believe it, but now . . ."

"Let's not jump to any conclusions just yet," Stone said. "Let's wait until we know more."

Wilkes nodded. "You're right," he said.

"And please don't do anything that might make Bartlett feel that your relationship with him has changed, or that you don't want to see or talk to him."

"I'll try," Wilkes said. "Margaret will, too."

As they left the party, Stone called Chief Dan Griggs.

"Dan, can you meet me at your office?" Stone asked. "There's something I need to talk to you about."

"Sure, Stone. I'll be there in ten minutes."

Stone took a minute to bring Griggs up to date on what he had learned that evening.

Griggs nodded as he heard the story. "So, if Bartlett is Manning, and if he killed his wife for her money, he *has* committed a crime, after all. We'd have grounds for an arrest."

"I think you'd have to have a long talk with the Minneapolis police department before we'd know about that," Stone said. "After all, if they'd suspected him, they'd probably have already arrested him."

"Good point," Griggs admitted.

"We may be able to confirm his identity anyway," Stone said. "Callie, the glass?"

Callie removed the liqueur glass from her purse and set it on the table.

Stone picked it up by the stem and held it against the light. "There's at least one good print on here," he said.

Griggs picked up the phone and pressed a couple of buttons. "Sam, it's Griggs," he said. "I want you to lift some prints from a drinking glass and run them through the computer." He hung up, and almost immediately, a detective came into the room, took the glass and went away with it.

"Well," Stone said, rising, "let me know what results you get."

"Hang on," Griggs said. "This won't take as long as you think." He got up and left the office for a few minutes, then returned. "A good right thumbprint and two partials," he said. "My guy is running them through the FBI computer now. Come on, let's go see what he comes up with."

Stone and Callie followed Griggs down a hallway to another office, where the detective was sitting at a computer.

"Got anything yet, Sam?" Griggs asked.

Sam hit the return key and sat back. "Shouldn't take long," he said. "Hang on," he said, "what's this?"

The group walked around the computer and looked over the detective's shoulder. The screen displayed a message:

ACCESS TO THIS FILE DENIED.
ENTRY REQUIRES APPROVAL
AT DIRECTOR LEVEL
UNDER PROTOCOL 1002.

"You ever seen anything like that before, Sam?"

"No, Chief, I haven't."

"What's protocol ten-oh-two?"

"I don't have the slightest idea," Sam said.

"Who the hell is this guy?" Griggs muttered.

"I'd really like to know that," Stone replied.

⤜ **Chapter 24** ⤛

The next morning, Stone called Dino. "How are you?"

"Not bad. Where the hell are you now?"

"In Palm Beach."

"You rotten bastard."

"Yeah, I sure am."

"And if I know you, you're getting paid for it."

"Right again."

"Why didn't I go to law school?"

"Listen, I want to run something by you."

"Okay, shoot."

"I'm trying to identify a guy down here who isn't who he says he is. You remember our friend Paul Manning that you arrested for me?"

"Sure, he's dead."

"Nope." Stone took Dino through what he knew about Manning/Bartlett thus far. "Then last night, I got his prints off a glass, and the local cop shop ran them for me."

"And he turns out to be the Lindbergh baby?"

"Nope. At least, I don't think so. But something weird happened: We're logged onto the FBI print database, and when we transmit the print, we get a message saying access is denied without approval from the director level, and it mentions something called 'protocol ten-oh-two.' What it sounds like to me is some sort of national security thing, like maybe he has a CIA connection."

"Nah," Dino said. "I'll tell you what I think it is, and I'll give you five-to-one odds I'm right. The guy is in the witness protection program."

This stopped Stone in his tracks. "But that doesn't make any sense. Manning's background is not that of somebody the government would want to protect. In fact, he doesn't even exist, in a legal sense."

"Maybe he testified against somebody in a criminal trial somewhere."

"I suppose it's possible, but I would think that Manning would do everything he could to avoid putting himself in such a position. Also, Bob Berman checked out Bartlett, and he says the man's identity is thin, that he has no financial background to speak of. Even his driver's license is recent. That doesn't sound like the kind of identity the Department of Justice would create for somebody in the program."

"No, it doesn't, but there's another possibility."

"What's that?"

"Let's say that Manning or Bartlett, or whoever whatever the fuck his name is, gets involved in some criminal deal, and he gets busted and rats out his partners in return for immunity and the program."

"Possible, but it seems unlikely."

"Go with me, here, Stone. Anyway, they put him in the program and he finds himself stuck in Peoria or someplace, running a Burger King, and he doesn't like it. So he bails out of the program—happens all the time. Once the government gets these people in the program, the feds run their lives, and they've got fuck-all to say about it. Lots of them go overboard."

"True enough."

"So our guy is on the street, now. Maybe he sells the business and the house the government bought him, so he's got a few bucks. He finds someplace he likes, in this case, Minneapolis, though God knows why anybody would want to be stuck there in the winter, but he can't use his old name because whoever he ratted on still wants to cut his heart out and eat it for dinner. So he has to make up his own new identity, and he doesn't do the greatest job in the world. After all, he's not Justice; he can't call up the State Department and tell them to issue him a new passport, so he does the best he can. He gets a local driver's license, picks up a credit card and finds a business partner who's real and who can deal with the banks."

"Makes sense."

"Then he meets the rich widow, and pretty soon he's living in a much nicer house, and he doesn't need the business anymore, or, for that matter, the wife, so he sells one and does away with the other, and he gets away with it. Now he's rich, footloose and fancy fucking free, and he's house-hunting in Palm Beach and shopping for a Bentley."

"Okay, I buy it."

"I don't," Dino said. "I don't buy it for a minute."

"What? Why not? You just convinced me."

"Yeah, well, you're a pushover for a good story, Stone. You always were."

"What are you talking about, Dino? Have I missed something?"

"You usually do, pal, and this time it's this: If Bartlett is Manning, why would he hunt down his ex—well, his *previous* wife and start harassing her? He risks bringing himself to the attention of the local police, which he has already done, and exposing himself—in the fully clothed sense of the expression. Why would he want to do that?"

"Because he's pissed off at her for running off with all the money he stole, and he's crazy as a fruit bat, and he knows how to hold a grudge."

Dino didn't say anything.

"Well?"

"Okay, maybe you're right. After all, you can't depend on criminals to behave sensibly. I got another question, though."

"Okay."

"He doesn't look enough like he used to look for anybody to ID him, even you. You didn't get a picture of the guy, so Allison can't identify him because she won't be in the same room with him, and the FBI won't tell you who his prints belong to. How are you going to know, once and for all, who he is?"

"I wish you hadn't asked that question."

"Because you don't know the answer?"

"That's pretty much it."

Dino sighed deeply. "It looks like I'm going to have to come down there and straighten this out for you."

Stone had sort of been hoping he would; he missed Dino.

"You'll have to bring Mary Ann."

"Nah, she won't come while the kid's in school."

"How is Ben?"

"Well, his grandfather hasn't turned him into a made man yet."

"And how is Eduardo?"

"As mean as ever. He never gets older, just meaner."

"And Dolce?"

"I don't know. Mary Ann won't talk about her. I guess she's still nuts. Eduardo's got her locked up in farthest Brooklyn, and I don't see her ever getting out."

"When can you come?"

"Tomorrow, the next day, maybe. I can get the time off, I think. Can you find me a sack?"

"Sure, and a nice one, too."

"I'll call you with my flight number."

"I'll be there."

"See you."

"See you."

∽ Chapter 25 ∾

The following morning it was, to Stone's astonishment, raining, and raining hard. Juanito had put up clear curtains around the afterdeck, so Stone had breakfast alone there and checked with Joan for messages. He returned half a dozen calls, including one to Bill Eggers.

"I spoke to Thad yesterday," Eggers said, "and he is one happy client. I hope you're not thinking of coming back to New York before you clear up any remaining problems. If you do, I'll have you hit over the head in the airport and put you on the next airplane back to Palm Beach."

"Oh, I'm sticking it out," Stone said, "and it has turned interesting."

"How so?"

Stone went through the whole story once again.

"You know," Eggers said when Stone had finished, "being a partner in this firm is not nearly as interesting as what you do."

"Probably not. By the way, I sat next to one of your clients at dinner last night—a Lila Baldwin."

"Oh, God," Eggers groaned. "Be careful around her. Once, during a discussion of estate tax avoidance, she grabbed my crotch."

"I'm not surprised."

"*I* was, I can tell you."

"You've led a sheltered life."

"Right, and I'd better get back to it. Call me if you need any backup."

"Will do."

Stone had hardly hung up when the phone rang. He punched a button. "Shames residence."

"May I speak with a Mr. Stone Barrington, please?" A male voice.

"Speaking."

"Mr. Barrington, my name is Ebbe Lundquist. I'm with the Minneapolis Police Department."

"How are you?"

"Okay. Earlier this morning I had a very interesting conversation with Chief Griggs of the Palm Beach PD."

"Did you?"

"Yes, and I immediately checked our records on Mrs. Frances Bartlett."

"And what did you find?"

"I found that the smashup was handled as an accident by the traffic division of the sheriff's department, and since they didn't suspect foul play, we were never brought into it. Apart from reading about it in the papers, this was the first I've known about it."

"I'm glad Dan Griggs enlightened you."

"He said that you enlightened him. You're ex-NYPD, right?"

"Right."

"Ever work homicide?"

"For many years."

"You think this was a homicide?"

"It has that distinct odor."

"What makes you think so?"

"Griggs told you about Bartlett's little identity problem?"

"Yes, we're looking at that now."

"That's a tip-off. Then there's the fact that Mrs. Bartlett rescinded a prenuptial agreement and made a new will in Paul Bartlett's favor less than a month before she was killed. And I understand she was very rich."

"First I've heard of that," Lundquist said. "I'll check it out. We're looking for the wrecked car, too. Right now, I'm not sure where it is."

"I'd be very interested in what you learn," Stone said.

"Tell me, what's your interest in Paul Bartlett?"

"He may be harassing a client of mine."

"Enough harassment to put him in jail?"

"Not yet, not unless he tries to harm her."

"So, if we arrested him for the murder of his wife, that would be okay with you, huh?"

"Sure would. But please don't think I'm trying to frame him for it to get my client off the hook. The information that Griggs and I passed on to you is just what I came up with, almost by accident. If he's a murderer, I'd like to see him nailed for it, but I'm not positive he's the guy who's harassing my client. There's a physical resemblance, and that's as far as I've gotten. Griggs told you about the FBI hold on his fingerprint file?"

"Yeah. I've run into that once before. It's not going to help."

"I don't see how it would hurt a homicide investigation. You can convict him as Bartlett or as John Doe; you don't need his real identity. I'm the one who needs that, so if you come up with something along those lines, I'd really like to hear about it."

"Can I reach you at this number?"

"Yes, and I'll give you my cell phone number, too." He recited the number.

"Got it. I'll call you."

"Thanks."

"Do you know where this guy can be found?"

"No. He checked out of the Chesterfield Hotel yesterday and didn't leave a forwarding address. He says he's house-hunting, and that he bought a Bentley. So far, he doesn't seem to have any interest in leaving Palm Beach, unless he's worried about me. I did ask him a few pointed questions."

"Do me a favor and don't crowd him. If we get something on him, I want him where I can find him."

"Our interests may diverge there," Stone said. "I have to put my client's safety first."

"Okay, okay, just try not to scare him out of town."

"I won't, unless I have to."

"Thanks. I'll call you."

"Bye." Stone hung up and greeted Callie, who was still yawning. "Sleep late?"

"It's the rain," she said. "It's like a narcotic. You had breakfast?"

"Yep, but it wasn't as good as the ones you make."

"You're sweet."

"Are you going to talk to Thad today?"

"Maybe. I can, if necessary."

"Please tell him that I've asked a friend, a New York City detective lieutenant, to come down here and lend a hand. I'd like to put him up on the boat."

"I'm sure that will be all right. We're not expecting any other guests, and anyway, the house is ready now. Who is this fellow?"

"His name is Dino Bacchetti. He and I were partners for a long time when I was on the force. He's saved my ass more than once."

"I must remember to thank him. Will I like him?"

"Probably. He'll certainly like you," Stone said.

"Should I see if I can find him some female companionship while he's here?"

"Not unless you want his Sicilian wife to come after you with a sharp instrument."

"I think not."

"Don't worry, Dino will be fine on his own. Anyway, we can pair him with Liz at dinner."

"Does he know her?"

"He knows about her, but they've never met."

"Funny, I don't think I've ever met a cop before. I mean, except for you, and you're not a cop anymore."

"You'll find Dino charming at times, and blunt to the point of rudeness at others."

"I never mind bluntness in people, unless they're insulting. Sometimes I'm not sure whether they're trying to insult."

"When Dino is trying, you'll know."

"He sounds interesting."

"He is certainly that."

Liz came out of her cabin and made her way aft.

"Oh, Liz," Callie said. "Stone has got you a date."

"Huh?" Liz asked sleepily.

"Not a date, just a dinner companion," Stone explained.

"As long as it's not Paul Manning," she said, sitting down at their table.

"It's not," Stone said. "Callie, do you know where the Rolls-Royce dealership is in Palm Beach?"

"It's in West Palm, on the mainland," she said. "Hang on, I'll show you." She dug a map out of her purse and pointed at it. "There are a whole bunch of car dealers along this stretch of road; it's one of those. You thinking of buying a Rolls?"

"No, but they sell Bentley, too."

⤳ Chapter 26 ⤳

Stone crossed the bridge to the mainland. The heavy rain roiled the Inland Waterway, and his windshield wipers were on full blast. The Rolls-Royce showroom was on the same lot with the BMW dealership, but separate. He put up his borrowed umbrella, strolled into the showroom and began looking at the Rollses and Bentleys, new and used, on the floor. Shortly, a man whose clothes were a cut above those of the average car salesman left his glassed-in office and approached him.

"Good morning. May I answer any questions?"

"Just looking, really. What does the new Bentley sell for?"

"It starts at two hundred fifteen thousand," the man said. "And there are some options available."

"Very handsome car," Stone said. "You just sold one to an acquaintance of mine—yesterday, I believe."

The salesman wrinkled his brow. "Yesterday? And who would that be?"

"His name is Paul Bartlett."

"Tall gentleman?"

"Yes."

"Oh, he came in and had a test drive, but he didn't buy a car. I believe he went into the BMW showroom next door, though. Perhaps they had something rather more to his liking."

"Maybe so," Stone said.

"Would you like to drive a car?"

"On another occasion, perhaps. Thanks for your time."

"Please come back," the salesman said.

Stone left and went next door. The BMW showroom was less plush than its neighbor, and the salesmen were lined up along the window at steel desks. One of them leaped up and came toward Stone.

"Hi, there. Can I show you a car?"

"Oh, I'm just window-shopping at the moment. You sold a car to a friend of mine yesterday, though."

"Oh? Who's that? We sell cars every day."

"Paul Bartlett."

"Oh, yeah. We did the deal on the phone. I picked him up at the airport yesterday. He's from Minneapolis."

"That's the one."

"Paul got the black 750i, with the V-twelve engine. I've got another one on the lot. I could put you in it inside the hour. Why don't you take a test drive?"

"Oh, I'd just be wasting your time. I'm a couple of weeks away from buying. I just wanted to have a look. Say, where is Paul staying, do you know? He was at the Chesterfield, but he's checked out."

"He's at the Colony. I sent the paperwork over there yesterday afternoon."

"Oh, yes, the Colony. Say, I don't mean to cause you any concern, but how did Paul pay for the car?"

"He gave me a cashier's check from a local bank." He suddenly looked concerned. "Why? Do you think something might be wrong?"

"Not if he gave you a cashier's check," Stone said. "Thanks for your time." He walked out of the showroom, put up his umbrella and ran back to his car, avoiding the deeper puddles. Well, he thought, Mr. Bartlett has lied about his residence and his car. He is obviously now watching his back. Stone sat in the car and called the Minneapolis police department.

"Ebbe Lundquist, in homicide," he said to the operator.

"Homicide," a man's voice said.

"Ebbe Lundquist, please."

"Lieutenant Lundquist is out of the office for a few days."

"Might he have gone to Florida?"

"That's right. Can someone else help you?"

"No, thanks," Stone said. He broke the connection and called Dan Griggs.

"Hello?"

"Morning, Dan, it's Stone Barrington. I believe you talked to a Lieutenant Lundquist yesterday?"

"Right."

"I think he's on the way down here."

"He must have found out something that got him moving," Griggs said.

"I think he wants to talk to Paul Bartlett," Stone said. "I've learned that Bartlett didn't buy a Bentley but a black BMW 750i. Also, he's moved into the Colony Hotel. I think Lundquist might appreciate it if you put a man on him. He seems to be getting slippery."

"I can do that."

"Tell him not to crowd the guy. Our friend Mr. Bartlett is getting nervous, and we wouldn't want him to bail out before Lundquist has a crack at him."

"I'll tell my man to work wide. Thanks, Stone."

"And I'd appreciate a call if there are any developments."

"Sure. You learn anything about that protocol ten-oh-two thing?"

"I talked to my old partner in New York. His guess is that Bartlett is, or rather was, in the Justice Department's witness protection program, and that he jumped ship and set up a new identity on his own."

"That's an interesting theory," Griggs said. "Has he got anything to back it up?"

"No, it's just his hunch, but I think it's a good one. By the way, he's coming down here soon, and I'd like for you to meet him. His name is Dino Bacchetti, and he commands the detective squad at the Nineteenth Precinct."

"Love to greet him," Griggs said.

"I'll bring him by. Take care." Stone hung up. He pulled into traffic and headed back toward the yacht, and his cell phone rang again.

"Hello?"

"It's me," Dino said.

Stone could hear a police siren in the background. "Let me guess; you're on the way to the airport."

"That's right," Dino said. "My flight arrives at two-thirty." He gave Stone the flight number.

"I'll meet you. Dino, you've got to stop driving around with the siren on. A trip to the airport is not exactly an emergency call."

"It is if I say it is," Dino replied. "Traffic is hell on the FDR Drive right now."

"And the siren helps."

"You bet your ass it does. How's the weather down there?"

"Gorgeous," Stone said, peering through the driving rain at the road ahead, which was barely visible. "I hope you're bringing a swimsuit."

"Damn right I am; my golf clubs, too."

"Great. How about a tennis racket?"

"You know I'm a lousy tennis player."

"You're a lousy golfer, too, but you're bringing your clubs."

"If that sonofabitch doesn't get the fuck out of the way, ram him!" Dino shouted, apparently at his driver.

"Have you got another rookie detective at the wheel?"

"So what if I have?"

"Give the kid a break, Dino. He can't drive *over* the traffic."

"My flight leaves in twenty minutes."

"So what? You're not going through the airport; you're going to flash your badge and drive out onto the tarmac, right up to the airplane, aren't you?"

"You bet your ass, but I've still got to move to make it."

"So call the airline and tell them it's a police emergency, to hold the flight."

"Jesus, why didn't I think of that? Get off the phone!"

"I'll see you at Palm Beach Airport," Stone said, and pressed the end button. He laughed aloud at the thought of Dino holding the flight for a police emergency, then arriving at the airplane carrying his golf clubs.

He called the yacht, and Callie answered.

"Hi. Where are you?"

"On the way back from the Rolls dealer."

"Find out anything?"

"I'll tell you later. Have you heard a weather forecast for tomorrow?"

"Rain ends late tonight; sunny all day tomorrow."

"Thank God. Dino's arriving this afternoon, with golf clubs. He'd shoot me if he couldn't play. Can you find us some golf somewhere?"

"Sure. I'll book a tee time at the Breakers. Ten o'clock okay?"

"Perfect. Dino's bringing his own clubs. I'll need to rent some."

"You can use Thad's; he won't mind."

"Do you play?"

"I've got a twelve handicap. What's yours?"

"We'll make it a threesome, then," Stone said, avoiding an answer.

"Well," she said, laughing, "I'm glad you're interested in *some* kind of threesome."

~ **Chapter 27** ~

Stone drove to the airport, and the rain had still not let up. At times he was driving through three and four inches of water in the street, and the wind had started to get up, as well. At the airport, he parked at the curb and ran inside, and the hell with tickets.

He found Dino in baggage claim, just getting his golf clubs off the carousel.

"You didn't tell me it was hurricane season," Dino grumbled, handing Stone two bags and hoisting the clubs onto a shoulder. "I should have brought fucking scuba gear!"

"Oh, I just wanted you to see that Palm Beach is a city of contrasts," Stone said, running for the car and getting soaked while stowing the bags in the trunk. The golf clubs had to go in the backseat. Finally, they were under way, with the windshield wipers trying hard to keep up with the deluge, and losing.

"I'm soaked to the skin!" Dino complained. "You might as well put the top down!"

"I don't understand it," Stone said. "The weather was glorious, until you decided to come."

"Oh, right, I brought the weather with me; it's all my fault."

"Thank you for pointing that out. So, how are things at home?"

"Oh, just great. Dolce is out."

Stone nearly wrecked the car. "What do you mean, 'out'?"

"Out. She set a fire in her room, which set off the alarm, and while her nurses were preoccupied with that, she got out of the house, took one of Eduardo's cars and vanished into the world."

"When did this happen?"

"This morning, apparently. Mary Ann called me on my pocket phone just as I was getting on the airplane. Eduardo is going nuts."

"She won't get far. Eduardo will have her back in no time. What, is she running around in her nightgown?"

"She packed three bags, according to the housekeeper, who counted the luggage. I'd say she has clothes for any occasion. Dolce is nothing if not organized."

"But she doesn't have any money or credit cards; she can't travel."

"Dolce has money of her own, you know, and quite a lot of it. Eduardo settled two million bucks on each of the girls when they turned twenty-one. And she took her purse, too—credit cards, even her passport. There's nowhere you can run."

"Oh, shit," Stone said, his heart sinking. He dug out his cell phone and pressed the speed dial button for his office.

"The Barrington Practice," Joan said.

"Hi, it's me. You might get a call from Dolce sometime soon. Can you recognize her voice?"

"Sure I can. I heard it less than ten minutes ago."

"What did she want?"

"You, I expect."

"What did you tell her?"

"That you were out of town."

"Did you tell her where?"

"No."

"Thank God for that."

"Bill Eggers told her that."

"What?"

"As soon as she hung up I called Bill's office, but he was on the phone. I held, and when he came on the line, he told me Dolce had called, and they'd had a nice chat. I take it Bill isn't fully informed about Dolce's condition."

"Wonderful. If she calls back try and get a number where I can reach her."

"Okay."

Stone hung up and punched the button for Bill Eggers's office at Woodman & Weld.

"Bill?"

"I take it from Joan's reaction that I did something stupid?"

"It's not your fault, Bill, but just how stupid were you?"

"Stupid enough to tell her you were in Palm Beach, before I noticed something about her. I stopped just short of telling her where you're staying."

"Thank God for small favors," Stone muttered.

"What's the matter with her, Stone? I thought she was just sick, but she sounded . . ."

"Exactly how did she sound?"

"Well, not deranged, exactly, but sort of otherworldly."

"Does she know I'm doing work for Thad Shames?"

"I didn't mention that."

"Okay, Bill, thanks, and I'll be in touch." Stone punched off. "She doesn't know where I'm staying."

"Her sister does."

"Oh, no. Mary Ann wouldn't . . ."

"No, of course she wouldn't, not if she were tortured, and Dolce is perfectly capable of torturing somebody to find out where you are."

Stone turned into the driveway of the Shames mansion.

"Hey, pretty nice," Dino said. "Do we have it to ourselves?"

"We're not staying in the house; we're out back."

"Guest house?"

"Not exactly."

"Uh-oh," Dino said.

"Come on, let's get the car unloaded and make a run for it."

Two minutes later they had dashed up the gangplank of *Toscana* and were standing, panting, on the afterdeck, while puddles formed around them. Juanito appeared with some towels and two thick terry robes, and took the luggage.

"Maybe you could change into the robes here?" he said, as he padded off toward Dino's cabin.

Stone and Dino emptied their pockets onto the table, including Dino's badge and gun, and stripped. They had just kicked their clothing into a sodden pile when Callie appeared.

"Well, hi there, sailors!" she said to the two naked men.

Dino grabbed for his robe.

"This must be Dino," Callie said. "I can always recognize a naked policeman."

"Dino, this is Callie Hodges," Stone said, getting into his own robe.

"How do you do," Dino said, trying to muster some dignity.

"We have a ten-thirty tee time at the Breakers tomorrow," she said.

"Great," Dino said. "We can go there on the boat."

"Don't worry, the front will pass through tonight. Tomorrow will be beautiful, I promise. The greens may be a little slow, but Palm Beach is thirsty and will soak the rain right up. I'm surprised your plane was able to land."

"It took the pilot two tries," Dino said. "I was ready to bust into the cockpit with my gun and order them to fly back to New York."

"I'm glad you didn't," Callie said, smiling sweetly.

Juanito came back with a tray of steaming mugs.

"We fixed you a little toddy," Callie said. "Figured that, with the temperature thirty degrees below normal, you might need it."

Everybody sat down, and Stone and Dino gratefully sipped their drinks, which were laced with rum.

"Well," Dino said to Callie, "any more at home like you?"

Callie laughed. "Don't worry, we've got you a date for dinner."

"Oh?"

"Allison Manning," Stone said. "Although she's called Liz Harding these days; you might remember that."

"I'll try," Dino said.

"Callie, have there been any phone calls for me?"

"No."

"If anyone besides Thad, Bill Eggers, Chief Griggs or my secretary, Joan, calls, will you tell them I've gone back to New York?"

"Sure. Who are you avoiding?"

"Mrs. Stone Barrington," Dino said.

She turned and looked at Stone, and her eyes narrowed. *"Who?"*

Dino set down his cup. "Well, I think I'll go get into some dry clothes."

As soon as he was gone, Stone began explaining to Callie who Dolce was. When he had finished, he waited for a comment.

"Well," she said finally, "hanging around you is never dull."

⤜ **Chapter 28** ⤛

Because of the weather, they had dinner in the yacht's dining room, which was a symphony of mahogany and teak. Juanito had set a small table for the four of them, and candlelight gleamed on fine silver, as he served the dinner Callie had cooked for them. Dino had taken a shine not only to Callie, but to Liz as well, and they to him.

"What, exactly, do you do on the police force, Dino?" Liz asked him.

"Well, you know how on the TV cop shows there's always these two detectives who are out there busting their balls to solve the case?"

"Yes."

"That used to be Stone and me."

"Oh."

"And you know how the two detectives come back to the station house and report to their lieutenant, and he criticizes them and second-guesses them and ridicules them and sends them back out onto the street to do it all over again?"

"Yes."

"That lieutenant is me, now."

"Was Stone a good detective?" Callie asked.

Stone shifted his weight uncomfortably.

"He wasn't all that bad," Dino said, "but he was hard to keep alive. I was always having to shoot people so they wouldn't kill him."

"Nonsense! I was a *very* good detective," Stone said, "but that second part is perfectly true, which gives you a pretty good indication of what percentage of Dino's statements you can believe."

"Tell us about when you saved Stone's life," Liz said.

Dino took a big sip of his wine. "Well, let's see," he said. "The first time was when we had chased this guy down in a car, and he came out shooting, got Stone in the knee. I put one in the middle of his forehead."

"Goodness," Callie said. Both the women were rapt.

"Then there was the time Stone had to jump out of a helicopter because people were trying to kill him. I used a shotgun that time; didn't kill anybody. Then—oh, this is my favorite—this very strange guy had Stone strung up by his heels, naked, in this old slaughterhouse, about to cut him a few new orifices, and I put two in him."

Liz blinked rapidly. "Strung up by his heels, naked? Whew! If I had a folding fan, this is where I'd use it."

"And there were probably a couple of other times, but you get the idea."

Callie spoke up. "The idea seems to be that Stone needs his hand held." She took his hand and squeezed it.

"That's about it," Dino said. "Stone has good instincts, but he never listens to them. He's so curious that he doesn't notice when people are trying to kill him."

"Tell us about Stone and women," Callie said.

Dino rolled his eyes. "Don't get me started."

"No," Stone said, "don't get him started. You keep this up, Dino, and I'm going to start telling them the truth about you."

Dino held up a hand. "Peace," he said. "Anything else you girls want to know about Stone, you're going to have to ask him."

"Well, Stone," Callie said. "Will you sit still for some personal questions?"

"As long as you don't expect an honest answer," Stone replied.

Juanito suddenly appeared, the cordless phone in his hands. "Miss Callie," he said, then mouthed, "It's for him," pointing at Stone.

Callie took the phone. "May I help you? And who is this? I'm sorry, Mr. Barrington left this morning. I believe he was headed for California somewhere, before returning to New York. No, I'm sorry, I don't have his schedule. Why don't you call his New York office? Good-bye." She punched the off button.

"Was it a woman?" Stone asked.

"No, a man. He wouldn't give his name. He sounded a little like Paul Bartlett, but I can't be sure about that."

"That was a nice touch, about California," Stone said. "I'll have to remember what a good liar you are."

"I was lying for a good cause," Callie replied. "Dino needs help in keeping you alive."

"Like Regis says, 'I'm only one man,'" Dino said.

The phone rang again while still in Callie's hand. "Here we go again," she said. "Hello? Oh, yes, Chief, I'll put him on." She handed the phone to Stone.

"Hello, Dan."

"Hi, Stone. Our friend from the frozen tundra, Lieutenant Lundquist, has arrived. Could we have a word with you tonight?"

"Sure," Stone said. "Give me half an hour, then come over to the Shames house. We're on the yacht moored out back."

"See you then."

Stone hung up. "Well, ladies, you're going to have a couple more cops on your hands shortly."

"I'd better finish dessert," Callie said, rising and heading toward the galley.

"What cops?" Dino asked.

Stone explained about Griggs and Lundquist, and about Paul Bartlett's sojourn in Minneapolis.

"God, I love catching murderers," Dino said, "don't you?"

"Not as much as you, Dino, but I'll admit, it's satisfying. What I don't like about murderers is that time after you've figured out what they did but before you arrest them. They tend to be touchy during that period."

"So you think Bartlett is dangerous?"

"I certainly do. Griggs has assigned somebody to keep an eye on him, but Lundquist has asked us not to crowd him just yet."

"I hate not crowding them," Dino said.

Callie returned to the table, followed by Juanito carrying a tray of flaming desserts.

"Something old-fashioned," she said. "Baked Alaska. I thought, given the weather, we could use the extra warmth."

"Mmmmmmmm," Dino said, plunging into his. "We may keep you on here."

"Why, thank you, sir."

Liz was toying with her dessert. "Stone," she said, "am I ever going to be able to leave this boat again?"

"Sure you are, but right now is not a good time. Paul doesn't know you're here, at least not for sure."

"We could stake her out, like a goat for a lion," Dino said.

"Thank you, Dino," Liz said. "That was so beautifully put."

"Don't mention it," Dino said, grinning.

⤳ Chapter 29 ⤳

C hief Dan Griggs and Lieutenant Ebbe Lundquist arrived, sharing a golf umbrella. They were both dripping wet.

"Sorry to get you out this late, Chief," Stone said. "Couldn't this have waited for better weather?"

"Lundquist, here, insisted," Griggs replied.

Lundquist looked around at the yacht. "You live pretty well, Mr. Barrington."

"I'm sorry to disappoint you, but, unfortunately, the yacht is not mine. And please call me Stone." Stone introduced everybody, and Callie got the visitors a hot toddy, while everyone else had brandy.

"It's like this," Lundquist said. "We dug Bartlett's car out of a junkyard, where it was waiting to go into the compactor. Couple more days, it would have been gone. We have you to thank for that, Stone."

Stone shrugged. "I just happened to get lucky."

"The car was a 1991 Mercedes station wagon, and that year, a passenger-side air bag was an option, and Mrs. Bartlett, who owned the car, had not ordered the option. Everything about the car was normal, for one that had just collided with a tree, except that the seat belt latch had been tampered with."

"Tampered with how?" Dino asked.

"There's a steel eye that sticks up on a stalk, then there's the receptor end that latches onto that. We opened up the receptor, and the spring inside had been deformed, compared with the driver's side, so that it would not hook securely when fastened. Mrs. Bartlett would have heard a click when she put it on, but it would have come undone under pressure."

"And colliding with a tree would certainly be enough pressure," Stone said.

"This guy is very clever," Lundquist said. "That was the sort of technical thing that would have gone completely unnoticed if you hadn't given us a heads up to look for something."

"This same guy once rigged an airplane engine to fail, killing all three aboard," Stone said. "He's not stupid, and he has some skills."

"*What?*" Lundquist demanded. "He's murdered three *other* people?"

"If he's who I think he is," Stone said. He explained Paul Manning's background, not mentioning that he had been Liz's husband.

"So we couldn't charge him with those three killings, then?" Lundquist asked.

"No, he was tried and convicted, then the authorities were bought off."

"He might even have a pardon," Liz said.

Stone looked at her. "Was his wife pardoned?"

"In a manner of speaking. She was given a piece of paper."

"So, Lieutenant, do you have enough evidence to arrest him?"

"I can arrest him for obtaining a Minnesota driver's license under a false name, and I can probably get him extradited, but I'm not sure we have enough evidence to convict him of murder. Still, I'd like to get him back to Minneapolis and question him thoroughly. Maybe he'll even cop to it."

"Not a chance," Stone said. "He'd lawyer up in a heartbeat. I'd be willing to bet he's got the number in his pocket right now, just in case. And it sounds like you'd have a hell of a time proving that he tampered with the seat belt. His attorney would paint it as damaged in the accident or defectively manufactured, and Bartlett as a grieving husband."

"Maybe you're right," Lundquist said, "but I'm waiting for a call from my office, and when they come up with just a little more evidence, I'm going to bust him. At the very least I can expose his false identity and let the world know who he is."

"He's not going to tell you who he is," Stone said, "and that's the only way you're going to find out. The feds certainly aren't going to admit that he was in their program."

"If he's Paul, I can identify him in court," Liz said.

"I thought you were refusing to face him," Stone replied.

"I won't while he's free, but I'd be happy to testify as to his identity, if it would help put him away."

"I don't know that it would," Stone said. "Given the evidence we've got, I'd much rather defend him than prosecute."

"This is very convoluted," Dino said. "Not only do we not know if he was in the witness protection program, we don't even know what name he was using before he went in."

"I don't understand," Liz said.

"Okay, he gets out of being hanged in St. Marks, and he returns to this country. He's not going back to using Paul Manning for a name, he's going to pick another one. Then he gets involved in whatever ends up getting him into the program, and he gives the feds that name, not Manning. They change it to another name, then he skips out of the program and changes it again. And there may be a couple of other name changes that we don't even know about."

"Holy cow," Lundquist said. "I didn't know what I was getting into when I came down here."

"You probably wanted a little nice weather, like me," Dino said. He waved an arm. "And look what we got."

Lundquist gazed through the transparent curtains as lightning lit up Lake Worth. "I might as well have stayed in Minneapolis."

"Well," Chief Griggs said, "if it's any consolation, I think we've got enough to run him out of Palm Beach."

"You sound like an Old West sheriff," Callie said.

"It's a little different," Griggs replied. "In the Old West, I'd have threatened to shoot him if he showed his face in town again. Nowadays, I'd just make sure the local and Florida papers heard the whole story, and once everybody had heard about it and gossiped about it, he wouldn't be able to show his face in town again. We had a guy down here a few years back that had kidnapped his young kids when a divorce didn't go his way. Established himself here under another name and stayed for years until his wife caught up with him. Now he's persona non grata among the people he knew best. That, I can do to Bartlett, or whatever his name is."

"It isn't enough," Liz said. "He could still try to kill me."

Lundquist turned and stared at her. "Just when I thought I had a grip on this story . . ."

"Mrs. Harding was once married to Paul Manning," Stone said. "We didn't mention that before."

"Oh," Lundquist said, tonelessly. He was massaging his temples, like someone trying to hold on to his sanity.

"Maybe your lab will come up with something else in the car," Stone said.

"Maybe, but I'm not going to count on it," Lundquist replied. "We do have the fact that he got his wife to cancel the prenuptial agreement and make a new will. That's motive."

"Oh, you have both motive and opportunity," Stone said, "but a good lawyer would make a conviction very difficult to obtain. It's like this: I'm his lawyer, and I stand up in front of the jury. Ladies and gentlemen, my client had no criminal intent when he changed his name. Bad people were after him, and he had to protect himself. Why, it was the government itself that changed his name first. There's no evidence that he put pressure on his wife to change her will. No, she did that out of love and affection for my client, who is a very loveable and affectionate fellow, crushed by the loss of his bride. My client doesn't have the technical expertise to tamper with a finely made piece of German engineering, and after all, he was in the same car; he could have been just as easily killed. And on and on like that."

"This is very depressing," Lundquist said.

Dino spoke up. "It might help in court if you proved he was Paul Manning, who had already murdered three other people in St. Marks, even if he got away with it."

"I could get his past ruled out as evidence," Stone said, "on the grounds that it was irrelevant and prejudicial, and if I couldn't, I'd say he was rail-roaded by a corrupt foreign government. No, Mr. Bartlett has crafted himself a very nice little box to live in. And, Dan, if you got him run out of Palm Beach, he'd just go to Palm Springs, or some other place with an inviting climate, and establish himself all over again under another identity. And now he's got the money to make himself credible in a place like that."

Everybody was quiet for a while.

Finally, Dino spoke up again. "Unless we staked out Liz like a goat for a lion, then waited to see what happened."

⤳ Chapter 30 ⤶

The four of them got out of the two cars at the Breakers Golf Club and gave three bags of clubs to the attendant. The clubhouse was modest, in comparison to the grandeur of the hotel, Stone thought. The weather, as predicted, had cleared beautifully, and it was much cooler after the front had passed through.

"But I don't play golf," Liz complained. "What am I doing here?"

"Playing chauffeur," Stone said. "You can drive a cart. Also, you're playing the goat."

"I don't think I like the goat idea," she said. "Not when Paul is the lion."

"Dino's right," Stone said, "as much as I hate to admit it. This is the only way to smoke him out. We're not having much luck any other way. If we see him, you can identify him; if not, then at least *we'll* be seen, and word may get back to him that you're still around."

"All right," Liz said.

"This is a pretty chilly paradise you got here," Dino said, zipping up his jacket to the neck.

"In more ways than one," Callie said, as another group of golfers inspected them as they passed, staring hard.

They signed in at the clubhouse, then got into carts and drove to the first tee, where the starter cleared them to tee off.

The course was mostly flat and uninteresting. "It's not the most attractive golf course I've ever seen," Stone said.

"Don't worry, they're about to rip the whole thing up and completely rebuild it to new design," Callie said.

"Ladies first," Dino said, motioning Callie to drive.

Callie took a few practice swings, displaying good form, teed up a ball and struck it solidly. It flew down the middle of the fairway.

"About two hundred and twenty yards," Stone said. He teed up and sliced his drive into the next fairway.

"Take a mulligan," Callie said.

Stone took the mulligan and got it in the fairway, a good twenty yards short of Callie's ball.

Dino teed up and hooked the ball into the rough. "Mulligan," he said, teeing up another ball. He swung at that, and it landed no more than a yard from his first ball.

"Your grip is too strong," Callie said, showing him how to turn his right hand to the left. "That should cure your hook."

"Don't count on it," Stone said.

They trundled off down the fairway in their carts, playing at a good pace, now and then crossing South County Road.

"This is the most urban golf I've ever played," Stone said. "Usually, on a golf course, you don't have to worry about being hit by a car."

"The Breakers has another course west of here," Callie said. "Maybe we'll play that one next time."

They played on, occasionally running into a foursome in which Callie knew someone. Two people knew Liz and chatted with her.

"Word's getting out," Callie said. "You shouldn't even try to keep a secret in this town, but we're advertising. Liz, you're the subject of much conversation since being seen with Thad at his party."

"Grand," Liz said.

They finished their round, went back to the clubhouse, had a beer, stowed their clubs in the two cars and prepared to depart the Breakers. Stone opened his cell phone and tapped in a number. "Okay, Dan, we've made our appearance at the Breakers, and we're ready to move on to part two of our plan."

"My guys are parked just down the road," Griggs said.

"Tell them not to crowd the girls. We don't want Bartlett picking up on cops."

"Bartlett left the Colony half an hour ago, and he's having lunch on Worth Avenue."

"They'll go shopping, then," Stone said. "Dino and I will wait back at the yacht."

"Right," Griggs said.

Stone ended the call. "Okay, ladies, you are sentenced to Worth Avenue shopping for at least two hours. Liz, if you recognize Paul, don't let on, just tell Callie so she can confirm who he is. You've got my cell phone number if you need to reach me."

"I'd feel better if you and Dino came along," Liz said.

"He knows us both, so we can't do that. We'd just scare him off."

"Oh, all right," Liz said, disconsolately. She got into the car with Callie, and they drove off.

"There goes our goat," Dino said. "But even if she makes him, Griggs isn't going to have any grounds for an arrest."

"Lundquist does, though. He can always bust him for the driver's license, and that will at least get him out of our hair."

"For the time being," Dino said. "This guy ain't going to go away easy."

"You have a point," Stone agreed.

They drove back to the yacht and waited. Dino got into a swimsuit and took up a strategic position on a chaise on the afterdeck, a rum and tonic at his elbow.

"You got anything to read?" he asked Stone.

Stone went into the saloon and came back with the novel *Tumult* that he had read a few days before. "Try this," he said, handing it to Dino. "It's very good."

Dino was soon rapt, and Stone dozed on a nearby chaise, protecting his fair skin from the sun under an awning.

Stone woke up with Callie shaking him. "Huh?" he said, sleepily.

"We're back," Callie said.

Stone sat up. "Anything happen?"

"We saw him."

"You did?"

"Coming out of Verdura, the jewelry store."

Liz came up the gangplank.

"Liz, you saw him?"

She nodded. "Yes."

"And?"

"And I don't know."

"You don't know what?"

"I don't know if it's Paul."

"But you said you recognized him in Easthampton by the way he walked and his body language."

"It was different this time," she said. "Anyway, I only saw him for a minute."

"Liz," Callie said, "you had a very good look at him. I was there; I saw him, too."

"Well, I'm sorry," Liz said crossly, "but I just can't swear that he's Paul. He may be and he may not be."

Stone's cell phone vibrated, and he opened it. "Hello?"

"It's Dan Griggs. The two ladies got a real good look at the guy. What does Mrs. Harding say?"

"Inconclusive," Stone said, walking away from the group.

"How could it be inconclusive? She got a good look at him, and she used to be married to the guy."

"All I can tell you is what she told me," Stone said. "She seems pretty annoyed about our pressing her on it."

"I don't get it," Griggs said.

"Frankly, neither do I. I thought that if we just put Bartlett in front of her, she'd make him, and that would be that."

"You think she's not playing this straight?"

"I honestly don't know, Dan. She's protected him in the past, after all."

"But she's supposed to be scared of the guy. You'd think she'd want to be rid of him and would help us do it."

"I don't know what to tell you, Dan."

"Well, if Mrs. Harding can't identify the guy, and if Lundquist can't come up with enough evidence for a murder warrant, I'm not going to be able to keep men on this. We have other problems to deal with, you know."

"I know you do, Dan, and I don't blame you. Has Lundquist not heard from his office?"

"He's called them twice, but the lab is still working on the car."

"Okay. Ask him to call me when he gets word. If he's going to arrest Bartlett, I'd like to be there when he does it."

"I'll tell him."

Stone ended the call and stood there thinking for a moment. He was getting tired of this, too. He punched 411 into the phone, asked for the number of the Colony Hotel and waited while the operator connected him.

"The Colony, good afternoon," a woman's voice said.

"Paul Bartlett, please."

She connected him, and the phone rang and rang. Finally she came back on the line. "There's no answer. Would you like to leave a message?"

"Yes, please. Ask him to . . ."

"One moment, I'll connect you with the front desk." She did so.

"Reception," a man's voice said.

"I'd like to leave a message for Paul Bartlett," Stone said. He'd just arrange to meet the man and put Liz's proposition to him.

"I'm sorry, but Mr. Bartlett checked out just a few minutes ago, and I'm afraid he didn't leave a forwarding address."

Stone punched the end button. "Shit," he said aloud.

Chapter 31

Stone couldn't believe it. He and Dino got dressed and into a car and drove to the Colony Hotel; he wanted to question the desk man. As they pulled into the parking lot, he spotted Detective Riley and Lieutenant Lundquist sitting in an idling car thirty yards away. Stone walked over and rapped on the window, startling them both.

"What are you doing here, Stone?" Lundquist asked. "You're going to spook the guy."

"What guy?" Stone asked.

"Bartlett."

"Bartlett has decamped."

"*What?*"

"Come with me." Stone started for the hotel lobby.

Lundquist caught up and fell into step with Stone. "What do you mean, 'decamped'?"

"I mean, Bartlett has checked out of the hotel, and he didn't leave a forwarding address."

"How do you know that?"

"Because I telephoned him half an hour ago, and that's what the desk clerk told me. I want to find out if it's true, or if Bartlett simply bought the desk man, and I want you to flash your badge at him so he'll talk to me."

The desk clerk stared blankly at the badge. "You're a police officer? Where? Your badge doesn't look familiar."

"He's from Minneapolis," Stone said. "I can have a Palm Beach badge here in thirty seconds, if that will refresh your memory."

"My memory about what?"

"First of all, has Paul Bartlett really checked out?"

"Yes, I saw him go."

"What forwarding address did he give?"

"I'll show you his registration card," the clerk said, riffling through a stack of them. "Here." He held it up. The space for a forwarding address was blank.

"Did you check him out of the hotel?"

"In a manner of speaking. He didn't even wait for his bill, said he had to catch a plane and I should mail it to him."

"To where?"

"To the address on the card."

Lundquist checked the card. "It's his Minneapolis address. The guy's gone home."

"How much luggage did he have?" Stone asked.

"A lot; three or four bags."

"And where did the bellman load his car?"

"Down on the street," the clerk said, pointing at the side door.

"That's why he got past you," Stone said to Lundquist. "I'd like to see his room, please."

The man pressed a few buttons on a machine, and a plastic card was spat out. "It's suite four-oh-four. Help yourself," he said.

Stone led the way to the elevator and pressed four. A moment later they were standing outside the suite, and Stone got the door open.

"Easy there," Lundquist said, pushing past Stone. "I'd better go first."

"It's not a crime scene," Stone said, following him. "Unless there's a corpse stashed under the bed."

Lundquist looked under the bed. "Nothing."

"No kidding?" Stone looked around. The room had already been cleaned that morning, and the bed had not been used since. He went around the room, looking in closets and opening drawers.

"What are you looking for?" Lundquist asked.

"I don't know," Stone replied.

"Whatever he can find," Dino said.

Lundquist started opening drawers, too.

Stone went back into the sitting room and looked around. The place was neat as a pin, the wastebaskets were empty, and there was not so much as a trace of Paul Bartlett, or whoever he was.

"What now?" Lundquist asked.

"The airport," Stone replied. "He told the clerk he had to catch a plane."

The three men left the hotel, and Lundquist got into the rear seat of Stone's convertible.

"I should be wearing sunscreen," Lundquist said as they pulled out of the parking lot.

"Yeah, that pale Scandinavian skin will fry every time," Dino said, half to himself, chuckling. "World's whitest white men."

"That's what you call me," Stone said.

"You, too."

At the airport, they went to the nearest ticket counter, and Lundquist flashed his badge and asked about flights to Minneapolis.

"None of the airlines flies directly to Minneapolis from Palm Beach," the woman behind the counter said. "You'd have to change, probably in Atlanta."

"Will you check reservations for a Paul Bartlett?" Lundquist asked.

The woman turned to her computer terminal, tapped a few keys and looked at the screen. "I'll do a search for the name," she said, tapping more keys. "Nope, nobody by that name."

"Try Paul Manning," Stone said, because he couldn't think of anything else to do.

She tapped the keys again. "Nope, no Manning."

"Do you recall, in the past hour or so, a tall man, six-three or -four, mid-to-late forties, dark hair going gray, fairly good-looking?"

"No, and I think I'd have noticed," the woman said, smiling.

"Thanks for your help," Stone said. He turned to Lundquist and Dino. "Let's hit the charter services."

"How do we find those?" Lundquist asked.

"There's a big sign outside, pointing to them all," Stone replied.

They went outside and checked the sign; there were half a dozen.

"Ebbe, you go in the car with Riley and check the north side of the field; Dino and I will check the south side."

"Okay." Lundquist jumped into the car with Riley.

"Well," Dino said as they got into the Mercedes. "Lundquist isn't the brightest tulip in the garden, is he?"

"Tulips are Dutch, not Scandinavian, and remember, he's a lieutenant, like you."

"Well, he can't be all bad," Dino said.

They checked all four companies on the south side of the field and came up with nothing. As they left the last one, Lundquist and Riley drove up.

"Nothing on the north side," Riley said.

"Nothing over here, either," Stone said. "Where's the chief?"

"Probably in his office," Riley replied.

Stone punched the number into his cell phone and asked for Griggs.

"Chief, Bartlett has checked out of the Colony."

"Well, shit," Griggs said. "You think he's left town?"

"He told the desk clerk he had a plane to catch, but we're at the airport now, and he didn't fly out of here."

"I guess he could have driven to Miami," Griggs said. "It's only an hour and a half to the airport."

"Can you check the flights out of there for a Bartlett or Manning?"

"I'll put somebody on it. Where do you think he went?"

"The only address we have is Minneapolis, but I don't think he's there."

"Where do you think he is?"

"I think he's still in Palm Beach. Remember, he checked out of the Chesterfield, too, without leaving a forwarding address, and he went directly to the Colony. Maybe, before you check the Miami flights, you should alert the other hotels in town to call you if he checks in."

"Okay, Stone, I'll do that."

"It seems that every time we start to get a line on the guy, he changes hotels."

"I'll get back to you."

Stone hung up.

"You think he's in another hotel?" Dino asked.

"That's my guess," Stone said. Then he thought for a moment. "Unless . . ."

"Unless what?"

"Come on," Stone said, "let's get back to the yacht, quick."

⤳ **Chapter 32** ⤳

Stone drove as quickly as he could, without getting arrested, through West Palm and across the bridge. Traffic was heavy and frustrating, and it took them nearly half an hour to reach the Shames residence. The front door stood open, and he ran quickly through the central hall and out the open back door, with Dino close on his heels.

As he came up the gangplank he was presented with an uncharacteristic sight on *Toscana*: a mess. Towels and books were scattered indiscriminately across the afterdeck. Normally, Juanito made a mess disappear as soon as it presented itself.

Stone turned around and was not surprised to see a gun in Dino's hand. He put a finger to his lips, then motioned for Dino to follow him. He walked through the saloon and down the corridor toward his cabin. His cabin door was open, and so was every other door in the passageway. He went into his cabin to retrieve the 9mm automatic from under his pillow. It was gone. He went back into the passage and climbed a few steps to the bridge, and as he approached it, he could hear music. He stepped onto the bridge, ready for anything. A portable radio rested on the dash above the wheel, softly playing rock music.

Stone crossed the bridge and left it on the other side, returning along the port corridor. Again, every cabin door was open.

He heard a footstep from somewhere aft and tiptoed toward it. Dino brushed past him, the gun out in front. He was armed, and he would lead the way; there was no talk about it. Stone followed him into the saloon.

"What the hell!" a man's voice shouted. "Who are you?"

Stone stepped around Dino to find Thad Shames standing in the saloon. "Thad," he said. "It's all right, Dino."

"What's going on here, Stone?" Shames demanded, clearly startled. "Who is this?"

"Thad, I'm sorry we frightened you. This is Lieutenant Dino Bacchetti, of the New York Police Department. Dino, this is Thad Shames, our host here."

Dino put the gun away, and the two men shook hands.

Thad collapsed onto a sofa. "Tell me what's happened," he said.

"I don't know what's happened," Stone replied. "We came back to the yacht a few minutes ago to find it deserted, and all the cabin doors open."

"No Callie or Liz? No crew?"

"Nobody."

"There's nobody in the main house, either," Thad said, "but the front and rear doors were open."

"I know; we just came through there."

"Do you think Callie and Liz might have gone shopping or something?"

"I don't think so; they did that earlier today."

"Did you check the pool?"

"Pool? What pool?"

"There's a pool on the property, you know."

"No, I didn't know. It must be very well concealed."

"Come on, let's take a look." Thad led the way down the gangplank and into the gardens. Instead of taking the path to the house, he turned right and appeared to be about to walk through a hedge, when he turned and disappeared.

Stone followed and discovered a gap in the hedge, concealed by a quick left turn, followed by a right. He caught up with Thad, who had stopped and, with his hands on his hips, was staring ahead.

"Isn't that lovely?" Thad said softly.

Stone looked and saw a beautiful swimming pool, completely surrounded by the high hedge. Beside it, perhaps thirty feet away, lay two women, asleep on their backs, naked.

Thad motioned them back through the gap in the hedge. "Let's give them a little warning," he said. "Callie? Liz?" he called out loudly.

"Yes?" Callie's voice replied. "We're out here."

Shames led them through the hedge a second time. Callie and Liz were tying robes around themselves. "There you are," he said. "I thought you had both decamped." He pecked Callie on the cheek, then embraced Liz at more length.

"Not likely," Callie said. "We thought we'd be safe here."

"Where's the crew?" Stone asked.

"I gave them the afternoon off. We weren't expecting you, Thad."

"And why are all the doors on the yacht open?"

"I thought it would be good to air out the cabins; keeps the mildew down."

"You gave us a scare," Stone said.

Callie reached into a pocket of her robe and produced the 9mm automatic. "We're perfectly all right," she said, handing the weapon to Stone. "Come on, let's go back to the yacht."

The group returned to *Toscana,* and Callie got drinks for everybody, except Liz, who excused herself to change. Callie followed her.

"Oh, Callie?" Thad called after her.

She turned. "Yes, Thad?"

"Book us a table someplace gaudy tonight. We'll celebrate my return."

Callie nodded and went toward her cabin.

"Where have you come from?" Stone asked.

"California. I've been sort of barnstorming LA and San Francisco and Silicon Valley, talking up the new company."

"I hope it went well."

"It did. How are things going here?"

"It's gotten complicated," Stone said. "Let me bring you up to date."

"I'd appreciate that."

Stone told him, in detail, everything that had happened in his absence. When he was through, he stopped talking and waited.

"And you still don't know if this guy is really Manning?"

"No," Stone said. "Not even Liz can be sure."

"I find that hard to believe," Shames said.

"So do I, but that's the way it is. She saw him only briefly in Easthampton, and something about the way he moved made her think the man she saw was Paul Manning. But she can't be sure that Paul Bartlett is Manning."

"And this guy Bartlett is a friend of Frank and Margaret?"

"Yes, from Minneapolis."

"And you think he killed his wife for her money?"

"It seems a strong possibility."

Shames grinned. "Well, this has certainly turned out to be interesting, hasn't it?"

"That's one way to look at it," Stone said. "I'm sorry I don't have any definite answers for you."

"I'm sure you'll come up with them," Shames said. "Well, Dino, welcome to Palm Beach. Callie told me you were coming, and I'm glad you could join us. Have you been made comfortable?"

"Yes, thanks," Dino said. "She's a beautiful yacht."

"Thank you, I think so." Thad stood up. "Well, if you'll excuse me, I'm going to go to my room in the main house and have a nap. I've been traveling for days, and I'm a little tired. I'll bounce back for dinner, though." He gave a little wave and left the yacht.

"He's a pretty easygoing guy, isn't he?" Dino said.

"He certainly is."

"I mean, if I'd come aboard my yacht and found a stranger with a gun, I'd have freaked out, but he didn't."

"I thought he behaved very well, in the circumstances," Stone said. "Looks like our goat-and-lion plan didn't work. If anything, we're worse off than we were this morning."

"Well, there's still dinner," Dino said. "If we're going someplace gaudy, *anybody* could be there, right?"

"In Palm Beach, you're right."

Chapter 33

Callie's choice of a gaudy restaurant turned out to be the high-ceilinged, chandeliered, tapestried, velvet-seated La Reserve. Thad seemed particularly pleased with the choice, and he swept the group to a round table at the center of the single large room, slipping the maître d' a bill on the way, then ordering a Krug champagne for everybody.

"You have beluga, of course," Thad said to the captain.

"Of course, Mr. Shames," the man replied. "Fifty grams each?"

"Let's start with half a kilo for the table," Shames said. Glasses were filled, and Thad raised his. "To this group," he said. "I'm happy to be back with you all." He turned to Liz at his side. "Particularly you."

Everyone drank. A moment later, a crystal bowl of caviar arrived, and the waiter went around the table spooning large amounts onto each plate.

Dino tried his.

"Well?" Thad asked.

"Well, wonderful," Dino replied. "We don't see a lot of beluga at the precinct."

"I remember once when we did," Stone said. "Somebody on the squad busted up a smuggling outfit, and, among other things, there was a lot of caviar. Most of it disappeared immediately, but I remember a few small tins found their way to your desk and mine."

"You're right, Stone," Dino said. "Funny, I remember busts involving drugs and money, but you remember caviar."

Menus appeared and everyone pored over them. Eventually, decisions were made, and the captain took their orders. Thad lingered over the wine list. "Who's drinking red?" he asked. Everyone's hand went up. "Ah, good. We'll start with a magnum of the Opus One," he said to the sommelier. "The 'eighty-nine."

The sommelier scurried away and returned with the big bottle. Thad tasted it. "Marvelous! Go ahead and pour us a glass so it can breathe."

"I like your friends," Dino said to Stone, getting a laugh.

"Ah, Dino," Thad said, "you have to spend more time in Palm Beach. The yacht is yours whenever you want it."

"Nobody ever said that to me before," Dino said, drawing another laugh.

Stone thought the evening was going particularly well. Then he looked up and saw Frank and Margaret Wilkes come into the restaurant, followed closely by a woman Stone did not know, and then, by Paul Bartlett. No one else at the table had seen them, but Stone caught Dino's eye and nodded in their direction.

Dino watched the tall man hold a chair for his companion, then sit down. "I would never have made him as Manning," Dino whispered. "He must have done something to his face."

Stone slipped the little cell phone off his belt, cupped it in his hand to hide it as well as possible, and dialed Dan Griggs's direct office number, which also rang at his home.

"Yes?" Griggs said.

"Dan, it's Stone. I'm at La Reserve, and Bartlett is here with Frank Wilkes and his wife and another woman."

"Have you talked to Lundquist?" Griggs asked.

"No."

"The Minneapolis department arrested a known car thief and insurance scam artist who, for immunity, told them Bartlett had hired him to fix his wife's seat belt. Apparently, they met in prison, during Bartlett's earlier existence, and he'll testify against Bartlett. Have they just sat down to eat?"

"Yes."

"Good. I'll get ahold of Lundquist and put some people together, and we'll take him when they leave. I don't want to cause a scene in the restaurant. Let me give you my portable number."

Stone wrote it down.

"Call that number when they get their check. That way I won't have to send people in to watch him. He's pretty edgy; he might catch on to that."

"I'll do it," Stone said. "I imagine you have a good hour and a half."

"See you later."

Stone put the phone away and saw Thad looking at him inquiringly. "It's nothing," he said.

Their dinner arrived, and everyone ate heartily, still in high spirits from the champagne. They had just finished their dessert, and their dishes were being taken away, when Stone looked up to see Lieutenant Ebbe Lundquist enter the restaurant, flash his badge at the maître d' and take up a position at the bar. Stone looked at Bartlett. He had seen the badge and was now staring at Lundquist, who in his plaid polyester suit looked out of place in the elegant restaurant.

Stone glanced at Dino, who had already taken this in.

"That's one really stupid cop," Dino said quietly.

Stone looked over at Bartlett's table and saw the waiter approaching with the check. "Excuse me a minute," Stone said to the table. "I'll be right back."

He rose and made his way across the restaurant to where the Wilkeses and Bartlett were sitting.

Frank Wilkes rose to greet him. "Stone," he said, "how good to see you."

Stone shook his hand as Bartlett, too, rose, buttoning his jacket.

"Hello, Stone," he said. "How are you?" He introduced his companion.

"How do you do? Good evening, Paul. Please sit down." Stone caught sight of the bulge under Bartlett's jacket.

"Frank, Margaret, I just wanted to thank you for such a delightful dinner the other evening," Stone said. "It was very kind of you to ask Callie and me."

"We were very glad to have you," Margaret Wilkes said, "and we hope you'll come again."

Stone caught sight of Lundquist moving down the bar.

"I see you're about to leave," Stone said to Wilkes. "Please let me send over some after-dinner drinks before you go." He didn't wait for an answer, but summoned a nearby waiter and told him to bring the Wilkes party whatever they wanted and to send the bill to him. That would keep them in their seats for another few minutes, Stone thought. He made his good-byes and, instead of returning to his table, walked toward the front of the restaurant and the men's room, dialing Dan Griggs's cell phone number on the way. He caught Dino's eye and patted his side, where Bartlett was wearing the gun. As he passed the bar, he caught Lundquist's eye, frowned and shook his head, whispering loudly, "Stay where you are."

He pressed the send button on the phone as he turned a corner, out of sight of Bartlett. Griggs answered immediately.

"It's Stone. I've bought them an after-dinner drink, so they'll be a few minutes."

"Okay."

"But listen. I think Bartlett is armed, and he's already seen Lundquist flash his badge. Why did you let him come in here?"

"I didn't. He just ignored me and walked in before I could stop him. I feel like arresting *him.*"

"I'm going back to my table. When they leave you'd better take Bartlett quickly, before he gets to his car, and you'd better be ready to disarm him. He's packing on the left side, at his belt."

"Got it. Are you armed?"

"No, but Dino is. Don't worry, he won't do anything stupid."

"Okay, just go back to your table, and we'll handle it."

"I'm on my way." Stone punched off the phone and put it away. He stepped back into the dining room, and as he did, he was horrified to see Lundquist moving toward Bartlett's table. He looked back at his own group, and Dino was suddenly on his feet, making his way across the room and unbuttoning his jacket. Then everything seemed to slow down.

Bartlett turned to see Lundquist coming toward him and began to rise. Lundquist, who didn't know Bartlett was armed, had his hands at his sides, empty. Bartlett unbuttoned his jacket as he rose, and his right hand went inside it to his belt.

Stone saw his hand close around the butt of the pistol. He turned toward Dino and yelled, "Gun!" Dino stopped in his tracks, perhaps a dozen feet from the Wilkeses' table.

Bartlett never saw Dino; his attention was riveted on Lundquist, who now began to understand what was happening and went for his own gun. Four shots came in rapid succession.

Lundquist left his feet, the gun flying from his hand and knocking over a wine bottle on a nearby table. A woman at that table screamed as Dino fired. Bartlett was hit in his left upper arm, then a second time in the side of his neck, falling backward and out of sight, knocking over his chair.

Dino began running toward the table, his gun out in front of him, yelling, "Police, Police!"

Stone began running, too.

ᦇ Chapter 34 ᦇ

Pandemonium. A mass of diners abandoned their tables and rushed for the main entrance, knocking over chairs and elaborate flower arrangements. Women were screaming, and men were shouting at them.

Stone was swept sideways toward the door. In front of him a woman fell, and Stone grabbed her and yanked her to her feet before she could be trampled in the rush. He could see Dino at the Wilkeses' table, standing over Bartlett, who was out of sight on the floor behind the table. Dino was still pointing the gun.

He looked toward the front door and saw three uniformed Palm Beach police officers, one of them Dan Griggs, vainly trying to fight their way through the onrushing crowd. Stone grabbed a post next to the bar and hung on for dear life. Finally, when most of the crowd had fled the restaurant, he was able to make his way through the stragglers to Dino, who was now bending over Bartlett, feeling at his throat for a pulse.

Frank and Margaret Wilkes stood huddled against the wall, Frank cradling his sobbing wife's head on his shoulder. Margaret was spattered with blood. Bartlett's date was nowhere in sight.

"He's dead," Dino said, holstering his weapon.

Stone looked around the restaurant for Lundquist but did not see him. Thad and his party were standing against the opposite wall of the restaurant, having wisely not joined the panicked crowd. Thad waved and called out, "We're okay. Do what you have to do."

Stone resumed his search for Lundquist and found him under an overturned table. Lundquist had taken a round in the chest, and he had been trampled by the crowd. His nose was badly broken where someone had stepped on it, and there was blood everywhere, but Stone found a pulse.

Griggs and his men finally got into the restaurant and rushed toward Stone.

"We need an ambulance," Stone said as Griggs arrived. "Lundquist is still alive, but he's bad. Bartlett is dead. Dino shot him almost at the same time Bartlett shot Lundquist."

"There's an ambulance outside," Griggs said. He spoke into a handheld radio.

"There are probably some injured people in the crowd, too," Stone said. "It got pretty ugly."

A pair of EMTs made their way into the ruined room, toting a stretcher and equipment, and immediately began working on Lundquist. Stone stepped away to let them do their work. He followed Griggs over to where Dino stood.

Dino handed Griggs his gun. "You're going to want this."

Griggs nodded and examined Bartlett closely, picking up his weapon by its trigger guard and handing both guns to one of his officers.

Stone went to the Wilkeses, picking up a stray napkin along the way. He dabbed at the blood on Margaret's face, and she barely seemed to notice.

"I want to get her home," Wilkes said.

Stone turned to Griggs, who had heard, and nodded.

"Chief Griggs will want to talk to you in the morning," Stone said.

"I saw it all," Frank said. "Paul had a gun; it was all his fault."

"Griggs and his men were waiting outside the restaurant to arrest him quietly, but the Minneapolis cop ruined it all."

"Is he dead?"

"No, but he's pretty bad. His office had called to say that they have a witness who says Bartlett hired him to fix the seat belt on the car, so that Frances would be unprotected. It doesn't matter now, of course, but he would almost certainly have been convicted."

"We'll go, then."

"Do you need any help?"

"No, I can manage."

Stone watched them leave, then he crossed the restaurant to where Thad, Liz and Callie waited. "Everybody all right?"

They all nodded.

"I'm sorry you had to see that."

"See what?" Liz said. "I didn't see anything. I just heard a lot of noise."

"Paul shot a Minneapolis policeman, and Dino shot Paul. The cop is alive, but Paul is dead."

"Which Paul?" she asked.

"Aren't they the same?" Stone asked.

"I wish I knew," Liz said.

"Thad, why don't you take Liz and Callie home. Dino and I will need to give statements to the Palm Beach police. We'll probably be quite late."

"Sure," Thad said. "I hope to God the guy is Manning."

"We'll see," Stone said.

Thad ushered the women out of the restaurant, and Stone rejoined Dino and Griggs.

Griggs righted a table and motioned for Dino and Stone to pull up a chair. "You two are the best witnesses I've got. We might as well do this right now, then you two can go home." He pulled a small tape recorder from a pocket, turned it on and set it on the table.

"Okay, Stone, you first."

Dino stood up. "I'm going to go to the john. It's better if you interview us separately."

"Right," Griggs said. "All right, Stone, tell me what happened, and don't leave anything out."

Stone began at the beginning, and when he had finished, Dino came and took his place. Stone waited at the bar and discovered that one of Bartlett's rounds had hit some liquor bottles and the mirror behind the bar. A cop was digging it out of the wall behind the mirror.

When Griggs had Dino's statement, they stood up, and Stone joined them. "Frank Wilkes saw the whole thing," he said. "He'll back us up on what happened."

"I'm going to let my people finish here," Griggs said. "I'm going to the hospital to see how Lundquist is doing. I've got to call his department and his family, if he has one."

"Let's talk in the morning, then," Stone said.

"By the way," Griggs said, "I talked to the Minneapolis department earlier this evening. The guy who rigged Bartlett's car says the name he knew Bartlett by was Douglas Barnacle. They shared a cell in the Chicago federal detention center when they were both awaiting trial. He says Barnacle was a stockbroker in Chicago who got mixed up in a mob-backed stock scam and turned state's evidence. That was a little over five years ago. I'm running a check on the Barnacle name now, and I'll let you know what I turn up."

"Thanks," Stone said. "I want to hear about it." They shook hands and parted.

In the car on the way home Stone and Dino were both quiet for a while.

"You thinking what I'm thinking?" Dino asked.

"Yes. If Barnacle was in jail in Chicago five years ago, he couldn't be Paul Manning."

"Right."

They drove the rest of the way to the Shames house in silence.

⤜ Chapter 35 ⤛

One by one, Thad Shames's guests straggled in for breakfast on the afterdeck at midmorning. Stone thought everybody looked tired, maybe a little shell-shocked. Not much was said, and he didn't feel ready to tell Thad and Liz what little he knew about Bartlett's background. He would wait for more information.

Stone was finishing his coffee when Juanito arrived with a fax of a dozen or so pages. Stone flipped through them, with Dino looking over his shoulder, occasionally pointing out something.

"What is that?" Thad finally asked.

"It's a copy of the criminal record of Paul Bartlett, aka Douglas Barnacle, William Wilfred, Edgar Chase and Terence Keane."

"He was all those people?" Liz asked.

"Those and maybe more. I'll summarize for you: He was born Robert Trent Smith, in Providence, Rhode Island, where he attended the public schools and the Rhode Island School of Design, which, incidentally, is very highly thought of. He was kicked out of school a month before graduation for running some kind of swindle that bilked nearly a hundred thousand dollars out of other students and faculty. After that, he chalked up half a dozen arrests for various confidence games. He was, apparently, a real bunco artist, and not averse to the use of violence, when he was caught. Five years ago, he got involved in a mob-backed boiler-room operation, selling worthless stocks at high prices. He ended up in jail and traded his testimony against his cohorts for his freedom and the federal witness protection program. While he was there, he shared a cell with a car thief and insurance scam artist. After that, he apparently left the program and took up a new identity as Paul Bartlett, in Minneapolis, where he eventually married a wealthy widow. Then he got his former cell mate to tamper with the seat belt on his car, and he wrecked it, killing her, but only after she changed her will in his favor."

"Then he's not Paul Manning?" Thad asked.

"No. Five years ago, Paul Manning and his wife were sailing in Europe, right, Liz?"

"That's right."

"And Bartlett was in jail at the time."

"So Bartlett was just a waste of your time?" Callie asked.

"Not entirely," Stone said. "At least you and I managed to get him caught for murdering his wife."

Dino spoke up. "And I managed to save the State of Minnesota the cost of a trial."

"I don't want you to feel you've wasted *my* time, Stone," Thad said. "You were perfectly right to follow that lead, and I'm glad that it came to some good."

"But now we're right back where we started," Stone said. "Liz, let's talk about this sighting of Paul Manning in Easthampton."

"All right," she said.

"Tell me exactly the circumstances under which you saw him."

"I was in a shop on Main Street, pointing to something in the window for the saleslady to get for me, and I saw him outside the window."

"Did you see his face?"

"Not entirely, just partly. I caught a glimpse of his nose, which was straight, and that threw me off for a moment. Then, as he was walking away, he did this thing with his shoulders that he used to do." She demonstrated with a sort of shrug. "As if his jacket weren't resting comfortably on his shoulders."

"I remember his doing that in St. Marks," Stone said. "What else?"

"That was it. I waited until he had gone on down the street, then I got into my car, made a U-turn and got out of there. You're looking at me as though it were my imagination."

"No, no," Stone said. "I believe you. I just wanted the details."

"And," Thad said, "there is the matter of the vandalizing of Liz's house."

"Of course," Stone said. "I know the threat is real, and I think Paul Manning is just as dangerous as Paul Bartlett was."

"So," Thad said, "where do we go from here?"

"I'll have to give that some thought," Stone said. "I'd feel better if we had some bit of information that would give us a basis for a search."

"What sort of information?" Thad asked.

"Well, for instance, a man made several phone calls to my office and wouldn't give his name, making my secretary suspicious. Caller ID told us the calls came from a Manhattan hotel." He pointed to the stack of computer paper that rested on a deck chair nearby. "A friend of mine managed to print out the guest list, and Liz and I went through it carefully. I was hoping a name might ring some sort of bell. One name seemed plausible, but it didn't work out, and neither of us saw another familiar name on the list."

"I did," Callie said.

"You did what?" Stone asked.

"I saw a familiar name on the list." She got up, went to the stack of paper, riffled through it and ripped off a page. "Here," she said, handing it to Stone.

Stone looked at the sheet. "Frederick James? Does that mean anything to you, Liz?"

Liz shook her head. "No."

"It should mean something to you, Stone, and you, too, Dino," Callie said.

"Doesn't ring a bell," Dino said.

Callie picked up the novel Dino had been reading and tossed it to him.

"*Tumult,* by Frederick James," Dino read aloud.

"I'd forgotten the name," Stone said.

"And he's a novelist, like Paul," Liz said.

"Why didn't you mention this before, Callie?"

She shrugged. "I meant to, but somebody changed the subject, and I forgot about it until you mentioned the hotel guest list just now."

Stone looked at the sheet. "His home address is on Gin Lane, in East-hampton. That's interesting." Stone took the book from Dino and turned it over, opened the back cover. "No photograph. All the dust jacket says is, 'Frederick James travels widely around the world, never staying in one place for long. This is his first novel.'"

"Usually there's some sort of biography," Thad said. "Who published it?"

Stone looked at the book jacket. "Hot Lead Press. Linotype machines used to use hot lead to set type. Never heard of this outfit."

"Liz," Dino asked, "have you read this book?"

"No."

"Read it, or at least some of it. See if you think Paul Manning wrote it." Stone handed her the book.

"All right," she said. "God knows I've read all of Paul's earlier novels; I ought to know his work."

"Well," Stone said, "now we've got some information—James's home address and his publisher's name. We couldn't ask for a better start. Dino, while Liz reads the book, let's you and I make some phone calls."

They went into the saloon, where there were two extensions. Stone was about to pick up a phone, but Dino stopped him.

"Listen, want to make a little bet?"

"About what?"

"I'll bet you a hundred bucks that after Liz reads the novel she won't be sure of whether Manning wrote it."

"I'm not sure I'd take that bet," Stone said. "She's been equivocal every time she was in a position to nail something down. I mean, you'd have thought she could tell us right away that Bartlett wasn't Manning."

"Yeah, I would have thought that," Dino agreed. "Of course, there could be a really strong resemblance. I mean, you knew Manning, and you weren't much help."

"You knew him, too, and you were no help at all, until shooting was required."

"You saying I'm trigger happy?"

"Dino, as far as I'm concerned, you can shoot anybody anytime you feel like it, because usually, when you shoot somebody, he's trying to shoot me."

"I'm glad you noticed."

"So, you suspect Liz of something?"

Dino shrugged. "Not yet. I'd just like to have a straight answer from her now and then."

"So would I," Stone said, half to himself.

Chapter 36

Dino picked up a phone. "I know a guy on the Easthampton force; let's start with the home address. Maybe we won't have to go any further." Dino made the call and waited. "I'm on hold," he said, then waited patiently. "Hey, yeah, I'm here." Dino listened and asked a couple of questions, then hung up and turned to Stone. "Frederick James rented a house on Gin Lane up until a week ago. He spoke to the real estate agent, and they didn't have a forwarding address. His address when he rented the place was a Manhattan hotel, the Brooke."

"Dead end," Stone said. "I'll call the publisher." He called New York information and was connected.

"Good morning, Hot Lead Press," a young woman's voice said.

"Good morning," Stone said. "This is Lieutenant Bacchetti, NYPD. I'd like to speak to the editor of Frederick James. Can you find out for me which of your editors that is?"

"That's easy," she replied. "We've only got one editor. I'll connect you."

This time, a man, also young: "Pete Willard."

"Good morning, Mr. Willard. This is Lieutenant Bacchetti of the NYPD. I'd—"

"No kidding? A real live cop?"

"That's right. I'd—"

"Listen, I'll bet you've got some great stories to tell. Have you got an agent?"

"No, and—"

"Great. And no publisher, either?"

"Mr. Willard, I'm calling on police business."

"Oh, okay, shoot. Not really. I mean, go ahead."

"I understand that you edit Frederick James?"

"Edit and publish. He was our first author."

"I take it you're new in business?"

"That's right. Opened our doors ten months ago, and already we've got a bestseller. That is, this Sunday we will. Frederick James's novel *Tumult* opens at number eleven on the *Times* list."

"Congratulations."

"Thanks. We're very excited."

"Who's we?"

"Molly and me. And baby makes three. No, Molly is . . . Well, she does everything I don't. And she's my wife, and she's pregnant."

"Congratulations again."

"Thanks. We're very excited."

Back where I started, Stone thought. "Mr. Willard, I need to get in touch with Frederick James."

"Oh, I'll bet you're one of his cop sources. He has all kinds of sources."

"Not yet," Stone said. "I'd just like to find him."

"Well, Mr. James is pretty reclusive," Willard said. "I'm not supposed to give out any information."

"This is a very serious police matter," Stone said. "I'd rather not have to come down there with a search warrant."

"Hey, just like on *Law and Order,* huh? Except they always screw up the warrant, and the judge throws out the evidence from the search."

"I won't screw up the warrant, Mr. Willard. And believe me, it will be much simpler for you just to give me Mr. James's address and phone number than for us to come down there and start tearing your office apart."

"Actually, I don't have either an address or a phone number for him. I know it's peculiar, but like I said, he's reclusive."

"How do you communicate with Mr. James?"

"E-mail," Willard said. "And through his agent."

"What's his e-mail address?"

"FJ at frederickjames dot com."

"And his agent's name?"

"Tom Jones."

"The singer or the novel?" Stone asked dryly.

"No kidding, that's his name. I'll give you his number."

Stone wrote it down. "By the way, Mr. Willard, if Mr. James should communicate with you, please don't tell him I called. It might make you a co-conspirator."

"Oh, jeez," Willard said. "I won't say a word."

Stone hung up, laughing. "This is some kind of publishing house," he said to Dino. "Just a kid and his pregnant wife. But I've got his agent's name." He dialed the number.

"Tom Jones," a voice said—middle-aged, husky from booze and cigarettes. No operator, no secretary, just Jones.

"Mr. Jones, this is Lieutenant Bacchetti of the NYPD."

"I didn't do it!" Jones cackled. "She swore she was over eighteen, anyway." He roared with laughter. It took him a moment to recover himself.

"Mr. Jones, I'm trying to find a client of yours."

"And which client would that be?" Jones asked, clearing his throat loudly.

"Frederick James."

"What a coincidence," Jones said. "He's my only client!" This time, he nearly collapsed with laughter.

The man has to be drunk, Stone thought. "Mr. Jones . . ."

Jones continued to laugh, cough and clear his throat. "Yeah?" he said finally.

"It's very important that I see Mr. James."

"Well, if you can do that, pal, you're way ahead of me. I've never seen him."

"He's your client, and you've never seen him?"

"He's reclusive."

"And how do you communicate with him?"

"E-mail," Jones said. "FJ at frederickjames dot com."

"How about a phone number?"

"Don't have one. I've never even spoken with him."

"And how did you become his agent?"

"Manuscript came in over the transom," he said. "Literally. I came to work one morning—I was just about to close up the shop for good—and the manuscript was lying on the floor. Tell you the truth, Lieutenant, I was all washed up as an agent. But when I read *Tumult,* I knew I had a winner. Trouble was, nobody in any established house would even take my calls, let alone read the manuscript. So I called my nephew, who was an editorial assistant at Simon and Schuster, and he read it and went nuts. His dad loaned him some money, and he packaged the book and got S and S to distribute it for him. He's making out like a bandit."

"Would that be Pete Willard?"

"That would be he."

"Mr. Jones, did you ever know a writer named Paul Manning?"

"Sure, I knew him for twenty years; got him started and I represented him right up until his untimely death."

"You haven't heard from him lately, then?"

"Not likely. I don't have those kind of connections!" Jones laughed hysterically again.

Stone waited him out. When Jones had recovered himself, Stone tried again. "Mr. Jones, how do you send Mr. James contracts to sign, checks from his publisher, that sort of thing? You must have some kind of address."

"You promise not to tell him where you got it?"

"I promise."

"He lives at One Vanderbilt Avenue, right here in New York."

"Phone number?"

"Doesn't have one; not even an unlisted one."

"Mr. Jones, when you hear from Mr. James, it's important that you don't tell him I called."

"But he's my client. I represent him."

"Believe me, Mr. Jones, you don't want to get in the middle of this."

"Has he done something wrong?"

"Not that I know of. We just want to talk to him."

"Well, okay. Whatever you say."

"Thank you, Mr. Jones, and if you do hear from him, please call me at this number." Stone gave him the cell phone number and hung up.

"What?" Dino said.

"This looks real good," Stone said. "This guy Jones was Manning's agent before he 'died.' Jones has no idea who he is, I think."

"Did you get an address?"

"Yep. One Vanderbilt Avenue."

Dino looked at Stone as if he were a retarded child. "Stone, One Vanderbilt Avenue is Grand Central Station."

"I knew that," Stone replied.

∾ Chapter 37 ∾

Dino looked thoughtful. "Haven't we run across One Vanderbilt Avenue as an address before? It sounds familiar."

Stone slapped his forehead. "Mail drop! I tracked it down once, roamed around Grand Central until I found this wall of mailboxes. They're unattended, except when somebody shows up to sort the mail. Can you call the precinct and detail a man to watch it?"

"Stone, Frederick James has committed no crime that we know of, and he's not a suspect in any case. You trying to get me fired? Why don't you get Bob Berman to do it?"

"That's a thought, but I just had another one. If I were James, and I didn't want to be located, for whatever reason, I'd rent a box at One Vanderbilt, then I'd go to the post office and have the mail forwarded to another address, and then, if I *really* don't want to be found, I'd have it forwarded from that address. I might get my mail a week late, but what the hell?"

"So it would be a waste of Berman's time."

"Yes, it would. Mr. James has built himself a firewall, and I can't think of a way around it."

"He must get paid," Dino said.

"Yes, but the checks go to the mailbox."

"But they have to be deposited, or the guy gets no money, right?"

"Right!" Stone said. He called Tom Jones back.

"Tom Jones."

"This is Lieutenant Bacchetti again."

"We've got to stop meeting like this. My wife will catch on." He roared with laughter.

Once again, Stone waited. "Mr. Jones," he said when he could get past the laughter. "How do you pay Frederick James?"

"He takes checks," Jones said. "If *I* were dealing with me, I'd demand cash!" This time it was a high-pitched giggle.

"Mr. Jones, when was the last time you paid Mr. James any money?"

"Last month, when *Tumult* came out. His contract calls for a payment on publication."

"All right. Dig out your most recent bank statement."

"It's right here in my bottom drawer, with all my bank statements," Jones said.

Stone heard the man struggling with a desk drawer.

"Got it," Jones said.

"Now, go through the canceled checks until you find the one to James."

"Okay, let's see: laundry, phone bill, liquor store—hey, that's a big one!" More laughter. "Here it is!"

"Turn the check over."

"It's over."

"There is a bank's name stamped on the back. That always happens when a check is deposited."

"Right, there is. It's kind of dim, though. Let me turn on a light and get my glasses."

Stone had visions of the man sitting in a dark office strewn with empty liquor bottles.

"Okay, I can see it now. It says, 'First Cayman Bank.'"

"Swell," Stone said.

"You like that, do you?"

"It's no help at all, I'm afraid. Mr. Jones, imagine for a moment that you absolutely *had* to get in touch with Mr. James. How would you go about it?"

"I'd e-mail him," Jones said. "I'm not much on computers, but my nephew set it up so that I can get to my e-mail without screwing it up. You want the e-mail address?"

"Thanks, but you already gave it to me."

"I did? Well, okay. Good luck finding him." Jones hung up.

"What?" Dino asked.

"His bank is in the Cayman Islands, well known for banking secrecy. We're not going to find him that way."

"What about his e-mail address? We could call his provider. Who is it? AOL or Hotmail? One of those?"

"Nope. He's got a domain of his own: frederickjames dot com."

"Then it's got to be registered somewhere."

"Yeah, but even if we could track it down, we'd find that his address is One Vanderbilt, or some hotel where he stayed for a few days."

"We could see if he has a phone number in New York."

"If he does, it will be unlisted."

"If it's unlisted, I can find out the number."

"I just had a thought," Stone said. He picked up a phone and called Dan Griggs.

"Griggs."

"It's Stone. How's Lundquist doing?"

"He made it through the night, and he's stable. The doctor says we can probably ship him home in a few days."

"Good. Listen, Dan, we've got another line on Paul Manning. He may be using the name Frederick James. James is a novelist with a new, best-selling book out, and he's something of a will-o'-the-wisp. Can you check the local hotels and see if he's registered?"

"Okay, Stone, but I have to tell you, I'm wearying of Mr. Manning, and I can't keep putting resources into finding somebody who did nothing but trash somebody's house."

"I understand, Dan, and I appreciate your help."

"I'll get back to you." Griggs hung up.

Stone called Bob Berman. "How you doing?"

"Okay. What's up?"

"The hotel guest list turned up the name of one Frederick James, an author. Can you do the whole skip-trace thing—address, phone number, credit report?"

"I don't suppose you've got a Social Security number?"

"No, but hang on." Stone dialed Jones again.

"Tom Jones."

"Mr. Jones, I need Frederick James's Social Security number. I know you've got it. You can't pay him without it."

"Sorry, the checks are made out to a corporation."

"Why didn't you tell me that before?"

"You didn't ask me." Jones laughed loudly.

"What's the name of the corporation?"

"Frederick James, Limited; it's a Cayman Islands firm."

"Thanks," Stone said, and hung up. He punched the button for Berman. "Sorry for the delay. No SSN; he deals through a Cayman Islands corporation. I don't suppose you can get anything on that."

"Probably not. You have any idea where the guy lives?"

"Until recently, he lived in Easthampton, New York. That's all I've got."

"Okay, I'll get back to you."

Stone hung up to see Liz appear in the doorway, holding the copy of *Tumult.* "What do you think?" he asked.

"Well, I've read enough of it to say that it *could* be Paul's work. But you have to understand, he was something of a chameleon as a writer. He changed styles from book to book, depending on the plot and characters."

"Thanks for trying, Liz."

She returned to the afterdeck, leaving Stone and Dino alone.

"What'd I tell you?" Dino said. "She's going to be useless in finding this guy."

"I'm feeling pretty useless myself," Stone said.

"I don't think we're going to get anywhere with the Frederick James name," Dino said. "My guess is, he's just using it as a pen name, that he's living his life under an entirely different name, maybe even more than one."

"That's a depressing thought," Stone said.

As if on cue, Dan Griggs called back. "I've had a whole squad calling around to the hotels," he said, "and there's no Frederick James registered anywhere."

"Thanks for your help again, Dan. I won't bother you unless we turn up something concrete." Stone hung up, and the phone rang.

"Hello?"

"It's Berman."

"Anything?"

"Mr. James has an American Express card, and that's it—no debts, not even a bank account."

"American Express wouldn't give somebody a card who had no credit record," Stone said.

"Then he must have applied under a name that does have a record, then asked them to put another name on the card. By the way, I have a friend at American Express. I called him and he looked up James's address."

"Great! What is it?"

"One Vanderbilt Avenue, New York City."

"Thanks, Bob." Stone hung up. "Another dead end."

"You got any other ideas?" Dino asked.

"No."

"Neither have I."

"Well, we're just going to have to wait until he has another go at Liz," Stone said.

Chapter 38

Everybody seemed to be taking a nap, except Dino.

"I need some things from the drugstore," Stone said. "You want to come?"

"Nope," Dino replied. "Married men don't need things from the drug-store."

"Toothpaste and dental floss," Stone said.

"Whatever you say."

"I'll be back in half an hour, if anybody calls."

"See ya."

Stone walked to the parking lot and got into his borrowed Mercedes convertible, putting the top down. He pulled out of the driveway, behind a passing Ford, which was driving rather slowly. Stone edged up behind the car, hoping to pass, when, suddenly, the Ford came to a screeching halt, and Stone plowed into it with a crash.

"Oh, shit," he said aloud. Now he had smashed up Thad's car, and it was his own fault. He got out of the car and walked toward the Ford. As he did, a man got out of the Ford, and to Stone's surprise, he was smiling.

"I'm sorry I hit you," Stone said, "but why did you slam on your brakes like that?"

The man looked like a salesman of some sort. He was dressed in a white short-sleeved shirt and necktie, and his shirt pocket contained a plastic pen guard and several writing instruments. "Don't worry about it," the man said, and very quickly, there was a gun in his hand.

Stone looked over his shoulder for some way out of this, but as he did, a silver Lincoln Town Car with darkly tinted windows screeched to a halt beside him.

The man with the gun opened the rear door. "Inside," he said, "and don't let's get blood on this pretty street."

Stone got in, followed by the man with the gun, and the car moved forward, leaving the other two cars stopped in the middle of the street. The whole thing had taken less than thirty seconds, he figured, and more disturbing than the gun in the man's hand was the fact that he was wearing rubber gloves. "What's this about?" he asked.

"First, let's get you all secured, and then I'll tell you," the man said. "Get down on your knees, rest your head on the armrest and put your hands behind you." He nudged Stone's ribs with the gun barrel for emphasis.

Stone did as he was told, and in a moment, he was handcuffed.

"All right, now you can sit back up here," the man said.

His accent was Southern, sort of educated redneck, Stone thought. "So what's this about?" he asked again.

"First, let's get the introductions out of the way," the man said. "You can call me Larry, and the feller driving is Ernest. And you would be one Mr. Stone Barrington."

"How do you do?" Stone said.

"I do pretty good," Larry replied. "Now, as to what this is about, we're going to take a little drive out in the country, and then we're gonna make a phone call." His tone was pleasant, conversational. "I don't enjoy putting violence on folks, so I'd 'preciate it if you wouldn't make that necessary. I *can* do it, if the need arises."

"All right, I'll behave," Stone lied. He was going to get out of this at the first opportunity, and he was beginning to regret that he had gotten into the car without a fight. The rubber gloves were weighing heavily on his mind.

Shortly, they were in West Palm, driving west on one of its broad boulevards. "You were saying?" Stone asked.

"Oh, yeah. A friend of mine called me a couple of days ago and asked me to come down here and shoot your ass."

"What friend is that?"

"Does it matter? He's paying me and Ernest, here, fifty big ones to deal with you, and that's the most I ever got for a hit."

They stopped at a traffic light, and a police car pulled up next to them.

Larry stuck the gun in Stone's crotch. "Don't you even think about it," he said. "They can't see us, and if they hear something, then I'm going to have to do you *and* the cop. Besides, wouldn't you rather die with your dick still on?"

Stone didn't answer that. "I'd like to know who your friend is," he said.

"I don't think you'd recognize the name," Larry said. "He uses a lot of them."

"What does he look like, then?"

"Tall feller, going gray."

"Ah, yes, Mr. Manning."

"Manning? If you say so."

"Funny thing is, I was about to try and give Mr. Manning a whole lot of money. Tell you what: Why don't you call him right now and tell him that? It might have an effect on the outcome of your day and mine."

"And why would you want to give him a lot of money?" Larry asked.

"I'm a lawyer. I represent a lady he knows. She's willing to pay a large sum to get him to go away."

"How much money we talking about?" Larry asked, clearly interested.

"She's willing to give him a million dollars," Stone said, "maybe more." *But not now,* Stone thought. *She won't give him a fucking penny, if I have anything to say about it.*

"You really expect me to believe that."

"You don't have to. Just make the call, and I'll make *him* believe it."

"What's in it for me?" Larry asked.

"How much has he paid you so far?" Stone asked.

"Twenty-five thousand," Larry replied. "There's another twenty-five due when he shoots you."

"When *he* shoots me? I thought he hired you to do that."

"Well, yeah, but only if you give me any trouble. He wants to do it himself, if he has the time. Something personal, I don't know."

"Tell you what. You make the call. If I can get him to agree to a settlement, I'll give you another fifty, on top of the twenty-five he's already given you."

"I don't know," Larry said.

"What have you got to lose? Tell you what. Drive me to the nearest bank, and I'll give you the fifty right now, in cash. Any bank will do. I just have to make a phone call."

"Well, see, I've got a lot of problems with that," Larry said. "You could make all sorts of trouble for me in a bank."

"You've got a point," said Stone, who had been planning on making a lot of trouble for him.

"And that wouldn't be the honorable thing to do, see? I mean, my deal is with Doug, not with you. Word got around about that, and I'd be short of clients."

"So, call him and let me speak to him."

"What the hell, why not? Ernest, give me the phone."

Ernest passed back a cell phone, and Larry dialed, mouthing the numbers from memory.

Stone heard the electronic shriek from the phone, and the announcement that the cellular customer being called was unavailable or out of the calling area.

"No luck," Larry said.

"Try him again in a minute," Stone replied. They were out of West Palm, now, headed west on a narrowing, increasingly empty road that seemed to be heading straight into the Everglades. He didn't want to go there.

"Okay," Larry said.

"You do a lot of this work?" Stone asked.

"You bet. Make a nice living at it, too."

"How'd you get into it?"

"Fellow offered me five grand once, when I was broke, so I got myself a mail-order book that tells you how to do it and get away with it."

"The work doesn't bother you?"

"Naw, it's just business. I mean, I don't have anything against the people I hit."

"You know, in my line of work, I have clients who sometimes have need of somebody with your skills. Maybe you should give me your number?"

Larry grinned broadly. "Well, first, let's see how this goes, okay?"

"Why don't you try the number again?" Stone said.

"Sure thing." Larry punched redial, then held the phone away from his ear, so Stone could hear the recorded message again. "Hey, Ernest," Larry said. "It's your next left, right?"

"Right," Ernest said, and a moment later, he turned left onto a dirt road. A moment later, they were winding down a track that ran through scrub pines. To their right, mangrove grew in swamp water. Shortly, they came to a small clearing, and Ernest made a U-turn and stopped.

"Okay, out of the car," Larry said, opening the door and helping Stone out of the rear seat.

"Let's try the number again," Stone said.

Larry punched redial, and again, the dreaded message repeated.

"Well, I guess you're just shit out of luck," Larry said, pocketing the phone. He pushed Stone toward the mangrove. "My instructions were, if I couldn't reach him, to do the deed and meet him tonight."

"You're doing this on credit, then?" Stone asked, trying not to panic.

"Don't worry," Larry said, "me and Mr. Barnacle go way back. We did a little stretch together."

Suddenly the name rang a bell. "Barnacle? *Douglas Barnacle?*"

"That's his name."

Stone realized that he was about to be murdered by a dead man. "Hang on," he said.

"Listen, Mr. Barrington, there's no use stretching this out. You don't want to think about this any more than you have to."

"Don't you read the papers? Watch television? Listen to the radio?"

"What are you talking about?"

"Didn't you hear about the shoot-out in a Palm Beach restaurant last night?"

Ernest, who had gotten out of the car, walked up. "Yeah, I heard something about that," he said.

"What shoot-out?"

"The guy you call Doug Barnacle was living in Palm Beach under the name of Paul Bartlett. The police killed him last night."

That brought Larry up short. "Ernest, that was the name, wasn't it? Paul Bartlett?"

"That's what he was using yesterday," Ernest said.

"Turn on the car radio," Stone said. "Find an all-news station."

"Do it, Ernest," Larry said.

Ernest went to the car, turned on the radio and found a station. Farm report, bank robbery in West Palm, weather.

Larry looked at his watch. "Ernest, we got a plane to catch."

"I know it," Ernest said.

Larry turned and marched Stone back to the mangrove. He put a foot against his backside and shoved him into the swamp. Stone kept his balance and ended up thigh-deep in the black water. A large snake slithered past no more than a yard away. "Mr. Barrington, that was a real nice try. I admire it, but it's time for you to say bye-bye." He raised the pistol and pointed it at Stone's forehead, no more than five feet away.

"Hey, Larry!" Ernest called.

"What?"

"Listen!" He turned up the radio.

". . . chaotic scene at La Reserve, a Palm Beach restaurant last night, ended up with one dead, and a Minneapolis police officer seriously wounded."

"Don't Doug live in Minneapolis?" Ernest asked.

"Shhhh."

". . . have identified the police officer as Lieutenant Ebbe Lundquist, of the Minneapolis PD, and the dead suspect as Paul Bartlett, also of Minneapolis. Bartlett had been wanted in Minnesota for the murder of his wife, Frances Simms Bartlett, nearly a year ago, and Lieutenant Lundquist was trying to effect an arrest in the restaurant, backed up by the Palm Beach Police Department."

"Well, shit," Larry said. "You're not lying, Mr. Barrington."

"No," Stone said, "I'm not."

"I mean, you got no idea what some folks will tell you in circumstances like this, you know?"

"I'm sure. But the fact remains, Larry, that you're not going to get paid for this one, so why do it? You've already got the twenty-five thousand, so you haven't wasted your time, but Bartlett isn't going to pay off, now." Stone did *not* like standing in this swamp, with *things* slithering around in it.

"He's got a point, Larry," Ernest said.

"Maybe," Larry said, thoughtfully.

Ernest looked at his watch. "And we haven't got all that much time before our plane."

Larry looked at Stone. "I don't guess you'd really pay me the fifty grand, would you?"

"Give me your address, and I'll send you a check," Stone replied.

Larry burst out laughing. "Come on, Ernest, let's get outta here!" He got into the car, and Ernest drove off, spinning the wheels and throwing mud everywhere.

Stone stood in the swamp for a minute, trying to get his heart rate down, then the snake appeared again, and he started struggling for the shore.

Once on dry land, he lay down and, with the greatest possible effort, got his handcuffed hands under his ass and finally over his feet. Now, with his hands in front of him, he was able to get to the cell phone under his sweater on his belt. He punched in the number.

"The Shames yacht," Dino said.

"Dino," Stone said, "I need you to come and get me, and bring your handcuffs key."

⤚ Chapter 39 ⤙

Dino found the whole story hilarious. "I don't believe it," he cackled. "Bartlett bites you on the ass from the grave! I wish I had been there!"

"Dino, it wouldn't have been funny, even if you were there."

"And you thought it was Manning who bought the hit!" He cackled again.

"And it *still* isn't funny."

Stone went to his cabin, showered and changed, retrieved his laptop computer and brought it into the saloon.

"What are you doing with that?" Dino asked.

"The only address we have for Frederick James is an e-mail address, so I'm going to e-mail him."

"Will he be able to tell you're in Palm Beach?"

"No. The return address will be the same as if I'd sent it from New York."

"Okay, why not?"

Stone made some adjustments in his telephone dialing program, logged on to his Internet provider and went to e-mail.

TO: FREDERICK JAMES
FROM: STONE BARRINGTON

DEAR MR. JAMES:

I UNDERSTAND YOU HAVE BEEN TRYING TO GET IN TOUCH WITH ME. IF SO, YOU MAY REACH ME AT THE ABOVE E-MAIL ADDRESS, OR TELEPHONE ME AT (917) 555-1455. I THINK YOU AND I MAY HAVE SOMETHING TO DISCUSS THAT WOULD REACT TO YOUR BENEFIT.

Stone sent the e-mail. "Let's see if that raises him."

"And what if it does?"

"All I want to do is buy the guy off. Maybe he'll listen to reason."

"You think he's interested in money?"

"I don't think he's interested in anything else. He's doing this because he's pissed off at his wife for taking all his money. I'm going to propose that she give some of it back."

"I think the guy's a fruitcake, Stone, and . . ."

A chime from Stone's computer interrupted him. "You have mail," a notice on the screen said.

"That was quick. The guy must have been working on his computer." Stone opened the e-mail.

TO: STONE BARRINGTON
FROM: FREDERICK JAMES

DEAR MR. BARRINGTON:

WHY DO YOU THINK I AM TRYING TO GET IN TOUCH WITH YOU? I DON'T EVEN KNOW WHO YOU ARE.

Stone was annoyed. He immediately wrote back.

TO: PAUL MANNING
FROM: STONE BARRINGTON

PAUL:

ALLISON HAS ASKED ME TO REPRESENT HER IN COMING TO TERMS WITH YOU.
SHE IS WILLING TO PART WITH A SUBSTANTIAL SUM OF MONEY IN ORDER TO AM-
ICABLY END ALL TIES WITH YOU. LET ME KNOW IF YOU ARE INTERESTED.

"Let's see if that has any effect," Stone said.

Considerable time passed while they waited. Stone and Dino chatted
about nothing in particular for a while, then the computer chimed again,
and Stone opened the mail.

TO: STONE BARRINGTON
FROM: FREDERICK JAMES

SIR:

YOU SEEM TO BE SUFFERING UNDER THE DELUSION THAT I AM SOMEONE ELSE.
HOW DID YOU GET THIS E-MAIL ADDRESS?

Stone immediately wrote back:

PAUL, THERE IS NO POINT IN CONTINUING WITH THIS. IF YOU HAVE NO INTER-
EST IN A SUBSTANTIAL SETTLEMENT, THEN YOU AND ALLISON CAN GO YOUR SEP-
ARATE WAYS, WITH YOU EMPTY-HANDED AND EXPOSED.

There was an immediate return message:

SIR:

JUST WHAT DO YOU THINK YOU CAN EXPOSE ABOUT ME? YOU DON'T EVEN KNOW
WHO I AM.

Stone wrote back:

PAUL, OF COURSE I KNOW WHO YOU ARE. HOW ABOUT THIS: I CALL SOMEBODY
I KNOW AT *60 MINUTES* AND SUGGEST THEY DO A PIECE ON PAUL AND ALLISON
MANNING, WHO EVERYBODY THINKS WERE HANGED IN ST. MARKS A WHILE BACK.
THEY COULD INTERVIEW ALLISON, WHO COULD TELL THEM HOW SHE BRIBED

GOVERNMENT OFFICIALS FOR HER OWN RELEASE AND YOURS. THEN SHE COULD TELL THEM HOW YOU ARE NOW CALLING YOURSELF FREDERICK JAMES, AND AS SOON AS THE SHOW IS OVER, EVERY JOURNALIST IN AMERICA WILL BE TRYING TO FIND YOU, WHICH SHOULD MAKE YOUR LIFE FUN. YOU SEEM TO HAVE MADE A NICE NEW LIFE FOR YOURSELF, WITH A BOOK ON THE *TIMES* LIST. WOULDN'T YOU LIKE TO CONTINUE TO LIVE THAT LIFE, UNDISTURBED?

ALL WE ASK IS THAT YOU TAKE SOME MONEY AND LEAVE ALLISON UNDIS- TURBED. TALK TO ME.

James's answer:

SIR: I DON'T KNOW WHAT KIND OF MANIAC YOU ARE, BUT YOU ARE FLIRTING WITH THE BIGGEST LAWSUIT YOU EVER HEARD OF, PLUS MAYBE CRIMINAL CHARGES OF EXTORTION. THIS CORRESPONDENCE IS AT AN END. I DON'T WANT TO HEAR FROM YOU AGAIN.

Dino, looking over Stone's shoulder, read the e-mail. "Well, that was certainly indignant. You think he's bluffing?"

"Yes," Stone said. "What's more, I think we may have smoked him out. I don't think we've heard the last of Mr. James."

⤳ Chapter 40 ⟿

Stone was reading the papers the following morning, when Thad appeared on deck, carrying two briefcases. He gave them to Juanito. "Put these in the car, will you, please?"

"You leaving?" Stone asked.

"Yes. I've got to go back to New York, then back to the Coast again."

"Thad, it might be a good idea if you took Liz with you."

"Why?"

"Well, I don't know if or when Paul Manning is going to turn up, but if he does, it might be better if Liz weren't here."

"What am I going to do with her in New York, lock her in a hotel suite? I'm going to be very busy for the next week or so, and I'd have little time to spend with her. And from what she tells me, I think she'd be afraid to go out shopping or anywhere else on her own."

"You have a point," Stone said.

"I'd feel much better if she were here with you and Callie and Dino."

"For how long?" Stone asked.

"For as long as you'll stay, or until you reach some sort of accommodation with Manning."

"Thad, I can't stay forever, but I'll give it another week or two. Maybe we'll hear from this Frederick James again. If he really is Manning, I can't think why he wouldn't want to talk to me. After all, he's already called my office three or four times."

"Does James know where you are?"

"No. At least, I don't think so."

"You want me to hire some private security to back you up?"

"No, not at the moment. If it gets bad we can always do that."

"If you want help, just tell Callie. She'll know who to call."

"All right."

The two men shook hands, and Thad left the yacht.

Dino, who had been having breakfast during this conversation, now spoke up. "Listen, Stone, I'm beginning to think you're taking this too seriously. I mean, all that's happened is the lady's house has been messed up a little. That's kid stuff; it's hardly a threat on her life. And if James is really Manning, then he can't be completely a fruitcake. He's made a life for himself, he's writing again, and if his book is on the best-seller list, he must be doing okay at it."

"Dino, you only met this guy when you arrested him. I got to know him a little in St. Marks, and he made this very angry scene in New York right before you picked him up. He wanted his money, and he wanted it bad. I've got a feeling he still does."

"A feeling? What's that? Your hunches were never all that good, you know."

"Liz feels the same way, and she knows him better than anybody."

"So now we're operating on *Liz's* hunches? Don't get me wrong, I'm getting used to living on a big yacht and having my every wish catered to; I always knew I could. I'll stay here until the chief of detectives sends somebody down here for me with an extradition warrant."

"She's not a stupid woman. She and Paul pulled off quite an insurance fraud, you know."

"Pulled off? You think nearly getting herself hanged is pulling it off? The whole thing completely backfired on them. They're stupid, both of them."

"Okay, so it didn't work out. She's still pretty smart," Stone said stubbornly.

"Anyway, she may not be your only problem."

"What are you talking about?"

"I haven't mentioned this, but yesterday we got followed around town by a car."

"*What?*"

"You heard me. Somebody is tailing us."

"Why didn't you tell me?"

"It didn't seem related to Liz and her problems."

"And what do you think it's related to?"

"I think it could be the former Mrs. Barrington."

"Oh, shit," Stone said. He had nearly forgotten about Dolce. "What kind of a car?"

"Sort of an anonymous-looking sedan, probably Japanese. The windows were tinted dark. I couldn't see who was inside."

"Everybody's windows are tinted dark down here; keeps out the heat."

"I think you should take Dolce seriously."

"You think I don't?"

"I think you don't take her seriously enough."

"And how do I do that? Carry an automatic weapon at all times?"

"You could do worse. And I'm worried about Callie."

"What about Callie?"

"If Dolce sees you with her, she could be in trouble."

"Oh, God," Stone moaned. "When is this going to be over?"

"As far as Dolce is concerned, it'll be over when one of you is dead, and she might want that sooner than later."

"You think she's suicidal?"

"Homicidal, more likely."

"Thanks, I needed that."

"Anytime."

The cell phone on Stone's belt vibrated. "Hello?"

"Mr. Barrington?"

"Yes."

"This is Frederick James."

"Good morning, Mr. James," Stone said loudly, so that Dino would get it. "I didn't think I'd hear from you again."

"I changed my mind. I want you to answer a question."

"Go ahead."

"How did you know that I know Paul Manning?"

"Let's not be cute, Mr. James. I think you *are* Paul Manning."

"Well, I'm not, but I've been in touch with him."

"When?"

"Recently."

"How recently?"

"Recently enough. I know about his past with Allison, and the business with the insurance company. Quite frankly, I know more about him than I want to know."

"Don't we all?"

"I got to thinking about what you said in your e-mail. Does Allison really want to buy him off?"

"Yes, she does."

"For how much?"

"I don't know that I can discuss that with you, since you claim not to be Paul Manning."

"Tell me this, then. Why do you think I've been trying to get in touch with you?"

"You really don't know?"

"No, I don't, or I wouldn't have asked you."

"A man called my office several times and wouldn't leave his name. I suspected it was Paul Manning. I managed to trace the call back to a Manhattan hotel, and you were the only guest whose name I recognized."

"That's pretty tenuous, isn't it?"

"Is it? Wasn't I right?"

"Actually, you may well be. Paul Manning was in my hotel suite a couple of times, and he made some phone calls."

"Well, I'm glad you admit, at least, to being in the same room with Manning."

"Have you ever met Manning, Mr. Barrington?"

"I got to know him rather well, but he was using another name at the time."

"Listen to my voice. Does it sound like the voice of Paul Manning?"

Stone admitted to himself that it did not. "Manning's is deeper," he said.

"Exactly. I have rather a light voice, wouldn't you say?"

"I suppose."

"And Manning's is a sort of bass-baritone."

"Yes."

"Does that do nothing to convince you that Manning and I are not the same person?"

"It helps. Of course, we can resolve the question of identity very easily."

"How?"

"We can meet, face-to-face."

"Where are you, at the moment, Mr. Barrington?"

"I'd rather not say."

"I'd rather not say, too."

"Then we might as well be on different continents."

"We may very well be."

"How are we going to resolve this?"

"I may be able to help you deal with Manning."

"Deal, how?"

"You're trying to buy him off, aren't you?"

"Let's just say that I'm trying to bring a difficult situation to an amicable close."

"Then I'll take him your offer."

"You know how to get in touch with him?"

"How could I take him your offer, otherwise?"

"All right. Tell him that Allison wants to come to an arrangement with him to get out of her life. If he agrees in principle, then we can discuss it in more detail. Or just get him to call me."

"I don't think he'll do that."

"Why not?"

"He's very shy these days, and he's not fond of you."

"Tell him I can arrange for him to live his life more openly, without fear of legal difficulties."

"Now *that* might appeal to him. Can I reach you at this number?"

"Yes. How can I reach you?"

But Frederick James had hung up.

Stone turned to Dino. "You heard that?"

"I heard it."

"What do you think?"

"I think this is getting very weird," Dino said.

Chapter 41

Callie came on deck. "And what have you two planned for the day?" she asked Stone and Dino.

"Zip," Dino said. "But I wouldn't mind some golf."

"I'll book you a tee time at the Breakers," she said.

"I don't want to leave you and Liz alone," Stone replied. "We'd better stick close."

"Liz and I will be just fine," Callie said. "I have your gun, and Juanito and a couple of crew members will be around. Besides, if you have to spend all your time here, you might get tired of me."

Stone snaked an arm around her and kissed her on the neck. "Not much chance of that," he said.

"I know," she replied, "but unless you and Dino get out of here and allow Liz and me some girl time, I'm going to start getting sick of you both."

Stone threw his hands up. "Golf, it is. Come on, Dino."

The starter cleared them from the first tee. Stone drove his usual slice into the next fairway, and Dino hooked his into yet another fairway.

"How're we going to handle the cart on this?" Dino asked, getting in.

"Well, I'm not giving it to you. You're away, so we'll go to your ball first."

Dino addressed the ball with a fairway wood, took a practice swing and sent the ball two hundred yards over a stand of palm trees, back into the fairway. "Take that!" he said.

Stone drove to his own ball, took a long iron and hit it to within five yards of Dino's ball.

"Looks like we're back in the game," Dino said.

"Back in the fairway, anyway."

They both parred the hole. A bit later, as they were crossing South County Road, Dino spoke up. "You are the most unobservant person I know."

"What brought that on?" Stone asked. "And how does being observant help my golf game?"

"Nothing can help your golf game," Dino replied, "but if somebody had told *me* that my former wife and lover was hunting me down to kill me, I'd take a look around me once in a while."

Stone tensed. "Where?"

"Over your left shoulder, parked at the curb, about two hundred yards down. Don't look yet!"

Stone tried to keep his eyes ahead. They stopped to tee off, and he took his driver out of the bag and tried a couple of practice swings, which allowed him to look at the car. "I can't see who's inside," he said.

"That's kind of the point, isn't it?" Dino asked. "If she'd wanted you to see her, she could have parked twenty yards from us."

"We've already made the local papers this week, as a result of the scene in the restaurant," Stone said. "I don't think I want to read a story that says I was shot dead on the golf course at the Breakers."

"Don't worry," Dino said, "you won't. I may, but not you."

"How do you know she doesn't want to kill you, too?"

"Because *I* never married her, then dumped her when an old girlfriend called," Dino said. "I've always been nice to Dolce."

Stone teed up and swung at the ball, hitting it straight, for a change. "I remember your telling me once that Eduardo was the devil, and that Dolce was his handmaiden. Is that what you call being nice?"

"I didn't say it to *her,* " Dino pointed out. "You think I have a death wish?"

"But she must know what you think of her."

"I don't know how she could. I've certainly never told her."

"What about Mary Ann?"

"Mary Ann and I have not yet come to the point in our marriage where she wants me dead. Someday, maybe, but not yet." Dino drove the ball, and they got back into the cart.

"What is it with Sicilians, anyway?" Stone asked.

"Well, speaking as a scion of the more elegant north of Italy, it has always been my opinion that all Sicilians are totally batshit crazy. I mean, the vendetta thing would be counterproductive anywhere else but Sicily, but they've made an art of it. Do you have any idea how many more Sicilians there would be in the world, not to mention in this country, if there were no vendetta? If you took all of them who've been knifed, shotgunned, garrotted, blown up, and poisoned, married them off and had them produce, say, four point five children each? Millions."

"And you're saying that's not counterproductive?"

"Nah. It just concentrates more ill-gotten wealth in fewer hands, and it prevents a Sicilian population explosion. And that can't be a bad thing."

"But you married a Sicilian."

"How do you think I know all this? It's been an education, I can tell you." Dino curled a thirty-foot, breaking, downhill putt into the cup.

"How'd you do that?" Stone asked, astonished.

"I just thought about how a Sicilian would do it, if the ball would kill somebody."

Stone laughed. "How can I make it up with Dolce, without getting killed?" he asked, serious again.

"Make it up? You mean marry her again?"

"No, no, no," Stone sputtered. "I mean just make peace with her."

"You don't make peace with Sicilians, unless there is a threat of death on both sides. You know, like the nuclear thing: mutually assured destruction. Where do you think the Pentagon and the Kremlin got the idea?"

"There has to be another way."

"Eduardo could call her off."

"Yeah? He could do that?"

"If she wasn't crazy. Nobody can call off a crazy person, not even with a threat of death."

"You're such a pleasure to be around, sometimes, Dino."

"I'm just telling you the way things are. No use kidding yourself."

"I guess not," Stone said glumly. They were on a tee that faced the road, now, some four hundred and fifty yards away. Stone hit his first true drive, now, two hundred and sixty yards straight down the fairway.

"Everybody gets lucky sometime," Dino said.

"That's the thing about this game," Stone said, getting into the cart. "Even the worst duffer can go out and, maybe two or three times in a round, he can hit a shot that's the equal of anything a pro could do under the circumstances. And it gives you the entirely irrational hope that, if you worked at it, you might get pretty good at this game."

"That's what keeps us coming back," Dino said. He hit a good drive, too, but short of Stone's.

"I like you keeping a respectful twenty yards back," Stone said. "Shows a certain deference."

Stone chunked his second shot, hitting the ground before striking the ball. It fell short, some forty yards from the green.

Dino hit the green. "Sorry about the lack of deference," he said.

Stone got out of the cart and looked toward the green, lining up his shot. Then he saw the car, sitting and idling at the side of the road, a hundred yards away.

"What club do you want?" Dino asked, standing at the rear of the cart beside the bags.

"Give me the two-iron," Stone said.

"Yeah, sure," Dino laughed. "You mean a wedge, don't you?"

"Give me the two-iron," Stone said again.

"Even you will hit the two-iron a hundred and eighty yards," Dino said. "I'd use a lob wedge, myself, to clear the bunker."

"Give me the two-iron," Stone said, an edge in his voice.

Dino gave him the two-iron.

Stone took the club and lined up on his target.

"You're aiming twenty yards to the left of the pin," Dino said, standing behind him.

Stone took a practice swing.

"Stone, if you take a full swing, you're going to hit the ball onto a neighboring golf course."

"No, I'm not," Stone said.

"Then you can kiss that ball good-bye."

Stone lined up with the ball. He took a short backswing and abbreviated his follow-through to keep the shot low. He connected solidly, and the ball flew straight and true, twenty yards to the left of the pin, across the road, narrowly missing a passing Rolls-Royce, and straight at the idling car with the blacked-out windows. The ball struck the driver's window with a *thwack,* but it did not shatter. Instead, it cracked into a hundred pieces, held together by the safety glass and the tinting film applied to the window.

Stone hoped somebody would get out, but instead, the car sped away, its tires squealing on the pavement, leaving a puff of black smoke.

"Nice shot!" Dino yelled.

⤳ **Chapter 42** ⤳

Dino watched the car speed away and laughed aloud. "That ought to make the guy keep his distance!"

"Guy? What guy? You said it was Dolce."

"I said I *thought* it was Dolce. For all I know, it may be one of your groupies."

"I don't have groupies," Stone said.

"Okay, maybe it's one of your many enemies."

"Come on, let's finish the round," Stone said. "I assume you're going to let me take a mulligan on that one."

"Yeah, I guess."

Stone took his sand wedge, choked down on it, opened the face and flopped the ball onto the green, within three feet of the pin.

"You should have taken my advice in the first place," Dino said.

They were driving back to the Shames estate, with Dino at the wheel, when Stone's cell phone vibrated. "Hello?"

"This is Frederick James."

"Good day, Mr. James."

"I've spoken with Paul, and he's willing to deal, through me."

"Not through you," Stone said.

"Why not? He's chosen me as his representative."

"How can I trust you?" Stone asked. "You've already lied to me at least once."

"When did I ever lie to you?" James asked, sounding offended.

"You told me you'd never heard of Paul Manning, and then you told me you knew him. One of those was a lie."

"But—"

"I'll deal directly with Manning."

"For whatever reason, Paul doesn't wish to deal with you."

"Then I'll deal with a reputable lawyer who represents him."

James was silent for a moment. "I am Paul Manning's attorney," he said finally.

"You're a novelist," Stone said.

"So is Scott Turow, but he's a lawyer, too."

"I take it your name is not Frederick James, then?"

"A *nom de plume.*"

"What is your real name?"

"I'm not prepared to divulge that."

"And you think I'm going to deal with somebody who says he's an attorney but won't tell me his name? Either get serious, or go away."

"But I—"

"I don't know who you are, where you are, if you're an attorney or even if you really know Paul Manning."

"I assure you, I do."

"That's not good enough."

"What exactly do you want, Mr. Barrington?"

"I want to know that I'm dealing with the real Paul Manning and that he's represented by an attorney whose identity I can confirm."

"And what proof of those things would you accept?"

"Bring Manning to a meeting, and let him authorize you to represent him in my presence."

"Paul won't meet with you."

"Then I'm not going to remove the threat of his arrest on insurance fraud, and I'm certainly not going to give him any of my client's money."

"There must be some way we can resolve this."

"I think you understand my concerns, Mr. James. Why don't you go away and think about it for a bit, discuss it with your client and get back to me?"

"All right," James said and hung up.

"He's playing games?" Dino asked.

"I don't know what the hell he's doing."

"Manning's afraid you're going to set him up for an arrest."

"A reasonable fear," Stone said.

"Can you really get him off on the insurance fraud charge, or are you just blowing smoke up his ass?"

"I've *already* gotten him off," Stone said. "But I'm not going to tell *him* that."

"How did you get him off?"

"I negotiated a deal for Allison with the insurance company, whereby they agreed not to prosecute in order to get some of the money back."

"And the deal includes Manning? Why?"

"I didn't want to admit to them that Allison was still alive, so I wrote the agreement without reference to names. Now they can't prosecute *anybody*."

"That's pretty slick, Stone."

"I'm a pretty slick lawyer," Stone replied.

"Yeah, sometimes," Dino admitted.

They were back on the yacht, having a drink with Callie, when Stone's phone buzzed again. "Hello?"

"It's Frederick James."

"What did you come up with?"

"I propose that you and I meet, in order for me to establish my credentials."

"Okay, where?"

"Where are you?"

"Where are *you*?"

"I'm in New York, but I have to go to Miami on business later in the week. Is there someplace between New York and Miami we can meet? Preferably in an airport?"

"I'm on the west coast of Florida," Stone said. "How about Palm Beach International? It's a couple of hours' drive for me."

"Agreed. Now, what do you need from me?"

"In what state are you licensed to practice?"

"New York."

"Okay. Bring a copy of your New York law license, your New York driver's license and your United States passport. Also, I'll need a photograph of you with Paul Manning, taken no earlier than today and no later than tomorrow, and I want a copy of the day's *New York Times* prominently displayed in the photograph."

"I can do all that, I think, although Paul doesn't like to be photographed."

"I can imagine. Then I'll need a copy of Manning's U.S. passport, with his current identity recorded therein, and I want that clearly visible in the photograph, too."

"Whoa, whoa, he's not going to go for that."

"I'm giving him nothing unless I'm convinced he's who he says he is, and in order to do that, I'll need to know who he says he is. He's going to have to prove it to me."

"You're throwing in a whole lot of stuff, here," James said.

"If you're a lawyer, you'll know very well that I have to protect my client, just as you have to protect yours. That's all we're talking about."

"I'll get back to you," James said and hung up.

"Any progress?" Liz asked.

"By inches," Stone said. "Manning is being *very* cautious."

"He's got a lot to be cautious about," Liz replied.

An hour later, Stone's phone vibrated again. "All right," James said. "The day after tomorrow at one P.M., at Signature Aviation, Palm Beach International."

"Fine," Stone said. "I'll see you then, but if my concerns are not met, there'll be no discussion of terms."

"I understand," James said.

Stone hung up. "We're on."

⟡ Chapter 43 ⟡

Late that night, after a big dinner and more wine than he had intended to drink, Stone fell into bed, exhausted. He had barely fallen asleep, when he was wakened by a knock on the door—at first, softly, then loudly. Annoyed, he got out of bed, put on a robe and went to the door.

"Good evening," Dolce said. She stood there with two brandy snifters in one hand and a pistol in the other. "May I come in?" she asked, unnecessarily.

Stone looked at the gun and backed into the room. "Of course," he said.

Dolce kicked the door shut and offered him a snifter. "I brought you a drink," she said.

"Thanks, but I've already had too much to drink this evening," he replied.

"I said, *I brought you a drink,*" she said, through clenched teeth.

Stone took the glass.

"Sit on the bed," she said, "where I can see you."

Stone sat on the bed.

Dolce lifted her glass. "To many more happy moments like this," she said.

Stone sipped at his brandy. It had an uncharacteristically bitter taste.

"Drink it!" she said, tossing down her own drink.

Stone tossed down his own. "To what do I owe this pleasure?" he asked.

Dolce smiled, revealing her startlingly white teeth against her olive skin. "A pleasure, is it? I had somehow gotten the impression that seeing your wife was no longer such a pleasure. How long has it been?"

"Too long," Stone said. He felt dreadful; the brandy on top of everything else he had had to drink at dinner was too much. He moved to set down his glass on the bedside table, and to his astonishment, he missed the table entirely. The glass dropped to the floor, missing the rug, shattering into tiny pieces. "I'm drunk," he said.

"Not exactly," Dolce replied. "You're just feeling the first effects of the Thorazine."

"What's Thorazine?" Stone asked, and he had to try hard to pronounce the words.

"It's a little something that an enlightened medical profession has devised to help those of us who are—how shall I put this?—*psychiatrically challenged* easier to manage. Do you know that one of Papa's doctors actually said those words to me? *Psychiatrically challenged!* You have no idea what those of us who do not meet society's standards of behavior have to endure at the hands of those who wish to make our company more acceptable." She smiled. "But you're about to find out."

"Huh?" Stone said, dully. His mind seemed fairly sharp—certainly, he could understand her—but there was something blocking the connection between his brain and his lips, something that slowed everything to a molasseslike flow.

"Don't worry, my darling, it won't last long," she said, rising and approaching the bed. Her shoes ground the broken snifter into the floor with a loud noise. She placed a finger in the middle of Stone's forehead and pushed gently.

Stone fell back onto the bed. It was where he had always wanted to be, here on this bed, staring at the beautifully crafted ceiling of his beautifully crafted cabin.

Dolce lifted his feet onto the bed, untied his robe, then rolled him over and stripped it off his body. She rolled him onto his back again and tucked two pillows under his head.

Stone lay there, naked, indolent to a degree he would not have dreamed possible. He had no wish to do anything except lie there and let this happen.

Dolce went back to her chair, picked up the handbag that had hung on her arm, opened it, took out a wad of something and returned to the bed. She sat down on the edge and shook the little bundle into long lengths. "You know," she said, smoothing them out, "science has never solved the problem of what to do with old nylon stockings. There's no recycling of them, and they seem too good to throw away. One little run, and they're use-less." She smiled again. "Or are they?" She rolled Stone's limp form through three hundred and sixty degrees, until he was centered on the bed, then she tied one end of a stocking to a wrist and the other end to a bedpost.

Stone watched her do it, unconcerned, and continued to watch as she tied his other hand and both feet to bedposts. He was spread-eagled, naked, on the bed, before a trickle of concern made its way from some-where in his brain to his forehead, where it manifested itself in beads of sweat that popped out. *Wait a minute,* he thought, *something is wrong here.* He tugged at the bedposts, but the sturdy mahogany bed would not move, and neither could he.

"Well," Dolce said, "I believe your tiny dose of Thorazine is beginning to wear off. A psychiatric dose would have lasted much longer. It took me several months to learn to control my dosage—without the knowledge of my nurses, of course—to the point where I could manage a clear thought sooner, rather than later." She drew back a hand and slapped him smartly across the face. "There, feel that?"

"Yes," he said, and his lips moved better than they had a few minutes before.

"Oh, good, because I want you to be wide awake and feeling everything that is going to happen now."

"Dolce," Stone said, "what are you doing?"

"I thought it would be good," she said, "if you had some personal experi-ence of a loss of control over what happens to you, and, particularly, if you experienced a sense of loss over, oh, I don't know, maybe a body part or two?" She opened her handbag and removed an old-fashioned straight razor.

Stone tried harder to free himself from the stockings and the bedposts, but to no avail.

"You're wasting your time, my dearest," she said, daubing the sweat from his brow with a corner of the sheet. "Nylon stockings make excellent restraints; they're extremely strong, stronger than you, in fact." She opened the razor, and the blade caught the light.

"There's a very nice little shop in town," she said, "that sells men's shav-ing products, and they had this very beautiful example of German steel-making." She pulled a hair from Stone's head and let it fall on the blade. It separated into two pieces and fell to the floor.

"It has never been used," she said, "and it will never be sharper than it is at this moment. Just as well, too, since I didn't manage to steal a local anesthetic from my captors, only the drug. You'll hardly feel a thing, just the warm trickle—or rather, gush—of blood as it flows across what I be-lieve the poets call the loins." She reached out and took hold of the tip of his penis. "Let's get it excited," she said. "It makes a better target." She drew back the hand holding the razor and swung it in a slow arc toward its destination.

Then Stone was screaming, and someone was hammering on the door.

"Stone, open the door!" a woman's voice called.

Stone was sitting straight up in bed, still dressed in his robe. He stumbled to the door and opened it.

"What's wrong?" Callie asked, alarmed. "You've been screaming at the top of your lungs."

Dino appeared behind Callie. "You all right, Stone?"

Stone went and sat on the edge of the bed, while Callie got a towel and wiped the sweat from his face and upper body.

"I had a dream," he panted.

"More like a nightmare," Callie said.

"Yes, more like a nightmare."

⤳ Chapter 44 ⤳

The following morning, Stone made the call he had been dreading and could no longer postpone.

"Hello, Stone," Eduardo Bianchi said.

"Good morning, Eduardo. I hope you're well."

"I have been better," Eduardo said, then was silent.

It was up to Stone. "I understand that Dolce has . . . left your house."

"I am afraid that is so," Eduardo replied.

"Do you have any idea of where she might be?"

"Stone, my friend, I think she would *like* to be wherever you are."

"I'm in Palm Beach, Florida, on business," Stone said. "Dino is with me, and he feels that Dolce may be in Palm Beach; that she may have been following me."

Eduardo heaved a sigh. "I will send people at once," he said.

"Eduardo, I cannot guarantee you that she is here. It's just a feeling."

"I respect what you feel, Stone, and if there is any chance at all that she is in Palm Beach, then that is where I must look for her."

"Eduardo, speaking as an attorney, I must ask if you have taken any legal steps toward guardianship?"

"No. This is a family problem, you understand, and I have no wish to bring the courts into it."

"I understand your feelings, but simply sending people to find her and return her could present legal difficulties that might be more invasive of your family privacy than taking steps to have her declared incompetent."

"She is not an incompetent person," Eduardo said stiffly.

"I'm sorry, I meant incompetent in the legal sense, not otherwise. Unless you are willing to make a case to a court that she is not currently able to account for herself and her actions, then she is legally entitled to do and go as she pleases. Removing her to New York from another state could pose problems."

"Stone, I understand this, and I am grateful for your advice, but you must understand that, in my family, we are accustomed to solving our problems without the help of, ah, public officials. If I can locate Dolce, I can achieve the reunification I desire."

"Of course, Eduardo. I don't doubt for a moment that you can."

"You say that Dino is with you? I had not heard this."

"Dino came down to help me with another matter, one not connected to Dolce."

"I see. Well, it is good that he is there; you may well need his help. I need hardly tell you that Dolce may be a danger to herself and to you."

"I hope you are wrong, but I understand," Stone said. "If I should locate Dolce, what would you have me do?"

"Simply call me, and I will do the rest," Eduardo said. "Please don't try to deal with her yourself. From what her doctors have told me, she could be very dangerous."

"Eduardo, if Dolce should be traveling under a name not her own, is there a name she might choose to use?"

Eduardo was silent while he thought. "Once, when she was sixteen, she ran away after a quarrel with me. At that time, she used the name Portia Buckingham. It was a ridiculous name for a schoolgirl to choose, I know, but it was a kind of fantasy identity she made up as a child. She might possibly use it again."

"Would you like me to make some discreet inquiries?" Stone asked.

"Only if you can do so without involving the local police," Eduardo replied. "I do not wish for Dolce to be brought to the attention of the authorities, unless she tries to harm someone."

"There's not much I can do on my own," Stone said, "but I'll try."

"Ask Dino for his help. She is his sister-in-law, after all."

"I'll do that." Stone told Eduardo how he could be contacted.

"Good-bye, Stone, and thank you for your concern for Dolce."

"Good-bye, Eduardo." Stone hung up.

Dino sat down beside him. "You called Eduardo?"

"I felt I had to. He's sending people down here."

"Great, now we'll have goombahs roaming the streets of this piss-elegant town."

"Dino, you know Eduardo is more subtle than that."

"We'll see."

"He wants your help in finding her."

"What can I do?"

Stone handed him a Palm Beach classified directory. "Start calling hotels. Flash your badge. Inquire about her under her own name and under the name Portia Buckingham."

"*Portia Buckingham?* Give me a break!"

"It's a name she used to fantasize about having when she was a child, Eduardo says."

Dino shook his head and took the phone book. "I'll use the phone in the saloon," he said.

"Don't alarm anybody, just find out if she's registered."

"Thanks, Stone. I needed that advice." Dino went into the saloon.

"Leave a description with the desk clerk, too," Stone called after him.

Stone called his office. "Hi, Joan, it's me. What's happening?"

"Amazingly little," she said.

"Patch me into the dictator," he said. "I have some documents I'd like you to type up and FedEx to me today."

"Sure. Anything else?"

"Not at the moment."

"Here you go."

Stone heard the beep and began to dictate. When he had finished and given Joan her instructions, he hung up and went into the saloon. Dino was just hanging up the phone.

"I need the phone book for a minute," Stone said.

Dino tossed it to him. "I've called half a dozen places, starting with the Breakers."

"No luck, I suppose?"

"She's already checked in and out of two—the Breakers and the Brazilian Court, under Rosaria Bianchi."

"You're kidding. That was easy."

"Not so easy, pal. She's moving every day, and that's going to make her harder to find."

"Oh. Well, at least we know she's really in town."

"That, we know."

"Will you call Eduardo and tell him that?"

"Okay, I guess." Dino did not like dealing directly with his father-in-law, but he seemed willing to make an exception this time. He picked up the phone and dialed the number.

Stone began looking in the phone book under airports, and when he found what he was looking for made the call.

Dino finished his conversation with Eduardo. "What are you up to?" he asked Stone.

"I told our friend Mr. James that I was on the west coast of Florida, a couple of hours' drive from Palm Beach airport. I want him to go on thinking that until we get this settled." He made the arrangements he required, then hung up. "There, I guess I've done what I can." He picked up the phone again. "I'll make some of the hotel calls. You don't mind if I use your name, do you?"

"When did I ever mind?" Dino asked. "When did you ever care if I mind?"

☞ Chapter 45 ☜

At mid-morning, Stone drove north on I-95 and took the well-marked exit. Soon he was at North Palm Beach County airport, a small general aviation field a few miles from Palm Beach International. He found North County Aviation and parked his car.

Inside, he told the receptionist why he was there, and she made a quick phone call. "Don will be right with you," she said. "You're taking the Warrior, is that right?"

"That's correct."

"Then if you'd like to give me a credit card we can take care of that while Don is on his way."

Stone gave her his American Express card and watched as a Piper Warrior taxied up to the apron of North County Aviation and a young man got out and came inside.

"Mr. Barrington?"

"That's right."

"I'm Don. There she is."

Stone looked at the neat little airplane. "Looks very nice."

"Can I see your license and medical, please?"

Stone handed the man his private pilot's license and his third-class medical certificate. They were inspected and returned to him.

"How many hours do you have in type?" Don asked.

"A little over a hundred, but it's been a while. I did most of my private ticket training in a Warrior, and I'm real comfortable with it."

"Come on, then, and let's do a little checkride."

Stone signed his credit card chit, pocketed the card and followed Don outside.

"You do the preflight," Don said, handing him a fuel cup.

Stone put his briefcase into the airplane and walked slowly around it, running through a mental checklist. He drained some fuel from each wing and inspected it for dirt or water, checked the oil and handed Don back the fuel cup. "Looks good to me," he said.

"Take the left seat, then."

Stone climbed into the airplane, followed by Don. He started the engine, listened to the recorded weather from PBI, checked the wind sock and taxied to the active runway. He pulled into the runup pad and did his final check of the airplane, then, looking for traffic, he announced his intentions over the unicom frequency and taxied onto the runway. He pushed the throttle forward and, watching his airspeed, started down the center line. At rotation speed he pulled back on the yoke and left the ground. It was a fixed-gear airplane, so he didn't have to bother retracting the landing gear. Announcing his intentions at every turn, he climbed crosswind.

"Just stay in the pattern," Don said, watching his every move closely.

Stone turned downwind, reduced power and prepared to land. He turned onto the base leg, then onto final and set the airplane lightly down on the runway.

"Okay," Don said. "You can fly it. Just drop me back at the FBO, and you're on your way. How long will you be gone?"

"Just a couple of hours," Stone said.

"You understand there's a four-hour minimum on the rental?"

"Yes."

Don hopped out of the airplane, and Stone taxied back to the runway and repeated his takeoff. He climbed to a thousand feet, listened again to the recorded weather, then called the PBI tower. "Palm Beach Tower, this is November One-two-three Tango Foxtrot," he said, reading the airplane's registration number from a plaque on the instrument panel. "I'm ten miles to the northwest, VFR, looking for landing instructions. I have the ATIS."

The tower called back. "Enter a right base for runway niner. Traffic's light today. You're cleared to land."

Stone followed the instructions and ten minutes later he was taxiing up to Signature Aviation, between a Gulfstream III and a G-IV. He wondered how long it had been since anything as small as his rental had parked here.

He got out of the airplane. "The brakes are off," he told the lineman, knowing they wouldn't leave it where it was. "No fuel. I'll be about an hour."

He went inside the handsome lobby and walked up to the huge desk. "I'm looking for Mr. Frederick James," he said to the young lady behind it.

"Oh, yes, you must be Mr. Barrington," she said. "Mr. James and his associate are in the conference room, right over there." She pointed. "You won't be disturbed."

"Thank you." He walked across the reception room to the door and knocked on it.

"Come in," a man's voice said.

Stone opened the door and entered the room. A man, who had been seated alone at the conference table, stood up to greet him. Stone recognized him immediately.

"Mr. Barrington, I'm Edward Ginsky," he said, offering his hand. He was dressed in a beautifully tailored, double-breasted blue blazer and white linen slacks, his shirt open at the collar.

Stone shook it. "Of course. I'm glad to meet you." Ginsky was a famous New York lawyer, known mostly for his expertise in representing women in divorce cases. He had handled a number of high-profile divorces, and his clients had always done very well from his representation.

"I've heard of you, too," Ginsky said, sitting down and motioning Stone to a chair. "Bill Eggers speaks well of you, in fact."

"That's kind of Bill," Stone said.

"Well," Ginsky said, "enough chitchat. Shall we get to it?"

"Let's," Stone replied.

"I trust that now you won't need the identification you requested."

"No, not for you, but for your client."

"Ah, yes. Trust me when I tell you that, before our meeting is concluded, you will have adequate proof that I represent Paul Manning. May we proceed on that basis?"

"For the moment," Stone said, "but I should tell you that I will not come to any agreement until I am satisfied who I am dealing with."

"Understood," Ginsky said. "Now, what do you have to propose?"

"Are you acquainted with Mr. Manning's activities with regard to the island of St. Marks some years ago?"

"I believe I have all the relevant facts."

"Then you will know that your client and mine were married at that time and, in the absence of a divorce, still are."

"You could put that light on it," Ginsky said.

"I hardly know what other light to put on it."

"I think you are aware that my client is, if not dead, then no longer legally alive."

"You could put that light on it," Stone said.

Ginsky allowed himself a smile.

"Still, he exists, my client exists and legally, as I'm sure you're aware, their marriage still exists."

"I assume your client would like that marriage to end," Ginsky said.

"You assume correctly. She wishes the marriage to end and she wishes not to see her husband again or hear from him."

"I think that could be arranged," Ginsky said. "Under appropriate circumstances. What is your offer?"

"My client is willing to pay your client one million dollars in cash, wire-transferred to any bank in the United States, in return for a signed property settlement to that effect and a contractual agreement that your client will never contact her again, nor knowingly inhabit the same city at the same time as my client." Stone knew that he had already put several stumbling blocks in the way of a settlement, one by omission. The two lawyers were circling each other, metaphorically, feeling each other out.

"I see," Ginsky said. "Of course, hardly anything you've said is acceptable."

"Tell me what you're willing to accept, and let's go on from there."

Ginsky threw his first punch. "Your client achieved a windfall of twelve million dollars as a result of my client's efforts. He wants half that."

"Your client masterminded a criminal conspiracy, and when it went wrong, left my client to hang by the neck until she was dead," Stone parried.

"She did not hang," Ginsky said.

"Neither did your client," Stone reminded him. "And, when your client murdered three people and was arrested in New York and extradited for his crimes, and was sentenced to hang himself, my client interceded on his behalf, paying half a million dollars to save his life. She could have done nothing, and we would not be having this conversation." Stone heard the door behind him close; he had not heard it open. He did not turn around. "It seems to me that your client is deeply in my client's debt."

"I don't owe her a fucking thing," Paul Manning's deep voice said from the door. "And don't turn around."

Stone felt cold steel pressed to the back of his neck.

∽ Chapter 46 ∾

Stone didn't move, nor did he allow himself to show any concern.

"Paul," Ginsky said, "that is entirely unnecessary, and moreover, unacceptable. If you want me to represent you in this matter, put it away and sit down."

"I'll put it away," Manning replied, "but I'll stay where I am. And, Barrington, if you turn around I'll use it on your skull."

"Mr. Ginsky," Stone said, "perhaps it would help if you explained your client's tenuous position to him."

"Let me explain something to you, Barrington," Manning said.

"Shut up," Stone said. "I will not deal with you, but with your attorney. If you can't accept that, then I'll leave now."

"Get in your little airplane and fly away, huh? Maybe I should have a look at that airplane. You know how good I am at fixing them."

"Paul, be quiet," Ginsky said. "If you say another word I will withdraw from this meeting, and we'll all be right back where we started. Mr. Barrington, you have not mentioned your previous offer to resolve any legal difficulties Mr. Manning might have."

"No, and I won't mention that until we are agreed on all other points, except to say that to resolve the legal difficulties is within my power."

"Very well," Ginsky said. "The offer on the table is for one million dollars in cash, a signed property settlement and, I assume, a divorce, and an undertaking not to see or speak to Mrs. Manning again. Is that correct?" He looked toward the door and held up a hand to stop Manning from speaking.

Ginsky had not mentioned that the transaction would take place through a U.S. bank. "You left out a couple of points, but I won't quibble," Stone said. "That's substantially it."

"The money is not enough," Ginsky said. "Let's cut to the chase. Make your best offer."

"A million and a half dollars," Stone said.

"If you will offer two million dollars, I think I can recommend the deal to my client."

"My client has already paid half a million dollars for his benefit; that makes a total of two million."

Ginsky looked at his client, then back at Stone. "Surely she can do better. She walked away with twelve million, tax free."

"My client has had many expenses over the years, and she has paid her taxes." He had advised her to, anyway.

"A U.S. bank is not acceptable for the transaction," Ginsky said.

"Then we'll wire it to your firm's trust account, and you can disburse it."

"Still not acceptable."

"What's the matter, doesn't your client want to pay *his* taxes?"

"That's beside the point."

"Speaking of points, you haven't addressed all of mine," Stone said.

"He can hardly agree not to be in the same city with her; he won't know her movements."

"All right, he stays out of Florida and New York City, except to change airplanes."

Ginsky looked at his client, then back at Stone. "We won't give you New York, but you can have Florida."

"Let me enumerate," Stone said, counting off on his fingers. "Two million dollars. I won't wire it abroad, but to your trust account. You can disburse it abroad, if you want to. He stays out of Florida, or he goes to jail for contempt of court. He signs a property settlement and a document acceding to a divorce petition, here and now."

"Let me see the papers," Ginsky said.

Stone unlatched his briefcase, selected the set of documents with the two-million-dollar figure typed in, then slid them across the table.

There was five minutes of silence while Ginsky speed-read the documents. He looked at his client. "This is good," he said.

"I expect there's a notary at this FBO," Stone said, "and I want him to sign twice, once as Manning and once as whatever his current passport says."

Ginsky nodded.

"Let me see the passport."

Ginsky spoke to his client. "Paul, please ask the girl at the desk to send a notary in here."

Stone heard the door open and close.

Ginsky slid a U.S. passport across the table.

Stone opened it, anxious to see the photograph. A postage stamp covered the face. He looked up at Ginsky. "How do I know this is Paul's passport, if I can't see the face on the photograph?"

"Do you doubt that the man who was just in this room was Paul Manning?"

"No, I know the voice."

"Then you don't need to see the face for purposes of identification, do you?"

"Your client is very shy."

"He has his reasons," Ginsky said.

Stone copied down the information on the passport: William Charles

Danforth, a Washington, D.C., address. He riffled through the visa pages and saw a number of entry and exit stamps—London, Rome, other European cities. "He's pretty well traveled." He slid the passport back across the table.

Manning returned with the notary, and Stone pulled out additional copies of the agreement.

"Both names," Ginsky said to his client.

Manning signed the documents on a credenza behind Stone, and the woman notarized them.

"When do we get your client's signature?" Ginsky asked.

"She'll sign today, and the documents will be FedExed to your New York office right away."

Ginsky gave Stone his business card.

The notary left. "What about the money?" Manning asked.

"To be wire-transferred as soon as the judge signs the divorce decree," Stone said.

"It's in the documents, Paul. He'll provide a release from the insurance company at the same time. The deal won't be final until we're in receipt of those two items."

"I don't like waiting," Manning said.

"It can't be helped," Ginsky replied. "It's how these things are done. Trust me."

Stone heard the door open and close behind him.

"Sorry, my client's a little edgy today," Ginsky said.

"How'd you get mixed up in this, Ed?" Stone asked.

"I've known him since college. He popped up in my life only a short time ago, when he got the e-mails from you."

"Can you make him hew to the terms of the agreement?"

"I think so. He wants out of the marriage, and he wants the insurance matter off his back."

"I'll tell you, off the record," Stone said, "that if he doesn't stick to the letter and the spirit of the agreement, I'll take it upon myself to expose him for who he is, and in a very public way."

"Are you threatening me, Stone?" Ginsky asked.

"No, Ed, I'm threatening Paul Manning, and I mean it. You should know that he's a dangerous man, and my advice to you is, when this matter is concluded, to stay as far away from him as you can."

"That may be good advice," Ginsky admitted.

Stone put his copies of the document into his briefcase and stood up.

Ginsky stood up, too. "We saw you taxi up and get out of the airplane," he said. "I was expecting you to drive in. Where are you flying back to?"

"I'd rather not say," Stone said.

"I don't think you'll have any more trouble from Paul. Where do you want to do the divorce?"

"Anywhere in Florida will do."

"I know a judge here in Palm Beach, and I'm licensed to practice here."

"Fine with me. I'm not licensed here, so I'll get Bill Eggers to find somebody. He'll be in touch."

"I'll look forward to receiving the signed documents tomorrow." Ginsky held out his hand.

Stone shook it. "Thanks for getting him to see sweet reason, Ed."

"See you around the courts in New York, I expect."

"I expect so."

The two lawyers walked out of the conference room and into the lobby. Paul Manning was nowhere in sight.

They walked out to the ramp together, shook hands again, and Ginsky got into a Hawker 125, parked near the door.

Stone assumed Manning was already on it. He walked a hundred yards to where his less imposing aircraft had been parked by the lineman. He did an especially thorough preflight inspection before climbing into the airplane.

He remembered Manning's remark about knowing how to fix airplanes, and he wanted to be sure the one he was flying would keep flying. He started the engine, and he listened to it carefully before starting to taxi.

All the way back to North County airport, he listened to the engine. It got him back safely.

Chapter 47

When Stone arrived back aboard the yacht, Liz, Callie and Dino were all waiting for him.

"Did you see him?" Liz asked.

"Not exactly," Stone said, "but we were in the same room."

"Did he sign the papers?" she asked anxiously.

"Yes."

"How much am I giving him?"

"Two million dollars."

Liz collapsed in his arms, laughing. "Oh, Stone, you are a wonder. You saved me three million dollars!"

"Don't ever tell Paul that," he said.

"I hope I won't ever have to talk to him."

"I think we can avoid a court appearance for the divorce."

"Where will we do the divorce?"

"Here in Palm Beach. I'll find you a Florida lawyer for that, but since we have a signed settlement, there won't be much work for him to do. Now you have to sign the documents, and we have to find a notary."

"I'm a notary," Callie said. "I have to witness stuff for Thad all the time."

"Great. Go get your seal."

Callie left them, then returned with her seal and stamp. Stone handed Liz a pen, she signed and Callie notarized.

"That's it," Stone said, handing the documents to Callie, along with Ed Ginsky's card. "Will you FedEx these to him right away?"

"Sure. I'll call for a pickup now." She picked up a phone.

"I have to call Thad and tell him," Liz said, running for the phone in the saloon.

Stone sat down beside Dino.

"Is this all over, Stone?"

"I hope so," Stone replied.

"But you're not sure?"

"It's not going to be over until it's over." He thought about that for a moment. "And maybe not even then."

"What's the problem?"

"The problem is Manning. He's still just as angry and, apparently, as nuts as he was the day you arrested him in New York. He's got a good lawyer—Ed Ginsky—but I don't know if Ed can control him."

"I know who Ginsky is," Dino said. "He's had a lot of experience dealing with angry spouses."

"I wonder how much experience he's had in dealing with crazy ones?"

"Everybody who's getting a divorce is crazy for a while," Dino said.

Stone picked up the phone. "I'd better call Bill Eggers and find Liz a local lawyer."

Liz came running back from the saloon. "Thad's coming back tonight!" She ran toward her cabin.

Stone placed the call to Eggers and told him what he wanted.

"I don't know the Florida law offhand," Eggers said, "but it sounds pretty straightforward."

"That's what I think. You know somebody in Palm Beach?"

"No, but somebody here in the shop will. I'll have somebody call you."

"Okay."

"How's everything going?"

Stone gave him a recap of recent events.

"This is kind of messy, isn't it?"

"As divorces go, yes; but we might conclude a nasty case as well."

Thad Shames came aboard his yacht late in the afternoon in high spirits. He swept Liz into his arms, kissed her, then shook hands with Stone and Dino, then he turned back to Liz. "Right here, in front of these witnesses, I want to ask you: Will you marry me?"

"Oh, yes!" she cried, and they kissed again.

Dino glanced at Stone and rolled his eyes.

"Isn't this romantic?" Callie asked Stone.

"Oh, yeah," Stone replied.

"Let's do it this weekend," Thad said enthusiastically.

"I'd love that!" Liz said, tears of happiness streaming down her cheeks.

Stone and Dino exchanged glances. Stone was horrified, Dino amused.

Liz went to repair her makeup, and Stone made Thad sit down with him and Dino.

"Thad," Stone said seriously, "don't you think you ought to wait until Liz is divorced before you get married?"

"Oh, that's just paperwork," Thad said. "You've already got the signed property settlement and divorce papers, and anyway, legally, she's a widow—twice, in fact. Both deaths are a matter of public record."

"Thad, rushing into this could make your life a lot more complicated. Why do that? I haven't looked into the Florida law, but with signed papers and a settlement, it shouldn't take long to get a decree. Relax and enjoy being engaged for a while."

"Listen, Stone," Thad said. "I've waited a long time for this girl, and I'm not going to let her get away. I'm not going to relax until we're married and on our honeymoon."

Callie came with drinks for all of them.

"Callie, we're having a Sunday afternoon wedding," Thad said. "Invite everybody who was at the housewarming, plus the New York list. Call the caterers—and find out how I get a marriage license and, if necessary, a blood test."

Callie grabbed a pad and started taking notes.

"And, Stone, Dino, I want you both to stay for the wedding," Thad said.

Stone looked at Dino, and they nodded.

"I wouldn't miss it," Dino said.

"And, Thad," Stone said, "we're going to need some outside security for this occasion."

"Callie, take care of it," Thad said. He got up. "I'm going to get a shower and change for dinner. Please book us a table somewhere, Callie." He departed for the house.

Callie sat down next to Stone. "How much security are you going to want?"

"Let's see," Stone said, looking toward the house. "We'll want two men, dressed like the car parkers, out in front of the house. There should be two men in each public room in the house, dressed as guests, four in the garden and two on the yacht. How many is that?"

"Eighteen."

"Ask for twenty-four, and I want them to have radios."

"Do you want them armed?"

Stone thought about that.

Dino spoke up. "I'm not sure it's a good idea, having that many armed men in a crowd. After all, we don't know these guys, don't know how good they are."

"We'll have one armed man in each room, in the garden and on the yacht," Stone said. "Tell them we want only their best-trained and most experienced men carrying."

"All right," Callie said.

"And I want them here an hour before the party, so I can brief them."

"Okay." She made a note of that.

"Anything else you can think of?" Stone asked Dino.

"Well, let's see," Dino said, "we could have a couple of machine guns mounted on the roof, and maybe a bazooka or two."

Callie laughed.

"Why do you think he's kidding?" Stone asked.

She laughed again. "I'd better go book us a dinner table," Callie said, "and I've got a lot of phone calls to make." She headed toward her cabin.

"Thad is completely nuts, isn't he?" Dino asked.

"He's nuts about Liz, no doubt about it."

"I've never seen anybody move so fast."

"It's the money. The superrich are accustomed to having what they want, when they want it, and that usually means *right now.*"

"It's a pretty short time to put together a big wedding."

"Frankly, I'm surprised we're not doing it tonight. But don't worry, this is what Callie does, and she's used to doing it Thad's way."

"Sounds like it's going to be a hell of a party," Dino said.

"Or a hell of a mess," Stone said.

They had dinner at an Italian restaurant, Luccia, on a covered terrace, and Stone was gratified that gunfire did not break out. He did not enjoy himself very much, though. He was preoccupied with Paul Manning, and he didn't even understand why.

Everything Manning was doing made sense. He was making money, he was removing the possibility of prosecution for insurance fraud, he was getting on with his life. So why was Stone so worried?

When he got back to the yacht that night, he started to crawl into bed with Callie, then stopped and went to the phone.

"This is Berman," the voice said.

"Bob, it's Stone. I hope I didn't wake you."

"Nah, what's up?"

"Got a pencil?"

"Shoot."

"I want everything you can find—and I mean *everything*—on a William Charles Danforth." He read him the P Street Washington address. "I want a full bio, and I want to know how far his credit history goes back. Do a criminal record check, too, and I want a photograph. I especially want a photograph."

"Will do. How soon?"

"Tomorrow, as early as possible."

"I'll call you." Berman hung up.

Stone got into bed and snuggled up to Callie. Now that he felt he was doing something, he could pay her the proper attention.

⟶ Chapter 48 ⟵

Dino finished his coffee. "How are we dressing for this shindig on Sunday?" he asked.

"Black tie," Callie replied.

"In the afternoon?"

"The wedding's at six, with a small group of invited guests. Everybody else arrives at seven."

"Oh, good, for a minute I thought we were going to be gauche and wear black tie in the afternoon."

Callie laughed. "You gauche, Dino? Never!"

Dino gave her a sweet smile. "Stone, I gotta go shopping. You come with me."

Stone looked at Callie.

"We'll be all right," she said. "I've already got two security men in the main house."

"You anticipate me," Stone said.

"I try."

"Okay, Dino, let's go shopping." He led the way toward where the cars were parked. A man who was obviously a security guard paid a lot of attention to them.

"You're one of the two men on duty?" Stone asked.

"That's right."

"My name is Barrington. This is Lieutenant Bacchetti, NYPD. You armed?"

"Yes, sir."

"Try not to shoot anybody, if you can help it."

"I'll try."

They got into the car and drove away.

"What are you shopping for?" he asked Dino.

"A dinner jacket."

"Why don't you ask Mary Ann to ship yours down here? There's time."

"That's a question only a lifelong bachelor could ask," Dino said. "If you're in Palm Beach, and she's not, you don't call home and say, 'Honey, send my dinner jacket, will you?' It would take too long to explain why to her, and in the end, she'd never believe you. Besides, I need a new one, anyway. Somebody threw up on the last one at a wedding last year, and the cleaners could never get it all out."

"Where you want to shop?"

"They got an Armani here?"

"They do."

"Giorgio always does my dinner jackets."

Stone found a parking spot on Worth Avenue. He put the top up to keep the sun from overheating the black leather upholstery, and they walked to the shop.

Dino conferred with a salesman, and shortly, a fitter was marking up a white dinner jacket. "You like the white?" he asked Stone.

"I like. Very elegant."

"I thought you would. I'm getting this just for you."

"You're sweet."

The fitter looked at them oddly. "What about the lump, sir?" he said, nodding toward the pistol on Dino's belt.

"Allow for that," Dino said. "I'll be wearing it to the party."

"Well, this is a first for Palm Beach," the man muttered, but he did his work.

When they returned to the car, the driver's side window was a web of pieces, held together by the lamination.

"Looks like a golf ball hit it," Dino said.

Stone looked up and down the street. "That's not funny."

"Sure it is," Dino laughed.

"You see her anywhere?"

"No, but a silver Volvo sedan has been following us."

"Why didn't you mention it sooner?"

"What good would it have done? It would have just ruined your day."

"You're right about that," Stone said, flicking small shards of glass out of the driver's seat.

They drove back to the house and walked to the yacht.

"A message for you, Stone," Callie said, handing him Bob Berman's number.

Dino glanced at the piece of paper. "What have you got Berman on?"

Stone led him into the saloon and picked up a phone. "One William Charles Danforth of Washington, D.C."

"Who's that?"

"It's the passport Paul Manning is using these days."

"Oh."

Stone called Berman. "It's me. You got something?"

"I got a lot," Berman said. "You want me to FedEx it to you, or you want to hear it now?"

"Let's hear it."

"Okay. Mr. Danforth is all over the Internet, just like you'd expect a substantial person to be. He's got a credit history going back only four years. It's little stuff, credit cards, couple of department stores—Saks, Macy's. There's apparently no Mrs. Danforth, and there are no mortgages on the reports. He rents an apartment in the P Street house in Georgetown, has for four years."

"So Mr. Danforth is only four years old."

"Right."

"What does he do?"

"He lists his occupation as business consultant."

"Whatever that means."

"Yeah. His credit card spending is consistent with a man making less than a hundred thousand dollars a year. I got one of the credit card statements for the past year, and he's traveled to Europe and Florida."

"Where in Florida?"

"Miami, twice; last time ten days ago. He rented a car there, too."

"Okay, what else?"

"He seems pretty ordinary. His phone number is listed. Nothing jumps out at you."

"Did you find a photograph?"

"Nope, wasn't available from any of my sources."

"What about a driver's license photo?"

"I checked D.C., Virginia and Maryland. Nothing there."

"If he rented a car, he must have a license; if he has a license, there should be a photograph on file somewhere."

"You want me to check all the states?"

"The contiguous forty-eight will do."

"Okay, but it's going to take a few days. There's no federal registry of driver's licenses; it's purely a state thing."

Stone had a thought. "How about a pilot's license? He knows something about airplanes."

"There's no photograph on pilots' licenses; you ought to know that."

"Oh, right," Stone said, thinking of the license in his own pocket.

"You suspect this guy of being wonky in any way?" Berman asked. "There's no criminal record."

"Yes."

"Well, if he's wonky, he wouldn't have any trouble picking up a driver's license that would get him a rental car."

"Good point, but do the search anyway."

"Whatever you say, Stone."

"Does he own a car?"

"Yes, a six-year-old BMW 320i, registered at the P Street address."

"Strange that he has a car and a passport with that address, but no driver's license."

"Maybe he doesn't want his picture taken any more than necessary. Does he know you're looking at him?"

"Probably not, but he might guess."

"Maybe, if he's wonky, he figured that someday, somebody would be looking for a photograph of him."

"He has a passport, and you need a photograph for that."

"Yeah, but the State Department is a lot harder to get a photograph out of than a state driver's license office."

"Once again, you have a point."

"Anything else?"

"Not that I can think of at the moment. Let me know about the license."

"Will do," Berman said.

"And, Bob?"

"Yeah?"

"Put your mind to other ways to find a photograph."

"I already did." Berman hung up.

Chapter 49

Stone sat on the afterdeck and nursed a gin and tonic. "Dino," he said finally, "when you arrested Manning that time in New York, you finger-printed him, didn't you?"

"Yeah, why?"

"Because that gives us a possible way to find out what Manning has been doing for the past four years to earn a living. I can't see him doing it honestly."

"What do you need?"

"I need for you to run his prints against unsolved crimes with no sus-pects."

"Stone, you're about to be rid of the guy. Why do you want to press this?"

"Because I have the awful feeling I'm *never* going to be rid of him. If he's committed a crime somewhere in this country, and I can prove it, then I'd have something on him, something that would either keep him in line or put him in jail."

Dino picked up a phone, called his office and asked them to run the Manning prints against unsolved crimes. "Shouldn't take long," he said. "Why do you think he might have committed a crime?"

"Because he's apparently been earning less than a hundred thousand dollars a year, and I don't think that's enough to keep Paul Manning in the style to which he long ago became accustomed."

The phone rang, and Stone picked it up.

"Mr. Barrington?"

"Yes."

"My name is Fred Williamson. Somebody in Bill Eggers's office at Woodman and Weld in New York asked me to call you about some divorce work."

"Yes, of course. How do you do, Fred?"

"Very well, thanks, and divorce is a specialty of mine."

"Glad to hear it. What I've got here is a petition from a Mrs. Allison Manning against Paul Manning. Mr. Manning has already waived a re-sponse, and we have a signed property settlement."

"Where do the Mannings live?"

"In Palm Beach." Stone gave him Liz's West Indies Drive address.

"Shouldn't be a problem, then. It'll probably take a month to get it heard."

"Do the Mannings have to appear?"

"Not necessary, as long as they're in agreement on the terms and they're both represented by counsel. Who's his lawyer?"

"Edward Ginsky, of New York, but he's licensed to practice in Florida." Stone gave him Ginsky's address and phone number.

"I'll call him and get us on the court calendar."

"Fred, is there any way to get this heard right away? And in chambers, if possible? I don't want it to make the papers, even in the legal notices."

"I know a judge who might hear it in chambers sooner, rather than later," Williamson said.

"I'd appreciate it if you could handle it that way. Ginsky has his own jet. I'm sure he could appear on short notice, or appoint someone local to do it."

"Who's got the paperwork?"

"I have. Can you send a messenger for it?"

"Sure. Where?"

Stone gave him the address.

"I'll have somebody there inside an hour."

"Thanks, Fred. Call me if you need any further information." Stone hung up. He went to his briefcase, extracted the documents, stuffed them into a manila envelope, wrote Williamson's name on it and gave it to Juanito to leave with the security man guarding the front door.

"Maybe I can get them divorced before Sunday," Stone said.

"Would that make you feel better?" Dino asked.

"Yes, indeed. I'm uncomfortable about witnessing a client—two clients, in this case—committing bigamy in front of the crumbs of Palm Beach's upper crust."

"When they get to that part about 'if anybody can show just cause why these two people shouldn't get married,' shouldn't you, as an officer of the court, stand up and yell, 'It's bigamy!'?"

"Probably, but this lawyer says he might be able to get it heard quickly."

The phone rang again, and this time it was for Dino.

"Hello? Yeah, this is Bacchetti. Hang on, let me get something to write with." He motioned to Stone for a pen.

Stone handed him one, and a pad.

"Yeah, yeah. Where? How many? And there's no other clue? Why the hell didn't this match pop up before? Oh, yeah, I see. Thanks. I don't know yet. Sit on it until I get back to you." He hung up.

"What?" Stone asked.

"You were right, pal. Our Mr. Manning knocked over a branch bank in Arlington, Virginia, four years ago."

"I knew it!" Stone said.

"He left a thumbprint on a note that he handed a teller."

"Why didn't the match turn up at the time?"

"I asked about that. It seems that when we printed the guy at the Nineteenth, whoever did it didn't put the prints into the system because he figured, what the hell, the guy's being prosecuted in another country. It was stupid, but it happens."

"This is wonderful," Stone said, meaning it.

"It gets better. A man answering the description—at least height and weight—knocked over three other branches within fifty miles of D.C. Two in Maryland and one more in Virginia. He was smart enough not to leave any prints on those jobs."

"What sort of money did he get?"

"Between a hundred and a hundred and fifty thousand at each bank; never more than that. Still, he had to do some planning or have some inside information to get that much out of a walk-in-and-hand-the-teller-a-note job. Usually those bring more like twenty-five or thirty grand a pop, and the banks don't even bother to prosecute if there was no violence involved." Dino stopped and looked at Stone.

"Why the smug little smile?"

"Gee, I don't know. I just have this warm fuzzy feeling inside."

"You've got the guy by the balls."

"You bet your sweet ass I have," Stone said with satisfaction.

"So what are you going to do?"

"I'm going to get Liz and Manning divorced and see her and Thad married, then I'm going to call the FBI and sic them on Paul Manning, and I'm going to take the greatest pleasure in doing it."

"I hope it's that easy, pal," Dino replied.

᪥ Chapter 50 ᪥

Stone was woken from a sound sleep by the phone next to his bed. He picked it up. "Hello," he said, sleepily. He looked at the bedside clock. It was shortly after ten A.M.

"Stone? It's Fred Williamson. Can you have Mrs. Manning at the courthouse at three o'clock this afternoon?"

"Why?"

"We've got a hearing before Judge Coronado in his chambers at that time."

"Why does Mrs. Manning have to be there?"

"This is an unusual situation, and the judge wants to talk to the couple face-to-face."

"But why? I thought we could do it with just their attorneys."

"He wants to know what the big rush is, I guess; whether these people are for real."

For real? Stone thought. *They are definitely not for real.* "Have you spoken to Ed Ginsky?"

"Yes. He says he can have his client there."

"Well, okay," Stone said. "We'll be there."

"The judge is going to ask some questions, like how long have the Mannings lived in Florida. You know the answer to that one?"

"I'll have to ask Mrs. Manning."

"This whole petition is based on the fact that they're Florida residents. Be sure you tell her that."

"All right. Have you told Ginsky about this?"

"Yes. He says his client will bring proof of Florida residency. The judge is going to ask these people why they want a divorce, and there shouldn't be any disagreement between them about that."

"You told Ginsky that, too?"

"Yes."

"All right."

"I'll see you at three o'clock in Judge Coronado's chambers, which are behind courtroom A."

"Good, see you then."

Stone got dressed and found Liz and Thad having breakfast on deck. "Good news," he said.

"I'm always up for good news," Thad said.

"Liz, you're getting divorced this afternoon."

"Wonderful!" she nearly shouted.

"You and I have to appear in the chambers of a Judge Coronado this afternoon at three. Paul and his attorney will be there, too."

"I don't want to do that," she said.

"I'm afraid you have no choice in the matter," Stone said.

"I won't be in the same room with him."

"Look, this is not the first divorce this judge has heard. He's accustomed to people who aren't speaking to each other."

"Liz," Thad said, "Stone has gone to a lot of trouble to get this thing resolved this week. This is only going to take a few minutes, right, Stone?"

"That's right. I shouldn't think it would take more than half an hour, at the most."

"Oh, all right," Liz said. "I don't have to talk to him, do I?"

"No, but you'll have to talk. The judge will ask you both some questions, and be warned, he's not going to like it if you argue about the answers. Just don't disagree with Paul."

"That may be difficult," she said.

"Liz, this is the quickest, quietest way possible to get you out of this marriage. Just do what you have to do," Thad said.

"All right, darling," she said, and put her hand on his.

"Can I be there?" Thad asked. "Liz might feel better."

"Absolutely not," Stone said. "You're a very recognizable figure in Palm Beach, and I don't want you anywhere near that courthouse."

"Oh, all right," Thad said. "Sit down and have some breakfast."

Juanito appeared, and Stone ordered. "Now, Liz, tell me: How long have you been a Florida resident?"

"Since I married Winston, I guess. Three years. He was a Florida resident well before that, for tax reasons."

"The judge will ask you that."

"What about Paul? He's not a Florida resident. At least, I don't think he is."

"His lawyer says he can show proof of residency. The judge will ask you things like how long you've been married, and he's going to ask you why you want a divorce. What are you going to tell him?"

"That my husband led me into a life of crime and that, when he murdered three people, I didn't want to live with him anymore."

"No, no, no," Stone said. "You want to be general, not specific."

"You mean like, we just grew apart over the years?"

"That's better. And if he asks Paul first, just go along with whatever he says. Don't worry, he has a very good lawyer, and he will have been well briefed."

"Whatever you say," she said.

"That's the right answer, too. Now, another thing. Your agreement with Paul requires you to wire-transfer the money into his lawyer's trust account as soon as the divorce is final. What I'd like is for you to transfer the money to my trust account today, and I'll take it from there."

"The two million dollars?" she asked.

"That's right."

"God, but I hate to give that son of a bitch any money."

"Liz, get a grip. You've already signed an agreement to that effect. Yesterday, you were delighted to get off so cheaply."

"Liz, honey," Thad said, "two million dollars is small change to me. Let me take care of that."

"I couldn't let you do that," Liz replied.

"No, really. I'd consider it a great favor if you'd let me do that."

"Oh, Thad," she said, putting her hand on his cheek. "You're so sweet."

Thad turned to Stone. "I'll move the money this morning."

"You're sure that's the way you want to do this?"

"Yes, I am."

Stone watched, amazed, as they kissed.

Later, when they were driving to the golf course, Stone brought Dino up to date.

Dino's mouth fell open. "He's giving her two million bucks?"

"Like Thad says, it's small change to him."

"Holy mother! She's good, isn't she? She meets this guy, what, three weeks ago, and now he's paying her ex-husband two million bucks to go away?"

"You've got it."

"Well, Thad is either the sweetest guy in the world or the dumbest, or both," Dino said.

"Don't talk about my client that way," Stone said.

"Yeah, yeah, I know; he pays his legal bills."

"That's very important," Stone said.

"And you don't even know if he's really going to go away."

"Oh, I know that," Stone said. "When the FBI takes him away, he'll be gone."

"How do you know they can get a conviction?" Dino asked. "After all, when he gets Thad's two million, he's going to be able to afford a *very* good lawyer."

"I thought you said they have his fingerprint on a note he handed a teller."

"Sure they do," Dino said. "Gee, I hope the FBI hasn't misplaced it during the years that have passed since the robbery. They would never do that, would they?"

"They'll have the tellers' identification of Manning," Stone said.

"How do you know? Maybe he dressed up like Ronald McDonald. And it's been four years since the last robbery. I'd be willing to bet you that at least one of the four tellers is dead, and a couple more are retired and living in Costa Rica or someplace, and that the remaining one has come down with Alzheimer's. And even if one of them is still around and can identify Manning, Ginsky is going to turn him inside out on the witness stand. 'But, sir, it's been four years since you say you saw the robber, and you also say he was wearing a red wig, a big nose and floppy shoes. How could you possibly say that man is my client?'"

"You're starting to annoy me, Dino."

"Oh, yeah? Well, you're not nearly as annoyed as you're going to be when Manning gets off scot-free and hires somebody to put his ex-wife at the bottom of Lake Worth in a concrete bikini."

Stone ran a red light, thinking about that.

∽ **Chapter 51** ∾

Stone got Liz to the courthouse half an hour early. He wanted to talk to Ed Ginsky before they went into the judge's chambers. There was too much happening this morning over which he had no control, and he didn't like it.

They had been sitting in the empty courtroom A for ten minutes, when a balding man in his mid-thirties came in.

"Are you Stone Barrington?"

"Yes."

"I'm Fred Williamson."

"Hello, Fred. This is Mrs. Manning."

"Don't call me that," Liz snapped.

"Everybody's going to call you that today, Liz. Just get used to it." Williamson shook her hand as if he were afraid she might bite it.

"I want to speak to Ginsky before we go into chambers," Stone said.

"Why?" Williamson asked. "I think we've got all our ducks in a row." He took a sheaf of papers from his briefcase and handed them to Stone. "I've taken the liberty of making a few changes so that they more closely follow the Florida form."

Stone flipped quickly through the papers. Ten minutes to three. Where the hell was Ed Ginsky and his client? "They look fine to me, but everybody will have to sign again. We'll need a notary."

"The judge's clerk can notarize them," Williamson said. "I've also written the decree for his signature. Judge Coronado is leaving on vacation today, and I don't want to have to wait for his signature."

"Neither do I," Stone said. He was looking forward to seeing Paul Manning's face at last, and he wished to hell the man would arrive.

At one minute before three, Ed Ginsky and his client strolled into the courtroom. Paul Manning looked like hell. He was wearing bandages that covered his nose and much of his face, and at the edges, both his eyes seemed blackened. Surgery, Stone thought as he stood up. He and Ginsky shook hands. "I'm glad you're here, Ed. I want to . . ."

At that moment a door behind the bench opened and a solidly built, handsome Hispanic man stepped into the courtroom. His hair was completely white, and he was not wearing a jacket but sporting loud braces. "Everybody here, Fred?"

"Yes, Judge. All present and accounted for." He shepherded everyone into the chambers and made the introductions. Coronado waved them all to chairs.

"Now," the judge said, "you have a request, Fred?"

"Yes, Judge. We're here in the matter of a divorce between Paul C. Manning and Allison S. Manning. Mr. Manning is represented by Mr. Ginsky, and I am representing Mrs. Manning, with the consultation of Mr. Barrington, who is a member of the New York bar and Mrs. Manning's attorney in that state." He handed the judge a stack of documents. "The parties have agreed on a property settlement. Mrs. Manning's petition and Mr. Manning's waiver of response are all in order. We ask for a decree based on their mutual desire for a divorce."

The judge glanced through the papers, then returned them to his desktop and leaned back in his chair.

"Mr. Manning, are you a legal resident of the State of Florida?"

"Yes, Your Honor," Manning replied.

Ed Ginsky offered a sheet of paper. "Judge, this is a copy of Mr. Manning's declaration of residency, filed at the Dade County courthouse two and a half years ago."

"This seems to be in order." The judge turned to Liz. "Mrs. Manning, are you a legal resident of the State of Florida?"

"Yes, Your Honor, for three years. I own a house in Palm Beach."

The judge nodded. "Mrs. Manning, Mr. Manning, you're both obviously mature adults. Mrs. Manning, is it your desire to end your marriage?"

"Yes, Your Honor," Liz replied.

"Mr. Manning?"

"Yes, Your Honor."

"Are you both completely satisfied with the terms of the property settlement on my desk? Mrs. Manning?"

"Yes, I am, Your Honor."

"Mr. Manning?"

"Yes, Your Honor."

"I would certainly assume that you are satisfied, since you are receiving a settlement of two million dollars. Mrs. Manning, does that sum represent a part of your net worth that you can afford to part with?"

"It does, Your Honor."

Especially since she isn't parting with it, Stone thought.

"Has any duress been brought upon you to part with such a sum?"

"No, Your Honor," Liz replied.

"Very well, then, I . . ." The judge stopped and looked oddly at Liz. "I beg your pardon, but have we met before, Mrs. Manning?"

"No, Your Honor," Liz replied. "I think I would remember," she added, flatteringly.

"Wait a minute," the judge said. "Aren't you Winston Harding's widow?"

Uh-oh, Stone thought. *Here's trouble.*

"Yes, Your Honor," Liz replied, as if it were the most natural question in the world, in the circumstances.

"I'm confused," the judge said. "Mr. Harding died only late last year, didn't he?"

"That's right, Your Honor," Liz said, still not getting it.

"And when were you married to Mr. Manning?"

Stone opened his mouth to speak, but nothing came out.

Liz had no such problem. "Oh, Paul and I were married before Winston and I." Then she realized what she had said and froze.

Stone still couldn't think of anything to say, and Fred Williamson was looking at him in panic.

Then Paul Manning spoke up. "Your Honor, may I explain?"

"I wish to God somebody would," the judge replied.

"Your Honor, Mrs. Manning and I were married eight years ago. Then, four years ago, I was accused of murder in a Caribbean country—unjustly, I might add. I was tried, convicted and sentenced to death. Then, at the last moment, the truth came out, and I was pardoned."

Stone looked at Ed Ginsky and thanked God it was Ginsky's client who was lying to the judge and not his own. Ginsky seemed, as well, to have lost the power of speech.

"Congratulations," said the judge, but he still looked baffled.

"Mrs. Manning had already left the island, having done everything she could, and she was under the impression that I had been executed. By the time I was released, we had lost touch, and it was only recently that she learned that I was still alive. So, you see, she married Mr. Harding in good faith, believing that I was dead. In fact, she had been given a death certificate."

The judge looked back and forth between Paul and Allison Manning as if they were escaped lunatics. "So this divorce is merely a matter of legal housekeeping, is that what you're telling me?"

None of the lawyers would speak, so Liz did. "Yes, Your Honor. I think you can see what a horrible series of events this was and how Paul and I, having parted long ago, would not like this hanging over our heads."

"Yes, I can see that," the judge said. "Fred, I hope you brought a decree for me to sign, because after today, I never want to hear about this again."

Williamson set the decree on the desk, and the judge signed it. "I'd like your clerk to notarize the property settlement, please," Williamson said.

The judge pressed an intercom button and spoke: "Amy, come in here, please." A woman entered the room. "I want you to notarize some documents for these people." He stood up and put on his jacket. "I've just signed a divorce decree, and I want you to see that nothing is published about it, do you understand?"

"No, Judge," the woman said, baffled.

He handed her a copy of the decree. "Just give these people copies of this and file it, and forget you ever saw it. I intend to." He turned to the group. "Fred, you can use my chambers to sign these papers, then get these people out of here. I don't ever want to hear a word about this again. Is that clear?"

"Perfectly clear, Judge," Williamson said.

The judge walked out of his chambers, slamming the door behind him. Williamson whipped out a pen, and everybody started signing. Five minutes later, the group broke up.

As they were leaving, Paul Manning approached his ex-wife. "Well, nice knowing you, Allison."

"There was nothing nice about it," Allison said, and stalked away.

"Wait for me in the car," Stone called out. He shook Fred Williamson's hand. "Thanks, Fred, for all your help."

"Can you tell me what the hell that was all about?" Williamson asked softly.

"Just forget it and send us your bill," Stone said. "Ed, Paul, a moment, please?"

The two men stopped. Stone waited until Williamson had left the room. "I've got something to say to you, Paul, and I want to say it to you in front of your attorney."

"Do I have to listen to this, Ed?" Manning asked.

"Give Stone a minute, Paul."

"First of all, the two million dollars will be wired into your trust account immediately, Ed."

"Thank you, Stone."

Stone removed a sheet of paper from his pocket. "And this is a release from the insurance company."

Ginsky looked at it. "Why, this is dated . . ."

"Yes, it is," Stone said.

Manning snatched the paper and read it. "You mean, I was already . . ."

"Yes, you were, Paul, but you're not out of the woods yet."

"What do you mean?" Ginsky asked.

"Ed, your client participated in four transactions in Virginia and Maryland a while back that you don't know about and don't want to know about. But I know about them, Paul, and I'm happy to tell you that you left a fingerprint on a note you handed somebody. I've never expected you to adhere voluntarily to the terms of the agreement you signed, so let's just call this insurance."

"It sounds a lot more like blackmail," Ginsky said.

"That's exactly what it is, Ed. Paul, if you ever so much as speak to Allison again," Stone said, ignoring the attorney and speaking directly to his client, "one phone call will make you a fugitive again. On the other hand, if you keep your word, you're in no jeopardy."

"I don't know what he's talking about, Ed," Manning said.

"Sure you do, Paul, and Ed shouldn't know. But I know, and don't you ever forget it. Ed, thanks for handling this so well. Paul, you can go fuck yourself."

Stone turned and walked away.

Chapter 52

Stone drove Liz back to the yacht, feeling relieved and relaxed for the first time since he had arrived in Palm Beach. His relief lasted only until he walked up the gangplank.

A short, stocky man with iron-gray hair, wearing slacks and some kind of Cuban or Filipino shirt, stood up from a chair, where he had been sitting next to Dino. "Are you Stone Barrington?" he asked.

"That's right," Stone replied.

The man didn't offer his hand. "My name is Guido. A friend of yours sent me." As he spoke, a puff breeze blew the loose shirt against his body, revealing the outline of a pistol at his waist.

It took Stone a second to register what the man had said and to interpret it. He looked at Dino questioningly.

"Yeah, that friend," Dino said.

"Oh, sorry. What can I do for you, Guido?"

Guido looked around at the other people. "Can we talk?"

"Let's go into the garden," Stone said, leading the way off the yacht and to a bench among some flowers. "Okay," he said, "tell me."

"I'm here to bring the lady in question home."

"All right," Stone said.

"Where is she?"

"Did you talk to Dino about this?"

"He didn't seem too interested in talking to me."

"She's moving from hotel to hotel, every day," Stone said. "We know she's already been to the Breakers and the Brazilian Court."

"How many hotels in this burg?" Guido asked.

"Lots."

"Anything else you can tell me?"

"She may be driving a silver Volvo sedan, but I can't swear to that."

"That ain't much," Guido said.

"I know, but it's all I've got. Do you have any help?"

"I got a couple guys and a Lear waiting at the airport with a doctor and a nurse."

"Good. Want some advice?"

"Why not?"

"She seems to have been following me. I suggest you follow me, too, but from a distance."

"Yeah, that sounds good."

"Do you know her?"

"Since she was in diapers; I used to change them."

"She knows you, then?"

"Oh, yeah; since she's old enough to talk she's called me Uncle Guido."

"Well, Guido, if she's that fond of you, she might not be so inclined to take a shot at you."

Guido nodded solemnly. "And she's a hell of a shot," he said. "I know. I taught her in her papa's basement, when she was fourteen."

"I noticed you're carrying," Stone said.

Guido threw up his hands. "Don't worry, I'm not here to off her. Those are not my instructions."

Stone didn't doubt that if those were his instructions, Guido would carry them out with alacrity. "I'm glad to hear it," he said. "Suppose you see her? How are you going to handle this?"

"Decisively," Guido said. "I'm not here to fuck around."

"Are the people with you good?"

"The best. They'd do anything for the old man."

"I suggest you lose the hardware. If I can spot it, anybody can spot it, and the local cops aren't going to take kindly to out-of-towners packing iron on their streets."

"What are the local cops like?" Guido asked.

"Professional. They've got a smart chief, and you don't want to mess with him or any of his men."

"We'll play it cool, then," Guido said.

"Guido, please don't take this the wrong way, but on the streets of Palm Beach, you're going to stand out."

"Don't worry, I tan fast."

Stone sighed. "I'm not talking about your lack of a tan. People around here can spot an outsider in a split second, and any cop in town would make you as a foreigner from a block away."

"I ain't a foreigner," Guido said hotly. "I was born in Brooklyn."

"My point is, Guido, nobody else in Palm Beach was born in Brooklyn.

And if they were, they'd have learned long ago to look like they were born on Park Avenue. I hope you're getting my drift."

"Yeah, I get your drift," Guido said, "and if you were anybody but a friend of my friend I wouldn't take it too good."

"I'm trying to help you, Guido. Your friend would not like it if I had to bail you and your pals out of the local can, would he?"

"I guess not," Guido admitted. "How can we fit in better here?"

Stone thought about an honest answer to that question, but thought better of giving it. "Go down to Worth Avenue, to the Polo store or Armani and buy some nice quiet sports clothes. Jackets, too, like blue blazers with brass buttons?"

Guido nodded, but he was watching Stone closely to see if he was being had. "You think that'll do it, huh?"

Stone bit his tongue. "It can't hurt."

"Okay. How can I get in touch with you?"

Stone gave Guido his cell phone number. "And you? Where are you staying?"

"I don't expect to be here that long," Guido said, and gave Stone his own cell phone number. "Listen," he said, looking around as if he might be overheard. "My people are not going to feel good about shedding their hardware, you know?"

"Guido, nobody in Palm Beach is going to give you a hard time, let alone shoot at you—with the possible exception of the young lady. And if that were to happen, I think you'd be better off taking a round or two than shooting her. Her father would not think well of that."

Guido nodded. "You got a point," he said.

"One other thing," Stone said. "What kind of cars are you driving?"

"Cadillacs," Guido replied.

"You might rent something more anonymous."

"Why? Don't nobody drive Cadillacs in Palm Beach? I thought we'd fit right in."

"I'm not thinking about the general public, I'm thinking about the young lady. I think it will be to your advantage if you see her before she sees you."

Guido nodded slowly. "I get you," he said.

"Another thing," Stone said. "There's going to be a wedding here on Sunday evening, starting at six o'clock. There'll probably be a couple hundred people. If you haven't found her by then, you should probably have your people here."

"Yeah, okay, we can do that."

"It's going to mean renting or buying some evening clothes."

"You mean, like, suits?"

"I mean, like, tuxedos. It's going to be that kind of wedding."

"Yeah, okay, I'll look into that."

"And tell your guys no pastel tuxedos or ruffled shirts. Keep it discreet."

Guido looked at Stone closely. "You think we don't know how to dress?"

"I thought we already covered that point, Guido. This is Palm Beach; it's different."

He nodded. "Different from Brooklyn."

"Different from anywhere you've ever been before. Give me the names of your people, and I'll get them on the guest list."

Guido took a notebook from one of his many shirt pockets and jotted down some names, then ripped off the sheet and gave it to Stone.

Stone read them aloud: "Mr. Smith, Mr. Jones, Mr. Williams and Mr. Edwards?"

"I'm Mr. Edwards," Guido said.

"Got it." Stone put the piece of paper into his pocket and stood up. "Thanks for checking in, Guido. I appreciate your help with this."

"I ain't doing it for you," Guido said, then walked away.

Stone watched him go, then walked back to the yacht and found Callie. "Please add these names to the guest list for Sunday," he said, handing her the paper.

Callie looked at it. "Do these people have first names?"

"No," Stone said.

⤙ Chapter 53 ⤚

Stone walked down Worth Avenue with Dino at his side, trying not to look behind him or at the reflections in windows.

"What are we doing, Stone?" Dino asked.

"We're trolling."

"For Dolce?"

"Yes."

"Which one of us is the bait on the hook?"

"I am."

"So what am I?"

"You're the cork."

"I must remember to stay out of the line of fire," Dino said.

"Don't worry, Guido and his buddies are on the job."

"Oh, that *really* makes me feel better: protection from goombahs."

"You're a goombah," Stone said.

"You say that again, and I'll shoot you myself."

"Come on, Dino, the only thing separating your life from Guido's and his chums' is the entrance exam to the police academy."

"You're really trying to piss me off, aren't you?"

"Can't you take a joke?"

"I'm going to sic the Italian-American Defamation League onto your ass," Dino said.

"Didn't the people who ran that fine organization all get gunned down while eating clams?"

"Only some of them. Are we trolling for Paul Manning, too?"

"No, I think Mr. Manning has retired from the field."

"And what makes you think that?"

"I explained to him that I knew about his little bank escapades, and that I could very easily cause the FBI to know about them, too, if he should annoy me."

"And you think that will get rid of him."

"I do."

"I expect it pissed him off, too."

"Oh, yes, I took some pleasure in pissing him off."

"Stone, you don't want to piss off crazy people with homicidal tendencies."

"I think he's smart enough to stay out of my way, now."

"Smart doesn't enter into it," Dino said. "Revenge has a way of doing away with smart."

Stone stopped and looked into a jewelry shop window. "See if you can spot Guido and his friends."

Dino didn't even turn around. "You mean the three goombahs in the red Cadillac, parked across the street?"

Stone sighed. "Tell me you're just saying that to annoy me."

"I'm just saying that to annoy you," Dino said. "They're really parked about fifty feet up the street."

"I told him to stay well away from me," Stone said.

"Goombahs like Guido don't listen, unless it involves an illegal profit, or the fun of shooting somebody in the head."

"I don't understand why Eduardo would send people like that to do this."

"Who else is he going to trust?" Dino asked. "They're his people. He's not going to ask his fellow board members at the Metropolitan Opera to come to Palm Beach and bring his crazy daughter home."

Stone started to walk again. "Once again, you have a point, but couldn't he have hired some private security people? Somebody with a little more discretion?"

"Then strangers would know his business," Dino said, "and Eduardo doesn't want anybody outside the family to know his business. To tell you the truth, I'm a little surprised he hasn't had *you* capped. After all, you're not exactly family, although you almost were."

"I guess I dodged that bullet," Stone said.

"Not yet, pal," Dino replied. "But at least you're not bound to them by a Catholic marriage and family obligations."

"I still feel obligated to Dolce."

"Eduardo doesn't feel you have any obligation to her, so why do you?"

"He has been very apologetic about this," Stone said.

"You're lucky he's Italian," Dino said. "If you'd been through the same experience with the daughter of some high Episcopalian, the old man would be out there ruining your reputation, even as we speak. He wouldn't have you shot, but you'd never get invited to dinner again by anybody with an Anglo-Saxon name, and you'd be kicked out of your clubs—if you belonged to any clubs."

"Yeah, keep telling me how lucky I am," Stone said. He turned into Tiffany & Company. "Come on, I've got to find a wedding present for Thad and Liz."

"Listen, those people ought to be giving *you* a wedding present," Dino said.

"Nevertheless." Stone looked, first at crystal, then moved up to sterling. "What do you think of this?" he asked, holding up a handsome silver bowl.

"What would they keep in that, their money?"

"Fruit."

"Oh."

"I'll take this," Stone said to a saleslady. "Could you gift wrap it?"

"Of course," the woman said. "I'll just be a moment." She vanished into a back room.

Dino went rigid. "Don't turn around," he said. "Dolce's looking in the window."

Involuntarily, Stone turned around and looked. He saw a disappearing flash of color.

"You stay right here," Dino said. "Don't move." He walked quickly to the front door and outside, looking up and down the street.

Stone waited impatiently until the saleswoman returned, then waited even more impatiently while she rang up the sale and had his credit card authorized. Finally, blue shopping bag in hand, he hurried to the front door. He looked up and down the street as far he could see, then stepped outside. Dino was nowhere in sight, and neither was the red Cadillac.

Stone stood in the bright sunlight, feeling helpless, not knowing which way to turn. He waited for five long minutes, then made a decision: He turned right and walked rapidly along the street, checking shopwindows for Dolce and looking up and down the street for the red Cadillac.

Suddenly, Dino stepped out of a doorway and ran head-on into Stone. "Didn't I tell you to stay where you were?" he demanded.

"I did, for a very long time," Stone said. "Did you lose her?"

"Yeah, and I don't understand it."

Then, from not too great a distance, they heard three rapid reports.

"Gun!" Dino said, and started running toward the noise.

Stone followed, and the two of them turned a corner and ran toward a parking lot behind Worth Avenue. Stone could see the trunk of the red Cadillac protruding into the street.

Dino got there first. Women were screaming, and people in cars were trying desperately to get out of the parking lot. The Cadillac sat, blocking the entrance, three of its four doors open, with three bullet holes in the windshield. It was empty.

Dino flashed his badge at a parking attendant, who was crouching in a booth at the entrance. "What happened?" he asked the trembling man.

"I don't know, exactly," he said. "I was about to give the man in the Cadillac his parking check when the windshield seemed to explode."

"Anybody hit?"

"I don't know. I dove in here in about half a second."

"Call nine-one-one," Dino said, then he turned to Stone. "Let's get out of here."

As they walked quickly away, Stone looked around the lot and the street for a familiar face, but Dolce was gone, and so were Guido and his two goombahs.

Chapter 54

They got back to the yacht without sighting Dolce, and Stone was in his cabin, putting away his wedding gift, when Juanito knocked on the door.

"Yes?" Stone called.

"Mr. Barrington, there's somebody to see you on the afterdeck."

"Be right there," Stone said. He retrieved the 9mm automatic from under his pillow and tucked it into his waistband in the small of his back. He wasn't expecting visitors.

His visitor turned out to be Dan Griggs, and Stone was relieved until Griggs started to talk. He looked very serious. "Stone, there was an attempted shooting in a parking lot downtown, and one of my people saw you leaving the scene. You want to tell me about that?"

"Don't worry, Dan, they weren't shooting at me."

Griggs didn't smile. "I thought maybe it was you doing the shooting."

Stone shook his head. "No, Dino and I were shopping on Worth Avenue, when we heard gunfire. Dino was armed, and we ran around the corner and saw the car with the bullet holes in it. That's all we saw. We told the parking lot attendant to dial nine-one-one, then left."

"Did you see the occupants of the car?"

"No."

"Did you see the shooter?"

"No."

"Witnesses said there were three men in the car, out-of-towners, by the look of them, and the shooter was a good-looking woman."

Stone said nothing.

"Why did you leave the scene?" Griggs asked.

"We didn't see anything. It's not like we were witnesses. There was nothing there for us to do." Stone was relieved that he could tell the truth about this, even if he was withholding information.

Griggs sighed.

Stone was about to say something, when he looked over Griggs's shoulder and saw Dolce standing in the garden, maybe two hundred feet away. Griggs was about to turn and follow his gaze, but Stone took him by the shoulder and led him toward the afterdeck banquette. "How about a drink, Dan?" he said.

Griggs pulled away from his grasp, but did not look toward Dolce. "Are you nuts? I'm on duty. I thought that was obvious."

"How's Lundquist?" Stone asked, desperate to keep Griggs looking in his direction instead of Dolce's. He couldn't allow himself to look that way, either.

"I put him on a medivac plane for Minneapolis this morning. He's recovering, and his department sent the aircraft."

"He's going to be all right, then?"

"Didn't I just say that?" Griggs asked, irritated.

"Sorry, Dan. I just wanted to be sure."

"Something else: You still looking for that Manning fellow?"

"Not really," Stone said. "I pretty much straightened that out in a favorable manner."

"Favorable? Did you shoot him?"

"No, no, I just sorted out the differences between him and Liz, and I think he's out of our hair now."

"Maybe not," Griggs said.

"What do you mean?"

"I've had two reports from my men of a man answering his description being in town."

"Well, if he's in town, I've got no quarrel with him, nor him with me."

"Does he have any quarrel with Liz?"

"Not anymore. That's all settled."

"Then you don't want me to pick him up?"

For a moment, Stone considered blowing the whistle on Paul Manning, and the hell with their agreement. "No. You wouldn't have a charge, anyway. He's clean."

"How do you know that? I thought you said he was the criminal type."

"As a result of our settlement, he's now too rich to be criminal."

"You paid him off?"

"Let's say he walked away in very good shape."

"Well, I'll leave him alone, if that's the way you want it, but I intend to keep an eye on him."

"That can't hurt, I suppose, if you have the manpower."

Stone thought of something. "Tell me, Dan, did the description of the man include a bandage on his face?"

"A bandage? No, nobody said anything about that. He's clean-shaven, with dark hair, going gray."

"Oh."

"Why did you think he might be wearing a bandage?"

"When I saw him he was. I thought maybe he'd had an accident or something."

"Well, I've got to get going," Griggs said, turning back toward the house.

Stone looked up to see that Dolce was nowhere in sight. "I'll walk with you," Stone said.

"Don't bother, I can find my way," Griggs replied.

"I was going to the house, anyway."

"Suit yourself."

They walked down the gangplank and toward the house, with Stone casing every shrub and tree they passed.

"Did I tell you it was stolen?" Griggs asked.

"What was?"

"The Cadillac, the one that was shot at."

"Sounds like a drug deal gone wrong," Stone said.

"Maybe, but we don't get a whole lot of drug dealing in broad daylight around the Worth Avenue shopping district."

"I guess not," Stone said, still looking for Dolce.

They reached the house and walked through the central hallway and outside to where Griggs had parked his car.

Stone looked around for the silver Volvo, or for any other strange car, but saw nothing.

"You know, Stone," Griggs said, his mood still somber, "I've got a strong feeling that you know something I ought to know."

"Me? I can't imagine what."

"When I find the guys in the Cadillac, I hope I don't find out that they know you."

"Since I left the force there are no drug dealers in my life," Stone said honestly.

"We didn't find any drugs in the car," Griggs said. "It was stolen from the airport, by the way."

"I guess they couldn't get a cab."

"I hear Thad Shames is getting married on Sunday," Griggs said. "You want me to send a few people down here to help with the traffic?"

"Couldn't hurt," Stone said. "Thad has hired some security for the wedding and the reception, but I don't think he's done anything about traffic."

"I'll send a couple of men," Griggs said. He was about to get into the car, but he stopped. "Why does Mr. Shames need private security?" he asked.

"Gate-crashers, that sort of thing."

"Oh." Griggs got into his car. "I'll see you around, Stone."

"Thanks for stopping by, Dan."

Griggs drove away, and Stone began to walk slowly through the gardens, expecting at any moment for Dolce to pop up. He passed through the hedge and had a look around the swimming pool, then walked back to the yacht.

Dino was having a drink on the afterdeck.

"Has Griggs put two and two together?" Dino asked.

"Just one and one. Apparently, a cop saw us leaving the area, and he thought we might be involved. He doesn't really know anything."

"I wish I didn't know anything," Dino said. "I'd really be happier that way."

"I'll devote my life to keeping you ignorant," Stone replied.

"I wish you would. It's tiring, knowing too much."

"Tell me about it."

"When are we getting out of here?"

"After the wedding, I guess. How about bright and early Monday morning?"

"Sounds good to me. It's too cold down here."

"I know what you mean," Stone said truthfully.

⟨⟩ Chapter 55 ⟨⟩

Stone and Dino were having dinner alone together on the yacht. The crew had been given the night off, and Callie, after preparing dinner for them, had gone to work in her new office in the main house. Stone had seen little of her since Thad and Liz had decided to get married on short notice; there didn't seem to be enough hours in the day for her to get her work done.

"Gee, it's kind of nice here, just you and me," Dino said. "We never get to have dinner alone anymore."

"Oh, shut up," Stone said. "You're worse than a wife."

"That's something only a bachelor could say," Dino replied.

"You know, Dino, I've been thinking about marriage."

"Oh, no," Dino groaned. "Not again."

"What kind of crack is that?"

"Stone, every time you start thinking about marriage, you get into terrible trouble."

"Nonsense," Stone snorted.

"Stone, when you were thinking about marrying Arrington, look what happened: She married somebody else, and you got involved with this flake Allison—excuse me, Liz. And look at all the trouble that came out of that."

"Well, that time, yes."

"Then there was the English girl—what was her name?"

"Sarah."

"You sure?"

"I'm sure."

"That didn't go so good, either, right?"

"Not so good."

"And then you actually *married* Dolce—well, sort of, and against all the advice I could muster. And now she's out there stalking you with a gun, and frankly, I wouldn't give you good odds on making it back to New York without taking along some excess baggage in the form of lead in your liver. Now, I ask you, what happens when you start thinking about marriage?"

"All right, I get into trouble," Stone said gloomily.

"Stone, you're my friend, and I love you, and that's why I can say this to you: You're not cut out to be married. Never in my life have I known anybody who was *less* cut out to be married. Marriage is very, very hard, and believe me, you're not tough enough to handle it."

"Callie is an awfully nice girl," Stone said mistily.

"I'll grant you that."

"I think it would be nice to be married to her."

"I'll even grant you that, up to a point. As far as I can see, the only thing wrong with Callie is that you're thinking about marrying her."

"What, you think I'm the kiss of death, or something?"

"I didn't say that, you did."

"The sex is wonderful."

"I'm glad to hear it," Dino said. "Let me tell you something somebody told me when I was young and single. This was a man who had been married three times. He said to me, 'Dino, tell you what you do: When you get married, you keep a piece of chalk in your bedside table drawer, and every time you make love to your wife, you take out the chalk and make a hash mark on the wall. Then, after you've been married for a year, throw away the chalk and keep an eraser in your bedside drawer, and every time you make love, take out the eraser and erase a hash mark.'"

"What was his point?" Stone asked.

"His point was this: 'It'll take you ten years to erase all the hash marks.'" Stone laughed in spite of himself.

"So, pal, my point is, if you're going to get married, you'd better have something going on in the relationship besides sex."

"I knew that," Stone said.

"No, you didn't," Dino sighed. "You still don't."

"No, I do, I really do."

"Tell me this," Dino said. "What makes you think she'd marry you?"

"Well . . ."

"You think all she's looking for is a great lay? Not that you're all that great."

"I could offer her a pretty good life," Stone said.

"Yeah, sure. You're traipsing all over the country, doing this very strange but oddly entertaining work. You think she's going to like that? You going to take her along when you have to drop everything and go to Podunk, Somewhere?"

"Why not?"

"Because women get rooted in their homes. I guarantee you, a month after you're married, you're going to find that your house has been totally redecorated."

"I like the way my house is decorated," Stone said. "I did it myself."

"Yeah, but Callie doesn't like it."

"She hasn't even seen it."

"You think that matters? She doesn't like it because *you* decorated it, dumbo. She won't think of it as her home until she's changed all the wallpaper and carpets and had a big garage sale and sold everything you love most in the house."

"You really know how to make marriage attractive, Dino."

"I'm telling you the truth, here."

"Did Mary Ann redecorate your place?"

"No, she *sold* my place one day when I was at work, and I had nothing to say about it. Then we bought one *she* liked."

"Oh."

"Yeah."

"This conversation is making me tired," Stone said.

"I don't blame you. Reality is always tiring."

Stone drained the last of the wine from his glass. "I'm going to bed."

"Good idea. The very least you should do about this marriage idea is to sleep on it. For about a month."

"I think I could sleep for a month," Stone said, yawning. "I could do that."

"Then go do it, pal," Dino said. "I'm going to finish my wine and look out at the night." He settled himself in a big leather chair and turned on the TV.

"Good night, then." Stone went to his cabin, undressed and got into bed. He stared at the ceiling, thinking about Callie redecorating his beloved house, until he fell asleep.

Then, seconds later, it seemed, Dino was shaking him.

"What?" Stone mumbled sleepily.

"Get up. You gotta see something."

"Jesus, Dino, what time is it?"

"A little after two."

"Don't you ever sleep?"

"I *was* sleeping, in the chair in front of the TV. Then I woke up."

Stone turned over and fluffed his pillow. "Then go back to sleep."

"Stone, get out of the fucking bed right now and come with me."

Stone turned over and tried to focus on Dino, then he realized that his friend had a gun in his hand. He sat bolt upright, now fully awake. "What's wrong?"

"Put your pants on and come with me."

Stone got out of bed and put his pants on, then padded along behind Dino as he led the way to the afterdeck.

"Look," Dino said, waving an arm.

"Look at what?"

"Look at the shore."

"What about the shore?"

"We aren't tied up to it anymore."

"Huh?" Stone looked quickly toward where the seawall behind Thad Shames's house should have been. It wasn't there. "We're adrift," he said.

"*That's* the word I was looking for," Dino said. "Adrift!"

"Why?"

"How the hell do you think *I* know? What do I know about boats?"

"This is crazy," Stone said. "The engines aren't running. Where's the crew?"

"Ashore, probably drunk," Dino said. "What do we do?"

Stone grappled with that problem for a minute. "We stop the yacht," he said.

"Great. How do we do that?"

"Come on," Stone said, "let's get up to the bridge."

"The bridge," Dino said, following Stone at a trot. "I like that. It sounds real nautical."

Chapter 56

Stone ran up to the bridge, which was completely dark. "Find a light somewhere," he said to Dino.

"I'm looking, I'm looking."

Stone began feeling along the bulkheads for a switch. Suddenly, the lights came on, but dimly.

"I found it, but it's not very bright," Dino said.

"That's okay, it won't ruin our night vision."

"What do we do now?"

"We've got to get the engines started," Stone said. "Look for the ignition switch."

"Right here," Dino said, pointing. "Trouble is, there's no key in it."

"Then look for the key," Stone said, starting to open drawers in the cabinetwork. He found no key. "We've got to get an anchor out."

"How do we do that?"

Stone looked over the instrument panel. "On a yacht this size, there's probably an electric windlass. Here it is!" He pressed the button, but nothing happened. "We need engine power for that, too."

"What about the radio?" Dino asked. "Call somebody."

"Good idea." Stone found the VHF radio, switched it on and picked up the microphone. "Channel sixteen is the calling channel." He changed the channel to 16 and pressed the switch on the microphone. "Coast Guard, Coast Guard, this is the yacht *Toscana, Toscana.* Do you read?"

Instantly a voice came back. *"Toscana,* this is the U.S. Coast Guard. What is your request?"

What was his request? He thought about it for a moment. "Coast Guard, *Toscana.* We're adrift in the Intracoastal Waterway, and we need a tow. We have no power."

"Toscana, Coast Guard. Sorry, you'll have to call a commercial towing service for that kind of help."

Stone looked at the ship's clock on the bulkhead. "But it's three o'clock in the morning," he said. "Where am I going to get a tow at this time of night?"

"Sorry, but we can't be of any help," the Coast Guard operator said. "Good night, and have a good trip." Then he was gone.

"Now what?" Dino asked.

"I'm not sure."

"Well, why don't we just wait until morning and flag somebody down?"

Stone pointed out the windshield. "See that?" he asked.

"What, the bridge? Sure, I see it; you think I'm blind?"

"We're drifting down on it."

"So what? We hit it, we'll stop. Isn't that what we want?"

"Dino, this is a two-hundred-and-twenty-foot yacht, and it weighs God knows how much. If we hit that bridge, either the yacht or the bridge is going to be very badly damaged, maybe both."

Dino blinked. "Well, do something, for chrissakes!"

Stone pressed the button on the microphone again. "Any ship, any ship, this is the yacht *Toscana,* in need of assistance. Anybody read me?"

Nothing. Silence.

"It's three o'clock in the morning," Dino said. "What did you expect?"

Then a voice came over the radio. *"Toscana, Toscana,* this is *Winddrifter.* Do you read?"

"Winddrifter, Toscana. I read you loud and clear."

"What's your problem?"

"We're adrift in the Waterway with no power, and we need a tow, fast, to keep from hitting a bridge."

"Sorry, *Toscana,* I'm halfway to the Bahamas. Afraid I can't be of any help. Good luck."

"You get the feeling we're all alone?" Dino asked.

"Well, shit, we've got to do *something,"* Stone said.

"I'm wide open to suggestions."

Stone looked outside the bridge and saw a large inflatable dinghy on deck. "There," he said. "We've got to get that thing launched right now."

"You mean we're going to abandon ship?" Dino asked.

"No, no. Come on, follow me." Stone opened the outside door and left the bridge. He ran forward to the dinghy, which appeared to be a good seventeen feet long. A big outboard motor was bolted to the stern. "Look, it's already hooked up to the davit," Stone said.

"To the what?"

"The davit, the cranelike thing." Stone yanked a cover off a pedestal. "Here we go," he said, switching on the electric motor. He tried the up switch, and the dinghy rose six inches, bringing its cradle with it. "Thank God it's got its own power." He set it back down on deck. "Quick, let's get this thing unlashed." He glanced at the bridge. It was beginning to look very large.

Dino fumbled with the ties. "Got this side undone," he said.

"Mine, too," Stone said. "Now, I'm going to get into the dinghy. You raise it higher than the rail, there, and use this joystick thing to swing it over the side. Then you push the down button."

"I've never operated anything like this before," Dino said.

"Think of it as a computer game."

"I can't do those, either."

Stone hopped into the dinghy. "Okay, let's go."

Dino started to work the controls. He raised the dinghy three feet off the deck.

"Right, now use the joystick."

Dino did something, and the dinghy began to move sideways at an alarming rate. Stone nearly fell out. "Slowly!" he yelled.

"I thought you were in a hurry," Dino said.

"Gently. Don't throw me out of the dinghy."

Dino tried again, and this time the dinghy moved smoothly over the rail and hung, suspended, six or eight feet above the water.

"Great, now with the down button."

Dino found the switch, and in a moment the dinghy was in the water. Stone unhooked the cable and was adrift. "Put the davit back in the same position we found it in," he called to Dino.

Dino followed Stone's instructions. "Now what?" he called.

A light breeze had sprung up, and Stone was drifting rapidly away from the yacht. "Find a long rope!" he yelled, "and go to the bow!"

"Where?"

"Up front to the pointed end." Stone felt around the instrument panel for the ignition key and found it. He tried starting the engine. It turned over but didn't start. He made his way to the stern of the dingy, found a gas tank with a fuel line leading to the engine, and pumped the attached rubber bulb a few times. Then he returned to the controls and tried again. The engine started.

Stone put the thing in gear and headed for the bows of the yacht, which was now turning sideways. Then he glanced over his shoulder and found that, in the time it had taken to launch the dingy, they were nearly to the bridge. The yacht was about to hit not one, but two of the bridge's supports.

He did the only thing he could think of. He gunned the engine and attacked the bows of the big yacht, as if the dinghy were a tugboat. Gradually, the bows of the yacht began to turn upstream, and a moment later she passed, backward, under the bridge.

Stone could see Dino standing on deck. "Did you find a rope?"

"Yeah, a big one, too."

"Make one end fast and throw me the other end." A moment later, a large coil of heavy rope hit Stone in the back of the head, knocking him down.

"You trying to kill me?" he yelled at Dino. He struggled back to his feet.

"You said throw you the other end."

"I didn't mean two hundred feet of it!" Stone paid out forty feet of rope, then made it fast to a stern cleat. "Okay, I've got it," he yelled.

"What do I do now?"

"Go back to the bridge and steer the boat."

"Steer it where?"

"Just keep it headed upstream behind the dinghy!"

"Okay, okay." Dino went aft toward the bridge.

"And when we pass back under the bridge, don't let the yacht hit it!" Stone screamed.

"Thanks," Dino called back. "I needed to be told that!"

Stone put the engine in gear and slowly went forward until the rope was taut. For a long moment nothing happened. He applied more power and finally, the dinghy began to move forward an inch at a time, then a foot. The bows of the yacht fell into line behind him, and he aimed at the center of the bridge.

Slowly, with the outboard engine making a loud racket, the yacht moved under, then away from the bridge.

"What now?" Dino yelled from the bows.

"Go back to the wheel! I'm going to try to bring the yacht alongside where we were tied up before. Find some more ropes, and as soon as we're by the seawall, make one end fast to the yacht and jump ashore with the other end!"

"Okay!" Dino yelled, and went aft again.

The seawall came into sight now, illuminated by a dock light and the lights on the garden paths ashore. Stone could see Juanito and the yacht's skipper standing on the wall, looking at them. He towed the yacht past the seawall, then, very slowly, made a 180-degree turn and started back toward the yacht's berth.

"Easy!" somebody yelled from ashore. "Cut your power, and she'll drift in."

Stone did as he was told. Gradually, the big yacht drifted toward the seawall, then Dino was throwing ropes to the men ashore. Five minutes later, the yacht was secure.

Stone scrambled up a ladder to shore and tied the dinghy to the ladder.

The skipper approached. "What the hell happened? Did you decide to go for a cruise?"

"Don't be ridiculous," Stone said. "I was asleep, and somebody cut our lines."

"Untied them," the skipper said.

Dino walked over. "Yeah, they were just hanging in the water."

"I tried to start the engines," Stone said, "but we couldn't find the ignition key."

"In my pocket," the skipper said, holding up the key. "Well, she's secure, now. Why don't you go back to bed, and we'll try to figure this out in the morning."

"Good idea," Stone said, and he and Dino trudged back aboard.

"Are you thinking Dolce?" Dino asked as he paused at his cabin door.

"Maybe. Or maybe our friend Manning."

"Some friend."

"Yeah."

The two men said good night and went to bed. It took Stone a long time to get to sleep.

⌐ Chapter 57 ⌐

Stone and Dino barely made it on deck in time for lunch the following day. They had the afterdeck to themselves, and they had just finished their omelettes when two men in suits emerged from the house and made their way toward the yacht.

"Ten to one they're FBI," Dino said.

"No bet," Stone replied. He knew how Dino hated FBI agents, and his own experience with them as a cop had not been wonderful.

"Nobody else looks quite like that. What the hell do they want?"

"I think we're about to find out," Stone said, as the two men came up the gangplank.

"Either one of you Lieutenant Dino Bacchetti of the NYPD?" one of them asked without preamble.

"Who wants to know?" Dino asked.

Both men whipped out ID.

"Wow, I'm impressed. I'm Bacchetti. Why are you disturbing my vacation?"

"We want to ask you some questions," the first agent said.

"See me in my office in New York," Dino said. "I'll be back next week."

"It's in connection with a bank robbery in Arlington, Virginia, four years ago," the man said.

"I didn't do it," Dino said, "and I can probably come up with an alibi."

The man turned to Stone. "Who are you?" he demanded.

Stone started to reply, but Dino interrupted. "None of your fucking business," he said. "Now get off my yacht."

The agent looked around. "Yours, huh? Pretty fancy for a New York cop. I wonder what your Internal Affairs people would have to say about this."

Dino began laughing, and so did Stone.

"What's so funny?" the agent asked, annoyed.

"You be sure and mention my yacht to Internal Affairs," Dino said. "I'd enjoy their reaction. Now, will you people go away?"

"Look," the agent said, "maybe we got off on the wrong foot, here. My name is Miles, and this is my partner, Nevins. We'd really appreciate your help, Lieutenant Bacchetti."

"Why didn't you say so?" Dino said expansively. "Have a seat." He kicked chairs in the agents' direction, and they both sat down.

"Can I get you something?" Dino asked, the generous host, now that he had brought the two men into line.

"No, thanks," Miles said.

"What can I do for you?" Dino asked.

"A couple of days ago, your office in New York ran a match on some fingerprints in our computer."

Dino said nothing.

"Isn't that right?"

"If you say so. We probably run prints a dozen times a day."

"You ran a set of prints that matched with a thumbprint we got from a note passed to a teller in a bank robbery in Virginia."

"So?"

"We want to know where you got the prints."

"Didn't you ask my office?"

"They wouldn't tell us. They said we had to talk to you, and you were in Palm Beach, so we drove up here from Miami this morning."

"How much did the bank robber get?" Dino asked.

"About thirty thousand, I think. I'm not sure."

"Let me get this straight," Dino said. "You two guys got into your government car and drove all the way up here from Miami, using government gas, in pursuit of a guy who got thirty grand from a bank four years ago?"

"That's right," Miles replied.

"Well, Agent Miles, I'm not too sure I approve of the way you people are spending my tax dollars," Dino said.

"I don't understand," Miles replied.

Stone spoke up. "Neither does Lieutenant Bacchetti. He can't figure out why you fellows are making this kind of effort to track down a penny-ante, walk-in bank robber who the bank won't even make the effort to prosecute."

"I'm sorry, I didn't get your name," Miles said.

"Stone Barrington."

"Well, Mr. Barrington, bank robbery is a very serious crime."

"Gee, the bank doesn't think so. When you catch this guy, they won't even send somebody down to court to testify against him."

"No matter what the banks think, the FBI considers bank robbery to be a very serious crime," Miles said. "It eats away at the roots of our economic system, if we let people get away with stealing even what you consider a small amount from a bank."

"No kidding?" Stone said.

"What else did this guy do?" Dino asked.

"I'm sorry?"

"Come on, Agent Miles, you're not here about a bank robbery. What did the guy do?"

"That's confidential."

"I'm a police officer. Mr. Barrington, here, used to be a police officer, and now he's a distinguished member of the bar. You can tell us."

"Those are not my instructions."

"What *are* your instructions?"

"I'm, ah, not at liberty to say."

"Well, Agent Miles, if you want information from me, you'd better be at liberty to trade a little information."

"Lieutenant, why are you being so difficult about this? All we want is to catch a bank robber."

"No, that's not all you want. You want to catch an entirely different animal, and I want to know the species."

Miles took out a handkerchief and wiped his brow. "Lieutenant, you're interfering with an FBI investigation."

"Oh? Well, I'm terribly sorry. Did it ever occur to you that you might be interfering with *my* investigation?"

"I think a federal investigation takes precedence."

"That's what you guys always think," Dino said. "You never think that something the NYPD is investigating might be as important as what the FBI is investigating."

"That's not true," Miles insisted.

"They're not going to tell us anything, are they?" Dino asked.

"Doesn't look like it."

"Then why should *we* tell *them* anything?"

"I can't think of a good reason," Stone said.

"This is obstruction," Miles said indignantly. "You obviously know something about this perpetrator."

"I didn't say that," Dino replied.

"Neither did I," Stone said.

"Look, Lieutenant, I could take this to your superior," Miles said.

"Oh, my captain would love that," Dino said. "Assuming you could even get him on the phone, he'd love you wasting his time about some dime-a-dozen bank job. He'd really call me in on the carpet about that."

"How about this, Agent Miles," Stone said. "Why don't you just tell us why the checking of this guy's prints would raise a flag on the FBI's computer system? It can't be just this bank robbery."

"If I told you that . . ." Miles stopped and thought better. "I can't tell you that," he said.

"Agent Miles," Dino said, "I'm trying hard to see some reason why I should help out the FBI, which wouldn't cross the street to help *me* out on an investigation."

Miles produced his card. "Here's my number," he said, handing the card to Dino. "I'll owe you one. A big one. Anytime you need a favor from the Bureau, you can call me."

Dino took the card. "How about you, Agent Nevins? Are you going to owe me one, too?"

Nevins produced a card and handed it over. "Yes, yes, I am."

"Well, now we're getting somewhere," Dino said. "Stone, tell the agents what you know about this guy."

"His name—or at least, one of his names—is William Charles Danforth, of a P Street address in Washington, D.C., a town with which you are no doubt familiar. Some years ago his name was Paul Manning, and he was a well-known author."

"Have you ever seen this man?" Miles asked.

"Yes, a couple of days ago."

"Can you give me a description?"

"Late forties, six-three or -four, two hundred pounds, dark hair going gray."

"Facial characteristics?"

"I haven't a clue."

"But you say you saw him a couple of days ago."

"That's right, but he had a big bandage right in the middle of his face. I had the distinct impression that he didn't want me to know what he looked like. Maybe he was afraid I might be talking to the FBI."

"Do you know his present whereabouts?"

"A man answering his description has been seen in Palm Beach, but I've no idea if it's the same man."

"Anything else you can tell me?"

"Nope."

Miles and Nevins stood up. "Thank you very much, Mr. Barrington, Lieutenant Bacchetti. We owe you one."

"You already said that," Dino pointed out.

"We'll be going, then," Miles said.

"Don't let the doorknob hit you in the ass on your way out," Dino said.

Miles looked at the gangplank. "There isn't a doorknob," he said.

Dino looked at Stone. "You can't fool the FBI, can you?"

"Nope," Stone agreed.

The two agents left.

When they had gone, Stone turned to Dino. "I'm surprised you cooperated. Why did you want me to tell them about Manning?"

"The sonofabitch set my yacht adrift," Dino said.

ꙮ Chapter 58 ꙮ

N o sooner had the FBI men left than Liz came out of the house and walked to the yacht. She came aboard and gave both Stone and Dino a big kiss. She was carrying an envelope and two gift-wrapped boxes.

"I just want to thank you both so much," she said, sitting down.

"You're welcome," Stone said. "Glad to be of service."

"Same here," Dino echoed. "Only I haven't been of all that much service."

"Of course you have," Liz said. "And I want to thank you. First of all," she said, handing Stone the envelope, "here's a check for your legal services."

Stone slipped the envelope into a pocket without looking inside. "Thank you, Liz."

"Second," she said, handing Stone the larger of the two packages, "this is to express my personal thanks for your friendship and your concern for me. Even though your job as my lawyer is done, I think of you as my friend."

"Thank you again," Stone said, accepting the box.

"And, Dino," she said, handing him the smaller of the two boxes, "this is for you, for taking the time and trouble to come down here and help out Stone. And for stopping that horrible man from hurting anyone else in that restaurant shoot-out."

"Thank you, ma'am," Dino said.

"Don't open them yet," she said, holding up a hand. "I'd be embarrassed." She stood up. "I have to run, now. Callie and I are going to town to look for dresses for the wedding." With a little wave, she departed the yacht and headed back toward the house.

"You first," Dino said.

"No, you."

Dino opened his gift. Inside was a handsome gold pen from Cartier. "Very nice," he said. "I'll be the envy of the precinct. What'd she get you?"

Stone opened the package to find a large, red Cartier box inside. He opened it and held the contents up for Dino to see.

Dino took the box from Stone and gave a low whistle. "Hey, now, that's *really* nice."

Stone took back the box and removed the wristwatch from it. "Certainly is," he said. He took off his steel Rolex, put it into his pocket and slipped on the new watch.

Dino picked up the red booklet that came with the watch. "Cartier Tank Francaise," he read. "You pick the best clients."

"I guess I do."

Juanito approached with the telephone. "For you, Mr. Barrington."

"Hello?"

"Stone, it's Dan Griggs. Did some FBI agents come see you?"

"Yes, they just left."

"Now I've got a guy from the Houston PD wants to talk to you."

"Houston, Texas?"

"One and the same. What the hell is going on down there?"

"I don't have the foggiest, Dan."

"I'm sending the guy to you right now. His name is Fritz Parker."

"Okay. I'll be here." Stone hung up.

"What?" Dino asked.

"A Houston cop wants to talk to me."

"You committed any crimes in Houston?"

"I've never even been to Houston."

Twenty minutes later a middle-aged man in a seersucker suit walked up the gangplank. "Lieutenant Bacchetti?" he asked.

"That's me," Dino said.

"I'm Fritz Parker, Houston PD. Can I have a word with you?"

"Sure, pull up a chair. This is Stone Barrington."

"How do you do?" Parker said, shaking hands. "Lieutenant, do you mind if we talk alone?"

"You can talk in front of Stone," Dino said. "He used to be my partner, before he became a rich lawyer."

"All right." Parker sat down.

"In fact, Dan Griggs said you wanted to see Stone."

"No, I wanted to see you. Chief Griggs told me you were Mr. Barrington's guest."

"Okay, what can I do for you?"

"A couple of days ago, your precinct ran some fingerprints that matched an unknown perpetrator from a bank robbery in Virginia, four years ago."

"Jesus," Dino said. "The FBI was just here about that."

"They were? I asked for their help, but I didn't know they were coming."

"Typical," Dino said. "They liked what you told them, so they're poaching on your territory."

"It's what they do," Stone said.

"What's this about?" Dino asked. "Can't be the bank robbery."

"No. At least my department has no interest in that; the FBI might. I'm here about a possible homicide."

Dino and Stone looked at each other.

"Manning has been a busy guy," Stone said.

"Manning?" Parker asked.

"The fingerprint belongs to a man named Paul Manning. Or, at least, that used to be his name."

"Tell us about the homicide," Dino said.

"It was last year," Parker said. "A Houston businessman died of an apparent heart attack, but our medical examiner wasn't entirely satisfied with that as a cause of death."

"What did he suspect?" Stone asked.

"Poisoning, of a very special kind. Apparently, there are two common household products which, when mixed, create a poison that can't be analyzed."

"I've heard about that poison," Stone said, "but I don't know what the household products are."

"Neither do I," Parker said, "and the ME wouldn't tell me. Said it's not the sort of knowledge that should be spread around, and I think I agree. He did look around the house and said both products were present."

"But why do you think Manning had anything to do with this?"

"Because this guy Manning, if that's who he is, left a thumbprint on a bedside glass, right next to the body."

"And these two chemicals were in the glass?"

"No, the glass was clean, except for the thumbprint. The ME theorizes that the murderer removed the glass containing the poisons and substituted a clean one."

"And what was the outcome of the case?"

"It's still open," Parker said, "until we can find the owner of the fingerprint and question him. Do you have any idea where I can find Paul Manning?"

"He may be in Palm Beach," Stone said. "Two of Chief Griggs's men have seen a man in town answering his description. Lately, he has also gone by the name of William Charles Danforth." Stone gave Parker the Washington address. "I gave that to the FBI agents, too." He gave him Manning's description.

Parker made a note of everything.

"I'd suggest you tell Chief Griggs that you have a good reason for him to pick up the guy," Stone said. "We didn't have a reason before now."

"I'll do that right away," Parker said. Stone handed him the phone, and he made the call. Parker spoke to Dan Griggs, then handed the phone to Stone. "He wants to talk to you."

"Hello?"

"Stone, I hear you've finally got something on this guy."

"Well, Parker has, anyway."

"It will give me the greatest pleasure to put out an APB on him."

"He may be carrying ID saying that he's William Charles Danforth, of Washington, D.C."

"Got it. I'll let you know if we pick him up."

"Thanks, Dan." He hung up the phone. "Fritz, you're doing me a very great favor."

"Glad to be of service. Lieutenant, running those prints was a very great favor to us. I'd love to clear this case."

"I hope you clear it before the weekend," Stone said.

"Why the weekend?"

"Because there's going to be a big wedding here, and Mr. Manning might just try to crash the party."

"I'll see what I can do," Parker said. He stood up and shook Stone's and Dino's hands. "Thanks for your help. I'll let you know if we find the guy." He turned to leave.

"Fritz," Stone said, "what was your victim's name?"

"Winston Harding," Parker replied.

Chapter 59

Stone watched Thad Shames leave the house and walk through the gardens toward the yacht.

"Maybe I should talk to him alone," Stone said.

Dino got up. "I'll be in my cabin if you need me."

As Dino departed, Thad came up the gangplank and walked to the afterdeck, where Stone waited for him. "Hello," he said.

"Hello, Thad. Have a seat." Stone wasn't going to enjoy this.

"What's up? Why did you want to see me alone?"

"Because what I have to tell you is for your ears only. You must not share this with Liz, or even Callie."

"You sound very serious," Thad said.

"This *is* very serious."

"Tell me."

"Today, Dino and I have had visits from two FBI agents and a detective from the Houston, Texas, police department."

"About Liz?"

"No, about Paul Manning."

"What about Manning?"

"One of the problems with finding Manning was that, for a long time, he had never been fingerprinted. Lots of people haven't. If you have never been arrested, applied for a security clearance or served in the armed forces, then you've probably not been fingerprinted. The Bureau maintains a huge database of everyone who has ever been fingerprinted, and it can be accessed by authorized law enforcement agencies."

"I understand. And Manning has never been fingerprinted?"

"He has, once. After the business on St. Marks, Manning paid me a visit in New York. He wanted money. Fortunately, I had been expecting him, and Dino showed up shortly after his arrival and arrested him on charges of insurance fraud. Since he was wanted in St. Marks on three murder charges, and since the insurance company had no hope of retrieving any funds from him, they waived their claim on Manning and allowed him to be extradited to St. Marks. But first, he was taken to Dino's precinct, the Nineteenth, in Manhattan, and routinely fingerprinted."

"And then his prints went into the FBI computer?"

"No. Whoever handled the fingerprinting at the Nineteenth considered Manning's arrest as a foreign matter and didn't forward his prints to the FBI. But they remained on file at the precinct, and earlier this week, I remembered that Manning had been printed.

"The FBI also maintains a database of fingerprints that are associated with unsolved crimes. If a perpetrator leaves a print at a crime scene, it's run against all known prints, and if there's no match, it goes into the unsolved crimes database under a file number that relates to the case. I asked Dino to run a match of Manning's prints against that database, and it turned up a match with a bank robbery in Arlington, Virginia, four years ago. That crime was also matched by modus operandi and description of the perpetrator to three other bank robberies in Maryland. All the robberies took place near Washington, D.C., where Manning kept an apartment under the name of William Charles Danforth."

"So Manning is a bank robber, as well as a murderer?"

"Yes. It appears that he had been supporting himself in that manner while he was writing a novel, which has now been published and has become a bestseller."

"Busy guy."

"Yes, he has been. Which brings us to today's visit from the FBI and the Houston detective. The FBI told us they were interested in the Virginia bank robbery, which was patently nonsense because the Bureau would never spend its resources on such a small crime, especially when they know the banks won't even prosecute small robberies unless violence was employed."

"So what were they really interested in?"

"The Houston PD, in investigating a suspected homicide, also came up with a fingerprint, which they ran against the FBI's databases. They turned up the Virginia bank robbery, too, and then, when Dino's precinct turned up the same thing, it alerted both the FBI and the Houston department that somebody else had a match. What's more, Dino could attach an identity to the prints, as well, and that's why we had these visits today."

"Did you or Dino tell them who the prints belonged to?"

"Yes, we did."

"So they're looking for Manning, now?"

"Yes. And we think he may be in Palm Beach."

"Well, this is very good news, Stone."

"It is. I hope they'll have him in custody soon, which would prevent Manning's trying to disrupt the wedding."

"Why do you think he would try to do that?"

"Last night, while the yacht's crew was off duty, and Dino and I were asleep on the yacht, somebody let go all her mooring lines and removed the gangplank. If Dino hadn't woken up, the yacht would almost certainly have collided with a bridge south of here and done great damage; maybe even have sunk the yacht."

"Jesus. And you think it was Manning?"

Stone avoided mention of Dolce. "He seems the likely candidate. It was hardly the prank of a roving band of juvenile delinquents."

"And you think he might try to disrupt the wedding?"

"Yes. We've taken security precautions against that possibility."

"So everything that can be done has been done?"

"Yes."

Thad stood up. "Then I'm going to put it out of my mind."

"Please sit down, Thad. I'm not finished."

Thad sat down.

"The Houston PD is interested in Manning because one of his fingerprints was found on a bedside glass of a man they believe may have been poisoned."

"So he killed somebody in Houston, too? Good God, the man's a maniac."

"That certainly appears to be so. But what's important to us here, today, is that the man the police think may have been poisoned was Winston Harding, Liz's late husband."

Thad seemed to freeze in place. "Oh, my God," he said, finally.

Stone felt he had finally made his point.

"The poor girl. This man has made her life hell, and now we learn he murdered her husband, too?"

Maybe he hadn't made his point, after all, Stone thought. He was going to have to spell it out. "That is a very distinct possibility," Stone said. "And it has implications for you."

"You mean, you think Manning may try to kill me?"

Stone nodded. "It's a possibility we can't ignore."

"But you've already taken security precautions."

"Yes, but how long are you willing to live under those circumstances?"

"I see," Thad said. "You mean that he might try to kill me at some time in the future?"

"Yes." Stone was having trouble getting the rest of it out. "Thad, I think that, under the circumstances, you should postpone the wedding."

Thad looked alarmed. "For how long?"

"Until Manning is caught and . . . interrogated."

"Gosh, I don't know if we could do that at this point without causing a major hullabaloo in town. We've already invited two hundred people from Palm Beach and all over the country. Some of them have already arrived."

"Of course, Manning may be arrested today or tomorrow."

"That would certainly solve the problem, wouldn't it?"

Stone took a deep breath. "Not necessarily."

Thad looked at him for a long moment. "You mean Manning might have help? An accomplice?"

"It's a very real possibility." Thank God, Stone thought, he's got it at last.

"Do you have any idea who it might be?"

No, he hadn't gotten it. "Thad, I want you to understand that what I'm about to say is conjecture, but it's a conjecture that has to be made."

"So, make it."

"There's only one person that we're aware of who knows both Manning and you."

Thad's brow wrinkled, then his face relaxed, and his mouth fell open. "You can't mean . . ."

"As I say, it's only conjecture at this point. We won't know more until Manning is arrested, and it's entirely possible that he won't say anything then."

"But that's completely crazy," Thad said.

"You may be right. But ask yourself this: Who profited from Winston Harding's death?"

"Well, Manning, I guess. In some way. Revenge against Liz, maybe."

"That's a possibility. But there's only one person who actually profited from Harding's death."

Thad didn't seem to be able even to think it.

Stone finally said it aloud. "That person is Liz."

"No, no, no, no . . ." Thad's voice trailed off.

"And if the two of you are married and anything should happen to you, she would profit a great deal more than she did from Winston Harding's death."

Thad's body sagged as if air had been let out of it. He seemed unable to speak.

"So, I think you should postpone the wedding until all this has been resolved."

Thad seemed to collect himself. He sat up straight. "No," he said. "I love her, and she loves me. If I know nothing else, I know that. The wedding goes on as scheduled. Do what you can to protect us from Manning, but you are not to say a word about this to Liz, is that understood?"

"Thad . . ."

"Stone, you have to either do as I wish in this matter, or leave. There's no in between. What's it going to be? Are you with me?"

Stone sighed. "All right," he said.

Chapter 60

Stone watched Callie leave the main house and, with a man in tow, come toward the yacht. She looked particularly beautiful today, he thought, and he had missed seeing her the past few days, when she had been so busy with the wedding.

She came up the gangplank. "Stone, this is Jeff Collender of Rightguard Security Services. He'll be helping us with the wedding, and I thought you'd better brief him."

"Yeah, I know," Collender said, shaking hands. "The name sounds like a deodorant; it was my wife's idea."

"Glad to meet you, Jeff. Have a seat."

"I hear you're throwing quite a shindig, here," Collender said.

"That describes it very well," Stone said.

"So, what do we need, here? You want us to keep out the gate-crashers, and like that?"

"Jeff, we may have more of a problem than gate-crashers," Stone said.

"Oh? You expecting a lot of big drinkers, then? We've had experience with that. We know how to quietly eject the drunks."

"Let me explain as fully as I can," Stone said. "We have to be ready to handle an armed intruder."

Collender blinked. *"Armed?* You mean with a gun?"

"Well, yes. You do have the capability of supplying armed security people, don't you?"

"Sure we do, but we've never had to actually shoot anybody."

"And I hope you won't on this occasion, but we have to be prepared for anything."

"Okay, we'll be prepared."

"Earlier, I had estimated that we'd need only a few armed men, but now I think they'll all have to be armed. I assume your men have had some standard training?"

"Well, most of them are ex-law enforcement, so they've been trained by whatever department they worked for."

"Are there any that haven't had training?"

"Maybe one or two."

"Let's drop them. We need men who know how to handle weapons in a crowd."

"Mr. Barrington, why don't you tell me exactly who you're expecting?"

"His name is Paul Manning. He's tall and slender—six-three or -four, two hundred pounds, dark hair going gray."

"Would you recognize him on sight?"

"Only by his size and shape. I haven't seen his current face."

"His *current* face?"

"We believe he's had some cosmetic surgery."

"So you don't have a photograph?"

"No."

"Ooookay, no photograph."

"There aren't too many people that tall. He should stand out in a crowd."

"How big a crowd are we expecting?"

"About two hundred," Callie said.

"There'll be a tight guest list?"

"Pretty tight. If a guest wants to bring someone along, we're not going to make a big thing of it."

"And how many of these guests are likely to be armed?"

"Just the one," Stone said dryly.

Dino came out of his cabin, and Stone introduced him to Collender.

"Nice to meet a fellow officer," Collender said. "I used to be the sheriff of Palm Beach County."

"Mmmm," Dino said. "Don't let me interrupt, just keep going."

"So," Collender said, "how many people do you want here?"

"Twenty-four ought to do it," Stone said.

"All armed?"

"Yes. Can you manage that?"

"Yeah, I can manage it. How do you want me to manage this Manning character, if we spot him?"

"Isolate him as quickly as possible, pat him down, check whatever name he gives you against the guest list and do it all very, very politely and apologetically. There are going to be some important people here, and we don't want to annoy them any more than absolutely necessary."

"Believe me," Collender said, "we're used to dealing with the rich and powerful in this town. We know how it's done."

"Good."

"How do you want my people dressed?"

"Black tie. I don't want them immediately identifiable as security. Do you have any women?"

"I've got four, all ex-officers and good."

"Put them with men. Couples are less noticeable than single men."

"Got it," Collender said, taking notes. "If Manning starts shooting, what do you want done?"

Stone and Dino exchanged a glance. "Stop him in the most expedient way possible."

Collender nodded sagely. "I get you."

"I hope so," Stone said. "I don't want Manning to be able to hurt any-body. I think you can imagine how big a mess that would be."

"Oh, yeah, I read you completely. Are we going to have any cops here?"

"I'm talking to Chief Griggs in a few minutes about that. I'll let you know."

Collender stood up. "Anything else?"

Stone shook his head.

"I'll be going, then." He gave Stone his card. "Call me if you think of anything else; there's office, home and cell phone on the card."

"Thanks, and it was good to meet you," Stone said.

Callie escorted Collender off the yacht.

"You think this guy knows what he's doing?" Dino asked.

"I hope to God he does. Callie says he's the best around here."

"Twenty-four guys with guns at a party? Let's hope they don't shoot each other."

"Let's hope," Stone said.

Dan Griggs sounded amenable on the phone. "I'm glad we've got a charge against this guy, now," he said. "I'd like it if we could snatch him off the street before the wedding."

"I'd like that, too, Dan," Stone said.

"I think we ought to have a meeting of all the security people and my people the afternoon of the wedding, and we're going to need some kind of lapel pin to identify everybody. I'll bring some."

"Good idea," Stone agreed. "There's no way everybody is going to know everybody else on sight."

"You know, we've covered a lot of parties in this town, mostly off duty, but this is the first time we're actually expecting an armed intruder."

"I hope we're being overly cautious," Stone said, "but we've got to be ready for anything. The more I learn about Manning, the more he wor-ries me."

"Let's meet at four tomorrow afternoon, then," Griggs said. "I know Jeff Collender. I'll call him."

"See you then, Dan." Stone hung up.

Dino called to him from the saloon, where he was watching a golf tour-nament on television. "Quick, come here."

Stone hurried into the saloon.

"Edward Ginsky was a prominent attorney in both New York and Miami legal circles," a television reporter was saying. He was standing in front of a large house. "He leaves a widow and two grown children."

"What happened?" Stone asked.

"Ed Ginsky got himself shot."

"Any details?"

"Maid found him on his front steps this morning. He took two in the head."

Stone sank into a chair. "Where is this going to end?"

"It's not going to end until Manning is dead," Dino said. "And I think you and I ought to do whatever we can to see that that happens, if he shows up at the wedding."

"Dino, are you suggesting we just shoot him down on sight?"

"As much as I'd like to, I think we have to be a little more subtle than that," Dino said. "But not much."

Chapter 61

Stone stood in front of the living room fireplace in Thad Shames's house and regarded the decidedly mixed group of men and women who stood around him, dressed—or half-dressed—in what each of them understood to be evening clothes.

Behind him, propped on the marble mantel, was a crude drawing of the house and grounds that he had done himself with a Magic Marker in black, with other colors for various personnel. He felt quite proud of it, in fact.

"Okay, everybody listen up," he said. "You see here an outline of the place—house, gardens and yacht. There are sixteen small circles, in red, denoting employees of Rightguard Security. Jeff Collender will assign each of you to stations, and, once we've swept the grounds, you are to maintain those stations. Pick up a drink from the bar so you'll look at least a little like a guest, and the drink will be iced water, soda, tonic or soft drink—no booze. Eight of you, four men and four women, will roam the house and grounds as couples. Jeff will assign you areas to patrol.

"The green circles denote Palm Beach police officers—two at the curb to control traffic, one at the door to display a little authority to anyone contemplating gate-crashing, especially unauthorized members of the press, and to handle the metal detector. Authorized press people will be wearing photo IDs on strings around their necks. If you see anybody taking notes or photographs who is not wearing this tag, firmly request the ID card and, if it is not immediately forthcoming, escort him or her from the premises. If possible, take such people either through the center hall of the house or around the sides to the street. If they become obstreperous, turn them over to a police officer on the street, who will arrest them for trespassing and place them in a police van."

He pointed to his colleagues as he listed their names. "Chief Dan Griggs, Jeff Collender of Rightguard, Lieutenant Bacchetti and I will be known as the 'management group' and will be roaming the house and grounds. Everybody has been issued a lapel pin—green for Rightguard Security, red for Palm Beach Police, black for management group. You may also see some people with yellow lapel pins, but they are separate. Each of you has been issued a two-way radio, tuned to channel six. You understand that the use of radios is to be confined to sightings of Paul Manning. There is to be no unnecessary chat on the radios; there are too many of us for that. Paul Manning is six-feet-three or -four, two hundred pounds, dark hair, going gray, moderately long. We have no photographs or sketches of him. If you spot a man answering that description, say the word 'bogey' into your microphone and give the specific location. If you see a weapon, either in his hand or on his person, say, 'gun' into the radio. Keep it as short as you can while conveying the information you need to. After that, speak into the radio only if the subject changes position or if you are asked questions by one of the management group.

"Each of you has two sheets of paper with the entire guest list printed on them. If you have reason to suspect that a visitor is uninvited, politely request his or her name and refer to the list. If the name does not appear, ask the person to accompany you to the front door by one of the routes already mentioned, and turn him or her over to a police officer, who will determine if that person is, in fact, invited. It is possible that some invited guest may bring along another, uninvited guest. If an invited guest intercedes on behalf of such a person, do nothing, but make a note of the name on your guest list. Apologize for any inconvenience.

"Everybody insert the radio earplug for a sound check." He waited while they did this. "This is a test," he said into the microphone concealed in his left hand. "Anybody didn't hear that, raise your hand." No hands went up. Thank God the equipment was working.

"Now, let me tell you the policy on firearms. You are all carrying concealed weapons. You are not to take out that weapon, unless you see a weapon in the hand of someone not in this room now, such as the subject, Paul Manning. If you do see a weapon and produce your own weapon, you are not to fire unless you feel sure that the subject is threatening to fire. You are not to fire unless you have a clear shot. You are not to shoot any guest. I hope that is perfectly clear." That got a laugh. "You might remember that if you fire a weapon this evening, you are going to have to answer to the police and, maybe, the courts for your actions. If you are in doubt about whether to fire your weapon, keep that in mind.

"Finally, if you spot the subject or any other threat, do not head for the bride and groom. Four Palm Beach detectives will be assigned to accompany them everywhere they go. Instead, head for the subject, and be ready to use physical force to disarm or disable him. Any questions?" Stone looked around at each face. Nobody spoke.

"All right, if you don't already have an assigned station, get one from the management group. As soon as you have your assignments, we're going to start at the seawall, and in a straight line, at arm's length, we're going to sweep the entire property, check every bush, every flower bed for any unwelcome person or weapon." *Or bomb,* he thought, but didn't say. He walked over to where Jeff Collender stood. "Jeff, the man standing over to the side of the group, there." He nodded toward a man in his twenties, barely encased in a white dinner jacket, with a head that had recently been shaved.

"Yeah, he's one of mine. Jason."

"Assign him to the seawall, to watch for anyone approaching the property in a boat. I don't want him mingling with the guests. He'll scare them to death."

"Will do."

"All right, everybody, let's go out to the seawall and start back toward the house." Stone led them out of the house and toward the yacht. When they were stretched out at arm's length, he called to them, "Commence your search, and when you get to the house, re-form farther down that way and come back to the seawall. When that's done, take up your assigned positions." He looked at his watch. "It's ten minutes to five. Guests will start to arrive at six, so move quickly but carefully."

"Dan, Jeff, Dino, the four of us will search the house, starting at the top floor. When we get downstairs, Dino and I will take the kitchen."

The four men walked back to the house, climbed the stairs to the third floor and went down hallways, knocking on every door, checking every room.

"Dan, your men at the door know that nobody enters the house except through the metal detector?"

"They know."

"Okay, Dino, let's check the kitchen." Stone led the way, and they walked into a large, restaurant-style facility, teeming with people. He found the caterer, spooning caviar into a crystal bowl. "Mr. Weems?"

"That's me."

"My name is Barrington. I'm in charge of security."

"How do you do?"

"I'd like you to walk around the room with me and confirm that every one of these people is known to you as a member of your staff."

"Okay," the man said.

Stone walked him around the room, then took him into the dining

room, where a bar was being set up. "Do you know every one of these people?" he asked.

"Every one of them. They're all mine. At the reception, we'll have half
a dozen people serving drinks who are not my regular employees, but they
all come well recommended."

"Thanks for your time."

"Don't mention it." The man returned to his work.

"Looks like you've got it covered," Dino said.

"I hope so," Stone replied. "Can you think of anything we haven't done?"

"Nope, not yet, anyway. If Manning gets in and shoots Thad or Liz, then
I'm sure I'll think of a couple of things we should have done."

"Great," Stone said.

"By the way," Dino said, "have you read the guest list?"

"I glanced at it. I don't know anybody who's coming except Bill Eggers
and a couple named Wilkes."

"Check it again," Dino said, "under C."

Stone removed the list from an inside pocket and ran a finger down to
the C's. He felt a light sweat break out on his forehead. "Mrs. Arrington
Calder," he read aloud.

"Did you know about that?" Dino asked.

"No, I didn't."

"I didn't think so. You've been too cool."

"And why do you think her name on this list would make me less than
cool?" Stone demanded.

"Well, you're raising your voice," Dino said, "and, all of a sudden,
you're sweating."

⁌ Chapter 62 ⁌

Stone and Dino took one more walk around the property, then, at six
o'clock, they headed for the front door to check out the arrival proce-
dures. Guests were already pulling up in Bentleys, Rollses and Mercedes-
Benzes, and Stone was pleased with the efficiency with which the cars were
being taken away and parked by the attendants.

He watched as a couple moved through the metal detector, which had been disguised as a rose arbor. A quiet beep was heard, and a smiling police officer approached the couple.

"Excuse me, sir," he said, and quickly ran a handheld wand over the man's clothes.

"Probably my house keys," the man said, holding up a large clump.

"I expect so, sir," the cop replied. "Sorry for the inconvenience."

"That was handled well," Dino said quietly.

"That's the Palm Beach Police Department for you," Stone replied.

The three dozen wedding guests had been asked to arrive early, and by six-thirty they were all present with drinks in their hands. At six thirty-five, there was a murmur from the group as Liz descended the main staircase, resplendent in a beautiful ivory lace wedding dress. She was met at the bottom of the stairs by Thad, who towered over her a good eighteen inches, Stone reckoned. He escorted her into the living room to the fireplace, where a judge was waiting to perform the ceremony.

"Let's go out back," Stone said.

"What, you want to miss the wedding?"

"Nobody in that room is going to bother them. If there's a threat, it'll come from outside."

"Okay."

They walked into the garden and had a look around until Stone was satisfied. There was applause from inside, and Stone turned in time to see, through a tall window, the bride and groom kissing. "That's one possibility down," Stone said.

"What do you mean?"

"If Manning wanted to stop the wedding, he'd have already made his move."

"I guess so," Dino replied. "But if he wants to create a very rich widow, he's got all evening."

"That's the scary part," Stone agreed. He looked up to see Guido and two other men approaching. They were carefully dressed in rented tuxedos, and Stone was relieved to see that the jackets were sufficiently loose-fitting not to reveal any weapons. "Evening, Guido," he said.

"Yeah, you, too," Guido said. "Everything cool?"

"So far." Stone dug into a pocket and came up with three yellow lapel pins. "Put these into your buttonholes," he said. "They will let security know you're okay."

The three men complied.

"Where you want us?" Guido asked.

"Wherever you think best. All the security people are looking for a tall man, but not for a beautiful woman, so you're on your own, if she turns up."

"Way I figure it," Guido said, "if she's coming, she's coming for you. We'll stick close."

"Not too close," Stone said. He didn't want to have to explain to anybody who they were.

"Got it." They wandered off.

At seven, the reception guests started to arrive, and the crowd became thicker.

"Jesus," Dino said, "this is a hell of a lot of people."

"Just two hundred of their closest friends," Stone said. A big dance band began to play tunes from the thirties and forties in the garden. Stone liked the music. It was a beautiful night, and a handsome crowd of people. They wandered through the house and gardens, sipping champagne and chatting with people they knew, and everybody seemed to know everybody. Stone began to relax a little.

The party wore on into the evening. The guests talked, danced, congratulated the bride and groom and did all the other things people did at parties. Some were drunk, but not too drunk. Then, late in the evening, Stone turned toward the house and saw Arrington. She was leaving the main house on the arm of a tall, handsome man of about forty, beautifully dressed. After the shock of recognition, Stone's next reaction was jealousy.

"Easy, pal," Dino said. "You look like you want to shoot the guy."

The tall man had already attracted the attention of a couple of security people, who looked at Stone inquiringly. He shook his head.

"Yeah, that's all we need," Dino said. "For security to shoot Arrington's date."

"Yes, that would be too bad," Stone said. Arrington saw him and started toward him, leaving her companion at the bar.

"Hello, Dino," she said, beaming at him and giving him a kiss on the lips.

"Hiya, kiddo," Dino said, beaming back.

"Hello, Stone," she said, almost shyly. She leaned forward and kissed him on the cheek. "I behaved badly the last time we saw each other," she whispered. "I know we can work this out. I'm at the Breakers. Call me late tonight, I don't care how late."

Stone nodded, then a voice entered his ear.

"Crasher at the front door," the voice said.

"Arrington, please excuse me," Stone said. "I have to attend to something. I'll call you later, I promise." He made his way toward the front door, closely followed by Dino.

"Don't you want me to handle the thing at the front door?" Dino asked. "Wouldn't you rather stay here and talk to Arrington?"

"I just want to see what's going on," Stone said. They arrived at the front door in time to see two Palm Beach PD officers hustling a man into a van.

Another cop approached. "Unauthorized photographer," he sad. "We know him. He's a stringer for one of the tabloids."

"Good work," Stone said. "You had any other problems at the front door?"

"Not really. We've had to frisk a few people, but no problems. Nobody as tall as the guy you're looking for. An old man in a wheelchair set off all the alarms, but he was on the guest list."

"Wheelchair?" Stone asked. "What kind of wheelchair?"

"One of those electric jobs, almost like a scooter. He arrived in a van and had to be helped with it."

"What's his name?"

The cop consulted his list. "Walter Feldman."

"Describe him."

"White hair, kind of hunched over and frail-looking."

Stone turned to look at Dino.

"A wheelchair is a good way not to look tall," Dino said.

Stone lifted his left hand to his mouth. "Everybody, listen up. This is Barrington. Without leaving your stations, find a man in an electric wheelchair and report his position." He released the talk switch. "Come on, Dino."

They quickly checked inside the house, but did not see the man. "He must be in the gardens," Stone said. He spoke into the microphone again. "This is Barrington. Anybody got a position on the man in the wheelchair yet?"

Nothing.

"Jesus, how hard can he be to find?" Stone asked.

Then a voice came over the radio. "Mr. Barrington, I've got the wheelchair."

"Where?" Stone asked.

"At the pool, behind the hedge."

"Describe the occupant."

"There's no occupant. The wheelchair is sitting empty by the pool."

"Everybody, listen up," Stone said. "Our subject has arrived. Locate him quickly."

They were near the seawall, now. Dino spoke up. "Where's the guard you put on the seawall, the bald guy?"

"Nowhere in sight," Stone said. He arrived at the wall, walked to the stern of the yacht and looked at the water. The big security guard, Jason, was floating facedown in Lake Worth, a trickle of red coloring the water around him.

"Oh, shit," Dino said.

Then gunfire broke out.

⮑ Chapter 63 ⮐

Stone turned around to find a mob of people rushing toward him, many of them screaming.

"Shots fired!" he said into the microphone. "Secure the bride and groom in the master suite now!" Then he and Dino did what cops always do, and other people don't: They ran toward the gunfire.

They had trouble making headway against the onrushing crowd, but after a couple of minutes they were nearing the house. A man and woman were huddled behind a huge shrub. "On the roof!" the man yelled at Stone, pointing.

"Detail at the front of the house," Stone said into the mike. "Subject on the roof of the house. Watch the front drainpipes and apprehend."

"He's not coming this way," Dino said. "There must be a way from the roof into the house."

"Oh, God," Stone said. He spoke into the mike. "Bride and groom detail. Where are you?"

"On the main stairs," a voice replied. "We'll have them secured in a minute."

"Oh, no," he said to Dino, "we've been suckered. Let's get up there." They started to run. "Don't take the bride and groom upstairs!" he said into the microphone. He raced into the house and headed for the stairs. From the bottom, he could just see the wedding party disappearing down the upstairs hallway. "Wedding group," he said into the mike. "Stop, and come downstairs." No one came down. He ran up the stairs.

At the top he came to a sudden halt because the stairs were blocked by the bride, the groom, several guests and four Palm Beach police officers. They were standing there, rigidly, and Stone couldn't see past them. He stopped a few steps from the top and listened.

"Step away from the bride and groom," a man's deep voice said.

Manning. Stone tiptoed up the remaining stairs. Then, blocked from Manning's view by the group above him, he clambered onto the stair handrail and grabbed the banister built around the stairwell. He was holding onto the banister's vertical risers, trying to pull himself up, and it wasn't working very well.

"I said, clear away from the bride and groom," Manning's voice commanded.

Stone could see a couple of guests peel off from the group, but the cops stood their ground.

"Listen, Mr. Manning," a cop said. "There's more of us than you. More firepower, too. Why don't you—"

"If any of you touches a gun, I'll start firing," Manning said, "and I've got thirteen rounds left. The happy couple will be the first to go."

Stone swung his legs sideways and got a toe on the landing. Slowly, painfully, he muscled his way up until he could get a grip on the handrail. Then, as silently as he could, he pulled himself to the top of the railing and let himself down on the other side, striking the floor with a muffled thud.

"What was that?" Manning demanded.

"What was what?" the cop said. "Come on, Mr. Manning, you're not getting out of here. Just drop the gun."

"For the last time, step away from the couple, or I'm going to start shooting."

Stone had the 9mm automatic in his hand by now, and he slowly pumped the first round into the chamber. On his hands and knees, he crawled to the edge of the group and, very quickly, stuck his head out and withdrew it. What he remembered seeing was a white-haired man in a dinner jacket who had assumed the combat position, pistol in both hands, at arm's length.

The odds were not good on hitting Manning before he could fire, Stone reflected. He crouched, ready to leap to one side of the group and start firing.

Then Manning changed everything. He fired a single shot into the group, and everybody scattered. The women were screaming, and a cop had thrown Liz to the floor and was lying on top of her. The group parted like the Red Sea, leaving Stone exposed, but also leaving him a clear shot at Manning. He took it, firing four rapid rounds down the hallway.

Manning fired twice more as he was spun backward, but Stone was sure the rounds had gone into the ceiling. Stone rushed him, pistol out before him, yelling, "Freeze, Manning!" He could hear people moving behind him.

As he ran down the hallway, he saw Manning struggle to one knee and start to raise his gun. Stone stopped and aimed. "Don't!" he yelled.

But Manning wasn't listening. His hand kept moving upward.

Stone fired once more, and Manning fell backward. Two Palm Beach officers were all over him, kicking his gun away, rolling him over and handcuffing him. Stone put his gun away and walked forward. "Is he alive?" he asked.

An officer knelt beside the man, his hand at Manning's throat. "I've got a pulse," he said.

Stone looked down at Manning. He reached out and pulled the white wig off, then turned his head. At last, he had a full frontal view of the man's face. It was unrecognizable, and for a moment he thought he had the wrong man, but he remembered that voice. He held the mike to his lips. "The subject is secured. He needs an ambulance, now." He turned and looked back down the hallway. Liz and Thad were sitting on the floor, a Palm Beach officer leaning against Thad, holding his upper arm. "Make that two ambulances," Stone said into the mike. He walked over to where the three sat, moved the cop's hand and looked at his arm. He found a clean handkerchief and pressed it onto the wound. "Hold that," he said to the man.

Then he turned to Thad and Liz. "Is either of you hurt?"

"No," they both said, simultaneously.

"I'm okay," the cop said. "Get them out of here."

Stone helped them up and led them to the master suite.

"Is anyone else hurt?" Thad asked.

"A security guard is dead, back at the seawall," Stone said. "And Manning doesn't look so good. He got into the house in a wheelchair, then abandoned it at the pool. From there, hidden by the hedge, he must have gotten to a kitchen door and made his way up the back stairs. He fired a couple of shots into the garden to cause chaos and to get us to bring you two upstairs. You'll be all right here. There's no danger now. I want to get back downstairs and make sure no one else was hurt."

"You go ahead, Stone," Thad said. "We'll be fine."

"Is Paul dead?" Liz asked.

Tears were streaming down her cheeks, and Stone thought she looked very worried. "No," he said, "but he took two or three bullets. An ambulance is on the way. Don't go out into the hall." He left the room and closed the door behind him, then he started down the stairs. Where the hell was Dino? Stone had been sure he was right behind him when he entered the house.

He walked into the back garden and surveyed the damage. The members of the band had abandoned their bandstand, and a couple of instruments lay on the ground beside it. A large table used as a bar had been overturned, and the air smelled of spilled booze.

He saw Arrington and her date come from behind a huge banyan tree, where they had apparently been hiding. Then he saw Dolce.

Chapter 64

She looked very beautiful, he thought. She was wearing a short, tight dress of dark green silk. Her hair, nails and makeup were perfectly done, and she was smiling slightly, showing the tips of her perfect, white teeth. For a moment, he thought she had an evening bag in her hand, but on further examination it turned out to be a small semiautomatic pistol with a short silencer affixed to it. *Where the hell did she get that?* he wondered.

She was not looking at Stone but at Arrington, and her smile became broader. Stone squeezed his left arm against his side, to be sure the pistol was still there. *I could shoot her right now, and this would all be over,* he thought. Instead, he managed the best smile he could, in the circumstances. "Hello, Dolce," he said, trying to work some delight into his voice. He held out his arms and walked toward her. *I'll just hug her, then I'll take away the gun,* he thought.

She turned toward him, and her face lit up with a burst of recognition. "Stone!" she said. "It's you!"

Then, to Stone's horror, she brought the pistol up before her and aimed it at him.

"I could shoot you, and this would all be over," she said.

Where have I heard that before? Stone wondered. "I'm glad to see you," he said. "Don't shoot me."

"Why not?" she said. "I don't want *her* to have you." She nodded toward Arrington.

"I don't want him, Dolce!" Arrington cried.

Stone looked at Arrington. Her handsome escort was edging away from her toward the banyan tree.

"Of course you do, Arrington," Dolce said. "You've always wanted him. You only married Vance because you thought I wanted *him.*"

"That's crazy, Dolce," Arrington said, then realized her choice of words was poor. She pressed on, though. "I didn't even know you knew Vance, when we were married. Come to think of it, I didn't even know *you.*"

Stone took the opportunity to edge closer to Arrington, his arms still outstretched.

"That's a gorgeous dress," Arrington said. "Where did you get it?"

Trust Arrington to bring up fashion at a time like this, Stone thought.

"At a little place on Worth Avenue. The shopping is very good in this town," Dolce replied conversationally.

Stone edged closer.

Without taking her eyes from Arrington, Dolce said, "Stone, if you come any closer, I'm going to have to make a decision."

Stone stopped moving, but he was afraid to lower his arms.

"You really don't want Stone, Arrington?" Dolce asked, wrinkling her brow.

"I wouldn't have him on a silver platter," Arrington said with conviction. "I'm with Barry, here." She turned to introduce her escort and discovered that he had vanished. "He must have had to go to the powder room," she explained.

Stone was beginning to wonder which of them was the crazier.

"Did you get the shoes here, too?" Arrington asked.

"Oh, yes," Dolce replied. "At Ferragamo."

What's going to happen when they run out of clothes to talk about? Stone wondered.

"And those earrings are a knockout," Arrington said.

"I got those at Verdura," Dolce said. "It's down a little alley off Worth Avenue, and up a flight."

"Wonderful shop," Arrington said. "I know them from New York."

"Dolce," Stone said, "can we—"

"Shut up, Stone," she replied. "Arrington and I are discussing shopping. I'll get to you in a minute."

"I'm so sorry," Stone said.

"Yes, you are, and we have to talk about that." She turned back to Arrington. "I love your handbag."

"Oh, thank you," Arrington said. "I got it at Bergdorf's, at that little boutique just inside the Fifty-eighth Street door. I can't think of the name at the moment."

Dolce pointed the pistol at her. "Think of it, or I'll shoot you."

Arrington thought desperately. "Suarez!" she said, looking relieved. "That's it." She held out the handbag. "Would you like to have mine? Please take it as a gift."

"Why, that's very kind of you, Arrington," Dolce said.

I've got to do something, Stone thought, but he couldn't think what. If he rushed her, she'd shoot him, and then only Arrington would be left, and Dolce would shoot her, too. He remembered what Guido had said about Dolce's shooting skills. *Where the hell is fucking Guido?*

Then Stone saw a movement behind Dolce. He dared not take his eyes from hers and look at it. Instead, he tried to identify it with his peripheral vision.

Dolce swung the pistol back to Stone. "I may as well get this over with, so Arrington and I can talk seriously about clothes," she said, raising the pistol.

"But . . ." Stone started to say, then the pistol in Dolce's hand went off, with an evil *pffft*, and he staggered backward. Almost simultaneously, the shape behind Dolce turned into a billowing sail, which fell over her head, and Dino, who had thrown a tablecloth over her, wrestled her to the ground.

Stone felt a searing pain in his left armpit and put his hand under his jacket. It came back covered in blood. Stone had always disliked the sight of his own blood.

"Will somebody give me a fucking hand?" Dino yelled.

Guido and his two friends materialized from behind a bush and went to Dino's aid. Or, that was the way it seemed at first. As Stone watched, the largest of the three men grabbed Dino by the collar and tossed him a few yards into a flower bed, as if he were an oddly shaped bowling ball. Guido picked up the shrouded Dolce, wrestled her gun away and threw her over a shoulder. Then he started toward the house, followed by his cohorts.

He nodded at Stone's bloody hand. "You oughta get that looked at," he said to Stone as he passed.

"Thanks," Stone said, and watched them walk through the house and out the front door. Painfully, Stone put the microphone to his lips. "Detail at the front of the house: Three men are coming out with a woman in a sack. Do not detain them. Repeat, do not detain." Then he fainted.

⮑ Chapter 65 ⮐

Stone came to in the backseat of a car. His head was in Dino's lap, and Dino was pressing something against his armpit.

"You awake?" Dino asked.

"Yes," Stone murmured.

"You want to know what happened?"

"I think I know what happened," Stone said.

Thad Shames spoke up from the driver's seat. "How are you feeling?"

"I'm not sure," Stone said. "Why aren't you with Liz?"

"Liz left the house," Thad said. "I came downstairs and went out into the garden to look for you, and she must have left the master suite then."

Dino spoke up. "The cop at the door said she insisted on getting into the ambulance with Manning."

"Are you sure I'm not still unconscious?" Stone asked, then he passed out again.

He came to again on a bed surrounded by curtains. Dino and Thad were standing beside the bed. Stone was not wearing a shirt anymore, there was a wad of gauze and tape in his armpit and his arm was in some sort of rubber sling, which seemed to be filled with ice. On a stand next to the bed, a plastic bag of blood dripped into a tube attached to Stone's other arm. He tried to sit up and started to speak.

Dino held a finger to his lips. He found a switch and the bed rose until Stone was in a sitting position. Dino pointed to the curtain and cupped a hand behind his ear.

Stone tried to focus. He could hear a woman's voice from behind the curtain.

"Don't you die on me, goddammit," she was saying. "Don't you leave me in this mess. We're going to get out of this together."

Stone recognized the voice, and he looked at Thad, whose face was drawn and whiter than usual.

"I'm going to need some time to heal," Paul Manning's voice rumbled, surprisingly strong.

"They're taking you to surgery in a minute," Allison Manning said. "But I've got to talk to you first. Thad told me they know about Winston."

"Do they know about you, or just me?" Manning asked.

"I don't know, but I can get Thad to tell me. Don't worry, I can deal with Thad. He'll believe whatever I tell him."

Stone looked at Thad. *He looks worse than I do,* he thought.

"The money is already in the Caymans," Manning said. "You know the account number. Wait until I've recovered; but before they move me to some jail ward, find a way to get me out of here. Charter a plane and bring me a gun."

"All right," Allison said. "I hear a gurney. They're coming for you."

"Better get out of here and back to Shames."

"I love you," she said.

Thad stepped over to the curtain and drew it back. Allison spun around and looked at her husband and the other two men. It took her only a moment to recover. "Thad! Thank God you're here!"

"Hello, Liz," he said. "Or, perhaps I should say, Allison."

"Did you hear all that?" she asked. "Paul is crazy, you know. I was trying to find out what he did with your two million dollars."

Dino left the cubicle.

"Were you?" Thad asked. "Well, I guess you found out, didn't you? It's in the Cayman Islands, and you know the account number."

"Thad . . ."

Thad held up a hand. "Don't. You'll just embarrass us both."

Dino returned with Dan Griggs and the Houston detective, Fritz Parker.

"Mrs., ah, Shames, I guess it is," Griggs said. "You're going to have to come with me. This detective has some questions he'd like to ask you, and I have a few, myself."

Allison looked at Thad. "You've got to help me," she said.

"I don't see how I can," Thad replied. Then he turned and walked away.

"Stone," she said, "you've got to represent me. I need your help."

"You don't need me, Allison," Stone said. "You can afford the very best. Paul probably has a phone number in his pocket."

"Please, please," she begged.

"Goodbye, Allison," Stone said. "I expect I'll see you in court."

They led her away, then Griggs came back. "We took a nine-millimeter away from Manning," he said, "but it looks like the security guard was shot with a smaller caliber. You have any thoughts on that?"

Stone thought about that for a moment, then he shook his head and closed his eyes.

"We didn't recover the slug."

Good, Stone thought.

"I understand there was some sort of scuffle in the garden after Manning was stopped. You know anything about that?"

Stone opened his eyes. "A drunken guest," he said. Apparently Griggs thought he'd been shot by Manning. "She had to be removed." He closed his eyes again and kept them closed until Griggs went away.

Stone was comfortable in a reclining seat on the G V. His arm was still numb, and he was still in a slight morphine haze.

Callie put a pillow behind his head. "Anything else I can do for you?" she asked.

"Yes," he said, "but not right now. Could I have a telephone, please?"

"I'll get you one."

Stone looked at his watch. Just past seven A.M. He had been taken to the airplane on a stretcher, but he had managed to walk up the airstair steps on his own. Callie had packed his clothes. They had been in the air for half an hour, and Dino was dozing across the aisle.

Callie brought him the phone. "After your call, you should get some sleep."

"Have you got the phone number for the Breakers Hotel?" he asked.

She took the phone, dialed the number for him, handed the phone back and walked toward the front of the airplane.

"The Breakers," an operator said.

"Please connect me with Mrs. Vance Calder," Stone said.

"One moment." The phone began ringing.

"Hello," a sleepy voice said.

Stone thought for a second, then pressed the off button on the phone.

Dino stirred and turned toward Stone. "Who was that?" he asked.

"Good question," Stone said.

"Why did you hang up?"

"Isn't that what you're supposed to do?"

"When?"

"When a man answers."

❧ AUTHOR'S NOTE ❧

I am happy to hear from readers, but you should know that if you write to me in care of my publisher, three to six months will pass before I receive your letter, and when it finally arrives it will be one among many, and I will not be able to reply.

However, if you have access to the Internet, you may visit my Web site at www.stuartwoods.com, where there is a button for sending me e-mail. So far, I have been able to reply to all of my e-mail, and I will continue to try to do so.

If you send me an e-mail and do not receive a reply, it is because you are one among an alarming number of people who have entered their e-mail return address incorrectly in their mail software. I have many of my replies returned as undeliverable.

Remember: e-mail, reply; snail mail, no reply.

When you e-mail me, please do not send attachments, as I never open these. They can take twenty minutes to download, and they often contain viruses.

Please do not place me on your mailing list for funny stories, prayers, political causes, charitable fund-raising, petitions, or sentimental claptrap. I get enough of that from people I already know. Generally speaking, when I get e-mail addressed to a large number of people, I immediately delete it without reading it.

Please do not send me your ideas for a book, as I have a policy of writing only what I myself invent. If you send me story ideas, I will immediately delete them without reading them. If you have a good idea for a book, write it yourself, but I will not be able to advise you on how to get it published. Buy a copy of *Writer's Market* at any bookstore; that will tell you how.

Anyone with a request concerning events or appearances may e-mail it to me or send it to: The Publicity Department, G. P. Putnam's Sons, 375 Hudson Street, New York, NY 10014.

Those ambitious folk who wish to buy film, dramatic, or television rights to my books should contact Matthew Snyder, Creative Artists Agency, 9830 Wilshire Boulevard, Beverly Hills, CA 90212-1825.

Those who wish to conduct business of a more literary nature should contact Anne Sibbald, Janklow & Nesbit, 445 Park Avenue, New York, NY 10022.

If you want to know if I will be signing books in your city, please visit my Web site, www.stuartwoods.com, where the tour schedule will be published a month or so in advance. If you wish me to do a book signing in your locality, ask your favorite bookseller to contact his Putnam representative or the G. P. Putnam's Sons Publicity Department with the request.

If you find typographical or editorial errors in my book and feel an irresistible urge to tell someone, please write to David Highfill at Putnam, address above. Do not e-mail your discoveries to me, as I will already have learned about them from others.

All my novels are still in print in paperback and can be found at or ordered from any bookstore. If you wish to obtain hardcover copies of earlier novels or of the two nonfiction books, a good used-book store or one of the online bookstores can help you find them. Otherwise, you will have to go to a great many garage sales.

ABOUT THE AUTHOR

Stuart Woods is the author of the bestselling Stone Barrington and Holly Barker series. He lives on the Treasure Coast of Florida, on a Maine Island, and in New York City. Readers may learn more about him and his work, read an interview, and correspond with him on his Web site at www.stuartwoods.com.